John Grisham

THE PARTNER

THE RUNAWAY JURY

ARROW

Also by John Grisham

A TIME TO KILL
THE FIRM
THE PELICAN BRIEF
THE CLIENT
THE CHAMBER
THE RAINMAKER
THE RUNAWAY JURY

This edition published in 1998 by Cresset Editions,
an imprint of Random House UK Ltd,
20 Vauxhall Bridge Road, London SW1V 2SA

Printed and bound in Germany
by Elsnerdruck, Berlin

ISBN 0 0918 6684 7

For David Gernert
friend, editor, agent

THE PARTNER

One

THEY FOUND HIM in Ponta Porã, a pleasant little town in Brazil, on the border of Paraguay, in a land still known as the Frontier.

They found him living in a shaded brick house on Rua Tiradentes, a wide avenue with trees down the center and barefoot boys dribbling soccer balls along the hot pavement.

They found him alone, as best they could tell, though a maid came and went at odd hours during the eight days they hid and watched.

They found him living a comfortable life but certainly not one of luxury. The house was modest and could've been owned by any local merchant. The car was a 1983 Volkswagen Beetle, manufactured in São Paulo with a million others. It was red and clean, polished to a shine. Their first photo of him was snapped as he waxed it just inside the gate to his short driveway.

They found him much thinner, down considerably from the two hundred and thirty pounds he'd been carrying when last seen. His hair and skin were darker, his chin had been squared, and his nose had been slightly pointed. Subtle changes to the face. They'd paid a steep bribe to the surgeon in Rio who'd performed the alterations two and a half years earlier.

They found him after four years of tedious but diligent searching, four years of dead ends and lost trails and false tips, four years of pouring good money down the drain, good money chasing bad, it seemed.

But they found him. And they waited. There was at first the desire to snatch him immediately, to drug him and smuggle him to a safe house in Paraguay, to seize him before he saw them or before a neighbor became suspicious. The initial excitement of the finding made them consider a quick strike, but after two days they settled down and waited. They loitered at various points along Rua Tiradentes, dressed like the locals, drinking tea in the shade, avoiding the sun, eating ice cream, talking to the children, watching his house. They tracked him as he drove downtown to shop, and they photographed him from across the street as he left the pharmacy. They eased very near him in a fruit market and listened as he spoke to the clerk. Excellent Portuguese, with the very slight accent of an American or a German who'd studied hard. He moved quickly downtown, gathering his goods and returning home, where he locked the gate behind him. His brief shopping trip yielded a dozen fine photos.

He had jogged in a prior life, though in the months before he disappeared his mileage shrunk as his weight ballooned. Now that he teetered on the brink of emaciation, they were not surprised to see him running again. He left his house, locking the gate behind him, and began a slow trot down the sidewalk along Rua Tiradentes. Nine minutes for the first mile, as the street went perfectly straight and the houses grew farther apart. The pavement turned to gravel on the edge of town, and halfway into the second mile his pace was down to eight minutes a mile and Danilo had himself a nice sweat. It was midday in October, the temperature near eighty, and he gained speed as he left town, past a small clinic packed with young mothers, past a small church the Baptists had built. The roads became dustier as he headed for the countryside at seven minutes a mile.

The running was serious business, and it pleased them mightily. Danilo would simply run into their arms.

THE DAY after the first sighting, a small unclean cottage on the edge of Ponta Porã was rented by a Brazilian named Osmar, and before long the rest of the pursuit team poured in. It was an equal mix of Americans and Brazilians, with Osmar giving the orders in Portuguese and Guy barking in English. Osmar could handle both languages, and had become the official interpreter for the team.

Guy was from Washington, an ex-government type who'd been hired to find Danny Boy, as he'd been nicknamed. Guy was considered a genius at some levels and immensely talented at others, and his past was a black hole. He was well into his fifth one-year contract to find Danny Boy, and there was a nice bonus for snagging the prey. Though he hid it well, Guy had been slowly cracking under the pressure of not finding Danny Boy.

Four years and three and a half million dollars, with nothing to show for it.

But now they'd found him.

Osmar and his band of Brazilians had not the slightest hint of Danny Boy's sins, but a fool could see that he'd disappeared and taken a trainload of money. And, although he was very curious about Danny Boy, Osmar had learned quickly not to ask questions. Guy and the Americans had nothing to say on the subject.

The pictures of Danny Boy were enlarged to eight by tens, and tacked along a wall in the kitchen of the dirty little cottage where they were studied by grim men with hard eyes, men who chain-smoked strong cigarettes and shook their heads at the photos. They whispered among themselves and compared the new photos to the old ones, the ones from his previous life. Smaller man, odd chin, different nose. His hair was shorter and his skin darker. Was it really him?

They had been through this before, in Recife, on the northeastern coast, nineteen months earlier when they'd rented an apartment and looked at photos on the wall until the decision was made to grab the American and check his fingerprints. Wrong prints. Wrong American. They pumped some more drugs in him and left him in a ditch.

They were afraid to dig too deeply into the current life of Danilo Silva. If he was in fact their man, then he had plenty of money. And cash always worked wonders with the local authorities. For decades, cash had bought protection for Nazis and other Germans who'd smuggled themselves into Ponta Porã.

Osmar wanted to grab him. Guy said they'd wait. He vanished on the fourth day, and the dirty little cottage was in chaos for thirty-six hours.

They saw him leave home in the red Beetle. He was in a hurry, came the report. He raced across town to the airport, jumped on a small commuter at the last moment, and was gone. His car was parked in the only lot, and they watched it every second of every hour. The plane was headed in the general direction of São Paulo, with four stops in between.

There was instantly a plan to enter his home and catalog everything. There had to be records. The money had to be tended to. Guy dreamed of finding bank statements, wire transfer reports, account summaries; all sorts of documents arranged in a neat portfolio which would lead him directly to the money.

But he knew better. If Danny Boy ran because of them, then he would never leave behind the evidence. And if he was in fact their man, then his home would be carefully secured. Danny Boy, wherever he was, would probably know the instant they opened his door or window.

They waited. They cursed and argued and strained even more under the pressure. Guy made his daily call to Washington, a nasty one. They watched the red Beetle. Each arrival brought out the binoculars and cell phones. Six flights the first day. Five the second. The dirty little cottage grew hot and the men settled outdoors—the Americans napping under a scrawny shade tree in the backyard and the Brazilians playing cards along the fence in the front.

Guy and Osmar took a long drive and vowed to grab him if he ever returned. Osmar was confident he would be back. Probably just out of town on business, whatever his business was. They'd snatch him, identify him, and if he happened to be the wrong man they'd simply throw him in a ditch and run. It had happened before.

He returned on the fifth day. They trailed him back to Rua Tiradentes, and everybody was happy.

□ □ □ □

ON THE EIGHTH DAY, the dirty cottage emptied as all the Brazilians and all the Americans took their positions.

The course was a six-miler. He had covered it each day he'd been home, leaving at almost the same time, wearing the same blue and orange runner's shorts, well-worn Nikes, ankle socks, no shirt.

The perfect spot was two and a half miles from his house, over a small hill on a gravel road, not far from his turning-around point. Danilo topped the hill twenty minutes into his run, a few seconds ahead of schedule. He ran harder, for some reason. Probably the clouds.

A small car with a flat tire was just over the hill, blocking the road, trunk opened, its rear jacked up. Its driver was a burly young man who pretended to be startled at the sight of the skinny racer sweating and panting as he topped the hill. Danilo slowed for a second. There was more room to the right.

"*Bom dia*," the burly young man said as he took a step toward Danilo.

"*Bom dia*," Danilo said, approaching the car.

The driver suddenly pulled a large shiny pistol from the trunk and shoved it into Danilo's face. He froze, his eyes locked onto the gun, his mouth open with heavy breathing. The driver had thick hands and long, stout arms. He grabbed Danilo by the neck and yanked him roughly toward the car, then down to the bumper. He stuck the pistol in a pocket and with both hands folded Danilo into the trunk. Danny Boy struggled and kicked, but was no match.

The driver slammed the trunk shut, lowered the car, tossed the jack into the ditch, and drove off. A mile away, he turned on to a narrow dirt path where his pals were anxiously waiting.

They tied nylon ropes around Danny Boy's wrists and a black cloth over his eyes, then shoved him into the back of a van. Osmar sat to his right, another Brazilian to his left. Someone removed his keys from the Velcro runner's pouch stuck to his waist. Danilo said nothing as the van started and began moving. He was still sweating and breathing even harder.

When the van stopped on a dusty road near a farm field, Danilo uttered his first words. "What do you want?" he asked, in Portuguese.

"Don't speak," came the reply from Osmar, in English. The Brazilian to Danilo's left removed a syringe from a small metal box and deftly filled it with a potent liquid. Osmar pulled Danilo's wrists tightly toward him while the other man jabbed the needle into his upper arm. He stiffened and jerked, then realized it was hopeless. He actually relaxed as the last of the drug entered his body. His breathing slowed; his head began to wobble. When his chin hit his chest, Osmar gently, with his right index finger, raised the shorts on Danilo's right leg, and found exactly what he expected to find. Pale skin.

The running kept him thin, and it also kept him brown.

Kidnappings were all too common in the Frontier. Americans were easy targets. But why him? Danilo asked himself this as his head wobbled and his eyes closed. He smiled as he fell through space, dodging comets and meteors, grabbing at moons and grinning through entire galaxies.

THEY STUFFED HIM under some cardboard boxes filled with melons and berries. The border guards nodded without leaving their chairs, and Danny Boy was now in Paraguay, though he couldn't have cared less at the moment. He bounced happily along on the floor of the van as the roads grew worse and the terrain steeper. Osmar chain-smoked and occasionally pointed this way and that. An hour after they grabbed him, they found the last turn. The cabin was in a crevice between two pointed hills, barely visible from the narrow dirt road. They carried him like a sack of meal and poured him onto a table in the den where Guy and the fingerprint man went to work.

Danny Boy snored heavily as prints were made of all eight fingers and both thumbs. The Americans and the Brazilians crowded around, watching every move. There was unopened whiskey in a box by the door, just in case this was the real Danny Boy.

The print man left abruptly and went to a room in the back where he locked the door and spread the fresh prints before him. He adjusted his lighting. He removed the master set, those freely given by Danny Boy when he was much younger, back when he was Patrick and seeking admission to the State Bar of Louisiana. Odd, this fingerprinting of lawyers.

Both sets were in fine shape, and it was immediately obvious they were a perfect match. But he meticulously checked all ten. There was no hurry. Let them wait out there. He rather enjoyed the moment. He finally opened the door and frowned hard at the dozen faces searching his. Then he smiled. "It's him," he said, in English, and they actually clapped.

Guy approved the whiskey, but only in moderation. There was more work to do. Danny Boy, still comatose, was given another shot and carried to a small bedroom with no window and a heavy door which locked from the outside. It was here that he would be interrogated, and tortured, if necessary.

THE BAREFOOT BOYS playing soccer in the street were too involved in their game to look up. Danny Boy's key ring had only four keys on it, and so the small front gate was unlocked quickly, and left open. An accomplice in a rented car came to a stop near a large tree four houses down. Another, on a motorbike, parked himself at the other end of the street and began tinkering with his brakes.

If a security system started howling upon entry, the intruder would simply run and never be seen again. If not, then he would lock himself in and take inventory.

The door opened without sirens. The security panel on the wall informed whoever might be looking that the system was disarmed. He breathed lightly and stood perfectly still for a full minute, then began to move around. He removed the hard drive from Danny Boy's PC, and collected all the disks. He rummaged through files on his desk, but found nothing but routine bills, some paid, others waiting. The fax was cheap and featureless, and declared itself to be out of order. He took photos of clothing, food, furniture, book-shelves, magazine racks.

Five minutes after the door opened, a silent signal was activated in Danilo's attic and a phone call was placed to a private security firm eleven blocks away, in downtown Ponta Porã. The call went unanswered because the security consultant on duty was swaying gently in a hammock out back. A recorded message from Danilo's house informed whoever was supposed to be listening that there was a break-in. Fifteen minutes passed before human ears heard the message. By the time the consultant raced to Danilo's house, the intruder was gone. So was Mr. Silva. Everything appeared to be in order, including the Beetle under the carport. The house and gate were locked.

The directions in the file were specific. On such alarms, do not call the police. Try first to locate Mr. Silva, and in the event he cannot be found at once, then call a number in Rio. Ask for Eva Miranda.

WITH BARELY suppressed excitement, Guy made his daily call to Washington. He actually closed his eyes and smiled when he uttered the words, "It's him." His voice was an octave higher.

There was a pause on the other end. Then, "You're certain?"

"Yes. Prints are a perfect match."

Another pause while Stephano arranged his thoughts, a process that usually took milliseconds. "The money?"

"We haven't started yet. He's still drugged."

"When?"

"Tonight."

"I'm by the phone." Stephano hung up, though he could've talked for hours.

Guy found a perch on a stump behind the cabin. The vegetation was dense, the air thin and cool. The soft voices of happy men drifted up to him. The ordeal was over, for the most part.

He had just earned an extra fifty thousand dollars. Finding the money would mean another bonus, and he was certain he'd find the money.

TWO

DOWNTOWN RIO. In a small neat office on the tenth floor of a high-rise, Eva Miranda squeezed the phone with both hands and slowly repeated the words she had just heard. The silent alarm had summoned the security guard. Mr. Silva wasn't at home, but his car was parked in the drive and the house was locked.

Someone had entered, tripped the alarm, and it couldn't be a false one because it was still activated when the security guard arrived.

Danilo was missing.

Maybe he'd gone jogging and neglected the routine. According to the guard's account, the silent alarm had been activated an hour and ten minutes ago. But Danilo jogged for less than an hour—six miles at seven to eight minutes per, total of fifty minutes max. No exceptions. She knew his movements.

She called his home on Rua Tiradentes, and no one answered. She called the number to a cell phone he sometimes kept nearby, and no one answered.

He had accidentally tripped the alarm three months ago, and scared them both badly. But a quick phone call from her had cleared up the matter.

He was much too careful about the security system to get careless. It meant too much.

She made the calls again, with the same results. There is an explanation for this, she told herself.

She dialed the number to an apartment in Curitiba, a city of a million and a half, and the capital of the state of Paraná. To their knowledge, no one knew of the apartment. It was leased under another name and used for storage and infrequent meetings. They spent short weekends there occasionally; not often enough to suit Eva.

She expected no answer at the apartment, and got none. Danilo would not go there without first calling her.

When the phone calls were finished, she locked her office door and leaned against it with her eyes closed. Associates and secretaries could be heard in the hallway. The firm had thirty-three lawyers at the moment, second largest in Rio with a branch in São Paulo and another in New York. Telephones and faxes and copiers blended together in a busy distant chorus.

At thirty-one, she was a seasoned five-year associate with the firm; seasoned to the point of working the long hours and coming in on Saturdays. Fourteen partners ran the firm, but only two were women. She had plans to change that ratio. Ten of the nineteen associates were female, evidence that in Brazil, as in the United States, women were rapidly entering the profession. She studied law at the Catholic University in Rio, one of the finer schools, in her opinion. Her father still taught philosophy there.

He had insisted she study law at Georgetown after studying law in Rio. Georgetown was his alma mater. His influence, along with her impressive résumé, striking looks, and fluent English made finding a top job with a top firm a quick chore.

She paused at her window and told herself to relax. Time was suddenly crucial. The next series of moves required steady nerves. Then she would have to disappear. There was a meeting in thirty minutes, but it would have to be postponed.

The file was locked in a small fireproof drawer. She removed it and read again the sheet of instructions; directions she and Danilo had covered many times.

He knew they would find him.

Eva had preferred to ignore the possibility.

Her mind drifted as she worried about his safety. The phone rang and startled her. It was not Danilo. A client was waiting, her secretary said. The client was early. Apologize to the client, she instructed, and politely reschedule the appointment. Do not disturb again.

The money was currently parked in two places: a bank in Panama, and an offshore holding trust in Bermuda. Her first fax authorized the immediate wire transfer of the money out of Panama and into a bank in Antigua. Her second fax scattered it among three banks on Grand Cayman. The third yanked it out of Bermuda and parked it in the Bahamas.

It was almost two in Rio. The European banks were closed, so she would be forced to skip the money around the Caribbean for a few hours until the rest of the world opened.

Danilo's instructions were clear but general. The details were left to her discretion. The initial wires were determined by Eva. She decided which banks got how much money. She had made the list of the fictitious corporate names under which the money was hidden; a list Danilo had never seen. She divided, dispersed, routed, and rerouted. It was a drill they had rehearsed many times, but without the specifics.

Danilo couldn't know where the money went. Only Eva. She had the unbridled discretion, at this moment and under these extreme circumstances, to move it as she saw fit. Her specialty was trade law. Most of her clients were Brazilian businessmen who wanted to develop exports to the United States and Canada. She understood foreign markets, currencies, banking. What she hadn't known about zipping money around the world, Danilo had taught her.

She glanced repeatedly at her watch. More than an hour had passed since the phone call from Ponta Porã.

As another fax rolled through the machine, the phone rang again. Certainly it was Danilo, finally, with a wild story and all of this was for nothing. Perhaps just a dry run, a rehearsal to test her mettle under pressure. But he was not one to play games.

It was a partner, quite perturbed that she was late for yet another meeting. She apologized with short words and returned to her fax.

The pressure mounted with each passing minute. Still no word from Danilo. No answers to her repeated calls. If they had in fact found him, then they wouldn't wait long before they tried to make him talk. That was what he feared the most. That was why she had to run.

An hour and a half. Reality was settling hard on her shoulders. Danilo was missing, and he would never disappear without first telling her. He planned his movements too carefully, always fearful of the shadows behind him. Their worst nightmare was unfolding, and quickly.

At a pay phone in the lobby of her office building, Eva made two calls. The first was to her apartment manager, to see if anyone had been to her apartment in Leblon, in Rio's South Zone, where the wealthy lived and the beautiful played. The answer was no, but the manager promised to watch things. The second call was to the office of the FBI in Biloxi, Mississippi. It was an emergency, she explained as calmly as possible with her best effort at accentless American English. She waited, knowing that from this moment forward there was no turning back.

Someone had taken Danilo. His past had finally caught him.

"Hello," came the voice, as if it were only a block away.

"Agent Joshua Cutter?"

"Yes."

She paused slightly. "Are you in charge of the Patrick Lanigan investigation?" She knew perfectly well that he was.

A pause on his end. "Yes. Who is this?"

They would trace the call to Rio, and that would take about three minutes. Then their tracking would drown in a city of ten million. But she looked around nervously anyway.

"I'm calling from Brazil," she said, according to script. "They've captured Patrick."

"Who?" Cutter asked.

"I'll give you a name."

"I'm listening," Cutter said, his voice suddenly edgy.

"Jack Stephano. Do you know him?"

A pause as Cutter tried to place the name. "No. Who is he?"

"A private agent in Washington. He's been searching for Patrick for the past four years."

"And you say he's found him, right?"

"Yes. His men found him."

"Where?"

"Here. In Brazil."

"When?"

"Today. And I think they might kill him."

Cutter pondered this for a second, then asked, "What else can you tell me?"

She gave him Stephano's phone number in D.C., then hung up and wandered out of the building.

GUY CAREFULLY FLIPPED through the assorted papers taken from Danny Boy's house, and marveled at the invisible trail. A monthly statement from a local bank listed a balance of three thousand dollars, not exactly what they had in mind. The only deposit was for eighteen hundred, debits for the month of less than a thousand. Danny Boy lived quite frugally. His electric and phone bills were unpaid but not past due. A dozen other small bills were marked paid.

One of Guy's men checked all the phone numbers on Danny Boy's bill, but turned up nothing interesting. Another scoured the hard drive from his little computer and quickly learned that Danny Boy was not much of a hacker. There was a lengthy journal about his adventures in the Brazilian outback. The last entry was almost a year old.

The scarcity of paperwork was in itself very suspicious. Only one bank statement? Who on the face of the earth keeps only last month's bank statement in the house? What about the month before? Danny Boy had a storage place somewhere, away from his home. It all fit nicely with a man on the run.

At dusk, Danny Boy, still unconscious, was stripped to his underwear, tight cotton briefs. His dirty running shoes and sweaty running socks were pulled off, revealing feet that nearly glowed in their whiteness. His new dark skin was counterfeit. He was placed on a one-inch-thick sheet of plywood next to his bed. Holes had been cut in the board and nylon ropes were used to tightly secure his ankles, knees, waist, chest, and wrists. A wide black plastic belt was strapped tightly across his forehead. An IV drip bag hung directly above his face. The tube ran to a vein above his left wrist.

He was poked with another needle; a shot in his left arm to wake him up. His labored breathing grew more rapid, and when his eyes opened they were red and glazed and took a while to study the drip bag. The Brazilian doctor stepped into the picture, and without saying a word stuck a needle into Danny Boy's left arm. It was sodium thiopental, a crude drug sometimes used to make people talk. Truth serum. It worked best if the captive had things he wanted to confess. A perfect tell-all drug had yet to be developed.

Ten minutes passed. He tried to move his head, without success. He could see a few feet on either side. The room was dark except for a small light somewhere in a corner behind him.

The door opened, then closed. Guy entered alone. He walked straight to Danny Boy, placed his fingers on the edge of the plywood, and said, "Hello, Patrick."

Patrick closed his eyes. Danilo Silva was behind him now, gone forever. An old trusted friend vanished, just like that. The simple life on Rua Tiradentes faded away with Danilo; his precious anonymity ripped away from him with the pleasant words, "Hello, Patrick."

For four years, he had often wondered how it would feel if they caught him. Would there be a sense of relief? Of justice? Any excitement at the prospect of going home to face the music?

Absolutely not! At the moment, Patrick was terror-stricken. Practically naked and strapped down like an animal, he knew the next few hours would be insufferable.

"Can you hear me, Patrick?" Guy asked, peering downward, and Patrick smiled, not because he wanted to but because an urge he couldn't control found something amusing.

The drug was taking effect, Guy noted. Sodium thiopental is a short-acting barbiturate that must be administered in very controlled doses. It was extremely difficult to find the proper level of consciousness where one would be susceptible to interrogation.

Too small a dose, and the resistance is not broken. A bit too much, and the subject is simply knocked out.

The door opened and closed. Another American slipped into the room to listen, but Patrick could not see him.

"You've been sleeping for three days, Patrick," Guy said. It was closer to five hours, but how could Patrick know? "Are you hungry or thirsty?"

"Thirsty," Patrick said.

Guy unscrewed the top from a small bottle of mineral water, and carefully poured it between Patrick's lips.

"Thanks," he said, then smiled.

"Are you hungry?" Guy asked again.

"No. What do you want?"

Guy slowly sat the mineral water on a table and leaned closer to Patrick's face. "Let's settle something first, Patrick. While you were sleeping, we took your fingerprints. We know precisely who you are, so can we please forgo the initial denials?"

"Who am I?" Patrick asked with another grin.

"Patrick Lanigan."

"From where?"

"Biloxi, Mississippi. Born in New Orleans. Law school at Tulane. Wife, one daughter, age six. Missing now for over four years."

"Bingo. That's me."

"Tell me, Patrick, did you watch your own burial service?"

"Is that a crime?"

"No. Just a rumor."

"Yes. I watched it. I was touched by it. Didn't know I had so many friends."

"How nice. Where did you hide after your burial?"

"Here and there."

A shadow emerged from the left and a hand adjusted the valve at the bottom of the drip bag. "What's that?" Patrick asked.

"A cocktail," Guy answered, nodding at the other man, who retreated to the corner.

"Where's the money, Patrick?" Guy asked with a smile.

"What money?"

"The money you took with you."

"Oh, that money," Patrick said, and breathed deeply. His eyelids closed suddenly and his body relaxed. Seconds passed and his chest moved slower, up and down.

"Patrick," Guy said, gently shaking his arm. No response, just the sounds of a deep sleep.

The dosage was immediately reduced, and they waited.

THE FBI FILE on Jack Stephano was a quick study; former Chicago detective with two degrees in criminology, former high-priced bounty hunter, expert marksman, self-taught master of search and espionage, and now the owner of a shady D.C. firm which apparently charged huge fees to locate missing people and conduct expensive surveillance.

The FBI file on Patrick Lanigan filled eight boxes. It made sense that one file would attract the other. There was no shortage of people who wanted Patrick found and brought home. Stephano's group had been hired to do it.

Stephano's firm, Edmund Associates, occupied the top floor of a nondescript building on K Street, six blocks from the White House. Two agents waited in the lobby by the elevator as two others stormed Stephano's office. They almost scuffled with a heavy secretary who insisted Mr. Stephano was too busy at the moment. They found him at his desk, alone, chatting happily on the phone. His smile vanished when they barged in with badges flashing.

"What the hell is this!" Stephano demanded. The wall behind his desk was a richly detailed map of the world, complete with little red blinking lights stuck on green continents. Which one was Patrick?

"Who hired you to find Patrick Lanigan?" asked Agent One.

"That's confidential," Stephano sneered. He'd been a cop for years, and was not easy to intimidate.

"We got a call from Brazil this afternoon," said Agent Two.

So did I, thought Stephano, stunned by this but desperately trying to appear unfazed. His jaw dropped an inch and his shoulders sagged as his mind raced wildly through all the possible theories that would bring these two thugs here. He'd talked to Guy and no one else. Guy was utterly dependable. Guy would never talk to anyone, especially the FBI. It couldn't be Guy.

Guy used a cell phone from the mountains of eastern Paraguay. There was no way the call could have been intercepted.

"Are you there?" asked Two smartly.

"Yeah," he said, hearing but not hearing.

"Where's Patrick?" asked One.

"Maybe he's in Brazil."

"Where in Brazil?"

Stephano managed a shrug, a stiff one. "I dunno. It's a big country."

"We have an outstanding warrant for him," One said. "He belongs to us."

Stephano shrugged again, this time a more casual one as if to say, "Big deal."

"We want him," demanded Two. "And now."

"I can't help you."

"You're lying," snarled One, and with that both of them joined together in front of Stephano's desk and glared down. Agent Two did the talking. "We have men downstairs, outside, around the corner, and outside your home in Falls Church. We'll watch every move you make from now until we get Lanigan."

"Fine. You can leave now."

"And don't hurt him, okay? We'll be happy to nail your ass if anything happens to our boy."

They left in step and Stephano locked the door behind them. His office had no windows. He stood before his map of the world. Brazil had three red lights, which meant little. His head shook slowly, in complete bewilderment.

He spent so much time and money covering his tracks.

His firm was known in certain circles as the best at taking the money and disappearing into the shadows. He'd never been caught before. No one ever knew who Stephano was stalking.

Three

ANOTHER SHOT to rouse him. Then a shot to sensitize the nerves.

The door opened loudly and the room was suddenly lit. It filled with the voices of many men, busy men, all with a purpose, all with heavy feet, it seemed. Guy gave orders, and someone growled in Portuguese.

Patrick opened and closed his eyes. Then he opened them for good as the drugs found their mark. They hovered over him, busy hands everywhere. His underwear was cut off, without much finesse, and he lay bare and exposed. An electric razor began buzzing, hitting his skin sharply at points on the chest, groin, thighs, and calves. He bit his lip and grimaced, his heart hammered away, though the pain had yet to start.

Guy hovered above him, his hands still but his eyes watching everything.

Patrick made no effort to speak, but just to be safe, more hands appeared from above and slapped a thick strip of silver duct tape over his mouth. Cold electrodes were stuck to the shaved points with alligator clips, and he heard a loud voice ask something about "current." Tape was then applied over the electrodes. He thought he counted eight sharp spots on his flesh. Maybe nine. His nerves were jumping. In his darkness, he could feel the hands moving above him. The tape stuck hard to skin.

Two or three men were busy in a corner, adjusting a device Patrick could not see. Wires were strung like Christmas lights across his body.

They were not going to kill him, he kept telling himself, though death might be welcome at some point in the next few hours. He had imagined this nightmare a thousand times in four years. He had prayed it would never happen, but he always knew it would. He always knew they were back there, somewhere in the shadows, tracking and bribing and looking under rocks.

Patrick always knew. Eva was too naive.

He closed his eyes, tried to breathe steadily and tried to control his thoughts as they scurried above him, preparing his body for whatever lay ahead. The drugs made his pulse race and his skin itch.

I don't know where the money is. I don't know where the money is. He almost chanted this aloud. Thank God for the tape across his mouth. I don't know where the money is.

He called Eva *every* day between 4 P.M. and 6 P.M. Every day. Seven days of the week. No exceptions unless one was planned. He knew in his pounding heart that she had moved the money by now, that it was safely hidden in two dozen places around the world. And he didn't know where it was.

But would they believe him?

The door opened again, and two or three figures left the room. The activity around his plywood cot was slowing. Then it was quiet. He opened his eyes and the IV drip bag was gone.

Guy was looking down at him. He gently took one corner of the silver duct tape and pulled it free so Patrick could talk, if he so chose.

"Thanks," Patrick said.

The Brazilian doctor appeared again from the left and stuck a needle in Patrick's arm. The syringe was long and filled with nothing but colored water, but how could Patrick know?

"Where is the money, Patrick?" Guy asked.

"I don't have any money," Patrick replied. His head ached from being pressed into the plywood. The tight plastic band across his forehead was hot. He hadn't moved in hours.

"You will tell me, Patrick. I promise you'll tell me. You can do it now, or you can do it ten hours from now when you're half-dead. Make it easy on yourself."

"I don't want to die, okay?" Patrick said, his eyes filled with fear. They will not kill me, he told himself.

Guy lifted a small, simple, nasty device from beside Patrick and displayed it close to his face. It was a chrome lever with a black rubber tip, mounted on a small square block with two wires running from it. "See this," Guy said, as if Patrick had a choice. "When the lever is up, the circuit is broken." Guy delicately gripped the rubber tip with his thumb and index finger, and slowly lowered it. "But when it moves down to this little contact point here, the circuit is closed and the current moves through the wires to the electrodes attached to your skin." He stopped the lever just centimeters from the contact point. Patrick held his breath. The room was still.

"Would you like to see what happens when the shock is delivered?" Guy asked.

"No."

"Then where's the money?"

"I don't know. I swear."

Twelve inches in front of Patrick's nose, Guy pushed the lever down to the contact point. The shock was instant and horrific—hot bolts of current ripped into his flesh. Patrick jerked and the nylon ropes stretched. He closed his eyes fiercely and clamped his teeth together in a determined effort not to scream, but gave up after a split second and let out a piercing shriek that was heard throughout the cabin.

Guy lifted the lever, waited a few seconds for Patrick to catch his breath and open his eyes, then said, "That's level one, the lowest current. I have five levels, and I'll use them all if necessary. Eight seconds of level five will kill you, and I'm perfectly willing to do that as a last resort. Are you listening, Patrick?"

His flesh still burned from his chest to his ankles. His heart pumped furiously and he exhaled quickly.

"Are you listening?" Guy repeated.

"Yes."

"Your situation is really quite simple. Tell me where the money is, and you leave this room alive. Eventually, we'll take you back to Ponta Porã, and you can carry on as you see fit. We have no interest in notifying the FBI." Guy paused for drama and toyed with the chrome lever. "If, however, you refuse to tell me where the money is, then you'll never leave this room alive. Do you understand, Patrick?"

"Yes."

"Good. Where's the money?"

"I swear I don't know. If I knew, I'd tell you."

Guy snapped the lever down without a word, and the currents hit like boiling acid. "I don't know!" Patrick screamed in anguish. "I swear I don't know."

Guy raised the lever, and waited a few seconds for Patrick to recover. Then, "Where's the money?" he asked calmly.

"I swear I don't know."

Another scream filled the cabin, and escaped through the open windows, into the crevice between the mountains where it echoed lightly before losing itself in the jungle.

THE APARTMENT in Curitiba was near the airport. Eva told the cabdriver to wait in the street. She left her overnight bag in the trunk, but carried her thick briefcase with her.

She took the elevator to the ninth floor where the hallway was dark and quiet. It was almost 11 P.M. She moved slowly, eyes looking in all directions. She unlocked the door to the apartment, then quickly disarmed the security system with another key.

Danilo was not in the apartment, and though this was not a surprise it was still a disappointment. No message on the phone recorder. No sign of him whatsoever. Her anxiety reached another level.

She could not stay long, because the men who had Danilo might be coming there. Though she knew exactly what to do, her movements were forced and slow. The apartment had only three rooms, and she searched them quickly.

The papers she wanted were in a locked file cabinet in the den. She opened the three heavy drawers and neatly placed the paperwork in a handsome leather suitcase he kept in a nearby closet. The bulk of the files contained financial records, though not much for such a large fortune. His paper trail was as narrow as possible. He came here once a month to hide records from his home, and at least once a month he shredded the old stuff.

And for the moment, Danilo couldn't know where his papers were.

She rearmed the security system and made a hasty exit. No one in the cramped building had noticed her. She found a room in a small hotel downtown, near the Museum of Contemporary Arts. The Asian banks were open, and it was almost four in Zurich. She unpacked a compact fax and rigged it to the phone jack in her room. The small bed was soon covered with sheets of instructions and wire authorizations.

She was tired, but sleep was out of the question. Danilo said they'd come looking for her. She could not go home. Her thoughts were not on money, but on him. Was he alive? If so, how much was he suffering? How much had he told them, and at what price?

She wiped her eyes and began to arrange the papers. There was no time for tears.

WITH TORTURE, the best results come after three days of episodic abuse. The more obstinate wills are slowly broken. The pain is dreamed of, and looms larger as the victim waits for the next session. Three days, and most people break and crumble into small pieces.

Guy didn't have three days. His prisoner was not one taken in war, but a U.S. citizen wanted by the FBI.

Around midnight, they left Patrick alone for a few minutes to suffer and think about the next round. His body was drenched with sweat; his skin red from the voltage and the heat. Blood trickled from under the tape on his chest where the electrodes had been stuck too tightly and were burning into his flesh. He gasped for breath and licked his dry shriveled lips. The nylon ropes on his wrists and ankles had rubbed the skin raw.

Guy returned alone, and sat on a stool next to the sheet of

plywood. For a minute the room was quiet, the only sound was Patrick breathing and trying to control himself. He kept his eyes closed tightly.

"You're a very stubborn man," Guy said, finally.

No response.

The first two hours had yielded nothing. Every question had been about the money. He didn't know where it was, he'd said a hundred times. Did it exist? No, he had said repeatedly. What happened to it? He didn't know.

Guy's experience with torture was extremely limited. He'd consulted an expert, a really twisted freak who seemed to actually enjoy it. He'd read a crude how-to manual, but finding practice time was difficult.

Now that Patrick knew how horrible things could get, it was important to chat him up.

"Where were you when your funeral took place?" Guy asked.

There was a slight relaxing of Patrick's muscles. Finally, a question not about the money. He hesitated and thought about it. What was the harm? He was caught. His story was about to be told. Maybe if he cooperated they'd lay off the voltage.

"In Biloxi," he said.

"Hiding?"

"Yes, of course."

"And you watched your graveside service?"

"Yes."

"From where?"

"I was in a tree, with binoculars." He kept his eyes closed and his fists clenched.

"Where did you go after that?"

"Mobile."

"Was that your hiding place?"

"Yes, one of them."

"How long did you stay there?"

"Off and on, coupla months."

"That long, huh? Where did you live in Mobile?"

"Cheap motels. I moved around a lot. Moved up and down the Gulf. Destin. Panama City Beach. Back to Mobile."

"You changed your appearance."

"Yeah. I shaved, colored my hair, dropped fifty pounds."

"Did you study a language?"

"Portuguese."

"So you knew you were headed here?"

"Where's here?"

"Let's say it's Brazil."

"Okay. Yeah, I figured this was a good place to hide."

"After Mobile, where did you go?"

"Toronto."

"Why Toronto?"

"I had to go somewhere. It's a nice place."

"Did you get new papers in Toronto?"

"Yeah."

"You became Danilo Silva in Toronto?"

"Yeah."

"Did you take another language course?"

"Yeah."

"Dropped some more weight?"

"Yeah. Another thirty pounds." He kept his eyes closed and tried to ignore the pain, or at least live with it for the moment. The electrodes on his chest were smoldering and cutting deeper into his skin.

"How long did you stay there?"

"Three months."

"So you left there around July of '92?"

"Something like that."

"And where did you go next?"

"Portugal."

"Why Portugal?"

"Had to go somewhere. It's a nice place. Never been there."

"How long were you there?"

"Coupla months."

"Then where?"

"São Paulo."

"Why São Paulo?"

"Twenty million people. A wonderful place to hide."

"How long did you stay there?"

"A year."

"Tell me what you did there."

Patrick took a deep breath, then grimaced when he moved his ankles. He relaxed. "I got lost in the city. I hired a tutor and mastered the language. Lost a few more pounds. Moved from one small apartment to another."

"What did you do with the money?"

A pause. A flinch of the muscles. Where was the wretched little chrome lever? Why couldn't they continue chatting about the chase and lay off the money?

"What money?" he asked, with a passable effort at desperation.

"Come on, Patrick. The ninety million dollars you stole from your law firm and its client."

"I told you. You got the wrong guy."

Guy suddenly yelled at the door. It opened instantly and the rest of the Americans rushed in. The Brazilian doctor emptied two more syringes into Patrick's veins, then left. Two men huddled over the device in the corner. The tape recorder was turned on. Guy hovered over Patrick with the chrome lever in an upright position, scowling and angry and even more determined to kill him if he didn't talk.

"The money arrived by wire to your law firm's account offshore in Nassau. The time was exactly ten-fifteen, Eastern Standard. The date was March 26, 1992, forty-five days after your death. You were there, Patrick, looking fit and tanned and posing as someone else. We have photos taken from the bank's security camera. You had perfect forged papers. Shortly after the money arrived it was gone, sent by wire to a bank in Malta. You stole it, Patrick. Now, where is it? Tell me, and you'll live."

Patrick took a last look at Guy, and a last glance at the lever, then he closed his eyes tightly, braced himself, and said, "I swear I don't know what you're talking about."

"Patrick, Patrick—"

"Please don't do it!" he begged. "Please!"

"This is only level three, Patrick. You're halfway there." Guy pushed the lever down, and watched the body bolt and straighten.

Patrick screamed with no restraint, a scream so fierce and horrible that Osmar and the Brazilians froze for a second on the front porch. Their conversation stopped in the darkness. One of them offered a silent prayer.

Down the road, a hundred yards away, a Brazilian with a gun sat by the dirt trail and watched for approaching cars. None were expected. The nearest dwelling was miles away. He too offered a small prayer when the screaming started again.

Four

IT WAS EITHER the fourth or fifth call from the neighbors that sent Mrs. Stephano over the edge, and it also forced Jack to tell his wife the truth. The three men in dark suits loitering outside the car parked in the street directly in front of their house were FBI agents. He explained why they were there. He told her most of the Patrick story, a serious breach of professional etiquette. Mrs. Stephano never asked questions.

She didn't care what her husband did at the office. She did, however, hold some rather strong feelings about what the neighbors might think. This was, after all, Falls Church, and, well, people would talk.

She went to bed at midnight. Jack napped on the sofa in the den, rising every half-hour to peek through the blinds and see what they were doing out there. He happened to be asleep at 3 A.M. when the doorbell rang.

He answered it in his sweatsuit. Four of them were at the door, one of whom he immediately recognized as Hamilton Jaynes, Deputy Director, FBI. The number-two man at the Bureau, who just happened to live four blocks over and belong to the same golf club, though the two had never met.

He allowed them into his spacious den. Stiff introductions were made. They sat while Mrs. Stephano wandered down in her bathrobe, then scurried back up at the sight of a room full of men in dark suits.

Jaynes did all the talking for the FBI. "We're working nonstop on this Lanigan discovery. Our intelligence informs us that he's in your custody. Can you confirm or deny?"

"No." Stephano was as cool as ice.

"I'm holding a warrant for your arrest."

The ice melted a bit. Stephano glanced at another stone-faced agent. "On what charges?"

"Harboring a federal fugitive. Interference. You name it, we'll include it. What difference does it make? I'm not interested in convicting you. All I want is to haul your ass off to jail, then later we'll get the rest of your firm, then we'll lock up your clients. Take about twenty-four hours to round up everybody. We'll get the indictments later, depending on whether or not we get Lanigan. You get the picture?"

"Yeah. I think so."

"Where's Lanigan?"

"Brazil."

"I want him. And now."

Stephano blinked a couple of times, and things fell into place. Under the circumstances, handing over Lanigan was not a bad move. The feds had ways of making him talk. Faced with life in prison, Patrick just might snap his fingers and make the money appear. There would be enormous pressure from all angles to produce it.

Later, Stephano would again ponder the incredible question of how anyone in the world knew he had captured Lanigan.

"All right, here's the deal," Stephano said. "Give me forty-eight hours, I'll give you Lanigan. And you burn my warrant and drop the threats of future prosecution."

"It's a deal."

There was a moment of silence as both sides savored the victory. Jaynes said, "I need to know where to pick him up."

"Send a plane to Asunción."

"Paraguay? What happened to Brazil?"

"He has friends in Brazil."

"Whatever." Jaynes whispered to an associate, who then left the house. "Is he in one piece?" he asked Stephano.

"Yeah."

"He'd better be. One bruise on his body, and I'll hound you to hell."

"I need to make a phone call."

Jaynes actually managed a grin. He scanned the walls and said, "It's your house."

"Are my lines tapped?"

"No."

"You swear?"

"I said no."

"Excuse me." Stephano stepped into the kitchen, then to a utility room where he kept a hidden cell phone. He walked onto the rear patio where he stood in the wet grass by a gaslight. He called Guy.

THE SCREAMING had stopped for the moment when the Brazilian guarding the van heard the phone ringing. It rested on its power unit in the front seat of the van, its antenna shooting fifteen feet beyond the roof. He answered it in English, then ran to get an American.

Guy rushed from the cabin and grabbed it.

"Is he talking?" Stephano asked.

"A little. He broke about an hour ago."

"What do you know?"

"The money still exists. He doesn't know where. It's controlled by a woman in Rio, a lawyer."

"Do you have her name?"

"Yes. We're making calls now. Osmar has people in Rio."

"Can you get any more out of him?"

"I don't think so. He's half-dead, Jack."

"Stop whatever you're doing. Is the doctor there?"

"Sure."

"Get the boy treated and spruced up. Drive him toward Asunción as soon as possible."

"But why—"

"Don't ask questions. There's no time for it. The feds are all over us. Just do as I say, and make sure he's not hurt."

"Not hurt? I've been trying to kill him for five hours."

"Just do as I say. Put him back together. Drug him. Start toward Asunción. Call me every hour, on the hour."

"Whatever."

"And find the woman."

Patrick's head was lifted gently and cool water was poured on his lips. The ropes were cut from his wrists and ankles, and they very slowly removed the tape and the wires and the electrodes. He jerked and twitched, moaning words no one could understand. A shot of morphine was pumped into his well-worn veins, then a light depressant, and Patrick floated away again.

At dawn, Osmar was in the airport at Ponta Porã waiting for a flight that would eventually get him to Rio by the end of the day. He had made contact with people in Rio. He had pulled them out of bed with promises of big bucks. They were supposed to be on the streets.

SHE CALLED her father first, just after sunrise, a time of the day he always enjoyed on his small terrace with his newspaper and his coffee. He lived in a small apartment in Ipanema, three blocks from the shore, not far from his beloved Eva. His apartment building was over thirty years old, making it one of the oldest in the poshest section of Rio. He lived alone.

He knew from her voice something was wrong. She assured him she was safe and would remain so, that a client in Europe suddenly needed her for two weeks, and that she would call every day. She went on to explain that this particular client was perhaps a bit shady and very secretive, and therefore he might send representatives to poke around in her past. Don't be alarmed. It was not unusual in international trade.

He had several questions, but he knew there would be no answers.

The call to her supervising partner was much more difficult. The story she had rehearsed delivered well, but there were huge gaps in it. A new client had called late yesterday, a referral from an

American lawyer she went to school with, and she was needed immediately in Hamburg. She was taking an early flight. The client was in telecommunications, with plans for a large expansion in Brazil.

The partner was half-asleep. He asked her to call later with more details.

She called her secretary with the same story, and asked her to postpone all appointments and meetings until she returned.

From Curitiba, she flew to São Paulo, where she boarded an Aerolineas Argentinas flight to Buenos Aires, nonstop. For the first time, she used her new passport, one Danilo had helped her acquire a year earlier. She had kept it hidden in the apartment, along with two new credit cards and eight thousand dollars in U.S. cash.

She was Leah Pires now, same age but different birthday. Danilo didn't know these details; he couldn't know.

She certainly felt like someone else.

There were many scenarios. He could've been shot by bandits making a routine heist along a rural road. Happened occasionally along the Frontier. He could've been grabbed by the shadows from his past, tortured, killed, buried in the jungle. Maybe he talked, and if he did maybe her name got mentioned. She could spend the rest of her life on the run. At least he had warned her of this in the beginning. Maybe he didn't talk, and she could remain Eva.

Perhaps Danilo was still alive somewhere. He had promised her they wouldn't kill him. They might make him beg for death, but they couldn't afford to kill him. If the American authorities found him first, it would be a matter of extradition. He'd picked Latin America because of its historical reluctance to extradite.

If the shadows found him first, they would beat him until he told them where the money was. That's what he feared most—the coercion.

She tried to nap in the Buenos Aires airport, but sleep was impossible. She called his home again in Ponta Porã, then the cell phone and the apartment in Curitiba.

In Buenos Aires, she boarded a flight to New York, where she waited three hours then caught another one to Zurich on SwissAir.

□ □ □ □

THEY LAID HIM across the rear seat of the Volkswagen van, and wrapped a seat belt around his waist so he wouldn't bounce off. The roads ahead were rough. He was dressed in his running shorts only. The doctor checked the heavy gauze bandages—eight of them in all. He had covered the burns with ointments and shot antibiotics into Patrick's blood. The doctor took the seat in front of his patient, and tucked his little black bag between his feet. Patrick had suffered enough. He would protect him now.

A day or two of rest and more painkillers, and Patrick would be on his way to recovery. The burns would leave small scars, which would probably fade with time.

The doctor turned around and patted him on the shoulder. He was so pleased they hadn't killed him. "He's ready," he said to Guy in the front seat. A Brazilian driver started the van and backed away from the cabin.

They stopped every hour, precisely every sixty minutes, so the antenna could be raised and the cell phone could work around the mountains. Guy called Stephano, who was in his D.C. office with Hamilton Jaynes and a top official with the State Department. The Pentagon was being consulted.

What the hell was going on, Guy wanted to ask. Where did the feds come from?

In the first six hours they traveled a hundred miles. At times, the roads were almost impassable. They often fought with the phone trying to get Washington. At two in the afternoon, the roads improved as they left the mountains.

THE EXTRADITION ISSUE was sticky, and Hamilton Jaynes wanted no part of it. Important diplomatic strings were pulled. The Director of the FBI called the President's Chief of Staff. The American Ambassador to Paraguay got involved. Promises and threats were made.

A suspect with cash and resolve can stifle extradition from Paraguay for years, if not forever. This suspect had no money on him, and didn't even know what country he was in.

The Paraguayans reluctantly agreed to ignore extradition.

At four, Stephano instructed Guy to find the airport at Concepción, a small city three hours by car from Asunción. The Brazilian driver cursed, in Portuguese, when told to turn around and head north.

IT WAS DUSK when they entered Concepción, and it was dark when they finally found the airport, a small brick building next to a narrow asphalt strip. Guy called Stephano, who instructed him to leave Patrick in the van, with the keys in the ignition, and walk away from it. Guy, the doctor, the driver, and another American eased away slowly while looking over their shoulders at the van. They found a spot a hundred yards away, under a large tree where they couldn't be seen. An hour passed.

Finally, a King Air with American registration landed and taxied to the small terminal. Two pilots emerged, and went inside the terminal. A moment later, they walked to the van, opened the doors, got inside, and drove it to a spot near their airplane.

Patrick was gently removed from the back of the van and loaded onto the turboprop. An Air Force medic was on board, and he immediately took possession of the prisoner. The two pilots returned the van to its original spot in the parking lot. Minutes later, the plane took off.

The King Air refueled in Asunción, and while it was on the ground there Patrick began to move. He was too weak and sore and groggy to sit up. The medic gave him cold water and crackers.

They refueled again in La Paz and Lima. In Bogotá, they transferred him to a small Lear, which flew at twice the speed of the King Air. It refueled on Aruba, off the coast of Venezuela, then flew nonstop to a U.S. Navy base outside San Juan, Puerto Rico. An ambulance took him to the base hospital.

After almost four and a half years, Patrick was back on American soil.

Five

THE LAW FIRM Patrick worked for before he died filed for bankruptcy protection a year after his funeral. After his death, the firm's letterhead properly included him: Patrick S. Lanigan, 1954–1992. He was listed up in the right-hand corner, just above the paralegals. Then the rumors got started and wouldn't stop. Before long, everyone believed he had taken the money and disappeared. After three months, no one on the Gulf Coast believed he was dead. His name came off the letterhead as the debts piled up.

The four remaining partners were still together, attached unwillingly at the hip by the bondage of bankruptcy. Their names had been joined on the mortgages and the bank notes, back when they were rolling and on the verge of serious wealth. They had been joint defendants in several unwinnable lawsuits; thus the bankruptcy. Since Patrick's departure, they had tried every possible way to divorce one another, but nothing would work. Two were raging alcoholics who drank at the office behind locked doors, but never together. The other two were in recovery, still teetering on the brink of sobriety.

He took their money. Their millions. Money they had already spent long before it arrived, as only lawyers can do. Money for their richly renovated office building in downtown Biloxi. Money for new homes, yachts, condos in the Caribbean. The money was on the way, approved, the papers signed, orders entered; they could see it, smell it, almost touch it when their dead partner snatched it at the last possible second.

He was dead. They buried him on February 11, 1992. They had consoled the widow and put his rotten name on their handsome letterhead. Yet six weeks later, he somehow stole their money.

They had brawled over who was to blame. Charles Bogan, the firm's senior partner and its iron hand, had insisted the money be wired from its source into a new account offshore, and this made sense after some discussion. It was ninety million bucks, a third of which the firm would keep, and it would be impossible to hide that kind of money in Biloxi, population fifty thousand. Someone at the bank would talk. Soon everyone would know. All four vowed secrecy, even as they made plans to display as much of their new wealth as possible. There had even been talk of a firm jet, a six-seater.

So Bogan took his share of the blame. At forty-nine, he was the oldest of the four, and, at the moment, the most stable. He was also responsible for hiring Patrick nine years earlier, and for this he had received no small amount of grief.

Doug Vitrano, the litigator, had made the fateful decision to recommend Patrick as the fifth partner. The other three had agreed, and when Lanigan was added to the firm name, he had access to virtually every file in the office. Bogan, Rapley, Vitrano, Havarac, and Lanigan, Attorneys and Counselors-at-Law. A large ad in the yellow pages claimed "Specialists in Offshore Injuries." Specialists or not, like most firms they would take almost anything if the fees were lucrative. Lots of secretaries and paralegals. Big overhead, and the strongest political connections on the Coast.

They were all in their mid- to late forties. Havarac had been raised by his father on a shrimp boat. His hands were still proudly calloused, and he dreamed of choking Patrick until his neck snapped. Rapley was severely depressed and seldom left his home, where he wrote briefs in a dark office in the attic.

BOGAN AND VITRANO were at their desks just after nine when Agent Cutter entered the building on Vieux Marche, in the old section of Biloxi. He smiled at the receptionist and asked if any of the lawyers were in. It was a fair question. They were known as a bunch of drunks who occasionally showed up for work.

She led him to a small conference room and gave him coffee. Vitrano came first, looking remarkably starched and clear-eyed. Bogan was just seconds behind. They mixed sugar in the coffee and talked about the weather.

In the months immediately following the disappearance of both Patrick and the money, Cutter would drop in periodically and deliver the latest update on the FBI's investigation. They became pleasant acquaintances, though the meetings were always disheartening. As the months became years, the updates grew further apart. And the updates had the same endings: no trace of Patrick. It had been almost a year since Cutter had spoken to any of them.

And so they figured he was simply being nice, happened to be downtown for something, probably wanted a cup of coffee, and this would be routine and quick.

Cutter said, "We have Patrick in custody."

Charlie Bogan closed his eyes and displayed every one of his teeth. "Oh my God!" he exclaimed, then buried his face in his palms. "Oh my God."

Vitrano's head fell back, his mouth too fell open. He gazed in utter disbelief at the ceiling. "Where?" he managed to ask.

"He's at a military base in Puerto Rico. He was captured in Brazil."

Bogan stood and walked to a corner, next to some bookcases, where he hid his face and tried to hold back the tears. "Oh my God," he kept repeating.

"Are you sure it's him?" Vitrano asked in disbelief.

"Positive."

"Tell me more," Vitrano said.

"Like what?"

"Like how did you find him? And where? And what was he doing? What does he look like?"

"We didn't find him. He was given to us."

Bogan sat down at the table, a handkerchief over his nose. "I'm sorry," he said, embarrassed.

"Do you know a man named Jack Stephano?" Cutter asked.

They both nodded with some reluctance.

"Are you part of his little consortium?"

They both shook their heads in the negative.

"You're lucky. Stephano found him, tortured him, damned near killed him, then gave him to us."

"I like the part about the torture," Vitrano said. "Tell us about that."

"Skip it. We picked him up last night in Paraguay, flew him to Puerto Rico. He's in the hospital there. He'll be released and sent here in a few days."

"What about the money?" Bogan managed to ask, his voice scratchy and dry.

"No sign of it. But then, we don't know what Stephano knows."

Vitrano stared at the table, his eyes dancing. Patrick had stolen ninety million dollars when he disappeared four years earlier. It would be impossible to spend all of it. He could have bought mansions and helicopters and lots of women and still have tens of millions left. Surely they could find it. The firm's fee was a third.

Maybe, just maybe.

Bogan worked on his moist eyes and thought of his ex-wife, a congenial woman who'd turned vicious when the sky fell. She had felt disgraced after the bankruptcy, and so she took their youngest child and moved to Pensacola where she filed for divorce and made ugly accusations. Bogan was drinking and using coke. She knew it and beat him over the head with it. He couldn't offer much resistance. He eventually cleaned himself up, but was still denied access to the child.

Oddly enough, he still loved his ex-wife; still dreamed of getting her back. Maybe the money would get her attention. Maybe there was hope. Surely they could find it.

Cutter broke the silence. "Stephano's in all sorts of trouble. There were burns all over Patrick's body where they tortured him."

"Good," Vitrano said with a smile.

"You expect sympathy from us?" Bogan asked.

"Anyway, Stephano is a side issue. We'll watch him, maybe he'll lead us to the money."

"The money will be easy to find," Vitrano said. "There was a dead body. Somebody got killed by our boy Patrick. It's a death penalty case, open and shut. Murder for the sake of money. Patrick will sing when the pressure is applied."

"Better yet, give him to us," Bogan said, without a smile. "Ten minutes, and we'll know everything."

Cutter glanced at his watch. "I gotta go. I have to go to Point Clear and break the news to Trudy."

Bogan and Vitrano snorted in perfect unison, then laughed. "Oh, she doesn't know?" Bogan said.

"Not yet."

"Please video it," Vitrano said, still laughing quietly. "I'd love to see her face."

"I'm actually looking forward to it," Cutter said.

"The bitch," Bogan said.

Cutter stood and said, "Tell the other partners, but sit on it until noon. We've scheduled a press conference then. I'll be in touch."

They didn't say a word for a long time after he left. There were so many questions, so much to say. The room spun with possibilities and scenarios.

THE VICTIM of a fiery one-car collision, on a rural road with no witnesses, Patrick was laid to rest by his lovely wife Trudy on February 11, 1992. She was a striking widow, dressed in black Armani, and as they shoveled dirt onto his casket she was already spending the money.

His will left everything to her. It was simple and had been recently updated. Hours before the funeral mass, Trudy and Doug Vitrano had carefully opened the lockbox in Patrick's office and inventoried the contents. They found the will, two car titles, the deed to the Lanigan home, a life insurance policy in the amount of half a million dollars that Trudy knew about, and another policy for two million that she'd never heard of.

Vitrano had quickly scanned the unexpected policy. It had been purchased by Patrick eight months earlier. Trudy was the sole beneficiary. The same company had sold both policies, and it was huge and solvent.

She swore she knew nothing about it, and the smile on her face convinced Vitrano she was genuinely shocked. Funeral or no funeral, Trudy was quite thrilled about her good fortune. With her pain eased considerably, she somehow managed to suffer through the funeral service and burial without a serious breakdown.

The life insurance company balked, as they all do initially, but Vitrano made sufficient threats to force payment. Four weeks after the burial, Trudy got her two and a half million.

A week later, she was driving a red Rolls-Royce around Biloxi, and people began to hate her. Then the ninety million vanished in thin air, and the rumors got started.

Perhaps she wasn't a widow.

Patrick was the first suspect, and eventually the only one. The gossip grew vicious, so Trudy loaded her small daughter and her boyfriend, Lance, a holdover from high school, into the red Rolls and fled to Mobile, an hour east of Biloxi. She found a slick lawyer who gave her lots of advice on how to protect the money. She bought a beautiful old home in Point Clear, overlooking Mobile Bay, and put it in Lance's name.

Lance was a strong, handsome loser she'd first slept with at the age of fourteen. He'd been convicted of smuggling pot at nineteen, and spent three years in prison while she was having a wonderful time at college, playing cheerleader and seducing football players, a legendary party girl who also managed to graduate with honors. She married a wealthy fraternity boy, and divorced him after two years. Then she enjoyed the single life for a few years until she met and married Patrick, a promising young lawyer who was new to the Coast. Their courtship had been long on passion and short on planning.

Through college, both marriages, and various short careers, Trudy had always kept Lance nearby. He was an addiction, a strapping, lusty boy she could never get enough of. She knew when she was fourteen that she would never be without Lance.

□ □ □ □

LANCE OPENED THE DOOR, bare-chested, black hair pulled back tightly into the obligatory ponytail, a large diamond earring in the left lobe. He sneered at Cutter as he sneered at the world, and didn't say a word.

"Is Trudy in?" Cutter asked.

"Maybe."

The badge flashed, and for a second the sneer vanished. "Agent Cutter, FBI. I've talked to her before."

Lance imported marijuana from Mexico with a large, fast boat Trudy had purchased for him. He sold the pot to a gang in Mobile. Business was slow because the DEA was asking questions.

"She's in the gym," Lance said, nodding past Cutter. "What do you want?"

Cutter ignored him and walked across the drive to a converted garage where the music was booming. Lance followed.

Trudy was in the midst of a high-level aerobics challenge being dictated to her by a supermodel on a large-screen TV at one end of the room. She bounced and gyrated and mouthed the words to a nameless song, and looked damned good doing it. Tight yellow spandex. Tight blond ponytail. Not an ounce of fat anywhere. Cutter could've watched for hours. Even her sweat was cute.

She did this two hours a day. At thirty-five, Trudy still looked like everybody's high school sweetheart.

Lance hit a switch and the video stopped. She twirled, saw Cutter, and gave him a look that would melt cheese. "Do you mind?" she snapped at Lance. Evidently, this workout was not to be disturbed.

"I'm Special Agent Cutter, FBI," he said, whipping out his badge and walking to her. "We met once before, a few years back."

She dabbed her face with a towel, a yellow one that matched the spandex. She was hardly breathing.

She flashed perfect teeth, and everything was okay. "What can I do for you?" Lance stood beside her. Matching ponytails.

"I have some wonderful news for you," Cutter said with a broad smile.

"What?"

"We've found your husband, Mrs. Lanigan, and he's alive."

A slight pause as it registered. "Patrick?" she said.

"He would be the one."

"You're lying," Lance sneered.

"Afraid not. He's in custody in Puerto Rico. Should make it back here in a week or so. Just thought you should hear the good news before we release it to the press."

Stunned and staggering, she backed away and sat on a workout bench next to a weight machine. Her glistening bronze flesh was growing pale. Her pliant body was crumbling. Lance scurried to help her. "Oh my God," she kept mumbling.

Cutter threw a card in front of them. "Call me if I can be of any help." They said nothing as he left.

It was obvious to him that she held no anger at having been duped by a man who faked his death. Nor was there the smallest hint of joy at his return. No relief whatsoever at the end of an ordeal.

There was nothing but fear; the horror of losing the money. The life insurance company would sue immediately.

WHILE CUTTER was in Mobile, another agent from the Biloxi office went to the home of Patrick's mother in New Orleans, and delivered the same news. Mrs. Lanigan was overcome with emotion, and begged the agent to sit for a while and answer questions. He stayed for an hour, but had few answers for her. She cried for joy, and after he left she spent the rest of the day calling friends with the wonderful news that her only child was alive after all.

Six

JACK STEPHANO was arrested by the FBI in his D.C. office. He spent thirty minutes in jail, then was rushed to a small courtroom in the federal courthouse where he faced a U.S. Magistrate in a closed hearing. He was informed that he would be released immediately on his own recognizance, that he couldn't leave the area, and that he would be watched by the FBI around the clock. While he was in court, a small army of agents entered his office, seized virtually every file, and sent the employees home.

After being dismissed by the Magistrate, Stephano was driven to the Hoover Building on Pennsylvania Avenue where Hamilton Jaynes was waiting. When the two were alone in Jaynes' office, the Deputy Director offered a lukewarm apology for the arrest. But he had no choice. You can't snatch a federal fugitive, drug him, torture him, and damned near kill him without being charged with something.

The issue was the money. The arrest was the leverage. Stephano swore Patrick had told them nothing.

As they spoke, the doors to Stephano's office were being chained shut and ominous federal bulletins were being taped to the windows. His home phones were being bugged while Mrs. Stephano played bridge.

After the brief and fruitless meeting with Jaynes, he was dropped off near the Supreme Court. Since he'd been ordered to stay away from his office, he flagged a cab and told the driver to go to the Hay-Adams Hotel, corner of H and Sixteenth. He sat in traffic, calmly reading a newspaper, occasionally rubbing the tracking device they'd sewn in the hem of his jacket when they booked him. It was called a tracing cone, a tiny but powerful transmitter used to monitor movements of people, packages, even automobiles. He'd frisked himself while chatting with Jaynes, and had been tempted to rip out the cone and toss it on his desk.

He was an expert at surveillance. He stuffed his jacket under the seat of the cab, and walked quickly into the Hay-Adams Hotel, across from Lafayette Park. There were no rooms, he was told. He asked to see the manager, a former client, and within minutes Mr. Stephano was escorted to a suite on the fourth floor, with a splendid view of the White House. He stripped to his socks and shorts and carefully placed each item of clothing on the bed where he examined and even caressed every inch of fabric. He ordered lunch. He called his wife, but there was no answer.

Then he called Benny Aricia, his client, the man whose ninety million got diverted just minutes after it had arrived at the bank in Nassau. Aricia's take was to have been sixty million, with thirty going to his lawyers, Bogan and Vitrano and the rest of those filthy crooks in Biloxi. But it had vanished, just before it reached Benny.

He was at the Willard Hotel, also near the White House, hiding and waiting to hear from Stephano.

They met an hour later at the Four Seasons Hotel in Georgetown, in a suite Aricia had just reserved for a week.

Benny was almost sixty, but looked ten years younger. He was lean and bronze, with the perpetual tan of an affluent South Florida retiree who played golf every day. He lived in a condo on a canal with a Swedish woman who was young enough to be his daughter.

When the money was stolen, the law firm owned an insurance policy covering fraud and theft by its partners and employees. Embezzlement is common in law firms. The policy, sold by Monarch-Sierra Insurance Company, had a limit of four million dollars, payable to the firm. Aricia sued the law firm with a vengeance. His lawsuit demanded sixty million; all that he was entitled to.

Because there was little else to collect, and because the firm was about to run to bankruptcy court, Benny had settled for the four million paid by Monarch-Sierra. He'd spent almost half of that searching for Patrick. The fancy condo in Boca had cost a half a million. Other expenditures here and there, and Benny was down to his last million.

He stood in the window and sipped decaffeinated coffee. "Am I going to be arrested?" he asked.

"Probably not. But I'd keep low anyway."

Benny placed his coffee on the table and sat across from Stephano. "Have you talked to the insurance companies?" he asked.

"Not yet. I'll call later. You guys are safe."

Northern Case Mutual, the life insurance company which had made Trudy rich, had secretly set aside half a million for the search. Monarch-Sierra had put up a million. In all, Stephano's little consortium had pledged and spent over three million dollars in the hunt for Patrick.

"Any luck with the girl?" Aricia asked.

"Not yet. Our people are in Rio. They found her father, but he wouldn't talk. Same at her law firm. She's out of town on business, they say."

Aricia folded his hands and calmly said, "Now tell me, what exactly did he say?"

"I haven't heard the tape yet. It was supposed to be delivered to my office this afternoon, but now things are complicated. Plus, it was sent from the jungles of Paraguay."

"I know that."

"According to Guy, he broke after five hours of shock. He said the money was still intact, hidden in various banks, none of which he could name. Guy damned near killed him when he couldn't, or wouldn't, name the banks. By then, Guy figured, correctly, that someone else had control of the money. A few more jolts, and the girl's name came out. Guy's men immediately called Rio, and confirmed her identity. She had already vanished."

"I want to hear that tape."

"It's brutal, Benny. The man's skin is burning and he's screaming for mercy."

Benny couldn't stop the smile. "I know. That's what I want to hear."

THEY PUT PATRICK at the end of a wing on the base hospital. His was the only room with doors which could be locked from the outside and windows that wouldn't open. The blinds were closed. Two military guards sat outside the hallway, for whatever reason.

Patrick wasn't going anywhere. The voltage had severely bruised the muscles and tissue in his legs and chest. Even his joints and bones were tender. The burns had laid open his flesh in four places, two on his chest, one on his thigh, one on his calf. Four other spots were being treated as second-degree burns.

The pain was intense, and so his doctors, all four of them, had made the simple decision to keep him sedated for the time being. There was no rush to move him. He was a wanted man, but it would take a few days to determine who got him first.

They kept the room dark, the music low, the IV full of delightful narcotics, and poor Patrick snored away the hours dreaming of nothing and oblivious to the storm brewing back home.

IN AUGUST of 1992, five months after the money vanished, a federal grand jury in Biloxi indicted Patrick for the theft. There was sufficient evidence that he had pulled the heist, and there was not the slightest hint that anyone else might be a suspect. It occurred internationally, thus the feds had jurisdiction.

The Harrison County Sheriff's Department and the local District Attorney had started a joint investigation into the murder, but had long since moved on to other, more pressing matters. Suddenly they were back in business.

The noon press conference was delayed while the authorities met in Cutter's office in downtown Biloxi to sort things out. It was a tense meeting, attended by people with competing interests. On one side of the table sat Cutter and the FBI, who took their orders from Maurice Mast, the U.S. Attorney for the Western District of Mississippi, who had driven in from Jackson. On the other side sat Raymond Sweeney, the Sheriff of Harrison County, and his right-hand man, Grimshaw, both of whom despised the FBI. Their spokesman was T.L. Parrish, the District Attorney for Harrison and surrounding counties.

It was federal versus state, big budgets versus low, with serious egos around the room and everyone wanting most of the Patrick show.

"The death penalty is crucial here," D.A. Parrish said.

"We can use the federal death penalty," U.S. Attorney Mast said, a little timid, if that was possible.

Parrish smiled and cast his eyes down. The federal death penalty had just recently been passed by a Congress with little clue of how to implement it. It certainly sounded good when the President signed it into law, but the kinks were enormous.

The state, on the other hand, had a rich and proven history of legal executions. "Ours is better," Parrish said. "And we all know it." Parrish had sent eight men to death row. Mast had yet to indict one for capital murder.

"And then there is the issue of prison," Parrish continued. "We send him to Parchman, where he's locked down twenty-three hours a day in a steam room with bad food served twice a day, two showers a week, lots of roaches and rapists. If you get him, he gets a country club for the rest of his life while the federal courts pamper him and find a thousand ways to keep him alive."

"It won't be a picnic," Mast said, on the ropes and covering badly.

"A day at the beach maybe. Come on, Maurice. The issue is leverage. We have two big mysteries, two questions that must be answered before Lanigan is put to rest. The big one is money. Where is it? What did he do with it? Can it be recovered and given to its owners? The second is just exactly who is buried out there. I gotta hunch that only Lanigan can tell us, and he won't unless he's forced to. He's gotta be scared, Maurice. Parchman is terrifying. I promise you, he's praying for a federal indictment."

Mast was convinced but he couldn't agree. The case was simply too big to hand over to the locals. Cameras were arriving at the moment.

"There are other charges, you know," he said. "The theft happened offshore, a long way from here."

"Yeah, but the victim was a resident of this county at the time," Parrish said.

"It's not a simple case."

"What are you proposing?"

"Perhaps we should do it jointly," Mast said, and the ice melted considerably. The feds could preempt at any time, and the fact that the U.S. Attorney was offering to share was the best Parrish could hope for.

Parchman was the key, and everyone in the room knew it. Lanigan the lawyer had to know what awaited him there, and the prospect of ten years in hell prior to death could loosen his tongue.

A plan was devised to divide the pie, with both men, Parrish and Mast, tacitly agreeing to share the spotlight. The FBI would continue its search for the money. The locals would concentrate on the murder. Parrish would hastily summon his grand jury. A united front would be presented to the public. Such sticky matters as the trial and its subsequent appeals were glossed over with a hasty promise to address them later. It was important now to reach a truce so that one side wouldn't be worrying about the other.

Because a trial was in progress in the federal building, the press was herded directly across the street into the Biloxi courthouse, where the main courtroom on the second floor was available. There were dozens of reporters. Most were wild-eyed locals, but others were from Jackson, New Orleans, and Mobile. They pressed forward and bunched together like children at a parade.

Mast and Parrish walked grim-faced to a podium laden with microphones and wires. Cutter and the rest of the cops made a wall behind them. Lights came on and cameras flashed.

Mast cleared his throat, and said, "We are pleased to announce the capture of Mr. Patrick S. Lanigan, formerly of Biloxi. He is indeed alive and well, and now in our custody." He paused for dramatic effect, savoring his moment in the sun, listening as a ripple of excitement played through the throng of vultures. He then gave a few details of the capture—Brazil, two days ago, assumed identity—without giving the slightest hint that neither he nor the FBI had had anything to do with the actual locating of Patrick. Next, some useless details about the arrival of the prisoner, the pending charges, the swift and sure hand of federal justice.

Parrish was not as dramatic. He promised a quick indictment for capital murder, and for any other charge he might think of.

The questions came in torrents. Mast and Parrish declined comment on just about everything, and managed to do so for an hour and a half.

SHE INSISTED that Lance be allowed to sit through the appointment with her. She needed him, she said. He was quite cute in his tight denim shorts. His muscular legs were hairy and brown. The lawyer was scornful, but then, he'd seen everything.

Trudy was dressed to the nines—tight short skirt, tasteful red blouse, full complement of makeup and jewelry. She crossed her shapely legs to get the lawyer's attention. She patted Lance on the arm as he massaged her knee.

The lawyer ignored her legs as he ignored their groping.

She had to file for divorce, she declared, though she had already given the short version on the phone. She was mad and bitter. How could he do this to her? And to Ashley Nicole, their precious daughter? She had loved him dearly. Their lives together had been good. Now this.

"The divorce is no problem," the lawyer said, more than once. His name was J. Murray Riddleton, an accomplished divorce practitioner with many clients. "It's an easy case of abandonment. Under Alabama law, you'll get the divorce, full custody, all assets, everything."

"I want to file as fast as possible," she said, looking at the Ego Wall behind the lawyer.

"I'll do it first thing in the morning."

"How long will it take?"

"Ninety days. Piece of cake."

This did nothing to relieve her anxiety. "I just don't see how a person could do this to someone he loved. I feel like a fool." Lance's hand moved slightly upward, still massaging.

The divorce was the least of her worries. The lawyer knew it. She could try to fake a broken heart, but it wasn't working.

"How much did you get in life insurance?" he asked, flipping through the file.

She looked absolutely shocked at the mention of her life insurance. "Why is that relevant?" she snapped.

"Because they're gonna sue you to get it back. He isn't dead, Trudy. No death, no life insurance."

"You must be kidding."

"Nope."

"They can't do that. Can they? Surely not."

"Oh yes. In fact, they'll do it quickly."

Lance withdrew his hand and slumped in his chair. Trudy's mouth opened and her eyes watered. "They just can't."

He took a fresh legal pad and uncapped his pen. "Let's make a list," he said.

She paid a hundred and thirty thousand dollars for the Rolls, and still owned it. Lance drove a Porsche, which she'd bought for eighty-five thousand. The house had been purchased for nine hundred thousand, cash, no mortgage, and it was in Lance's name. Sixty thousand for his dope boat. A hundred thousand for her jewelry. They figured and pondered and pulled numbers from the air. The list stopped at about a million and a half. The lawyer didn't have the heart to tell them that these precious assets would be the first to go.

Like pulling teeth without Novocain, he made Trudy estimate their monthly living expenses. She reckoned it was around ten grand a month, for the past four years. They had taken some fabulous trips, money spilled down the drain that no life insurance company could ever recover.

She was unemployed, or retired, as she preferred to call it. Lance was not about to mention his narcotics business. Nor did they dare reveal, even to their own lawyer, that they had hidden three hundred thousand in a bank in Florida.

"When do you think they'll sue?" she asked.

"Before the week is out," said the lawyer.

IT WAS, in fact, much faster. In the middle of the press conference, when the news of Patrick's resurrection was being made, attorneys for Northern Case Mutual quietly entered the clerk's office downstairs and sued Trudy Lanigan for the full two and a half million dollars, plus interest and attorneys' fees. The lawsuit also included a petition for a temporary restraining order to prevent Trudy from moving assets now that she was no longer a widow.

The attorneys carried their petition down the hall to the chambers of an accommodating judge, one they had spoken to hours earlier, and in an emergency and perfectly proper closed hearing, the judge granted the restraining order. As an established member of the legal community, the judge was very familiar with the saga of Patrick Lanigan. His wife had been snubbed by Trudy shortly after she took delivery of the red Rolls.

As Trudy and Lance pawed each other and schemed with their lawyer, a copy of the restraining order was driven to Mobile and enrolled with the county clerk. Two hours later, as they sipped their first drink on their patio and gazed forlornly across Mobile Bay, a process server intruded long enough to hand Trudy a copy of the lawsuit filed by Northern Case Mutual, a summons to appear in court in Biloxi, and a certified copy of the restraining order. Among its list of prohibitions was an order for her not to write another check until the judge said so.

Seven

ATTORNEY ETHAN RAPLEY left his dark attic, showered and shaved and poured eye drops into his bloodshot retinas, and sipped strong coffee as he found a semiclean navy blazer to wear downtown. He hadn't been to the office in sixteen days. Not that he was missed, and he certainly didn't miss anyone there. They faxed him when they needed him, and he faxed them back. He wrote the briefs and memos and motions the firm needed to survive, and he did the research for people he despised. He was occasionally forced to put on a tie and meet a client or attend some hideous conference with his fellow partners. He hated his office; he hated the people, even the ones he barely knew; he hated every book on every shelf and every file on every desk. He hated the photos on his wall, and the smell of everything—the stale coffee in the hall, the chemicals near the copier, the perfume of the secretaries. Everything.

Yet, he caught himself almost smiling as he eased through the late afternoon traffic along the Coast. He nodded at an old acquaintance as he walked rather briskly down the Vieux Marche. He actually spoke to the receptionist, a woman he helped pay but whose last name he couldn't recall.

In the conference room, a crowd mingled; mostly lawyers from nearby offices, a judge or two, some courthouse types. It was after five, and the mood was loud and festive. Cigar smoke filled the air.

Rapley found the liquor on a table at one end of the room, and spoke to Vitrano as he poured a Scotch and tried to appear pleased. At the other end, a variety of bottled waters and soft drinks was being ignored.

"It's been like this all afternoon," Vitrano said as they looked at the crowd and listened to the happy talk. "Soon as word got out, this place started hopping."

The Patrick news raced through the legal community along the Coast in a matter of minutes. Lawyers thrive on gossip, tend even to embellish it, and repeat it with amazing rapidity. Rumors were heard, collected, invented. He weighs a hundred and thirty pounds and speaks five languages. The money was found. The money is gone forever. He lived in near poverty. Or was it a mansion? He lived alone. He has a new wife and three kids. They know where the money is. They haven't a clue.

All rumors eventually got back to the money. As the friends and the curious gathered in the conference room and chatted about this and that, everything drifted back to the money. Secrets were scarce among this crowd. For years now everyone knew the firm lost one third of ninety million. And the remotest chance of collecting that money brought in the friends and the curious for a drink or two and a story or a rumor and an update and the inevitable, "Damn, I hope they find the money."

Rapley disappeared into the crowd with his second drink. Bogan slugged down sparkling water and chatted with a judge. Vitrano worked the crowd and confirmed or denied as much as possible. Havarac huddled in a corner with an aging court reporter who suddenly found him cute.

The liquor flowed as night fell. Hopes were raised and raised as the gossip got recycled.

PATRICK essentially *was* the evening news on the Coast station. It reported little else. There were Mast and Parrish staring grimly at the bank of microphones as if they'd been whipped and dragged there against their wills. There was a close-up of the front door of the law office, with no comments from anyone inside. There was a drippy little chronicle from Patrick's gravesite, complete with brooding possibilities of what may have happened to the poor soul whose ashes were buried down there. There was a flashback to the fiery crash four years earlier, with shots of the site and the burned hulk of Mr. Patrick Lanigan's Chevy Blazer. No comments from the wife, the FBI, the Sheriff. No comments from the players, but lots of wild speculation from the reporters.

The news also played well in New Orleans, Mobile, Jackson, and even Memphis. CNN picked it up mid-evening, and ran it nationally for an hour before sending it abroad. It was such an irresistible story.

It was almost 7 A.M., Swiss time, when Eva saw it in her hotel room. She had fallen asleep with the TV on sometime after midnight, and had slept on and off throughout the night, waiting as long as possible for news of Patrick before drifting away. She was tired and scared. She wanted to go home but knew she couldn't.

Patrick was alive. He had promised her a hundred times they would never kill him if and when they found him. For the first time, she believed him.

How much had he told them? That was the question.

How badly was he hurt? How much did they get from him?

She whispered a short prayer and thanked God that Patrick was still alive.

Then she made a checklist.

UNDER THE INDIFFERENT GAZE of two uniformed guards, and with the feeble assistance of Luis, his ancient Puerto Rican orderly, Patrick shuffled down the hallway in his bare feet and baggy white military boxer shorts. His wounds needed air—no clothing or bandages now. Just ointments and oxygen. His calves and thighs were painfully tender, and his knees and ankles quivered with each step.

He wanted to clear his head, dammit. He welcomed the pain from the open burns because it sharpened his brain. Only God knew what vile blend of chemicals had been pumped into his blood during the past three days.

The torture was a dense, horrible fog, but it was lifting now. As the chemicals broke down and dissolved and were flushed out, he began to hear his anguished screams. How much had he told them about the money?

He leaned on the windowsill in the empty canteen while the orderly fetched a soft drink. The ocean was a mile away, with rows of barracks in between. He was on some type of military base.

Yes, he'd admitted the money still existed, he remembered that because the shocks had ceased for a moment when this came out. Then he'd passed out, it seemed now, because there was a long break before he was awakened with cold water splashed in his face. He remembered how soothing the water felt, but they wouldn't allow him a drink. They had kept poking him with needles.

Banks. He'd almost given his life for the names of some lousy banks. With hot current running through his body, he had tracked the money for them from the moment he stole it from the United Bank of Wales in the Bahamas, onward to a bank in Malta, then to Panama, where no one could find it.

He didn't know where the money was once they'd snatched him. It still existed, all of it plus interest and earnings, he had most certainly told them that, he remembered now, remembered quite clearly because he had figured what the hell—they know I stole it, know I've got it, know it would be impossible to blow ninety million in four years—but he honestly didn't know precisely where the money was as his flesh melted.

The orderly handed him a soda and he said, *"Obrigado."* Thanks in Portuguese. Why was he speaking Portuguese?

There had been a blackout then, after the money trail stopped. "Stop!" someone had yelled from the corner of the room, someone he never saw. They thought they'd killed him with the current.

He had no idea how long he was unconscious. At one point he woke up blind; the sweat and drugs and the horrific screaming had blinded him. Or was it a blindfold? He remembered that now—thinking that maybe it was a blindfold because maybe they were about to implement some new, even more hideous means of torture. Amputation of body parts, maybe. And he lay there naked.

Another shot in the arm, and suddenly his heart raced away and his skin jumped. His buddy was back with his little play toy. Patrick could see again. So who's got the money? he asked.

Patrick sipped his soda. The orderly loitered nearby, smiling pleasantly, the way he did for every patient. Patrick was suddenly nauseous, though he'd eaten little. He was light-headed and dizzy, but determined to remain on his feet so the blood would move and maybe he could think. He focused on a fishing boat, far on the horizon.

They'd blasted him a few times, wanting names. He had screamed his denials. They taped an electrode to his testicles, and the pain soared to a different level. Then there were blackouts.

Patrick couldn't remember. He simply couldn't remember the last stage of his torture. His body was on fire. He was near death. He had called her name, but was it to himself? Where was she now?

He dropped the soda and reached for the orderly.

STEPHANO WAITED until one in the morning before leaving the house. He drove down his dark street in his wife's car. He waved at the two agents sitting in a van at the intersection. He drove slowly so they could turn around and follow him. By the time he crossed the Arlington Memorial Bridge, there were at least two cars trailing.

The little convoy slid through empty streets until it reached Georgetown. Stephano held the advantage of knowing where he was going. He took a sudden right off K Street on to Wisconsin, then another on M. He parked illegally, and quickly, and walked half a block to a Holiday Inn.

He took the elevator to the third floor, where Guy was waiting in a suite. Back in the United States for the first time in months, he'd slept little in three days. Stephano couldn't have cared less.

There were six tapes, all labeled and neatly arranged, sitting on a table next to a battery-operated player. "The rooms next door are empty," Guy said, pointing in both directions. "So you can listen at full volume."

"It's nasty, I take it," Stephano said, staring at the tapes.

"Pretty sick. I'll never do it again."

"You can leave now."

"Good. I'm down the hall if you need me."

Guy left the room. Stephano made a call, and a minute later Benny Aricia knocked on the door. They ordered black coffee, and spent the rest of the night listening to Patrick scream in the jungles of Paraguay.

It was Benny's finest hour.

Eight

TO SAY it was Patrick's day in the papers would be an understatement. The Coast morning daily ran *nothing* on the front page but Patrick.

LANIGAN BACK FROM THE DEAD

shouted the headline in thick block letters. Four stories with no less than six photos covered the front page and continued inside. He also played well on the front page in New Orleans, his hometown, as well as in Jackson and Mobile. Memphis, Birmingham, Baton Rouge, and Atlanta also ran photos of the old Patrick with small front-page stories.

Throughout the morning, two television vans kept a vigil outside his mother's home in Gretna, a New Orleans suburb. She had nothing to say, and was protected by two vigorous ladies from down the street who took turns walking to the front door and glaring at the vultures.

The press also congregated near the front of Trudy's home on Point Clear, but were kept at bay by Lance, who sat under a shade tree with a shotgun. He wore a tight black tee shirt, black boots and trousers, and looked very much the part of a successful mercenary. They yelled banal questions at him. He only scowled. Trudy hid inside with Ashley Nicole, the six-year-old, who'd been kept home from school.

They flocked to the law office downtown and waited on the sidewalk. They were denied entrance by two beefy security guards who'd been hurriedly pressed into action.

They loitered around the Sheriff's office, and Cutter's office, and anywhere else they might pick up a scent. Someone got a tip, and they gathered at the Circuit Clerk's office just in time to see Vitrano, in his finest gray suit, hand the clerk a document which he described as a lawsuit the firm was filing against Patrick S. Lanigan. The firm wanted its money back, plain and simple, and Vitrano was perfectly willing to discuss this with the press for as long as he could hold an audience.

It would prove to be a litigious morning. Trudy's lawyer leaked the earth-shattering news that at 10 A.M. he would stride over to the clerk's office in Mobile and file a petition for divorce. He performed this task admirably. Though he'd filed a thousand divorces, this was the first time he'd done it in front of a TV news crew. He reluctantly agreed to be interviewed, at length. The grounds were abandonment, and the petition alleged all sorts of heinous sins. He posed for some pictures in the hallway outside the clerk's office.

Word spread quickly about yesterday's lawsuit, the one in which Northern Case Mutual sued Trudy Lanigan for the return of the two-point-five million. The court file was ransacked for details. The attorneys involved were contacted. A leak here, a casual word there, and before long a dozen reporters knew Trudy couldn't write a check for groceries without court approval.

Monarch-Sierra Insurance wanted its four million dollars back, plus interest and attorneys' fees, of course. Its Biloxi lawyers hurriedly threw together a suit against the law firm for receiving the policy limit and against poor Patrick for defrauding everyone. As was becoming customary, the press got tipped off, and copies of the lawsuit were in hand only minutes after its filing.

Not surprisingly, Benny Aricia wanted his ninety million from Patrick. His new lawyer, a flamboyant mouthpiece, had a different approach in dealing with the media. He called a press conference for 10 A.M., and invited everyone into his spacious conference room to discuss every insignificant aspect of his client's claim *before* he filed suit. Then he invited his new pals in the press corps to stroll with him down the sidewalk as he went to file it. He talked every step of the way.

The capture of Patrick Lanigan did more to create legal work on the Coast than any single event in recent history.

WITH THE Harrison County Courthouse bustling to a near frenzy, seventeen members of the grand jury quietly entered an unmarked room on the second floor. They had received urgent phone calls during the night from the District Attorney himself, T.L. Parrish. They knew the nature of this meeting. They got coffee and took their designated seats around the long table. They were anxious, even excited to be in the middle of the storm.

Parrish said hello, apologized for the emergency session, then welcomed Sheriff Sweeney and his chief investigator, Ted Grimshaw, and Special Agent Joshua Cutter. "Seems we suddenly have a fresh murder on our hands," he said, unfolding a copy of the morning paper. "I'm sure most of you have seen this." Everyone nodded.

Pacing slowly along one wall with a legal pad in hand, Parrish recited the particulars: background on Patrick; his firm's representation of Benny Aricia; Patrick's death, faked now, of course; his burial; most of the details they'd read in the morning paper Parrish had just laid on the table.

He passed around photos of Patrick's burned-out Blazer at the site; photos of the site the next morning without the Blazer; photos of the charred brush, soil, the burned weeds and trunk of a tree. And, quite dramatically and with a warning, Parrish passed around color eight by tens of the remains of the only person in the Blazer.

"We, of course, thought it was Patrick Lanigan," he said with a smile. "We now know we were wrong."

There was nothing about the blackened hulk to suggest it was human remains. No distinguishable body parts, except for a protruding pale bone which Parrish gravely explained came from the pelvis. "A human pelvis," he added, just in case his grand jurors got confused and thought that perhaps Patrick had murdered a hog or some other beast.

The grand jurors took it well, mainly because there was little to see. No blood, tissue, or gore. Nothing to get sick over. He, or she, or whatever it was, had come to rest in the right front passenger seat, which had been burned to the frame, like everything else.

"Of course it was a gasoline fire," Parrish explained. "We know that Patrick had filled his tank eight miles up the road, so twenty gallons exploded. Our investigator did, however, make a note that the fire seemed unusually hot and intense."

"Did you find the remains of any containers in the vehicle?" asked one grand juror.

"No. Plastic containers are typically used in fires such as this. Gallon milk jugs and antifreeze containers seem to be the favorite of arsonists. They don't leave a trace. We see it all the time, though rarely in a car fire."

"Are the bodies always this bad?" asked another.

Parrish answered quickly, "No, as a matter of fact they are not. I've never seen a corpse burned this badly, frankly. We would try to exhume it, but, as you probably know, it was cremated."

"Any idea who it is?" asked Ronny Burkes, a dockworker.

"We have one person in mind, but it's only speculation."

There were other questions about this and that, nothing of significance, just little inquiries served up in hopes of taking something from the meeting that the papers had left out. They voted unanimously to indict Patrick on one count of capital murder—murder committed in the perpetration of another crime, to wit, grand larceny. Punishable by death, by lethal injection up at the state penitentiary at Parchman.

In less than twenty-four hours, Patrick managed to get himself indicted for capital murder, sued for divorce, sued for ninety million by Aricia, plus punitive damages, sued for thirty million by his old law firm buddies, plus punitive, and sued for four million by Monarch-Sierra Insurance, plus another ten million in punitive, for good measure.

He watched it all, compliments of CNN.

□ □ □ □

THE PROSECUTORS, T.L. Parrish and Maurice Mast, once again stood glumly before the cameras and announced, jointly, though the feds had nothing to do with this indictment, that the good people of Harrison County, acting by and through the office of its grand jury, had now moved swiftly to lay charges against Patrick Lanigan, a murderer. They deflected the questions they could not answer, evaded the ones they could, and hinted strongly that more charges would follow.

When the cameras left, the two men met quietly with the Honorable Karl Huskey, one of the three circuit judges for Harrison County, and a close friend of Patrick's, before the funeral. Cases were supposedly assigned at random, but Huskey, as well as the other judges, knew how to manipulate the filing clerk so that he could receive, or not receive, any particular case. Huskey wanted Patrick's case, for now.

WHILE EATING a tomato sandwich in the kitchen, alone, Lance saw something move in the rear yard, near the pool. He grabbed his shotgun, eased from the house, around some shrubs on the patio, and spotted a chubby photographer squatting by the pool house, three bulking cameras dangling from his neck. Lance tiptoed barefoot around the pool house, gun at the ready, and crouched to within two feet of the man's back. He leaned forward, placed the gun near the man's head with the barrel pointed upward, and pulled the trigger.

The photographer lurched forward and fell on his face, screaming frightfully and floundering on top of his cameras. Lance kicked him between the legs, then again as he rolled over and finally got a glimpse of his assailant.

Lance ripped off the three cameras and threw them into the pool. Trudy was on the patio, horrified. Lance yelled at her to call the police.

Nine

I'M GOING to scrape the dead skin away now," the doctor said, gently probing a chest wound with a pointed instrument. "I really think you should consider some pain medication."

"No thanks," Patrick said. He was sitting on his bed, naked, with the doctor, two nurses, and the Puerto Rican orderly, Luis, huddled around him.

"It's gonna hurt, Patrick," said the doctor.

"I've been through worse. Besides, where would you stick me?" he asked, lifting his left arm. It was covered with purple and dark blue bruises where the Brazilian doctor had relentlessly poked him during his ordeal. His entire body was a rainbow of bruises and scar tissue. "No more drugs," he said.

"Okay. As you wish."

Patrick reclined and gripped the side rails to his bed. The nurses and Luis held his ankles as the doctor began scraping the raw, third-degree burns on his chest. With surgical scalpels, he pulled the dead skin off the wound, then cut it free.

Patrick flinched and closed his eyes.

"How about a shot, Patrick?" asked the doctor.

"No,." he grunted.

More scalpels. More dead skin.

"These are healing nicely, Patrick. I tend to think you might not need skin grafts after all."

"Good," he said, then flinched again.

Four of the nine burns were severe enough to be considered third degree; two on the chest, one on the left thigh, and one on the right calf. The rope burns on his wrists, elbows, and ankles were raw and covered with ointments.

The doctor finished in half an hour, and explained that it would be best to remain still, unclothed and unbandaged, at least for now. He applied a cool antibacterial salve, and again offered pills for the pain. Patrick again declined.

The doctor and the nurses left, and Luis loitered long enough to see them off. He closed the door behind them, and pulled down the blinds. From a pocket under his white orderly's jacket, he produced a disposable Kodak camera, with a flash.

"Start there," Patrick said, pointing to the foot of the bed. "Get the entire body, including my face." Luis stuck the camera to his head, fiddled with it, backed to the wall, then pushed the button. The camera flashed.

"Again, from there," Patrick directed.

Luis did as he was told. At first, he'd been reluctant to agree to this venture, said his boss might need to approve it. Living on the border of Paraguay, Patrick not only had perfected his Portuguese but he'd also learned to handle Spanish. He could understand almost everything Luis said. Luis had more trouble understanding Patrick.

The language of money prevailed, with Luis eventually comprehending the offer of five hundred U.S. dollars in return for his services as a photographer. He agreed to purchase three disposable cameras, take almost a hundred shots, get them developed overnight, and to hide them far from the hospital until further orders.

Patrick didn't have five hundred dollars on him, but he persuaded Luis that he was an honest man, regardless of what he might have heard, and that he would send the money as soon as he got home.

Luis wasn't much of a photographer, but then he didn't have much of a camera. Patrick coordinated every shot. There were close-ups of the serious burns on his chest and thigh, close-ups of his badly bruised limbs, full-length shots from every angle. They worked fast so they wouldn't get caught. It was almost time for lunch and another round of busy nurses with charts and incessant chatter.

Luis left the hospital on his lunch break and dropped the film off at a camera shop.

IN RIO, Osmar convinced a low-paid secretary at Eva's law firm to accept a thousand dollars in cash in exchange for all the current in-house gossip. There wasn't much. Things were very quiet among the partners. But the phone records revealed two calls to the firm from a number in Zurich. It was a hotel, Guy determined from Washington, but no other information was available. The Swiss were so discreet.

Her partners had no patience with her disappearance. Their quiet gossip about her soon changed to daily meetings about what to do. She'd called once the first day, once the second, then no word. The mysterious client she had flown off to see could not be verified. Meanwhile, her legitimate clients were making demands and threats. She missed appointments, meetings, deadlines.

Finally, they decided to temporarily remove her from the firm, and deal with her later when she returned.

Osmar and his men stalked Eva's father until the poor man was unable to sleep. They watched his apartment lobby and followed him in traffic and along the busy sidewalks of Ipanema. There was talk of snatching him and roughing him up a bit, forcing him to talk, but he was careful and never allowed himself to be isolated.

ON HIS THIRD TRIP to her bedroom, Lance finally found the door unlocked. He entered quietly with another Valium and her favorite bottled sparkling water, from Ireland, four bucks a bottle, and he sat next to her on the bed without a word and held out the pill. She took it, her second in an hour, and she sipped the water.

The police car carrying the chubby photographer had left an hour ago. Two cops hung around for twenty minutes, asking their questions, apparently not anxious to press charges since it was private property, and the press had been told to stay away, the publication was a sleazy magazine from up North anyway. The cops seemed quite sympathetic, even respectful of the way Lance handled the situation. They were given the name of Trudy's attorney downtown in case charges were to be pressed. Lance threatened to press charges of his own if hauled into court.

Trudy snapped after the cops left. She threw cushions from a sofa into the fireplace as the nanny raced off with the child. She yelled obscenities at Lance because he was the nearest target. It was just too much—the news about Patrick, the lawsuit by the insurance company, the restraining order, the horde of vultures out front, and then Lance had caught a photographer by the pool.

But she was quiet now. He'd had a Valium too, and he sighed relief that she was under control. He wanted to touch her, to pat her on the knee and say something nice, but such gestures never worked on her in these situations. A wrong move and she would snap again. Trudy would cool down, but only on her own terms.

Trudy reclined on the bed, closed her eyes, placed the back of her wrist on her forehead. The room was dark, like the rest of the house—blinds and shades pulled tight, lights off or dimmed. There were a hundred people loitering out by the road taking pictures and shooting film to be used with all those wretched Patrick stories. At noon, she'd seen her house on the local news, in the background as some silly orange-faced woman with large teeth gushed on about Patrick this and Patrick that, and the divorce filed by Patrick's wife that very morning.

Patrick's wife! The thought made her numb with disbelief. She hadn't been Patrick's wife for almost four and a half years. She'd buried him right properly, then tried to forget about him as she waited for the money. By the time she received it, he was a fading memory.

The only painful moment had come when she sat down with Ashley Nicole to inform the child, then barely two, that her father would no longer be around, that he had gone on to heaven where he would certainly be happier. The child was puzzled for a while, then shook it off as only a toddler can. No one was allowed to mention Patrick's name in the presence of the child. This was to protect her, Trudy had explained. She doesn't remember her father, so please don't try and make her.

Other than that one brief episode, she had shouldered the weight of widowhood with remarkable resiliency. She shopped in New Orleans, ordered health foods from California, sweated two hours a day in designer spandex, and treated herself to expensive facials and treatments. She had a nanny to keep the kid so she and Lance could travel. They loved the Caribbean, especially St. Barts with its nude beaches. They stripped and strutted with the French.

Christmas was in New York at the Plaza. January was in Vail with the rich and beautiful. May meant Paris and Vienna. They longed for a private jet like some of the wonderful people they'd met in the fast lane. A small, used Lear could be bought for a million, but for now was out of the question.

Lance claimed to be working on this idea, and she worried anytime he grew serious about business matters. She knew he smuggled dope, but it was just pot and hash from Mexico and there was little risk. They needed the income, and she liked him out of the house occasionally.

She didn't hate Patrick, not the dead one anyway. She just hated the fact that he wasn't dead, that he had been resurrected and was back to complicate things. She'd first met him at a party in New Orleans, during a period of time when she was pouting with Lance and looking for another husband, preferably one with money and promise. She was twenty-seven, four years out of a bad marriage and restless for stability. He was thirty-three, still single and ready to settle down. He had just accepted a job with a nice firm in Biloxi, which was where she happened to be living at the time. After four months of nonstop passion, they were married in Jamaica. Three weeks after the honeymoon, Lance sneaked into their new apartment and spent the night while Patrick was away on business.

She couldn't lose the money, that was for certain. Her lawyer would simply have to do something, find some loophole which would allow her to keep it. That's what he got paid to do. Surely the insurance company couldn't get the house, the furniture and cars and clothes, the bank accounts, the boat, the fabulous things she'd bought with the money. It just didn't seem fair. Patrick had died. She'd buried him. She'd been a widow now for over four years. That must count for something.

It wasn't her fault he was alive.

"We'll have to kill him, you know," Lance said in the semidarkness. He had moved to a cushioned chair between the bed and the window, his bare feet draped over an ottoman.

She didn't move, didn't flinch in the smallest way, but thought about it for a second before saying, "Don't be stupid." This she offered with little conviction.

"There is no alternative, you know that."

"We're in enough trouble."

She only breathed, her wrist still stuck to her forehead, eyes closed, perfectly still, and actually quite happy that Lance had broached the subject. She, of course, had thought about this within minutes of being told that Patrick was headed home. She had walked through various scenarios, each leading to the same inescapable conclusion: to keep the money, Patrick must be dead. It was, after all, an insurance policy on his life.

She couldn't kill him; that was a ridiculous notion. Lance, on the other hand, had lots of shadowy friends in dark places.

"You wanna keep the money, don't you?" he asked.

"I can't think about it now, Lance. Maybe later." Perhaps real soon. She couldn't seem eager or Lance would get too excited. As usual, she would manipulate him, string him along into some devilish plot until it was too late for *him* to back out.

"We can't wait too long, baby. Hell, the life insurance company's already got us choked."

"Please, Lance."

"There ain't no way around it. You wanna keep this house, the money, everything we've got, then he's gotta die."

She didn't speak or move for a long time, but his words delighted her soul. In spite of half a brain and many other flaws, Lance was the only man she'd ever loved. He was nasty enough to take care of Patrick, but was he smart enough not to get caught?

THE AGENT'S NAME was Brent Myers, from the office in Biloxi, sent by Cutter to make contact with their prize. He intro-

duced himself and flashed a badge at Patrick, who hardly acknowl-
edged it while reaching for the remote. "A pleasure," he said as he
pulled the sheets over his boxer shorts.

"I'm from the office in Biloxi," Myers said, genuinely trying to
be nice.

"Where's that?" Patrick asked, poker-faced.

"Yes, well, I thought we should meet and get to know each
other. We'll be spending some time together during the next few
months."

"Don't be so sure of that."

"Do you have a lawyer?"

"Not yet."

"Do you plan to hire one?"

"Absolutely none of your business."

Myers was obviously no match for a seasoned lawyer like Lanigan. He placed his hands on the railing across the foot of the bed,
and stared at Patrick with his best effort at intimidation. "Doc says
you might be ready to transport in two days," he said.

"So. I'm ready now."

"There's quite a party waiting on you in Biloxi."

"I've been watching," Patrick said, nodding at the television.

"Don't suppose you'd want to answer some questions."

Patrick snorted his contempt at this ludicrous suggestion.

"Didn't think so," Myers said, and took a step for the door.
"Anyway, I'll be escorting you home." He tossed a card on the
sheets. "Here's my hotel number, in case you want to talk."

"Don't sit by the phone."

Ten

SANDY McDERMOTT had read with great interest the news accounts of the amazing discovery of his old pal from law school. He and Patrick had studied and partied together for three years at Tulane. They had clerked for the same Judge after they passed the bar exam, and they had spent many hours in their favorite pub on St. Charles plotting their assault upon the legal world. They would build a firm together—a small but powerful firm of hard-charging trial lawyers with impeccable ethics. They would get rich in the process, and they would donate ten hours a month to clients who couldn't afford to pay. It was all planned.

Life intervened. Sandy took a job as an assistant federal prosecutor, primarily because the pay was good and he was a newlywed. Patrick got lost in a firm with two hundred lawyers in downtown New Orleans. Marriage eluded him because he worked eighty hours a week.

Their plans for their perfect little firm lasted until they were about thirty. They tried to meet for a quick lunch or a drink whenever possible, though the meetings and the phone calls happened less frequently as the years passed. Then Patrick escaped to a calmer life in Biloxi, and they hardly spoke once a year.

Sandy's big break in the suing game came when the friend of a cousin was maimed on an offshore oil rig in the Gulf. He borrowed ten thousand dollars, opened his own shop, sued Exxon and collected close to three million dollars, one third of which he kept. He was in business. Without Patrick, he built a nice little firm of three lawyers whose specialty was offshore injuries and deaths.

When Patrick died, Sandy actually sat down with his calendar and determined that it had been nine months since he'd talked to his buddy. Of course he felt lousy about this, but he was also realistic. Like most college friends, they had simply gone their separate ways.

He sat with Trudy through the ordeal, and he helped carry the casket to the grave.

When the money disappeared six weeks later, and the gossip started, Sandy had laughed to himself and wished his buddy well. Run Patrick run, he'd thought many times over the past four years, and always with a smile.

Sandy's office was off Poydras Street, nine blocks from the Superdome, near the intersection of Magazine, in a beautiful nine-teenth-century building he'd bought with an offshore settlement. He leased the second and third floors, and kept the bottom one for himself, his two partners, three paralegals, and half a dozen secretaries.

HE WAS VERY BUSY when his secretary entered his office with a grim face and said, "There's a lady here to see you."

"Does she have an appointment?" he asked, glancing at one of three daily-weekly-monthly planners on the edge of his desk.

"No. She says it's urgent. She's not leaving. It's about Patrick Lanigan."

He looked at her curiously. "She says she's a lawyer," the secretary said.

"Where's she from?"

"Brazil."

"Brazil?"

"Yes."

"Does she look, you know, Brazilian?"

"I guess."

"Show her in."

Sandy met her at the door and greeted her warmly. Eva gave her name as Leah, with nothing behind it.

"I didn't catch your last name," Sandy said, all smiles.

"I don't use one," she said. "Not yet, anyway."

Must be a Brazilian thing, Sandy thought. Like Pelé, the soccer player. Just a first name with no last.

He escorted her to a chair in the corner and sent for coffee. She declined and sat slowly. He glanced at her legs. She was dressed casually, nothing flashy. He sat across the coffee table from her and noticed her eyes—beautiful eyes, light brown, but very tired. Her long dark hair fell past her shoulders.

Patrick always had a good eye. Trudy was a mismatch, but she could certainly stop traffic.

"I'm here on behalf of Patrick," she said, haltingly.

"Did he send you?" Sandy asked.

"Yes, he did."

She spoke slowly, her words soft and low. The accent was very slight.

"Did you study in the States?" he asked.

"Yes. I have a degree in law from Georgetown."

That would explain the near perfect American-English.

"And you practice where?"

"In a firm in Rio. My work is in international trade."

She had yet to smile, and this bothered Sandy. A visitor from afar. A beautiful one at that; one with a brain and nice legs. He wanted her to relax in the warmth of his office. This was, after all, New Orleans.

"Is that where you met Patrick?" he asked.

"Yes. In Rio."

"Have you spoken to him since—"

"No. Not since he was taken." She almost added that she was desperately worried about him, but that would seem unprofessional. She was not to divulge much here; nothing about her relationship with Patrick. Sandy McDermott could be trusted, but he was to be fed information in small doses.

There was a pause as they both looked away, and Sandy instinctively knew that there were many chapters to this story he would never know. But, oh, the questions! How did he steal the money? How did he get to Brazil? How did he pick her up along the way?

And the big one: Where's the money?

"So what am I supposed to do?" he asked.

"I want to retain you, for Patrick."

"I'm available."

"Confidentiality is crucial."

"It always is."

"This is different."

Got that right. Different to the tune of ninety million bucks.

"I assure you that anything you and Patrick tell me will be held in the strictest of confidence," he said with a reassuring smile, and she managed a very slight one in return.

"You might be pressured to divulge client secrets," she said.

"I'm not worried about that. I can take care of myself."

"You might be threatened."

"I've been threatened before."

"You might be followed."

"By whom."

"Some very nasty people."

"Who?"

"The people chasing Patrick."

"I think they've caught him."

"Yes, but not the money."

"I see." So the money was still around; that was not surprising. Sandy, and everyone else for that matter, knew Patrick couldn't go through such a fortune in four years. But how much was left?

"Where is the money?" he asked, somewhat tentatively, not for a moment expecting an answer.

"You can't ask that question."

"I just did."

Leah smiled, and quickly moved on. "Let's settle some details. How much is your retainer?"

"For what am I being retained?"

"To represent Patrick."

"For which batch of sins? According to the newspapers, it'll take an entire army of lawyers to cover his flanks."

"A hundred thousand dollars?"

"That'll do for starters. Am I doing the civil as well as the criminal?"

"Everything."

"Just me?"

"Yes. He wants no other lawyer."

"I'm touched," Sandy said, and he meant it. There were dozens of lawyers Patrick could turn to now, bigger lawyers with more death penalty experience, connected lawyers on the Coast with local clout, lawyers in bigger firms with more resources, and, undoubtedly, lawyers who'd been closer friends than Sandy had been for the past eight years.

"Then I'm hired," he said. "Patrick's an old friend, you know."

"I know."

How much did she really know? he wondered. Was she more than a lawyer?

"I'd like to wire the money today," she said. "If you could give me wiring instructions."

"Of course. I'll prepare a contract for legal services."

"There are some other things Patrick is concerned about. One is publicity. He wants you to say nothing to the press. Never. Not a word. No press conferences unless approved by him. Not even a casual 'no comment.'"

"No problem."

"You can't write a book about it when it's over."

Sandy actually laughed, but she missed the humor. "I wouldn't think of it," he said.

"He wants it in the contract."

He stopped laughing, and scribbled something to that effect on the legal pad. "Anything else?"

"Yes, you can expect your office and home to get wired. You should hire a surveillance expert to protect you. Patrick is willing to pay for this."

"Done."

"And it will be best if we don't meet here again. There are people trying to find me, because they think I can lead them to the money. So we'll meet in other places."

There was nothing Sandy could say to this. He wanted to help, to offer protection, to question her about where she would go and how she would hide, but Leah seemed to have things very much under control.

She glanced at her watch. "There's a flight to Miami in three hours. I have two first-class tickets. We can talk on the plane."

"Uh, where might I be going?"

"You'll fly on to San Juan, to see Patrick. I've made arrangements."

"And you?"

"I'll go another direction."

SANDY ORDERED more coffee and muffins while they waited for the wiring instructions to be finalized. His secretary canceled his appointments and court appearances for the next three days. His wife brought an overnight bag to the office.

A paralegal drove them to the airport, and at some point along the way Sandy noticed she had no luggage, nothing but a small brown leather satchel, well used and quite handsome.

"Where are you staying?" he asked as they sipped a cola in an airport deli.

"Here and there," she said, looking out the window.

"How do I contact you?" he asked.

"We'll work that out later."

They sat next to each other in the third row in first class, and for twenty minutes after takeoff she said nothing as she skimmed a fashion magazine and he tried to read a thick deposition. Sandy didn't want to read the deposition—it could wait. He wanted to talk, to fire away the endless questions, the same questions everyone else wanted to ask.

But there was a wall between them, a rather thick one that went far beyond gender and familiarity. She had the answers, but she was perfectly willing to keep them to herself. He tried his best to match her coolness.

Salted peanuts and pretzels were distributed. They declined the complimentary champagne. Bottled water was poured. "So how long have you known Patrick?" he asked, cautiously.

"Why do you ask?"

"Sorry. Look, is there anything you can tell me about what's happened to Patrick in the past four years? I am, after all, an old friend. And now I'm his lawyer. You can't blame me for being curious."

"You'll have to ask him," she said, with a trace of sweetness, then returned to her magazine. He ate her peanuts.

She waited until they started their descent into Miami before speaking again. It came fast, clearly well rehearsed. "I won't see you again for a few days. I have to keep moving because of the people after me. Patrick will give you instructions, and for the time being he and I will communicate through you. Watch for the un-usual. A stranger on the phone. A car behind you. Someone hang-ing around your office. Once you're identified as his lawyer, you will attract the people who are looking for me."

"Who are they?"

"Patrick will tell you."

"You have the money, don't you?"

"I can't answer that question."

He watched the clouds get closer below the wing. Of course the money had grown. Patrick wasn't an idiot. He'd stashed it away in a foreign bank where pros handled it. Probably earned at least twelve percent a year.

There was no more conversation until they landed. They hur-ried through the terminal to catch his flight to San Juan. She shook his hand firmly, and said, "Tell Patrick I'm fine."

"He'll ask where you are."

"Europe."

He watched her disappear into the mass of hustling travelers, and as he did he envied his old friend. All that money. A gorgeous lady with exotic charm and class.

A boarding call woke him up. He shook his head and asked himself how he could envy a man who now faced the possibility of spending the next ten years on death row waiting to be executed. And a hundred hungry lawyers anxious to peel away his skin in search of the money.

Envy! He took his seat, first class again, and began to feel the magnitude of representing Patrick.

EVA TOOK A CAB back to the trendy hotel on South Beach where she had spent the night. She would be there for a few days, depending on what happened in Biloxi. Patrick had told her to move around, and not to stay in one place more than four days. She was registered under the name of Leah Pires, and now had a gold credit card issued to her in that name. Her address was in São Paulo.

She quickly changed and went to the beach. It was mid-afternoon, the beach was crowded, and that suited her fine. Her beaches in Rio were crowded, but there were always friends around. Now she was a stranger, another nameless beauty in a small bikini baking in the sun. She wanted to go home.

Eleven

I T TOOK SANDY an hour to bully his way through the outer walls of the Navy base. His new client had not made things easy. No one seemed to know he was expected. He was forced to rely upon the attorney's usual repertoire: threats of instantaneous lawsuits, threats of ominous phone calls to senators and others in high places, and loud and angry complaints of all sorts of rights violations. He made it to the hospital office at dark, and hit another line of defense. But this time a nurse simply called Patrick.

His room was dark, lit only by the bluish light of the muted television hanging high in a corner—a soccer game from Brazil. The two old pals shook hands gently. They had not seen each other in six years. Patrick kept a sheet pulled to his chin, hiding his wounds. For the moment, the soccer game seemed more important than serious conversation.

If Sandy was hoping for a warm reunion, he quickly adjusted to a subdued one. While trying not to stare, he studied Patrick's face. It was thin, almost gaunt, with a newly squared chin and a sharper nose. He could pass for someone else, but for the eyes. And the voice was unmistakable.

"Thanks for coming," Patrick said. All of his words were very soft, as if the act of speaking required great effort and thought.

"Sure. Didn't have much of a choice, you know. Your friend is very persuasive."

Patrick closed his eyes and bit his tongue. He said a quick prayer of thanks. She was out there and she was fine.

"How much did she pay you?" he asked.

"A hundred thousand."

"Good," Patrick said, and then said no more. A long pause, and Sandy slowly realized that their conversations would be built around long silent intervals.

"She's fine," he said. "She's a beautiful woman. She's smart as hell and fully in control of whatever she's supposed to be in control of. In case you're wondering."

"That's nice."

"When was the last time you saw her?"

"Couple of weeks. I've lost track of time."

"Is she the wife, girlfriend, mistress, hooker—"

"Lawyer."

"Lawyer?"

"Yes, lawyer." Sandy was amused by this. Patrick shut down again, no words, no movement anywhere under the sheet. Minutes passed. Sandy took a seat in the only chair, content to wait for his friend. Patrick was reentering an ugly world where the wolves were waiting, and if he wanted to lie there and stare at the ceiling then that was fine with Sandy. They would have lots of time to talk. And no shortage of topics.

He was alive, and right now nothing else mattered. Sandy amused himself by recalling images of the funeral and burial, of the casket being lowered on a cold and cloudy day, of the priest's last words and Trudy's controlled sobs. It was downright funny, to think that old Patrick had been hiding in a tree not far away watching them grieve, as had been reported for three days now.

He laid low somehow, then snatched the money. Some men crack up when they near forty. The midlife crisis drives them to a new wife, or back to college. Not old Patrick. He celebrated his angst by killing himself, stealing ninety million dollars, and disappearing.

The real dead body in the car suddenly erased the humor, and Sandy wanted to talk. "There's quite a welcome committee back home, Patrick," he said.

"Who's the chairman?"

"Hard to say. Trudy filed for divorce two days ago, but that's the least of your problems."

"You're right about that. Let me guess, she wants half of the money."

"She wants many things. The grand jury has indicted you for capital murder. State not federal."

"I've watched it on television."

"Good. So you know about all the lawsuits."

"Yeah. CNN has been quite diligent in keeping me up to date."

"You can't blame them, Patrick. It's such a wonderful story."

"Thanks."

"When do you want to talk?"

Patrick rolled to his side and gazed past Sandy. There was nothing to look at but the wall, painted antiseptic white, but he wasn't looking at it. "They tortured me, Sandy," he said, his voice even quieter, and breaking.

"Who?"

"They taped wires to my body and shot current through me until I talked."

Sandy stood and walked to the edge of the bed. He placed his hand on Patrick's shoulder. "What did you tell them?"

"I don't know. I can't remember everything. They were shooting drugs in me. Here, look." He lifted his left arm so Sandy could inspect the bruises.

Sandy found a switch and flipped on the table lamp so he could see. "Good Lord," he said.

"They kept on about the money," Patrick said. "I blacked out, then I came to and they shocked some more. I'm afraid I told them about the girl, Sandy."

"The lawyer?"

"Yeah, the lawyer. What name did she give you?"

"Leah."

"Okay, good. Her name is Leah then. I might have told them about Leah. In fact, I'm almost certain I did."

"Told who, Patrick?"

He closed his eyes and grimaced as the pain returned to his legs.

The muscles were still raw and the cramping had begun. He gently rolled again and rested on his back. He pulled the sheet down to his waist. "Look, Sandy," he said, waving his hand across the two nasty burns on his chest. "Here's the proof."

Sandy leaned a bit closer and inspected the evidence—the red sores surrounded by shaved skin. "Who did this?" he asked again.

"I don't know. A bunch of people. There was a whole room full of them."

"Where?"

Patrick felt sorry for his friend. He was so eager to know what had happened, and not just about the torture. Sandy, as well as the rest of the world, wanted the irresistible details. It was indeed a wonderful story, but he wasn't sure how much he could tell. No one knew the details of the car crash that burned John Doe. But he could tell his lawyer and friend about his seizure and torture. He shifted his weight again and pulled the sheet up to his neck. Drug free for two days now, he was coping with the pain and trying mightily to avoid more injections. "Pull that chair closer and take a seat, Sandy. And turn off that switch. The light bothers me."

Sandy hurriedly followed orders. He sat as close to the bed as possible. "This is what they did to me, Sandy," Patrick said, in the semidarkness. He started in Ponta Porã, with the jogging and the small car with a flat tire, and told the entire story of how they grabbed him.

ASHLEY NICOLE was twenty-five months old when her father was buried. She was too young to remember Patrick. Lance was the only man who lived in the house, the only man she'd ever seen with her mom. He took her to school occasionally. They sometimes ate dinner as a family.

After the funeral, Trudy hid all photos and other evidence of her life with Patrick. Ashley Nicole had never heard his name mentioned.

But after three days of reporters camping on their street, the child naturally was asking questions. Her mother was acting strange. There was so much tension around the house that even a six-year-old could feel it. Trudy waited until Lance left for a visit with the lawyer, then she sat her daughter on her bed for a little chat.

She began by admitting that she had been married before. Actually, she had been married twice before, but she figured Ashley Nicole wouldn't need to know about the first husband until she was much older. The second husband was the issue for the moment.

"Patrick and I were married for four years, and then he did a very bad thing."

"What?" Ashley Nicole asked, wide-eyed and absorbing more than Trudy wanted.

"He killed a man, and he made it look like, well, there was a big car wreck, you see, a big fire, and it was Patrick's car, and the police found a body inside the car, once the fire was out, and the police figured it was Patrick. Everybody did. Patrick was gone, burned up in his car, and I was very sad. He was my husband. I loved him dearly, and he was suddenly gone. We buried him in the cemetery. Now, four years later, they found Patrick off hiding on the other side of the world. He ran away and hid."

"Why?"

"Because he stole a bunch of money from his friends, and since he's a very bad man he wanted to keep all of this money for himself."

"He killed a man and he stole money."

"That's right, honey. Patrick is not a nice person."

"I'm sorry you were married to him, Mommy."

"Yes. But look, honey, there's something you need to understand. You were born when Patrick and I were married." She let the words drift through the air, and watched the little eyes to see if she caught the message. Evidently not. She squeezed Ashley Nicole's hand, and said, "Patrick is your father."

She looked blankly at her mother, the wheels turning rapidly in her head. "But I don't want him to be—"

"I'm sorry, honey. I was gonna tell you when you were much older, but Patrick is about to come back now, and it's important for you to know."

"What about Lance? Isn't he my father?"

"No. Lance and I are just together, that's all." Trudy had never allowed her to refer to Lance as her father. And Lance, for his part, had never shown the slightest interest in approaching the arena of fatherhood. Trudy was a single mom. Ashley Nicole had no father. This was perfectly common and acceptable.

"Lance and I have been friends for a long time," Trudy said, keeping the initiative and trying to prevent a thousand questions. "Very close friends. He loves you very much, but he is not your father. Not your real father anyway. Patrick, I'm afraid, is your real father, but I don't want you to worry about him."

"Does he want to see me?"

"I don't know, but I'll fight forever to keep him away from you. He is a very bad person, honey. He left you when you were two years old. He left me. He stole a bunch of money and disappeared. He didn't care about us then, and he doesn't care about us now. He wouldn't be coming back if they hadn't caught him. We would never have seen him again. So don't worry about Patrick and what he might do."

Ashley Nicole crawled across the end of the bed and cuddled in her mother's lap. Trudy squeezed and patted her. "It's going to be all right, honey. I promise. I hated to tell you this, but with all those reporters out there and all the stuff on television, well, I just thought it best."

"Why are those people out there?" she asked, clutching her mother's arms.

"I don't know. I wish they would leave."

"What do they want?"

"Pictures of you. Pictures of me. Pictures they can put in the newspapers when they talk about Patrick and all the bad things he's done."

"So they're out there because of Patrick?"

"Yes, honey."

She turned and looked at Trudy square in the eyes, and said, "I hate Patrick."

Trudy shook her head as if the child were naughty, then she clutched her tightly, and smiled.

□ □ □ □

LANCE WAS BORN and raised on Point Cadet, an old fishing community on a small peninsula jutting into the Bay of Biloxi. The Point was a working neighborhood where the immigrants landed and the shrimpers lived. He grew up in the streets on the Point, and still had many friends there, one of whom was Cap. It was Cap who had been behind the wheel of the van loaded with marijuana when the narcs stopped them. They had awakened Lance, who'd been asleep with his shotgun amid the thick blocks of cannabis. Cap and Lance had used the same lawyer, received the same sentence, and at nineteen been sent away together.

Cap ran a pub and loan-sharked money to cannery workers. Lance met him for a drink in the rear of the pub, something they tried to do at least once a month, though Cap saw less and less of Lance now that Trudy had become wealthy and they had moved to Mobile. His friend was troubled. Cap had read the papers, had in fact been waiting for Lance to appear with a long face, looking for a sympathetic ear.

They caught up on the gossip over beer—who had won how much at the casinos, where the newest crack source was, who was being shadowed by the DEA—the usual idle chitchat of small-time Coast crooks still dreaming of riches.

Cap despised Trudy, and in the past he had often laughed at Lance for trailing behind her wherever she might go. "So how's the whore?" he asked.

"She's fine. Worried, you know, since they've caught him."

"She oughta be worried. How much life insurance did she collect?"

"Coupla mill."

"Paper said two point five. Way that bitch spends it, though, I'm sure there ain't much left."

"It's safe."

"Safe my ass. Paper said she's already been sued by the life insurance company."

"We got lawyers too."

"Yeah, but you ain't here 'cause you got lawyers, Lance, are you? You're here 'cause you need help. Lawyers can't do what she needs."

Lance smiled and sipped his beer. He lit a cigarette, something he could never do around Trudy. "Where's Zeke?"

"That's exactly what I figured," Cap said angrily. "She gets in trouble, her money is threatened, and so she sends you down here looking for Zeke or some other klutz you can grease to do something stupid. He gets caught. You get caught. You take the fall and she forgets your name. You're a dumbass, Lance, you know that."

"Yeah, I know. Where's Zeke?"

"In jail."

"Where?"

"Texas. Feds got him running guns. You're stupid, you know that. Don't do this. When they bring your guy back, there'll be cops crawling all around him. They'll lock him away some place, his mother can't even get near him. There's serious money at stake here, Lance. They gotta protect this guy until he breaks and tells where he's buried it, you know. You try to hit him, and you'll kill half a dozen cops. And die tryin'."

"Not if it's done right."

"And I suppose you know how to do it. Could that be because you ain't ever done it before? When did you get so damned smart?"

"I can find the right people."

"For how much?"

"Whatever it takes."

"You got fifty grand?"

"Yeah."

Cap took a deep breath and glanced around his pub. Then he leaned forward on his elbows and glared at his friend. "Lemme tell you why it's a bad idea, Lance. You never were too bright, you know. Girls always liked you because they think you're cute, but thinking was never your strong suit."

"Thanks, pal."

"Everybody wants this guy alive. Think about it. Everybody. Feds. The lawyers. The cops. The guy whose money got stolen. Everybody. Except, of course, that fleabag who lets you live in her house. She needs him dead. If you pull this, and somehow knock him off, the cops go straight to her. She, of course, will be completely innocent because you'll be there to take the fall. That's what little stud puppies are for. He's dead. She keeps the money, which you and I know is the only thing that matters to her, and you go back to Parchman because you've got a record, remember? For the rest of your life. She won't even write you."

"Can we get it done for fifty?"

"We?"

"Yeah. Me and you."

"I can give you a name, that's all. I'm not touching this. It won't work, and there's nothing in it for me."

"Who is it?"

"A guy from New Orleans. He hangs around here some."

"Can you make the call?"

"Yeah, but that's it. And remember, I told you not to mess with this."

Twelve

EVA LEFT MIAMI on a flight to New York where she boarded the Concorde and flew to Paris. The Concorde was an extravagance, but she now considered herself to be a wealthy woman. From Paris to Nice, and from there across the countryside by car to Aix-en-Provence, a journey she and Patrick had made almost one year earlier. It was the only time he'd left Brazil since he'd arrived. He was terrified of crossing borders, even with a perfect new phony passport.

Brazilians love all things French, and virtually all with education know the language and culture. They had taken a suite at the Villa Gallici, a beautiful inn on the edge of town, and spent a week strolling the streets, shopping, eating, and occasionally venturing into the villages between Aix and Avignon. They also spent a lot of time in their room, like newlyweds. Once, after too much wine, Patrick referred to it as their honeymoon.

SHE FOUND a smaller room at the same hotel, and after a nap had tea on the patio in her bathrobe. Later, she dressed in jeans and took a casual walk into town, to the Cours Mirabeau, the main avenue of Aix. She sipped a glass of red wine at a crowded sidewalk café and watched the college kids parade back and forth. She envied the young lovers strolling aimlessly hand in hand, nothing to worry about. She and Patrick had made these walks, arm in arm, whispering and laughing as if the shadows behind him had vanished.

It was in Aix, during the only week they had ever spent together without interruption, that she first realized how little he slept. Regardless of when she awoke, he was already awake, lying still and quiet and staring at her as if she were in danger. A table lamp was on. The room would be dark when she fell asleep, but a light would be on when she awoke. He would turn it off, rub her gently until she fell asleep, then sleep himself for half an hour before turning the light on again. He was up well before dawn, and usually had read the newspapers and several chapters of a mystery by the time she ambled forth and found him on the patio.

"Never more than two hours," he answered when she asked how long he could sleep. He seldom napped and never went to bed early.

He didn't carry a weapon or peek around corners. He wasn't overly suspicious of strangers. And he seldom talked about life on the run. Except for his sleeping habits, he seemed so perfectly normal that she often forgot he was one of the most wanted men in the world.

Though he preferred not to talk about his past, there were times in their conversations when it became unavoidable. They were together, after all, only because he had fled and re-created himself. His favorite topic was his boyhood in New Orleans; not the adult life he was running from. He almost never mentioned his wife, but Eva knew she was a person Patrick deeply despised. It had become a miserable marriage, and as it deteriorated he became determined to flee it.

He had tried to talk about Ashley Nicole, but the thought of the child brought tears to his eyes. His voice quit him, and he said he was sorry. It was too painful.

Because the past was not yet complete, the future was difficult to contemplate. Plans were impossible as long as shadows were moving back there somewhere. He would not allow himself to speculate on the future until the past was settled.

The shadows kept him awake, she knew that. Shadows he couldn't see. Shadows only he could feel.

□ □ □ □

THEY HAD MET in her office, in Rio, two years earlier, when he presented himself as a Canadian businessman who now lived in Brazil. He said he needed a good lawyer to advise him on import and taxation matters. He was dressed for the part in a handsome linen suit with a white starched shirt. He was lean and tanned and friendly. His Portuguese was very good, though not as good as her English. He wanted to speak in her language; she insisted on his. They had a business lunch that lasted three hours, with the languages switching back and forth, and both realized there would be others. Then there was a long dinner, and a barefoot walk on the beach at Ipanema.

Her husband was an older man who'd been killed in a plane crash in Chile. No children. Patrick, or Danilo, as he was at first called, claimed to be happily divorced from his first wife, who still lived in Toronto, their home.

Eva and Danilo saw each other several times a week during the first two months, as the romance flourished. Finally, he told the truth. All of it.

After a late dinner in her apartment, and a bottle of good French wine, Danilo confronted his past and bared his soul. He talked nonstop until the early hours of the morning, and went from a confident businessman to a frightened man on the run. Frightened and anxious, but extremely wealthy.

The relief was so forceful he almost cried, but caught himself. This was, after all, Brazil, and men simply did not cry. Especially in front of beautiful women.

She loved him for it. She embraced him and kissed him and cried when he couldn't, and promised to do everything in her power to hide him. He had given her his darkest, deadliest secret, and she promised to always protect it.

During the next weeks, he told her where the money was and taught her how to move it quickly around the world. Together, they studied offshore tax havens and found safe investments.

He had been in Brazil for two years by the time they met. He had lived in São Paulo, his first home there, and Recife and Minas Gerais and half a dozen other places. He had spent two months working on the Amazon, sleeping on a floating barge under a thick mosquito net, the insects so thick he couldn't see the moon. He had cleaned wild game killed by rich Argentines in the Pantanal, a mammoth preserve the size of Great Britain in the states of Mato Grosso and Mato Grosso do Sul. He had seen more of her country than she; he'd been to places she'd never heard of. He had carefully selected Ponta Porã as his home. It was small and remote, and in a land of a million perfect hiding places, Danilo decided Ponta Porã was the safest. Plus, it had the tactical advantage of being on the Paraguayan border—an easy place to run to if a threat occurred.

She didn't argue with this. She preferred that he stay in Rio, close to her, but she knew nothing about life on the run, and she reluctantly deferred to his judgment. He promised many times that they would be together someday. They occasionally met at the apartment in Curitiba; brief little honeymoons that never lasted much more than a few days. She longed for more, but he was unwilling to make plans.

As the months passed, Danilo—she never called him Patrick—became more convinced that he would be found. She refused to believe this, especially given the meticulous steps he took to avoid his past. He worried more; slept even less; talked more about what she should do in this scenario, or that one. He stopped talking about the money. His premonitions were haunting him.

SHE WOULD STAY in Aix for a few days, watching CNN International and reading what she could find in American newspapers. They would move Patrick shortly, take him home and put him in jail and file all sorts of hideous charges against him. He knew he would be locked up, but he'd assured her he would be fine. He would cope; he could handle anything as long as she promised to wait for him.

She'd probably return to Zurich and tidy up her affairs. Beyond that, she wasn't certain. Home was out of the question, and this weighed heavy on her mind. She had talked to her father three times, always calling from airport pay phones, always reassuring him she was okay. She just couldn't come home now, she explained.

She and Patrick would communicate through Sandy, but weeks would pass before she would actually see him.

HE CALLED for the first pill just before 2 A.M., after waking with a sharp pain. It felt like the voltage returning to his legs. And the cruel voices of his captors were taunting him. "Where's the money, Patrick?" they chanted like a demonic chorus. "Where's the money?"

The pill arrived on a tray carried by a lethargic night orderly who forgot to bring cold water. He demanded a glass, then swallowed the pill and washed it away with warm soda from a leftover can.

Ten minutes, and nothing happened. His body was covered with sweat. The sheets were drenched. The sores burned from the salt in the sweat. Another ten minutes. He turned on the television.

The men who had tied him down and burned him were still out there, looking for the money, no doubt fully aware of where he was at this moment. He felt safer in daylight. Darkness and dreams brought them back. Thirty minutes. He called the nurses' station, but no one answered.

He drifted away.

At six, he was awake when his doctor entered, smileless today, all business as he poked the wounds quickly, then declared, "You're ready to go. They have good doctors waiting for you where you're going." He scribbled in his chart and left without another word.

Thirty minutes later, Agent Brent Myers sauntered into the room with a nasty smile and a flash of the badge, as if he needed to practice its delivery. "Good morning," he said. Patrick didn't look at him, but said, "Couldn't you knock first?"

"Sure, sorry. Look, Patrick, I just talked to your doc. Great news, man, you're going home. You'll be released tomorrow. I've got orders to bring you back. We'll leave in the morning. Your government is giving you a special flight back to Biloxi on a military plane. Isn't that exciting? And I'll be with you."

"Could you leave now?"

"Sure. See you early in the morning."

"Just leave."

He bounced from the room and closed the door. Luis was next, arriving quietly with a tray of coffee and juice and sliced mangoes. He slid a package under Patrick's mattress, and asked if he needed anything else. No, Patrick said, thanking him softly.

An hour later, Sandy arrived for what he thought would be a long day of digging through the past four years and finding answers to his countless questions. The television went off, the shades opened, the room brightened up as the day began.

"I want you to go home, immediately," Patrick said. "And take these with you." He handed over the package. Sandy sat in the only chair, flipping through the photos of his naked friend, taking his time.

"When were these taken?" he asked.

"Yesterday." Sandy made a note of this on a yellow legal pad.

"By whom?"

"Luis, the orderly."

"Who did this to you?"

"Who has custody of me, Sandy?"

"The FBI."

"So, I think the FBI did it to me. My own government tracked me down, caught me, tortured me, and is now hauling me back. The government, Sandy. The FBI, Justice Department, and the locals—the D.A. and the rest of my welcoming party. Just look at what they've done to me."

"They should be sued for this," Sandy said.

"For millions. And quickly. Here's the plan: I'm leaving in the morning on some type of military flight to Biloxi. You can imagine the reception I'll get. We should take advantage of it."

"Take advantage?"

"Exactly. We should file our lawsuit late this afternoon so it'll be in the paper tomorrow. Leak it to the press. Show them two of the photos, the two I've got marked there on the back."

Sandy shuffled until he picked out the photos. One was a close-up of the burns on Patrick's chest, with his face visible. The other showed the third-degree burn on his left thigh. "You want me to give these to the press?"

"Only to the Coast paper. That's the only one I'm worried about. It's read by eighty percent of Harrison County, where I'm sure our jury will come from."

Sandy smiled, then chuckled. "You didn't sleep much last night, did you?"

"I haven't slept in four years."

"This is brilliant."

"No, but it's one of the few tactical advantages we can spring on those hyenas circling my carcass. We broadside them with this, and we soften up the sentiment a bit. Think of it, Sandy. The FBI torturing a suspect, an American citizen."

"Brilliant, just brilliant. We sue only the FBI?"

"Yes, keep it simple. Me versus the FBI, the government—for permanent physical and psychological injuries sustained during a brutal torture and interrogation session somewhere in the jungles of Brazil."

"Sounds wonderful to me."

"It'll sound even better when the press gets finished with it."

"How much?"

"I don't care. Ten million in actual damages, a hundred million in punitive."

Sandy scrawled notes and flipped to the next page. Then he stopped and studied Patrick's face. "It wasn't really the FBI, was it."

"No," Patrick said, "it wasn't. I was delivered to the FBI by some faceless thugs who've been chasing me for a long time. And they're still lurking out there somewhere."

"Does the FBI know about them?"

"Yes."

The room went silent, as Sandy waited for more and Patrick became tight-lipped. Nurses could be heard prattling in the hall-way.

Patrick shifted his weight. Three days on his back, and he was ready for a change of scenery. "You need to hurry home, Sandy.

We'll have plenty of time to talk later. I know you have questions, just give me some time."

"Okay, pal."

"File the lawsuit with as much noise as possible. We can always amend it later to bring in the real defendants."

"No problem. This won't be the first time I've sued the wrong defendants."

"It's strategy. A little sympathy won't hurt."

Sandy placed his legal pad and the photos into his briefcase.

"Be careful," Patrick said. "As soon as you're identified as my lawyer, you'll attract all sorts of strange and nasty people."

"The press?"

"Yeah, but not exactly what I had in mind. I've buried a lot of money, Sandy. There are people who'll do anything to find it."

"How much of the money is left?"

"All of it. And then some more."

"It may take that to save you, pal."

"I have a plan."

"I'm sure you do. See you in Biloxi."

Thirteen

THROUGH THE VAST WEB of leaks and sources, word came that yet another lawsuit would be filed late in the day, just before the clerk closed her office. The web had already been electrified with the confirmed reports that Patrick himself would be arriving around noon tomorrow.

Sandy asked the reporters to wait in the foyer of the courthouse while he filed the suit. He then distributed copies to the dozen or so bloodhounds gathered and jostling for position. Most were newspaper reporters. There were two minicams. One radio station.

At first, it appeared to be just another lawsuit, filed by another lawyer anxious to see his face in print. Things changed dramatically when Sandy announced he represented Patrick Lanigan. The crowd grew and bunched together—curious office clerks, local lawyers, even a janitor stopped to listen. Calmly, he informed them that his client was filing suit against the FBI for physical abuse and torture.

Sandy took his time with the allegations, then answered the barrage of questions thoughtfully, fully, looking directly at the cameras. He saved the best for last. He reached into his briefcase and removed the two color photos, now enlarged to twelve by sixteen inches, and mounted on foam board. "This is what they did to Patrick," he said dramatically.

The cameras lunged in for close-ups. The group teetered on the verge of unruliness.

"They drugged him, then stuck wires to his body. They tortured him until his flesh burned because he wouldn't, and couldn't, answer their questions. This is your government at work, ladies and gentlemen, torturing an American citizen. Government thugs who call themselves FBI agents."

Even the most jaded reporters were shocked. It was a splendid performance.

The Biloxi affiliate ran it at six, after announcing it with a sensational lead-in. Almost half the newscast was Sandy and the photos. The other half was Patrick's return tomorrow.

By early evening, CNN began running it every half-hour, and Sandy was the lawyer of the moment. The allegations were just too juicy to downplay.

HAMILTON JAYNES was enjoying a quiet drink with the boys in the lounge of a posh country club near Alexandria when he saw the news clip on a corner TV. He had played eighteen holes, during which he had forbidden himself from thinking about the Bureau and the countless headaches there.

Another headache had just found him. The FBI sued by Patrick Lanigan? He excused himself and walked to the empty bar where he punched numbers on his cell phone.

Deep inside the Hoover Building on Pennsylvania Avenue is a hallway lined with windowless rooms where technicians monitor television news broadcasts from around the world. In another set of rooms they listen to and record radio news programs. In another, they read magazines and newspapers. Within the Bureau, the entire operation is known simply as Accumulation.

Jaynes called the supervisor on duty in Accumulation, and within minutes had the full story. He left the country club and drove back to his office, on the third floor of the Hoover Building. He called the Attorney General, who, not surprisingly, had been trying to reach him. A vicious ass-chewing ensued, with Jaynes on the receiving end and being allowed to say little. He did manage to reassure the Attorney General that the FBI had absolutely nothing to do with the alleged abuse of Patrick Lanigan.

"Alleged?" asked the Attorney General. "I've seen the burns, haven't I! Hell, the whole world has seen the burns."

"We didn't do it, sir," Jaynes said calmly, armed with the knowledge that this time he was repeating the truth.

"Then who did?" the Attorney General snapped back. "Do you know who did?"

"Yes sir."

"Good. I want a three-page report on my desk at nine in the morning."

"It will be there."

The phone was hung up loudly on the other end, and Jaynes cursed and gave his desk a hard kick. Then he made another call, the effect of which was that two agents emerged from the darkness and stood before the front door of Mr. and Mrs. Jack Stephano.

Jack had watched the reports throughout the night, and was not surprised to get a reaction from the feds. As the story unfolded, he sat on the patio chatting with his lawyer on a cell phone. It was actually funny, he'd decided; the FBI getting blamed for acts committed by his men. And it was a brilliant move by Patrick Lanigan and his lawyer.

"Good evening," he said politely as he stood in the door. "Lemme guess. You're selling doughnuts."

"FBI, sir," one said, fumbling for his pocket.

"Save it, kid. I recognize you boys by now. Last time I saw you, you were parked down at the corner reading a tabloid and trying to duck behind your steering wheel. Did you honestly think you'd be doing such exciting work when you were in college?"

"Mr. Jaynes would like to see you," the second one said.

"Why?"

"Don't know. He told us to come get you. He wants you to ride with us to his office."

"So Hamilton is working late, is he?"

"Yes sir. Can you come with us?"

"Are you arresting me again?"

"Well, no."

"Then what exactly are you doing? I have lots of lawyers, you know. Wrongful arrest or detention, and you boys could get yourselves sued."

They looked at each other nervously.

Stephano was not afraid of meeting with Jaynes, or anybody else for that matter. He could certainly handle anything Jaynes could throw at him.

But he reminded himself that there were criminal charges pending against him. A little cooperation might help.

"Give me five minutes," he said, then disappeared inside.

JAYNES STOOD behind his desk holding a thick report and flipping its pages when Stephano entered. "Have a seat," he said abruptly, waving at the chairs opposite his desk. It was almost midnight.

"A pleasant evening to you, Hamilton," Stephano said with a grin.

Jaynes dropped the report. "What on earth did you do to that boy down there?"

"I don't know. I guess one of the Brazilian boys got a little rough. He'll survive."

"Who did it?"

"Do I need my lawyer here, Hamilton? Is this an interrogation?"

"I'm not sure what this is, okay? The Director is at home, on the phone, consulting with the Attorney General, who by the way is not taking this very well, and they call me every twenty minutes and peel off some more skin. This is serious stuff, okay, Jack? These allegations are hideous, and right now the whole country is looking at those damned pictures and wondering why we tortured an American citizen."

"I'm terribly sorry."

"I can tell. Now, who did it?"

"Some locals down there. A gang of Brazilians we hired when we got a tip he was there. I don't even know their names."

"Where'd the tip come from?"

"Wouldn't you like to know?"

"Yes, I would." Jaynes loosened his tie and sat on the edge of his desk, looking down at Stephano, who was looking up without the slightest trace of concern. He could bargain his way out of any trouble the FBI might send him. He had very good lawyers.

"I have a deal for you," Jaynes said. "And this just came down from the Director."

"I can't wait."

"We're prepared to arrest Benny Aricia tomorrow. We'll make a big deal out of it, leak it to the press and all, tell them how this guy who lost ninety million hired you to track down Lanigan. And when you caught him, you worked him over but still didn't find the money."

Stephano listened hard, but revealed nothing.

"Then we'll arrest the two CEO's—Atterson at Monarch-Sierra Insurance and Jill at Northern Case Mutual. Those are the other two members of your little consortium, as we understand it. We'll march into their fancy offices with storm troopers, cameras won't be far behind, and we'll haul them out in handcuffs and throw them in black vans. Lots of leaks to the media, you understand. And we'll make sure that it's well reported that these guys helped Aricia fund your little mission into Brazil to drag out Patrick. Think of it, Stephano, your clients will all be arrested and placed in jail."

Stephano wanted to ask just exactly how in hell the FBI identified the members of his little Patrick consortium, but then he figured it wasn't too difficult. They isolated the people who'd lost the most.

"It'll kill your business, you know," Jaynes said, feigning sympathy.

"So what do you want?"

"Well, here's the deal. It's quite simple. You tell us everything—how you found him, how much he told you, etc., everything. We have lots of questions—and we'll drop the charges against you and lay off your clients."

"It's nothing but harassment then."

"Exactly. We wrote the book. Your problem is that we can humiliate your clients and put you out of business."

"Is that all?"

"No. With a bit of luck on our end, you could also go to jail."

There were lots of reasons to grab this deal, not the least of which was Mrs. Stephano. She felt disgraced because word was out the FBI was watching her house at all hours. Her phones were bugged; she knew this for a fact because her husband made his calls in the backyard near the rosebushes. She was on the verge of a nervous breakdown. They were respectable people, she kept telling her husband.

By implying he knew more than he did, Stephano had placed the FBI precisely where he wanted them. He could get his charges dismissed. He could protect his clients. And, most importantly, he would enlist the considerable resources of the feds to track down the money.

"I'll have to talk to my attorney."

"You have until 5 P.M. tomorrow."

PATRICK SAW his ghastly wounds on a late edition of CNN, in full color, as his man Sandy waved the pictures around like a boxer showing the world his newly won belt. It was about halfway through an hour wrap-up of the day's stories. There was no official response from the FBI, said a correspondent who was poised outside the Hoover Building in Washington.

Luis happened to be in the room when the report ran. He froze, listening to it, looking from the television to the bed where Patrick sat smirking. Things connected quickly. "My pictures?" he asked in heavily accented English.

"Yes," Patrick replied, ready to laugh.

"My pictures," he repeated proudly.

THE STORY about the American lawyer who faked his death, watched his burial, stole ninety million from his firm and got caught four years later living quietly in Brazil made for good light reading in most of the Western world. Eva read the latest episode in an American paper while sipping coffee under a canopy at Les Deux Garçons, her favorite sidewalk café in Aix. It was raining, a steady mist that soaked the tables and chairs not far from her.

The story was buried deep inside the front section. It described third-degree burns but did not run the photos. Her heart broke and she put on sunglasses to hide her eyes.

Patrick was going home. Wounded and chained like an animal, he would make the one journey he always knew was inevitable. And she would go. She would linger in the background, hiding and doing what he wanted, and praying for the safety of both of them. She would roam her room at night, just like Patrick, asking herself what had become of their future.

Fourteen

FOR HIS RETURN HOME, Patrick chose a pair of aqua surgeon's scrubs, very baggy and loose-fitting because he wanted nothing to aggravate his burns. The flight would be non-stop, but still more than two hours, and he needed to be as comfortable as possible. The doctor gave him a small bottle of pain pills, just in case, and also a file with his medical records. Patrick thanked him. He shook hands with Luis and said good-bye to a nurse.

Agent Myers waited outside his door with four large uniformed Military Police. "I'll make a deal with you, Patrick," he said. "If you behave, no handcuffs and leg chains now. Once we land, though, I have no choice."

"Thanks," Patrick said, and began walking gingerly down the hallway. His legs ached from toe to hip, and his knees were weak from lack of use. He held his head high, shoulders back, and nodded politely to the nurses as he walked past. Down the elevator to the basement, where a blue van waited with two more MP's, armed and scowling at the empty cars parked nearby. A strong hand under the arm, and Patrick was helped up and onto the middle bench. An MP handed him a pair of cheap aviator sunglasses. "You'll need these," he said. "It's bright as hell out there."

The van never left the base. It moved slowly over blistering asphalt, through half-guarded checkpoints, never reaching thirty miles per hour. Not a word was spoken inside the van. Patrick looked through the thick shades and through the tinted windows at rows of barracks, then rows of offices, then a hangar. He had been there four days, he thought. Maybe three. He couldn't be sure because the drugs blurred the earlier hours. An air conditioner roared from the dash and kept them cool. He gripped his medical file, the only physical thing he owned at the moment.

He thought of Ponta Porã, his home now, and wondered if he had been missed. What had they done to his house? Was the maid cleaning it? Probably not. And what about his car, the little red Beetle he loved so much? He knew only a handful of people in town. What were they saying about him? Probably nothing.

What difference did it make now? Regardless of the gossip in Ponta Porã, the folks in Biloxi had certainly missed him. The prodigal son returns. The most famous Biloxian on the planet comes home, and how will they greet him? With leg chains and subpoenas. Why not a parade down Highway 90, along the Coast, to celebrate this local boy who made good? He put them on the map; he made their town famous. How many of them had beer shrewd enough to own ninety million dollars?

He almost chuckled at his own silliness.

What jail would they put him in? As a lawyer, he had, at various times, seen all the local jails—City of Biloxi, Harrison County, even a federal holding cell at Keesler Air Force Base in Biloxi. He wouldn't be that lucky.

Would he get a cell to himself, or share it with common thieves and crackheads? An idea hit. He opened the file and quickly scanned the doctor's release notes. There it was, in bold letters—

PATIENT SHOULD REMAIN HOSPITALIZED
FOR AT LEAST ANOTHER WEEK

God bless him! Why hadn't he thought of this before? The drugs. His poor system had been subjected to more narcotics in the past week than he'd taken in a lifetime. His lapses in memory and judgment could be blamed on the chemicals.

He needed desperately to get a copy of his release to Sandy so that a nice little bed could be prepared for him, preferably in a private room with nurses running back and forth. That was the incarceration he had in mind. Put ten cops by the door, he didn't care. Just fix him up with an adjustable bed and remote control, and by all means keep him away from the common criminals.

"I need to make a phone call," he said, past the MP's, in the general direction of the driver. There was no response.

They stopped at a large hangar with a cargo jet parked in front of it. The MP's waited outside, in the sun, while Patrick and Agent Myers went inside the small office and haggled over whether there existed a constitutional right for an accused to not only make a phone call to his attorney but also to fax along a document.

Patrick prevailed after calmly threatening all sorts of vile litigation against Brent, and the doctor's release instructions were faxed to the law office of Sandy McDermott in New Orleans.

After a long visit to the men's room, Patrick rejoined his escorts and slowly climbed the steps into the Air Force cargo plane.

IT LANDED at Keesler Air Force Base at twenty minutes before noon. Much to Patrick's surprise, and a little to his dismay, there were no festivities awaiting his arrival. No throng of cameras and reporters. No mob of old friends rushing forth to offer assistance in his hour of need.

The landing field had been sealed off for the moment by higher orders. The press had been excluded. A large group congregated near the front gate, a mile and a half away, and for good measure taped and photographed the plane as it flew over. They were greatly disappointed, too.

Frankly, Patrick wanted the press to see him as he emerged from the plane in his carefully selected surgeon's scrubs, and awkwardly limped his way down the steps to the tarmac, and then shuffled like a crippled dog in leg chains and handcuffs. It could have been a powerful image, the first seen by all those potential jurors out there.

As expected, the Coast's morning paper had run the story of his lawsuit against the FBI on the front page, as the lead story, with the pictures large and in color. Only the meanest of souls couldn't muster a trace of sympathy for Patrick, at least at this moment.

The other side—the government, the prosecutors, the investigators—had been softened by the blow. It was to have been a glorious day for law enforcement; the return of a master thief, and a lawyer at that! Instead, the local office of the FBI had its phones unplugged and doors locked to keep reporters out. Only Cutter ventured forth, and he did so secretively. It was his duty to meet Patrick as soon as he touched ground.

Cutter was waiting with Sheriff Sweeney, two Air Force officers from the base, and Sandy.

"Hello, Patrick. Welcome home," the Sheriff said.

Patrick extended his hands, cuffed at the wrist, and tried to shake hands. "Hello, Raymond," he answered with a smile. They knew each other well, a common acquaintance between local cops and local lawyers. Raymond Sweeney had been the chief deputy of Harrison County nine years earlier when Patrick arrived in town.

Cutter stepped forward to introduce himself, but as soon as Patrick heard "FBI" he turned his face and nodded at Sandy. A navy van, one remarkably similar to the van that had just deposited him at the plane in Puerto Rico, was nearby. They piled in, with Patrick in the back next to his lawyer.

"Where are we going?" Patrick whispered.

"To the base hospital," Sandy whispered back. "For medical reasons."

"Good job."

The van puttered along at a snail's pace, past a checkpoint where the guard lifted his eyes from the sports page just for a second, then down a quiet street with officers' quarters on both sides.

Life on the run was filled with dreams, some at night during sleep, real dreams, and some when the mind was awake but drifting. Most were terrifying, the nightmares of the shadows growing bolder and larger. Others were pleasant wishes of a rosy future, free of the past. These were rare, Patrick had learned. Life on the run was life in the past. There was no closure.

Other dreams were intriguing musings of the return home. Who would be there to greet him? Would the Gulf air feel and smell the same? When would he return, in what season? How many friends would seek him, and how many would avoid him? He could think of a handful of people he wanted to see, but he was not sure if they wanted to see him. Was he a leper now? Or a celebrity to be embraced? Probably neither.

There was a certain, very small comfort in the end of the chase. Horrendous problems lay ahead, but for now he could ignore what was behind. The truth was, Patrick had never been able to completely relax and enjoy his new life. Not even the money could calm his fears. This very day was inevitable; he'd known it all along. He had stolen too much money. A lot less, and the victims might not have been so determined.

He noticed small things as he rode along. The driveways were paved, which was quite rare in Brazil, at least in Ponta Porã. And the children wore sneakers as they played. In Brazil, they were always barefoot, the soles of their feet as tough as rubber. He suddenly missed his quiet street, Rua Tiradentes, with the groups of boys dribbling soccer balls in search of a game.

"Are you okay?" Sandy asked.

He nodded, still wearing the aviator shades.

Sandy reached into his briefcase and removed a copy of the Coast paper. The headline screamed,

LANIGAN SUES FBI FOR TORTURE AND ABUSE

The two photos consumed half the front page.

Patrick admired it for a moment. "I'll read it later."

Cutter sat directly in front of Patrick, and of course he was listening to his prisoner breathe. Conversation was out of the question, which suited Patrick fine. The van entered the parking lot of the base hospital, and stopped at the emergency entrance. They took Patrick through a service door, then along a hallway where the nurses were waiting for a quick inspection of their new patient. Two lab technicians stopped ahead of them, and one actually said, "Welcome home, Patrick." A real smartass.

No red tape here. No preadmission forms. No questions about insurance or who's paying for what. He was taken straight to the third floor and placed in a room at the end of the hall. Cutter had a few banal comments and instructions, as did the Sheriff. Limited phone use, guards by the door, meals in the room. What else can you say to a prisoner? They left, and only Sandy remained.

Patrick sat on the edge of his bed, his feet dangling. "I'd like to see my mother," he said.

"She's on her way. She'll be here at one."

"Thanks."

"What about your wife and daughter?"

"I'd like to see Ashley Nicole, but not now. I'm sure she doesn't remember me. By now, she thinks I'm a monster. For obvious reasons, I'd rather not see Trudy."

There was a loud knock on the door, and Sheriff Sweeney was back, now holding a rather thick stack of papers. "Sorry to disturb, Patrick, but this is business. I thought it best to get this over with."

"Sure, Sheriff," Patrick said, bracing for the onslaught.

"I need to serve these on you. First, this here is an indictment returned by the grand jury of Harrison County for capital murder."

Patrick took it and, without looking at it, handed it to Sandy.

"This here is a summons and a complaint for divorce, filed by Trudy Lanigan over in Mobile."

"What a surprise," Patrick said, as he took it. "On what grounds?"

"I haven't read it. This is a summons and complaint filed by a Mr. Benjamin Aricia."

"Who?" Patrick asked, in a flat effort at humor. The Sheriff didn't crack a smile.

"This is a summons and complaint filed by your old law firm."

"How much are they after?" Patrick asked, taking the summons and complaint.

"I haven't read it. This is a summons and complaint filed by Monarch-Sierra Insurance Company."

"Oh yes. I remember those boys." He passed it to Sandy, whose hands were now full while the Sheriff's were empty.

"Sorry, Patrick," Sweeney said.

"Is that all?"

"For now. I'll stop by the clerk's office in town to see if any more suits have been filed."

"Send 'em over. Sandy here works fast."

They shook hands, this time without the intrusion of cuffs, and the Sheriff left.

"I always liked Raymond," Patrick said, hands on hips, slowly bending at the knees. He made it halfway down before stopping and easing up. "A long way to go, Sandy. I'm bruised to the bone."

"Great. Helps our lawsuit." Sandy flipped through the papers. "Seems Trudy is really upset with you. She wants you out of her life."

"I've tried my best. What are the grounds?"

"Abandonment and desertion. Mental cruelty."

"Poor thing."

"Are you planning to contest it?"

"Depends on what she wants."

Sandy flipped another page. "Well, just scanning here, it appears she wants a divorce, full custody of the child with the termination of all your parental rights, including the right of visitation, all real and personal property jointly owned at the time of your disappearance—that's what she's calling it, your disappearance—plus, oh yes, here it is, a fair and reasonable percentage of the assets you may have acquired since your disappearance."

"Surprise, surprise."

"That's all she wants, for now anyway."

"I'll give her the divorce, Sandy, and gladly. But it won't be as easy as she thinks."

"What do you have in mind?"

"We'll talk about it later. I'm tired."

"We have to talk sometime, Patrick. Whether you realize it or not, we have many things to discuss."

"Later. I need to rest now. Mom will be here in a minute."

"Fine. By the time I drive, fight New Orleans traffic, park and walk, it takes two hours to get from here to my office. When, exactly, might you want to meet again?"

"I'm sorry, Sandy. I'm tired, okay? How about tomorrow morning? I'll get rested up, and we'll work all day."

Sandy relaxed and placed the papers in his briefcase. "Sure, pal. I'll be here at ten."

"Thanks, Sandy."

He left, and Patrick rested comfortably for about eight minutes before his room was suddenly filled with all sorts of health care professionals, an all-female team. "Hi, I'm Rose, your head nurse. We need to examine you. Can we take off your shirt here?" It was not a request. Rose was already pulling on the shirt. Two other nurses, equally as thick as Rose, appeared on each side and began to undress Patrick. They seemed to enjoy it. Another nurse stood ready with a thermometer and a box of other dreadful instruments. A technician of some variety gawked from the end of the bed. An orderly in an orange coat hovered near the door.

They had invaded as a team, and for fifteen minutes performed various tasks upon his body. He closed his eyes and simply took it. They left as fast as they had come.

PATRICK AND HIS MOTHER had a tearful reunion. He apologized only once, for everything. She lovingly accepted, and forgave him, as only a mother can do. Her joy at seeing him displaced any ill will and bitterness that had naturally crept up during the past four days.

Joyce Lanigan was sixty-eight years old, in reasonably good health with only high blood pressure to struggle with. Her husband, Patrick's father, had left her for a younger woman twenty years earlier, then promptly died of a heart attack. Neither she nor Patrick attended his funeral in Texas. The second wife was pregnant at the time. Her child, Patrick's half brother, killed two undercover narcotics officers when he was seventeen, and now sat on death row in Huntsville, Texas. This little bit of dirty family laundry was unknown in New Orleans and Biloxi. Patrick had never told Trudy, his wife of four years. Nor had he told Eva. Why should he?

What a cruel twist. Both sons of Patrick's father were now charged with capital murder. One had been convicted. The other was well on his way.

Patrick was in college when his father left, then died. His mother adjusted badly to the life of a divorced middle-aged woman with no professional skills and no history of employment. The divorce settlement allowed her to keep the house and provided her with barely enough money to live on without having to find a job. She occasionally worked as a substitute teacher in a local elementary school, but she preferred to stay at home, puttering in the garden, watching soap operas, drinking tea with old ladies in the neighborhood.

Patrick had always found his mother to be a depressing person, especially after his father left, an event that didn't particularly bother him because he wasn't much of a father anyway. And he wasn't much of a husband either. Patrick had encouraged his mother to get out of the house, find a job, find a cause, live a little. She had a new lease on life.

But she enjoyed the misery too much. Over the years, as Patrick got busier and busier with his lawyering, he spent less time with her. He moved to Biloxi, married a woman his mother couldn't tolerate, and on and on.

HE ASKED about aunts and uncles and cousins, people he had lost contact with long before his death; people he had hardly thought of in the past four years. He asked only because he was expected to ask. For the most part, they were doing fine.

No, he did not want to see any of them.

They were anxious to see him.

Odd. They'd never been anxious to see him before.

They were very concerned about him.

Odd, too.

They chatted warmly for two hours, and the passage of time was quickly erased. She scolded him about his weight. "Sickly" was her word. She quizzed him about his new chin and nose, and his dark hair. She said all sorts of motherly things, then she left for New Orleans. He promised to keep in touch.

He had always promised that, she thought to herself as she drove away. But he'd rarely kept in touch.

Fifteen

OPERATING FROM A SUITE at the Hay-Adams Hotel, Stephano spent the morning playing telephone tag with harried corporate executives. It had been easy to convince Benny Aricia that he was about to be arrested, photographed, printed, and otherwise harassed by the FBI. Convincing egos like Paul Atterson at Monarch-Sierra Insurance and Frank Jill at Northern Case Mutual was another matter. Both were typical CEO's, serious white men with huge salaries and large staffs to keep away anything unpleasant. Arrests and prosecutions were for the lower classes.

The FBI proved quite helpful. Hamilton Jaynes dispatched agents to both headquarters—Monarch's in Palo Alto and Northern Case Mutual's in St. Paul—with instructions to call on both men and ask a bunch of questions about the search and capture of one Patrick Lanigan.

Both threw in the towel by lunch. Call off the dogs, they said to Stephano. The search is over. Cooperate fully with the FBI, and for heaven's sakes do something to get these agents out of our headquarters. It was very embarrassing.

And so the consortium unraveled. Stephano had kept it together for four years, and in doing so earned himself almost a million dollars. He'd spent another 2.5 million of his client's, and he could claim success. They'd found Lanigan. They had not found the ninety million, but it was still around. It had not been spent. There was a chance of recouping it.

BENNY ARICIA was in the suite with Stephano throughout the morning, reading papers, making calls of his own, listening as Stephano worked the phones. At one, he called his attorney in Biloxi and got the news that Patrick had arrived. And amid almost no fanfare. The local TV ran the story at noon, complete with a shot of the Air Force cargo plane roaring overhead as it landed at Keesler. That was as close as they were allowed. The local Sheriff confirmed that the boy was back.

He had listened to the torture tape three times, often stopping it to replay his favorite spots. Once, two days ago on a flight to Florida, he had listened to it with earphones as he sipped a drink in first class and smiled at the blood-curdling sounds of a man begging for mercy. But the smiles were rare for Benny these days. He was certain Patrick had told what he knew, and it wasn't enough. Patrick knew he would someday get caught; that's why he shrewdly placed the money with the girl, who then hid it from everyone, including Patrick. Brilliant. Nothing short of it.

"What will it take to find her?" he asked Stephano, as the two lunched on soup sent up by room service. The question had been asked many times already.

"What, or how much?"

"How much, I guess."

"Can't answer that. We have no idea where she is, but we know where she's from. And we know she'll likely surface somewhere around Biloxi, now that her man's there. It can be done."

"How much?"

"Just guessing, I'd say a hundred thousand, with no guarantees. Put up the money, and when it's gone, we quit."

"Any chance the feds will know we're still looking?"

"Nope."

Benny stirred his soup—tomatoes and noodles. Down one point nine million already, it seemed foolish not to give it one last shot. The odds were long, but the reward could be enormous. It was the same game he'd played for four years now.

"And if you find her?" he asked.

"We'll make her talk," Stephano said, and they exchanged grimaces at the unpleasant thought of doing to a woman what they'd done to Patrick.

"What about his lawyer?" Aricia finally asked. "Can't we bug his office, tap his phones, somehow listen in when he talks to his client. Surely they'll talk about my money."

"It's a possibility. Are you serious?"

"Serious? I got ninety million out there, Jack. Minus a third for those bloodsucking lawyers. Of course I'm serious."

"It could be tricky. The lawyer's not stupid, you know. And his client's a cautious fellow."

"Come on, Jack. You're supposed to be the best. You're certainly the most expensive."

"We'll do a preliminary—trail him for a couple of days, see his layout. There's no rush. His client isn't moving for a while. Right now I'm more concerned with getting the feds outta my hair. I need to do a few trivial things like reopen my office and get the bugs outta my phones."

Aricia waved him off. "How much will it cost me?"

"I don't know. We'll talk about it later. Finish your lunch. The lawyers are waiting."

Stephano left first, on foot, and waved politely to the two agents parked illegally on I Street, down from the hotel. He walked briskly to his lawyer's office, seven blocks away. Benny waited ten minutes and caught a cab.

They spent the afternoon in a conference room crowded with lawyers and paralegals. The agreements were faxed back and forth between the lawyers—Stephano's and the FBI's. Eventually both sides got what they wanted. The criminal charges against Stephano were dropped and would not be pursued against his clients. The FBI received his written promise to divulge everything he knew about the search and capture of Patrick Lanigan.

Stephano truly planned to tell most of what he knew. The search was over; thus there was no longer anything to hide. The interrogation had produced little, just the name of a Brazilian lawyer who had the money. Now she had vanished, and he seriously doubted the FBI had the time and desire to pursue her. Why should they? The money didn't belong to them.

And though he worked hard not to show it, he desperately wanted the FBI out of his life. Mrs. Stephano was severely rattled, and the pressure at home was enormous. If he didn't reopen his office quickly, he'd be out of business.

So, he planned to tell them what they wanted to hear, most of it anyway. He'd take Benny's money, what was left of it, and chase the girl some more, maybe get lucky. And he'd send a crew to New Orleans to watch Lanigan's lawyer. The FBI didn't need to know these little details.

SINCE THERE WASN'T an available square inch in the federal building in Biloxi, Cutter asked Sheriff Sweeney to find a spot at the county jail. Sweeney reluctantly agreed, though the idea of the FBI spending time in his offices was unsettling. He cleaned out a storage room and installed a table and some chairs. The Lanigan Room was christened.

There was little to store there. No one suspected murder when Patrick died, and so there was no effort at gathering physical clues, at least not for the first six weeks. When the money vanished, suspicions grew, but by then the trail was cold.

Cutter and Ted Grimshaw, the chief investigator for Harrison County, carefully examined and inventoried their meager evidence. There were ten large color photos of the burned-out Chevy Blazer, and they tacked these on one wall. They had been taken by Grimshaw.

The fire had been extremely hot; now they knew why. Patrick no doubt had loaded the interior with plastic containers of gasoline. That would account for the melted aluminum seat frames, the blown-out windows, the disintegrated dashboard, and the scant remains of the body. Six photos were of the corpse, such as it was—a small pile of charred matter with half a pelvic bone protruding. It had come to rest on the floorboard of the passenger's side. The Blazer had flipped several times after it left the highway and barreled down a ravine. It burned on its right side.

Sheriff Sweeney had kept it for a month, then sold it for scrap with three other abandoned wrecks. Later, he wished he hadn't.

There were half a dozen photos of the site around the vehicle, trees and shrubs burned black. The volunteers had fought the fire for an hour before extinguishing it.

How convenient that Patrick wanted to be cremated. According to Trudy (and they had a typed statement given by her a month after the funeral), Patrick had suddenly decided he wanted to be cremated with his ashes buried in Locust Grove, the loveliest cemetery in the county. This decision was made almost eleven months before he disappeared. He'd even changed his will and included language directing his executor, Trudy, or in the event she died with him his alternate executor, Karl Huskey, to carry out the cremation. He also included specific details about his funeral and burial.

His excuse for doing this had been the death of a client who had not planned well. The family had fought viciously about how to bury the client, and Patrick had been pulled into the fray. He even made Trudy pick out her cemetery plot. She picked one next to his, but both knew she would quickly move it if something happened to him first.

The mortician later told Grimshaw that ninety percent of the cremating had been done in the Blazer. When he weighed the ashes after cooking the remains for an hour at two thousand degrees, the scales registered just four ounces, by far the smallest amount he'd ever registered. He could tell nothing about the body—male, female, black, white, young, old, alive or dead before the fire. There was simply no way. He didn't really try, to be honest about the whole thing.

They had no corpse, no autopsy report, no idea who John Doe was. Fire is the surest way to destroy evidence, and Patrick had done a splendid job of covering his tracks.

HE'D SPENT the weekend in an old hunting cabin near the small town of Leaf, up in Greene County, at the edge of the De Soto National Forest. He and a law school friend from Jackson had bought the cabin two years earlier with modest plans to make small improvements. It was quite rustic. They hunted deer in the fall and winter, and turkeys in the spring. With the ups and downs of his marriage, he was spending more and more weekends at the cabin. It was only an hour and a half away. He claimed to be able to work there. It was very remote and quiet. His friend, the co-owner, had all but forgotten about it.

Trudy pretended to resent his weekends away, but Lance was usually lurking nearby, just waiting for Patrick to leave town.

Sunday night, February 9, 1992, Patrick called to tell his wife he was leaving the cabin. He'd finished a complicated brief for an appeal, and he was tired. Lance lingered for another hour before easing into the darkness.

Patrick stopped at Verhall's Country Store on Highway 15 at the divide between Stone and Harrison counties. He bought twelve gallons of gas for fourteen dollars and twenty-one cents and paid for it with a credit card. He chatted with Mrs. Verhall, an older lady he'd become acquainted with. She knew many of the hunters who passed through, especially the ones who liked to linger and brag of their exploits in the woods, like Patrick. She said later that he was in good spirits, though he claimed to be tired because he had worked all weekend. She remembered thinking that this was odd. An hour later she heard the police and fire trucks race by.

Eight miles down the road, Patrick's Blazer was found engulfed in a raging fire at the bottom of a steep ravine, eighty yards from the highway. A truck driver saw the fire first, and managed to get to within fifty feet of it before his eyebrows were singed. He radioed for help, then sat on a stump and watched helplessly as it burned. The Blazer was on its right side with its top facing away, and so it was impossible to see if anyone was in the vehicle. It wouldn't have made any difference. A rescue was utterly impossible.

By the time the first county deputy arrived, the fireball was so intense it was difficult to distinguish the outline of the Blazer. The grass and shrubs began to burn. A small volunteer pumper arrived, but it was low on water. More traffic stopped, and soon a nice crowd stood mutely, watching and listening to the roar down below. Since the driver of the Blazer was not among them, everyone believed that he or she was in there getting incinerated along with everything else.

Two larger trucks arrived, and the fire was eventually extinguished. Hours passed as Sheriff Sweeney waited for things to cool. It was almost midnight when he first spotted a blackened clump of something he thought might be a body. The coroner was nearby. The pelvic bone ended the speculation. Grimshaw took his photographs. They waited for the corpse to cool even more, then collected it and placed it in a cardboard box.

The raised lettering and numerals on the license plates were traced by flashlight, and at 3:30 A.M. Trudy received the phone call that made her a widow. For four and a half years, anyway.

The Sheriff decided not to move the car during the night. At dawn, he returned with five of his deputies to comb the area. They found ninety feet of skid marks on the highway, and they speculated that perhaps a deer had run in front of poor Patrick, causing him to lose control. Because the fire had spread in all directions, any possible clues as to what might have happened were destroyed. The only surprise was the discovery of a shoe a hundred and thirty-one feet from the Blazer. It was a lightly worn Nike Air Max running shoe, size ten, and Trudy readily identified it as being Patrick's. She wept profusely when they showed it to her.

The Sheriff speculated that the vehicle rolled and flipped a few times as it crashed through the ravine, and perhaps in the midst of all this the body was thrown around inside. The shoe came off, got thrown out during a flip, etc. It made as much sense as anything else.

They loaded the Blazer on a flatbed truck and took it away. By late afternoon, what was left of Patrick had been cremated. His memorial service was the next day, and it was followed by a brief graveside service, the one he watched through binoculars.

CUTTER AND GRIMSHAW looked at the lonely shoe in the center of the table. Beside it were various statements taken from witnesses—Trudy, Mrs. Verhall, the coroner, the mortician, even Grimshaw and the Sheriff—all saying exactly what they were expected to say. Only one surprise witness came forward in the months after the disappearance of the money. A young lady who lived near Verhall's store gave a sworn statement in which she claimed to have seen a red 1991 Chevy Blazer parked beside the road, precisely near the point where the fire occurred. She saw it twice. Once on Saturday night, then about twenty-four hours later around the time of the fire.

Her statement was taken by Grimshaw at her home in rural Harrison County, seven weeks after Patrick's funeral. By then, the death was shrouded in suspicion because the money had disappeared.

Sixteen

THE DOCTOR was a young Pakistani resident named Hayani, who by nature was a caring and compassionate soul. His English was heavily accented, and he seemed content to simply sit and chat with Patrick for as long as the patient wanted. The wounds were healing fine.

But the patient was deeply troubled. "The torture was something I could never accurately describe," Patrick said, after they had been talking for almost an hour. Hayani had brought the conversation around to this topic. It was all over the papers, since the filing of the lawsuit against the FBI, and from a medical standpoint it was a rare opportunity to examine and treat one injured in such an awful manner. Any young doc would enjoy being this close to the center of the storm.

Hayani nodded gravely. Just keep talking, he pleaded with his eyes.

Today, Patrick was certainly willing to do so. "Sleep is impossible," he said. "Maybe an hour at the most before I hear voices, then I smell my flesh burning, then I wake up in a pool of sweat. And it's not getting better. I'm here now, home and safe, I guess, but they're still out there, still after me. I can't sleep. I don't want to sleep, Doc."

"I can give you some pills."

"No. Not yet, anyway. I've had too many chemicals."

"Your blood looks fine. Some residue, but nothing significant."

"No more drugs, Doc. Not now."

"You need some sleep, Patrick."

"I know, but I don't want to sleep. I'll get tortured again."

Hayani wrote something on the chart he was holding. A long silence followed in which both men occupied themselves with thoughts about what to say next. Hayani found it difficult to believe that this kind man was capable of killing another, and especially in such a ghastly way.

The room was lit only by a narrow ray of sunshine along the edge of the window. "Can I be honest with you about something, Doc?" Patrick asked, his voice even lower.

"Of course."

"I need to stay here as long as I can. Here, in this room. In a few days, they'll start making noises about moving me to the Harrison County Jail where I'll get a bunk in a small cell with two or three street punks, and there's no way I can survive."

"But why do they want to move you?"

"It's pressure, Doc. They have to slowly increase the pressure on me until I tell them what they want. They put me in a bad cell with rapists and drug dealers, and the message will be conveyed that I'd better start talking because that is what I'm faced with for the rest of my life. Prison, at Parchman, the worst place in the world. You ever been to Parchman, Doc?"

"No."

"I have. I had a client there once. It's hell, literally. And the county jail isn't much better. But you can keep me here, Doc. All you have to do is keep telling the Judge that I need to remain under your care, and I stay here. Please, Doc."

"Of course, Patrick," he said, then made one more entry on his chart. Another long pause as Patrick closed his eyes and breathed rapidly. Just the thought of jail and prison had upset him mightily.

"I'm going to recommend a psychiatric evaluation," Hayani said, and Patrick bit his lower lip to suppress a smile.

"Why?" he asked, feigning alarm.

"Because I'm curious. Do you object?"

"I guess not. When?"

"Perhaps in a couple of days."

"I'm not sure if I can do it so soon."

"There's no hurry."

"That's more like it. We shouldn't hurry anything around here, Doc."

"I see. Of course. Perhaps next week."

"Maybe. Or the week after."

THE BOY'S MOTHER was Neldene Crouch. She now lived in a trailer park outside Hattiesburg, but at the time of her son's disappearance she lived, with him, in a trailer park outside Lucedale, a small town thirty miles from Leaf. According to her recollection, her son had been missing since Sunday, February 9, 1992, precisely the same day Patrick Lanigan died on Highway 15.

But according to Sheriff Sweeney's records, Neldene Prewitt (her married name then) had first called his office on February 13, 1992, with the news that her son was missing. She was calling all the surrounding sheriffs, as well as the FBI and the CIA. She was quite disturbed and at times near hysterics.

Her son's name was Pepper Scarboro—Scarboro being the name of her first husband, Pepper's alleged father, though she'd never been certain precisely who the father was. As for his first name, no one could remember exactly where Pepper came from. She had named him LaVelle at the hospital, a name he'd always hated. He'd picked up Pepper at a young age, and had vigorously asserted it as his legal name. Anything but LaVelle.

Pepper Scarboro was seventeen at the time of his disappearance. After successfully completing the fifth grade, after three attempts, he dropped out of school and pumped gas at a local station in Lucedale. An odd child who stuttered badly, Pepper discovered the great outdoors as a young teenager, and loved nothing better than to camp and hunt for days, usually alone.

Pepper had few friends, and his mother rode him constantly for

an assortment of shortcomings. She had two smaller children and
various men friends, and she lived with the rest of her family in a
dirty trailer with no air conditioning. Pepper preferred to sleep in
a pup tent deep in the woods. He saved his money and bought his
own shotgun and camping gear. So Pepper spent as much time as
possible in the De Soto National Forest, twenty minutes but a
thousand miles away from his mother.

There was no clear evidence that Pepper and Patrick had ever
met. Coincidentally, Patrick's cabin was situated in the general
vicinity of the forest where Pepper liked to hunt. Patrick and Pepper were both white males, roughly the same height, though Patrick was much heavier. Of much greater interest was the fact that
Pepper's shotgun, tent, and sleeping bag were found in Patrick's
cabin in late February of 1992.

The two disappeared at approximately the same time, from
about the same area. In the months after their joint disappearances, Sweeney and Cutter had determined that no other person in
the state of Mississippi had turned up missing around February 9
and remained so for more than ten weeks. Several, most of them
troubled teens, had been reported missing in February of 1992, but
by late spring all had been accounted for. In March, a housewife
up in Corinth evidently fled a violent marriage and had yet to be
seen.

Working with FBI computers in Washington, Cutter had determined that the nearest person reported missing shortly before Patrick's fire was a shiftless truck driver from Dothan, Alabama, seven
hours away. He had simply vanished on Saturday, February 8,
leaving behind a miserable marriage and lots of bills. After investigating this case for three months, Cutter was certain there was no
connection between the truck driver and Patrick.

Statistically, there was strong evidence that the disappearances
of Pepper and Patrick were related. If, by some chance, Patrick
didn't perish in his Blazer, Cutter and Sweeney were now almost
positive Pepper did. This evidence, of course, was much too specu-
lative to be admitted in a court of law. Patrick could've picked up a
hitchhiker from Australia, a hobo from parts unknown, a drifter
from a bus station.

They had a list with eight other names, ranging from an elderly gentleman in Mobile who was last seen driving errantly out of town, in the general direction of Mississippi, to a young prostitute in Houston who told friends she was moving to Atlanta to start a new life. All eight had been declared missing months and even years before February of 1992. Cutter and the Sheriff had long since declared the list worthless.

Pepper remained their strongest prospect; they just couldn't prove it.

Neldene, however, thought she could, and she was quite anxious to share her views with the press. Two days after Patrick was caught she went to a lawyer, a local sleazeball who'd handled her last divorce for three hundred dollars, and asked his assistance in guiding her through the media maze. He quickly obliged, said in fact he'd do it for free, then did what most bad lawyers do when presented with a client with a story—he called a press conference at his office in Hattiesburg, ninety miles north of Biloxi.

He displayed his weeping client to the media, and said all sorts of vile things about the local Sheriff down there in Biloxi and the FBI and their lame efforts at locating Pepper. Shame on them for dragging their feet for over four years while his poor client lived in sorrow and uncertainty. He ranted and raved and made the most of his fifteen minutes of fame. He hinted at legal action against Patrick Lanigan, the man who obviously killed Pepper and burned his body to hide the evidence so he could make off with ninety million bucks, but he was vague on specifics.

The press, disregarding whatever caution it may have collectively possessed, if any, ate it up. They were given pictures of young Pepper, a simple-looking boy with nasty peach fuzz around his mouth and unkempt hair. A face was thus given to the faceless victim, and he became human. This was the boy Patrick had killed.

THE PEPPER STORY played well in the press. He was properly referred to as the "alleged victim," but the word "alleged" was invariably mumbled under the breath. Patrick watched it alone in his dark room.

Shortly after Patrick disappeared, he learned that Pepper

Scarboro was rumored to have been lost in the fire. He and Pepper had hunted deer together in January of 1992, and had eaten beef stew over a fire late one cold afternoon in the woods. He had been surprised to learn that the boy practically lived in the forest, preferring it to home, which he spoke of sparingly. His camping and survival skills were extraordinary. Patrick offered the use of the cabin porch in the event of rain or bad weather, but to his knowledge the kid had never used it.

They had met several times in the woods. Pepper could see the cabin from the top of a wooded hill a mile away, and when Patrick's car was there he would hide nearby. He enjoyed tracking behind Patrick as he took long walks or made his way into the woods to hunt. He would toss pebbles and acorns at him until Patrick would yell and curse. They would then sit for a short talk. Conversation was not something Pepper thrived on, but he seemed to enjoy the break in solitude. Patrick took him snacks and candy.

He wasn't surprised by the assumption, then or now, that he had killed the kid.

DR. HAYANI watched the evening news with great interest. He read the papers and talked in great detail to his new wife about his famous patient. They sat in bed and watched it all again on the late news.

The phone rang as they were turning off the lights and preparing for sleep. It was Patrick, full of apologies, but in pain, and scared, and just needing someone to talk to. Since he was technically a prisoner, his calls were restricted to his lawyer and his doctor, and only twice a day each. Did the doctor have a minute?

Of course. Another apology for calling so late, but sleep was impossible now, and he was deeply upset by all the news and especially the suggestion that he killed that young kid. Did the doctor see it on TV?

Yes, of course. Patrick was in his room with the lights off, huddled in his bed. Thank God those deputies were in the hallway because he was scared, he had to admit. He was hearing things, voices and noises that made no sense. The voices were not coming from the hall but from within the room. Could it be the drugs?

It could be a number of things, Patrick. The medicine, the fatigue, the trauma of what you've been through, the shock both physically and psychologically.

They talked for an hour.

Seventeen

H E DIDN'T WASH his hair for the third straight day. He wanted the oily look. He didn't shave either. For his outfit, he switched from the light cotton hospital gown he'd slept in back to the aqua surgeon's scrubs, which were very wrinkled. Hayani promised to get him new ones. But for today, he needed the wrinkles. He put a white sock on his right foot but there was a nasty rope burn just above his left ankle, and he wanted people to see this. No sock there. Just a matching black rubber shower sandal.

He would be displayed today. The world was waiting.

Sandy arrived at ten with two pairs of cheap pharmacy sunglasses, per his client's instructions. And a black New Orleans Saints cap. "Thanks," Patrick said, as he stood before the mirror in the bathroom and admired the sunglasses and prepared the cap.

Dr. Hayani arrived minutes later, and Patrick introduced one to the other. Patrick was suddenly nervous and light-headed. He sat on the edge of his bed, ran his fingers through his hair, and tried to breathe slowly. "I never thought this day would happen, you know," he mumbled to the floor. "Never." His doctor and his lawyer looked at each other with nothing to say.

Hayani ordered a strong depressant, and Patrick gulped down both pills. "Maybe I'll sleep through it all," he said.

"I'll do all the talking," Sandy said. "Just try and relax."

"He's about to," Hayani said.

A knock on the door, and Sheriff Sweeney entered with enough deputies to quell a riot. Stiff pleasantries were exchanged. Patrick put on his Saints cap and his new shades, large dark ones, and held out his wrists to be handcuffed.

"What are those?" Sandy demanded, pointing to a set of ankle irons a deputy was holding.

"Ankle irons," said Sweeney.

"I don't think so," Sandy said harshly. "The man has burns on one ankle."

"He certainly does," Dr. Hayani said boldly, anxious to enter the fray. "See," he insisted, pointing to Patrick's left ankle.

Sweeney pondered this for a moment, and his hesitation cost him. Sandy charged ahead: "Come on, Sheriff, what are his chances of escape? He's injured, handcuffed, surrounded by all these people. What the hell's he gonna do? Break and run? You guys aren't that slow, are you?"

"I'll call the Judge, if necessary," Dr. Hayani said angrily.

"Well, he came here with ankle irons," the Sheriff said.

"That was the FBI, Raymond," Patrick said. "And they were leg chains, not ankle irons. And they hurt like hell anyway."

The ankle irons were put away, and Patrick was led into the hallway, where men in matching brown uniforms grew silent at the sight of him. They gathered around him and the mob moved slowly toward the elevator. Sandy stayed to his left, gently holding him by the elbow.

The elevator was too small for his entire entourage. The ones who didn't make it scurried down the staircase and met them in the lobby where they reorganized and shuffled past the front reception and through the glass doors, into the warm autumn air, where a regular parade of freshly waxed vehicles awaited them. They put him in a sparkling new black Suburban with Harrison County insignia plastered from bumper to bumper, and away they went, followed by a white Suburban carrying his armed protectors. It, in turn, was followed by three freshly cleaned patrol cars. In front, two more patrol cars, the newest additions to the fleet, led the invasion as it cleared military checkpoints and entered the civilian world.

Through the cheap thick sunglasses, Patrick saw everything outside. Streets he'd driven a million times. The houses looked familiar. They turned on to Highway 90 and there was the Gulf, its calm brown waters seemingly unchanged since he left. There was the beach, a narrow strip of sand between the highway and the water, too far from the hotels and condos on the other side of the highway.

The Coast had prospered during his exile, thanks wholly to the surprising arrival of casino gambling. There had been rumors of its coming when he left town, and now he was riding past large Vegas-style casinos with glitz and neon. The parking lots were filling, at nine-thirty in the morning.

"How many casinos?" he asked the Sheriff, seated to his right.

"Thirteen at last count. With more on the way."

"Hard to believe."

The depressant was quite effective. His breathing became heavy and his body relaxed. He felt like nodding off for a moment, then they turned on to Main Street and he was anxious again. Just a couple of blocks now. A few more minutes, and his past would come roaring back to greet him. By City Hall, to the left, quickly now, for a glimpse of the Vieux Marche, and in the middle of the old street lined with shops and stores, a fine large white building he once owned a piece of as a partner in Bogan, Rapley, Vitrano, Havarac, and Lanigan, Attorneys and Counselors-at-Law.

It was still standing, but the partnership was crumbling within.

Ahead was the Harrison County Courthouse, only a three-block walk from his old office. It was a plain, brick two-story building with a small green lawn in the front next to Howard Street. The lawn was covered with people milling about. The streets were lined with cars. Pedestrians hurried along the sidewalks, all headed for the courthouse it seemed. Cars ahead pulled over as Patrick and his caravan came through.

The horde in front of the courthouse moved in a frantic wave around both sides, but was stopped by police barricades at the rear where a section was cordoned off. Patrick had seen several notorious murderers rushed to and from court through the back door, and so he knew exactly what was happening. The parade stopped. Doors flew open and a dozen deputies spilled forth. They crowded around the black Suburban. Its door slid open slowly. Patrick eventually appeared, his aqua garb quite the contrast to the dark brown uniforms squeezing around him.

An impressive mob of reporters, photographers, and cameramen gathered breathlessly along the nearest barricade. Others behind them ran to catch up. Patrick was immediately aware of the spotlight, and he lowered his head and crouched among the deputies. They walked him quickly to the rear door, a barrage of idiotic questions flying over his head.

"Patrick, what's it like to be home!?"

"Where's the money, Patrick!?"

"Who burned up in the car, Patrick!?"

Through the door and up the back stairway, a brief journey Patrick had sometimes taken when he was in a hurry to catch a judge for a quick signature. The smell was suddenly familiar. The concrete steps had not been painted in four years. Through a door, through a short hallway with a crowd of courthouse clerks gathered at one end gawking at him. They put him in the jury room, which was next to the courtroom, and he took a seat in a padded chair by a coffeepot.

Sandy hovered over him, anxious to make sure he was okay. Sheriff Sweeney dismissed the deputies, and they moved into the hall to wait for the next transfer.

"Coffee?" Sandy asked.

"Please, black."

"You okay, Patrick?" Sweeney asked.

"Yeah, sure, Raymond, thanks." He sounded meek and scared. His hands and knees shook and he couldn't make them stop. He ignored the coffee, and despite both hands cuffed together adjusted his black sunglasses and pulled the bill of his cap further down. His shoulders sagged.

There was a knock on the door, and a pretty girl named Belinda eased her head through just long enough to say, "Judge Huskey would like to meet with Patrick." The voice was so familiar. Patrick raised his head, looked at the door, and said softly, "Hello, Belinda."

"Hello, Patrick. Welcome back."

He turned away. She was a secretary in the clerk's office, and all the lawyers flirted with her. A sweet girl. A sweet voice. Had it really been four years?

"Where?" the Sheriff asked.

"In here," she said. "In a few minutes."

"Do you want to meet with the Judge, Patrick?" Sandy asked. It was not mandatory. Under normal circumstances, it would be downright unusual.

"Sure." Patrick was desperate to see Karl Huskey.

She left and the door clicked behind her.

"I'll step outside," Sweeney said. "I need a cigarette."

Finally, Patrick was alone with his lawyer. He suddenly perked up. "Couple of things. Any word from Leah Pires?"

"No," Sandy said.

"She'll get in touch soon, so be ready. I've written her a long letter, and I'd like for you to get it to her."

"Okay."

"Second. There's an antibugging device called a DX-130, made by LoKim, a Korean electronics outfit. Costs about six hundred dollars; about the size of a portable Dictaphone. Get one, and bring it with you whenever we meet. We'll disinfect the room and the phones before each little conference. Also, hire a reputable surveillance firm in New Orleans to check your office twice a week. It's very expensive, but I'll pay for it. Any questions?"

"No."

Another knock, and Patrick slouched again. Judge Karl Huskey entered the room alone, robeless, in shirt and tie with reading glasses perched halfway down his nose. His gray hair and wrinkled eyes made him appear much older and wiser than forty-eight, which was exactly what he wanted.

Patrick was looking up and already smiling when Huskey offered his hand. "Good to see you, Patrick," he said warmly as they shook hands, the cuffs rattling. Huskey wanted to reach down and hug him, but with judicial restraint he limited the contact to a soft handshake.

"How are you, Karl?" Patrick said, keeping his seat.

"I'm fine. And what about you?"

"I've had better days, but it is good to see you. Even under these circumstances."

"Thanks. I can't imagine—"

"Guess I look different, don't I?"

"You certainly do. I'm not sure I would recognize you on the street."

Patrick only smiled.

Like a few others who still professed some level of friendship for Patrick, Huskey felt betrayed, but even more so he felt great relief in knowing that his pal was not dead. He was deeply worried about the capital murder charge. The divorce and the civil suits could be dealt with, but not murder.

Because of their friendship, Huskey would not preside over the trial. He planned to handle the preliminary matters, then step aside long before the important rulings were due. There had already been a story about their history.

"I assume you will enter a plea of not guilty," he said.

"Yes, that's correct."

"Then it will be a routine first appearance. I'll deny bail since it's capital murder."

"I understand, Karl."

"Whole thing won't take ten minutes."

"I've been here before. The chair will be different, that's all."

In twelve years on the bench, Judge Huskey had often been astonished at the amount of sympathy he could muster for average people who'd committed heinous crimes. He saw the human side of their suffering. He saw guilt eat them alive. He'd sent to prison hundreds of people who, if given the chance, would have left his courtroom and never sinned again. He wanted to help, to reach out, to forgive.

But this was Patrick. His Honor was almost moved to tears at the moment. His old friend—bound and dressed in a clown suit, eyes covered, face altered, nervous and twitchy and scared beyond words. He'd like to take him home, feed him some good food, let him rest, and help him pull his life together.

He kneeled next to him, and said, "Patrick, I can't hear this case, for obvious reasons. Right now I'll handle the preliminary stuff to make sure you're protected. I'm still your friend. Don't hesitate to call." He patted him very gently on the knee, hoping he didn't touch a raw spot.

"Thanks, Karl," Patrick said, biting his lip.

Karl wanted eye contact, but it was impossible with the sunglasses. He stood and headed for the door. "Everything's routine today, Counselor," he said to Sandy.

"Are there a lot of people out there?" Patrick asked.

"Yes, Patrick. Friends and enemies alike. They're all out there." He left the room.

THE COAST had a long and rich history of sensational murders and notorious criminals, so crowded courtrooms were not uncommon. No one could remember, though, such a packed house for a simple *first appearance.*

The press had arrived early and taken the good seats. Since Mississippi was one of the remaining few states with the good sense to ban cameras from the courtroom, the reporters would be forced to sit and watch and listen, then put in their own words what they saw. They would be forced to be real reporters, a task for which most of them were ill-equipped.

Every big trial attracted the regulars—clerks and secretaries from courthouse offices, bored paralegals, retired cops, local lawyers who hung around most of the day, sipping free coffee in the clerks' offices, gossiping, examining real estate deeds, waiting for a judge to sign an order, doing anything to stay away from the office—and Patrick attracted all these and more.

In particular, there were many lawyers present just to get a glimpse of Patrick. The papers had been filled with stories about him for four days now, but no one had seen a current photo. Rumors were rampant about his appearance. The torture story had elevated curiosity even more.

Charles Bogan and Doug Vitrano sat together in the middle of the pack, as close to the front as they could get. The damned reporters beat them to the courthouse. They wanted to be on the front row, near the table where the defendant always sat. They wanted to see him, to make eye contact, to whisper threats and vulgarities if at all possible, to spit as much bile as they could in this civilized setting. But they were five rows back, waiting patiently for a moment they thought would never come.

The third partner, Jimmy Havarac, stood along the back wall and chatted quietly with a deputy. He ignored the stares and glances from people he knew, many of whom were other lawyers who secretly had been delighted when the money vanished and the firm lost its fortune. It would have been, after all, the largest single fee earned by any firm in the history of the state. Jealousy was the natural tendency. He hated them, as he hated virtually everyone else in the courtroom. A bunch of vultures waiting for a carcass.

Havarac, the son of a shrimper, was still stout and crude and not beyond a barroom brawl. Five minutes alone with Patrick in a locked room, and he'd have the money.

The fourth partner, Ethan Rapley, was at home in the attic, as usual, working on a brief in support of some insipid motion. He would read about it tomorrow.

A handful of the lawyers were old buddies who came to cheer Patrick on. Escape was a common, usually unspoken, dream of many small-town lawyers trapped in an overcrowded, boring profession where expectations were too high. At least Patrick had the guts to chase the dream. There was an explanation for the dead body, they were sure of that.

Arriving late and pushed into a corner was Lance. He had loitered around back with the reporters, taking the measure of the security. It was quite impressive, at least for now. But could the cops keep it up every day during a long trial? That was the question.

Many acquaintances were present, people Patrick had known only in passing but who now suddenly claimed to have been his dearest friends. Some in fact had never met Patrick, but that didn't stop their idle chatter about Patrick this and Patrick that. Likewise, Trudy suddenly had new friends who had stopped by to scowl at the man who had broken her heart and abandoned precious little Ashley Nicole.

They read paperbacks and scanned newspapers and tried to look bored, as if they didn't really want to be there. There was movement among the deputy clerks and bailiffs near the bench, and the courtroom instantly grew quiet. The newspapers were lowered in unison.

The door next to the jury box opened and brown uniforms poured into the courtroom. Sheriff Sweeney entered, holding Patrick by the elbow, then two more deputies, then Sandy brought up the rear.

There he was! Necks strained and stretched and heads bobbed and weaved. The courtroom artists went to work.

Patrick walked slowly across the courtroom to the defense table, his head down, though from behind the sunglasses he was searching the spectators. He caught a glimpse of Havarac on the rear wall, his scowling face speaking volumes. And just before he sat he saw Father Phillip, his priest, looking much older but just as amiable.

He sat low, his shoulders sagging, chin down, no pride here. He did not look around because he could feel the stares from every direction. Sandy put his arm on his shoulder and whispered something meaningless.

The door opened again, and T.L. Parrish, the District Attorney, entered, alone, and walked to his table next to Patrick's. Parrish was a bookish sort with a small ego, contained ego. No higher office was calling him. His trial work was methodical, absent of any trace of flamboyance, and lethal. Parrish currently carried the second-highest conviction rate in the state. He sat next to the Sheriff, who had moved from Patrick's table to where he belonged. Behind him were agents Joshua Cutter, Brent Myers, and two other FBI types Parrish couldn't even name.

The stage was set for a spectacular trial, yet it was at least six months away. A bailiff called them to order, made them stand while Judge Huskey entered and assumed his perch on the bench. "Please sit," were his first words, and everyone obeyed.

"The matter of *State versus Patrick S. Lanigan*, case number 96-1140. Is the defendant present?"

"Yes, Your Honor," Sandy said, half-standing.

"Would you please rise, Mr. Lanigan?" Huskey asked. Patrick, still handcuffed, slowly pushed his chair back and got to his feet. He was semi-bent at the waist, with his chin and shoulders down. And it was no act. The depressant had deadened most parts of his body, including his brain.

He stiffened a bit.

"Mr. Lanigan, I'm holding a copy of an indictment returned against you by the grand jury of Harrison County, in which it is alleged you murdered one John Doe, a human being, and for this you have been charged with capital murder. Have you read this indictment?"

"Yes sir," he announced, chin up, voice as strong as he could make it.

"Have you discussed it with your attorney?"

"Yes sir."

"How do you wish to plead?"

"Not guilty."

"Your plea of not guilty is accepted. You may sit down."

Huskey shuffled some papers, then continued: "The Court, on its own motion, hereby imposes a gag order on the defendant, the attorneys, the police and investigating authorities, any and all witnesses, and all court personnel, effective now and lasting until the trial is over. I have copies of this order for everyone to read. Any violation of it will result in contempt of court, and I will deal harshly with any violators. Not one word to any reporter or journalist without my approval. Any questions from the attorneys?"

His tone left little doubt that the Judge not only meant what he said, but relished the thought of going after violators. The lawyers said nothing.

"Good. I have prepared a schedule for discovery, motions, pretrial, and trial. It's available in the clerk's office. Anything else?"

Parrish stood and said, "Just one small matter, Your Honor. We would like to get the defendant in our detention facility as soon as possible. As you know, he's now at the base in a hospital, and, well, we—"

"I just talked to his doctor, Mr. Parrish. He's undergoing medical treatment. I assure you that as soon as he is released by his doctor, then we'll transfer him to the Harrison County Jail."

"Thank you, Judge."

"If nothing else, then we stand adjourned."

He was rushed from the courtroom, down the back stairs, into the black Suburban as the cameras clicked and rolled. Patrick nodded then napped as he was returned to the hospital.

Eighteen

THE ONLY CRIMES Stephano possibly committed were the kidnapping and assault of Patrick, and convictions were unlikely. It happened in South America, far from U.S. jurisdiction. The actual assault was conducted by others, including some Brazilians. Stephano's lawyer was confident that they would prevail if pressed to trial.

But there were clients involved, and a reputation to protect. The lawyer knew all too well the FBI's ability to harass without actually prosecuting. It was his advice that Stephano cut the deal—agree to spill his guts in return for the government's promise to grant immunity to him and his clients. Since no other crimes were involved, what was the harm?

The lawyer insisted on sitting with Stephano while his statement was taken. The sessions would last for many hours over several days, but the lawyer wanted to be there. Jaynes wanted it done in the Hoover Building, by his men. Coffee and pastries were served. Two video cameras were aimed at the end of the table where Stephano sat calmly in his shirtsleeves, his lawyer by his side.

"Would you state your name?" asked Underhill, the first of the interrogators, each of whom had memorized the Lanigan file.

"Jonathan Edmund Stephano. Jack."

"And your company is?"

"Edmund Associates."

"And what does your company do?"

"Lots of things. Security consulting. Surveillance. Personnel research. Locating of missing persons."

"Who owns the company?"

"I do. All of it."

"How many employees do you have?"

"It varies. As of now, eleven full-time. Thirty or so part-time, or freelancers."

"Were you hired to find Patrick Lanigan?"

"Yes."

"When?"

"March 28, 1992." Stephano had files packed with notes, but he didn't need them.

"Who hired you?"

"Benny Aricia, the man whose money was stolen."

"How much did you charge him?"

"The initial retainer was two hundred grand."

"How much has he paid you to date?"

"One point nine million."

"What did you do after you were hired by Benny Aricia?"

"Several things. I immediately flew to Nassau in the Bahamas to meet with the bank where the theft occurred. It was a branch of the United Bank of Wales. My client, Mr. Aricia, and his former law firm, had established a new account there to receive the money, and, as we now know, someone else was waiting on the money, too."

"Is Mr. Aricia a U.S. citizen?"

"Yes."

"Why did he establish an account offshore?"

"It was ninety million dollars, sixty for him, thirty for the lawyers, and nobody wanted the money to appear in a bank in Biloxi. Mr. Aricia lived there at the time, and it was agreed by all that it would be a bad idea for anyone locally to see the money."

"Was Mr. Aricia trying to avoid the IRS?"

"I don't know. You'll have to ask him. That was none of my business."

"Who did you talk to at the United Bank of Wales?"

The lawyer snorted his disapproval, but said nothing.

"Graham Dunlap, a Brit. A vice president of some sort with the bank."

"What did he tell you?"

"Same thing he told the FBI. That the money was gone."

"Where did it come from?"

"Here, in Washington. The wire began at nine-thirty on the morning of March 26, 1992, originating from D.C. National Bank. It was a priority wire, meaning it would take less than an hour for it to land in Nassau. At fifteen minutes after ten, the wire hit the United Bank, where it sat for nine minutes before it was wired to a bank in Malta. From there, it was wired to Panama."

"How did the money get wired out of the account?"

The lawyer was irritated by this. "This is a waste of time," he interrupted. "You guys have had this information for four years now. You've spent more time with the bankers than my client has."

Underhill was unfazed. "We have a right to ask these questions. We are simply verifying what we know. How did the money get wired out of the account, Mr. Stephano?"

"Unknown to my client and his lawyers, someone, Mr. Lanigan we presume, had accessed the new offshore account, and had prepared the Malta wiring instructions in anticipation of the money coming in. He prepared bogus wiring instructions from my client's lawyers, his old firm, and rerouted the money nine minutes after it landed. They, of course, thought he was dead, and had no reason to suspect anyone was after the money. The settlement which produced the ninety million in the first place was extremely secret, and no one, with the exception of my client, his lawyers, and a handful of people at the Justice Department, knew exactly when or where the money was wired."

"As I understand it, someone was actually at the bank when the money arrived."

"Yes. We're almost certain it was Patrick Lanigan. On the morning the money was wired, he presented himself to Graham Dunlap as Doug Vitrano, one of the partners in the law firm. He had perfect identification—passport, driver's license, etc.—plus he was well dressed and knew all about the money which was about to be wired from Washington. He had a notarized partnership resolution authorizing him to accept the money on behalf of the firm, then wire it to the bank in Malta."

"I know damned well you have copies of the resolution and the wire transfer authorizations," the lawyer said.

"We do," Underhill said, flipping through his notes and paying little attention to the lawyer. The FBI had tracked the money to Malta, and from there to Panama, where all trails vanished. There was a blurred still shot taken from the bank's security camera of the man who presented himself as Doug Vitrano. The FBI and the partners were certain it was Patrick, though he was wonderfully disguised. He was much thinner, his hair was short and very dark, he had grown a dark mustache and worn stylish horn-rimmed glasses. He had flown in, he explained to Graham Dunlap, to personally monitor the receiving and transferring of the money because the firm and the client were quite nervous about the transaction. That was certainly not unusual in Dunlap's view, and he was happy to oblige. He was sacked a week later and returned to London.

"So we went to Biloxi, and spent a month there looking for clues," Stephano continued.

"And you found the law offices to be wired?"

"We did. For obvious reasons, we were immediately suspicious of Mr. Lanigan, and our task was twofold: first, to find him and the money, and, second, to determine how he had pulled the heist. The remaining partners granted us access to their offices for one weekend, and our technical people picked the place apart. It was, as you say, infested. We found bugs in every phone, in every office, under every desk, in the hallways, even in the men's rest room on the first floor. There was one exception. The office of Charles Bogan was completely clean. He was fastidious about locking it. The bugs were high in quality; twenty-two in all. Their signals were gathered by a hub we found hidden in a storage file box in the attic, in a spot no one had touched in years."

Underhill listened but didn't hear. This was, after all, being recorded on video, and his superiors could study it later. He was quite familiar with these preliminaries. He pulled out a technical summary which analyzed, in four dense paragraphs, the bugging scheme installed by Patrick. The microphones were state of the art—tiny, powerful, costly, and manufactured by a reputable firm in Malaysia. Illegal to buy or possess in the United States, they could be purchased with relative ease in any European city. Patrick and Trudy had spent New Year's in Rome, five weeks before his death.

The hub found in the attic storage box had impressed even the FBI experts. It was less than three months old when Stephano found it, and the FBI reluctantly admitted it was at least a year ahead of their latest wizardry. Made in Hungary, it could receive signals from all twenty-two bugs hidden in the offices below, keep them separate, then transmit them, one at a time or all at once, to a satellite dish nearby.

"Did you determine where the signals were being relayed to?" Underhill asked. It was a fair question because the FBI certainly didn't know.

"No. It has a range of three miles, in all directions, so it would be impossible to tell."

"Any ideas?"

"Yes, a very good one. I doubt Lanigan was foolish enough to set up a receiving dish anywhere within three miles of downtown Biloxi. He would have to rent space, hide the dish, spend lots of time there monitoring hours of conversations. He has proven to be quite methodical. I've always suspected he used a boat. It would be much simpler and safer. The office is only six hundred yards from the beach. There are a lot of boats in the Gulf. A man could drop anchor two miles out and never speak to another soul."

"Did he own a boat?"

"We couldn't find one."

"Any evidence he used a boat?"

"Maybe." Stephano paused here because he was now entering territory unknown to the FBI.

The pause quickly irritated Underhill. "This is not a cross-examination, Mr. Stephano."

"I know. We talked to every charter outfit along the Coast, from Destin to New Orleans, and found only one possible suspect. A small company in Orange Beach, Alabama, leased a thirty-two-foot sailboat to a man on February 11, 1992, the day Lanigan was buried. Their rate was a thousand dollars a month. This guy offered twice that if the transaction could be done in cash with nothing in writing. They figured he was a doper, and said no way. The guy then offered a five-thousand-dollar deposit, plus two thousand a month for two months. Business was slow. The boat was insured against theft. They took a chance."

Underhill listened without blinking. He took no notes. "Did you show them a picture?"

"Yeah. Said it could've been Patrick. But the beard was gone, the hair was dark, baseball cap, eyeglasses, overweight. This was before he discovered Ultra Slim-Fast. Anyway, the guy couldn't make a positive ID."

"What name did he use?"

"Randy Austin. Had a Georgia driver's license. And he refused to provide more identification. He was offering cash, remember, five thousand. The guy would've sold it to him for twenty."

"What happened to the boat?"

"They got it back, eventually. The guy said he got real suspicious because Randy didn't seem to know much about sailboats. He asked questions, fished around. Randy said he was in the process of drifting south after a bad marriage in Atlanta, tired of the rat race, lots of money, that routine. Used to sail a lot, and now wanted to float down to the Keys and practice his skills along the way. Said he'd always keep the shore in sight. It was a nice story, and the guy felt somewhat better, but he was still suspicious. Next day, Randy appeared from nowhere, no car, no cab, as if he had walked or hitchhiked somehow to the dock, and, after a lot of preliminaries, he left with the boat. It had a big diesel engine of some sort and it would cruise at eight knots, regardless of the wind. He disappeared, going east, and the owner had nothing else to do, so he eased down the Coast, stopped at a couple of favorite bars along the way, and managed to keep an eye on Randy, who was a quarter of a mile out and doing a decent job of handling the boat. He docked it at a marina at Perdido Bay, and left in a rented Taurus with Alabama registration. This went on for a couple of days. Our guy kept an eye on the boat. Randy played with it, a mile out at first, then he ventured farther. On the third or fourth day, Randy took it west, toward Mobile and Biloxi, and was gone for three days.

"He came back, then left, going west again. Never east or south, in the direction of the Keys. The guy stopped worrying about his boat because Randy stayed close to home. He would leave for a week at a time, but he always came back."

"And you think it was Patrick?"

"I do. I'm convinced of it. Makes perfect sense to me. He was isolated on the boat. He could go for days without speaking to another person. He could gather his intelligence from a hundred different spots along the Biloxi-Gulfport shore. Plus, the boat was a perfect place to starve himself."

"What happened to it?"

"Randy left it at the dock, and simply vanished without a word. The owner got his boat back, plus the five grand."

"Did you examine the boat?"

"With a microscope. Nothing. The guy said the boat had never been so clean."

"When did he disappear?"

"The guy wasn't certain because he stopped checking on the boat every day. He found it at the dock on March 30, four days after the money was stolen. We talked to a kid who was on duty at the dock, and, to the best of his recollection, Randy docked on either March 24 or March 25, and was never seen again. So the dates match up perfect."

"What happened to the rental car?"

"We tracked it down later. It was rented from the Avis desk at the Mobile Regional Airport on Monday morning, February 10, about ten hours after the fire was put out. Rented by a man with no beard, clean-shaven, short dark hair, horn-rimmed glasses, wearing a coat and tie and claiming he just stepped off a commuter flight from Atlanta. We showed pictures to the clerk on duty, and she made a very tentative ID of Patrick Lanigan. Evidently, he used the same Georgia driver's license. He used a phony Visa Card, one with the name of Randy Austin and a number he stole from a legitimate account in Decatur, Georgia. Said he was a self-employed real estate developer in town to look at land for a casino. So he had no company name to put on the form. He wanted the car for a week. Avis never saw him again. Didn't see the car for fourteen months."

"Why wouldn't he return the car?" Underhill asked, musing.

"Simple. When he rented it, his death had just happened, and had not been reported. But the next day, his face was on the front page of both the Biloxi and Mobile papers. He probably figured it was too risky to take the car back. They found it later in Montgomery, wrecked and stolen."

"Where did Patrick go?"

"My guess is that he left the Orange Beach area on March 24 or 25. He assumed the identity of Doug Vitrano, his former partner. We learned that on the twenty-fifth he flew from Montgomery to Atlanta, then first class to Miami, then first class to Nassau. All tickets were in the name of Doug Vitrano, and he used the passport when he left Miami and again when he entered the Bahamas. The flight arrived in Nassau at eight-thirty on the morning of the twenty-sixth, and he was at the bank when it opened at nine. He presented the passport and other papers to Graham Dunlap. He diverted the money, said good-bye, caught a flight to New York, and landed at La Guardia at 2:30 P.M. At that point, he ditched the Vitrano papers and found some others. We lost him."

WHEN THE BIDDING got to fifty thousand dollars, Trudy said yes. The show was "Inside Journal," a slash-and-burn tabloid with solid ratings and, apparently, lots of cash. They set up lights and covered windows and ran wires throughout the den. The "journalist" was Nancy de Angelo, flown straight in from L.A. with her own band of hairdressers and makeup artists.

Not to be outdone, Trudy spent two hours in front of the mirror, and looked absolutely glorious when she appeared. Nancy said she looked too good. She was supposed to be wounded, hurt, broke, besieged, handcuffed by the court, angry at what her husband had done to her and her daughter. She retreated in tears and

Lance had to console her for half an hour. She looked almost as good when she returned in jeans and a cotton pullover.

Ashley Nicole was used as a prop. She sat close to her mother on the sofa. "Look real sad now," Nancy told her as the technicians checked the lights. "We need tears from you," she said to Trudy. "Genuine tears."

They chatted for an hour about all the horrible things Patrick was doing to them. Trudy cried when she recalled the funeral. They had a picture of the shoe found at the site. She suffered through the months and years afterward. No, she had not remarried. No, she had not heard from her husband since he had returned. Wasn't sure if she wanted to. No, he had made no effort to see his daughter, and she broke down again.

She hated the thought of divorce, but what was she to do? And the lawsuit, how horrible! This nasty insurance company hounding her like she was a deadbeat.

Patrick was such a horrible person. If they found the money, did she expect to get any of it? Of course not! She was shocked by the suggestion.

It was edited to twenty minutes, and Patrick watched it in his dark hospital room. It made him smile.

Nineteen

SANDY'S SECRETARY was clipping his photo and the story of yesterday's brief court appearance from the New Orleans paper when the call came. She immediately found him, extracted him from a crowded deposition, and put him on the phone.

Leah Pires was back. She said hello and immediately asked if he'd had his office checked for bugs. Sandy said yes, just yesterday. She was in a hotel suite on Canal, a few blocks over, and she suggested the meeting take place there. A suggestion from her carried more weight than a directive from a federal judge. Whatever she wanted. He was excited just to hear her voice.

She was in no hurry, so Sandy strolled leisurely down Poydras, then to Magazine, then to Canal. He refused to watch his back. Patrick's paranoia was understandable—poor guy had lived on the run until the ghosts finally caught him. But no one could ever convince Sandy that the same people would shadow him. He was a lawyer in a high-profile case. The bad guys would be crazy to tap his phones and stalk him. One bungled move, and serious damage could be done to the case against Patrick.

But he had contacted a local security firm and made an appointment to have his offices swept for bugs. This was his client's wish, not his.

Leah greeted him with a firm handshake and a quick smile, but he could tell instantly that she had many things on her mind. She was barefoot, in jeans and a white cotton tee shirt, very casual, the way most Brazilians probably are, he thought. He'd never been down there. The closet door was open; there weren't many clothes hanging. She was moving around quickly, living out of a suitcase, probably on the run just as Patrick had been until last week. She poured coffee for both of them, and asked him to sit at the table.

"How is he?" she asked.

"He's healing. The doctor says he'll be fine."

"How bad was it?" she asked quietly. He loved her accent, slight as it was.

"Pretty rough." He reached into his briefcase, removed a folder, and slid it to her. "Here."

She frowned at the sight of the first photo, then mumbled something in Portuguese. Her eyes watered as she looked at the second one. "Poor Patrick," she said to herself. "Poor baby."

She took her time with the photos, gently wiping tears with the back of her hand until Sandy found the presence of mind to get her a tissue. She wasn't ashamed to cry over the pictures, and when she was finished with them she placed them in a neat stack and put them back in the folder.

"I'm sorry," Sandy said. He could think of nothing else to offer. "Here's a letter from Patrick," he finally said.

She finished her crying and poured more coffee. "Are any of the injuries permanent?" she asked.

"The doctor thinks probably not. There will be scarring, but with time everything should heal."

"Mentally, how is he?"

"He's okay. He's sleeping even less. He has nightmares constantly, both day and night. But with medication, he's getting better. I honestly can't imagine what he's going through." He took a sip of coffee, and said, "I guess he's lucky to be alive."

"He always said they wouldn't kill him."

There was so much to ask her. The lawyer in Sandy almost screamed out an endless barrage: Did Patrick know they were close behind him? Did he know the chase was about to end? Where was she when they were closing in? Did she live with him? How did they hide the money? Where is the money now? Is it safe? Please, tell me something. I'm the lawyer. I can be trusted.

"Let's talk about his divorce," she said, abruptly changing the subject. She could sense his curiosity. She stood and walked to a drawer where she removed a thick file and placed it before him. "Did you see Trudy on TV last night?" she asked.

"Yes. Pathetic, wasn't it?"

"She's very pretty," Leah said.

"Yes, she is. I'm afraid Patrick made the mistake of marrying her for her looks."

"He wouldn't be the first."

"No, he wouldn't."

"Patrick despises her. She is a bad person, and she was unfaithful to him throughout their marriage."

"Unfaithful?"

"Yes. It's all in the file there. The last year they were together, Patrick hired an investigator to watch her. Her lover was a man named Lance Maxa, and they were seeing each other all the time. There are even some photographs of Lance coming and going from Patrick's house when he was away. There are pictures of Lance and Trudy sunbathing by Patrick's pool, naked of course."

Sandy took the file and flipped quickly until he found the photographs. Naked as newborns. He smiled wickedly. "This will add something to the divorce."

"Patrick wants the divorce, you understand. He will not contest it. But she needs to be silenced. She's having a nice time saying all those bad things about Patrick."

"This should shut her up. What about the child?"

Leah took her seat and looked him squarely in the eyes. "Patrick loves Ashley Nicole, but there is one problem. He is not the father."

He shrugged as if he heard this every day. "Who is?"

"Patrick doesn't know. Probably Lance. It seems as if Lance and Trudy have been together for some time. It goes back to high school even."

"How does he know he's not the father?"

"When the child was fourteen months old, Patrick obtained a

small blood sample by pricking her finger. He sent it, along with a sample of his, to a lab where DNA tests were run. His suspicions were correct. He is definitely not the father of the child. The report is in the file."

Sandy had to walk around a bit to sort things out. He stood in the window and watched the traffic on Canal. Another clue in the Patrick puzzle had just fallen into place. The question of the moment was this: How long had Patrick planned his departure from his old life? Bad wife, bastard child, horrible accident, no corpse, elaborate theft, take the money and run. The planning was astonishing. Everything had worked perfectly, until now of course.

"Then why fight the divorce?" he asked, still looking below. "If he doesn't want the child, why bring up the trash?"

Sandy knew the answer, but he wanted her to explain it. In doing so, she would give the first glimpse of the rest of the master plan.

"You bring up the trash only to her lawyer," she said. "You show him the file, all of it. At that point, they'll be anxious to settle."

"Settle, as in money."

"Correct."

"What type of settlement?"

"She gets nothing."

"What is there to get?"

"Depends. It could be a small fortune, or a large one."

Sandy turned and glared at her. "I cannot negotiate a property settlement if I don't know how much my client has. At some point, you guys have to clue me in."

"Be patient," she said, thoroughly unruffled. "With time, you'll know more."

"Does Patrick really think he can buy his way out of this?"

"He'll certainly try."

"It won't work."

"Do you have a better idea?"

"No."

"I didn't think so. It's our only chance."

Sandy relaxed and leaned against the wall. "It would be helpful if you guys would tell me more."

"We will. I promise. But first, we'll take care of the divorce. Trudy has to relinquish all claims to his assets."

"That should be easy. And fun."

"Get it done, and we'll chat again next week."

It was suddenly time for Sandy to leave. She was on her feet, gathering papers. He took his files and placed them in his briefcase. "How long will you be here?" he asked.

"Not long," she said, and handed him an envelope. "That's a letter for Patrick. Tell him I'm fine, I'm moving around, and so far I haven't seen anyone behind me."

Sandy took the envelope and tried to make eye contact. She was nervous and anxious for him to leave. He wanted to help her, or at least to offer, but he knew whatever he said at this point would be dismissed.

She forced a smile, and said, "You have a job to do. So do it. Patrick and I will worry about the rest."

WHILE STEPHANO TOLD his story in Washington, Benny Aricia and Guy set up camp in Biloxi. They leased a three-bedroom condo on the Back Bay, and installed phones and a fax.

The theory was that the girl would have to surface in Biloxi. Patrick was confined, and for the foreseeable future his life was fairly predictable. He wasn't going anywhere. She would have to come to him. And they had to catch her when she did.

Aricia had budgeted a hundred thousand for this last little campaign, and that would be the end of it, he swore to himself. Down almost two million, he simply had to stop burning money while he had some left. Northern Case Mutual and Monarch-Sierra, the other two members of his shaky partnership, had thrown in the towel. Stephano would keep the FBI happy with his tall tales, while hopefully Guy and the rest of the organization could find the girl. It was a longshot.

Osmar and his boys were still loitering in the streets of Rio, watching the same places each day. If she came back, they would see her. Osmar used a lot of men, but they worked cheap down there.

□ □ □ □

RETURNING to the Coast brought back bitter feelings in Benny Aricia. He had moved there in 1985 as an executive of Platt & Rockland Industries, a mammoth conglomerate which had sent him around the world for twenty years as a troubleshooter. One of the company's more profitable divisions was New Coastal Shipyards in Pascagoula, between Biloxi and Mobile. In 1985, New Coastal received a twelve-billion-dollar Navy contract to build four Expedition Class nuclear submarines, and someone upstairs decided Benny needed a permanent home.

Raised in New Jersey, educated in Boston, and the husband, at the time, of a repressed socialite, he was miserable living on the Gulf Coast of Mississippi. He considered it a serious diversion from the corporate hierarchy he longed for. His wife left him after two years in Biloxi.

Platt & Rockland was a public company with twenty-one billion in stockholders' equity, eighty thousand employees in thirty-six divisions in a hundred and three countries. It retailed office supplies, cut timber, made thousands of consumer products, sold insurance, drilled for natural gas, shipped containerized cargo, mined copper, and among many other ventures, built nuclear submarines. It was a sprawling mass of decentralized companies, and as a rule, the left hand seldom knew what the right one was doing. It amassed huge profits in spite of itself.

Benny dreamed of streamlining the company, of selling off the junk and investing in the prosperous divisions. He was unabashedly ambitious, and through the ranks of upper managers it was well known that he wanted the top job.

To him, life in Biloxi was a cruel joke, a pit stop from the fast lane orchestrated by his enemies within the company. He detested contracting with the government, detested the red tape and bureaucrats and arrogance from the Pentagon. He hated the snail's pace with which the submarines were built.

In 1988, he asked to be transferred, and was denied. A year later, the rumors of serious cost overruns on the Expedition project surfaced. Construction came to a halt as government auditors and Pentagon brass descended on New Coastal Shipyards. Benny was on the hot seat, and the end was near.

As a defense contractor, Platt & Rockland had a rich history of cost overruns, overbilling, and false claims. It was a way of doing business, and when discovered, the company typically fired everybody near the controversy and negotiated with the Pentagon for a small repayment.

Benny went to a local attorney, Charles Bogan, the senior partner in a small firm which included a young partner named Patrick Lanigan. Bogan's cousin was a U.S. Senator from Mississippi. The Senator was a rabid hawk who chaired the subcommittee on military appropriations, and was dearly loved by the armed services.

Lawyer Bogan's mentor was now a federal judge, and thus the small firm was as politically well connected as any in Mississippi. Benny knew this, and carefully selected Bogan.

The False Claims Act, also known as the Whistle-Blower Law, was designed by Congress to encourage those with knowledge of overbilling in government contracts to come forward. Benny studied the act thoroughly, and even had an in-house lawyer dissect it for him before he went to Bogan.

He claimed he could prove a scheme by Platt & Rockland to overbill the government some six hundred million dollars on the Expedition project. He could feel the ax dropping, and he refused to be the fall guy. By squealing, he would lose any chance of ever finding comparable work. Platt & Rockland would flood the industry with rumors of his own wrongdoing. He would be blacklisted. It would be the end of Benny's corporate life. He understood very well how the game was played.

Under the act, the whistle-blower *may* receive fifteen percent of the amount repaid to the government by the offending corporation. Benny had the documentation to prove Platt & Rockland's scheme. He needed Bogan's expertise and clout to collect the fifteen percent.

Bogan hired private engineers and consultants to review and make sense of the thousands of documents Aricia was feeding him from inside New Coastal Shipyards. The scheme was tied together nicely, and it turned out not to be so intricate after all. The company was doing what it had always done—charging multiple prices for the same materials, and fabricating paperwork. The practice was so ingrained at Platt & Rockland that only two upper managers at the shipyards knew it existed. Benny claimed to have stumbled upon it by accident.

A clear and convincing case was assembled by the lawyers, and they filed suit in federal court in September of 1990. The lawsuit alleged six hundred million dollars in fraudulent claims submitted by Platt & Rockland. Benny resigned the day the suit was filed.

The lawsuit was meticulously prepared and researched, and Bogan pressed hard. So did his cousin. The Senator had been placed in the loop long before the actual filing, and monitored it with great interest once it arrived in Washington. Bogan did not come cheap; nor did the Senator. The firm's fee would be the standard one third. One third of fifteen percent of six hundred million dollars. The Senator's cut was never ascertained.

Bogan leaked enough dirt to the local press to keep the pressure on in Mississippi, and the Senator did the same in Washington. Platt & Rockland found itself besieged by hideous publicity. It was pinned to the ropes, its money cut off, its stockholders angry. A dozen managers at New Coastal Shipyards were fired. More terminations were promised.

As usual, Platt & Rockland negotiated hard with Justice, but this time made no progress. After a year, it agreed to repay the six hundred million dollars, and to sin no more. Because two of the subs were half-built, the Pentagon agreed not to yank the contract. Thus, Platt & Rockland could finish what was planned as a twelve-billion-dollar project, but was now well on its way to twenty billion.

Benny got set to receive his fortune. Bogan and the other partners in the firm got set to spend theirs. Then Patrick disappeared, followed by their money.

Twenty

PEPPER SCARBORO'S shotgun was a Remington .12 gauge pump he purchased from a pawnshop in Lucedale when he was sixteen, too young to buy from a licensed dealer. He paid two hundred dollars for it, and, according to his mother, Neldene, it was his most beloved possession. Sheriff Sweeney and Sheriff Tatum, of Greene County, found the shotgun, along with a well-worn sleeping bag and a small tent, a week after Patrick's death as they were making a routine inventory of his cabin. Trudy had given permission for the search, which in itself was a major problem since she had no ownership interest in the cabin. Any effort to use the shotgun, sleeping bag, and tent as evidence in Patrick's murder trial would be met with fierce resistance since they were found without a search warrant. A valid argument could be made that the sheriffs weren't searching for evidence since there wasn't, at that time, a crime. They were simply gathering up Patrick's personal effects to hand over to his family.

Trudy didn't want the sleeping bag and the tent. She was adamant in her belief that they didn't belong to Patrick. She had never seen them before. They were cheap, unlike items Patrick would buy. And, besides, he didn't camp. He had the cabin to sleep in. Sweeney put labels on them and stored them in his evidence room, for lack of a better place. He planned to wait a year or two, then sell them at one of his annual Sheriff's sales. Six weeks later,

Neldene Crouch burst into tears when confronted with Pepper's camping gear.

The shotgun was handled differently. It was found under a bed, along with the tent and the sleeping bag, in the room Patrick slept in. Someone had hurriedly slid the items under the bed, in Sweeney's opinion. His curiosity was immediately aroused because of the presence of the shotgun. An avid hunter himself, he knew that no hunter with a brain would leave a shotgun or hunting rifle in a remote cabin for thieves to take at their convenience. Nothing of value was ever left in a hunting cabin in these parts. He had carefully examined it on the spot, and noticed the serial number had been filed off. The gun had been stolen at some point since its manufacture.

He discussed it with Sheriff Tatum, and they made the decision to at least have it checked for fingerprints. Nothing would come of it, they were sure, but both were experienced and patient cops.

Later, after repeated promises of immunity, the pawnbroker in Lucedale admitted he had sold the gun to Pepper.

SWEENEY AND TED GRIMSHAW, the chief investigator for Harrison County, politely knocked on Patrick's hospital door, and entered only when invited in. Sweeney had called ahead to alert Patrick of their visit, and to inform him of its purpose. Just routine procedures. Patrick had yet to be properly booked.

They photographed his face while he was sitting in a chair, wearing a tee shirt and gym shorts, his hair unruly and his expression sour. He held the booking numbers they had brought along. They took his fingerprints, with Grimshaw doing the work as Sweeney handled the conversation. Patrick insisted on standing over the small table while Grimshaw took the prints.

Sweeney asked a couple of questions about Pepper Scarboro, but Patrick quickly reminded him he had a lawyer, and his lawyer would be present during any interrogation. Furthermore, he had nothing to say about anything, with or without a lawyer.

They thanked him and left. Cutter and an FBI fingerprint expert from Jackson were waiting in the Lanigan Room at the jail. At the time it was found, Pepper's .12 gauge yielded more than a dozen full, usable prints. They had been lifted by Grimshaw after dusting, filed away in a vault, and now were spread on the table. The shotgun was on a shelf, next to the tent and the sleeping bag, and the jogging shoe and the photographs, and the few other sparse items of evidence to be used against Patrick.

They drank coffee from plastic cups and talked about fishing while the print expert compared the old with the new through a magnifying glass. It didn't take long.

"Several of these are perfect matches," he said, still working. "The gun stock was covered with Lanigan's prints."

Certainly good news, they thought. Now what?

PATRICK INSISTED on a different room for all future meetings with his attorney, and Dr. Hayani was quick to make the necessary arrangements. He also requested a wheelchair to transport him to the room on the first floor. A nurse pushed him, past the two deputies sitting benignly in the hall outside his door, past Special Agent Brent Myers, and onto the elevator for the brief ride to the first floor. One of the deputies trailed along.

The room was one used by doctors for staff meetings. The hospital was small and the room appeared to be used sparingly. Sandy had ordered the antibugging scanner Patrick had mentioned, but it wouldn't be in for a few days.

"Please rush it," Patrick said.

"Come on, Patrick. Surely you don't think they would bug this room. No one knew we would use it until an hour ago."

"We can't be too careful." Patrick stood from the wheelchair and walked around the long conference table, walked without any limp whatsoever, Sandy noted.

"Look, Patrick, I think you should try and relax a little. I know you've been on the run for a long time. You've lived in fear, always looking over your shoulder, I know all that. But those days are over. They caught you. Relax."

"They're still out there, okay? They have me, but not the money. And the money is much more important. Don't forget that, Sandy. They won't rest until they have the money."

"So who might be bugging us here? Good guys or bad? Cops or crooks?"

"The people who lost the money have spent a bloody fortune trying to find it."

"How do you know?"

Patrick merely shrugged as if it were time to play games again.

"Who are they?" Sandy asked, and there was a long pause, one similar to those used by Leah when she wanted to change the subject.

"Sit down," Patrick said. They sat on opposite sides of the table. Sandy removed the thick file Leah had given him four hours earlier; the dirt-on-Trudy file.

Patrick recognized it immediately. "When did you see her?" he asked anxiously.

"This morning. She's fine, sends her love, says nobody's stalking her yet, and asked me to deliver this." He slid the envelope across the table where Patrick grabbed it, ripped it open, and pulled out a three-page letter. He then proceeded to read it slowly, oblivious to his lawyer.

Sandy flipped through the file and settled on the nudie pictures of Trudy reclining by the pool with her gigolo sprawled nearby. He couldn't wait to show these to her lawyer in Mobile. They had a meeting scheduled in three hours.

Patrick finished the letter, carefully refolded it, and placed it in the envelope. "I have another letter for her," he said. He glanced across the table and saw the photos. "Pretty good work, huh?"

"It's amazing. I've never seen this much proof in a divorce case."

"Well, there was a lot to work with. We'd been married almost two years when I bumped into her first husband, quite by accident. It was at a party before a Saints game in New Orleans. We had a few drinks, and he told me about Lance. He's the tomcat in the pictures there."

"Leah explained it."

"Trudy was very pregnant at the time, so I said nothing. The marriage was slowly unraveling, and we hoped the child would make things perfect. She has an amazing capacity for deceit. I decided to play along, be a proud daddy and all that, but a year later I started gathering evidence. I wasn't sure when I would need it, but I knew the marriage was over. I left town every chance I got—business, hunting, fishing, weekends with the boys, whatever. She never seemed to mind."

"I meet with her lawyer at 5 P.M."

"Good. You'll have a great time. It's a lawyer's dream. Threaten everything, but walk away with the settlement. She has to sign away all rights, Sandy. She gets none of my assets."

"When do we talk about your assets?"

"Soon. I promise. But there is something more pressing."

Sandy removed his obligatory legal pad and poised himself to take notes. "I'm listening," he said.

"Lance is a nasty character. He grew up in the bars along Point Cadet, never finished high school, and served three years for smuggling dope. A bad seed. He has friends in the underworld. He knows people who'll do anything for money. There's another thick file, this one on him. I take it Leah didn't give it to you."

"No. Just this one."

"Ask her about it next time. I gathered dirt on Lance for a year with the same private detective. Lance is a small-time hood, but he's dangerous because he has friends. And Trudy has money. We don't know how much is left, but she probably hasn't spent it all."

"And you think he's coming after you?"

"Probably. Think about it, Sandy. Trudy is the only person right now who still needs me dead. If I'm out of the way, she keeps the money she has left, and she doesn't worry about the insurance company getting what she now owns. I know her. The money and the lifestyle mean everything."

"But how could he—"

"It can be done, Sandy. Believe me. It can be done."

He said this with the calm assurance of one who had committed murder and gotten by with it, and for a second Sandy's blood ran cold.

"It can easily be done," he said for the third time, his eyes glaring, the wrinkles around them pinched tightly.

"Okay, what am I supposed to do? Sit with the deputies in the hallway?"

"You create the fiction, Sandy."

"I'm listening."

"First, you tell her lawyer that your office has received an anonymous tip that Lance is in the market for a hit man. Do this at the end of your meeting today. By then, the guy will be shell-shocked and he'll believe anything you say. Tell him you plan to meet with the cops and discuss this. He'll no doubt call his client, who'll deny it vehemently. But her credibility with him will be shot. Trudy will recoil at the very idea that someone else suspects she and Lance have entertained such thoughts. Then, meet with the Sheriff and the FBI and tell the same story. Tell them why you're worried about my safety. Insist that they chat with Trudy and Lance about these rumors. I know her very well, Sandy. She'll sacrifice Lance to keep the money, but not if there's the chance she'll get caught too. If the cops are suspicious now, she'll back off."

"You've given this some thought. Anything else?"

"Yes. The last thing you do is leak it to the press. You need to find a reporter—"

"That shouldn't be hard to do."

"One that you can trust."

"Much harder."

"Not really. I've been reading the papers, and I have a couple of names for you. Check them out. Find one you like. Tell him to print the rumors, off the record, and in return you'll give him first shot at the real stories. That's the way these guys operate. Tell him the Sheriff is investigating reports of the wife attempting to procure the services of a contract killer so she can keep the money. He'll eat it up. He won't have to validate the story. Hell, they print rumors all the time."

Sandy finished his notes and marveled at his client's preparation. He closed his file, tapped it with his pen, and asked, "How much of this stuff do you have?"

"Dirt?"

"Yeah."

"I'd guess fifty pounds. It's been locked in a mini-storage in Mobile ever since I disappeared."

"What else is there?"

"More dirt."

"On who?"

"My former partners. And others. We'll get to it later."

"When?"

"Soon, Sandy."

TRUDY'S LAWYER, J. Murray Riddleton, was a jovial, thick-necked man of sixty who specialized in two types of law: big, nasty divorces, and financial advice aimed at cheating the government. He was a quick study in contrasts; successful but badly dressed, intelligent but plain-faced, smiling but vicious, mild-spoken but sharp-tongued. His large office in downtown Mobile was strewn with long neglected files and out-of-date law books. He politely welcomed Sandy, indicated a chair, and offered a drink. It was, after all, a few minutes after five. Sandy declined, and J. Murray drank nothing.

"So how's our boy?" J. Murray asked, flashing teeth.

"That would be?"

"Come on. Our boy Patrick. Have you found the money yet?"

"Didn't know I was looking for any."

J. Murray found this hilarious and laughed a few seconds. There was no doubt in his mind that he was thoroughly in control of this meeting. The cards were heavily stacked on his side of the desk.

"I saw your client on TV last night," Sandy said. "That sleazy tabloid, what's it called?"

" 'Inside Journal.' Wasn't she marvelous? And the little girl, what a doll. Those poor people."

"My client would like to request that your client refrain from any further public comment about their marriage and divorce."

"Your client can kiss my client's ass. And you can kiss mine."

"I'll pass, as will my client."

"Look, son, I'm a First Amendment hawk. Say anything. Do anything. Publish anything. It's all protected right there by the Constitution." He pointed to a wall of cobwebbed law books next to his window. "Request denied. My client has the right to go public with anything she wants, anytime she wants. She's been humiliated by your client, and now faces a very uncertain future."

"Fair enough. Just wanted to clear the air."

"Is it clear enough?"

"Yes. Now, we really have no problems with your client's desire to get a divorce, and she can have custody of the child."

"Gee thanks. You guys are being generous."

"In fact, my client has no plans to seek visitation rights with the child."

"Smart man. After abandoning the child for four years, he'd be hard-pressed to see her."

"There is another reason," Sandy said, as he opened the file and picked out the DNA test. He handed a copy across to J. Murray, who had stopped smiling and was squinting at the papers.

"What's this?" he asked, suspiciously.

"Why don't you read it?" Sandy said.

J. Murray yanked his reading glasses from a coat pocket, and stuck them to his rather round head. He pushed the report away, got it just right, then read it slowly. He glanced up with a blank look after page one, and his buoyant shoulders sagged a bit at the end of page two.

"Disastrous, isn't it?" Sandy said when J. Murray had finished.

"Don't patronize me. I'm sure this can be explained."

"I'm sure it cannot. Under Alabama law, the DNA is conclusive proof. Now, I'm not quite the First Amendment hawk you are, but if this got published it would be very embarrassing for your client. Imagine, having someone else's child while pretending to be happily married to another. Wouldn't play well along the Coast, I'm afraid."

"Publish it," J. Murray said, with no conviction. "I don't care."

"Better check with your client first."

"It's insignificant, under our law. Even if she committed adultery, he continued to live with her after he knew. Therefore, he accepted it. He's barred from using it as grounds for divorce."

"Forget the divorce. She can have that. Forget the kid too."

"Oh, I see then. It's extortion. She releases her claim to his assets, and he doesn't go public."

"Something like that."

"Your client's crazy as hell and so are you." J. Murray's cheeks turned red and his fists clenched for a second.

Sandy, coolly, flipped through the file and extracted the next bit of damage. He slid a report across the desk.

"What is it?" J. Murray demanded.

"Read it."

"I'm tired of reading."

"Okay, it's a report by the private detective who followed your client and her boyfriend for a year prior to my client's disappearance. They were together, alone, at various places but primarily at my client's home, indoors, and we presume in bed, on at least sixteen occasions."

"Big deal."

"Check these out," Sandy said, and flung two eight-by-ten color photos, two of the nude ones, on top of the report. J. Murray glanced, then grabbed them for a more in-depth study.

Sandy decided to be helpful. "Those were taken by the pool at my client's home while he was attending a seminar in Dallas. Recognize anyone?"

J. Murray managed a slight grunt.

"There are many more," Sandy promised, then waited for J. Murray to stop his gawking. "And I also have three other reports from private detectives. Seems my client was quite suspicious."

Before Sandy's eyes, J. Murray was transformed from a hard-nosed advocate to a soulful mediator, a chameleon-like conversion common among lawyers who suddenly found themselves stripped of ammunition. He exhaled heavily, defeated, and sat low in his leather swivel. "They never tell us everything, do they," he said. It was suddenly us versus them. Lawyers versus their clients. He and Sandy were really together now, and what were they to do?

Sandy, though, was not ready for the tag team. "Again, I'm not the First Amendment hawk you claim to be, but if these found their way into the tabloids, then it sure would be embarrassing for Trudy."

J. Murray waved him off, and glanced at his watch. "Sure you don't want a drink?"

"I'm sure."

"What's your boy got?"

"I honestly don't know, yet. And that's not the important question. What matters is what he will have left when the dust settles, and right now no one knows."

"Surely he's got most of the ninety million."

"He's being sued for much more than that. Not to mention the possibility of a long prison sentence and maybe an execution. This divorce, Mr. Riddleton, is the least of his worries."

"Then why are you threatening us?"

"He wants her to shut up, to get her divorce and go away, and to release all future claims against him. He wants it done now."

"If not?" J. Murray loosened his tie and sunk an inch lower. The day was suddenly late; he needed to go home. He thought for a long minute, then said, "She'll lose everything, does he know that? The life insurance company will wipe her out."

"There are no winners here, Mr. Riddleton."

"Let me speak to her."

Sandy gathered his things and made a slow retreat to the door. J. Murray managed another sad smile, and just as they were shaking hands to depart, Sandy, as if he had almost forgotten it, mentioned the anonymous tip his office had received in New Orleans about Lance searching for a hit man. He didn't know if he believed it, but he felt compelled to discuss it with the Sheriff and the FBI anyway.

They discussed it briefly. Riddleton promised to mention it to his client.

Twenty-one

D R. HAYANI'S LAST STOP was Patrick's room. It was almost dark, long past time to leave for the day, and he found his famous patient sitting in his gym shorts in a chair at a makeshift desk in the only empty corner of his room. The desk was a small table, with a lamp Patrick had conned out of an orderly. A plastic water cup held pens and pencils. Another held the beginning of a collection of paper clips, rubber bands, push pins, all donated by the nursing staff. He even had three legal pads.

Patrick was in business. An impressive collection of legal documents occupied one corner, and he was reviewing one of the numerous lawsuits filed against him when his doc popped in, for the third time of the day.

"Welcome to my office," Patrick said. A bulky TV hung not far above his head. The back of his chair was a foot from the end of his bed.

"Nice," Hayani said. Rumors in hospitals flew faster than in law offices, and throughout the last two days there had been amused whispers about the new firm being established in Room 312. "I hope you don't sue doctors."

"Never. In thirteen years of practicing law, I never sued a doctor. Nor a hospital." He stood as he said this and turned to face Hayani.

"I knew I liked you," the doctor said as he gently examined the burns on Patrick's chest. "How are you doing?" he asked, for the third time that day.

"I'm fine," Patrick repeated, for the umpteenth time that day. The nurses, starstruck and curious, barged in at least twice an hour with any one of a hundred errands, and always with a chirping, "How ya feeling?"

"I'm fine," he always answered.

"Did you nap today?" Hayani asked, squatting and poking along the left thigh.

"No. It's hard to sleep without pills, and I really hate to take anything during the day," Patrick answered. In truth, napping was impossible with the parade of nurses and orderlies.

He sat on the edge of the bed and looked sincerely at his doctor. "Can I tell you something?" he asked.

Hayani stopped scribbling on a chart. "Certainly."

Patrick cast his eyes to the left and to the right as if there could be ears everywhere. "When I was a lawyer," he began softly, "I had this client, a banker, who got caught embezzling. He was forty-four years old, married, three teenaged kids, a great guy who did a dumb thing. He was arrested at home, late at night, and taken to the county jail. It was crowded, and he got thrown into a cell with a couple of young street punks, black guys, mean as hell. They gagged him first so he couldn't scream. They beat him, then they did things you don't want to know about. Two hours after he was sitting in his den watching a movie, he was half-dead in a jail cell three miles from his home." Patrick's chin hit his chest and he pinched the bridge of his nose.

Dr. Hayani touched his shoulder.

"You can't let that happen to me, Doc," Patrick said, his eyes watery, his voice strained.

"Don't worry, Patrick."

"The thought of it horrifies me, Doc. I have nightmares about it."

"You have my word, Patrick."

"God knows I've been through enough."

"I promise, Patrick."

□ □ □ □

THE NEXT INTERROGATOR was a squirrely little man named Warren, who chain-smoked and viewed the world through thick, dark glasses. His eyes were invisible. His left hand worked the cigarette, his right one handled the pen, and nothing else moved, except his lips. He crouched behind his neat little piles of paper and shot questions to the other end, where Stephano fiddled with a paper clip and his lawyer fought with a laptop.

"When did you form your consortium?" Warren asked.

"After we lost his trail in New York, we pulled back and waited. We listened where we could listen. We covered old tracks. Nothing happened. The trail quickly ran cold, and we settled in for the long run. I'd met with Benny Aricia, and he was willing to finance the search. Then I also met with people from Monarch-Sierra and Northern Case Mutual, and they gave their tentative approval. Northern Case Mutual had just forked over two point five million to the widow. They couldn't sue to get it back because there was no conclusive evidence he was still alive. They agreed to put up a half a million. Monarch-Sierra was more complicated because they had not paid, at that time. Their exposure was four million."

"Monarch carried the law firm's malpractice insurance?"

"Close. It was a separate crime rider, in addition to the customary Errors and Omissions policy. It protected the law firm from fraud and theft by its employees and partners. Since Lanigan stole from the firm, Monarch-Sierra was forced to pay up, to the tune of four million dollars."

"But your client, Mr. Aricia, received this money, correct?"

"Yes. He first sued the law firm for the entire sixty million he lost, but the firm had few assets. The firm agreed to hand over the proceeds from the policy. We all sat down at the table and struck a deal. Monarch-Sierra agreed to pay the money without a fight if Mr. Aricia would use up to a million of it to find Lanigan. Mr. Aricia agreed, but only if Monarch-Sierra would kick in another one million to finance the search."

"So Aricia was in for a million, Monarch-Sierra for a million, and Northern Case Mutual for half a million. Total of two point five."

"Yes, that was the initial agreement."

"Where was the law firm?"

"They chose not to participate. Frankly, they didn't have the money, and they were too shocked to respond. Initially, they helped in other ways."

"And the players paid up?"

"Yes. The money was wired to my firm's account."

"Now that the search is over, how much of the money is left?"

"Almost none."

"How much was spent?"

"Three and a half million, give or take a little. About a year ago, the funds ran out. The insurance companies said no. Mr. Aricia kicked in another half a million, then another three hundred thousand. His total to date is one point nine."

Actually, it was an even two million, now that Benny had reluctantly decided to go after the girl. The FBI, of course, would not know this.

"And how was the money spent?"

Stephano referred to his notes, but only for a glimpse.

"Almost a million in payroll, travel, and other expenses related to the search. One point five million in rewards. And an even million to my firm as fees."

"You've been paid a million dollars?" Warren asked, still with no movement of muscle but with a slightly raised voice.

"Yes. Over a four-year period."

"Tell me about the rewards."

"Well, it goes to the heart of the search."

"We're listening."

"One of the first things we did was to establish a reward for any information about the disappearance of Patrick Lanigan. You guys knew about the reward, but you thought the law firm was backing it. We quietly went to the law firm and convinced Charles Bogan to announce the formation of a reward for information. He went public and promised fifty thousand, at first. Our deal with Bogan was that he would secretly notify us if there was any response."

"The FBI was not informed of this."

"No. The FBI knew about the reward, and approved it. But our agreement with Bogan was kept quiet. We wanted the first shot at any information. We didn't distrust the FBI, we simply wanted to find Lanigan and the money ourselves."

"How many men did you have working on the case at this point?"

"Probably a dozen."

"And where were you?"

"Here. But I went to Biloxi at least once a week."

"Did the FBI know what you were doing?"

"Absolutely not. To my knowledge, the FBI never knew we were involved, until last week."

The file in front of Warren certainly reflected this. "Continue."

"We heard nothing for two months, three months, four. We raised the reward money to seventy-five, then to a hundred. Bogan got hammered with all the nuts out there, and he passed this along to the FBI. Then in August of '92, he got a call from a lawyer in New Orleans who claimed to have a client who knew something about the disappearance. The guy sounded very legitimate, and so we went to New Orleans to meet with him."

"What was his name?"

"Raul Lauziere, on Loyola Street."

"Did you meet with him?"

"I did."

"And who else from your firm?"

Stephano glanced at his lawyer, who had frozen for the moment and was deep in thought. "This is a secretive business. I'd rather not mention the names of my associates."

"He doesn't have to," the lawyer pronounced loudly, and that was the end of the matter.

"Fine. Continue."

"Lauziere appeared to be serious, ethical, and believable. He was also very prepared. He seemed to know everything about the disappearance of Patrick and the money. He had a file of all the press clippings. Everything was indexed and at his fingertips. He handed us a four-page, double-spaced narrative of what his client knew."

"Just summarize it in detail. I'll read it later."

"Certainly," Stephano said, and recounted the narrative from memory: "His client was a young woman named Erin who was struggling through med school at Tulane. She was recently divorced, broke, etc., and to help make ends meet she worked the late shift in a large bookstore in a mall, one of those big chains. Sometime in January of '92 she noticed a customer milling around the travel and language section. He was heavyset, dressed in a suit, neat black and gray beard, and appeared to be somewhat nervous. It was almost nine at night, and the store was practically deserted. He finally picked out a language course with twelve cassettes, workbooks, etc., all in one slick box, and he was easing toward the checkout area where Erin worked when another man entered the store. The first man immediately withdrew between the racks and placed the language course back on the shelf. He then emerged on the other side, and attempted to slip past the second man, a person he obviously knew and didn't want to speak to. But he didn't make it. The second man glanced up, and said, "Patrick, it's been a long time." A brief conversation ensued in which the two men talked about their law careers. Erin puttered around the checkout stand and listened because there was nothing else to do. Evidently, she was keenly curious and watched everything.

"Anyway, the one called Patrick was anxious to leave, so he finally found the right moment and made a graceful getaway. Three nights later, at about the same time, he came back. Erin was putting up stock, not checking out. She saw him enter, recognized him, remembered he was called Patrick, and watched him. He made a point to look at the checkout clerk, and when he realized she was a different one, he loitered around the store until he stopped in the language and travel section. He picked out the same language course, slid to the counter, paid for it in cash, and left quickly. Almost three hundred bucks. Erin watched him leave. He never saw her, or if he did, he didn't recognize her."

"So what's the language?"

"That, of course, was the big question. Three weeks later Erin saw in the paper where Patrick Lanigan was killed in a terrible auto accident, and she recognized his picture. Then, six weeks later the story broke about the stolen money from his old firm, the same picture was in the papers, and Erin saw it again."

"Did the bookstore have security cameras?"

"No. We checked."

"So what was the language?"

"Lauziere wouldn't tell us. At least at first he wouldn't. We were offering a hundred thousand dollars for solid information about Lanigan's whereabouts. He, and his client, quite naturally wanted all of the money for the name of the language. We negotiated for three days. He wouldn't budge. He allowed us to interrogate Erin. We spent six hours with her, and every aspect of her story checked out, so we agreed to pay the hundred grand."

"Brazilian Portuguese?"

"Yes. The world suddenly shrunk."

LIKE EVERY LAWYER, J. Murray Riddleton had been through it many times before, unfortunately. The airtight case suddenly springs leaks. The tables get turned in the blink of an eye.

Just for the fun of it, and with no small measure of enjoyment, he allowed Trudy to puff and posture for a bit before he lowered the ax.

"Adultery!" she gasped, with all the self-righteousness of a Puritan virgin. Even Lance pulled off a look of shock. He reached across and took her hand.

"I know, I know," J. Murray said, playing along. "Happens in almost every divorce. These things do get nasty."

"I'll kill him," Lance grunted.

"We'll get to that later," J. Murray said.

"With whom?" she demanded.

"With Lance here. They claim the two of you were getting it on before, during, and after the marriage. In fact, they claim it goes all the way back to high school."

Ninth grade, actually. "He's an idiot," Lance said, without conviction.

Trudy nodded and agreed with Lance. Preposterous. Then she asked nervously, "What proof does he claim to have?"

"Do you deny it?" J. Murray asked, completing the setup.

"Absolutely," she snapped.

"Of course," added Lance. "The man is a living lie."

J. Murray reached into a deep drawer and withdrew one of the reports Sandy had given him. "Seems Patrick was suspicious throughout most of the marriage. He hired investigators to snoop around. This is a report from one of them."

Trudy and Lance looked at each other for a second, then realized they had been caught. Suddenly, it was difficult to deny a relationship that was now more than twenty years old. They both became smug at the same instant. So what? Big deal.

"I'll just summarize it," J. Murray said, then clicked off dates, times, and places. They weren't ashamed of their activities, but it was discomforting to know that things were so well documented.

"Still deny it?" J. Murray asked when he finished.

"Anybody can write that stuff," Lance said. Trudy was silent.

J. Murray pulled out another report, this one covering the seven months prior to Patrick's disappearance. Dates, times, places. Patrick left town, bam, Lance moved in. Every time.

"Can these investigators testify in court?" Lance asked when J. Murray finished.

"We're not going to court," J. Murray said.

"Why not?" Trudy asked.

"Because of these." J. Murray slid the eight-by-ten color glossies across his desk. Trudy grabbed one and gasped at the sight of herself lounging by the pool, naked, her stud next to her. Lance was shocked too, but managed a tiny grin. He sort of liked them.

They swapped the photos back and forth without a word. J. Murray relished the moment, then said, "You guys got too careless."

"Skip the lecture," Lance said.

Predictably, Trudy started to cry. Her eyes watered, her lip quivered, her nose sniffled, and then she cried. J. Murray had seen it a thousand times. They always cried, not for what they had done, but for the wages of their sins.

"He's not getting my daughter," she said angrily through the tears. She lost it, and they listened to her bawl for a while. Lance, ever vigilant, pawed at her and tried to console.

"I'm sorry," she finally said, wiping tears.

"Relax," J. Murray said without the slightest trace of compassion. "He doesn't want the kid."

"Why not?" she asked, the tear ducts shutting down instantly.

"He's not the father."

They squinted, thought hard, tried to assemble things.

J. Murray reached for yet another report. "He took a blood sample from the child when she was fourteen months old, and had a DNA test run on it. No way he's the father."

"Then who . . ." Lance started to ask, but couldn't complete the thought.

"Depends on who else was around," J. Murray said, helpfully.

"No one else was around," she said, mocking him angrily.

"Except me," Lance volunteered, then slowly closed his eyes. Fatherhood descended heavily upon his shoulders. Lance despised children. He tolerated Ashley Nicole only because she belonged to Trudy.

"Congratulations," J. Murray said. He reached into a drawer, pulled out a cheap cigar and tossed it to Lance. "It's a girl," he said, and laughed loudly.

Trudy fumed and Lance toyed with the cigar. When J. Murray finished humoring himself, she asked, "So where are we?"

"It's simple. You waive any right to his assets, whatever they may be, and he gives you the divorce, the kid, everything else you want."

"What are his assets?" she asked.

"His lawyer is not sure right now. We may never know. The man is headed for death row, and the cash might stay buried forever."

"But I'm about to lose everything," she said. "Look at what he's done to me. I got two and a half million when he died, now the insurance company is ready to bankrupt me."

"She deserves a helluva lot of money," Lance piped in on cue.

"Can I sue him for mental distress, or fraud, or something like that?" she pleaded.

"No. Look, it's very simple. You get the divorce and the kid, and Patrick keeps whatever money is out there. And everything is kept quiet. Otherwise, he'll leak all this to the press." J. Murray tapped

the reports and the photos when he said this. "And you'll be humiliated. You've gone public with your dirty laundry; he's quite
anxious to return the favor."

"Where do I sign?" she said.

J. MURRAY fixed them all a vodka, and before too long he was
mixing another round. He finally brought up the subject of those
silly rumors about Lance looking for a hit man. The denials came
fast and furious, and J. Murray confessed that he really didn't believe the trash anyway.

There were so many rumors racing up and down the Coast.

Twenty-two

T HEY BEGAN TRACKING Sandy McDermott as he left New Orleans at 8 A.M. and worked his way through the traffic on Interstate 10. He was followed until the congestion thinned near Lake Pontchartrain. They called ahead and reported he was on his way to Biloxi. Following him was easy. Listening would be another matter. Guy had bugs for Sandy's office and home phones, even one for his car, but the decision to install them had not yet been made. The risks were significant. Aricia especially was wary. He argued with Stephano and with Guy that Sandy might well expect his phones to get tapped, and might feed them all sorts of useless or even damaging gossip. His client had so far proved quite proficient at seeing around corners. And so they argued.

Sandy wasn't looking over his shoulder. Nor was he seeing much in front of him. He was simply driving, moving forward while avoiding contact, his mind, as usual, many miles away.

From a strategic point of view, the various Lanigan battles were in good shape. The civil suits filed by Monarch-Sierra, the law firm, and Aricia had been placed on dockets already densely crowded. Formal responses by Sandy were a month away. Discovery wouldn't start for three months and would last for a year. Trials were two years away at the earliest. Likewise for Patrick's suit against the FBI; it would one day be amended to bring in Stephano and his consortium. It would be a delightful case to try, but Sandy doubted he would ever get the chance.

The divorce was under control.

The capital murder charge, clearly the center of attention, was another matter. Obviously the most serious of Patrick's problems, it was also the speediest. By law, the state had to try Patrick within two hundred and seventy days of the indictment, so the clock was ticking.

In Sandy's opinion, a conviction based on the evidence would be a longshot. For the moment, crucial elements of proof were missing—significant facts such as the identity of John Doe, and the manner in which he died, and the certainty that Patrick killed him. It was a tenuous circumstantial case at best. Large assumptions would be called for.

However, a conviction based on public sentiment was foreseeable. By now everyone within a hundred miles of Biloxi knew most of the details, and you couldn't find a literate breathing soul who didn't think Patrick killed someone to fake his death so he could lie in ambush and steal ninety million dollars. Patrick had a few admirers, those who also dreamed of a new life with a new name and plenty of dough. But they would not be on his jury. Most folks, it seemed through the informal polling of coffee shop talk and courthouse gossip, felt he was guilty and should spend time in prison. Very few favored the death penalty. Leave that for rapists and cop killers.

Most pressing, though, at the moment, was keeping Patrick alive. The file on Lance, hand-delivered last night by the lovely Leah in yet another hotel room, portrayed a quiet man with a hairtrigger temper and a penchant for violence. He liked guns, and had once been indicted by a federal grand jury for fencing them through a pawnshop. The charges were later dismissed. In addition to his three-year stint for smuggling pot, he had been sentenced to sixty days for his part in a barroom brawl in Gulfport, though the time was suspended due to an overcrowded jail. There were two other arrests—one for another fight and one for a DUI.

Lance could be cleaned up and made presentable. He was lanky and handsome, and well admired by the ladies. He knew how to dress and carry on amusing chitchat over cocktails. But his forays into society were temporary. His heart was always in the street, just above the gutter, where he hung out with loan sharks and bookies and fences and reputable drug dealers, the smart white-collar boys of local crime. These were his friends, the guys from his neighborhood. Patrick had found them too, and the file contained no fewer than a dozen little biographies of Lance's pals, all with criminal records.

Sandy at first had been skeptical of Patrick's paranoia. Now he believed it. Though he knew little of the underworld, the nature of his profession occasionally brought him into contact with criminals. He had heard many times that for five thousand bucks you could get anyone killed. Maybe even less along the Coast.

Lance certainly had more than five thousand bucks. And he had a wonderful motive to eliminate Patrick. The life insurance policies that made Trudy rich didn't exclude any particular causes of death, other than suicide. A bullet to the head was treated just like a car wreck, or a heart attack, or anything else. Dead was dead.

THE COAST was not Sandy's turf. He didn't know the sheriffs and their deputies, the judges and their quirks, the other members of the bar. He suspected this was precisely why Patrick picked him.

Sweeney had been less than hospitable on the phone. He was very busy, he said, and besides, meetings with lawyers were usually a waste of time. He could spare a few minutes, starting at nine-thirty and barring an emergency. Sandy arrived early, and poured his own coffee from a pot he found next to the watercooler. Deputies milled about. The sprawling jail was in the rear. Sweeney found him and led him through to his office, a spartan room with government hand-me-down furniture and fading photos of smiling politicians on the wall.

"Have a seat," Sweeney said, pointing to a ratty chair as he sat behind his desk. Sandy did as he was told.

"Mind if I record?" Sweeney asked, already punching the button on a large tape recorder in the center of his desk. "I tape everything," he said.

"Sure," Sandy said, as if he had a choice. "Thanks for working me in."

"No problem," Sweeney said. He had yet to smile or offer anything other than the impression of being bothered by this. He lit a cigarette and sipped steaming coffee from a Styrofoam cup.

"I'll get right to the point," Sandy said, as if idle conversation were an option. "My office has received a tip that Patrick's life may be in danger." Sandy hated the lying, but he had little choice under the circumstances. This was what his client wanted.

"Why would someone tip your office that your client was in danger?" Sweeney asked.

"I have investigators working on the case. They know lots of people. Some gossip got passed along, and one of my investigators tracked it down. That's the way these things happen."

Sweeney showed neither belief nor disbelief. He smoked his cigarette and thought about it. In the past week, he had heard every conceivable species of rumor about the adventures of Patrick Lanigan. People were talking about nothing else. The hit man stories were of several varieties. Sweeney figured his network was better than the lawyer's, especially one from New Orleans, so he would let him talk. "Got any suspects?"

"Yes. His name is Lance Maxa; I'm sure you know him."

"We do."

"He took Patrick's place with Trudy not long after the funeral."

"Some would say Patrick took his place," Sweeney said, with his first smile. Sandy was indeed on foreign turf. The Sheriff knew more than he.

"Then I guess you know all about Lance and Trudy," Sandy said, a little rattled.

"We do. We take good notes around here."

"I'm sure you do. Anyway, Lance, as you know, is a nasty sort, and my men got a rumor that he was looking for a contract killer."

"How much is he offering?" Sweeney asked skeptically.

"Don't know. But he has the money, and he has the motive."

"I've already heard this."

"Good. What do you plan to do?"

"About what?"

"About keeping my client alive."

Sweeney took a deep breath and decided to hold his tongue. He struggled with his temper. "He's on a military base, in a hospital room with my deputies guarding his door and FBI agents down the hall. I'm not sure what else you have in mind."

"Look, Sheriff, I'm not trying to tell you how to do your job."

"Really?"

"No. I promise. Please try and understand that my client is a very frightened man right now. I'm here acting on his behalf. He's been stalked for over four years. He's been caught. He hears voices we don't hear. He sees shadows we don't see. He's convinced people will try to kill him, and he expects me to protect him."

"He's safe."

"For now. What if you talked to Lance, and you grilled him pretty good and told him about the rumors. If he knew you were watching, he'd be stupid to try something."

"Lance is stupid."

"Maybe, but Trudy is not. If she thinks she might get caught, she'll yank Lance back where he belongs."

"Been yanking him all his life."

"Precisely. She will not run the risk."

Sweeney lit another cigarette, and glanced at his watch. "Anything else?" he asked, suddenly anxious to get up and leave. He was a Sheriff, not an office manager with a desk and Rolodex.

"Just one thing. And again, I'm not trying to tend to your business. Patrick has enormous respect for you. But, well, he thinks he's much safer where he is."

"What a surprise."

"Jail could be dangerous for him."

"He shoulda thought about that before he killed Mr. Doe."

Sandy ignored this, and said, "He'll be easier to protect in the hospital."

"Have you been to my jail?"

"No."

"Then don't lecture me about how unsafe it is. I've been doing this for a long time, got it?"

"I'm not lecturing."

"The hell you're not. You got five more minutes. Anything else?"

"No."

"Good." Sweeney bolted to his feet and left the room.

THE HONORABLE KARL HUSKEY arrived at Keesler Air Force Base late in the afternoon, and slowly made his way through security to the hospital. He was in the middle of a one-week drug trial, and he was tired. Patrick had called and asked him to stop by, if possible.

Himself a pallbearer, Karl had sat next to Sandy McDermott at Patrick's funeral. Unlike Sandy, though, Huskey had been a recent friend of Patrick's. The two had met during a civil case Patrick had tried not long after he arrived in Biloxi. They became friendly, the way lawyers and judges often do when they see each other every week. They chatted over bad food at the monthly bar luncheons, and once drank too much at a Christmas party. They played golf twice a year.

It was an easy acquaintance, but not a close friendship, at least not for the first three years Patrick was in Biloxi. But they grew closer in the months before he disappeared. With the benefit of hindsight, though, it was easy to look back and see a change in Patrick.

IN THE MONTHS after his disappearance, those in the legal community who knew him best, including Karl, liked to gather over drinks at the Lower Bar at Mary Mahoney's Restaurant on Friday afternoons and piece together the Patrick puzzle.

Trudy took her share of the blame, though she was too easy a target, in Karl's opinion. On the surface, the marriage didn't appear to be that bad. Patrick certainly didn't discuss it with anybody, at least no one who drank with them at Mary Mahoney's. Trudy's actions after the funeral, especially the red Rolls and the live-in toyboy and the go-to-hell attitude she adopted as soon as the life insurance was collected, had soured everyone and made objectivity impossible. No one was certain that she was sleeping around before Patrick left. In fact, Buster Gillespie, the Chancery

Clerk and a regular at those sessions, professed admiration for Trudy. She'd once worked with his wife at a charity ball of some variety, and he always felt compelled to say something nice about her. He was about the only one. Trudy was easy to talk about and easy to criticize.

Job pressure was certainly a factor in pushing Patrick to the brink. The firm was rolling in those days, and he desperately wanted to become a partner. He worked long hours, and he took the difficult cases his partners didn't want. Not even the birth of Ashley Nicole kept him home. He had made partner three years after joining as an associate, but few people outside the firm knew it. He had whispered it to Karl one day after court, but Patrick was not the least bit boastful.

He was tired and stressed, but then so were most of the lawyers who entered Karl's courtroom. The oddest changes in Patrick were physical. He was an even six feet tall, and he said he had never been thin. He claimed to have been quite a jogger in law school, at one point doing forty miles a week. But as a busy lawyer, who had the time? His weight crept up, then ballooned the last year he was in Biloxi. He seemed oblivious to the jokes and comments from the courthouse crowd. Karl had chided him more than once, but he kept eating. A month before he disappeared, he told Karl over lunch that he weighed two hundred and thirty pounds, and that Trudy was raising hell about it. She, of course, aerobicized two hours a day with Jane Fonda and was as thin as a model.

He said his blood pressure was up, and he promised to go on a diet. Karl had encouraged this. He found out later that Patrick's blood pressure had been normal.

The weight gain, and its overnight loss, made perfect sense now that they thought about it.

The beard too. He had grown it around November of 1990, said it was his deer hunting beard. Such growth was not unusual among non-rednecks and lawyers in Mississippi. The air was cool. The testosterone was up. It was a boy thing. He didn't shave it, and Trudy bitched about that too. The longer he kept it, the grayer it became. His friends got accustomed to it. She did not.

He let his hair a grow a bit and started wearing it thicker on top and halfway down the ears. Karl called it the Jimmy Carter look from 1976. Patrick claimed to have lost his hairstylist and couldn't find one he trusted.

He wore nice clothes and carried his weight well, but he was too young to let himself go.

Three months before he checked out of Biloxi, Patrick succeeded in convincing his partners that the firm needed its own brochure. It was a small project, but one he embraced with great vigor. Though Patrick wasn't supposed to know it, the firm was getting closer to the Aricia settlement, and the money was almost in sight. Egos were expanding daily. A very serious firm was about to become a very wealthy one, so why not impress themselves with a professionally done brochure. It was a way to humor Patrick. Each of the five sat for a professional photographer, then they spent an hour on the group shot. Patrick printed five thousand, and received high marks from the other partners. There he was on page two, fat, bearded, bushy-headed, and looking nothing like the Patrick they found in Brazil.

The photo was used by the press when his death was reported. It was by far the most recent, and coincidentally, Patrick had sent a brochure to the local paper, just in case the firm decided to advertise. They had laughed about this over drinks at Mary Mahoney's. They could envision Patrick orchestrating the photography in the firm's conference room. They could see Bogan and Vitrano and Rapley and Havarac in the darkest navy suits and their most serious smiles, and all the while Patrick was laying the groundwork for his exit.

In the months after he left them, the gang at Mary Mahoney's had toasted Patrick many times and played the game of "Where could he be?" They had wished him well and thought about his money. Time passed and so did the shock of his disappearance. Once they had thoroughly analyzed his life, the sessions came further apart and finally stopped. Months became years. Patrick would never be found.

KARL STILL FOUND IT difficult to believe. He entered the elevator in the lobby and rode alone to the third floor.

He wondered if he had ever given up on Patrick. The mysteries were too rich to escape. A bad day on the bench, and he would think of Patrick on a sun-drenched beach reading a novel, sipping a drink, watching the girls. Another year without a pay raise, and he would wonder what the ninety million was doing. The latest rumor on the demise of the Bogan firm, and he would shame Patrick for the misery he had caused. No, the truth was, Karl had thought of Patrick, for one reason or another, at least once a day, every day, since he left.

There were no nurses or other patients in the hall. The two deputies stood. One said, "Evenin', Judge." He greeted them and entered the darkened room.

Twenty-three

PATRICK WAS SITTING in bed watching "Jeopardy" with his shirt off and the blinds drawn. A dim table light was on. "Sit here," he told Karl, pointing to the end of his bed. He waited just long enough for Karl to see the burns on his chest, then quickly slipped on a tee shirt. The sheet was up to his waist.

"Thanks for coming," he said. He turned the TV off, and the room grew even darker.

"Pretty nasty burns, Patrick," Karl said as he sat on the edge of the bed, as far away as possible, his right foot hanging off the edge. Patrick pulled his knees to his chest. Under the sheet, he still looked painfully thin.

"It was ugly," he said, his hands wrapped tightly around his knees. "Doc says they're healing okay. But I'll need to stay here for a while."

"I have no problem with that, Patrick. No one is screaming for you to be moved to the jail."

"Not yet. But I bet the press will start soon."

"Relax, Patrick. That decision will be made by me."

He seemed relieved. "Thanks, Karl. You know I can't survive in jail. You've seen it."

"What about Parchman? It's a hundred times worse."

There was a long pause as Karl wished he could take back the words. It was instantaneous, and cruel. "I'm sorry," he said. "That was uncalled for."

"I'll kill myself before I go to Parchman."

"I don't blame you. Let's talk about something pleasant."

"You can't keep this case, can you, Karl?"

"No. Of course not. I'll have to recuse myself."

"When?"

"Pretty soon."

"Who'll get it?"

"Either Trussel or Lanks, probably Trussel." Karl stared at him intently as he spoke. Patrick was having trouble with eye contact. Karl was waiting for a telling flicker from the eyes, followed by a grin, then a laugh as Patrick broke down and bragged about his escapades. "Come on, Patrick," Karl wanted to say. "Let's hear it. Tell me the whole story."

But the eyes were distant. This was not the same Patrick.

Karl felt compelled to try. "Where'd you get that chin?"

"Bought it in Rio."

"And the nose?"

"Same place, same time. You like it?"

"It's handsome."

"In Rio, they have drive-through plastic surgery shops."

"I hear they have beaches."

"Unbelievable beaches."

"Did you meet any girls down there?"

"A couple."

Sex was not a subject Patrick had ever dwelt on. He enjoyed a long, admiring gaze at an attractive woman, but, to Karl's knowledge, he had remained faithful to Trudy throughout their marriage. Once, at deer camp, they had compared notes about their wives. Patrick had admitted it was a challenge to keep Trudy satisfied.

A long pause, and Karl realized Patrick was in no hurry to talk. The first minute passed in silence, and the second one dragged on. Karl was happy to visit, even delighted to see his friend, but there was a limit to how long he could sit in a dark room and stare at the walls.

"Look, Patrick, I will not hear your case, so I'm not here as your Judge. I'm not your lawyer. I'm your friend. You can talk to me."

Patrick reached for a small can of orange juice with a straw in it. "Would you like something to drink?"

"No."

He took a short drink, and put the can back on the table. "I guess it sounds romantic, doesn't it? The dream of simply walking away, vanishing into the night and when the sun comes up you're somebody new. All your problems are left behind—the drudgery of work, the heartbreak of a bad marriage, the pressure of becoming more and more affluent. You have that dream, don't you, Karl?"

"I guess everybody does at some point. How long did you plan it?"

"A long time. I seriously doubted that the baby was mine. I decided—"

"I beg your pardon."

"It's true, Karl. I'm not the father. Trudy slept around throughout our marriage. I loved the child as best I could, but I was miserable. I gathered evidence and promised myself I would confront Trudy, but it was easy to put off. Oddly enough, I sort of got used to the idea that she had a lover. I was planning to leave, but I just didn't know how to do it. So I read a couple of underground books on how to change identities and obtain new papers. It's not complicated. Just takes a little thought and planning."

"So you grew a beard and gained fifty pounds."

"Yeah, I was amazed at how different I looked with the beard. That was right about the time I made partner, and I was already burned out. I was married to a woman who wasn't faithful, playing with a child who wasn't mine, working with a bunch of people I couldn't stand. Something clicked, Karl. I was driving one day along Highway 90, headed somewhere important but stuck in traffic, and I looked out across the Gulf. There was a lonely little sailboat barely moving on the horizon. And I wanted so desperately to be on it, to sail away to some place where no one knew me. I sat there, watching it move, aching so badly to swim out to it. I cried, Karl. Can you believe that?"

"We all have days like that."

"Then I snapped, and I was never the same afterward. I knew I would vanish."

"How long did it take?"

"I had to be patient. Most people get in a hurry when they decide to disappear, and they make mistakes. I had time. I wasn't broke or running from creditors. I bought a two-million-dollar life insurance policy, and that took three months. I knew I couldn't leave Trudy and the baby with nothing. I started gaining the weight, eating like a maniac. I changed my will. I convinced Trudy that we should make our funeral and burial arrangements, and I did it without arousing suspicions."

"Cremation was a nice touch."

"Thanks. I highly recommend it."

"Makes it impossible to determine cause of death and identity, a few important things like that."

"Let's not talk about that."

"Sorry."

"Then I got wind of Mr. Benny Aricia, and his little war with the Pentagon and Platt & Rockland Industries. Bogan kept him under wraps. I dug deeper and found out that Vitrano and Rapley and Havarac were all in on the deal. All the partners but me. They changed, Karl, all of them. They became secretive and devious. Sure I was the new guy, but I was a partner after all. They had voted unanimously to make me a full partner, and two months later they were dodging me while they conspired with Aricia. Suddenly, I was the guy doing all the traveling, which worked out just beautifully for everyone. Trudy could arrange her little trysts. The partners could meet with Aricia without hiding. They sent me everywhere, which was fine with me too because I was making plans. Once I went to Fort Lauderdale for three days of depositions, and while I was there I found a guy in Miami who could do perfect papers. Two thousand bucks and I had a new driver's license, passport, Social Security card, and voter registration papers from right here in Harrison County. Carl Hildebrand was my name, in honor of you."

"I'm touched."

"In Boston, I tracked down a guy who can get you lost. For a thousand bucks I had my own one-day seminar on how to vanish. In Dayton, I hired a surveillance expert who taught me about bugs and mikes and dirty little devices like that. I was patient, Karl. Very patient. I stayed at the office at odd hours, and gathered as much of the Aricia story as I could get. I listened hard, quizzed secretaries, rummaged through the garbage. Then I began wiring offices, just a couple at first to learn how it's done. I wired Vitrano's, and I couldn't believe what I heard. They were going to kick me out of the firm, Karl. Can you believe it? They knew their cut from the Aricia settlement would be around thirty million, and they were planning to split it four ways. But the pieces would not be equal. Bogan, of course, would get more, something close to ten million. He had to take care of some people in Washington. The other three would get five million, and the rest would be spent on the firm. I, as it was planned, would be on the streets."

"When was this?"

"Throughout most of '91. Aricia's claim got tentative Justice approval to settle on December 14, 1991, and at that time it was taking about ninety days to get the money. Not even the Senator could speed things along."

"Tell me about the car wreck."

Patrick shifted his weight, then kicked his legs from under the sheet and got out of bed. "A cramp," he mumbled as he stretched his back and legs. He stood by the bathroom door, rocking gently from one foot to the other, looking down at Karl. "It was a Sunday."

"February ninth."

"Right. February ninth. I spent the weekend at my cabin, and as I was driving home I had a wreck, got killed, and went to heaven."

Karl watched him closely and never smiled. "Try it again," he said.

"Why, Karl?"

"Morbid fascination."

"Is that all?"

"I promise. It was such a masterful job of deceit, Patrick. How'd you do it?"

"I may have to skip a few of the details."

"I'm sure you will."

"Let's take a walk. I'm tired of this place."

They entered the hall, and Patrick explained to his guards that he and the Judge needed a stroll. The deputies followed at a distance. A nurse smiled and asked if she could bring anything. Two Diet Cokes, Patrick said politely. Patrick walked very deliberately, saying nothing until they came to the end of the hallway, where plate-glass windows overlooked the parking lot. They sat on a vinyl bench, looking back down the hall, where the deputies waited fifty feet away with their backs turned to them.

Patrick wore scrub pants, no socks, leather sandals. "Have you seen pictures of the crash site?" he asked, very quietly.

"Yes."

"I found it the day before. The ravine is fairly steep, and I thought it was the perfect place to have the accident. I waited until about ten, Sunday night, and left the cabin. I stopped at a little store at the county line."

"Verhall's."

"Right, Verhall's. I filled the tank."

"Twelve gallons, fourteen dollars and twenty-one cents, paid with a credit card."

"That sounds right. I chatted with Mrs. Verhall, then left. There wasn't much traffic. Two miles away, I turned onto a gravel road and went a mile to a spot I had picked out. I stopped, opened the trunk, and proceeded to get dressed. I had a set of gear used by dirt bikers—a helmet, shoulder pads, knee and hand pads, the works. I quickly put it on over my clothing, everything but the helmet, then returned to the highway, where I drove south. The first time, there was a car behind me. The second time, there was a car coming toward me in the distance. I braked hard anyway, leaving skid marks. There was no traffic the third time. I put the helmet on, took a deep breath, and left the road. It was scary as hell, Karl."

Karl figured that at this point there was another body somewhere in the car, either dead or alive, but he wouldn't ask. At least not now.

"I was only doing about thirty when I left the road, but thirty feels like ninety when you're airborne and trees are flying by. I was bouncing, snapping small trees. The windshield cracked. I was steering right and left, dodging as best I could, but a big pine tree caught the left front. The airbag exploded, and for a second I was knocked out. There was a tumbling sensation, then all was still. I opened my eyes, and felt a sharp pain in my left shoulder. No blood. I was dangling somehow, and I realized that the Blazer had come to rest on its right side. I began crawling out. By the time I got out of the damned thing, I knew I was lucky. My shoulder wasn't broken, just jammed. I walked around the Blazer and was amazed at how well I had wrecked it. The roof had caved in just above my head. Another six inches and I'm not sure I could've gotten out."

"That seems incredibly risky. You could've been killed or badly injured. Why not simply push the car down the ravine?"

"Wouldn't work. It had to look real, Karl. The ravine was not steep enough. This is flat country, remember."

"Why not put a brick on the accelerator and jump out of the way?"

"Bricks don't burn. If they'd found a brick in the car, maybe they would've been suspicious. I thought of everything, and I decided I could drive it into the trees and walk away. I had a seat belt, an airbag, a helmet."

"Evel Knievel himself."

The nurse brought the Diet Cokes, and wanted to chat for a moment. She finally left. "Where was I?" Patrick asked.

"I think you were about to torch it."

"Right. I listened for a moment. The left rear wheel was spinning, and that was the only sound. I couldn't see the highway, but I looked up in its direction and heard nothing. Absolutely nothing. It was a clean exit. The nearest house was a mile away. I was certain no one had heard the crash, but still I was in a hurry. I stripped off the helmet and the pads and threw them in the Blazer, then I ran farther down the ravine to a spot where I had hidden the gasoline."

"When?"

"Earlier in the day. Very early. At dawn. I had four two-gallon plastic jugs of gas, and I quickly hauled them up to the Blazer. It was dark as hell and I couldn't use a flashlight, but I had marked off a little path. I placed three of the containers in the Blazer, stopped, listened. Nothing from the highway. Not a sound anywhere. The adrenaline was pumping and my heart was in my throat. The last container I splashed inside and out, then threw it in with the rest. I backed off thirty feet or so, and lit a cigarette I had in my pocket. I threw it, backed up even farther, and ducked behind a tree. It landed on the Blazer, then the gas exploded. Sounded like a bomb. In an instant it was roaring from all the windows. I climbed up the steepest side of the ravine and found a vantage point probably a hundred feet away. I wanted to watch without getting caught. The fire was howling; I had no idea it would make so much noise. Some brush started to burn, and I thought maybe I had started a forest fire. Luckily it had rained on Friday, a hard rain that soaked the trees and ground cover." He took a drink of his soda. "I just realized I forgot to ask you about your family. I'm sorry, Karl. How's Iris?"

"Iris is fine. We can talk about the family later. Right now, I'd like to hear the story."

"Sure. Where was I? I'm so scatterbrained. It's all those drugs."

"Watching the car burn."

"Right. So the fire gets really hot, then the gas tank explodes and it's another bomb. I thought for a second I might get scorched. Debris flies through the air, and rattles through the trees as it falls. Finally, I hear something from the highway. Voices. People yelling. I can't see anybody, but there's a commotion. A long time passes and the fire spreads around the car. It's coming at me now, so I leave. I can hear a siren coming. I'm trying to find a creek I'd come across the day before a hundred yards or so through the woods. I'm going to follow it. And I'm looking for my dirt bike."

Karl hung on every word, absorbed every scene, made every step along the way with Patrick. This escape route had been the subject of many fierce debates in the months after the disappearance, and no one had a clue. "A dirt bike?"

"Yeah. An old one. I bought it for five hundred dollars cash from a used car dealer in Hattiesburg several months earlier. I played with it some in the woods. Nobody knew I had it."

"No title or registration?"

"Of course not. I gotta tell you, Karl, as I ran through the woods, looking for the creek, still scared but in one piece, and I heard the fire and voices fade behind me and the siren getting louder, I knew I was running to freedom. Patrick was dead, and he took with him a bad life. He would get honored and buried properly, and everyone would say good-bye. And before long people would start to forget about him. But me, I was running wildly to a new life. It was exhilarating."

What about the poor guy burning in the car, Patrick? While you were running joyously through the woods someone else was dying in your place. Karl almost asked. Patrick seemed oblivious to the fact that he had committed murder.

"Then suddenly, I'm lost. The woods are dense, and somehow I stumble the wrong way. I get a small flashlight, and I figure it's safe to use it. I roam and backtrack until I can no longer hear the siren. At one point, I sit down on a stump and make myself get a grip. I'm in a panic. Wouldn't this be great? Survive the wreck only to die of starvation and exposure. I start walking again, get lucky and find the creek. Before long, I find the dirt bike. I push it a hundred yards, up the side of a hill, to an old logging trail, and of course by now my two-hundred-and-thirty-pound lumbering fat ass is practically dead. There's not a house within two miles, so I start the bike and follow the logging trail. I've ridden the area several times on the bike, so I know it well. I find a gravel road, and see the first house. I've got the bike jerry-rigged with aluminum tubes that act to muffle the engine, so I'm not making much noise. Before long, I'm on a paved road in Stone County. I stay away from the main highway, and stick to the back roads. A couple of hours later, I make it back to the cabin."

"Why did you go back to the cabin?"

"I had to regroup."

"Weren't you afraid of being seen by Pepper?"

Patrick didn't flinch at the question. Karl had timed it perfectly, and he watched for a reaction. None. Patrick studied his feet for a few seconds, then said, "Pepper was gone."

Twenty-four

UNDERHILL WAS BACK. Fresh from eight hours of watching videos and reviewing notes in another room. He walked in, gave a generic hello in the general direction of Stephano and his lawyer, then got to work. "If we could pick up where you left off yesterday, Mr. Stephano."

"Where might that be?"

"Your invasion of Brazil."

"Right. Well, let's see. It's a big country. A hundred and sixty million people, more square miles than the lower forty-eight, and a history of being a marvelous place to hide, especially if you're on the run. Nazis favored it for years. We put together a dossier on Lanigan, had it translated into Portuguese. We had a police artist work with some computer people to develop a series of color-enhanced renderings of what Lanigan looked like now. We spent hours with the sailboat charter captain in Orange Beach, as well as with the bankers in Nassau, and together they helped us develop a series of detailed sketches of Lanigan. We even met with the partners in the firm and went over the sketches. They, in turn, showed them to the secretaries. One of the partners, Mr. Bogan, even took the best rendering to the widow Lanigan for her opinion."

"Now that you've caught him, were your photos close?"

"Fairly close. The chin and the nose threw us off a bit."

"Please continue."

"We hurried to Brazil, and found three of the best private investigative firms in the country. One in Rio, one in São Paulo, and one in Recife, in the northeast. We were paying top dollar, so we hired the very best. We put them together as a team, and gathered them in São Paulo for a week. We listened to them. They developed the story that Patrick should be an American fugitive wanted for the kidnap and murder of the daughter of a wealthy family, a family now offering a reward for information about his whereabouts. The murder of a child was, of course, designed to arouse more sympathy than stealing money from a bunch of lawyers.

"We went straight to the language schools, flashing pictures of Lanigan and offering cash. The reputable schools slammed their doors. Others looked at the pictures but couldn't help. By this time, we had a lot of respect for Lanigan, and we didn't think he'd run the risk of studying in a place where questions were asked and records were kept. So we targeted the private tutors, of which there are only about a million in Brazil. It was tedious work."

"Did you offer cash up front?"

"We did what our Brazilian agents wanted to do, which was to show the pictures, tell the story of the murdered child, then wait for a reaction. If there was a nibble, then we'd gently drop the hint about some reward money."

"Any nibbles?"

"A few, here and there. But we never paid any money, at least not to language tutors."

"To others?"

Stephano nodded as he glanced at a sheet of paper. "In April of '94, we found a plastic surgeon in Rio who showed some interest in Lanigan's pictures. He toyed with us for a month, and finally convinced us he had worked on Lanigan. He had some photos of his own, before and after shots. He played us perfectly, and we eventually agreed to pay him a quarter of a million dollars, cash, off-shore, for his entire file."

"What was in the file?"

"Just the basics. Clear frontal photos of our man before and after the surgery. It was really odd because Lanigan had insisted on no photos. He wanted no trail whatsoever, just hard cash for the alterations. Wouldn't give his real name, said he was a businessman from Canada who suddenly wanted to look younger. The surgeon heard this all the time, and he knew the guy was on the run. He kept a hidden camera in his office, thus the photos."

"Could we see them?"

"Certainly." The lawyer was aroused for the moment and slid a manila envelope down the table to Underhill, who opened it and only glanced at the photos.

"How did you find the doctor?"

"At the same time we were checking language schools and tutors, we were also pursuing other professions. Forgers, plastic surgeons, importers."

"Importers?"

"Yeah, there's a Portuguese word for these guys, but "importers" is a very rough translation. They're a shady group of specialists who can get you into Brazil and then get you lost—new names, new papers, the best places to live and hide. We found them to be impenetrable. We had pretty much the same bad luck with the forgers. They can't afford to talk about their clients. It's very bad for business."

"But the doctors were different?"

"Not really. They don't talk. But we hired a plastic surgeon as a consultant, and he gave us the names of some of his sleazier brethren who worked on the nameless. That's how we found the doctor in Rio."

"This was over two years after Lanigan disappeared."

"That's correct."

"Was this the first evidence that he was actually in the country?"

"The very first, yes."

"What did you do for the first two years?"

"Spent a lot of money. Knocked on a lot of doors. Chased a lot of worthless leads. As I said, it's a big country."

"How many men were working for you in Brazil?"

"At one point, I was paying sixty agents. Thankfully, they're not as expensive as Americans."

□ □ □ □

IF THE JUDGE wanted a pizza, then the Judge got a pizza. It was fetched from Hugo's, an old family bistro on Division Street, near the Point and far away from the fast-food places lining the beach. It was delivered by a deputy to Room 312. Patrick smelled it as it left the elevator. He stared at it when Karl opened the box at the foot of his bed. He closed his eyes and sucked in the heavenly aroma of black olives, portobello mushrooms, Italian sausage, green peppers, and six different cheeses. He had eaten a thousand pizzas from Hugo's, especially during the last two years of his old life, and he had been dreaming of this one for a week now. Home did have certain advantages.

"You look like death warmed over. Eat up," Karl said.

Patrick devoured his first slice of pizza without a word, then went for a second.

"How did you get so skinny?" Karl asked, chomping away.

"Can we get some beer?" Patrick asked.

"No. Sorry. You're in jail, remember."

"Losing weight is between the ears. Make up your mind, it's easy. I suddenly had plenty of motivation to starve myself."

"How fat did you get?"

"The Friday before I disappeared, I weighed two hundred thirty-six pounds. I dropped forty-seven pounds the first six weeks. This morning I weighed one-sixty."

"You look like a refugee. Eat."

"Thanks."

"You were at the cabin."

Patrick wiped his chin with a paper napkin and placed his slice back in the box. He sipped from his Diet Coke. "Yeah, I was at the cabin. It was around eleven-thirty. I entered through the front door, and didn't turn on any lights. There's another cabin a half a mile away, up on a ridge and visible from mine. It's owned by some people from Hattiesburg, and while I didn't think they were there that weekend, I had to be careful. I covered the small bathroom window with a dark towel, turned on the light, and quickly shaved. Then I cut my hair. Then I dyed it, a dark brown, almost black."

"Sorry I missed that."

"It was quite becoming. It was odd. I even felt like a different person as I stared at the mirror. Then I cleaned up my mess, wiped up all the hair and whiskers because I knew they would go through the place with a fine-tooth comb, and I packed away the dye box and tubes. I changed into heavy clothing. I made a pot of strong coffee, and drank half of it. The other half went in a thermos for my journey. At 1 A.M., I left the cabin in a hurry. I didn't expect the cops to show up that night, but there was always the chance. I knew it would take time to identify the Blazer and call Trudy, and someone might suggest that they go to the cabin for some reason. I didn't expect this to happen, but by 1 A.M. I was anxious to leave."

"Did you have any concern for Trudy?"

"Not particularly. I knew she would handle the shock well, and that she would do a marvelous job of getting me buried. She'd be a model widow for about a month, and then she would get the life insurance money. It would be her finest hour. Lots of attention, lots of money. No, Karl, I had no love for the woman. Nor any concern."

"Did you ever go back to the cabin?"

"No."

Karl could not, would not, hold the next question. "Pepper's shotgun and camping gear were found under one of the beds. How'd they get there?"

Patrick glanced up for a second as if surprised, then he looked away. Karl absorbed this reaction, because he would think about it many times over the next few days. A jolt, then a glance, and then unable to answer truthfully, a diversion to the wall.

The line from the old movie said, "When you commit a murder you make twenty-five mistakes. If you can think of fifteen of them, you're a genius." Perhaps Patrick, in all his meticulous scheming, had simply forgotten about Pepper's things. In the rush of the moment, he had hurried a bit too much.

"I don't know," he said, almost grunting it, still looking at the wall.

Karl had got what he wanted, and he pressed on. "Where did you go?"

"The bike ride from hell," Patrick said, perking up and anxious to move on. "It was forty degrees, which on a motorcycle going down a highway at night feels like twenty below. I stayed on the back roads, away from traffic, moving slowly because the wind cut through me like a knife. I crossed into Alabama, and again kept off the main roads. A dirt bike on a highway at three in the morning might give a bored cop something to do, so I avoided towns. I finally made it to the outskirts of Mobile around four in the morning. A month earlier I had found a small motel where they took cash and asked no questions. I sneaked into the parking lot, hid the bike behind the motel, and walked in the front door as if I had just gotten out of a cab. Thirty bucks for a room, cash, no paperwork. It took an hour to thaw out. I slept for two hours and woke up with the sun. When did you hear about it, Karl?"

"I guess about the time you were dirt-biking through the countryside. Doug Vitrano called me at a few minutes after three. Woke me up, which really ticks me off now. Losing sleep and grieving while you were playing Easy Rider and rambling off to the good life."

"I wasn't home free."

"No, but you certainly weren't worried about your friends."

"I feel bad about that, Karl."

"No you don't."

"You're right, I don't." Patrick was relaxed, animated, into his story, grinning now.

"You woke up with the sun. A new man in a new world. All your worries and problems left behind."

"Most of them. It was terribly exciting, and also frightening. Sleep was difficult. I watched television until eight-thirty, saw nothing about my death, then showered, changed into fresh clothes—"

"Wait. Where was the hair dye box and tubes?"

"I threw them in a dumpster somewhere in Washington County, Alabama. I called a cab, which in Mobile is not the easiest thing to do. The driver parked outside my room, and I left. No checkout. I left the dirt bike behind the motel and went to a mall which I knew opened at nine. I went to a department store and bought a navy jacket, some slacks, and a pair of loafers."

"How did you pay for them?"

"Cash."

"You didn't have a credit card?"

"Yes, I had a phony Visa I'd procured from a source in Miami. It was good for only a handful of charges, then it had to be discarded. I saved it for the rental car."

"How much cash did you have?"

"About twenty thousand."

"Where did it come from?"

"I'd been saving it for a while. I was making good money, though Trudy was doing her best to spend it faster than I could make it. I told the bookkeeper in the firm that I needed to reroute some money to keep it away from my wife. She said she did this all the time for the lawyers. It went to another account. I cashed it periodically, and stuffed it in a drawer. Satisfied?"

"Yes. You had just bought a pair of loafers."

"I went to another store and bought a white shirt and a tie. I changed in a mall rest room, and presto, I looked like any one of a million traveling salesmen. I bought some more clothes and accessories, put them in a new canvas bag, and called another cab. This one took me to the Mobile airport, where I ate breakfast and waited on a Northwest Airlink flight from Atlanta. It arrived. I fell in with the other commuters, all very busy and anxious to attack Mobile, and I stopped with two other guys at the Avis desk. They had reserved cars. Mine was a bit more complicated. I had a perfect driver's license from Georgia, along with my passport, just in case. I used the Visa, and I was very scared. The card number was a valid one—some poor guy in Decatur, Georgia, and I was terrified a computer would catch it and alarms would go off. But nothing happened. I filled out the paperwork, and left in a hurry."

"What was your name?"

"Randy Austin."

"Big question, Randy," Karl said as he took a bite of pizza and chewed it slowly. "You were in the airport. Why didn't you simply get on a plane and leave?"

"Oh, I thought about it. As I was eating breakfast, I watched two planes take off, and I wanted so badly to hop on and leave. But there was unfinished business. It was a very tough decision."

"What was the unfinished business?"

"I think you know. I drove to Gulf Shores, then along the Coast east to Orange Beach, where I rented a small condo."

"One you had already checked out."

"Of course. I knew they would take cash. It was February, and cold, business was slow. I took a mild sedative and slept for six hours. I watched the evening news and saw where I'd died a fiery death. My friends were just devastated."

"You ass."

"I drove to the grocery and bought a bag of apples and some diet pills. After dark, I walked the beach for three hours, something I did every night while I was hiding around Mobile. Next morning, I sneaked into Pascagoula and got a newspaper, saw my fat smiling face on the front page, read about the tragedy, saw the touching little blurb you offered, and also saw that the funeral would be that afternoon at three. I went to Orange Beach and rented a sailboat. Then drove to Biloxi in time for my service."

"The papers have said you watched your own burial."

"True. I hid in a tree in the woods beyond the cemetery, and watched through binoculars."

"That seems like an incredibly dumb thing to do."

"It was. Absolutely idiotic. But I was drawn to the place. I had to make certain, to see for myself that my trick had worked. And I guess by then, I was convinced I could get by with anything."

"I guess you had picked out the tree, the perfect spot."

"No. In fact, I wasn't sure I would do it. I left Mobile and drove west on the interstate, and I kept telling myself not to do it. Not to get near Biloxi."

"Your big ass climbed a tree?"

"I was motivated. It was an oak with thick branches."

"Thank God for that. I wish a limb had cracked and you'd fallen on your head."

"No you don't."

"Yes I do. We're huddled around the grave fighting back tears and consoling the widow, and you're perched on a limb like a fat frog laughing at us."

"You're just trying to be angry, Karl."

And he was right. Four and a half years had eliminated any anger Karl had felt. The truth was, he was delighted to be sitting there on the end of the hospital bed, eating pizza with Patrick and soaking up the coveted details.

However, the funeral was as far as they would get. Patrick had talked enough, and they were now back in his room, a place he didn't completely trust. "Tell me, how are Bogan and Vitrano and the boys?" he said, and relaxed on his pillows, already relishing what he was about to hear.

Twenty-five

PAULO MIRANDA'S last phone call from his daughter had been two days earlier. She was in a hotel in New Orleans, still traveling on her legal work for her mysterious new client, still warning him of people who might be looking for her and watching him because her client had enemies in Brazil. As with the previous calls, she was brief and vague and scared, though trying desperately not to show it. He had become angry and pressed for details. She had been more concerned with his safety. He wanted her to come home. He exploded and revealed for the first time that he had met with her former partners and knew that she had been terminated. She had calmly explained that she was on her own now, a solo practitioner with a rich client in international trading, and that extended travel like this would become routine.

He hated to argue with her on the phone, especially since he was so worried about her.

Paulo was also tired of the shady little men lurking around his street and following him as he walked to the market or drove to his office at the Pontifícia Universidade Católica. He watched for them; they were always nearby. He had nicknames for them. Paulo had spoken several times to the manager of Eva's apartment building, and the same shifty creatures were watching there too.

His last class, a survey of German philosophy, ended at one. He met in his office for thirty minutes with a struggling student, then left for the day. It was raining and he had forgotten his umbrella. His car was parked in a small faculty lot behind a classroom building.

Osmar was waiting. Paulo was deep in thought as he left the building, his eyes down, with a newspaper on top of his head, his mind a million miles away as he walked under a dripping shade tree and stepped in a puddle near his car. Next to it was a small red Fiat delivery van. The driver emerged, but Paulo didn't notice. The driver opened the rear door of the van, but Paulo neither heard nor saw anything. He was reaching for his keys when Osmar shoved him from the side, and knocked him roughly into the van. His briefcase fell to the ground.

The door slammed. In the darkness, the barrel of a gun was placed between Paulo's eyes, and a voice told him to be silent.

The driver's door of his car was opened, and papers from his briefcase were strewn from the front seat to the rear tires.

The van raced away.

A phone call to the police informed them of the kidnapping.

For an hour and a half, they drove Paulo out of the city, then into the countryside, though he had no idea where he was. The van was hot—no windows, no lights. There were the silhouettes of two men sitting close to him, both with guns. They stopped behind a sprawling farmhouse, and Paulo was led inside. His quarters were in the rear; a bedroom, a bath, a parlor with a television. There was plenty of food. He would not be harmed, he was told, unless of course he made the mistake of trying to escape. He would be held for a week or so, then released, if he behaved himself.

He locked his door and peeked from a window. Two men sat under a tree, laughing and drinking tea with submachine guns nearby.

Anonymous calls were made to Paulo's son in Rio, to the manager of Eva's apartment, to her old law firm, and to one of her friends who worked at a travel agency. The message was the same; Paulo Miranda had been kidnapped. The police were investigating.

EVA WAS IN NEW YORK, staying for a few days in a suite at the Pierre Hotel, shopping along Fifth Avenue, spending hours in museums. Her instructions were to keep on the move, to pop in and out of New Orleans. She had received three letters from Patrick, and she had written him twice, all correspondence being passed through Sandy. Whatever physical abuse he had suffered had certainly not affected his attention to details. His letters were specific—plans and checklists and emergency procedures.

She called her father, and there was no answer. She called her brother, and the sky came crashing down. She had to return immediately, he insisted. Her brother was a delicate type, unaccustomed to pressure and adversity. He cracked easily. The difficult family decisions were always left to Eva.

She kept him on the phone for half an hour as she tried to calm both of them. No, there had been no ransom demand. Not a word from the kidnappers.

AGAINST his specific instructions, she called him. Fidgeting at a pay phone in La Guardia, looking over her shoulder through thick sunglasses and tugging nervously at her hair, she dialed his room number, and spoke in Portuguese. If they were listening, at least they would have to find a translator.

"Patrick, it's Leah," she said, with as little emotion as possible.

"What's wrong?" he asked, also in Portuguese. He hadn't heard her wonderful voice for some time, and he was not pleased to hear it now.

"Can we talk?"

"Yes. What's the matter?" Patrick checked the phone in his room for bugs every three or four hours. He was bored. He also scanned every possible hiding place with the bugging sensor Sandy had found him. With guards posted around the clock, he had learned to relax somewhat. But the outside lines still worried him.

"It's my father," she said, then blurted out the story of Paulo's disappearance. "I have to go home."

"No, Leah," he said calmly. "It's a trap. Your father is not a wealthy man. They are not asking for money. They want you."

"I cannot abandon my father."

"And you can't find him either."

"This is all my fault."

"No. The blame lies with me. But don't make matters worse by rushing into their trap."

She twirled her hair and watched the parade of people rushing by. "So what do I do?"

"Go to New Orleans. Call Sandy when you get there. Let me think."

She bought a ticket, then walked to her gate and found a seat in a corner where she could hide her face next to the wall and behind a magazine. She thought of her poppa and the horrible things they could be doing to him. The only two men she loved had been kidnapped by the same people, and Patrick was still in the hospital because of his wounds. Her father was older and not as strong as Patrick. They were hurting him because of her. And there was nothing she could do.

AFTER A DAY of searching, a Biloxi policeman saw Lance's car leaving the Grand Casino at 10:20 P.M. Lance was stopped and detained for no valid reason until Sweeney arrived. He and Lance conferenced in the backseat of a flashing patrol car in the parking lot of a Burger King.

The Sheriff asked how the dope trade was going, and Lance said business was good.

"How's Trudy?" the Sheriff asked, toothpick between his lips. It was a massive struggle in the backseat to see who could be the coolest. Lance even put on his newest Ray-Bans.

"She's fine. How's your woman?"

"I don't have one. Look, Lance, we've picked up some pretty serious tips that you're in the market for a trigger."

"Lies, lies, total lies."

"Yeah, well, we don't think so. You see, Lance, all your pals are just like you. Either just off probation or working hard to get back on. Scum, you know. Just scum. Always looking for a dirty buck, always one step ahead of trouble. They hear a good rumor, they can't wait to whisper it to the feds. Might help them with their probation."

"That's nice, real nice. I like that."

"And so we know you got some cash, you got this woman who's

about to lose a bundle, and everything would be great if Mr. Lanigan sorta remained dead."

"Who?"

"Yeah. So here's what we're doing. Us and the feds. We're puttin' you under surveillance, you and the woman, and we're watching and listening real hard. You make a move, we'll get you. Both you and Trudy will get yourselves in more trouble than Lanigan's in."

"I'm supposed to be frightened by this?"

"If you had a brain you would be."

"Can I go now?"

"Please."

Both doors were opened from the outside, and Lance was taken back to his car.

AT THE SAME TIME, Agent Cutter rang Trudy's doorbell, hoping she was asleep. He had been sitting in a coffee shop in Fairhope, waiting for word that Lance had been detained.

Trudy was awake. She unbolted the front door and spoke through the chain. "What do you want?" she demanded as Cutter flashed his badge and emphasized the "FBI." She recognized him.

"Can I come in?"

"No."

"Lance is in police custody. I think we should talk."

"What!"

"The Biloxi police have him."

She unlocked the chain and opened the door. They stood in the foyer, facing each other. Cutter was thoroughly enjoying himself.

"What's he done?" she asked.

"I think he'll be released soon."

"I'll call my lawyer."

"Fine, but there's something I should tell you first. We have it from a good source that Lance has been trying to locate a hit man to take out your husband, Patrick Lanigan."

"No!" She covered her mouth with a hand. The surprise seemed real.

"Yes. And you could be implicated. It's your money Lance is

trying to protect, and I'm sure you'll be considered a co-conspirator. If something happens to Lanigan, we'll come here first."

"I haven't done anything."

"Not yet. We're watching you very closely, Mrs. Lanigan."

"Don't call me that."

"Sorry."

Cutter left her standing in the foyer.

SANDY PARKED in a lot off Canal around midnight, and darted down Decatur and into the heart of the French Quarter. His client had lectured him sternly about security, especially when meeting Leah. Only Sandy could lead them to her, and so he must be extremely cautious. "She's in grave danger, Sandy," Patrick had told him an hour before. "You can't be too careful."

He walked around one block three times, and when he was certain no one could possibly be behind him, he ducked into an open bar, where he drank a soda and watched the sidewalk. Then he walked across the street to the Royal Sonesta. He milled about the lobby with the tourists, then he rode the elevator to the third floor. Leah opened the door, and locked it behind him.

Not surprisingly, she looked tired and wrung out.

"I'm sorry about your father," Sandy said. "Have you heard anything?"

"No. I've been traveling." There was a tray of coffee on top of the television. Sandy poured a cup and stirred in sugar. "Patrick told me about it," he said. "Who are these people?"

"There's a file over there," she said, nodding at a small table. "Please sit." She was pointing at the end of the bed. Sandy sat with his coffee and waited. It was time for a talk.

"We met two years ago, in 1994, after his surgery in Rio. Patrick said he was a Canadian businessman who needed a lawyer with experience in trade matters. But he really needed a friend. I was a friend for two days, then we fell in love. He told me everything about his past, everything. He had done a perfect job of escaping, and he had lots of money, but Patrick could not forget his past. He was determined to know who was chasing him, and how close they were. In August of 1994, I came to the U.S., and I made contact with a private security firm in Atlanta. It's an odd name, the Pluto Group, a bunch of ex-FBI types Patrick had found before he disappeared. I gave them a false name, told them I was from Spain, and that I needed information about the search for Patrick Lanigan. I paid them fifty thousand dollars. They, in turn, sent people to Biloxi, where they at first made contact with Patrick's old law firm. They pretended to have some vague information about his whereabouts, and the lawyers very quietly referred them to a man in Washington named Jack Stephano. Stephano is a high-priced sleuth who specializes in corporate espionage and the locating of missing people. They met with him in Washington. He was very secretive and told them little, but it was obvious he was running the search for Patrick. They met with him several times, and the prospect of a reward popped up. They offered to sell their information, and Stephano agreed to pay fifty thousand dollars if it led to Patrick. In the course of these meetings, they learned that Stephano had good reason to believe Patrick was in Brazil. This, of course, terrified Patrick and me."

"This was Patrick's first hint that they knew he was in Brazil?"

"Absolutely. He had been there for over two years. When he told me the truth about his past, he had no idea if his pursuers were on the right continent. To learn they were in Brazil was devastating."

"Why didn't he run again?"

"Lots of reasons. He thought about it. We talked about it forever. I was willing to leave with him. But in the end, he was convinced he could disappear even farther into the country. He knew it well—the language, the people, the endless places to hide. Plus, he didn't want me to leave my home. I guess we should've run to China or some place."

"Maybe you couldn't run."

"Maybe. I kept in touch with the Pluto Group. They were hired to monitor the Stephano investigation as best they could. They contacted his client, Mr. Benny Aricia, with the same story about possible information. They also contacted the insurance companies. All calls were referred to Jack Stephano. I flew in every three or four months, always from some place in Europe, and they would tell me what they had discovered."

"How did Stephano find him?"

"I can't tell you that story now. Patrick will have to do it."

Another black hole, and a rather significant one. Sandy placed his coffee on the floor and tried to sort things out. It would certainly be easier if these two would tell him everything. Start at the beginning, bring it forward to the present, so that he, the lawyer, could help them with their immediate future. Perhaps they didn't need any help.

So Patrick knew how he'd been found.

She handed him the thick folder from the table. "These are the people who have my father," she said.

"Stephano?"

"Yes. I'm the only person who knows where the money is, Sandy. The kidnapping is a trap."

"How does Stephano know about you?"

"Patrick told them."

"Patrick?"

"Yes. You've seen the burns, haven't you?"

Sandy stood and tried to clear his head. "They why didn't Patrick tell them where the money is?"

"Because he didn't know."

"He gave it all to you."

"Something like that. I have control of it. Now I'm being chased, and my poor father is caught in the middle."

"What am I supposed to do?"

She opened a drawer and removed a similar but thinner file. "This contains information about the FBI investigation of Patrick. We didn't learn much, for obvious reasons. The agent in charge is a man named Cutter, in Biloxi. As soon as I knew Patrick had been captured, I called Cutter. It probably saved Patrick's life."

"Slow down. This is hard to follow."

"I told Cutter that Patrick Lanigan had been found, and that he was in the custody of people working for Jack Stephano. We assume the FBI went straight to Stephano and threatened him. His operatives in Brazil tortured Patrick for a few hours, almost killed him, then handed him over to the FBI."

Sandy absorbed every word with his eyes closed hard. "Go on," he said.

"Two days later, Stephano was arrested in Washington and his offices were locked up."

"How do you know this?"

"I'm still paying a lot of money to the men at Pluto. They're very good. We suspect that Stephano is talking to the FBI, while at the same time quietly pursuing me. And my father."

"What am I supposed to tell Cutter?"

"First, tell him about me. Describe me as a lawyer who is very close to Patrick, that I'm making decisions for him, and that I know everything. Then, tell him about my father."

"And you think the FBI will lean on Stephano?"

"Maybe, maybe not. But we have nothing to lose."

It was almost one, and she was very tired. Sandy gathered the files and headed for the door.

"We have a lot to talk about," she said.

"It would be nice to know everything."

"Just give us time."

"You'd better hurry."

Twenty-six

DR. HAYANI began his morning rounds promptly at seven. Because Patrick had such trouble sleeping, he eased into his dark room each morning just for a peek. The patient was usually asleep, though later in the day he would often explain the ordeals of the night. This morning, Patrick was awake, and seated in a chair before the window. He wore only his white cotton boxers. He stared at the blinds closed tightly before him, stared at nothing because there was nothing to see. The dim light came from the table by his bed.

"Patrick, are you okay?" Hayani asked as he stood beside him.

He didn't answer. Hayani glanced down at the table in the corner where Patrick did his legal work. It was neat, with no books open or files out of place.

Finally, he said, "I'm fine, Doc."

"Did you sleep?"

"No. Not at all."

"You're safe now, Patrick. The sun is up."

He said nothing; didn't move or speak. Hayani left him as he found him, gripping the chair arms and watching the shades.

Patrick heard the pleasant voices in the hallway, the doc speaking again to the bored deputies, and the nurses as they hurried by. Breakfast would arrive shortly, not that food held much interest for him. After four and a half years of near starvation, he had mastered his desire to eat. A few bites of this and that, with sliced apples and carrots when hunger hit. The nurses at first had felt challenged to fatten him up, but Dr. Hayani intervened and imposed a diet low in fat, free of sugar, and heavy on steamed vegetables and breads.

He rose from his chair and walked to the door. He opened it and quietly said good morning to the deputies, Pete and Eddie, two of the regulars.

"Did you sleep well?" Eddie asked, as he did every morning.

"I slept safe, Eddie, thanks," Patrick said, part of the ritual. Down the hall on a bench by the elevator he saw Brent Myers, the useless FBI agent who had escorted him from Puerto Rico. He nodded, but Brent was involved with the morning paper.

Patrick withdrew to his room, and began a set of gentle knee bends. His muscles were healed, but the burns were still sore and stiff. Push-ups and sit-ups were out of the question.

A nurse knocked on the door as she pushed it open. "Good morning, Patrick," she chirped happily. "It's time for breakfast." She sat the tray on a table. "How was your night?"

"Wonderful. Yours?"

"Wonderful. Anything I can get for you?"

"No thanks."

"Just call," she said, leaving. The routine varied little from day to day. As boring as it had become, Patrick had not lost sight of how bad things could be. Breakfast at the Harrison County Jail would be served on metal trays stuck through narrow slots in the bars and eaten in the presence of various cellmates, the mixture of which changed daily.

He took his coffee and entered his little office in the corner, under the television. He turned the lamp on and stared at his files.

He had been in Biloxi a week. His other life had ended thirteen days ago, on a narrow dusty road that was now a million miles away. He wanted to be Danilo again, Senhor Silva, with his quiet life in his simple house, where the maid spoke to him in melodic Portuguese heavily tinted with her Indian roots. He yearned for the long walks along the warm streets of Ponta Porã, and the long runs into the countryside. He wanted to speak again to the old men lounging under cool trees sipping their green tea and anxious to chat up anyone willing to linger. He missed the bustle of the market downtown.

He missed Brazil, Danilo's home, with its vastness and beauty and stark contrasts, its teeming cities and backward villages, its gentle people. He ached for his beloved Eva; the softness of her touch, the beauty of her smile, the wonders of her flesh, the warmth of her soul. He would not live without her.

Why can't a man have more than one life? Where was it written that you couldn't start over? And over? Patrick had died, and Danilo had been captured.

He had survived both the death of the first and the seizure of the second. Why couldn't he escape again? A third life was calling, this one, though, without the sorrow of the first or the shadows of the second. This would be the perfect life with Eva. They would live somewhere, anywhere, as long as they were together and the past couldn't catch them. They would live in a grand home and reproduce like rabbits.

She was strong, but she had limits, like everyone. She loved her father, and home was a powerful magnet. All true Cariocas love their city, and consider it specially created by the Almighty.

He had placed her in danger, and now he must protect her.

Could he do it again? Or had his luck run out?

CUTTER AGREED to an eight o'clock meeting only because Mr. McDermott insisted it was urgent. The federal building was creaking to life as a meager handful of bureaucrats arrived at such an early hour. The throng would get there at nine.

Cutter was not abrupt, but certainly not hospitable. Chats with pushy lawyers ranked low on his list of favorite chores. He fixed scalding coffee in Styrofoam cups, and cleared some of the debris from his tiny desk.

Sandy thanked him nicely for agreeing to see him, and Cutter softened a bit. "You remember that phone call you received thirteen days ago?" Sandy asked. "The lady from Brazil?"

"Sure."

"I've met with her a few times. She's a lawyer for Patrick."

"Is she here?"

"She's around." Sandy blew hard into his cup, then ventured a sip. He quickly explained most of what he knew about Leah, though he never called her by name. Then he asked how the Stephano investigation was proceeding.

Cutter grew cautious. He scribbled some notes with a cheap pen, and tried to arrange the players. "How do you know about Stephano?"

"My co-counsel, the lady from Brazil, knows all about Stephano. Remember, she gave you his name."

"How did she know about him?"

"It's a very long, complicated story, and I don't know most of it."

"Then why bring it up?"

"Because Stephano is still after my client, and I'd like to stop him."

More scribbling by Cutter, another sip of steaming coffee. A rough flow chart evolved as he tried to arrange who had said what to whom. He knew most of what was happening in Washington with the Stephano tell-all, but there were gaps. It had certainly been established that Stephano would stop his chase. "And how do you know this?"

"Because his men in Brazil have kidnapped the father of my co-counsel."

Cutter couldn't keep his lips together, nor his head exactly straight. His eyes wandered to the ceiling as this rattled around his brain. Then it made some sense. "Could it be that this Brazilian lawyer might possibly know where the money is?"

"That's a possibility."

Perfect sense now.

Sandy continued, "The kidnapping is an effort to lure her back to Brazil, where they'd like to snatch her and give her some of the same medicine they gave Patrick. It's all about money."

Cutter's words were ponderous, but not by choice. "When did the kidnapping occur?"

"Yesterday." A paralegal in Sandy's office had pulled a story off the Internet two hours earlier. It was a short report on page six of

O Globo, a popular Rio daily. It gave the victim's name as Paulo Miranda. Sandy still had no idea of Leah's real name, and it was safe to assume the FBI could identify her if and when it got the story. Frankly, he saw no harm in telling the FBI her name. Trouble was, he didn't know it.

"There's not much we can do about it."

"The hell there isn't. Stephano's behind it. Put pressure on him. Tell him my co-counsel is not about to be sucked into his trap, and that she's preparing to go to the Brazilian authorities with the name of Jack Stephano."

"I'll see what I can do." Cutter had not forgotten the fact that Sandy McDermott had filed a multi-million-dollar lawsuit against the Bureau for crimes it did not commit. Nothing would be gained by discussing the lawsuit at this point. Maybe later.

"Stephano cares about nothing but the money," Sandy said. "If the old man gets hurt, he'll never see a dime."

"Are you implying there's room for negotiation here?"

"What do you think? You're facing death row or life in prison, wouldn't you be willing to negotiate?"

"So what do we tell Stephano?"

"Tell him to release the old man, and then we might talk about the money."

STEPHANO'S DAY began early. The meeting, his fourth, was scheduled to last all day and bring to an end his tales of adventure in the search for Patrick. His lawyer was absent, away in court with an unavoidable conflict. Stephano didn't need a lawyer to hold his hand, and, frankly, he was tired of paying $450 an hour. The interrogator was a new one. Oliver something or other. It didn't matter. They were all from the same school.

"You were talking about the plastic surgeon," Oliver said, as if the two men had simply been interrupted by a phone call. The two men had never met, and it had been thirteen hours since Jack had spoken to anyone about Patrick.

"Yes."

"And that was April of '94?"

"Correct."

"Continue, then."

Stephano settled into his chair and got himself comfortable. "The trail ran cold for a while. For a long time, actually. We worked hard, but months passed with nothing, absolutely nothing. Not a clue. Then, late in '94, we were contacted by an investigative firm in Atlanta, the Pluto Group."

"Pluto?"

"Yes, the Pluto Group. We referred to them as the boys from Pluto. Good boys. Some of your ex-agents. They asked questions about the search for Patrick Lanigan, said they might have some information. I met with them a couple of times here in Washington. They had a mysterious client who claimed to know something about Lanigan. Obviously, I was interested. They were in no hurry because their client seemed quite patient. The client, not surprisingly, wanted lots of money. Oddly enough, this was encouraging."

"How so?"

"If their client knew enough to expect a fat reward, then the client had to know that Lanigan still had plenty of money. In July of '95, the boys from Pluto approached me with a scheme. What if, they said, their client could lead us to a place in Brazil where Lanigan had recently lived? I said sure. They said, how much? And we agreed on the sum of fifty thousand dollars. I was desperate. The money changed hands by way of a wire transfer to a bank in Panama. I was then told to go to the small city of Itajaí in the state of Santa Catarina, in the deep south of Brazil. The address they gave us led to a small apartment building in a nice part of town. The manager was cordial, especially after we greased his palm. We showed him our pictures of Lanigan post-op, and he said maybe. More grease in the palm, and he made a definite I.D. Jan Horst was the man's name, a German, he thought, with good Portuguese. He had rented a three-room apartment for two months, paid in cash, kept to himself, and spent little time there. He was friendly, and liked to drink coffee with the manager and his wife. She also made a positive I.D. Horst said he was a travel writer who was working on a book about the immigration of Germans and

Italians to Brazil. When he left, he said he was going to the city of
Blumenau to study the Bavarian architecture there."

"Did you go to Blumenau?"

"Of course we did. And quickly. We covered the town, but after
two months gave it up. After the initial excitement, we settled back
into the tedium of hanging around hotels and markets, showing
the photos and offering small bribes."

"What about the boys from Pluto, as you called them?"

"They cooled off considerably. I was anxious to talk to them,
but they had little to say. I think their client got scared, or maybe
was happy just to get the fifty grand. Anyway, six months passed
with little word from Pluto. Then, in late January of this year, they
came back in a rush. Their client needed money, and was finally
ready to sell out. We shadowboxed for a few days, then they
dropped the bomb that for a million dollars we could learn the
exact location of our man. I said no. It wasn't that I didn't have the
money, it was just too risky. Their client was not willing to talk
until the money was paid, and I was not willing to pay until their
client talked. There was no way whatsoever to ascertain whether
their client knew anything. In fact, for all I knew there wasn't a
client anymore. Tempers flared and talks broke down."

"But you kept talking?"

"Yes, eventually. We had to. Their client had to have the money.
We had to have Lanigan. Another deal was proposed whereby we
would, for another fifty thousand bucks, get the name and location
of a place Lanigan had lived after he left Itajaí. We agreed, because
from our point of view the fifty thousand was cheap and there was
always the chance of getting lucky and stumbling over another tip.
From their point of view, it was smart because it strengthened
their client's credibility. And, of course, it was another step toward
the million bucks. There was a brain at work behind Pluto, and I
was desperate to play ball. I would gladly pay the million bucks. I
just needed some reassurance."

"Where was the second town?"

"São Mateus, in the state of Espírito Santo, north of Rio on the
coast. It's a small town of sixty thousand, a pretty place with
friendly people, and we spent a month there mingling and showing

our photos. The apartment arrangement was similar to the one in
Itajaí—two months' cash paid by a man named Derrick Boone, a
Brit. Without being bribed, the owner positively identified Boone
as our man. Seems as if Boone stayed over for a week without
paying, so there was a bit of a grudge. Unlike Itajaí, though, Boone
kept to himself and the owner knew nothing about his doings.
Nothing else turned up, and we left São Mateus in early March of
this year. We regrouped in São Paulo and Rio, and made new
plans."

"What were the new plans?"

"We withdrew from the north and concentrated on the smaller
towns in the states near Rio and São Paulo. Here in Washington, I
got more aggressive with the boys from Pluto. Their client was
stuck on a million. My client was unwilling to pay without verifica-
tion. It was a logjam, with both sides playing hardball but willing
to keep talking."

"Did you ever learn how their client knew so much about Lanigan's movements?"

"No. We speculated for hours. One theory was that their client
was also chasing Lanigan, for some unknown reason. It could've
been someone in the FBI who needed cash. That, of course, was a
longshot, but we thought of everything. The second theory, and
the most likely, was that their client was someone Lanigan knew
and trusted, who was willing to sell him out. Regardless, my client
and I decided we could not allow the opportunity to escape. The
search was now almost four years old, and going nowhere. As we
had learned, there are a million wonderful places to hide in Brazil,
and Lanigan seemed to know what he was doing."

"Did you break the logjam?"

"They did. In August of this year, they ambushed us with another offer: current photos of Lanigan, in exchange for another
fifty grand. We said yes. The money was wired offshore. They
handed me the photos in my office here in Washington. There
were three, black-and-white eight-by-tens."

"Could I see them, please?"

"Sure." Stephano pulled them from his perfectly organized
briefcase, and slid them down the table. The first was a shot of

Lanigan in a crowded market, obviously taken at long range. He wore sunglasses, and was holding what appeared to be a tomato. The second was taken either a moment before or a moment after as he walked along a sidewalk with a bag of something in his hand. He wore jeans and looked no different from any Brazilian. The third was the most telling; Patrick in shorts and a tee shirt washing the hood of his Volkswagen Beetle. The license plates could not be seen, nor could much of the house. The sunglasses were off, and it was a clear shot of his face.

"No street names, no license plates," Oliver said.

"Nothing. We studied them for hours, but found nothing. Again, as I said, there was a brain at work."

"So what did you do?"

"Agreed to pay the million dollars."

"When?"

"In September. The money was placed in escrow with a trust agent in Geneva, to be held until both sides gave notice to move it. Under our deal, their client had fifteen days to give us the name of the town, and the street address where he lived. We chewed our nails for the entire fifteen days, then on the sixteenth, after verbal warfare, they came through. The town was Ponta Porã, the street was Rua Tiradentes. We raced to the town, then sneaked into it. We had great respect for Lanigan by now, and we figured he was brilliant at moving forward while watching his back. We found him, then watched him for a week just to make sure. His name was Danilo Silva."

"A week?"

"Yeah, we had to be patient. He picked Ponta Porã for a reason. It's a wonderful place to hide. Local officials are cooperative if the money is right. The Germans discovered it after the war. One bad move, the cops get tipped, and they step in to protect him. So we waited and schemed and finally grabbed him outside of town, on a small road with no witnesses. A clean getaway. We sneaked him into Paraguay to a safe house."

"And there you tortured him?"

Stephano paused, took a sip of coffee, and stared at Oliver. "Something like that," he said.

Twenty-seven

PATRICK PACED and stretched at one end of the doctors' conference room while Sandy sat and listened and doodled on a legal pad. A nurse had brought a tray of cookies, still untouched. Sandy admired the cookies and asked himself how many capital murder prisoners got cookies delivered to them? How many had their own team of bodyguards lurking nearby? How many had the Judge stopping by for pizza?

"Things are changing, Sandy," Patrick said without looking at him. "We have to move fast."

"Move where?"

"She won't stay here as long as her father is missing."

"As usual, I'm thoroughly confused. The gaps are getting wider and the two of you speak in tongues. But I'm just the lawyer. Why should I know anything?"

"She has the files and records, and the story. You have to go see her."

"I just saw her last night."

"She's waiting on you."

"Really? Where?"

"There's a beach house at Perdido. She's there."

"Let me guess. I'm supposed to drop everything, and race over right now."

"It's important, Sandy."

"So are my other clients," he said angrily. "Why can't you give me a little notice here?"

"I'm sorry."

"I have court this afternoon. My daughter's got soccer. Is it asking too much for some warning?"

"I couldn't anticipate a kidnapping, Sandy. You've got to admit the circumstances are somewhat unusual. Try and understand."

Sandy took a deep breath and scribbled something. Patrick sat on the edge of the table, very near him. "I'm sorry, Sandy."

"What might we discuss at the beach house?"

"Aricia."

"Aricia," he repeated, then looked away. He knew the basics, at least what he'd read in the papers.

"It will take some time, so I'd pack for overnight."

"Am I expected to stay at the beach house?"

"Yes."

"With Leah?"

"Yes. It's a big house."

"And what exactly am I supposed to tell my wife? That I'm shacked up in a beach house with a beautiful Brazilian woman?"

"I wouldn't. Just tell her you're meeting with the rest of my defense team."

"That's nice."

"Thanks, Sandy."

UNDERHILL joined Oliver after a coffee break. They sat next to each other with the video camera behind them, all eyes aimed down the table at Stephano.

"Who interrogated Patrick?" Underhill asked Stephano.

"I'm not required to give the names of my associates."

"Did this person have any experience with physical interrogation?"

"Limited."

"Describe the means used."

"I'm not sure—"

"We've seen the photos of the burns, Mr. Stephano. And we, the

FBI, have been sued for injuries inflicted by your men. Now, tell us how you did it."

"I wasn't there. I didn't plan the interrogation because I have little experience in that field. I knew in general terms that a series of electrical shocks would be applied to various points on Mr. Lanigan's body. That is what happened. I had no idea it would cause serious burns."

There was a pause as Underhill glanced at Oliver and Oliver glanced at Underhill. Blatant disbelief. Stephano simply sneered at them.

"How long did this go on?"

"Five to six hours."

They looked at a file and whispered something. Underhill asked him some questions about the identification process, and Stephano described the fingerprinting. Oliver struggled with the time sequences, and spent almost an hour pinning down exactly when they grabbed him and how far they drove him and how long they interrogated him. They grilled Stephano about the trip out of the jungle to the airstrip at Concepción. They probed and fished and covered everything else, then they huddled for a moment and returned to the crucial question.

"During the interrogation of Mr. Lanigan, what did you learn about the money?"

"Not much. He told us where the money had been, but it had been moved."

"Can we assume he told you this under extreme duress?"

"Safe assumption."

"Are you convinced he didn't know where the money was at that time?"

"I wasn't there. But the man who conducted the interrogation has told me that, without a doubt, he believes that Mr. Lanigan did not know the exact location of the money."

"The interrogation wasn't recorded either by video or audio?"

"Of course not," Jack said, as if he had never thought about it.

"Did Mr. Lanigan mention an accomplice?"

"Not to my knowledge."

"What does that mean?"

"Means I don't know."

"How about the man who conducted the interrogation? Did he hear Mr. Lanigan mention an accomplice?"

"Not to my knowledge."

"So, as far as you know, Mr. Lanigan never mentioned an accomplice?"

"That's correct."

They shuffled files again, and whispered between themselves, then took a long pause, one that became profoundly unsettling for Stephano. He had told two lies in a row—no recording and no accomplice—and he still felt safe with them. How could these guys know what was said in the jungles of Paraguay? But they were the FBI. So he fidgeted, and waited.

The door opened suddenly, and Hamilton Jaynes walked through it, followed by Warren, the third interrogator. "Hello, Jack," Jaynes said loudly as he took a seat on one side of the table. Warren sat near his buddies.

"Hello, Hamilton," Stephano said, fidgeting even more.

"Been listening in the next room," Jaynes said with a smile. "And I'm suddenly wondering if you're being truthful."

"Of course I am."

"Of course. Look, ever heard the name Eva Miranda?"

Stephano repeated it slowly, as if totally confused by it. "Don't think so."

"She's a lawyer in Rio. A friend of Patrick's."

"Nope."

"Well, see, that's what bothers me, Jack, because I think you know precisely who she is."

"I've never heard of her."

"Then why are you trying to find her?"

"I don't know what you're talking about," Stephano said, rather weakly.

Underhill spoke first. He was looking directly at Stephano, but he spoke to Jaynes. "He's lying."

"He certainly is," said Oliver.

"No question about it," Warren added.

Stephano's eyes darted from voice to voice. He started to say something, but Jaynes showed him his palms. The door opened, and one more comrade from the Underhill-Oliver-Warren school walked in just far enough to say, "The voice analysis shows sufficient proof of lying." His announcement over, he withdrew immediately.

Jaynes picked up a single sheet of paper and summarized from it. "This is a story appearing in a Rio paper this morning. It tells of the kidnapping of a Mr. Paulo Miranda. His daughter is Patrick's friend, Jack. We've checked with the authorities in Rio. No ransom demand. Nothing from the kidnappers." He slid the paper in the direction of Stephano, but it stopped out of his reach.

"So where is Mr. Miranda?"

"I don't know. I don't know what you're talking about."

Jaynes looked at the other end of the table.

"Still lying," Underhill said. Oliver and Warren nodded their agreement.

"We had a deal, Jack. You would tell us the truth, and we would drop the charges against you. And, as I recall, we agreed not to arrest your clients. Now what I am supposed to do, Jack?"

Stephano was looking at Underhill and Oliver, who seemed ready to pounce on his next utterance. They, in turn, stared coldly at him, missing nothing.

"She knows where the money is," Stephano said in resignation.

"Do you know where she is?"

"No. She fled Rio when we found Patrick."

"No sign of her?"

"No."

Haynes looked at his truth squad. Yes, he had stopped the lying.

"I agreed to tell you everything," Jack said. "I did not agree to do anything else. We can still look for her."

"We didn't know about her."

"Too bad. If necessary, we can review our agreement. I'll be happy to call my lawyer."

"Yes, but we've already caught you lying."

"I'm sorry. It won't happen again."

"Lay off the girl, Jack. And release her father."

"I'll think about it."

"No. You'll do it now."

THE BEACH HOUSE was a modern tri-level in a row of seemingly identical structures along a freshly developed strip of the Coast. October was off-season. Most of the houses appeared to be empty. Sandy parked behind a shiny generic four-door with Louisiana plates, a rental car, he presumed. The sun was low on the horizon, inches off the top of the flat water. The Gulf was deserted; not a boat or a ship could be seen. He climbed the steps and followed the wraparound deck until he found a door.

Leah answered his knock with a smile, a short one forced through because she was at heart a warm person, not given to the dark mood swings which now plagued her. "Come in," she said softly, and locked the door behind him. The living room was large and vaulted, with glass on three sides and a fireplace in the center.

"Nice place," he said, then caught a delicious aroma floating in from the kitchen. He had skipped lunch, thanks to Patrick.

"Are you hungry?" she asked.

"Starving."

"I'm cooking a little something."

"Wonderful."

The authentic hardwood floors creaked a little as he followed her to the dining room. On the table was a cardboard box, and beside it were papers neatly arranged. She had been working. She paused by the table and said, "This is the Aricia file."

"Prepared by whom?"

"Patrick, of course."

"Where has it been for the past four years?"

"In storage. In Mobile."

Her answers were short, and each gave rise to a dozen quick questions Sandy would have loved to throw at her. "We'll get to it later," she said, and dismissed it with a casual wave.

In the kitchen, there was a whole roasted chicken on the cutting board by the sink. A pan of brown rice mixed with vegetables was steaming on the stove. "It's pretty basic," she said. "I find it hard to cook in someone else's kitchen."

"Looks delicious. Whose kitchen is this?"

"It's just a rental. I have it for the month."

She sliced the chicken and directed Sandy to pour the wine, a fine pinot noir from California. They sat at a small table in the breakfast nook, with a splendid view of the water and the remains of the sunset.

"Cheers," she said, raising her glass.

"To Patrick," Sandy said.

"Yes, to Patrick." She made no effort to address her food. Sandy stuffed a large slice of chicken breast into his mouth.

"How is he?"

He chewed rapidly so he wouldn't disgust this delightful young woman with a mouthful of food. A sip of wine. Napkin to the lips. "Patrick's okay. The burns are healing nicely. A plastic surgeon examined him yesterday, and said that no grafts will be necessary. The scars will be with him for a few years, but they will eventually fade. The nurses bring him cookies. The Judge brings him pizza. No less than six armed men guard him around the clock, so I'd say Patrick is doing better than most capital murder defendants."

"This is Judge Huskey?"

"Yes, Karl Huskey. Do you know him?"

"No. But Patrick spoke of him often. They were good friends. Patrick told me once that if he was captured, he hoped it would happen while Karl Huskey was still the Judge."

"He's retiring soon," Sandy said. What fortunate timing, he thought.

"He can't hear Patrick's case, can he?" she asked.

"No. He'll recuse himself very soon." Sandy ate a much smaller piece of chicken, still eating alone because she had yet to touch her knife and fork. She held the glass of wine near her head, and looked at the orange and violet clouds on the horizon.

"I'm sorry. I forgot to ask about your father."

"No word. I talked to my brother three hours ago, and there's still no word."

"I'm very sorry, Leah. I wish I could do something."

"And I wish I could do something. It's frustrating. I can't go home, and I can't stay here."

"I'm sorry," Sandy said again, because he could think of nothing better to offer.

He continued his meal in silence. She played with her rice and watched the ocean.

"This is delicious," he said, twice.

"Thanks," she said with a sad grin.

"What does your father do?"

"He's a university professor."

"Where?"

"In Rio. At the Catholic University."

"Where does he live?"

"In Ipanema, in the apartment I grew up in."

Her father was a delicate subject, but at least Sandy was getting answers to his questions. Maybe it helped her to talk about him. He asked more questions, all very general and all far away from the kidnapping.

She never touched her food.

WHEN HE FINISHED, she asked, "Would you like some coffee?"

"We'll probably need it, won't we?"

"Yes."

They removed the plastic rental dishes from the table and left them in the kitchen. Leah made coffee while Sandy inspected the house. They met in the dining room, where the coffee was served and the polite talk, such as it was, came to an end. They sat facing each other across the glass table.

"How much do you know about the Aricia matter?" she asked.

"He was the client whose ninety million got snatched by Patrick, if you believe the papers. He was an executive with Platt & Rockland, who had squealed on the company for overbilling. He filed a charge under the False Claims Act. Platt & Rockland got caught to the tune of something like six hundred million. His reward, under the act, was fifteen percent of that. His lawyers were Bogan and company, where our pal Patrick worked. That's about it. The basics."

"That's pretty good. What I'm about to tell you can all be verified by these documents and tapes. We'll go through them, as it will be necessary for you to know this material inside and out."

"I've actually done this before, you know." He smiled, but she didn't. No more lame efforts at humor.

"The Aricia claim was fraudulent from the very beginning." She spoke deliberately; there was no hurry. She waited until he absorbed this, which took a few seconds. "Benny Aricia is a very corrupt man who conceived a scheme to defraud both his company and his government. He was assisted by some very capable lawyers, Patrick's old firm, and some powerful people in Washington."

"That would be Senator Nye, Bogan's first cousin."

"Primarily, yes. But, as you know, Senator Nye has considerable influence in Washington."

"So I've heard."

"Aricia carefully planned his scheme, then took it to Charles Bogan. Patrick was a new partner then, but he knew nothing of Aricia. The other partners were brought into the conspiracy, everyone but Patrick. The law firm changed, and Patrick knew something was different. He started digging and eavesdropping and eventually found out that this new client named Aricia was the cause for all the secrecy. He was patient. He pretended to notice nothing, and all the time he was gathering evidence. A lot of it is in here." She touched the box when she said this.

"Let's go back to the beginning," Sandy said. "Explain how the claim was fraudulent."

"Aricia ran New Coastal Shipyards in Pascagoula. It's a division of Platt & Rockland."

"I know all that. Big defense contractor with a shady past, a bad reputation for bilking the government."

"That's it. Aricia took advantage of its size to implement his plan. New Coastal was building the Expedition nuclear submarines, and things were already over budget. Aricia decided to make matters worse. New Coastal submitted fraudulent labor records, thousands of hours at union scale for work that was never done, for employees who never existed. It procured materials at grossly inflated prices—lightbulbs for sixteen dollars each, drinking cups at thirty dollars each, and on and on. The list is endless."

"Is the list in this box?"

"Only the big items. Radar systems, missiles, weapons, things I've never heard of. The lightbulbs are insignificant. Aricia had been with the company long enough to know exactly how to avoid detection. He created a ton of paperwork, little of it with his name on it. Platt & Rockland had six different divisions involved with defense contracting, and so the home office was a zoo. Aricia took advantage of this. For every bogus claim he submitted to the Navy, he had written authorization signed by some executive at the home office. Aricia would subcontract for the inflated materials, then request approval from a higher-up. It was an easy system to work, especially for a shrewd man like Aricia, who was planning on screwing the company anyway. He kept meticulous records, and later gave them to his lawyers."

"And Patrick got them?"

"Some of them."

Sandy looked at the box. The top flaps were closed. "And this has been in hiding since he disappeared?"

"Yes."

"Did he ever come back to check on it?"

"No."

"Did you?"

"I came two years ago to renew the rental at the storage facility. I looked in the box, but didn't have the time to examine the contents. I was scared and nervous, and I didn't want to come. I was convinced these materials would never be needed because he would never be caught. But Patrick always knew."

The cross-examiner in Sandy was ready to burst with another round of questions unrelated to Aricia, but he let the moment pass. Relax, he told himself, don't appear eager and maybe the questions will get answered eventually. "So Aricia's scheme worked, and at some point he approached Charles Bogan, whose cousin is an ass-kicker in Washington and whose old boss is a federal judge. Did Bogan know Aricia had caused the overruns?"

She stood, reached into the box, and removed a battery-operated tape player and a rack of neatly labeled mini-cassettes. She picked through the cassettes with a pen until she found the one she wanted. She inserted it in the tape player. It was obvious to Sandy that she had done this many times before.

"Listen," she said. "April 11, 1991. The first voice is Bogan, the second is Aricia. Aricia had placed the call, and Bogan took it in the conference room on the second floor of the firm's offices."

Sandy leaned forward on his elbows. The tape began to play.

BOGAN: I gotta call from one of Platt's New York lawyers today. A guy named Krasny.

ARICIA: I know him. Typical New York ass.

BOGAN: Yes, he wasn't very friendly. He said they might have proof that you knew about the double-billing on the Stalker screens New Coastal bought from RamTec. I asked him to show me the proof. He said it would be a week or so.

ARICIA: Relax, Charlie. There's no way they can prove that because I didn't sign anything.

BOGAN: But you knew about it?

ARICIA: Of course I knew about it. I planned it. I set it in motion. It was another one of my wonderful ideas. Their problem, Charlie, is that they can't prove it. There are no documents, no witnesses.

The cassette went silent, and Leah said, "Same conversation, about ten minutes later."

ARICIA: How's the Senator?

BOGAN: Doing well. Yesterday he met with the Secretary of the Navy.

ARICIA: How'd it go?

BOGAN: Went well. They're old friends, you know. The Senator expressed his strong desire to punish Platt & Rockland for its greed, yet not harm the Expedition project. The Secretary feels the same, and said he would push for a stiff penalty against Platt & Rockland.

ARICIA: Can he speed things up?

BOGAN: Why?

ARICIA: I want the damned money, Charlie. I can feel it. I can taste it.

Leah pushed a button and the recording stopped. She removed the cassette and placed it back in the rack. "Patrick started recording early in '91. Their plans were to cut him out of the firm at the end of February, on the grounds that he was not generating enough business."

"Is that box full of tapes?"

"There are about sixty of them, all carefully edited by Patrick, so you can listen to everything in three hours."

Sandy glanced at his watch.

"We have a lot of work to do," she said.

Twenty-eight

PAULO'S REQUEST for a radio was declined, but when they realized he simply wanted music they brought him a well-used tape player and two cassettes of the Rio Philharmonic Orchestra. Classical was his preference. Paulo turned the volume low and flipped through a stack of old magazines. His request for books had been taken under consideration. The food so far was more than adequate; they seemed anxious to keep him happy. His captors were young men working for someone else, someone Paulo knew he would never see. If they in fact released him, the young men would flee and prosecution would be impossible.

His second day passed slowly. Eva was too wise to rush into their trap. One day soon this would make sense. He could wait as long as they could.

HIS HONOR brought the pizza with him on the second night. He had enjoyed the first so much, he had called Patrick during the afternoon to see if they could do it again. Patrick was anxious for company.

Huskey reached into a small briefcase and withdrew a stack of envelopes which he tossed on Lawyer Lanigan's worktable. "A lot of people want to say hello, mostly the courthouse gang. I told them they could write."

"I didn't realize I had so many friends."

"You don't. These are bored office workers with plenty of time to write letters. It's as close as they can get to the action."

"Gee thanks."

Huskey pulled a chair close to Patrick's bed and propped his feet on a drawer opened from the night table. Patrick had eaten almost two pieces of pizza, and was now finished.

"I'll have to recuse myself soon," Huskey said, almost apologetically.

"I know."

"I talked with Trussel this morning at length. I know you're not crazy about him, but he is a good judge. He's willing to take the case."

"I prefer Judge Lanks."

"Yes, but unfortunately, you don't get your choice. Lanks is having trouble with his blood pressure, and we've tried to keep the big cases away from him. As you know, Trussel has more experience than Lanks and myself combined, especially in death penalty cases."

Patrick managed a slight flinch, a sudden squinting around the eyes, and a momentary sag of the bony shoulders when his friend finished the last sentence. A death penalty case. It seized him, as often happened when he dragged himself to the mirror for a long look. Huskey caught every tiny movement.

As they say, anybody is capable of murder, and Huskey had chatted with many killers during his twelve years as a judge. Patrick, however, just happened to be his first friend to face death row.

"Why are you leaving the bench?" Patrick asked.

"The usual reasons. I'm bored with it, and if I don't quit now I'll never be able to. Kids are getting closer to college, and I need to make more money." Huskey paused for a second, then asked, "Just curious, how did you know I was leaving the bench? It's not something I've broadcast."

"Word gets around."

"To Brazil?"

"I had a spy, Karl."

"Someone here?"

"No. Of course not. I couldn't run the risk of contacting anyone here."

"So it was someone down there?"

"Yes, an attorney I met."

"And you told him everything?"

"Her. And yes, I told her everything."

Huskey tapped his fingers together, and said, "I guess that makes sense."

"I highly recommend it, next time you're down there disappearing."

"I'll remember that. This attorney, where is she now?"

"Close by, I think."

"Now I see. She must be the one who has the money."

Patrick smiled, then chuckled. The ice was broken, finally. "What do you want to know about the money, Karl?"

"Everything. How'd you steal it? Where is it? How much is left?"

"What's the best courthouse rumor you've heard about the money?"

"Oh, there are hundreds. My favorite is that you've doubled the money and buried it in vaults in Switzerland, that you were just passing time in Brazil and in a few more years you would leave and go play with your cash."

"Not bad."

"Remember Bobby Doak, that little pimple-faced weasel who does divorces for ninety-nine bucks and resents any lawyer who charges more?"

"Sure, advertises in church bulletins."

"That's him. He was drinking coffee in the clerk's office yesterday and telling how he had it from an inside source that you'd blown the money on drugs and teenaged prostitutes, and that was why you were living like a peasant in Brazil."

"That sounds like Doak."

The levity passed quickly as Patrick grew quiet. Huskey wasn't about to lose the moment. "So where's the money?"

"I can't tell you, Karl."

"How much is left?"

"A ton."

"More than you stole?"

"More than I took, yes."

"How'd you do it?"

Patrick swung his feet from the other side of the bed, and walked to the door. It was closed. He stretched his back and legs, and took a drink from a bottle of water. Then he sat on the edge of the bed, looking down at Karl.

"I got lucky," he said, almost in a whisper. But Karl heard every syllable.

"I was leaving, Karl, with or without the money. I knew the money was coming to the firm, and I had a plan to get it. But if that had fallen through, I was still leaving. I couldn't take another day with Trudy. I hated my job, and I was about to get my throat cut at the firm anyway. Bogan and those boys were in the midst of a gigantic fraud, and I was the only person outside the firm who knew it."

"What fraud?"

"Aricia's claim. We'll talk about that later. So I slowly planned my escape, and I got lucky and got away. The luck followed me until two weeks ago. Incredible luck."

"We got as far as the burial."

"Right. I went back to the little condo I had rented at Orange Beach. I stayed there a couple of days, indoors, listening to language tapes and memorizing Portuguese vocabulary. I also spent hours editing the conversations I had recorded around the office. There were a lot of documents to organize. I actually worked quite hard. At night, I walked the beach for hours, working up a sweat, trying to melt the pounds off as quickly as possible. I completely disassociated myself from food."

"What kind of documents?"

"The Aricia file. I ventured out in the sailboat. I knew the basics, and suddenly I was motivated to become a good sailor. The boat was big enough to live on for days at a time, and soon I was hiding out there on the water."

"Here?"

"Yes. I'd anchor close to Ship Island, and watch the shoreline of Biloxi."

"Why did you want to do that?"

"I had the office wired, Karl. Every phone, every desk, except for Bogan's. I even had a mike in the men's room on the first floor between Bogan's office and Vitrano's. The mikes transmitted to a hub I had hidden in the attic. It's an old firm in an old building with a million old files stashed away in the attic. Nobody ever went up there. There was an old TV antenna attached to the chimney on top of the building, and I ran my wires through it. The receiver then transmitted to a ten-inch dish I had on the sailboat. This was high-tech, state-of-the-art stuff, Karl. I bought it on the black market in Rome, cost me a ton of money. With binoculars, I could see the chimney, and the signals were easy to collect. Every conversation within earshot of a mike was beamed to me on the sailboat. I recorded all of them, and did my editing at night. I knew where they were eating lunch and what moods their wives were in. I knew everything."

"That's incredible."

"You should've heard them trying to sound serious after my funeral. On the phone, they took all these calls, all these condolences, and sounded so grave and proper. But among themselves, they joked about my death. It saved a nasty confrontation. Bogan had been elected to deliver the news to me that I was being booted from the firm. The day after the funeral he and Havarac drank Scotch in the conference room and laughed about how lucky I was to have died at such an opportune time."

"Do you have these tapes?"

"Of course. Get this. I have the tape of the conversation between Trudy and Doug Vitrano, in my old office, just hours before my funeral, when they open my lockbox and find the surprise life insurance policy for two million dollars. It's hilarious. It took Trudy about twenty seconds before she asked, "When do I get the money?""

"When can I hear it?"

"I don't know. Soon. There were hundreds of tapes. The editing took twelve hours a day for several weeks. Imagine all the phone calls I had to wade through."

"Were they ever suspicious?"

"Not really. Rapley once made the remark to Vitrano that my timing was incredible, since I had purchased the two-million-dollar policy only eight months before my death. And there was a comment or two about how strange I had been acting, but it was harmless. They were so thrilled that I was gone and out of the way."

"Did you tap Trudy's phones?"

"I thought about it, but then why bother? Her behavior was predictable. She couldn't help me."

"But Aricia could."

"Certainly. I knew every move they made for Aricia. I knew the money was going offshore. I knew which bank, and when it would get there."

"So how'd you steal it?"

"Again, lots of luck. Though Bogan was calling the shots, Vitrano was doing most of the talking with the bankers. I flew to Miami with a fresh set of papers declaring me to be Doug Vitrano. I had his Social Security number and other vitals. This guy in Miami has a computer catalog with a million faces in it, and you simply point to the one you want, and presto, that face is on your driver's license. I picked a face that was somewhere between mine and Vitrano's. From Miami I flew to Nassau, and that's where it got sticky. I presented myself to the bank, the United Bank of Wales. The main guy Vitrano had been talking to was a chap named Graham Dunlap. I presented all my fake papers, including a forged partnership resolution, on firm stationery of course, which directed me to wire the money out as fast as it came in. Dunlap had not expected Mr. Vitrano, and he was quite surprised, even flattered, that someone from the firm would make the journey for such a routine matter. He fixed me coffee and sent a secretary out for croissants. I was eating one in his office when the wire came in."

"He never thought about calling the firm?"

"No. And listen, Karl, I was prepared to bolt. If Dunlap had been the least bit suspicious, I would have slugged him, run from the building, grabbed a cab, and raced to the airport. I had three different tickets for three different flights."

"Where would you have gone?"

"Well, I was still dead, remember. Probably to Brazil. I would've found a job as a bartender and spent the rest of my days on the beach. In retrospect, I might have been better off without the money. I had it, and they had to come after it. That's why I'm here now. Anyway, Dunlap asked the right questions and my answers came out beautifully. He confirmed the wire was in, and I immediately authorized the wire out, to a bank in Malta."

"All of it?"

"Almost all of it. Dunlap hesitated for a moment when he realized all the money was leaving his bank. I almost swallowed my tongue. He mentioned something about an administrative fee for his services, and I asked him what was customary. He turned into a slimy little twerp, said fifty thousand would be appropriate, and I said fine. Fifty thousand stayed in the account and was later transferred to Dunlap. The bank is in downtown Nassau—"

"Was in downtown Nassau. It folded six months after you robbed it."

"Yeah, so I heard. Too bad. When I left through the front door, my feet hit the sidewalk, and it was difficult to keep from sprinting like a madman through the traffic. I wanted to scream and leap from street to street, but I controlled myself. I jumped into the first empty cab, told the driver I was late for a flight, and off we went. The plane to Atlanta left in an hour. The one to Miami was an hour and a half. The one to La Guardia was boarding, so I flew to New York."

"With ninety million bucks."

"Minus fifty thousand for old Dunlap. It was the longest flight of my life, Karl. I knocked down three martinis and was still nothing but nerves. I would close my eyes and see customs agents with machine guns waiting on me at the gate. I just knew Dunlap had gotten suspicious and called the firm, and that somehow they had tracked me to the airport and onto the flight. I have never wanted to get off a plane so badly in my life. We landed, taxied to the terminal, got off the plane. A camera flashed as we stepped into the gate area, and I thought, This is it! They've got me! It was some kid with a Kodak. I practically ran to the men's room, where I sat on the toilet for twenty minutes. Next to my feet was a canvas overnight bag with all my worldly possessions."

"Don't forget the ninety million."

"Oh yeah."

"How'd the money get to Panama?"

"How do you know it went to Panama?"

"I'm the Judge, Patrick. The cops talk to me. It's a small town."

"It was in the wiring instructions from Nassau. The money went into a new account in Malta, then quickly on to Panama."

"How'd you become such a wizard at wiring money?"

"Just took a little research. I worked on it for a year. Tell me, Karl, when did you hear that the money was missing?"

Karl laughed and reclined even farther. He clasped his hands behind his head. "Well, your pals at the firm did a poor job of keeping their little settlement quiet."

"I'm shocked."

"In fact, the whole town knew they were about to be filthy rich. They acted so serious about the secrecy, yet they were spending money like crazy. Havarac bought the biggest, blackest Mercedes ever made. Vitrano's architect was in the final stage of designing their new home—eleven thousand square feet. Rapley signed a contract to buy an eighty-foot sailboat; said he was contemplating retirement. I heard the private jet talk a few times. Thirty million in legal fees would be hard to hide around here, but they didn't really try. They wanted people to know."

"Sounds like a bunch of lawyers."

"You struck on a Thursday, right?"

"Right. March twenty-sixth."

"The next day, I was preparing to proceed with a civil trial when one of the lawyers got a call from the office. The news was that there were problems with the big settlement over at Bogan, Rapley, Vitrano, Havarac, and Lanigan. The money vanished. All of it. Stolen by someone offshore."

"Was my name mentioned?"

"Not the first day. It didn't take long, though. Word got out that the bank's security cameras had captured someone vaguely resembling you. Other pieces fell into place, and the gossip roared around town."

"Did you believe I did it?"

"At first, I was too shocked to believe anything. All of us were. We had buried you, put you to rest, said our prayers. It was impossible to believe. But, as the days passed, the shock wore off and the puzzle came together. The new will, the life insurance, the cremated corpse—we started getting suspicious. Then they found the office crawling with bugs. The FBI was questioning everyone around here. A week after it happened, it was pretty well accepted that you had pulled it off."

"Were you proud of me?"

"I wouldn't say I was proud. Astonished maybe. Perhaps stunned. There was, after all, a dead body. Then, I was intrigued."

"Not the slightest hint of admiration?"

"I don't remember it that way, Patrick. No, an innocent person had been murdered so you could steal the money. Plus, you left behind a wife and daughter."

"The wife got a bundle. The child isn't mine."

"I didn't know that at the time. No one did. No, I don't think you were admired around here."

"What about my pals at the firm?"

"No one saw them for months. They got sued by Aricia. Other litigation followed. They had grossly overspent, so bankruptcy got them. Divorces, booze, it was awful. They self-destructed in textbook fashion."

Patrick crawled onto his bed and gently folded his legs. He savored this with a nasty smile. Huskey stood and walked to the window. "How long did you stay in New York?" he asked, peeking through the shades.

"About a week. I didn't want any of the money coming back into the States, so I arranged to have it wired to a bank in Toronto. The bank in Panama was a branch of the Bank of Ontario, so it was easy to wire in as much as I needed."

"You started spending?"

"Not much. I was a Canadian now, with good papers, a transplant from Vancouver, and the money allowed me to purchase a small apartment and obtain credit cards. I found a Portuguese instructor and studied the language six hours a day. I went to Europe several times so my passport would get used and scrutinized. Everything worked perfectly. After three months, I put the apartment on the market and went to Lisbon, where I studied the language for a couple of months. Then, on August 5, 1992, I flew to São Paulo."

"Your independence day."

"Absolute freedom, Karl. I landed in that city with two small bags. I got in a cab and I was soon lost in a sea of twenty million people. It was dark and raining, traffic was standing still, and I was in the back of a cab thinking to myself that no one in the world knew where I was. And no one would ever find me. I almost cried, Karl. It was sheer, unbridled freedom. I looked at the faces of the people racing down the sidewalks, and I thought to myself, I'm now one of them. I'm a Brazilian named Danilo, and I'll never be anybody else."

Twenty-nine

SANDY SLEPT THREE HOURS on a hard mattress in a loft somewhere above the den, far away from her, and awoke with the early sun beaming through slits beneath the blinds. It was six-thirty. They had said good night at three, after seven hours of intensely scouring documents and listening to dozens of surreptitious talks Patrick had amazingly captured.

He showered and dressed, and found his way down to the kitchen, where Leah sat in the breakfast nook with fresh coffee and a surprisingly alert face. She fixed him wheat toast with jam as he glanced at the newspapers. Sandy was ready to leave, to return to his office with the Aricia mess and sort it out on his own turf.

"Any word from your father?" he asked. The early voices were quiet, the words scarce.

"No. But I can't call from here. I'll go to the market later and use a pay phone."

"I'll say a prayer for him."

"Thanks."

They loaded the entire Aricia file into the trunk of his car, and said good-bye. She promised to call him within twenty-four hours. She would not be leaving anytime soon. Their client's problems had gone from serious to urgent.

The early air was cool. It was October after all, and even the Coast felt a hint of autumn. She put on a parka and went for a walk on the beach, barefoot and bare-legged, with one hand in a pocket and the other holding her coffee. She hid behind sunglasses, which annoyed her. The beach was deserted. Why was she compelled to hide her face?

Like all Cariocas, she had spent a great deal of her life on the beach, the center of culture. Her childhood home had been her father's apartment in Ipanema, the poshest of Rio's neighborhoods, where every kid grew up on the beach.

She was unaccustomed to long walks near the water without being surrounded by a million people happily sunning and playing. Her father had been one of the first to organize efforts against the unbridled development of Ipanema. He despised the increase of population and haphazard construction, and worked tirelessly with neighborhood groups. Such actions went against the typical Carioca attitude of live and let live, but with time came to be admired and even welcomed. As a lawyer, Eva still donated time to preservation groups in the neighborhoods of Ipanema and Leblon.

The sun crept behind clouds, and the breeze picked up. She returned to the house as the seagulls followed and squawked overhead. She locked every door and window, and drove two miles to a supermarket, where she planned to buy shampoo and fruit, and to find the nearest possible pay phone.

She didn't see the man at first, and when she finally noticed him he seemed to have been standing beside her forever. She was holding a bottle of hair conditioner when he sniffed, as if he had a cold. She turned, glanced from behind the sunglasses, and was startled by his sustained eye contact. He was thirty or forty, white, unshaven, but she didn't have time to notice anything else.

He was staring at her, with rabid green eyes that glowed in the middle of a beach-bronzed face. She coolly walked away, down the aisle with the conditioner. Maybe he was just a local character, a harmless pervert who lurked in the grocery and scared pretty vacationers. Perhaps everyone in the store knew his name and made excuses for him because he wouldn't harm an insect.

Minutes later, she saw him again, this time hiding near the bakery with his face behind a pizza crust but his metallic eyes watching every move she made. Why was he hiding, covering his face? He wore shorts and sandals, she noticed.

Panic hit hard through her chest and sent waves down her legs. Her first thought was to run, but she kept her cool long enough to find a small shopping basket. She had been spotted by whoever he was, and it was to her advantage to watch him as much as he was watching her. Who knew when she might see him again? She loitered in the produce department, next picked her way through the cheeses, and didn't see him for a long time. Then she saw him with his back to her, holding a gallon of milk.

A few minutes later, she caught sight of him through the large front windows, walking through the parking lot, his head cocked to one side, talking into a cell phone, carrying nothing. What happened to the milk? She would've raced through a back door, but her car was parked in the front. She paid for the items as calmly as possible, but her hands shook as she took her change.

There were thirty cars, including her rental, in the parking lot, and she knew she couldn't inspect them all. Not that she wanted to. He was in one of them. She simply wanted to leave without being followed. She quickly got in her car, left the lot, and turned in the direction of the beach house, though she knew she could never go back there. She drove a half a mile, then made an abrupt U-turn, just in time to see him behind her, three cars back, driving a new Toyota. His green eyes glanced away at the last second. Odd, she thought, that he wasn't covering them.

Everything seemed odd, at the moment. How odd that she was driving along a foreign highway in a foreign country with a fake passport proclaiming her to be someone she never wanted to be, and going to a place that she had yet to determine. Yes, everything was odd and blurred and frightening as hell, and what Eva needed and desperately wanted was to see Patrick so she could scream at him for an hour, and throw rocks as well. This was not part of the deal. It was one thing for Patrick to be hunted for his past, but she had done nothing wrong. Not to mention Paulo.

Being Brazilian, she normally drove with one foot on the gas and the other on the brake, and the traffic along the beach badly needed a good dose of her native driving. But she had to be calm.

You don't panic when you're on the run, Patrick had said many times. You think, you watch, you plan.

She watched the cars behind her. She obeyed all highway rules. "Always know where you are," Patrick had told her. She had studied the road atlas for hours. She turned north and stopped at a gas station to see what she attracted. Nothing. The man with the green eyes was not behind her, but this was of no comfort. He knew she had seen him. He'd been caught. He'd simply called ahead with his little cell phone and now the rest of them were watching.

An hour later, she entered the airport terminal in Pensacola and waited eighty minutes for a flight to Miami. Any flight would have suited her. The one to Miami happened to be the soonest. It would prove to be disastrous.

She waited behind a magazine in a coffee bar and watched everything that moved. A security guard enjoyed looking at her, and she found him difficult to ignore. Otherwise, the airport was almost devoid of human activity.

The flight to Miami was by turboprop commuter, and seemed to take forever. Eighteen of the twenty-four seats were vacant, and the other five passengers looked harmless. She even managed a brief nap.

In Miami, she hid in an airport lounge for an hour, sipping expensive water and watching the throngs come and go. At the Varig counter, she bought a first-class ticket to São Paulo, one way. She wasn't sure why. São Paulo wasn't home, but it was certainly in the right direction. Maybe she would hide there in a nice hotel for a few days. She'd be closer to her father, wherever he was. Planes were leaving for a hundred destinations. Why not visit her country?

AS IT ROUTINELY DOES, the FBI issued an alert to customs and immigration personnel, as well as to the airlines. This one specified a young woman, age thirty-one, traveling under a Brazilian passport, real name of Eva Miranda but probably using an alias. Having learned the identity of her father, getting her real name was a simple matter. When Leah Pires walked through a passport checkpoint at Miami International, she wasn't expecting trouble in front of her. She was still looking for the men behind her.

Her Leah Pires passport had proven quite reliable in the past two weeks.

But the customs agent had seen the alert an hour earlier during a coffee break. He pushed an alarm button on his scanner while he slowly examined every word of the passport. The hesitation at first was annoying, then Leah realized something was wrong. The travelers at the other booths were breezing through, barely slowing long enough to open their passports and having the approvals nodded back at them. A supervisor in a navy jacket appeared from nowhere and huddled with the agent. "Could you step in here, Ms. Pires?" he asked politely but with no room for discussion. He was pointing at a row of doors down the wide corridor.

"Is there a problem?" she insisted.

"Not really. Just a few questions." He was waiting for her. A uniformed guard with Mace and a gun on his waist was waiting too. The supervisor was holding her passport. Dozens of passengers behind her were watching.

"Questions about what?" she demanded as she walked with the supervisor and the guard to the second door.

"Just a few questions," he repeated, opening the door and escorting her into a square room with no windows. A holding room. She noticed the name of Rivera on his lapel. He didn't look to be Hispanic.

"Give me the passport," she demanded as soon as they were alone and the door was closed.

"Not so fast, Ms. Pires. I need to ask you a few questions."

"And I don't have to answer them."

"Please, relax. Have a seat. Can I get you some coffee or water?"

"No."

"Is this a valid address in Rio?"

"It certainly is."

"Where did you arrive from?"

"Pensacola."

"Your flight?"

"Airlink 855."

"And your destination?"

"São Paulo."

"Where in São Paulo?"

"Maybe that's a private matter."

"Business or pleasure?"

"Why does it matter?"

"It matters. Your passport lists your home in Rio. So where will you be staying in São Paulo?"

"A hotel."

"And the name of the hotel?"

She hesitated as she struggled to grab the name of a hotel, and the little interval was deadly. "Uh, the—the—Inter-Continental," she finally said, without the slightest hint of truthfulness.

He wrote it down, then said, "And we can assume the room there is reserved in the name of Leah Pires?"

"Of course," she said, snapping back nicely. But one quick phone call would prove she was lying.

"Where is your luggage?" he asked.

Another crack in the facade, and this one even more revealing. She hesitated, glanced away, and said, "I'm traveling light."

Someone knocked on the door. Rivera opened it slightly, took a sheet of paper, and whispered to his unseen colleague. Leah sat down and tried to relax. The door closed and Rivera studied his evidence.

"According to our records, you entered the country eight days ago, here in Miami, on a flight from London which originated in Zurich. Eight days, and no luggage. Seems odd, doesn't it?"

"Is it a crime to travel light?" she asked.

"No, but it is a crime to use a false passport. At least here, in the U.S."

She looked at the passport lying on the table near him, and she knew it was as phony as could be. "It's not a false passport," she said indignantly.

"Do you know a person by the name of Eva Miranda?" Rivera asked, and Leah couldn't keep her chin up. Her heart stopped and her face fell, and she knew the chase was over.

Rivera knew they had snared another one. "I'll have to contact the FBI," he said. "It will take some time."

"Am I under arrest?" she asked.

"Not yet."

"I'm a lawyer. I—"

"We know. And we have the right to detain you for questioning. Our offices are on the lower level. Let's go."

She was led away hurriedly, clutching her purse, her eyes still covered.

THE LONG TABLE was piled with papers and files, with crumpled sheets from legal pads and napkins and empty cups and even half-eaten sandwiches from the hospital cafeteria. Lunch had been five hours earlier but neither lawyer had thought of dinner. Time was being kept outside the room. Inside, it didn't matter.

Both men were barefoot. Patrick wore a tee shirt and gym shorts. Sandy wore a very wrinkled cotton button-down, khakis, no socks, the same attire he'd put on hours earlier in the beach house.

The Aricia box was empty in a corner, its contents all on the table.

The door opened while it was being knocked on, and Agent Joshua Cutter entered before he was asked. He stayed by the door.

"This is a private meeting," Sandy said, very near Cutter's face. The documents on the table could not be seen by anyone. Patrick walked to the door and helped shield the view.

"Why don't you knock before you enter?" he said angrily.

"Sorry," Cutter said calmly. "I'll just be a minute. Just thought you'd want to know that we have Eva Miranda in custody. Caught her sneaking through the Miami airport, on her way home to Brazil, fake passport and all."

Patrick froze and tried to think of something to say.

"Eva?" Sandy asked.

"Yeah, also known as Leah Pires. That's what her fake passport calls her." Cutter was looking at Patrick while answering Sandy.

"Where is she?" Patrick asked, stunned.

"Jail, in Miami."

Patrick turned and walked along the table. Jail would be horrible anywhere, but jail in Miami had a particularly ominous ring to it.

"Do you have a number where we can call her?" Sandy asked.

"No."

"She has the right to a telephone."

"We're working on it."

"Get me a number, okay."

"We'll see." Cutter continued to watch Patrick and ignore Sandy. "She was in a hurry. No luggage, not one bag. Just trying to sneak back to Brazil, leaving you behind."

"Shut up," Patrick said.

"You can leave now," Sandy said.

"Just thought you'd want to know," Cutter said with a smile, and left.

Patrick sat down and gently massaged his temples. His head had been aching before Cutter arrived, now it was splitting. He and Eva had gone over and over the three scenarios which she would face if they caught him. First, and the one according to plan, was that she would remain in the shadows, assisting Sandy and moving at will. Second, she might be caught by Stephano and Aricia, which was by far the most frightening possibility. Third, the FBI could catch her, which was not nearly as terrifying as the second, but did pose enormous problems. At least she was safe.

They had not discussed this fourth scenario, her return to Brazil without him. He would not believe it was abandonment.

Sandy quietly gathered files and cleaned up the table.

"What time did you leave her?" Patrick asked.

"About eight. She was fine, Patrick. I told you that."

"No mention of Miami or Brazil?"

"No. None whatsoever. I left with the impression she would be at the beach house for a while. She told me she leased it for a month."

"Then she got scared. Why else would she run?"

"I don't know."

"Find a lawyer in Miami, Sandy. And quickly."

"I know a couple."

"She must be scared to death."

Thirty

IT WAS AFTER SIX, so Havarac was probably in a casino at the blackjack table, sipping free whiskey and looking for women. Rumors about his gambling debts were abundant. No doubt Rapley was locked away in his attic, a place the rest of the world preferred him to be. The secretaries and paralegals were gone. Doug Vitrano locked the front door of the building and walked to the rear office, the largest and nicest one, where Charlie Bogan was waiting behind his desk with his sleeves rolled up.

Patrick had managed to bug every office except the senior partner's, a fact Bogan had relied on heavily during the roaring brawls that followed the loss of the money. If Bogan wasn't in his office, or somewhere in the very near vicinity, it was locked with a deadbolt. His partners had been much too careless, he had reminded them repeatedly. Especially Vitrano, whose phone had been used during those last fateful chats with Graham Dunlap offshore, which was how Patrick had learned the direction of the money. This had been rehashed to the point of near fistfights.

Bogan could not, in all fairness, claim he suspected espionage in his own firm. If so, why hadn't he warned his more indifferent partners? He'd simply been cautious, and lucky. Important conversations were held in Bogan's office. It took only seconds to engage the deadbolt. He kept the only key. Not even the janitors could get in without Bogan's presence.

Vitrano closed the door firmly and dropped into the soft leather chair across the desk.

"I saw the Senator this morning," Bogan said. "He called me to his house." Bogan's mother and the Senator's father were siblings. The Senator was ten years older than Bogan.

"Is he in a good mood?" Vitrano asked.

"I wouldn't call it that. He wanted an update on Lanigan, and I told him what I knew. Still no sign of the money. He's very nervous about what Lanigan might know. I assured him, as I've done many times, that all communications with him were done in this office, and that this office was clean. So, he shouldn't worry about what Lanigan might know."

"But he's worried?"

"Of course he's worried. He asked me again if there was any document tying him to Aricia, and I again said no."

"Which of course is true."

"Yes. There are no documents with the Senator's name. Everything with him was verbal. Most of it was done on the golf course. I've told him this a thousand times, but he wanted to hear it again, in light of Patrick's return."

"You didn't tell him about the Closet?"

"No."

They both watched the dust on Bogan's desk and relived what happened in the Closet. In January of 1992, a month after the Justice Department approved the Aricia settlement, and about two months before they were to receive the money, Aricia had popped in one day, unscheduled and unannounced and in a foul mood. Patrick was still around, though his funeral was only three weeks away. The firm had already begun an extensive renovation of its offices, and for this reason Bogan couldn't meet with Aricia in his office. Painters were on ladders. Drop cloths covered the furniture. They got the combative Aricia into a small meeting room across the hall from Bogan's, a room everyone referred to simply as the Closet because of its size. A small square table with a chair on each side. No windows. The ceiling was slanted because a stairway ran above it.

Vitrano was fetched because he was second in command, and a

meeting of sorts commenced. It didn't last long. Aricia was chafed because the lawyers were about to earn thirty million dollars. Now that his settlement had been approved, reality had hit hard, and he thought thirty million in legal fees was obscene. Things turned nasty quickly as Bogan and Vitrano held their ground. They offered to find their contract for legal services, but Aricia cared nothing for it.

In the heat of the moment, Aricia asked how much of the thirty million the Senator would get. Bogan grew hostile and said it was none of his business. Aricia claimed that it was his business, because, after all, the money was his, and then he launched into a windy diatribe attacking the Senator and all politicians in general. He made much of the fact that the Senator had been working so hard in Washington to pressure the Navy, the Pentagon, and the Justice Department to settle his claim. "How much will he get?" he kept asking.

Bogan kept slipping the punches. He would say only that the Senator would be taken care of. He reminded Aricia that he had carefully chosen the firm because of its political connections. And he hotly added that sixty million in Aricia's pocket was not such a bad deal, considering how the claim was bogus to begin with.

Too much was said.

Aricia proposed a fee of only ten million. Bogan and Vitrano rejected it outright. He stormed out of the Closet, swearing every step of the way.

There were no phones in the Closet, but two mikes were found. One was under the table, hidden in a corner where two brackets joined, stuck in place by black putty. The second was placed between two dusty ancient law books on the only shelf in the room. The books were for decorative purposes.

After the shock of the vanishing fortune, and the subsequent discovery by Stephano of all the bugs and wires, Bogan and Vitrano didn't discuss the Closet meeting for a long time. Maybe it would just disappear. They never spoke to Aricia about it, primarily because he had sued them so quickly and now hated the mention of their names. The incident faded from their memories. Maybe it never happened after all.

Now that Patrick was back, they had been forced to timidly confront it. There was always the chance that the mikes had malfunctioned or that Patrick in his haste had missed it. There were certainly enough other bugs for him to absorb and assimilate. In fact, they had decided there was a very good chance the Closet meeting had been missed by Patrick.

"Surely he wouldn't keep the tapes for four years, would he?" Vitrano asked.

But Bogan didn't answer. He sat with his fingers locked over his stomach and watched the dust settle on his desk. Oh, what could've been. He would get five million, the Senator the same. No bankruptcy, no divorce. He would still have his wife and family, his home and his stature. He could've taken the five and made it ten by now, and twenty before long, serious big money and the freedom to do anything. It was all there, a feast on a table, then Patrick snatched it.

The giddiness of finding Patrick had lasted a couple of days, then vanished slowly when it became obvious that the money was not following him back to Biloxi. With each passing day, the money actually seemed farther away.

"Do you think we'll get the money, Charlie?" Vitrano asked, barely audible, his eyes on the floor. He hadn't called him Charlie in years. Such familiarity was unheard of in a firm with so much hatred.

"No," he said. There was a long pause. "We'll be lucky if we're not indicted."

WITH AN HOUR of serious phone work ahead of him, Sandy made the most troubling one first. Sitting in his parked car in the hospital lot, he called his wife and told her he'd be in very late, so late that he might be forced to stay in Biloxi. His son was playing in a junior high football game. He apologized, blamed everything on Patrick, and said he'd explain later. She took it much better than expected.

He caught a secretary working late at his office, and collected phone numbers from her. He knew two lawyers in Miami, neither of whom happened to be at the office at seven-fifteen. The home number for one went unanswered. The other had a private listing. He made a series of calls to lawyers he knew in New Orleans, and finally got the home number of Mark Birck, a highly regarded criminal defense specialist in Miami. Birck was not delighted at receiving the call during dinner, but he listened anyway. Sandy gave the ten-minute version of the Patrick saga, including the latest development with Eva in jail somewhere in Miami. Thus the call. Birck showed an interest, and claimed a thorough knowledge of immigration law as well as criminal procedure. He would make two calls, after dinner. Sandy agreed to phone him back in an hour.

It took three calls to locate Cutter, and twenty minutes of wheedling before he would agree to meet for coffee at a doughnut shop. Sandy drove there, and while waiting for Cutter called Birck again.

Birck reported that Eva Miranda was indeed in custody in a federal detention center in Miami. She had not yet been formally charged with any crime, but it was early. There was no way to see her tonight, and it would be difficult to see her tomorrow. Under the law, the FBI and the U.S. Customs Service can hold an alien caught traveling under a bogus passport for up to four days before a release can be applied for. Makes sense, Birck explained, considering the circumstances. These people tend to disappear quickly.

Birck had been in the detention center several times visiting clients, and, as these places went, it was not bad. She was in her own private cell, and generally safe. With luck, she would have access to a telephone in the morning.

Without providing too much detail, Sandy stressed that there was no rush in getting her released. There were people looking for her on the outside. Birck promised to pull strings early in the morning, and try to see her.

His fee would be ten thousand dollars, which Sandy agreed to pay.

He hung up as Cutter swaggered into the doughnut shop and sat at a table by the front window, as promised. Sandy locked his car and followed him in.

□ □ □ □

DINNER was packaged food, microwaved and served on a well-worn plastic tray. Though she was hungry, the thought of eating it hardly crossed her mind. It was delivered to her cinder-blocked cell by two heavy women in uniform, keys dangling from chains around their waists. One asked how she was doing. She mumbled something in Portuguese and they left her alone. The door was thick metal with a small square hole in it. Voices of other women prisoners could occasionally be heard, but the place was generally quiet.

She had never been in jail before, not even as a lawyer. Other than Patrick, she couldn't recall a friend who'd been incarcerated. The initial shock yielded to fear, then to humiliation at being caged like a criminal. Only the thought of her poor father kept her focused during the first hours. No doubt his conditions were far worse than hers. She prayed that they were not hurting him.

The praying came easier in jail. She prayed for her father, and she prayed for Patrick. She resisted the temptation to blame him for her troubles, though it would've been easy. Most of the blame rested with her. She had panicked and run too quickly. Patrick had taught her how to move without leaving a trail, how to vanish. The mistake was her fault, not his.

The false passport charges were minor, she decided, and could be dealt with in short order. In a violent country without enough jail cells, surely such a simple offense from such a noncriminal could be handled swiftly with a small fine and a quick deportation.

She found comfort in the money. Tomorrow she would demand an attorney, a good one with clout. Phone calls would be made to officials in Brasília; she knew their names. If necessary, the money could be used to bully everyone in sight. She would be out before long, then back home to rescue her father. She would hide somewhere in Rio; it would be simple.

The cell was warm, and locked, and guarded by lots of people with guns. It was a safe place, she decided. The men who hurt Patrick and now had her father couldn't touch her.

She turned off the ceiling light and stretched out on the narrow bunk. The FBI would be anxious to tell Patrick that she was in custody, so he probably knew by now. She could see him with his legal pad, running lines here and there, analyzing this latest development from an amazing variety of angles. By now, Patrick had conceived no fewer than ten ways to rescue her. And he wouldn't sleep until he had the list pared down to the best three plans.

The fun was in the planning, he always said.

CUTTER ORDERED a caffeine-free soda and a chocolate doughnut. He was off-duty, so the standard dark suit and white shirt were replaced by jeans and short sleeves. Smirking came naturally for him. Now that they had found the girl and locked her up, he was especially cocky.

Sandy ate a ham sandwich in four bites. It was almost 9 P.M. Lunch had been hospital food with Patrick, a long time ago. "We need to have a serious talk," he said. The shop was packed and his voice was low.

"I'm listening," Cutter said.

Sandy swallowed, wiped his mouth, leaned even closer and said, "Don't take this the wrong way, but we need to include other people."

"Like who?"

"Like the people above you. People in Washington."

Cutter pondered this for a minute as he watched the traffic move along Highway 90. The Gulf was a hundred yards away.

"Sure," he said. "But I gotta tell them something."

Sandy glanced around. Not a single person was even casually looking their way. "What if I can prove that the Aricia claim against Platt & Rockland was completely fraudulent; that he conspired with the Bogan firm to defraud the government, and that Bogan's cousin, the Senator, was a part of the conspiracy and was to have received several million bucks under the table?"

"A wonderful story."

"I can prove it."

"And if we believe it, then we're supposed to allow Mr. Lanigan to make some type of restitution and walk away."

"Perhaps."

"Not so fast. There's still the matter of the dead body."

Cutter casually took a bite of his doughnut and chewed it thoughtfully. Then, "What kind of proof?"

"Documents, recorded phone calls, all sorts of things."

"Admissible in court?"

"Most of it."

"Enough for convictions?"

"A box full."

"Where's the box?"

"In the trunk of my car."

Cutter instinctively looked over his shoulder in the general direction of the parking lot. Then he stared at Sandy. "This is stuff Patrick gathered before he split?"

"Correct. He got wind of the Aricia matter. The firm was planning to kick him out, so he very patiently collected the dirt."

"Bad marriage, etc., etc., so he took the money and ran."

"No. He ran, then took the money."

"Whatever. So now he wants to cut a deal, huh?"

"Of course. Wouldn't you?"

"What about the murder?"

"That's a state matter, not really your concern. We'll deal with it later."

"We can make it our concern."

"I'm afraid not. You've got the indictment for the theft of the ninety million. The state of Mississippi has the indictment for the murder. Unfortunately for you, the feds can't come in now and charge murder."

Cutter hated lawyers for that very reason. They didn't bluff easily.

Sandy continued. "Look, this meeting is a formality. I'm just going through channels, don't want to overstep here. But I'm perfectly ready to start making calls to Washington first thing in the morning. I thought we'd have this chat, and I hoped you would be convinced we're ready to deal. Otherwise, I'm on the phone."

"Who do you want?"

"Someone with complete authority, FBI and Justice. We'll meet in a large room somewhere and I'll lay out the case."

"Let me talk to Washington. But this better be good."

They shook hands stiffly, and Sandy left.

Thirty-one

MRS. STEPHANO was sleeping again. Those bothersome young men in matching dark suits had left their street, and the neighbors had stopped calling with their nosy questions. The gossip over bridge had returned to more normal topics. Her husband was relaxed.

She was sleeping soundly when the phone rang at 5:30 A.M. She grabbed it from the night table. "Hello."

A stout, firm voice said, "Jack Stephano, please."

"Who's calling?" she demanded. Jack was moving under the covers.

"Hamilton Jaynes, FBI," came the reply.

And she said, "Oh my God!" She placed a hand over the receiver. "Jack, it's the FBI again."

Jack turned on a light, glanced at the clock, took the phone. "Who is it?"

"Good morning, Jack. This is Hamilton Jaynes. Hate to call so early."

"Then don't."

"Just wanted you to know that we've got the girl, Eva Miranda, in custody. She's safe and secure, so you boys can call off your dogs."

Stephano swung his feet out of the bed and stood next to the table. Their last hope was gone. The search for the money was finally over. "Where is she?" he asked, not expecting any meaningful answer.

"We have her, Jack. She's with us."

"Congratulations."

"Look, Jack, I've sent some men down to Rio to monitor the situation with her father. You have twenty-four hours, Jack. If he is not released by five-thirty tomorrow morning, then I'll have a warrant for your arrest, and the arrest of Aricia. Hell, I'll probably arrest Mr. Atterson at Monarch-Sierra and Mr. Jill at Northern Case Mutual, you know, just for the hell of it. I've really wanted to talk to those boys, along with Aricia."

"You enjoy the harassment, don't you?"

"Love it. We'll help the Brazilians extradite you guys down to Brazil, you know, and that should take a coupla months. No bail with an extradition, so you and your sleazy clients would spend Christmas in jail. Who knows, extradition might work for a change, and you'd get to go to Rio. I hear the beaches are lovely. Are you there, Jack?"

"I hear you."

"Twenty-four hours." The phone clicked and the line was dead. Mrs. Stephano was in the bathroom with the door locked, too rattled to face him.

Jack went downstairs and made coffee. He sat at the kitchen table, in the semidarkness, waiting for the sun to rise. He was tired of Benny Aricia.

He had been hired to find Patrick and the money, not to ask questions about how the money got created. He knew the basics of Benny Aricia's history with Platt & Rockland, and he had always suspected there was much more to the story. He had probed once or twice, but Aricia showed no interest in discussing the events which preceded Patrick's disappearance.

From the beginning, Jack had suspected the law firm's offices had been wired for two reasons. The first was to gather dirt on the other partners and their clients, specifically Aricia. The second was to lead Patrick to the money after his funeral. What was unknown to everyone, except to maybe Aricia and the partners, was how much damaging evidence had been taped and stored by Patrick. Stephano suspected that plenty of dirt had been gathered.

When the money vanished, and Stephano began his search, the law firm chose not to join the consortium. It had thirty million dollars at stake, yet chose to lick its wounds and go home. The reason given was lack of money. The partners were basically broke, things were about to get much worse, and they simply couldn't afford to participate. This had some logic at the time, but Stephano also sensed a reluctance to find Patrick.

Something was on the tapes. Patrick had caught them red-handed. As miserable as their lives had become, the actual capture of Patrick could be their worst nightmare.

Same for Aricia. He'd wait an hour, then call him.

BY SIX-THIRTY, the office of Hamilton Jaynes was crawling with people. Two agents sat on a sofa and studied the latest report from their contacts in Rio. One stood beside Jaynes' desk and waited to give an update on Aricia's whereabouts; he was still at the rented condo in Biloxi.

Another stood nearby with an update on Eva Miranda. A secretary carried a box of files into the office. Jaynes was in his chair, on the phone, haggard and coatless, ignoring everyone.

Joshua Cutter entered, also worn and wrinkled. He'd slept two hours in the Atlanta airport waiting for a flight to Washington, D.C., where an agent met him for the drive to the Hoover Building. Jaynes immediately hung up, and ordered everyone from his office.

"Get us some coffee, lots of it," he barked at the secretary. The room cleared and Cutter sat rigidly before the grand desk. Though mightily fatigued, he tried hard to be alert. He'd never been near the Deputy Director's office before.

"Let's hear it," Jaynes growled.

"Lanigan wants to cut a deal. He claims to have enough evidence to convict Aricia, the lawyers, and an unnamed U.S. Senator."

"What kind of evidence?"

"A box full of documents and tapes, stuff Lanigan accumulated before he skipped out."

"Did you see the box?"

"No. McDermott said it was in the trunk of his car."

"And what about the money?"

"We never got that far. He wants to meet with you and somebody at Justice to discuss settlement possibilities. I got the impression he thinks they can buy their way out of it."

"That's always a possibility when you steal dirty money. Where does he want to meet?"

"Down there, somewhere in Biloxi."

"Let me call Sprawling at Justice," Jaynes said almost to himself, as he lunged for the phone. The coffee arrived.

MARK BIRCK tapped his designer pen on the table as he waited in the visitors' room of the federal detention center. It was not quite nine, much too early for lawyers to see their clients, but he had a friend in administration. Birck explained it was an emergency. The table had privacy panels on both sides and a thick glass plate down the center. He would talk to her through a small screened opening.

For thirty minutes he tapped and fidgeted. She was finally brought from around the corner, dressed in a yellow one-piece jumpsuit with faded lettering stamped in black across the chest. The guard removed the handcuffs and she rubbed her wrists.

When they were alone, she sat in her chair and looked at him. He slid a business card through a tiny slot. She took it and examined every letter.

"Patrick sent me," he said, and she closed her eyes.

"Are you okay?" he asked.

She leaned forward on her elbows and spoke through the screened opening. "I'm fine. Thanks for coming. When do I get out?"

"Not for a few days. The feds can do one of two things. First, and the most serious, they can indict you for traveling under a false passport. This is a longshot because you're a foreigner and you have no criminal record. Second, and most likely, they'll simply deport you with your promise never to return. Either way, it'll take them a few days to decide. In the meantime, you're stuck here because we can't get bail right now."

"I understand."

"Patrick is very concerned about you."

"I know. Tell him I'm fine. And I'm very concerned about him."

Birck adjusted his legal pad, and said, "Now, Patrick wants a detailed account of exactly how you were caught."

She smiled and seemed to relax. Of course Patrick would want the details. She started with the man with the green eyes, and slowly told the story.

BENNY HAD ALWAYS laughed at the Biloxi beach. Just a narrow strip of sand bordered on one side by a highway too dangerous to cross on foot, and on the other by dull brown water too brackish to swim in. During the summer it attracted low-budget vacationers, and on weekends students threw Frisbees and rented jet-skis. The casino boom brought more tourists to the beach, but they seldom lingered long before returning to their gambling.

He parked at the Biloxi pier, lit a long cigar, removed his shoes, and walked the beach anyway. It was much cleaner now, another benefit from the casinos. It was also deserted. A few fishing boats drifted out to sea.

Stephano's call an hour earlier had ruined his morning, and, for the most part, altered the remainder of his life. With the girl locked away, he had no chance of finding the money. She couldn't lead him to it now, nor could she be used as leverage with Lanigan.

The feds had an indictment hanging over Patrick's head. Patrick, in turn, had the money and the evidence. One would be swapped for the other, and Aricia would get caught in the crossfire. When the pressure was applied to his co-conspirators, Bogan and the rest of those pansy-ass lawyers, they would sing in an instant. Benny was the odd man out, and he knew this perfectly well. Had known it, in fact, for a long time. His dream had been to somehow find the money, then disappear with it, just like Patrick.

But his dream was over now. He had a million bucks left. He

had friends in other countries, and contacts around the world. It was time to split, just like Patrick.

SANDY KEPT a scheduled 10 A.M. meeting with T.L. Parrish, in the D.A.'s office, though he'd been tempted to postpone it and spend the morning working on the documents. When he left his office at 8:30, his entire staff and both of his partners were making copies and enlarging crucial pages.

Parrish had requested the meeting. Sandy was certain he knew why. The state's case had major holes in it, and now that the thrill of the indictment had passed, it was time to talk business. Prosecutors tend to try the airtight cases, and there is never a shortage of them. But a high-profile case with gaping holes is serious trouble.

Parrish wanted to fish, but first he puffed and postured and talked about venue. A jury anywhere would not be sympathetic to a lawyer who murdered for money. Sandy just listened, at first. Parrish recited his favorite statistics about his conviction rate and the fact that he'd never lost a capital murder trial. Got eight of 'em on death row, he said, not bragging.

Sandy really had better things to do. He needed to have a serious conversation with Parrish, but not today. He asked how he would prove the murder occurred in Harrison County. And he followed it by the cause of death—how could that be proven? Patrick certainly wouldn't testify and help them out. And the big one, who was the victim? According to Sandy's research, there was not a single reported murder conviction in the state with an unidentified victim.

Parrish anticipated these troublesome inquiries, and did an adequate job of evading concrete answers. "Has your client considered a plea bargain?" he finally asked, as if in deep pain.

"No."

"Would he?"

"No."

"Why not?"

"You ran to the grand jury, got your capital murder indictment, waved it in front of the press, now you have to prove it. You didn't bother to wait and assess your evidence. Forget it."

JOHN GRISHAM

"I can get a conviction for manslaughter," Parrish said angrily. "That carries twenty years."

"Maybe," Sandy said nonchalantly. "But my client has not been charged with manslaughter."

"I can do that tomorrow."

"Fine. Go do it. Dismiss the capital murder charges, refile for manslaughter, then we'll talk."

Thirty-two

IT WAS LABELED the Camille Suite, and it occupied one third of the top floor of the Biloxi Nugget, the newest, gaudiest, largest, and most successful of all the Vegas-style casinos popping up along the Coast. The boys from Vegas thought it clever to name the Nugget's suites and banquet rooms after the worst hurricanes to hit the Coast. For an average Joe who came in from the street and simply wanted spacious quarters, it rented for $750 a day. That's what Sandy agreed to pay. For a high-roller flown in from afar, the suite would be complimentary. But gambling was the last thing on Sandy's mind. His client, less than two miles away, had approved the expense. The Camille had two bedrooms, a kitchen, den, and two parlors—plenty of places to meet with separate groups. It also had four incoming phone lines, a fax, and a VCR. Sandy's paralegal brought the PC and the technical machinery from New Orleans, along with the first batch of Aricia documents.

The first visitor to Mr. McDermott's temporary law offices was J. Murray Riddleton, Trudy's thoroughly defeated divorce lawyer. He sheepishly handed over a proposed settlement of property rights and child visitation. They discussed it over lunch. The terms of surrender were dictated by Patrick. And since he was now calling the shots, Sandy found numerous details to nitpick through. "This is a good first draft," he said repeatedly as he continued to mark it up with red ink. Riddleton took the thrashing like a pro. He argued every point, bitched about the amendments, but both lawyers knew the settlement would be changed to suit Patrick's whim. The DNA test and nude photos ruled supreme.

The second visitor was Talbot Mims, Biloxi counsel for Northern Case Mutual, a hyper and jovial man who traveled in a very comfortable van, complete with a fast driver, leather seats and interior, a small worktable, two phones, a fax, beeper, television and VCR so Mims could study video depositions, a laptop and a PC, and a sofa for quick naps, though he succumbed only after the most arduous days in court. His entourage included a secretary and a paralegal, both of whom kept cell phones in their pockets, and an obligatory associate hauled along for extra billing purposes.

The four hurriedly presented themselves at the Camille Suite, where Sandy met them in jeans and offered soft drinks from the mini-bar. All declined. The secretary and the paralegal immediately found matters to discuss on their cell phones. Sandy led Mims and the unnamed associate to a parlor, where they sat before a huge window with a splendid view of the Nugget's parking garage, and beyond that the first steel pillars of yet another garish casino.

"I'll get right to the point," Sandy said. "Do you know a man by the name of Jack Stephano?"

Mims thought quickly. "No."

"I didn't think so. He's a super-sleuth out of D.C. He was hired by Aricia, Northern Case Mutual, and Monarch-Sierra to find Patrick."

"So?"

"So take a look at these," Sandy said with a smile as he slid a set of gory color photos from a file. Mims spread them out on the table—Patrick's horrid burns in all their glory.

"These were in the newspaper, right?" he said.

"Some of them."

"Yeah, I think you spread them around when you sued the FBI."

"The FBI didn't do this to my client, Mr. Mims."

"Oh really." Mims released the photos and waited for Sandy.

"The FBI didn't find Patrick."

"Then why did you sue them?"

"Publicity stunt, designed to arouse some sympathy for my client."

"Didn't work."

"Maybe not with you, but you won't be on the jury, will you? Anyway, these injuries were the result of prolonged torture, inflicted by men working for Jack Stephano, who was working for several clients, one of whom happened to be Northern Case Mutual, a very proud publicly owned company with a solid reputation for corporate responsibility and six billion in stockholders' equity."

Talbot Mims was extremely practical. He had to be. With three hundred open files in his office and eighteen large insurance companies as clients, he didn't have time to play games. "Two questions," he said. "First, can you prove this?"

"Yes. The FBI can confirm it."

"Second. What do you want?"

"I want a high-ranking Northern Case Mutual executive here in this room tomorrow, someone with unquestioned authority."

"These are busy people."

"We're all busy. I'm not threatening a lawsuit, but think of how embarrassing this could be."

"Sounds like a threat to me."

"Take it any way you want."

"What time tomorrow?"

"Four P.M."

"We'll be here," Mims said, reaching forward to shake hands. He then left in a rush, his minions racing behind.

Sandy's own crew arrived mid-afternoon. A secretary answered the phone, which by then was ringing every ten minutes. Sandy had placed calls to Cutter, T.L. Parrish, Sheriff Sweeney, Mark Birck in Miami, Judge Huskey, a handful of lawyers in Biloxi, and Maurice Mast, the U.S. Attorney for the Western District of Mississippi. On a personal level, he called his wife twice to get reports on the family, and he called the principal of his third-grader's lower school.

He had spoken to Hal Ladd twice by phone, but met him for the first time at the Camille Suite. Ladd represented Monarch-Sierra.

He arrived alone, which Sandy found shocking because insurance defense lawyers *always* traveled in pairs. Regardless of the task at hand, there had to be two of them before the work began. Both listened, both looked, spoke, took notes, and, most important, both billed the client for the same work.

Sandy knew of two large, rich firms in New Orleans that, not surprisingly, had adopted a threesome approach to the practice of insurance defense.

Ladd was a serious sort in his late forties, and by reputation didn't need the assistance of another lawyer. He politely took a diet cola and sat in the same seat Mr. Mims had occupied.

Sandy asked him the same question. "Do you know a man by the name of Jack Stephano?"

He didn't, and so Sandy delivered the standard brief bio. Then he laid the color photos of Patrick's wounds on the table, and they discussed them for a moment. The burns were not inflicted by the FBI, Sandy explained. Ladd read between the lines. Having represented insurance companies for many years, he had long since ceased to be surprised by the depths to which they could sink.

Even so, this was shocking. "Assuming you can prove this," Ladd said, "I'm sure my client would prefer to keep it quiet."

"We're prepared to amend our lawsuit, drop the FBI, and name as defendants your client, Northern Case Mutual, Aricia, Stephano, and anybody else responsible for the torture. It's an American citizen intentionally wounded and scarred by American defendants. The case is worth millions. We'll go to trial right here in Biloxi."

Not if Ladd had anything to do with it. He agreed to call Monarch-Sierra immediately and demand that the chief in-house lawyer drop everything and fly to Biloxi. He appeared angry that his client had funded the search without informing him. "If it's true," he said, "I'll never represent them again."

"Trust me. It's true."

IT WAS ALMOST DARK when Paulo was blindfolded and handcuffed and led from the house. No guns were poked at him, no threats made. No voices whatsoever. He rode in the backseat of a small car, by himself, for an hour or so. The radio played classical music.

When the car stopped, the two front doors opened, and Paulo was helped from the back. "Come with me," came a voice at his shoulder, and a large hand took him by the elbow. The road under his feet was gravel. They walked a hundred meters or so, then stopped. The voice said, "You are on a road twenty kilometers from Rio. To your left, three hundred meters, is a farmhouse with a telephone. Go there for help. I have a gun. If you turn around, I will have no choice but to kill you."

"I won't turn around," Paulo said, his body shaking.

"Good. I will remove the handcuffs first, then I will remove the blindfold."

"I won't turn around," Paulo said.

The handcuffs were removed. "Now, I will remove the blindfold. Walk forward quickly."

The blindfold was yanked off, and Paulo lowered his head and began jogging down the road. There was no sound behind him. He didn't dare glance around. He called the police at the farmhouse, then he called his son.

Thirty-three

THE COURT REPORTERS arrived promptly at eight. Both were named Linda—one with an *i* and one with a *y*. They produced business cards and followed Sandy to the center of the suite, where the furniture had been shoved to the walls and chairs added. He placed Y at one end of the room, with her back to the window with the shades pulled tightly, and sat I at the other end, in a nook next to the bar with a clear view of all the players. Both desperately needed one last smoke. He sent them into the far bedroom.

Jaynes arrived next with his group. He had a driver, an aging FBI agent who also served as bodyguard, lookout, and errand boy; he had an FBI lawyer; and he had Cutter and Cutter's immediate supervisor. From the Attorney General's office, he had Sprawling, an intense dark-eyed veteran who said little but gathered every sound. All six men wore either black or navy suits; all produced business cards, which Sandy's paralegal collected. Sandy's secretary took their coffee orders while the men shuffled as a group through the small parlor and into the den.

Next came Maurice Mast, the U.S. Attorney for the Western District of Mississippi, traveling light with only one assistant. He was followed by T.L. Parrish, alone, and the meeting was ready to begin.

The pecking order took care of itself. Jaynes' driver and Mast's assistant stayed in the parlor, where they found a platter of dough-nuts and the morning papers.

Sandy closed the door, offered a cheerful "Good morning," and thanked them all for coming. They were seated around the room. No one smiled, yet they were not unhappy to be there. It was quite intriguing.

Sandy introduced both court reporters, and explained that their dual transcripts of the meeting would be kept by him and consid-ered extremely confidential. This seemed to satisfy everyone. There were no questions or comments at this point because they weren't sure what the meeting was about.

Sandy held a legal pad with his notes neatly arranged, his case organized for a dozen pages or so. He could've been in front of a jury. He sent greetings from his client, Patrick Lanigan, and said the burns were healing nicely. Then he recapped the charges pending against Patrick; capital murder levied by the state; theft, wire fraud, and flight charged by the United States. Capital mur-der could mean death. The others could tally up to thirty years.

"The federal charges are serious," he said gravely. "But they pale in comparison to capital murder. Frankly, and with all due respect, we'd like to get rid of the feds so we can concentrate on the murder charges."

"Do you have a plan to get rid of us?" Jaynes asked.

"We have an offer."

"Does it include the money?"

"It does indeed."

"We have no claim to the money. It wasn't stolen from the federal government."

"That's where you're wrong."

Sprawling was itching to say something. "Do you really think you can buy your way out of this?" It was more of a challenge. His gruff voice was flat, his words efficient.

The jury was barking back at him, but Sandy was determined to follow his script. "Just wait," he said. "If you'll allow me to present my case, then we'll discuss the options. Now, I'm assuming that we're all familiar with Mr. Aricia's 1991 claim against his former employer under the False Claims Act. It was prepared and filed by the Bogan firm here in Biloxi, a firm which, at that time, included a new partner by the name of Patrick Lanigan. The claim was fraudulent. My client found out about it, and then learned that the firm planned to kick him out after the claim was approved by Justice but before the money arrived. Over the course of many months, my client covertly gathered evidence which proves, clearly and convincingly, that Mr. Aricia and his lawyers conspired to screw the government out of ninety million dollars. The evidence is in the form of documents and taped conversations."

"Where is this evidence?" asked Jaynes.

"It's under the control of my client."

"We can get it, you know. We can get a search warrant and take the evidence anytime we want."

"And what if my client doesn't honor your search warrant? What if he destroys the evidence, or simply hides it again? What will you do then? Lock him up? Indict him for something else? Frankly, he's not afraid of you and your search warrants."

"And what about you?" asked Jaynes. "If it's in your possession, we can get a search warrant for you."

"I won't produce. Anything my client gives me is privileged and confidential, you know that. It's called attorney's work product. Don't forget that Mr. Aricia has sued my client. All documents in my possession are privileged. I will not, under any circumstances, hand over the documents until my client tells me to."

"What if we get a court order?" asked Sprawling.

"I'll ignore it, then I'll appeal it. You can't win on this one, gentlemen." And with that they seemed to accept their defeat. No one was surprised.

"How many people were involved?" asked Jaynes.

"The four partners at the firm and Mr. Aricia."

There was a heavy pause as they waited for Sandy to announce the name of the Senator, but he didn't. Instead, he looked at his notes and continued. "The deal is quite simple. We'll hand over the documents and tapes. Patrick will return the money, all of it. In exchange, the federal charges are dropped so we can concentrate on the state's. The IRS agrees to leave him alone. His Brazilian attorney, Eva Miranda, is released immediately." He clicked off these terms fluidly because they had been well rehearsed, and his jury absorbed every word. Sprawling took careful notes. Jaynes looked at the floor, neither smiling nor frowning. The rest were noncommittal, but each had many questions.

"And it has to be done today," Sandy added. "There is a sense of urgency."

"Why?" asked Jaynes.

"Because she's locked up. Because you're all here, and you have the authority to make the decision. Because my client has set a deadline of 5 P.M. today to strike the deal, or he'll just keep the money, destroy the evidence, serve his time, and hope one day he gets out."

With Patrick, they doubted nothing. He had thus far managed to spend his incarceration in a rather cushy private room with a staff at his beck and call.

"Let's talk about the Senator," Sprawling said.

"Great idea," Sandy said. He opened a door to the parlor and said something to a paralegal. A table with speakers and tape deck was rolled into the center of the room, and Sandy closed the door again. He looked at his notes, said, "The date was January 14, 1992, about three weeks before Patrick disappeared. The conversation took place in the law firm, on the first floor, in a room known as the Closet, sort of an all-purpose room sometimes used for very small meetings. The first voice you'll hear is that of Charlie Bogan, then Benny Aricia, then Doug Vitrano. Aricia had arrived at the firm unannounced, and, as you'll see, was not in a good mood."

Sandy stepped to the table and examined the various buttons. The tape deck was new and had two expensive speakers wired to it. They watched him carefully, most of them pushing forward just a little.

Sandy said, "Again, Bogan first, then Aricia, then Vitrano." He pushed a button. There was a ten-second gap of complete silence, then voices came sharply from the speakers. Edgy voices.

BOGAN: We agreed on a fee of one third, that's our standard fee. You signed the contract. You've known for a year and a half that our fee was a third.

ARICIA: You don't deserve thirty million dollars.

VITRANO: And you don't deserve sixty.

ARICIA: I want to know how the money will be split.

BOGAN: Two thirds, one third. Sixty, thirty.

ARICIA: No, no. The thirty million that comes in here. Who gets how much?

VITRANO: That's none of your business.

ARICIA: The hell it's not. It's money I'm paying as a fee. I'm entitled to know who gets how much.

BOGAN: No you're not.

ARICIA: How much does the Senator get?

BOGAN: None of your business.

ARICIA: (Shouting) It is my business. This guy's spent the last year in Washington twisting arms, leaning on people at Navy and the Pentagon and Justice. Hell, he's spent more time working on my file than he has working for his constituents.

VITRANO: Don't yell, okay, Benny.

ARICIA: I want to know how much the slimy little crook's getting. I have a right to know how much you're shoveling under the table, because it's my money.

VITRANO: It's all under the table, Benny.

ARICIA: How much?

BOGAN: He'll be taken care of, Benny, okay. Why are you so hung up on this? This is nothing new.

VITRANO: I think you picked this firm specifically because of our connections in Washington.

ARICIA: Five million, ten million? How expensive is he?

BOGAN: You'll never know.

ARICIA: The hell I won't. I'll call the sonofabitch up and ask him myself.

BOGAN: Go ahead.

VITRANO: What's with you, Benny? You're about to get sixty million bucks, and now you're getting greedy.

ARICIA: Don't preach to me, especially about greed. When I came here you guys were working for two hundred bucks an hour. Now look at you, trying to justify a fee of thirty million bucks. Already redoing your offices. Already ordering new cars. Next it'll be boats and airplanes and all the other toys of the seriously rich. And all with my money.

BOGAN: Your money? Aren't we missing something here, Benny? Help me out. Your claim was as bogus as a three-dollar bill.

ARICIA: Yeah, but I made it happen. I, not you, set the trap for Platt & Rockland.

BOGAN: Then why did you hire us?

ARICIA: A helluva question.

VITRANO: You got a bad memory, Benny. You came here because of our clout. You needed help. We put the claim together, spent four thousand hours working on it, and we pulled the right strings in Washington. All with your full knowledge, I might add.

ARICIA: Let's cut the Senator out. That should save us ten million. Shave another ten million, and that leaves you boys with ten million for yourselves. That's a much fairer fee, in my opinion.

VITRANO: (Laughing) That's a great deal, Benny. You get eighty, we get ten.

ARICIA: Yeah, and we screw the politicians.

BOGAN: No way, Benny. You're forgetting something very important. If not for us and the politicians, you wouldn't be getting a dime.

Sandy pushed the button. The tape stopped, but the voices seemed to rattle around the room for a full minute. The players looked at the floor, the ceiling, the walls, each trying to savor and record for later the best of what had been said.

With a vulgar smile, Sandy said, "Gentlemen, this is just a sample."

"When do we get the rest?" asked Jaynes.

"Could happen within hours."

"Will your client testify before a federal grand jury?" asked Sprawling.

"Yes, he will. But he won't promise to testify at trial."

"Why not?"

"He doesn't have to explain. That's just his position." Sandy rolled the table to the door, knocked, and gave it back to the paralegal. He addressed his group again. "You fellas should talk. I'll step outside. Make yourselves comfortable."

"We're not talking in here," Jaynes said, jumping to his feet. There were too many wires, and given Patrick's history, no room was safe. "We'll go to our room."

"Whatever," Sandy said. They were all rising and grabbing briefcases. They filed through the door, through the parlor, and finally out of the suite. Lynda and Linda raced to the rear bedroom for a smoke and a pee.

Sandy fixed a coffee, and waited.

THEY REASSEMBLED two floors below in a double room that immediately became cramped. Jackets were removed and thrown across the pillows of both beds. Jaynes asked his driver to wait in the hall with Mast's assistant. Matters too sensitive for their lowly ears were about to be discussed.

The deal's biggest loser would be Maurice Mast. If the federal charges were dropped, he would have nothing to prosecute. A rather grand trial would vanish, and he felt compelled to at least register his objection before the others got started. "We'll look foolish if we allow him to buy his way out," he said, primarily in the direction of Sprawling, who was trying vainly to relax in a flimsy wooden chair.

Sprawling was only one level down from the Attorney General himself, and this placed him several levels above Mast. He would listen politely for a few minutes to the opinions of the underlings, then he and Jaynes would make the decision.

Hamilton Jaynes looked at T.L. Parrish, and asked, "Are you reasonably confident you can convict Lanigan of murder?"

T.L. was a cautious type, and he knew full well any promises made to this group would be long remembered. "Murder might have some problems. Manslaughter is a lock."

"How much time on a manslaughter?"

"Twenty years."

"How much would he serve?"

"Five, more or less."

Oddly, this seemed to please Jaynes, a career man who thought trespassers should serve time. "You agree, Cutter?" he asked, pacing along the edge of the bed.

"There's not much evidence," Cutter said. "We can't prove who, how, what, when, or where as far as the murder goes. We think we know why, but the trial could be a nightmare. Manslaughter is much easier."

Jaynes asked Parrish, "How about the Judge? Will he sentence him to the maximum?"

"If convicted of manslaughter, I would expect the Judge to sentence him to twenty years. Parole is determined by the prison authorities."

"Can we safely assume that Lanigan will spend the next five years behind bars?" Jaynes asked, looking around the room.

"Yes, certainly," said Parrish, defensively. "And we're not backing off the capital murder. We intend to make a strong argument that Lanigan killed another person so he could steal the money. The death penalty is a longshot, but if he's convicted of simple murder, he could face life in prison."

"Does it really make any difference to us whether he spends time at Parchman prison or in a federal facility?" Jaynes asked. It was obvious it didn't make any difference to him.

"I'm sure Patrick has an opinion on the matter," Parrish said, and got a few weak grins.

T.L. especially liked the deal because he would become the sole remaining prosecutor. Mast and the FBI would make a hasty exit from the case. There was a gap, and he decided to shove Mast a bit closer to the edge of the cliff. "I have no doubt Patrick will serve time, at Parchman," he said, helpfully.

Mast wouldn't go quietly. He shook his head and frowned gravely. "I don't know," he said. "I think we look bad if we do this. You can't rob a bank, then get caught, then offer to give the money back if the charges are dropped. Justice is not for sale."

"It's a bit more complicated than that," Sprawling said. "We suddenly have bigger fish to catch, and Lanigan is the key. The money he stole was contaminated. We're simply retrieving it and returning it to the taxpayers."

Mast wasn't about to argue with Sprawling.

Jaynes looked at T.L. Parrish, and said, "With all due respect,

Mr. Parrish, could I ask you to step outside for just a moment. Us federal boys need to discuss something."

"Sure," Parrish said. He walked to the door and stepped into the hallway.

Enough of the chitchat. It was time for Sprawling to close the deal. "Gentlemen, it's very simple. There are some very important people in the White House who are watching things closely. Senator Nye has never been a friend of the President's, and, frankly, a good scandal down here would make the administration happy. Nye's up for reelection in two years. These allegations will keep him busy. And if they're true, then he's dead."

"We'll do the investigation," Jaynes said to Mast. "And you'll get to prosecute."

It was suddenly obvious to Mast that this meeting was for his benefit. The decision to cut a deal with Patrick had been made by people with far more clout than Sprawling and Jaynes. They were just trying to keep him happy, since he was, after all, the U.S. Attorney for the district.

The idea of indicting and prosecuting a U.S. Senator had enormous potential, and Mast warmed to it immediately. He could see himself in a crowded courtroom playing Patrick's tapes, the jurors and spectators hanging on every word. "So we're gonna take the deal?" he said, shrugging as if he couldn't have cared less.

"Yes," said Sprawling. "It's a no-brainer. We look good by getting the money back. Patrick stays in jail for a long time. We nail even bigger crooks."

"Plus the President wants it done," Mast said, smiling, though no one else did so.

"I didn't say that," Sprawling said. "I haven't talked to the President about this. My bosses talked to his people. That's all I know."

Jaynes retrieved T.L. Parrish from the hall, and they spent almost an hour walking through Patrick's offer and examining each of its components. The girl could be released with an hour's notice. Patrick would also have to pay interest on the money, they decided. What about the lawsuit he'd filed against the FBI? Jaynes made a list of points to cover with Sandy.

□ □ □ □

IN MIAMI, Mark Birck personally delivered to Eva the wonderful news that her father had been released. He had not been harmed; in fact, had been treated quite well.

He told her that with a little luck, she might be released herself in a day or two.

Thirty-four

SOLEMN-FACED and noncommittal, they returned to the Camille Suite and took their same seats. Most had left their jackets in the other room, and had rolled up their sleeves and loosened their ties, as if all manner of hard work was under way. By Sandy's watch, they had been gone for almost an hour and a half. Sprawling was now their spokesman.

"About the money," he began, and Sandy instantly knew they had a deal. It was just a matter of the details. "About the money, how much is your client willing to return?"

"All of it."

"All of it being?"

"All ninety million."

"What about interest?"

"Who cares about interest?"

"We do."

"Why?"

"Well, it's only fair."

"Fair to whom?"

"Uh, the taxpayers."

Sandy practically laughed at him. "Come on. You guys work for the federal government. Since when do you worry about protecting the taxpayers?"

"It's standard in cases involving theft and embezzlement," Maurice Mast added.

"How much?" Sandy asked. "At what rate?"

"Prime is nine percent," Sprawling said. "That would be fair, I think."

"Oh you do? What does the IRS pay when it determines I've paid too much and it sends me a refund?"

No one could answer. "Six percent," Sandy said. "Six lousy percent is what the government pays."

Sandy, of course, had had the benefit of planning this. He had anticipated the questions and had crafted the answers, and it was enormous fun watching them squirm as they tried to catch up.

"So, are you offering six percent?" Sprawling asked. His words were careful and slow.

"Of course not. We have the money; we'll determine how much we'll pay. It's the same principle used by the government. We figure the money'll simply go back into the black hole at the Pentagon."

"We can't control that," Jaynes said. He was already tired and in no mood for a lecture.

"Here's the way we see the money," Sandy said. "It would've been lost entirely, paid to some very slick crooks and never seen again. My client prevented this, has held the money, and is now willing to return it."

"So we give him a reward?" asked Jaynes.

"No. Just back off the interest."

"We have to sell this to some people in Washington," Sprawling said, not pleading but needing help. "Give us something to work with."

"We'll pay half the IRS rate, and not a penny more."

With a serious poker face, Sprawling said, "I'll run it by the Attorney General. I just hope he's in a good mood."

"Give him my regards," Sandy said.

Jaynes looked up from his notetaking, and asked, "Three percent, right?"

"That's right. From March 26, 1992, until November 1, 1996.

Total comes to a hundred and thirteen million, plus some change, which we'll ignore. One hundred thirteen million, even."

The figure had a nice ring to it, and it certainly sounded good to the government boys. They each wrote it on their legal pads. It looked large. Who could argue with a deal that brought so much back into the hands of the taxpayers?

To offer this much meant only one thing: Patrick had taken the ninety and invested well. Sprawling's boys had crunched some numbers earlier. Assuming Patrick placed all the money in investments earning eight percent a year, the loot would now be worth a hundred and thirty-one million. Ten percent, and the value would be one hundred and forty-four million. Tax free, of course. Apparently, Patrick hadn't spent much of it, so he would remain a very wealthy man.

"We're also concerned about this lawsuit you filed on behalf of Mr. Lanigan," Sprawling said.

"We'll dismiss the FBI from the lawsuit, but I'll need a quick favor from Mr. Jaynes. We can discuss it later. It's a minor point."

"All right. Moving right along. When will your client be prepared to testify before the grand jury?"

"Whenever you need him. Physically, he's able to do it anytime."

"We intend to move quickly with this."

"The sooner the better for my client."

Sprawling circled items on his checklist. "We will insist on confidentiality. No press whatsoever. This deal will be subject to a lot of criticism."

"We're not saying a word," Sandy promised.

"When would you like for Ms. Miranda to be released?"

"Tomorrow. And she needs to be escorted from the jail in Miami to the private air terminal. We would like FBI protection until she is on the plane."

Jaynes shrugged as if he didn't understand. "No problem," he said.

"Anything else?" Sandy asked, rubbing his hands together as if the fun was about to start.

"Nothing from the government," Sprawling said.

"Good. Here's what I suggest," Sandy said, as if they had a choice. "I have two secretaries here with PC's. We have already prepared a rough draft of a settlement agreement and order of dismissal. It shouldn't take too long to hammer out the finer points, then you guys can sign off. I will then drive it over to my client, and hopefully within a couple of hours we'll be finished. Mr. Mast, I suggest you contact the federal Judge and arrange a conference call as soon as possible. We'll fax him the order of dismissal."

"When do we get the documents and tapes?" asked Jaynes.

"If everything gets signed and approved in the next few hours, you can have them at 5 P.M. today."

"I need a phone," Sprawling said. So did Mast and Jaynes. They scattered throughout the suite.

REGULAR INMATES received an hour each day outdoors. It was late October, a cool and cloudy day, and Patrick decided to demand his constitutional rights. The deputies in the hallway said no; it had not been authorized.

Patrick called Karl Huskey and got everything approved. He also asked Karl if he could stop by Rosetti's on Division Street near the Point and pick up a couple of Vancleave Specials—crabmeat and cheese po'boys—and join him for lunch, outside. Karl said he would be delighted.

They ate on a wooden bench, not far from a small fountain and a sad little maple. The various wings of the hospital surrounded them. Karl had brought po'boys for the deputies as well, and they sat nearby, just out of earshot.

Karl knew nothing of the meeting under way at the hotel suite, and Patrick didn't tell him. Parrish was there, and before long he would tell His Honor.

"What are people saying about me?" Patrick asked after he finished a third of his sandwich and put it away.

"The gossip has died down. Things are back to normal. Your friends are still your friends."

"I'm writing letters to some of them. Would you deliver them?"

"Of course I will."

"Thanks."

"I hear they caught your lady friend in Miami."

"Yeah. But she'll be out soon. Just a small problem with her passport."

Huskey took a large bite of his sandwich and chewed in silence. He was growing accustomed to the long quiet intervals in their dialogue. He struggled with what to say next. Patrick did not.

"The fresh air is nice," he finally said. "Thanks."

"You have a constitutional right to fresh air."

"You ever been to Brazil?"

"No."

"You should go."

"Like you, or with my family?"

"No, no. Go visit sometime."

"The beaches?"

"No. Forget the beaches, and forget the cities. Go to the heart of the country, to the open spaces where the sky is clear and blue, the air is light, the land is beautiful, the people are gentle and uncomplicated. It's my home, Karl. I can't wait to go back there."

"Might be a while."

"Maybe, but I can wait. I'm not Patrick anymore, Karl. Patrick is dead. He was trapped and unhappy. He was fat and miserable and, thankfully, he went away. I'm Danilo now, Danilo Silva, a much happier person with a quiet life in another country. Danilo can wait."

And with a beautiful woman and a large fortune, Karl wanted to say, but he let it pass.

"How does Danilo get back to Brazil?" Karl asked.

"I'm still working on that."

"Look, Patrick—I guess it's okay if I call you Patrick and not Danilo."

"Sure."

"I think it's time for me to step down and give the case to Judge Trussel. Some motions will soon be due, and rulings will have to be issued. I've done all I can do to help you."

"Are you taking some heat?"

"A little, but nothing that worries me. I don't want to hurt you, and I'm afraid if I keep your case much longer, people might resent it. Everybody knows we're friends. Hell, you even picked me as one of your pallbearers."

"Did I ever thank you for serving?"

"No. You were dead at the time, so don't mention it. It was fun."

"Yeah, I know."

"Anyway, I've talked to Trussel, and he's ready to take the case. I've also told him about your heinous injuries, and how important it is for you to stay here for as long as possible. He understands."

"Thanks."

"But you have to be realistic. At some point, you're gonna be put in jail. And you might be there for a long time."

"Do you think I killed that boy, Karl?"

Karl dropped the remains of his sandwich into a bag and drank his iced tea. He was not inclined to lie about this. "It looks suspicious. First, there were human remains in the car, so somebody was killed. Second, the FBI has done an exhaustive computer analysis of all persons who became missing on or shortly before February 9, 1992. Pepper is the only person within three hundred miles who has not been heard from."

"But that's not enough to convict me."

"Your question was not about getting a conviction."

"Fine. Do you think I killed him?"

"I don't know what to think, Patrick. I've been a judge for twelve years, and I've seen people stand before me and confess to crimes that they still couldn't believe they committed. Under the right circumstances, a man can do just about anything."

"So you believe it?"

"I don't want to. I'm not sure what I believe."

"You think I could kill someone?"

"No. But I didn't think you could fake your death and swipe ninety million bucks either. Your recent history is full of surprises."

Another long pause. Karl glanced at his watch. Patrick left him on the bench and walked slowly around the courtyard.

☐ ☐ ☐ ☐

LUNCH in the Camille Suite was an array of bland sandwiches served on plastic trays, and it was interrupted by a return call from the federal Judge who had been assigned Patrick's case four years earlier. The Judge was in the middle of a trial in Jackson, and had only a minute. Mast described the cast of players assembled in the suite, and the Judge consented to being placed on a speakerphone. Mast then gave a hurried summary of the proposed agreement. The Judge wanted to hear Sandy's version next, and he delivered it. Sprawling was asked a few questions, and the short phone conference became a lengthy one. At one point, Sprawling left the room to chat privately with the Judge. He conveyed the urgent wishes of higher-ups in Washington to cut the deal with Mr. Lanigan so bigger fish could be caught. The Judge also talked privately with T.L. Parrish, who gave the same assurances that Lanigan was not walking away, that he would indeed face the more serious charges, and in all likelihood, though no guarantees were given, spend many years in jail.

The Judge was reluctant to act in such a hurry, but with pressure from those so intimately involved with the case, and given the stature of those present in Biloxi, he relented and agreed to sign the order dismissing all federal charges against Patrick. The order was promptly faxed to him, and he promptly signed it and faxed it back.

As they finished lunch, Sandy left them briefly for a quick drive to the hospital. Patrick was in his room, writing a letter to his mother, when Sandy burst in. "We did it!" He threw the agreement on Patrick's worktable.

"We got everything we wanted," he said.

"Full dismissal?"

"Yep. The Judge just signed it."

"How much money?"

"Ninety, plus three percent."

Patrick closed his eyes and clenched his fists. The fortune had just taken a major hit, but there was plenty left; enough for him and Eva to one day settle down somewhere safe and have a house full of kids. A large house. And many kids.

They scanned the agreement. Patrick signed it, then Sandy raced back to the hotel.

THE CROWD had thinned by 2 P.M., when the second meeting got started. Sandy welcomed Talbot Mims and his client, a senior VP for Northern Case Mutual named Shenault, who brought with him two in-house lawyers whose names Sandy missed. For good measure, Mims also brought one of his partners and an associate, both nameless too. Sandy collected their business cards and escorted them into the same parlor where the first meeting had taken place. The court reporters took their positions.

Jaynes and Sprawling were next door in the den, on the phone to Washington. They had sent the rest of their entourage down to the casino for an hour of leisure, no alcohol.

The squad from Monarch-Sierra was much smaller, just Hal Ladd, one of his associates, and the chief in-house lawyer for the company, a dapper little man named Cohen. Stiff introductions were made around the room, and they all settled in to listen to Sandy. He had packets for them, thin folders which he distributed and asked them to flip through. Each contained a copy of the lawsuit filed by Patrick against the FBI for his injuries, and each had a set of color pictures of the burns. The insurance boys had been prepped by their lawyers, so none of this was a surprise.

Sandy summarized what he had alleged yesterday—that the injuries to his client had not been inflicted by the FBI because the FBI didn't find Patrick. Stephano did. And Stephano was working for three clients: Benny Aricia, Northern Case Mutual, and Monarch-Sierra. All three had serious exposure in a civil liability suit to be filed by Patrick.

"How do you plan to prove this Stephano business?" asked Talbot Mims.

"Just a second," Sandy said. He opened the door that led to the den and asked Jaynes if he had a minute. Jaynes entered the room, and identified himself to the group. With great pleasure he described in detail the things Stephano had told them about the search for Patrick; the financing of the consortium, the rewards, the tips, the hunt in Brazil, the plastic surgeon, the boys from

Pluto, the capture, and the torture. Everything. And all done with money provided by Aricia, Monarch-Sierra, and Northern Case Mutual. And all done solely for their benefit.

It was a dazzling performance, one Jaynes himself enjoyed immensely.

"Any questions for Mr. Jaynes?" Sandy asked happily as the narrative came to a close.

There were none. In the past eighteen hours, neither Shenault of Northern Case Mutual nor Cohen of Monarch-Sierra had been able to determine who in their companies had authorized the hiring of Jack Stephano. It was unlikely they would ever know, now that tracks were being erased.

Both companies were large and rich, with lots of shareholders and big ad budgets used to protect their good corporate names. Neither wanted this headache.

"Thank you, Mr. Jaynes," Sandy said.

"I'm next door if you need me," Jaynes said, as if he would like nothing better than to return and do some more coffin-nailing.

His presence was baffling and ominous. Why was the Deputy Director of the FBI in Biloxi, and why did he seem so eager to place blame on them?

"Here's the deal," Sandy said when the door was shut. "It's simple, quick, non-negotiable. First, Mr. Shenault, as to Northern Case Mutual, your client's last assault in this little war is an effort to recoup its two and a half million paid to Trudy Lanigan. We prefer that you simply go back home. Dismiss the lawsuit, forget about Trudy, let her live in peace. She has a child to raise, and, besides, most of the money has been spent anyway. Dismiss, and my client will not pursue his claim for personal injuries against your company."

"Is that all?" Talbot Mims asked in disbelief.

"Yes. That's it."

"Done."

"We'd like a moment to consult," Shenault said, still hard-faced.

"No we don't," Mims said to his client. "It's a great deal. It's on the table. We take it. Just like that."

Shenault said, "I'd like to analyze—"

"No," Mims said, bristling at Shenault. "We take the deal. Now, if you want someone else to represent you, fine. But as long as I'm your lawyer, we're taking the deal, right now."

Shenault went speechless.

"We'll take it," Mims said.

"Mr. Shenault?" Sandy said.

"Uh, sure. I guess we'll agree to it."

"Great. I have a proposed settlement agreement waiting on you in the room next door. Now, if you gentlemen will leave us for a few minutes, I need to talk with Mr. Ladd and his client in private."

Mims led his crew out. Sandy locked the door behind them and turned to address Mr. Cohen, Hal Ladd, and his associate. "Your deal is a bit different from theirs, I'm afraid. They get off lightly because there is a divorce. It's messy and complicated, and my client can use his claim against Northern Case Mutual to his advantage in the divorce proceedings. You, unfortunately, are not in the same position. They put up a half a million for Stephano, you put up twice that much. You have more liability, more exposure, and, as we all know, a helluva lot more cash than Northern Case Mutual."

"How much do you have in mind?" Cohen asked.

"Nothing for Patrick. He's very concerned, however, about the child. She's six, and her mother burns money. That's one reason Northern Case Mutual collapsed so quickly—it'll be very difficult to collect from Mrs. Lanigan. Patrick would like a modest amount to go into a trust fund for the child, money out of the mother's reach."

"How much?"

"A quarter of a million. Plus the same amount to cover his legal fees. Total of a half a million, paid very quietly so your client won't be embarrassed by those pictures."

The Coast had a history of generous verdicts in personal injury and wrongful death cases. Hal Ladd had advised Cohen that he could see a multi-million-dollar verdict against Aricia and the insurance companies for what was done to Patrick. Cohen, from

California, certainly understood this. The company was quite anxious to settle and leave town.

"All litigation is dismissed," Cohen said. "And we pay a half a million?"

"That's it."

"We'll do it."

Sandy reached into a file and removed some papers. "I have a proposed settlement agreement, which I'll leave with you." He handed copies to them, and left them.

Thirty-five

THE PSYCHIATRIST was a friend of Dr. Hayani's. Patrick's second session with him lasted for two hours and was as unproductive as the first. It would be the last.

Patrick asked to be excused, and returned to his room in time for dinner. He ignored most of it as he watched the evening news. His name was not mentioned. He paced the floor and spoke to his guards. Sandy had called throughout the afternoon with updates, but he wanted to see documents. He watched "Jeopardy" and tried to read a thick paperback.

It was almost eight when he heard Sandy speak to the guards and ask how the prisoner was doing. Sandy enjoyed referring to him as "the prisoner."

Patrick met him at the door. His lawyer was exhausted, but smiling. "It's all done," he said as he handed Patrick a stack of paperwork.

"What about the documents and tapes?"

"We handed them over an hour ago. There must've been a dozen FBI agents swarming around. Jaynes told me they would work through the night."

Patrick took the settlement agreements and sat at his worktable in the corner, under the television. Carefully, he read every word. Sandy's dinner was fast food from a bag, and he ate it standing beside the bed, watching muted rugby from Australia on ESPN.

"Did they squawk at the half a million?" Patrick asked, without looking up.

"Not for a minute. Nobody squawked at anything."

"Guess we should've asked for more."

"I think you have enough."

Patrick flipped a page, then signed his name. "Good work, Sandy. A masterful job."

"We had a good day. Federal charges are all dismissed, the litigation is settled. Attorneys' fees are taken care of. The kid's future is secure. Tomorrow we'll finish with Trudy. You're on a roll, Patrick. Too bad you've got this dead body in your way."

Patrick left the papers on the table and stepped to the window, his back to the room. The shades were open, the window was cracked six inches.

Sandy kept eating and watching him. "You have to tell me sometime, Patrick."

"Tell you what?"

"Well, let's see. Why don't we start with Pepper?"

"Okay. I didn't kill Pepper."

"Did someone else kill Pepper?"

"Not to my knowledge."

"Did Pepper kill himself?"

"Not to my knowledge."

"Was Pepper alive when you disappeared?"

"I think so."

"Dammit, Patrick! I've had a long day! I'm not in the mood for games."

Patrick turned around and politely said, "Please, don't yell. There are cops out there, straining to hear every word. Sit down."

"I don't want to sit down."

"Please."

"I can hear better standing up. I'm listening."

Patrick shut the window, pulled the shades, checked the locked door, and turned off the television. He resumed his customary position on his bed, sitting, with the sheet pulled to his waist. Once situated, he said, in a low voice, "I knew Pepper. He came to the cabin one day asking for food. It was just before Christmas of '91.

He told me he lived in the woods most of the time. I cooked bacon and eggs for him and he ate like a refugee. He stuttered, and was very shy and uncomfortable around me. Obviously, I was intrigued. Here was this kid, he said he was seventeen but looked younger, who was reasonably clean and dressed and had a family twenty miles away, yet lived in the woods. I made him talk. I asked about his family, and got the sad story. When he finished eating, he was ready to go. I offered him a place to sleep, but he insisted on returning to his campsite.

"The next day, I was deer hunting, alone, and Pepper tracked me down. He showed me his little tent and sleeping bag. He had cooking utensils, an ice chest, a lantern, a shotgun. He said he hadn't been home in two weeks. Said his mother had a new boyfriend, who was the worst one in years. I followed him deep into the woods to a deer stand he'd found. An hour later, I killed a ten-point buck, my biggest ever. He said he knew the woods inside and out, and offered to show me the best places to hunt.

"A couple of weeks later, I was back at the cabin. Life with Trudy was unbearable, and she and I both lived for the weekends so I could leave. Pepper showed up not long after I arrived. I cooked a stew and we ate like hogs—I had an appetite back then. He said he'd gone home for three days, and left after a fight with his mother. The more he talked, the less he stuttered. I told him I was a lawyer and before long he told me his legal troubles. His last job had been pumping gas at a station in Lucedale. Some money came up missing from the cash register. Because everybody thought he was retarded, they blamed it on him. He, of course, had nothing to do with it. It was another very good reason to stay in the woods. I promised to check into the matter."

"And so the setup began," Sandy said.

"Something like that. We saw each other a few more times in the woods."

"It was getting close to February ninth."

"Yes, it was. I told Pepper that the cops were about to arrest him. This was a lie. I hadn't made a single call. Couldn't afford to. But the more we talked, the more convinced I became that he knew something about the missing money. He was scared, and leaning heavily on me. We discussed his options, one of which was to simply disappear."

"Gee, that sounds familiar."

"He hated his mother. Cops were after him. He was a scared boy who couldn't live in the woods for the rest of his life. He liked the idea of going out West and working as a hunting guide in the mountains. We hatched a plan. I watched the newspapers until I saw this terrible story of a high school sophomore getting killed in a train wreck outside New Orleans. His name was Joey Palmer; had a nice generic ring to it. I called a forger in Miami, who got Joey's Social Security number, and presto!—within four days I had a nice set of papers for Pepper. Louisiana driver's license, complete with a very close photo, Social Security number, birth certificate, even a passport."

"You make it sound so easy."

"No, it's easier than I make it sound. Just takes a little cash and some imagination. Pepper liked his new papers, and loved the idea of riding a bus off to the mountains. No kidding, Sandy, the kid had no hesitation whatsoever about leaving his mother in the dark. There was not one trace of concern."

"Your kinda guy."

"Yeah, well, anyway, on Sunday, February ninth—"

"The date of your death."

"Yes, as I recall it now. I drove Pepper to the Greyhound bus station in Jackson. I gave him every opportunity to turn back, but he was determined. No, he was excited. The poor kid had never left the state of Mississippi. Just the ride to Jackson was a thrill. I made it clear that he could never come back, under any circumstances. He never mentioned his mother. Three hours in the car, and he never mentioned his mother."

"Where was he headed?"

"I'd located a logging camp north of Eugene, Oregon, and I'd checked the bus routes and schedules. I wrote it all down for him, then we practiced it a dozen times on the way to the bus station. I gave him two thousand dollars in cash, and dropped him off two blocks from the bus station. It was almost 1 P.M., and I couldn't run the risk of being seen. The last time I saw Pepper he was jogging away with a smile on his face and a stuffed backpack slung over his shoulder."

"His shotgun and camping gear were found in the cabin."

"Where else could he put it?"

"Just another piece of the puzzle."

"Of course. I wanted them to think Pepper burned up in the car."

"Where is he now?"

"I don't know, and it's not important."

"That's not what I asked, Patrick."

"It's not important, really."

"Stop playing games with me, dammit. If I ask a question, then I deserve an answer."

"I'll give an answer when I feel like it."

"Why are you so evasive with me?"

Sandy's voice was louder, and edgy, and Patrick paused a moment to let him calm down. They both breathed slower, both tried to get a grip.

"I'm not being evasive, Sandy," Patrick said evenly.

"The hell you're not. I fight like hell to solve one riddle, and ten more mysteries hit me in the face. Why can't you tell me everything?"

"Because you don't need to know everything."

"It would certainly be nice."

"Really? When was the last time a criminal defendant told you everything?"

"Funny, I don't think of you as a criminal."

"Then what am I?"

"A friend, maybe."

"Your job will be easier if you think of me as a criminal."

Sandy lifted the settlement agreements from the table and started for the door. "I'm tired and I'm going to rest. I'll be back tomorrow, and you'll tell me everything."

He opened the door and left.

THE TAIL had first been noticed two days earlier by Guy as they were leaving a casino. A familiar face turned away a little too quickly. Then a car followed them a bit too aggressively. Guy had experience in such matters, and he mentioned it to Benny, who happened to be driving. "It's gotta be the feds," Guy had said. "Who else would care?"

They made plans to leave Biloxi. The phone lines were disconnected in the rented condo. They sent the other boys away.

They waited until dark. Guy left in one car, headed east to Mobile, where he would spend the night watching his rear and then catch a plane in the morning. Benny went west, along the Coast on Highway 90, then across Lake Ponchartrain into New Orleans, a city he knew well. He watched closely, but saw nothing behind him. He ate oysters in the French Quarter, then caught a cab to the airport. He flew to Memphis, then to O'Hare, where he hid most of the night in an airport lounge. Then on to New York at dawn.

The FBI was in Boca Raton, watching his home. His Swedish live-in was still there. She would bolt soon, they figured, and be much easier to follow.

Thirty-six

NO RELEASE had ever gone as smoothly. Eva walked out of the detention center a free woman at 8:30 A.M., in the same jeans and button-down she'd worn into the place. The guards were nice; the clerks were surprisingly efficient; the supervisor even wished her well. Mark Birck whisked her to his car, a handsome old Jaguar he'd scrubbed inside and out for the occasion, and nodded to their two escorts. "Those are FBI agents," he said to her, pointing with his head at two gentlemen waiting in a car nearby.

"I thought we were through with them," she said.

"Not quite."

"Am I supposed to wave hello or something?"

"No. Just get in the car." He opened the door for her, closed it gently, for a second admired the fresh wax job on the long, sloping hood, then scampered around to the driver's side.

"Here's a letter faxed to me from Sandy McDermott," he said as he cranked the engine and backed away. "Open it."

"Where are we going?" she asked.

"To the airport, general aviation. There's a small jet waiting for you there."

"To take me where?"

"New York."

"And then to where?"

"London, on the Concorde."

They were on a busy street, with the FBI agents behind them. "Why are they behind us?" she asked.

"Protection."

She closed her eyes and rubbed her forehead, and thought of Patrick in his small room at the hospital, bored, with little to do but think of places to send her. Then she noticed the car phone. "May I?" she said, lifting it.

"Sure." Birck was driving carefully, watching his mirrors as if he were chauffeuring the President.

Eva called Brazil and, switching to her native tongue, had a tearful reunion with her father, via satellite. He was well, and so was she. Both were liberated, though she didn't tell him where she'd spent the last three days. Kidnapping wasn't such a harsh ordeal after all, he joked. He had been treated superbly; not a single bruise. She promised to be home soon. Her legal work in the United States was almost over, and she was very homesick.

Birck listened without trying to, though he couldn't understand a word. When she hung up and finished wiping her eyes, he said, "There are some phone numbers in the letter, in case you get stopped again by customs. The FBI has lifted its alert, and they've agreed to allow you to travel under your passport for the next seven days."

She listened but said nothing.

"There's also a phone number in London, if something happens at Heathrow."

She finally opened the letter. It was from Sandy, on his letterhead. Things were proceeding nicely, and rapidly, in Biloxi. Call him at the hotel suite when she arrived at JFK. He would have further instructions.

In other words, he would tell her things Mr. Birck here shouldn't hear.

They arrived at the busy general aviation terminal on the north side of Miami International. The agents stayed with their car as Birck escorted her inside. The pilots were waiting. They pointed to a handsome little jet parked just outside, ready to take her anywhere she wanted. "Take me to Rio," she almost said. "Please, Rio."

She shook hands with Birck, thanked him for being so nice, and boarded her flight. No luggage. Not a stitch of extra clothing. Patrick would pay dearly for this. Let her get to London; give her a day along Bond and Oxford. She'd have more clothes than this little jet could carry.

AT SUCH an early hour, J. Murray looked especially tired and disheveled. He managed to grunt a hello to the secretary who opened the door, and he said yes to coffee, strong and black. Sandy greeted him, took his wrinkled blazer, and showed him to a parlor where they sat and reviewed the property settlement agreement.

"This is much better," Sandy said when he finished. Trudy had already signed off on the deal. J. Murray couldn't endure another visit by her and her slimy gigolo. She and Lance had fought yesterday in his office. J. Murray had been doing dirty divorces for years, and he'd bet good money that Lance's days were numbered. The financial strain was gnawing at Trudy.

"We'll sign it," Sandy said.

"Why wouldn't you? You're getting everything you want."

"It's a fair settlement, under the circumstances."

"Yeah, yeah."

"Look, Murray, there's been a significant development involving your client and her lawsuit with Northern Case Mutual."

"Do tell."

"Yes, there's a lot of background which is really not relevant to your client, but the bottom line is this: Northern Case Mutual has agreed to drop its lawsuit against Trudy."

J. Murray just sat there for a few seconds, then his bottom lip slowly departed from his top. Was this a joke?

Sandy reached for some papers, a copy of the settlement agreement with Northern Case Mutual. He had already blacked out sensitive paragraphs, but there was plenty for J. Murray to read.

"You're kidding," he mumbled as he took the agreement. He scanned past the blackened lines without the least bit of curiosity, and came to the heart of the matter, two paragraphs beautifully untouched by censors. He read clear and precise language which called for the immediate dismissal of the lawsuit against his client.

He didn't care why it was happening. An impenetrable shroud of mystery surrounded Patrick, and he wasn't about to start asking questions.

"What a pleasant surprise," he said.

"I thought you'd like it."

"She keeps everything?"

"Everything she has left."

J. Murray read it again, slowly. "Can I keep this?" he asked.

"No. It's confidential. But a motion to dismiss will be filed today, and I'll fax you a copy."

"Thanks."

"There's one other item," Sandy said. He handed J. Murray a copy of the Monarch-Sierra settlement, equally as censored. "Look on page four, third paragraph."

J. Murray read the sentences establishing a trust to be funded to the tune of two hundred and fifty thousand dollars, for the benefit of little Ashley Nicole Lanigan. Sandy McDermott would act as trustee. The money was to be used only for the health and education of the child, and any unused funds would be paid to the child upon her thirtieth birthday.

"I don't know what to say." But he was already thinking of how this might play back in his office.

Sandy waved him off as if it were nothing.

"Anything else?" J. Murray asked with a bright smile. Any more goodies?

"That's it. The divorce is settled. It's been a pleasure."

They shook hands and J. Murray left, his step a bit quicker. He rode the elevator alone, his mind racing wildly. He'd tell her how he'd played hardball with the rascals, how he'd finally just had it up to here with their outrageous demands, how he had barged into the meeting and threatened a vicious trial unless they yielded and made concessions. He had tried many such cases, was in fact known to be quite a courtroom brawler.

Damn the adultery charges! Damn the nudie pictures! His client was wrong but was still entitled to fairness. There was a poor innocent child to protect here!

He'd tell her how they'd broken and run in full retreat. He had demanded a trust fund for the child, and Patrick had collapsed under the weight of his own guilt. Here, they insisted, take a quarter of a million dollars.

And he'd fight like hell, fight them forever to protect the assets of his client, who had done nothing wrong by taking the two point five million. Out of fear, they had folded and scrambled to find a way to save Trudy's money. These details were murky at the moment, but he had an hour's worth of driving to work on the story.

By the time he got to his office, it would be a magnificent victory.

EYEBROWS WERE RAISED at the Concorde counter at JFK because she had no luggage. A supervisor was called and a huddle ensued as Eva fought to control her nerves. She couldn't take another arrest. She loved Patrick, but this was far above and beyond the call of romance. Not long ago she'd had a promising career as a lawyer in a city she loved. Then Patrick came along.

Suddenly there were warm British smiles everywhere. She was directed to the Concorde lounge, where she had coffee and called Sandy's number in Biloxi.

"Are you okay?" he asked when he heard her voice.

"I'm fine, Sandy. I'm at JFK, en route to London. How's Patrick?"

"Wonderful. We've cut the deal with the federal folks."

"How much?"

"A hundred and thirteen million," he replied, and waited to hear a response. Patrick had been perfectly noncommittal when he'd been told the size of the repayment. She followed the same script.

"When?" was all she said.

"I'll have instructions when you get to London. There's a room at the Four Seasons in the name of Leah Pires."

"That's me again."

"Call me when you get there?"

"Tell Patrick I still love him, even after going to jail."

"I'll see him tonight. Be careful."

"*Tchau.*"

WITH SUCH HEAVYWEIGHTS in town, Mast couldn't resist the opportunity to impress them. The evening before, after they had taken possession of the documents and tapes, he'd arranged for his staff to call every member of the sitting grand jury and inform them of an emergency session. With five of his assistant U.S. attorneys, he had worked with the FBI in scouring and indexing the documents. He had left his office at three in the morning, and returned five hours later.

The federal grand jury meeting was at noon, with lunch provided. Hamilton Jaynes decided to hang around long enough to sit through it, as did Sprawling from the Attorney General's office. Patrick would be the only witness.

Pursuant to their agreement, he was not transported in handcuffs. He was hidden in the back of an unmarked Bureau car, and sneaked through a side door of the federal courthouse in Biloxi. Sandy was at his side. Patrick wore large khakis, sneakers, a sweatshirt; clothing Sandy had purchased for him. He was pale and thin, but walked with no visible impairment. Actually, Patrick felt great.

The sixteen grand jurors sat around a long, square table, so that at least half of them had their back to the door when Patrick walked through with a smile. Those not facing him quickly turned around. Jaynes and Sprawling sat in a corner, intrigued by their first glimpse of Mr. Lanigan.

Patrick sat at the end of the table, in a chair used by witnesses, and seized the moment. He needed little prodding from Mast to tell his story, or at least some of it. He was relaxed and lively, in part because this panel could no longer touch him. He had managed to free himself of the tentacles of any federal law.

He started with the law firm, the partners, their personalities, clients, work habits, and slowly built his way to Aricia.

Mast stopped him, and handed over a document which Patrick identified as the contract between the firm and Aricia. It was four pages long, but could be reduced to a basic agreement of the firm getting one third of anything Aricia got by filing his claim against Platt & Rockland Industries.

"And how did you get this?" Mast asked.

"Mr. Bogan's secretary typed it. Our computers were interfaced. I simply pulled it off."

"Is that why this copy is unsigned?"

"That's correct. The original is probably in Mr. Bogan's file."

"Did you have access to Mr. Bogan's office?"

"Limited," Patrick answered, and explained Bogan's zealousness for secrecy. That led to a digression about access to the other offices, then to the fascinating story of Patrick's adventures in the world of sophisticated surveillance. Because he was very suspicious of Aricia, he set out to gather as much information as possible. He educated himself on electronic surveillance. He monitored the other PC's in the firm. He listened for gossip. He quizzed secretaries and paralegals. He went through the wastepaper in the copy room. He worked odd hours in hopes of finding open doors.

After two hours, Patrick asked for a soft drink. Mast declared a fifteen-minute break. The time had gone so fast because the audience was enthralled.

When the witness returned from the rest room, they settled in quickly, anxious to hear more. Mast asked some questions about the claim against Platt & Rockland, and Patrick described it in general terms. "Mr. Aricia was quite skillful. He set up a scheme for double billing, yet was able to pass the blame on to people in the home office. He was the secret moving force behind the cost overruns."

Mast placed a stack of documents at Patrick's side. He took one, and with only a glance knew everything about it. "This is a sample of the fictitious labor New Coastal Shipyards was paid for. It's a computerized labor summary for one week in June of 1988. It lists eighty-four employees, all bogus names, and gives their wages for the week. The total is seventy-one thousand dollars."

"How were these names selected?" asked Mast.

"At the time, there were eight thousand employees at New Coastal. They selected real names that were common—Jones, Johnson, Miller, Green, Young—and changed the first initial."

"How much labor was falsified?"

"According to Aricia's filing, it was nineteen million dollars over a four-year period."

"Did Mr. Aricia know it was falsified?"

"Yes, he implemented the scheme."

"And how do you know this?"

"Where are the tapes?"

Mast handed him a sheet of paper on which the tapes of over sixty conversations had been cataloged. Patrick studied it for a minute. "I think it's tape number seventeen," he said. The assistant U.S. attorney in charge of the box of tapes produced number seventeen, and inserted it into a player in the center of the table.

Patrick said, "This is Doug Vitrano talking to Jimmy Havarac, two of the partners, in Vitrano's office, on May 3, 1991."

The player was turned on, and they waited for the voices.

FIRST VOICE: How do you pad nineteen million dollars in bogus labor?

"That's Jimmy Havarac," Patrick said quickly.

SECOND VOICE: It wasn't difficult.

"And that's Doug Vitrano," Patrick said.

VITRANO: The labor was running fifty million a year. For four years it was over two hundred million. So they were just tacking on a ten percent increase. It got lost in the paperwork.

HAVARAC: And Aricia knew about it?

VITRANO: Knew about it? Hell, he implemented it.

HAVARAC: Come on, Doug.

VITRANO: It's all bogus, Jimmy. Every aspect of his claim is bogus. The labor, the inflated invoices, the double and triple billing for expensive hardware. Everything. Aricia planned this from the beginning, and he just happened to work for a company with a long history of screwing the government. He knew how the company worked. He knew how the Pentagon worked. And he was shrewd enough to set up the scheme.

HAVARAC: Who told you this?

VITRANO: Bogan. Aricia's told Bogan everything. Bogan's told the Senator everything. We keep our mouths shut and play along, and we'll all be millionaires.

The voices went silent as the tape, well edited by Patrick years ago, came to the end.

The grand jurors stared at the tape player.

"Could we hear some more?" one of them asked.

Mast shrugged and looked at Patrick, who said, "I think that's a marvelous idea."

With Patrick's play-by-play commentary and sometimes colorful analysis, it took almost three hours to listen to the tapes. The Closet tape was saved for last, and played four times before the grand jurors would let it go. At six, they ordered dinner from a nearby deli.

At seven, Patrick was allowed to leave.

While they ate, Mast discussed some of the more telling documents. He addressed the various federal laws involved. With the voices of the crooks captured so vividly on the tapes, the conspiracy was laid bare.

At eight-thirty, the grand jury voted unanimously to indict Benny Aricia, Charles Bogan, Doug Vitrano, Jimmy Havarac, and Ethan Rapley for conspiring to commit fraud under the False Claims Act. If convicted, each could face up to ten years, and be fined up to five hundred thousand dollars.

Senator Harris Nye was named as an unindicted co-conspirator, a temporary designation that would most likely change for the worse. Sprawling, Jaynes, and Maurice Mast fashioned a strategy of first indicting the smaller fish, then pressuring them to cut a deal and squeal on the big one. They would aggressively go after Rapley and Havarac because of their hatred of Charles Bogan.

The grand jury adjourned at nine. Mast met with the U.S. Marshal, and planned the arrests for early the next morning. Jaynes and Sprawling found late flights from New Orleans back to D.C.

Thirty-seven

"I HANDLED a car wreck once, just after I joined the firm. It happened on 49, up in Stone County, near Wiggins. Our clients were going north when a flatbed truck pulled out from a county road, right in front of them. A big wreck. Three people were in our car, the driver was killed, his wife was severely injured, a kid in the backseat had a broken leg. The flatbed truck was owned by a paper company, heavily insured, and so the case had potential. They gave it to me, and I jumped in gung ho because I was new. There was no doubt the truck was at fault, but its driver, who was not hurt, claimed our car was speeding. This became the big issue—how fast was our dead driver going? My accident reconstructionist estimated his speed at sixty miles per hour, which was not too bad. The highway was posted for fifty-five; everybody does at least sixty. My clients were driving to Jackson to visit family, and were in no hurry.

"The accident reconstructionist hired by the truck's insurance company estimated my guy's speed at seventy-five, and this, of course, would've seriously hurt our case. Any jury will frown on twenty miles over the speed limit. We found a witness, an old man who was either the second or third person on the scene. His name was Mr. Clovis Goodman, age eighty-one, blind in one eye and couldn't see out of the other."

"Seriously?" Sandy asked.

"No, but his vision was somewhat impaired. He was still driving, and on that day he was puttering down the highway in his 1968 Chevrolet pickup when our car passed him. Then, just over the next hill, old Clovis happened upon the wreck. Clovis was a very tender old man, lived alone, no close family, forgotten and neglected, and seeing this horrible accident moved him deeply. He tried to help the victims, and hung around for a while, then he left. He didn't say anything to anybody. He was too upset. He told me later he didn't sleep for a week.

"Anyway, we got word that one of the later arrivals had actually videoed the accident scene while the ambulances and cops and fire trucks were there. Traffic was backed up, people were bored, and, hell, they'll video anything, so we borrowed the tape. A paralegal analyzed it and took down all the license plate numbers. Then he found the owners, trying to find witnesses. That's how we found Clovis. He said he practically saw the wreck, but was too upset to talk about it. I asked him if I could come out for a visit, and he said yes.

"Clovis lived in the country, out from Wiggins, in a small white-frame house he and his wife had built back before the war. She had been dead for many years. So had his only child, a son who'd gone astray. He had two grandchildren; one lived in California and the other near Hattiesburg. He hadn't seen either in years. I learned all this within the first hour. Clovis was a lonely old man, gruff at first, as if he didn't trust lawyers and resented wasting time, but not long into the first visit he was boiling hot water for instant coffee and telling family secrets. We sat on the porch, in rocking chairs with a dozen old cats swarming under our feet, and talked about everything but the wreck. Fortunately, it was a Saturday, so I could waste time and not worry about the office. He was a wonderful storyteller. The Depression was a favorite topic, as was the war. After a couple of hours, I finally mentioned the car wreck, and he went quiet and looked pained and informed me softly that he just couldn't talk about it yet. Said he knew something important, but it wasn't the right time. I asked him how fast he was driving when our car went by. He said he never got above fifty. I asked him if he could estimate how fast our car was going, and he just shook his head.

"Two days later, I stopped by late one afternoon, and we settled back on the porch for another round of war stories. Promptly at six, Clovis said he was hungry, said furthermore that he loved catfish, and asked if I would like to join him for dinner. I was single at the time, and so Clovis and I left for dinner. I drove, of course, and he talked. We had greasy catfish at six bucks for all you can eat. Clovis ate real slow, his chin just inches above the pile of fish. The waitress put the check on the table and Clovis never saw it. It sat there for ten minutes. He kept talking with a mouthful of hush puppies. I figured the dinner was money well spent if Clovis ever came through with his testimony. We eventually left, and driving back to his house he announced he needed a beer, just one beer for his bladder, and at that moment we just happened to be nearing a country store. I parked. He didn't move, and so I bought the beer too. We drove and drank, and he said he'd like to show me where he grew up. It wasn't far away, he said. One county road led to the next, and after twenty minutes I had no idea where I was. Clovis couldn't see very well. He needed another beer, also for his bladder. I asked directions from a store clerk, and Clovis and I set sail again. He pointed this way and that, and we finally found the town of Necaise Crossing in Hancock County. Once we found it, he said we could turn around. He forgot the part about his childhood home. More beer. More directions from the store clerks.

"When we got near his house, I realized where we were, and I started asking questions about the car wreck. He said it was still too painful to talk about. I helped him into the house and he fell onto the sofa, snoring. It was almost midnight. This went on for about a month. Rocking on the front porch. Catfish on Tuesdays. Road trips for his bladder. The insurance policy had limits of two million. Our case was worth every bit of that, and, though Clovis didn't know it, his testimony was getting more crucial by the day. He assured me no one else had contacted him about the accident, so it was critical that I nail down his facts before the insurance boys found him."

"How much time had passed since the accident?" Sandy asked.

"Four or five months. I finally pressed him one day. I told him that we had reached an important point in the lawsuit, and it was time for him to answer some questions. He said he was ready. I asked him how fast our car was going when it passed him. He said it sure was awful, seeing those people hurt like that, crushed and bleeding, especially the little boy. The poor old man had tears in his eyes. A few minutes later, I asked him again, 'Clovis, can you estimate how fast the car was going when it passed you?' He said he sure would like to help the family. I said they would certainly appreciate that. And then he looked me square in the eyes, and said, 'How fast do you think it was going?'

"I said that in my opinion it was going about fifty-five miles an hour. Clovis said, 'Then that's what it was. Fifty-five miles an hour. I was doing fifty, and they just barely eased past me.'

"We went to trial, and Clovis Goodman was the best witness I've ever seen. He was old, humble, but wise and thoroughly believable. The jury ignored all the fancy accident reconstruction testimony and hung their verdict on Clovis. They gave us two point three million dollars.

"We kept in touch. I did his will for him. He didn't have much; just the house and six acres, seven thousand dollars in the bank. When he died, he wanted everything sold and the money given to the Daughters of the Confederacy. Not one relative was mentioned in his will. The grandson in California had been gone for twenty years. The granddaughter in Hattiesburg hadn't made contact since he received an invitation to her high school graduation in 1968. He neither attended nor sent a gift. He seldom mentioned them, but I knew Clovis longed for some connection with his family.

"He got sick and couldn't live by himself, so I moved him into a nursing home in Wiggins. I sold his house and farm, and handled all of his financial affairs. At the time, I was his only friend. I sent him cards and gifts, and every time I went to Hattiesburg or Jackson I would stop and visit for as long as I could. At least once a month, I would go get him and take him to the Catfish Cabin. Then we'd take a road trip. After a beer or two he'd start with his

1020100J O H N   G R I S H A M

stories. I took him fishing one day, just me and Clovis in a boat for eight hours, and I've never laughed so hard in my life.

"He caught pneumonia in November of '91, and almost died. It scared him. We fixed his will again. He wanted to leave some of the money to his local church, the rest to the remnants of the Confederacy. He picked out his cemetery plot, made his burial arrangements. I brought up the idea of a living will, so he wouldn't be kept alive by machines. He liked it, and he insisted that I be designated as the person to pull the plug, in consultation with his doctors, of course. Clovis was tired of the nursing home, tired of the loneliness, tired of life. He said his heart was right with God, and he was ready to go.

"The pneumonia came back with a fury in early January of '92. I had him transferred to the hospital here in Biloxi so I could watch him. I went by every day, and I was the only visitor old Clovis ever had. No other friends. No relatives. No minister. Not one single person but me. He deteriorated slowly, and it became apparent he would never leave. He lapsed into a coma, never to return. They put him on a respirator, and after about a week of that the doctors said he was brain dead. We, myself and three doctors, read his living will together, then turned off the respirator."

"What day was it?" Sandy asked.

"February 6, 1992."

Sandy exhaled, closed his eyes tightly, and slowly shook his head.

"He didn't want a church service because he knew no one would come. We buried him in a cemetery outside Wiggins. I was there, as a pallbearer. Three old widows from the church were there, crying, but you got the impression they had cried over every burial in Wiggins in the past fifty years. The minister was there, and he dragged with him five elderly deacons to act as pallbearers. Two other folks were there, for a total of twelve. After a brief service, Clovis was laid to rest."

"It was a pretty light casket, wasn't it?" Sandy said.

"Yes it was."

"Where was Clovis?"

"His spirit was rejoicing with the saints."

"Where was his body?"

"On the porch of my cabin, in a freezer."

"You sick puppy."

"I didn't kill anybody, Sandy. Old Clovis was singing with the angels when his remains got burned up. I figured he wouldn't mind."

"You have an excuse for everything, don't you, Patrick?"

Patrick's legs hung from the side of his bed. His feet were six inches from the floor. He didn't respond.

Sandy paced around a bit, then leaned on the wall. He was only slightly relieved to learn his friend had not killed anyone. The thought of burning a corpse seemed almost as repulsive.

"Let's hear the rest of it," Sandy said. "I'm sure you have everything mapped out."

"I've had time to think about it, yes."

"I'm listening."

"There's a Mississippi penal statute on grave-snatching, but it wouldn't apply to me. I didn't steal Clovis from the grave. I took him from his casket. There's another statute dealing with mutilating a corpse, and it's the only one Parrish can stick on me. It's a felony, and carries up to one year in jail. I figure that if that's all they can use, then Parrish will push very hard for the one year."

"He can't let you walk away."

"No, he can't. But here's the catch. He won't know about Clovis unless I tell him, but I have to tell him before he'll drop the murder charges. Now, telling him about Clovis is one thing, but testifying in court is another. He can't make me testify in court if he tries me for mutilation. He'll be pressured to try me for something, because, as you say, he can't allow me to walk away. He can try me, but he can't convict me because I'm the only witness and there's no way to prove the burned body was that of Clovis."

"Parrish is screwed from all sides."

"Correct. The federal charges are gone, and when we drop this bomb Parrish will feel enormous heat to nail me for something. Otherwise, I walk."

"So what's the plan?"

"Simple. We take the pressure off Parrish and allow him to save face. You go to Clovis' grandchildren, tell them the truth, offer them some money. They'll certainly have the right to sue me once the truth is known, and you can assume they'll do it. Their suit isn't worth much because they ignored the old man most of their lives, but it's a safe bet they'll sue anyway. We cut them off at the pass. We settle with them quietly, and in return for the money they agree to pressure Parrish not to press charges."

"You scheming bastard."

"Thank you. Why won't it work?"

"Parrish can prosecute you regardless of the family's wishes."

"But he won't because he can't convict me. The worst scenario for Parrish is to take me to trial and lose. It's much safer for him to hit the back door now, use the family as an excuse, and avoid the embarrassment of losing a high-profile case."

"Is this what you've been thinking about for the past four years?"

"It has crossed my mind, yes."

Sandy began pacing along the foot of the bed, deep in thought, his mind clicking away and trying to keep up with his client's. "We have to give Parrish something," he said, almost to himself, still walking.

"I'm more concerned with myself than Parrish," Patrick said.

"It's not just Parrish. It's the system, Patrick. If you walk away, then you've effectively bought your way out of jail. Everybody looks bad but you."

"Maybe I'm only concerned with me."

"So am I. But you can't humiliate the system and expect to ride off into the sunset."

"Nobody made Parrish run and get a capital murder indictment. He could've waited a week or two. No one made him announce it to the press. I have no sympathy for him."

"Neither do I. But this is a hard sell, Patrick."

"Then I'll make it a bit easier. I'll plead guilty to the mutilation, but with no jail time. Not one single day. I'll go to court, plead guilty, pay a fine, let Parrish get credit for a conviction, but then I'm outta here."

"You'll be a convicted felon."

"No, I'll be free. Who in Brazil will care if I get a slap on the wrist?"

Sandy stopped the pacing and sat on the bed beside him. "So you'll go back to Brazil?"

"It's home, Sandy."

"And the girl?"

"We'll either have ten kids, or eleven. We haven't decided."

"How much money will you have?"

"Millions. You gotta get me out of here, Sandy. I have another life to live."

A nurse barged through the door, flipped on a light switch, and said, "It's eleven o'clock, Patty. Visiting hours are over." She touched his shoulder. "You okay, sweetie?"

"I'm fine."

"You need anything?"

"No thanks."

She left as fast as she came. Sandy picked up his briefcase. "Patty?" he said.

Patrick shrugged.

"Sweetie?"

Another shrug.

Sandy thought of something else when he got to the door. "A quick question. When you drove the car off the road, where was Clovis?"

"Same place as always. Strapped in the passenger's seat. I put a beer between his legs and wished him farewell. He had a smile on his face."

Thirty-eight

BY 10 A.M. in London, the wiring instructions for the return of the loot had not yet arrived. Eva left her hotel and took a long walk along Piccadilly. With no particular destination and no schedule, she drifted with the crowd, gazed at the store windows, and enjoyed life on the sidewalk. Three days in solitary had sharpened her appreciation for the sounds and voices of people hurrying about. Lunch was a warm goat cheese salad in the corner of a crowded ancient pub. She absorbed the light, happy voices of people who had no clue as to who she was. And they didn't care.

Patrick had told her his first year in São Paulo was often exhilarating because not a single person knew his name. Sitting in the pub, she felt more like Leah Pires than Eva Miranda.

She began shopping on Bond Street, first for the necessities—undergarments and perfume—but before long it was Armani and Versace and Chanel, with little regard for price. She was a very wealthy woman at the moment.

IT WOULD have been simpler, and certainly less dramatic, to wait until nine and arrest them at the office. But then their work habits were erratic, and one, Rapley, seldom left home.

A predawn raid was chosen. So what if it scared them and humiliated them in front of their families. So what if the neighbors were drawn to the commotion. Catch 'em while they're sleeping or in the shower, that would be the best tactic.

Charles Bogan answered the door in his pajamas, and began crying quietly when a U.S. Marshal, a man he knew, produced handcuffs. Bogan had lost his family, so at least he was spared some of the shame.

Doug Vitrano's wife answered the door and was immediately hostile. She slammed it in the faces of two young FBI agents, who waited patiently as she ran upstairs to get her husband out of the shower. Thankfully, the kids were asleep when they put Doug in the back of the car, handcuffed like a common criminal, and left her on the front steps in her nightgown, cursing them and crying at the same time.

As usual, Jimmy Havarac had gone to bed blind drunk and the doorbell proved inadequate. They called him from a cell phone as they sat in his driveway, and he was eventually aroused and arrested.

Ethan Rapley was in the attic when the sun rose, working on a brief, oblivious to day or time. He heard nothing below. His wife was awakened by the knocking on the door, and she climbed the steps to deliver the bad news. First, though, she hid his gun. He kept it in a drawer in his dresser. He looked for it twice as he searched for the right pair of socks. But he wouldn't ask her for it. He was afraid she would tell him where it was.

The lawyer who founded the Bogan firm had been promoted to the federal bench thirteen years earlier. He had been nominated by Senator Nye, and once he left the firm Charles took over. The firm had strong connections with all five sitting federal judges, and so it was no surprise that the phones were ringing even before the partners were reunited at the jail. At eight-thirty, they were transported in separate cars to the federal courthouse in Biloxi for a hastily arranged appearance before the nearest federal Magistrate.

Cutter was irritated by the speed and ease with which Bogan pulled strings. While he didn't expect the four to stay in jail pending their trials, neither could he accept the sudden hearing before a Magistrate barely out of bed. And so Cutter tipped the local newspaper, and then he tipped the TV station.

The paperwork was prepared and signed quickly, and the four left the courthouse, on foot, unshackled, free to walk the three blocks to their offices. They were followed by a large, clumsy boy fumbling with a minicam and a young, green reporter who wasn't sure what the story was, but had been told it was huge. No comments from the stern faces. They made it to their office building on Vieux Marche, and locked the door behind them.

Charles Bogan went straight to the phone to call the Senator.

THE PRIVATE INVESTIGATOR, the one recommended by Patrick, found the woman in less than two hours, using nothing but the phone. She lived in Meridian, two hours north and east of Biloxi. Her name was Deena Postell, and she ran the deli and worked the second cash register of a brand-new convenience store on the edge of town.

Sandy found the place and walked inside. He pretended to admire a fresh rack of fried chicken breasts and deep-fried potato logs while he surveyed the employees hustling behind the counters. A wide, squatty woman with frosted hair and a loud voice caught his attention. Like all employees, she wore a red-and-white-striped shirt, and when she got close enough, Sandy could see her nameplate. It said Deena.

To build trust, he wore jeans and a navy blazer, no tie.

"Can I help you?" she said with a smile.

It was almost 10 A.M., much too early for a potato log. "A large coffee, please," Sandy said, also with a smile, and there was a twinkle in her eye. Deena enjoyed flirting. She met him at the cash register. Instead of handing over the money, Sandy gave her a business card.

She took one glance at it, then dropped it. For a woman who had raised three juvenile delinquents, a surprise like this only meant trouble. "A dollar-twenty," she said, punching buttons and glancing down the counter to see if anyone was watching.

"I have nothing but good news for you," Sandy said, reaching for the money.

"What do you want?" she said, almost under her breath.

"Ten minutes of your time. I'll wait over there at a table."

"But what do you want?" She took his money, and got the change.

"Please. You'll be happy you gave me the time."

She loved men, and Sandy was a nice-looking guy, much better dressed than most of the traffic she endured. She fiddled with the rotisserie chicken, made some more coffee, then told her supervisor she was taking her break.

Sandy was waiting patiently at a table in the small dining section, next to the beer cooler and the ice machine. "Thanks," he said as she sat down.

She was in her mid-forties, with a round face generously adorned with cheap cosmetics.

"A lawyer from New Orleans, huh?" she said.

"Yeah. I don't suppose you've read or heard about that case down on the Coast where they caught the lawyer who stole all that money?"

She was shaking her head before he finished. "I don't read nothin', honey. I work sixty hours a week here, and I got two grandbabies livin' with me. My husband keeps 'em. He's disabled. Bad back. I don't read nothin', watch nothin', do nothin' but work here and change dirty diapers when I'm home."

Sandy was almost sorry he asked. How depressing!

As efficiently as possible, he told Patrick's story. She found it amusing, but her interest waned toward the end.

"Give 'im the death penalty," she said during a pause.

"He didn't kill anybody."

"Thought you said there was a body in his car."

"There was. But the body was already dead."

"Did he kill it?"

"No. He just sort of stole it."

"Hummm. Look, I gotta get back to work. If you don't mind me askin', what's all this got to do with me?"

"The body he took was Clovis Goodman, your dear departed grandfather."

Her head rolled to the right. "He burned up Clovis!"

Sandy nodded.

Her eyes narrowed as she tried to arrange the proper emotions. "What for?" she asked.

"He had to fake a death, okay?"

"But why Clovis?"

"Patrick was his lawyer and friend."

"Some friend."

"Yeah, look, I'm not trying to make sense of all this. It was done four years ago, long before you and I entered the picture."

She tapped the fingers of one hand and chewed the nails of the other. The guy across from her seemed to be a pretty sharp lawyer, so the onset of drippy feelings about her beloved old gramps probably wouldn't work. This was confusing. Let him do the talking.

"I'm listening," she said.

"It's a felony to mutilate a corpse."

"It should be."

"It's also actionable at civil law. That means the family of Clovis Goodman can sue my client for destroying the corpse."

Ah, yes. Her back stiffened as she took a deep breath, then smiled, then said, "Now I see."

Sandy smiled too. "Yes. That's why I'm here. My client would like to offer a very quiet settlement with Clovis' family."

"What does family mean?"

"Surviving spouse, children, and grandchildren."

"I guess I'm the family."

"What about your brother?"

"Nope. Luther died two years ago. Drugs and alkyhall."

"Then you're the only person with a right to sue."

"How much?" she blurted out, unable to hold it, then was embarrassed by it.

Sandy leaned a bit closer. "We're prepared to offer twenty-five thousand dollars. Right now. The check's in my pocket."

She was leaning down too, getting lower and closer to his face, when the money hit and stopped her cold. Her eyes watered and her bottom lip quivered. "Oh my God," she said.

Sandy glanced around. "That's right, twenty-five thousand bucks."

She ripped a paper napkin from the holder and in doing so

knocked over the salt shaker. She dabbed her eyes, then blew her nose. Sandy was still glancing around, hoping to avoid a spectacle.

"All mine?" she managed to say. Her voice was hoarse and low, her breathing rapid.

"All yours, yes."

She wiped her eyes again, then said, "I need a Coke."

SHE DRANK a 44-ounce Big Gulp without a word. Sandy sipped his bad coffee and watched the foot traffic come and go. He was in no hurry.

"The way I figure it," she finally said, clear-eyed now, "is that if you walk in here and offer twenty-five thousand right off the bat, then you're probably willing to pay more."

"I'm in no position to negotiate."

"If I sue, it might look bad for your client, you know what I mean? The jury will look at me, and think about poor old Clovis getting burned up so your client could steal ninety million dollars."

Sandy sipped and nodded. He had to admire her.

"If I got me a lawyer, I could probably get a lot more money."

"Maybe, but it might take five years. Plus, you have other problems."

"Such as?" she asked.

"You were not close to Clovis."

"Maybe I was."

"Then why didn't you go to his funeral? That might be hard to sell to a jury. Look, Deena, I'm here ready to settle. If you don't want to, then I'll get in my car and go back to New Orleans."

"What's your top dollar?"

"Fifty thousand."

"It's a deal." She stuck forth her beefy right hand, still moist from the Big Gulp, and squeezed his.

Sandy pulled a blank check from his pocket and filled it in. He also produced two documents; one was a short settlement agreement, the other was a letter from Deena to the prosecutor.

The paperwork took less than ten minutes.

□ □ □ □

FINALLY, there was movement on the canal in Boca. The Swedish lady was seen hurriedly shoving luggage into the trunk of Benny's BMW. She sped away. They tracked her to Miami International, where she waited two hours before boarding a plane to Frankfurt.

They would be waiting in Frankfurt. They would patiently watch her until she made a mistake. Then they would find Mr. Aricia.

Thirty-nine

THE PRESIDING JUDGE'S last official act in the matter was an impromptu hearing of an undetermined variety, in his office, and without the accused's attorney present. Nor the prosecutor. The file would indicate no record of the meeting. Patrick was rushed through the rear of the courthouse by three escorts, up the back stairs, and quietly into Huskey's chambers, where His Honor waited, robeless. No trial was in session, and on an otherwise typical day the courthouse would have been peaceful. But four prominent lawyers had been arrested that morning, and the gossip was bouncing along the hallways at full throttle.

His wounds were still bandaged and prevented tight clothing. The aqua surgeon's scrubs were nice and baggy, and they also reminded people that he was hospitalized, not jailed like a criminal.

When they were alone and the door was locked, Karl handed him a single sheet of paper. "Take a look at this."

It was a one-paragraph order, signed by Judge Karl Huskey, in which he, upon his own motion, recused himself in the matter of *State versus Patrick S. Lanigan*. Effective at noon, an hour away.

"I spent two hours with Judge Trussel this morning. In fact, he just left."

"Will he be nice to me?"

"As fair as possible. I told him that, in my opinion, it's not a capital murder trial. He was very relieved."

"There's not going to be a trial, Karl."

Patrick looked at a calendar on the wall, the same kind Karl had always used. Each day for the month of October was packed with more hearings and trials than any five judges could handle. "Haven't you bought a computer yet?" he asked.

"My secretary uses one."

They had first met in this room, years earlier when Patrick arrived as a young, unknown lawyer representing a family devastated by a car wreck. Karl was presiding. The trial lasted for three days, and the two became friends. The jury awarded Patrick's client two point three million dollars, at that time one of the largest verdicts on the Coast. Against Patrick's wishes, the Bogan firm agreed to settle the case for an even two million dollars during appeal. The lawyers took a third, and after the firm paid some debts and made some purchases, the remaining fee was split four ways. Patrick was not a partner at the time. They reluctantly gave him a bonus of twenty-five thousand dollars.

It was the trial in which Clovis Goodman was the star.

Patrick picked at Sheetrock peeling in a corner. He examined a brown water spot on the ceiling. "Can't you get the county to paint this room. It hasn't changed a bit in four years."

"I'm leaving in two months. Why should I care?"

"Remember the Hoover trial? My first in your courtroom, and my finest hour as a trial lawyer."

"Of course." Karl crossed his feet on his desk, his hands locked behind his head.

Patrick told him the Clovis story.

A FIRM RAP on the door interrupted the narrative near the end. Lunch had arrived, and it would not wait. A deputy walked in with a cardboard box, and the aroma floated from it. Patrick stood close by as it was unloaded on Karl's desk: gumbo and crab claws.

"It's from Mahoney's," Karl said. "Bob sent it over. He said hello."

Mary Mahoney's was more than a Friday afternoon watering

hole for lawyers and judges. It was the oldest restaurant on the Coast, with delicious food and legendary gumbo.

"Tell him I said hello too," Patrick said, reaching for a crab claw. "I want to eat there soon."

At precisely noon, Karl turned on the small television mounted in the center of a set of bookshelves, and they watched without comment the frenzied coverage of the arrests. It was a mum bunch. No comments from anybody; certainly the lawyers, in fact their office doors were locked; Maurice Mast surprisingly had nothing to say; nothing from the FBI. Nothing of any substance, so the reporter did what she'd been trained to do. She lapsed into gossip and rumor, and that's where Patrick entered the piece. Unconfirmed sources told her that the arrests were part of an ever-widening investigation in the Lanigan matter, and to prove this she flashed up uncontroverted footage of Patrick entering the Biloxi courthouse for his appearance. An earnest colleague appeared on the screen, informed them in hushed tones that he was standing outside the door of the Biloxi office of Senator Harris Nye, first cousin to Charles Bogan, in case anybody had missed the connection. The Senator was off in Kuala Lumpur on a trade mission to bring more minimum-wage jobs back to Mississippi, and thus unavailable for comment. None of the eight people in the office knew anything about anything; thus they had nothing to say.

The story ran uninterrupted for ten minutes.

"Why are you smiling?" Karl asked.

"It's a wonderful day. I just hope they have the guts to nail the Senator."

"I hear the feds have dropped everything against you."

"That's correct. I testified before the grand jury yesterday. It was great fun, Karl, finally unloading all this baggage I've been keeping secret for years."

Patrick had stopped eating during the news story, and was suddenly bored with food. According to Karl's observations, he had eaten two crab claws and hardly touched the gumbo. "Eat. You look like a skeleton."

Patrick took a saltine and walked to the window.

"So let me get this straight," Karl said. "The divorce is settled.

The feds have dropped all charges and you've agreed to pay back the ninety million, plus a little interest."

"Total of a hundred and thirteen."

"The capital murder is about to collapse because there wasn't a murder. The state can't charge you with theft because the feds have already done so. The lawsuits filed by the insurance companies have been dismissed. Pepper is still alive, out there somewhere. Clovis took his place. That leaves one lousy little charge of grave tampering."

"Close. It's called mutilating a corpse, should you care to check the criminal code. You should know this stuff by now."

"Right. A felony, I believe."

"A light felony."

Karl stirred his gumbo and admired his skinny friend gazing out the window, nibbling on a cracker, no doubt plotting his next maneuver.

"Can I go with you?" he asked.

"To where?"

"To wherever you're going. You walk outta here, meet the girl, pick up the dough, hit the beach, live on a yacht. I'd just like to tag along for the ride."

"I'm not there yet."

"You're getting closer every day."

Karl turned off the television and moved his food aside. "There's a gap I'd like to fill in," he said. "Clovis died, then he was buried, or he wasn't buried. But what happened in between?"

Patrick chuckled, and said, "You like the details, don't you?"

"I'm a Judge. The facts are important."

Patrick took a seat and propped his bare feet on the desk. "I almost got caught. It's not easy to steal a corpse, you know?"

"I'll take your word for it."

"I had insisted that Clovis make his funeral arrangements. I even added a codicil to his will giving directions to the funeral home— no open casket, no visitation, no music, an overnight wake, a simple wood coffin, and a simple graveside service."

"A wooden coffin?"

"Yeah, Clovis was big on the ashes-to-ashes-dust-to-dust routine. Cheap wooden casket, no vault. That was the way his grandfather was buried. Anyway, I was at the hospital when he died, and I waited for the mortician from Wiggins to arrive with the hearse. Rolland was his name, a real card. Owns the only funeral home in town. Black suit, the works. I gave him a copy of Clovis' instructions. The will gave me authority to do what needed to be done, and Rolland didn't care. It was around three in the afternoon. Rolland said he would do the embalming in a few hours. He asked me if Clovis had a suit to be buried in. We hadn't thought of that. I said no, I had never seen Clovis in a suit. Rolland said he kept a few old ones around, and he'd take care of it.

"Clovis wanted to be buried on his farm, but I explained to him many times that in Mississippi you can't do that. Has to be in a registered cemetery. His grandfather fought in the Civil War, and had been quite the hero, according to Clovis. When he was seven years old his grandfather died, and they had one of those old-fashioned wakes that lasted for three days. They placed his grandfather's casket on a table in the front parlor and folks trooped by and looked at him. Clovis liked that. He was determined to do something similar. He made me swear that I would do a small wake for him. I explained this to Rolland. He said something to the effect that he'd seen everything. This was no surprise.

"Just after dark, I was sitting on Clovis' front porch when the hearse pulled up. I helped Rolland roll the casket down the driveway. We manhandled it up the steps, over the porch, and into the den, where we parked it in front of the television. I remember thinking how light it was. Clovis had shriveled up to a hundred pounds.

" 'You the only one here?' Rolland said, looking around.

" 'Yep. It's a small wake,' I said.

"I asked him to open the casket. He hesitated, and I told him that I had forgotten to include some Civil War memorabilia that Clovis wanted to be buried with. While I watched, he opened the casket with his church key, a small generic wrench which will open any casket in the world. Clovis looked the same. On his waist, I placed his grandfather's infantryman's cap and a tattered regimental banner from the Seventeenth Mississippi. Rolland closed the casket again, and left.

"No one showed up for the wake. Not a soul. I turned the lights off around midnight and locked the doors. Church keys are nothing more than Allen wrenches, and I had purchased a full set. It took less than a minute to open the casket. I removed Clovis; he was light, stiff as a board, and shoeless. I guess for three thousand bucks you don't get a pair of shoes. I laid him gently on the sofa, then I placed four concrete cinder blocks in the coffin, and closed it.

"Clovis and I left and drove to my hunting cabin. He was lying in the backseat, and I was driving very carefully. It would've been difficult to answer questions from a highway patrolman.

"A month earlier, I had bought an old freezer and put it on the screened porch of the cabin. I had just managed to get Clovis stuffed in the freezer when I heard something in the woods. It was Pepper, sneaking up on the cabin. Two o'clock in the morning, and Pepper caught me. I told him my wife and I had just finished a big fight, I was in a foul mood, and would he please leave. I don't think he saw me wrestling the corpse up the steps of the cabin. I locked the freezer with log chains, put a tarp over it, then some old boxes. I waited until dawn because Pepper was out there somewhere. Then I sneaked off, drove home, changed clothes, and was back at Clovis' by ten. Rolland arrived in a chirpy mood and wanted to know how the wake went. Just perfect, I said. The grieving had been held to a minimum. We pushed and pulled and loaded the casket back into the hearse, then went to the cemetery."

Karl listened with his eyes closed, his lips curled into a smile, his head shaking slowly in disbelief. "You devious bastard," he said, almost to himself.

"Thanks. On Friday afternoon, I went to the cabin for the weekend. I worked on a brief, scouted turkeys with Pepper, checked on old Clovis, who seemed to be resting comfortably. Sunday morning, I left before sunrise and positioned the dirt bike and the gasoline. Later, I drove Pepper to the bus station in Jackson. After dark, I removed Clovis from the freezer, sat him up next to the fireplace so he'd thaw, then around ten put him in my trunk. An hour later, I was dead."

"No remorse?"

"Of course. It was a terrible thing to do. But I made the decision to vanish, Karl, and I had to figure out a way. I couldn't kill anybody, but I needed a body. It actually makes sense."

"Perfectly logical."

"And when Clovis died, it was time for me to leave. A lot of it was luck. So many things could've gone wrong."

"Your luck continues."

"So far."

Karl looked at his watch, and took another crab claw. "How much of this do I tell Judge Trussel?"

"Everything but Clovis' name. We'll save that for later."

Forty

PATRICK SAT at the end of the table. His space was clear, unlike his attorney to the right, who had two files and a short stack of legal pads arranged like weapons poised for battle. To his left sat T.L. Parrish, with only one legal pad but also armed with a bulky tape recorder, which Patrick had allowed him to set up. No associates or flunkies to complicate things, but since all good lawyers need verifiers, they agreed to the taping.

Now that the federal charges had disintegrated, the pressure was on the state to extract justice from Patrick. Parrish felt it. The feds had dumped this defendant on him so they could chase a Senator; off to bigger things. But this defendant had new twists to add to the story, and Parrish was at his mercy.

"You can forget capital murder, Terry," Patrick said. Though nearly everyone called him Terry, it grated a bit coming from a defendant he'd barely known years before in a prior life. "I didn't kill anyone."

"Who burned in the car?"

"A person who had been dead for four days."

"Anybody we know?"

"No. It was an old person nobody knew."

"How did this old person die?"

"Old age."

"Where did this old person die of old age?"

"Here, in Mississippi."

Parrish drew lines and made squares on his pad. The door had opened when the feds collapsed. Patrick was walking through it; no shackles, no handcuffs, nothing, it seemed, could stop him.

"So you burned a corpse?"

"That's correct."

"Don't we have a statute on that?"

Sandy slid a sheet of paper across the table. Parrish read it quickly, and said, "Forgive me. It's not something we prosecute every day."

"It's all you have, Terry," Patrick said, with all the cool confidence of someone who'd planned this meeting for years.

T.L. was convinced, but no prosecutor folded this easily. "Looks like a year in jail," he said. "A year in Parchman should do you good."

"Sure, except that I'm not going to Parchman."

"Where do you plan to go?"

"Somewhere. And I'll get there with a first-class ticket."

"Not so fast. We have this body."

"No, Terry. You don't have a body. You have no clue who got cremated, and I'm not telling until we cut the deal."

"The deal being?"

"Drop the charges. Give it up. Both sides pack up and go home."

"Oh, that'll look nice. We catch the bank robber, he gives the money back, we drop the charges, and wave good-bye to him. That'll send the right message to the other four hundred defendants I have under indictment. I'm sure their lawyers will understand. A real shot in the arm for law and order."

"I don't care about the other four hundred, and they certainly don't care about me. This is the criminal process, Terry. It's every man for himself."

"But not everybody is on the front page."

"Oh, I see. You're worried about the press. When is reelection. Next year?"

"I'm unopposed. I'm not too worried about the press."

"Of course you are. You're a public official. It's your job to be worried about the press, which is precisely the reason why you should dismiss the charges against me. You can't win. You're worried about the front page? Imagine your picture there after you lose."

"The family of the victim does not wish to press charges," Sandy said. "And the family is willing to go public." He lifted a piece of paper and waved it. The message was delivered: we have the proof, we have the family, we know who they are and you don't.

"That'll look good on the front page," Patrick said. "The family begging you not to prosecute."

How much did you pay them, he started to ask, then let it go. It was not relevant. More doodling on the legal pad. More appraising his sinking options as the tape recorder captured the silence.

With his opponent on the ropes, Patrick moved in for the knockout. "Look, Terry," he said sincerely. "You can't prosecute me for murder. That's gone. You can't prosecute me for mutilating a corpse, because you don't know who got mutilated. You have nothing. I know it's a bitter pill to swallow, but you can't change the facts. You'll take some heat, but, hell, that's part of your job."

"Gee thanks. Look, I can indict you for mutilating the corpse. We'll call him John Doe."

"Why not Jane Doe?" Sandy asked.

"Whatever. And we'll pull the records of every old codger who died in early February of 1992. We'll go to the families, see if they've talked to you. We might even get a court order, dig up a few graves. We'll take our time. Meanwhile, you'll get transferred to the Harrison County Jail, where I'm sure Sheriff Sweeney will see the need to give you a few good cellmates. We'll oppose bail, and no judge will grant it because of your propensity to flee. Months will go by. Summer will come. The jail has no air conditioning. You'll lose some more weight. We'll keep digging, and with a little luck we'll find the empty grave. And in exactly nine months, two hundred and seventy days after the indictment, we'll go to trial."

"How are you going to prove I did it? There are no witnesses, nothing but some circumstantial evidence."

"It'll be close. But you miss my point. If I drag my feet getting the indictment, I could add two months to your sentence. That's almost a year you'll spend in the county jail before trial. That's a long time for a man with plenty of money."

"I can handle it," Patrick said, staring into Parrish's eyes, hoping he didn't blink first.

"Maybe, but you can't run the risk of getting convicted."

"What's your bottom line?" Sandy asked.

"You gotta look at the big picture," Parrish said, spreading his hands wide above his head. "You can't make fools out of us, Patrick. The feds have hit the back door. The state doesn't have much left. Give us a notch for our belts, something."

"I'll give you a conviction. I'll walk into a courtroom, face the Judge, listen to your routine, and I'll plead guilty to the felony charge of mutilating the corpse. But I get no jail time. You can explain to the Judge that the family does not want to prosecute. You can recommend a suspended sentence, probation, fines, restitution, credit for time served. You can talk about the torture and what I've been through. You can do all that, Parrish, and you'll look very good. Bottom line is this: no jail."

Parrish tapped his fingers and analyzed it. "And you'll reveal the name of the victim?"

"I will, but only after we have a deal."

"We have authorization from the family to open the casket," Sandy said, waving another document briefly before returning it to the file.

"I'm in a hurry, Terry. I have places to go."

"I need to speak with Trussel. He'll have to approve this, you know."

"He will," Patrick said.

"Do we have a deal?" Sandy asked.

"As far as I'm concerned we do," Parrish said, then turned off the recorder. He gathered his weapons and stuffed them into his briefcase. Patrick winked at Sandy.

"Oh, by the way," Parrish said as he stood. "I almost forgot. What can you tell us about Pepper Scarboro?"

"I can give you his new name and Social Security number."

"So he's still with us?"

"Yes. You can track him down, but you can't disturb him. He's done nothing wrong."

The D.A. left the room without another word.

HER TWO O'CLOCK APPOINTMENT was with a senior vice president of DeutscheBank, London branch. He was a German with perfect English, an impeccably tailored navy double-breasted suit, rigid manners, and a fixed smile. He gazed for one split second at her legs, then got down to business. The wire from his bank, Zurich branch, would be for one hundred and thirteen million dollars, sent immediately to the AmericaBank, Washington branch. She had the account numbers and routing instructions. Tea and biscuits were brought in as he excused himself to have a private chat with Zurich.

"No problem, Ms. Pires," he said, smiling warmly now as he returned and took a biscuit for himself. She certainly hadn't expected any problems.

His computer hissed with quiet efficiency, and a printout emerged. He handed it to her. After the wire, the balance in DeutscheBank would be one point nine million dollars and change. She folded it and put it in her purse, a sleek new Chanel.

Another Swiss account had a balance of three million. A Canadian bank on Grand Cayman held six point five million. A money manager in Bermuda was investing over four million for them, and seven point two million was currently parked in Luxembourg, but was about to be moved.

When her business was complete, she left the bank and found her car and driver parked nearby. She would call Sandy, and pass along her next movements.

BENNY'S STINT as a federal fugitive was brief. His girlfriend spent the night in Frankfurt, then flew to London, landing at Heathrow around noon. Since they knew she was coming, the customs officer double-checked her passport and made her wait. She wore dark sunglasses and her hands shook. It was all captured on video.

At the cab stand, she was unknowingly detained by a policeman who appeared to be in charge of whistling for taxis. He asked her to stand over there, next to those other two ladies, while he worked the traffic. Her driver was a true cabbie, but only seconds earlier had been briefed and given a small radio.

"Athenaeum Hotel on Piccadilly," she said. He eased away from the terminal in heavy traffic, and nonchalantly gave the destination on the radio.

He took his time. An hour and a half later, he deposited her at the door of the hotel. She waited again at the registration desk. The assistant manager apologized for the delay, but the computer was down.

When word came that the phone in her room was adequately tapped, they gave her a key and a bellman took her away. She tipped him lightly, locked and chained her door, and went straight for the phone.

The first words they heard her say were, "Benny, it's me. I'm here."

"Thank God," said Benny. "Are you okay?"

"I'm fine. Just scared."

"Did anyone follow you?"

"No. I don't think so. I was very careful."

"Great. Look, there's a little coffee bar on Brick Street near Down, two blocks from your hotel. Meet me there in an hour."

"Okay. I'm scared, Benny."

"Everything's fine, dear. I can't wait to see you."

Benny wasn't at the coffee bar when she arrived. She waited for an hour before panicking and running back to her hotel. He didn't call, and she didn't sleep.

The next morning, she gathered up the morning papers in the lobby and read them over coffee in the dining room. Deep in the *Daily Mail* she finally found a two-paragraph blip about the capture of an American fugitive, one Benjamin Aricia.

She packed her bags and booked a flight to Sweden.

Forty-one

WITH JUDGE KARL HUSKEY whispering into the ear of his colleague Judge Henry Trussel, it was established that the Lanigan matter should take precedence until it was put to rest. Rumors of a deal were floating throughout the legal community in Biloxi, rumors chased and being chased by even more gossip about the poor Bogan firm. In fact, nothing else was being discussed in the courthouse.

Trussel began the day by calling in T.L. Parrish and Sandy Mc-Dermott for a quick update, which eventually lasted for hours. Patrick was brought into the discussion on three occasions by use of Dr. Hayani's cell phone. The two, patient and doctor, were playing chess in the hospital cafeteria.

"I don't think he's cut out for jail," Trussel mumbled after the second call to Patrick. He was visibly and verbally reluctant to let Patrick off the hook with such ease, but a conviction was a longshot. With a docket filled with drug dealers and child molesters, he wasn't about to waste time with a high-profile corpse mutilator. All the evidence was circumstantial, and given Patrick's current reputation for meticulous planning, Trussel doubted a conviction.

The terms of the plea agreement were hammered out. The paperwork began with a joint motion to reduce the charges against Patrick. Then an agreed order to substitute new charges was prepared, followed by an agreed order accepting the guilty plea. In the course of the first meeting, Trussel spoke by phone to Sheriff Sweeney, Maurice Mast, Joshua Cutter, and Hamilton Jaynes in Washington. He also chatted twice with Karl Huskey, who was next door, just in case.

The two judges, along with Parrish, were subject to voter recall every four years in the general election. Trussel had never had an opponent and considered himself politically immune. Huskey was quitting. Parrish was sensitive, though being a good politician he presented the traditional facade of making the tough decisions without regard for public reaction. The three had been involved in politics for a long time, and each had learned a basic lesson: when contemplating an action which might be unpopular, do it quickly. Get it over with. Hesitation allows the issue to fester. The press grabs it, creates a controversy before the action, and certainly throws gasoline on the fire afterward.

The Clovis issue was simple, once Patrick explained it to everybody. He would submit the name of the victim, along with authorization from the family to dig up the grave, open the casket, look inside. If it was in fact empty, then the plea agreement would be complete. Since there would always be doubt until they opened the grave, if by some chance the casket was occupied, then the plea agreement would be ripped up and Patrick would still face capital murder charges. Patrick was supremely confident when he talked of the victim, and everyone believed without a doubt that the grave would be empty.

Sandy drove to the hospital, where he found his client in bed, surrounded by nurses as Dr. Hayani cleaned and dressed his burns. It was urgent, Sandy said, and Patrick apologized and asked them to leave. Alone, they walked through each motion and order, read every word aloud, then Patrick signed his approval.

Sandy noticed a cardboard box on the floor next to Patrick's temporary desk. In it were some of the books he'd loaned his client. The client was already packing.

For Sandy, lunch was a quick sandwich at the hotel suite, eaten while standing and watching over the shoulder as a secretary retyped a document. Both paralegals and a second secretary were back in the office in New Orleans.

The phone rang, and Sandy grabbed it. The caller identified himself as Jack Stephano, from D.C.; maybe Sandy had heard of him. Yes, in fact, he had. Stephano was in the lobby downstairs and would like to talk for a few minutes. Certainly. Trussel had asked the lawyers to return around two.

They sat in the small den and looked at each other across a cluttered coffee table. "I'm here out of curiosity," Stephano said, and Sandy didn't believe him.

"Shouldn't you start with an apology?" Sandy said.

"Yes, you're right. My men got a little carried away down there, and, well, they shouldn't have been so rough with your boy."

"Is that your idea of an apology?"

"I'm sorry. We were wrong." It lacked sincerity.

"I'll pass it along to my client. I'm sure it'll mean a lot to him."

"Yes, well, moving along here, I, of course, no longer have a dog in this fight. My wife and I are on our way to Florida for a vacation, and I wanted to take this little detour. I'll just be a minute."

"Have they caught Aricia?" Sandy asked.

"Yes. Just hours ago. In London."

"Good."

"I no longer represent him, and I had nothing to do with all that Platt & Rockland business. I was hired after the money disappeared. My job was to find it. I tried, I got paid, I've closed the file."

"So why this visit?"

"I'm extremely curious about something. We found Lanigan in Brazil only after someone squealed on him. Someone who knew him very well. Two years ago we were contacted by an Atlanta firm called the Pluto Group. They had a client from Europe who knew something about Lanigan, and this client wanted money. We happened to have some at the time, and so a relationship developed. The client would offer us a clue, we would agree to pay a reward, the money changed hands, and the client was always accurate. This person knew an awful lot about Lanigan—his movements, his habits, his aliases. It was all a setup—there was a brain at work. We knew what was coming, and, frankly, we were quite anxious. Finally, they popped the big one. For a million bucks, the client would tell us where he lived. They produced some very nice photos of Lanigan, one washing his car, a Volkswagen Beetle. We paid the money. We got Lanigan."

"So who was the client?" Sandy asked.

"That's my question. It's gotta be the girl, right?"

Sandy's reaction was delayed a bit. He grunted as if to laugh, but there was no humor in it. It came back to him slowly, her story about using Pluto to monitor Stephano, who of course was searching for Patrick.

"Where is she now?" Stephano asked.

"I don't know," Sandy said. She was in London, but it was certainly none of his business.

"We paid a total of one million, one hundred and fifty thousand dollars to this mysterious client, and she, or he, delivered. Just like Judas."

"It's over. What do you want from me?"

"As I said, I'm just curious. One of these days, if you learn the truth, I'd appreciate a call. I have nothing to gain or lose, but I won't rest well until I know if she took our money."

Sandy made a vague promise to perhaps one day give a call if he learned the truth, and Stephano left.

SHERIFF RAYMOND SWEENEY got wind of the deal during lunch, and didn't like it at all. He called Parrish and Judge Trussel, but both were too busy to talk to him. Cutter was out of the office.

Sweeney went to the courthouse to be seen. He parked himself in the hallway between the judges' offices, so that if a deal was struck he would somehow be in the middle of it. He whispered with the bailiffs and deputies. Something was coming down.

The lawyers showed up around two with tight lips and solemn faces. They gathered in Trussel's office behind a locked door. After ten minutes, Sweeney knocked on it. He crashed the meeting with a demand to know what was going on with his prisoner. Judge Trussel calmly explained that there would soon be a guilty plea, the result of a plea bargain, which, in his opinion, and in the collective opinions of everyone present, was in the best interests of justice.

Sweeney had his own opinion, which he readily shared. "It

makes us look like fools. Folks out there are hot about this. You catch a rich crook, and he buys his way outta jail. What are we, a bunch of clowns?"

"What do you suggest, Raymond?" Parrish asked.

"I'm glad you asked. First, I'd put him in the county jail and let him sit for a while, same as all prisoners. Then I'd prosecute him to the fullest extent."

"For what crime?"

"He stole the damned money, didn't he? He burned up that dead body. Let the boy serve ten years in Parchman. That's justice."

"He didn't steal the money here," Trussel explained. "We have no jurisdiction. It was a federal matter, and the federal boys have already dismissed the charges." Sandy was in a corner, his eyes fixed on a document.

"Then somebody screwed up, didn't they?"

"It wasn't us," Parrish said quickly.

"That's great. Go sell that to the people who elected you. Blame it on the feds because they don't run for office. What about burning the corpse? He gets to walk after admitting he did it?"

"You think he should be prosecuted for it?" Trussel asked.

"Damned right I do."

"Good. How do you think we should prove our case?" Parrish asked.

"You're the prosecutor. That's your job."

"Yeah, but you seem to know everything. Tell me, how would you prove the case?"

"He said he did it, didn't he?"

"Yeah, and do you think Patrick Lanigan will take the witness stand in his own criminal trial and confess to the jury that he burned a corpse? Is that your idea of trial strategy?"

"He won't," Sandy inserted helpfully.

Sweeney's neck and cheeks were red, and his arms were flailing in all directions. He glared at Parrish, then at Sandy.

And when he realized that these lawyers had all the answers, he brought himself under control. "When will this happen?" he asked.

"Late this afternoon," Trussel said.

Sweeney didn't like this either. He stuck his hands deep in his pockets and headed for the door. "You lawyers take care of your own," he said, just loud enough for everyone to hear.

"One big happy family," Parrish said, the sarcasm heavy.

Sweeney slammed the door and huffed down the hallway. He left the courthouse in his unmarked cruiser. Using his car phone, he called his own personal informant, a reporter with the Coast daily.

SINCE THE FAMILY, such as it was, had given blanket approval, as had Patrick, the executor of the estate, the digging up of the grave was a simple matter. Judge Trussel and Parrish and Sandy didn't miss the irony of having Patrick, Clovis' only friend, sign an affidavit granting permission to open the casket so that Patrick could be cleared. Every decision seemed to be layered with irony.

It was far different from an exhumation, a procedure that required a court order, after a proper motion and sometimes even a hearing. It was simply a look-see, a procedure unknown to the Mississippi Code, and therefore Judge Trussel took great latitude with it. Who could be harmed? Certainly not the family. Certainly not the casket; evidently it was serving little purpose anyway.

Rolland still owned the funeral home up in Wiggins. How well he remembered Mr. Clovis Goodman and his lawyer, and the odd little wake out there in the county, at the home of Mr. Goodman, where no one showed up but the lawyer. Yes, he recalled it well, he told the Judge on the phone. Yes, he'd read something about Mr. Lanigan, and no, he hadn't made the connection.

Judge Trussel gave him a quick summary, which led immediately to Clovis' involvement in the plot. No, he had not opened the casket after the wake, had had no need to, never did in those situations. While the Judge talked, Parrish faxed to Rolland copies of the consents signed by Deena Postell and by Patrick Lanigan, the executor.

Rolland was suddenly eager to help. He'd never had a corpse stolen before, folks just didn't do those things in Wiggins, and, well, yes, he could certainly have the grave opened in no time flat. He owned the cemetery too.

Judge Trussel sent his law clerk and two deputies to the cemetery. Under the handsome headstone:

CLOVIS F. GOODMAN
JANUARY 23, 1907, TO FEBRUARY 6, 1992
GONE ON TO GLORY

a backhoe carefully picked through the loamy soil as Rolland gave directions and waited with a shovel. It took less than fifteen minutes to reach the casket. Rolland and a helper stepped into the grave and shoveled away more dirt. The poplar had started to rot around the edges of the coffin. Rolland straddled the lower half of the casket and with dirty hands inserted the church key. He jerked and pried until the lid made a cracking sound, then he slowly opened it.

To no one's surprise, the casket was empty.

Except, of course, for the four cinder blocks.

THE PLAN was to do it in open court, as required by law, but to wait until almost five, when the courthouse was closing and many of the county employees were leaving. Five o'clock sounded fine to everyone, especially to the Judge and the District Attorney, who were convinced they were doing the right and proper thing, but were nervous about it nonetheless. Throughout the day, Sandy had pushed hard for a quick disposal once the plea agreement had been reached and the casket opened. There was no reason to wait. His client was incarcerated, though this received little sympathy. The court was in the middle of a scheduled term. The timing was perfect. What could be gained by waiting?

Nothing, His Honor finally decided. Parrish did not object. He had eight trials scheduled over the next three weeks, and unloading Lanigan was a relief.

Five was most satisfactory for the defense. With a bit of luck, they could be in and out of the courtroom in less than ten minutes. Another bit of luck, and no one would see them. Five was perfect for Patrick. What else did he have to do?

He changed into a pair of loose-fitting khakis and a large white cotton shirt. He wore new Bass loafers, no socks because of the rope-burned ankle. He hugged Hayani and thanked him for his friendship. He hugged the nurses and thanked the orderlies, and promised them all he'd be back soon to visit again. He wouldn't, and everyone knew it.

After more than two weeks as a patient and prisoner, Patrick left the hospital, his lawyer at his side, his armed escorts following dutifully behind.

Forty-two

EVIDENTLY five was a perfect time for everyone. Not a single courthouse employee left for home once word reached every corner of every office, a process that took only minutes.

A real estate secretary for a large law firm was busy checking a land title in the office of the Chancery Clerk when she overheard the latest Patrick report. She raced to the phone and called her office. Within minutes the entire legal community along the Coast knew that Lanigan was about to plead guilty in some strange deal, and would attempt to do so secretly at five in the main courtroom.

The notion of a clandestine hearing to complete a backroom deal made for a frenzy of phone calls; calls to other lawyers, to wives, to favorite reporters, to partners out of town. In less than thirty minutes, half the city knew Patrick was about to make an appearance and a deal, and most likely walk.

The hearing would have attracted less attention had it been advertised in the newspaper and posted on billboards. It was to be quick and secretive. Mystery engulfed it. It was the legal system protecting one of its own.

They grouped in pockets of hushed gossip in the courtroom, whispering while watching people stream in, and guarding their seats. The crowd grew and gave further credence to the hearsay.

All these people couldn't be wrong. And when the reporters arrived, the rumors were immediately confirmed as facts.

"He's here," someone said, a court clerk up near the bench, and the curious began finding seats.

Patrick smiled for the two cameramen rushing to meet him by the back door. He was led to the same jury room on the second floor, where the handcuffs were removed. His khakis were an inch too long, so he methodically rolled them up and cuffed them. Karl entered and asked the deputies to wait in the hall.

"So much for a quiet little appearance," Patrick said.

"Secrets are hard to keep around here. Nice clothes."

"Thanks."

"This reporter I know from the Jackson paper asked me to ask you—"

"Absolutely not. Not a word to anybody."

"That's what I figured. When are you leaving?"

"I don't know. Soon."

"Where's the girl?"

"Europe."

"Can I go with you?"

"Why?"

"Just want to watch."

"I'll send you a video."

"Gee thanks."

"Would you really leave? If you had the chance to walk away, to vanish right now, would you do it?"

"With or without ninety million?"

"Either way."

"Of course not. It's not the same. I love my wife, you didn't. I have three great kids, your situation was different. No, I wouldn't run. But I don't blame you."

"Everybody wants to run, Karl. At some point in life, everybody thinks about walking away. Life's always better on the beach or in the mountains. Problems can be left behind. It's inbred in us. We're the products of immigrants who left miserable conditions and came here in search of a better life. And they kept moving west, packing up and leaving, always looking for the pot of gold. Now, there's no place to go."

"Wow. I hadn't thought of it through a historical perspective."

"It's a stretch."

"I wish my grandparents had clipped someone for ninety million before they left Poland."

"I gave it back."

"I hear there might be a small nest egg left over."

"One of many unfounded rumors."

"So you're saying the next trend will be looting of clients' money, the burning of dead bodies, and the flight to South America, where, of course, there are beautiful women just waiting to be caressed?"

"It's working well so far."

"Those poor Brazilians. All these crooked lawyers coming their way."

Sandy entered the room with yet another sheet of paper for another signature. "Trussel is really edgy," he said to Karl. "The pressure is getting to him. His phone is ringing off the hook."

"What about Parrish?"

"Nervous as a whore in church."

"Let's get it done before they get cold feet," Patrick said as he signed his name.

A bailiff walked to the bar and announced that court was about to convene, so please have a seat. People hushed and moved hurriedly for empty spaces. Another bailiff closed the double doors. Spectators lined the walls. Every clerk in the courthouse had business near the bench. It was almost five-thirty.

Judge Trussel entered with his customary rigid dignity, and everybody stood. He welcomed them, thanked them for their interest in justice, especially at this late hour of the day. He and the District Attorney had agreed that a quick hearing would reek of a sleazy deal, so things would proceed deliberately. They had even discussed postponing it, but decided a delay would give the impression that they had been caught trying to sneak something through.

Patrick was led through the door by the jury box, and stood next to Sandy in front of the bench. He did not look at his audience. Parrish stood nearby, anxious to perform. Judge Trussel flipped through the file, inspecting every word on every page.

"Mr. Lanigan," he finally said, deeply and slowly. For the next thirty minutes, everything would be said in slow motion. "You have filed several motions."

"Yes, Your Honor," Sandy said. "Our first is a motion to reduce the charges from capital murder to mutilating a corpse."

The words echoed through the still courtroom. Mutilating a corpse?

"Mr. Parrish," His Honor said. It had been agreed that Parrish would do the bulk of the talking. The burden would be his to explain to the court, for the record, and, more important, for the press and the citizenry listening out there.

He did a wonderful job of detailing recent developments. Wasn't a murder, after all, but something far less. The state did not oppose the reduction of charges, because it no longer believed that Mr. Lanigan killed anyone. He paced around the courtroom in his best Perry Mason routine, unshackled by the customary rules of etiquette and procedure. He was the spin doctor for all sides.

"Next, we have a motion by the defendant for this court to accept a plea of guilty to the charge of mutilating a corpse. Mr. Parrish?"

The second act was similar to the first, with Parrish relishing the story of poor old Clovis. Patrick could feel the heated stares as Parrish delighted in as many details as Sandy had given them. "At least I didn't kill anyone!" Patrick wanted to scream.

"How do you plead, Mr. Lanigan?" His Honor asked.

"Guilty," Patrick said, firmly but with no pride.

"Does the state have a recommended sentence?" the Judge asked the prosecutor.

Parrish walked to his table, fumbled through his notes, paced back toward the bench, and along the way finally said, "Yes, Your Honor. I have a letter from a Ms. Deena Postell of Meridian, Mississippi. She is the only surviving grandchild of Clovis Goodman." He handed a copy to Trussel as if it were something brand-

new. "In the letter, Ms. Postell pleads with this court not to prosecute Mr. Lanigan for burning her grandfather's corpse. He's been
dead for over four years, and the family cannot survive any more
suffering and agony. Evidently, Ms. Postell was quite close to her
grandfather, and took his death very hard."

Patrick cut his eyes at Sandy. Sandy wasn't about to look at
Patrick.

"Have you spoken with her?" the Judge asked.

"Yes. About an hour ago. She became quite emotional on the
phone, and pleaded with me not to reopen this sad case. She
vowed that she would not testify in any trial, nor would she cooperate with the prosecution in any way." Parrish again walked to his
table and rifled through some more papers. He spoke to the Judge
but addressed the courtroom. "Given the feelings of the family, it
is the recommendation of the state that the defendant be sentenced
to serve twelve months in jail, that the incarceration be suspended
pending good behavior, that he pay a fine of five thousand dollars
and all court costs, and be placed on probation."

"Mr. Lanigan, do you agree with this sentence?" Trussel asked.

"Yes, Your Honor," Patrick said, barely able to lift his head.

"It is so ordered. Anything further?" Trussel picked up his gavel,
and waited. Both lawyers shook their heads.

"We are adjourned," he said, rapping it loudly.

Patrick turned and made a quick exit from the courtroom. Gone
again, vanished before their very eyes.

He waited with Sandy for an hour in Huskey's office while darkness settled in and the last of the courtroom stragglers reluctantly
gave it up and went home. Patrick was anxious to leave.

At seven, he said a long, fond good-bye to Karl. He thanked him
for being there, for standing by him, for everything, and he promised to keep in touch. On his way out the door, he also thanked
him again for serving as one of his pallbearers.

"Anytime," Karl said. "Anytime."

THEY LEFT BILOXI in Sandy's Lexus—Sandy at the wheel,
Patrick sitting low in the passenger's seat, subdued and taking in
for the last time the lights along the Gulf. They passed the casinos

on the beaches at Biloxi and Gulfport, the pier at Pass Christian, and then the lights spread out as they crossed the Bay of St. Louis.

Sandy handed him the phone number, and he called her hotel. It was 3 A.M. in London, but she grabbed the phone as if she were watching it. "Eva, it's me," he said, with restraint. Sandy almost stopped the car so he could get out while they talked. He tried not to listen.

"We're leaving Biloxi now, on the way to New Orleans. Yes, I'm fine. I've never felt better. And you?"

He listened for a long time, his eyes closed, his head leaning back.

"What's today?" he asked.

"Friday, November sixth," Sandy said.

"I'll meet you in Aix, at the Villa Gallici, on Sunday. Right. Yes. I'm fine, dear. I love you. Go back to sleep, and I'll call you in a few hours."

They crossed into Louisiana in silence, and somewhere over Lake Pontchartrain, Sandy said, "I had a very interesting visitor this afternoon."

"Really, who?"

"Jack Stephano."

"Here, in Biloxi?"

"Yes. He found me at the hotel, said he was finished with the Aricia case and was on his way to Florida for a vacation."

"Why didn't you kill him?"

"He said he was sorry. Said his boys got a little carried away down there when they caught you, wanted me to pass along his apologies."

"What a guy. I'm sure he didn't stop by just to apologize."

"No, he didn't. He told me about the mole in Brazil, about the Pluto Group and the rewards, and he asked me point-blank if the girl, Eva, was your Judas. I said I had no idea."

"Why does he care?"

"Good question. He said his curiosity has the best of him. He paid over a million bucks in rewards, got his man, but didn't get the money, and he said he won't be able to sleep until he knows. I sort of believed him."

"Sounds reasonable."

"He doesn't have a dog in the fight anymore, or something like that. His words, not mine."

Patrick put his left ankle on his right knee, and gently touched the burn. "What does he look like?" he asked.

"Fifty-five, very Italian, lots of groomed gray hair, black eyes, a handsome man. Why?"

"Because I've seen him everywhere. For the last three years, half the strangers I've seen in the outback of Brazil have been Jack Stephano. I've been chased in my sleep by a hundred men, all of whom turned out to be Jack Stephano. He has ducked in alleys, hidden behind trees, followed on foot at night in São Paulo, tagged behind me on motor scooters and chased me in cars. I've thought about Stephano more than I have my own mother."

"The chase is over."

"I finally got tired of it, Sandy. I gave up. Life on the run is quite an adventure, very thrilling and romantic, until you learn that someone is back there. While you're sleeping, someone is trying to find you. While you're having dinner with a wonderful woman in a city of ten million, someone is knocking on doors, quietly showing your photo to a clerk, offering small bribes for information. I stole too much money, Sandy. They had to come after me, and when I learned they were already in Brazil, I knew the end would come."

"What do you mean, you gave up?"

Patrick breathed heavily and shifted his weight. He looked through his window at the waters below, and tried to organize his thoughts. "I gave up, Sandy. I got tired of running, and I gave up."

"Yeah, I've already heard that."

"I knew they would find me, so I decided to do it on my terms, not theirs."

"I'm listening."

"The rewards were my idea, Sandy. Eva would fly to Madrid, then to Atlanta, where she would meet with the boys from Pluto. They were paid to contact Stephano and handle the flow of information and money. We milked the money out of Stephano, and eventually led him to me, to my little house in Ponta Porã."

Sandy turned slowly, his face blank, mouth open and crooked to one side, his eyes vacant.

"Watch where you're going," Patrick said, pointing to the road.

Sandy jerked the wheel and brought the car back into the right lane. "You're lying," he said, without moving his lips. "I know you're lying."

"Nope. We collected one million, one hundred fifty thousand bucks from Stephano, and it's hidden now, probably in Switzerland with the rest of it."

"You don't know where it is?"

"She's been taking care of it. I'll find out when I see her."

Sandy was too shocked to say anything else. Patrick decided to help. "I knew they would grab me, and I knew they would try to make me talk. But I had no idea this would happen." He pointed to the burn above his left ankle. "I thought it might get ugly, but they damned near killed me, Sandy. They finally broke me, and I told them about Eva. By then, she was gone, and so was the money."

"You could've easily been killed," Sandy managed to say. He was driving with his right hand, scratching his head with his left.

"That's true. Very true. But two hours after I was captured, the FBI in Washington knew Stephano had me. That's what saved my life. Stephano couldn't kill me, because the feds knew about it."

"But how—"

"Eva called Cutter in Biloxi. He called Washington."

Sandy wanted to stop the car, get out and scream. Lean over the side of the bridge, and let flow an endless string of blue profanities. Just when he thought he had been clued in to Patrick's past, this latest twist came crashing in.

"You were a damned fool if you let them catch you."

"Oh really. Did I not just walk out of the courtroom a free man? Did I not just talk with a woman I love dearly, a woman who happens to be keeping a small fortune for me? The past is finally gone, Sandy. Don't you see? There's no one looking for me anymore."

"So many things could've gone wrong."

"Yeah, but they didn't. I had the money, the tapes, the Clovis alibi. And I had four years to plan everything."

"The torture wasn't planned."

"No, but the scars will heal. Don't ruin the moment, Sandy. I'm on a roll."

Sandy dropped him off at his mother's house, his childhood home, where a cake was in the oven. Mrs. Lanigan asked him to stay, but he knew they needed time alone. Plus he hadn't seen his wife and kids in four days. Sandy drove away, his brain still swirling.

Forty-three

H E AWOKE before sunrise in a bed he hadn't slept in in almost twenty years, in a room he hadn't seen in almost ten. The years were distant, another lifetime. The walls were closer together now, the ceiling lower. Over the years his things had been removed, the boyhood memorabilia, the Saints banners, the posters of blond models in tight swimsuits.

As the product of two people who rarely spoke to each other, he had made his room his sanctuary. He'd kept the door locked long before his teen years. His parents entered only when he allowed them.

His mother was cooking downstairs; the smell of bacon drifted throughout the house. They had stayed up late; now she was up early, anxious to talk. And who could blame her?

He stretched slowly and carefully. The crusted skin around his burns cracked and pulled. Too much of a stretch and the skin broke, and the bleeding started. He touched the burns on his chest, desperately wanting to dig in with his fingernails and scratch with a fury. He crossed his feet and locked his hands behind his head. He smiled at the ceiling, an arrogant smile because life on the run was now over. Patrick and Danilo were gone, and the shadows behind them had been destroyed in a crushing defeat. Stephano and Aricia and Bogan et al., and the feds and Parrish with his insipid little indictment, all had been laid to waste. There was no one left to chase him.

Sunlight eased through the window, and the walls inched together. He showered quickly and treated his wounds with a cream
and fresh gauze.

He had promised his mother some new grandchildren, a fresh
batch of them to take the place of Ashley Nicole, a child she still
dreamed of seeing again. He told her wonderful things about Eva,
and promised to bring her to New Orleans in the very near future.
No definite plans to get married, but it was inevitable.

They ate waffles and bacon and drank coffee on the patio as the
old streets came to life. Before the neighbors could begin stopping
by to applaud the good news, they left for a long drive. Patrick
wanted to at least see his city again, if only briefly.

At nine, he and his mother walked into Robilio Brothers on
Canal, where he bought new khakis and shirts and a handsome
leather travel bag. They ate beignets at Café du Monde on Decatur, then a late lunch at a nearby café.

They sat at his gate at the airport for an hour, holding hands and
saying little. When his flight was called, Patrick hugged his mother
tightly and promised to call every day. She wanted to see the new
grandkids, and quickly, she said, with a sad smile.

He flew to Atlanta. Using his legitimate Patrick Lanigan passport, given to Sandy by Eva, he boarded a flight to Nice.

HE HAD LAST SEEN Eva a month earlier, in Rio, over a long
weekend in which they spent every moment together. The chase
was almost over and Patrick knew it. The end was near.

They clung to each other as they walked the crowded beaches of
Ipanema and Leblon, ignoring the happy voices around them.
They had late, quiet dinners in their favorite restaurants—Anti-
quarius and Antonio's—but they had little appetite for food. When
they spoke, the sentences were soft and short. The long conversations ended in tears.

At one point, she had convinced him to flee again, to leave with
her while he was still able, to hide in a castle in Scotland or a tiny
apartment in Rome, where no one would ever find them. But the
moment passed. He was simply tired of running.

Late in the afternoon, they rode a cable car to the top of Sugarloaf Mountain to watch the sunset over Rio. The view of the city at night was spectacular, but difficult to appreciate under the circumstances. He held her closely as the wind chilled them, and he promised her that some day, when it was all over, they would stand in this exact spot, and watch the sunset, and plan their future. She tried to believe him.

They said good-bye on a street corner, near her apartment. He kissed her on the forehead and walked away, into the crowd. He left her crying there because it was better than a messy scene at the crowded airport. He left the city, and flew west, changing flights as the planes and airports got smaller. He arrived in Ponta Porã after dark, found his Beetle parked where he'd left it at the airport, and drove the quiet streets to Rua Tiradentes, to his modest home, where he arranged his things, and began his wait.

He called her every day between 4 and 6 P.M., a coded call with different names.

And then his calls stopped.

They had found him.

THE TRAIN from Nice arrived in Aix on time, a few minutes after noon, Sunday. He stepped onto the platform, and looked for her in the crowd. He didn't really expect to see her. He was only hoping, almost praying. Carrying his new bag with his new clothes, he found a taxi for the short ride across town to the Villa Gallici, on the edge of the city.

She had reserved a room in both names, Eva Miranda and Patrick Lanigan. How nice to be in from the cold, to travel as real people without the cloak and dagger of false names and passports. She had not checked in yet, the clerk informed him, and his spirits sank. He had dreamed of finding her in the room, adorned in soft lingerie, ready for intimacy. He could almost feel her.

"When was the reservation made?" he asked the clerk, irritated.

"Yesterday. She called from London, and said she would arrive this morning. We haven't seen her."

He went to the room and showered. He unpacked his bag, and ordered tea and pastries. He fell asleep amid dreams of hearing her knock on the door, of pulling her into the room.

He left a message for her at the front desk, and went for a long walk through the lovely Renaissance city. The air was brisk and clear. Provence in early November was delightful. Perhaps they would live there. He looked at quaint apartments above the ancient, narrow streets and thought, yes, this would be a nice place to live. It was a university town where the arts were revered. Her French was very good and he wanted to become proficient. Yes, French would be his next language. They would stay here for a week or so, then go back to Rio awhile, but maybe Rio wouldn't be home. Flush with freedom, Patrick wanted to live everywhere, to absorb different cultures, to learn different languages.

He was set upon by a pack of young Mormon missionaries, but shook them off and walked along the Cours Mirabeau. He sipped espresso at the same sidewalk café where they had held hands and watched the students a year earlier.

He refused to panic. It was a simple matter of a late connecting flight. He forced himself to wait until dark, then strolled as casually as possible back to the hotel.

She wasn't there, nor was there a message. Nothing. He called the hotel in London, and was informed that she had left yesterday, Saturday, around mid-morning.

He went to the terrace garden next to the dining room, and found a chair in a corner which he turned so he could watch the front desk through a window. He ordered two double cognacs to fight the chill. He would see her when she arrived.

If she'd missed a flight, she would've called by now. If she'd been stopped by customs again, she would've called by now. Any problems with passports, visas, tickets, and she would've called by now.

No one was chasing her. All the bad guys had been either locked up or bought off.

More cognac on an empty stomach, and before long he was drunk. He switched to strong coffee to stay awake.

When the bar closed, Patrick went to his room. It was 8 A.M. in Rio, and he reluctantly called her father, whom he'd met twice. She had introduced him as a friend and a Canadian client. The poor man had been through enough, but Patrick had no choice.

He said he was in France, and needed to discuss a legal matter with his Brazilian lawyer. Apologies for disturbing him at home so early, but he couldn't seem to locate her. It was an important matter, even urgent. Paulo didn't want to talk, but the man on the phone seemed to know a lot about his daughter.

She was in London, Paulo said. He had talked to her on Saturday. He would say nothing more.

Patrick waited two agonizing hours, then called Sandy. "She's missing," he said, now very much in a panic. Sandy had not heard a word from her.

PATRICK ROAMED the streets of Aix for two days, taking long aimless walks, napping at odd hours, eating nothing, drinking cognac and strong coffee, calling Sandy and scaring poor Paulo with repeated calls. The city lost its romance. Alone in his room, he wept from a broken heart, and alone on the streets he cursed the woman he still madly loved.

The hotel clerks watched him come and go. At first he was anxious as he asked for his messages, but as the hours and days passed, he barely nodded at them. He didn't shave and he looked tired. He drank too much.

He checked out after the third day, said he was going back to America. He asked his favorite clerk to keep a sealed envelope at the desk in case Madame Miranda appeared.

Patrick flew to Rio. Why, he wasn't sure. As much as she loved Rio, it would be the last place she would be seen. She was much too smart to go to Rio. She knew where to hide, and how to disappear, and how to change identities, and how to move money instantly, and how to spend it without drawing attention.

She had learned from a master. Patrick had taught her all too well the art of vanishing. No one would find Eva, unless, of course, she wanted them to.

He had a painful meeting with Paulo, in which he told the entire story, every detail. The poor man crumbled before his eyes, crying and cursing him for corrupting his precious daughter. The meeting was an act of desperation, and utterly fruitless.

He stayed in small hotels close to her apartment, walking the streets, once again looking at every face, but for different reasons. No longer the prey, he was now the hunter, and such a desperate one at that.

Her face would not be seen, because he'd taught her how to hide it.

His money dwindled, and he was eventually reduced to calling Sandy and asking for a five-thousand-dollar loan. Sandy quickly agreed, and even offered more.

He gave up after a month, and traveled by bus across the country to Ponta Porã.

He could sell his house there, and maybe his car. Together, both would net thirty thousand U.S. dollars. Or maybe he would keep them and get a job. He could live in a country he loved, in a pleasant little town he adored. He could work perhaps as an English tutor, live peacefully on Rua Tiradentes, where the shadows were gone now but the barefoot boys still dribbled soccer balls along the hot street.

Where else could he go? His journey was over. His past was finally closed.

Surely, some day she would find him.

Acknowledgments

As always, I relied on the knowledge of friends while writing this book, and here I'd like to thank them. Steve Holland, Gene Mc-Dade, Mark Lee, Buster Hale, and R. Warren Moak lent their experience and/or went chasing after esoteric little facts. Will Denton again read the manuscript, and again kept it legally accurate.

In Brazil, I was assisted by Paulo Rocco, my publisher and friend. He and his charming wife Angela shared with me their beloved Rio, the most beautiful city in the world.

When asked, these friends gave me the truth. As usual, the mistakes are all mine.

The Runaway Jury

THE RUNAWAY
JURY

To the memory of
Tim Hargrove
(1953–1995)

Acknowledgments

ONCE AGAIN, I am indebted to my friend Will Denton, now of Biloxi, Mississippi, for providing much of the research and many of the stories upon which this one is based; and to his lovely wife Lucy, for the hospitalities extended to me while I was on the Coast.

Thanks also to Glenn Hunt of Oxford, Mark Lee of Little Rock, Robert Warren of Bogue Chitto; and to Estelle, for finding more mistakes than I care to think about.

One

T HE FACE of Nicholas Easter was slightly hidden by a display rack filled with slim cordless phones, and he was looking not directly at the hidden camera but somewhere off to the left, perhaps at a customer, or perhaps at a counter where a group of kids hovered over the latest electronic games from Asia. Though taken from a distance of forty yards by a man dodging rather heavy mall foot traffic, the photo was clear and revealed a nice face, clean-shaven with strong features and boyish good looks. Easter was twenty-seven, they knew that for a fact. No eyeglasses. No nose ring or weird haircut. Nothing to indicate he was one of the usual computer nerds who worked in the store at five bucks an hour. His questionnaire said he'd been there for four months, said also that he was a part-time student, though no record of enrollment had been found at any college within three hundred miles. He was lying about this, they were certain.

He had to be lying. Their intelligence was too good. If the kid was a student, they'd know where, for how long, what field of study, how good were the grades, or how bad. They'd know. He was a clerk in a Computer Hut in a mall. Nothing more or less. Maybe he planned to enroll somewhere. Maybe he'd dropped out but still liked the notion of referring to himself as a part-time student. Maybe it made him feel better, gave him a sense of purpose, sounded good.

But he was not, at this moment nor at any time in the recent past, a student of any sort. So, could he be trusted? This had been thrashed about the room twice already, each time they came to Easter's name on the master list and his face hit the screen. It was a harmless lie, they'd almost decided.

He didn't smoke. The store had a strict nonsmoking rule, but he'd been seen (not photographed) eating a taco in the Food Garden with a co-worker who smoked two cigarettes with her lemonade. Easter didn't seem to mind the smoke. At least he wasn't an antismoking zealot.

The face in the photo was lean and tanned and smiling slightly with lips closed. The white shirt under the red store jacket had a buttonless collar and a tasteful striped tie. He appeared neat, in shape, and the man who took the photo actually spoke with Nicholas as he pretended to shop for an obsolete gadget; said he was articulate, helpful, knowledgeable, a nice young man. His name badge labeled Easter as a Co-Manager, but two others with the same title were spotted in the store at the same time.

The day after the photo was taken, an attractive young female in jeans entered the store, and while browsing near the software actually lit up a cigarette. Nicholas Easter just happened to be the nearest clerk, or Co-Manager, or whatever he was, and he politely approached the woman and asked her to stop smoking. She pretended to be frustrated by this, even insulted, and tried to provoke him. He maintained his tactful manner, explained to her that the store had a strict no-smoking policy. She was welcome to smoke elsewhere. "Does smoking bother you?" she had asked, taking a puff. "Not really," he had answered. "But it bothers the man who owns this store." He then asked her once again to stop. She really wanted to purchase a new digital radio, she explained, so would it be possible for him to fetch an ashtray. Nicholas pulled an empty soft drink can from under the counter, and actually took the cigarette from her and extinguished it. They talked about radios for twenty minutes as she struggled with the selection. She flirted shamelessly, and he warmed to the occasion. After paying for the radio, she left him her phone number. He promised to call.

The episode lasted twenty-four minutes and was captured by a small recorder hidden in her purse. The tape had been played both times while his face had been projected on the wall and studied by the lawyers and their experts. Her written report of the incident was in the file, six typed pages of her observations on everything from his shoes (old Nikes) to his breath (cinnamon gum) to his vocabulary (college level) to the way he handled the cigarette. In her opinion, and she was experienced in such matters, he had never smoked.

They listened to his pleasant tone and his professional sales pitch and his charming chatter, and they liked him. He was bright and he didn't hate tobacco. He didn't fit as their model juror, but he was certainly one to watch. The problem with Easter, potential juror number fifty-six, was that they knew so little about him. Evidently, he had landed on the Gulf Coast less than a year ago, and they had no idea where he came from. His past was a complete mystery. He rented a one-bedroom eight blocks from the Biloxi courthouse—they had photos of the apartment building—and at first worked as a waiter in a casino on the beach. He rose quickly to the rank of blackjack dealer, but quit after two months.

Shortly after Mississippi legalized gambling, a dozen casinos along the Coast sprang forth overnight, and a new wave of prosperity hit hard. Job seekers came from all directions, and so it was safe to assume Nicholas Easter arrived in Biloxi for the same reason as ten thousand others. The only odd thing about his move was that he had registered to vote so quickly.

He drove a 1969 Volkswagen Beetle, and a photo of it was flashed on the wall, taking the place of his face. Big deal. He was twenty-seven, single, an alleged part-time student—the perfect type to drive such a car. No bumper stickers. Nothing to indicate political affiliation or social conscience or favorite team. No college parking sticker. Not even a faded dealer decal. The car meant nothing, as far as they were concerned. Nothing but near-poverty.

The man operating the projector and doing most of the talking was Carl Nussman, a lawyer from Chicago who no longer practiced law but instead ran his own jury consulting firm. For a small fortune, Carl Nussman and his firm could pick you the right jury. They gathered the data, took the photos, recorded the voices, sent the blondes in tight jeans into the right situations. Carl and his associates flirted around the edges of laws and ethics, but it was impossible to catch them. After all, there's nothing illegal or unethical about photographing prospective jurors. They had conducted exhaustive telephone surveys in Harrison County six months ago, then again two months ago, then a month later to gauge community sentiment about tobacco issues and formulate models of the perfect jurors. They left no photo untaken, no dirt ungathered. They had a file on every prospective juror.

Carl pushed his button and the VW was replaced with a meaningless shot of an apartment building with peeling paint; home, somewhere in there, of Nicholas Easter. Then a flick, and back to the face.

"And so we have only the three photos of number fifty-six," Carl said with a note of frustration as he turned and glared at the photographer, one of his countless private snoops, who had explained he just couldn't catch the kid without getting caught himself. The photographer sat in a chair against the back wall, facing the long table of lawyers and paralegals and jury experts. The photographer was quite bored and ready to bolt. It was seven o'clock on a Friday night. Number fifty-six was on the wall, leaving a hundred and forty still to come. The weekend would be awful. He needed a drink.

A half-dozen lawyers in rumpled shirts and rolled-up sleeves scribbled never-ending notes, and glanced occasionally at the face of Nicholas Easter up there behind Carl. Jury experts of almost every variety—psychiatrist, sociologist, handwriting analyst, law professor, and so on—shuffled papers and thumped the inch-thick computer printouts. They weren't sure what to do with Easter. He was a liar, and he was hiding his past, but still on paper and on the wall he looked okay.

Maybe he wasn't lying. Maybe he was a student last year in some low-rent junior college in eastern Arizona, and maybe they were simply missing this.

Give the kid a break, the photographer thought, but he kept it to himself. In this room of well-educated and well-paid suits, he was the last one whose opinion would be appreciated. Wasn't his job to say a word.

Carl cleared his throat while glancing once more at the photographer, then said, "Number fifty-seven." The sweaty face of a young mother flashed on the wall, and at least two people in the room managed a chuckle. "Traci Wilkes," Carl said, as if Traci was now an old friend. Papers moved slightly around the table.

"Age thirty-three, married, mother of two, doctor's wife, two country clubs, two health clubs, a whole list of social clubs." Carl clicked off these items from memory while twirling his projector button. Traci's red face was replaced by a shot of her jogging along a sidewalk, splendidly awash in pink and black spandex and spotless Reeboks with a white sun visor sitting just above the latest in reflective sport sunglasses, her long hair in a cute perfect ponytail. She was pushing a jogging carriage with a small baby in it. Traci lived for sweat. She was tanned and fit, but not exactly as thin as might be expected. She had a few bad habits. Another shot of Traci in her black Mercedes wagon with kids and dogs looking from every window. Another of Traci loading bags of groceries into the same car, Traci with different sneakers and tight shorts and the precise appearance of one who aspired to look forever athletic. She'd been easy to follow because she was busy to the point of being frazzled, and she never stopped long enough to look around.

Carl ran through the photos of the Wilkeses' home, a massive suburban trilevel with Doctor stamped all over it. He spent little time with these, saving the best for last. Then there was Traci, once again soaked with sweat, her designer bike nearby on the grass, sitting under a tree in a park, far away from everyone, half-hidden and—smoking a cigarette!

The same photographer grinned stupidly. It was his finest work, this hundred-yard shot of the doctor's wife sneaking a cigarette. He had had no idea she smoked, just happened to be nonchalantly smoking himself near a footbridge when she dashed by. He loitered about the park for half an hour until he saw her stop and reach into the pouch on her bike.

The mood around the room lightened for a fleeting moment as they looked at Traci by the tree. Then Carl said, "Safe to say that we'll take number fifty-seven." He made a notation on a sheet of paper, then took a sip of old coffee from a paper cup. Of course he'd take Traci Wilkes! Who wouldn't want a doctor's wife on the jury when the plaintiff's lawyers were asking for millions? Carl wanted nothing but doctors' wives, but he wouldn't get them. The fact that she enjoyed cigarettes was simply a small bonus.

Number fifty-eight was a shipyard worker at Ingalls in Pascagoula—fifty years old, white male, divorced, a union officer. Carl flashed a photo of the man's Ford pickup on the wall, and was about to summarize his life when the door opened and Mr. Rankin Fitch stepped into the room. Carl stopped. The lawyers bolted upright in their seats and instantly became enthralled by the Ford. They wrote furiously on their legal pads as if they might never again see such a vehicle. The jury consultants likewise snapped into action and all began taking notes in earnest, each careful not to look at the man.

Fitch was back. Fitch was in the room.

He slowly closed the door behind him, took a few steps toward the edge of the table, and glared at everyone sitting around it. It was more of a snarl than a glare. The puffy flesh around his dark eyes pinched inward. The deep wrinkles running the length of his forehead closed together. His thick chest rose and sank slowly, and for a second or two Fitch was the only person breathing. His lips parted to eat and drink, occasionally to talk, never to smile.

Fitch was angry, as usual, nothing new about that because the man even slept in a state of hostility. But would he curse and threaten, maybe throw things, or simply boil under the surface? They never knew with Fitch. He stopped at the edge of the table between two young lawyers who were junior partners and thus earning comfortable six-figure salaries, who were members of this firm and this was their room in their building. Fitch, on the other hand, was a stranger from Washington, an intruder who'd been growling and barking in their hallways for a month now. The two young lawyers dared not look at him.

"What number?" Fitch asked of Carl.

"Fifty-eight," Carl answered quickly, anxious to please.

"Go back to fifty-six," Fitch demanded, and Carl flicked rapidly until the face of Nicholas Easter was once again on the wall. Paperwork ruffled around the table.

"What do you know?" Fitch asked.

"The same," Carl said, looking away.

"That's just great. Out of a hundred and ninety-six, how many are still mysteries?"

"Eight."

Fitch snorted and shook his head slowly, and everyone waited for an eruption. Instead, he slowly stroked his meticulously trimmed black and gray goatee for a few seconds, looked at Carl, allowed the severity of the moment to filter in, then said, "You'll work until midnight, then return at seven in the morning. Same for Sunday." With that, he wheeled his pudgy body around and left the room.

The door slammed. The air lightened considerably, then, in unison, the lawyers and the jury consultants and Carl and everybody else glanced at their watches. They had just been ordered to spend thirty-nine out of the next fifty-three hours in this room, looking at enlarged photos of faces they'd already seen, memorizing names and birthdates and vital stats of almost two hundred people.

And there wasn't the slightest doubt anywhere in the room that they all would do exactly what they'd been told. Not the slightest.

FITCH TOOK THE STAIRS to the first floor of the building, and was met there by his driver, a large man named José. José wore a black suit with black western boots and black sunglasses that were removed only when he showered and slept. Fitch opened a door without knocking, and interrupted a meeting which had been in progress for hours. Four lawyers and their assorted support staff were watching the videotaped depositions of the plaintiff's first witnesses. The tape stopped just seconds after Fitch burst in. He spoke briefly to one of the lawyers, then left the room. José followed him through a narrow library to another hallway, where he barged through another door and frightened another bunch of lawyers.

With eighty lawyers, the firm of Whitney & Cable & White was the largest on the Gulf Coast. The firm had been handpicked by Fitch himself, and it would earn millions in fees because of this selection. To earn the money, though, the firm had to endure the tyranny and ruthlessness of Rankin Fitch.

When satisfied that the entire building was aware of his presence and terrified of his movements, Fitch left. He stood on the sidewalk, in the warm October air, and waited for José. Three blocks away, in the top half of an old bank building, he could see an office suite filled with lights. The enemy was still working. The plaintiff's lawyers were up there, all huddled together in various rooms, meeting with experts and looking at grainy photos and doing pretty much the same things his people were doing. The trial started Monday with jury selection, and he knew they too were sweating over names and faces and wondering who the hell was Nicholas Easter and where did he come from. And Ramon Caro and Lucas Miller and Andrew Lamb and Barbara Furrow and Delores DeBoe? Who were these people? Only in a backwater place like Mississippi would you find such outdated lists of prospective jurors. Fitch had directed the defense in eight cases before this one, in eight different states where computers were used and rolls were purged and where, when the clerks handed you your list of jurors, you didn't have to worry about who was dead and who wasn't.

He stared blankly at the distant lights and wondered how the greedy sharks would split the money, if they happened to win. How in the world could they ever agree to divide the bloody carcass? The trial would be a gentle skirmish compared to the throat-cutting that would ensue if they got their verdict, and their spoils.

He hated them, and he spat on the sidewalk. He lit a cigarette, squeezing it tightly between his thick fingers.

José pulled to the curb in a shiny, rented Suburban with dark windows. Fitch took his customary place in the front seat. José too looked up at the enemy lawyers' office as they drove past, but he said nothing because his boss did not suffer small talk. They drove past the Biloxi courthouse, and past a semi-abandoned dime store where Fitch and associates maintained a hidden suite of offices with fresh plywood dust on the floor and cheap rented furniture.

They turned west on Highway 90 at the beach and limped through heavy traffic. It was Friday night, and the casinos were packed with people gambling away grocery money with big plans to win it back tomorrow. They slowly made it out of Biloxi, through Gulfport, Long Beach, and Pass Christian. Then they left the coastline, and were soon passing through a security check-point near a lagoon.

Two

T HE BEACH HOUSE was modern and sprawling and built
    without the benefit of a beach. A white-board pier disap-
peared into the still and weedy waters of the bay, but the nearest
sand was two miles away. A twenty-foot fishing boat was moored
at the pier. The house had been leased from an oil man in New
Orleans—three months, cash, no questions. It was being temporarily used as a retreat, a hiding place, a sleep-over for some very
important people.

On a deck high above the water, four gentlemen enjoyed drinks
and managed small talk while waiting for a visitor. Though their
businesses normally required them to be bitter enemies, they had
played eighteen holes of golf this afternoon, then eaten shrimp
and oysters off the grill. Now they drank and looked into the
black waters below them. They loathed the fact that they were on
the Gulf Coast, on Friday night, far away from their homes.

But business was at hand, crucial affairs that necessitated a
truce and made the golf almost pleasant. Each of the four was the
CEO of a large public corporation. Each corporation was in the
Fortune 500, each was traded on the NYSE. The smallest had
sales last year of six hundred million, the largest, four billion.
Each had record profits, large dividends, happy stockholders, and
CEO's who earned millions for their performances.

Each was a conglomerate of sorts with different divisions and a
multitude of products, fat ad budgets, and insipid names such as

Trellco and Smith Greer, names designed to deflect attention from the fact that at the core they were little more than tobacco companies. Each of the four, the Big Four as they were known in financial circles, could easily trace its roots to nineteenth-century tobacco brokers in the Carolinas and Virginia. They manufactured cigarettes—together, ninety-eight percent of all cigarettes sold in the United States and Canada. They also manufactured such things as crowbars and corn chips and hair dye, but dig just below the surface and you'd find that their profits came from cigarettes. There had been mergers and name changes and various efforts at preening for the public, but the Big Four had been thoroughly isolated and vilified by consumer groups, doctors, even politicians.

And now the lawyers were after them. The survivors of dead people out there were actually suing and asking for huge sums of money because cigarettes cause lung cancer, they claimed. Sixteen trials so far, and Big Tobacco had won them all, but the pressure was mounting. And the first time a jury handed out a few million to a widow, then all hell would break loose. The trial lawyers would go berserk with their nonstop advertising, begging smokers and the survivors of smokers to sign up now and sue while the suing was good.

As a rule, the men talked of other matters when they were alone, but the liquor loosened their tongues. The bitterness began to ooze forth. They leaned on the railing of the deck, stared at the water, and began to curse lawyers and the American tort system. Each of their companies spent millions in Washington on various groups trying to reform tort laws so that responsible companies like themselves could be protected from litigation. They needed a shield from such senseless attacks by alleged victims. But, it seemed, nothing was working. Here they were somewhere in the backwaters of Mississippi sweating out yet another trial.

In response to the growing assault from the courts, the Big Four had created a pool of money known simply as The Fund. It had no limits, left no trail. It did not exist. The Fund was used for hardball tactics in lawsuits; to hire the best and meanest defense lawyers, the smoothest experts, the most sophisticated jury consultants. No restrictions were placed on what The Fund could do. After sixteen victories, they sometimes asked, among themselves, if there was anything The Fund couldn't do. Each company siphoned off three million a year and routed the cash circuitously until it landed in The Fund. No bean counter, no auditor, no regulator had ever caught wind of the slush money.

The Fund was administered by Rankin Fitch, a man they collectively despised but nonetheless listened to and even obeyed when necessary. And they waited for him. They gathered when he said to gather. They dispersed and returned at his command. They tolerated being at his beck and call as long as he was winning. Fitch had directed eight trials without a loss. He'd also engineered two mistrials, but of course there was no proof of this.

An assistant stepped onto the deck with a tray of fresh drinks, each mixed to exact specifications. The drinks were being lifted from the tray when someone said, "Fitch is here." In unison the drinks shot upward then downward as the four knocked back a stiff belt.

They quickly stepped into the den while Fitch was parking José just outside the front door. An assistant handed him a mineral water, no ice. He never drank, though in an earlier life he'd consumed enough to float a barge. He didn't say thanks to the assistant, didn't acknowledge his presence, but moved to the faux fireplace and waited for the four to gather around him on the sofas. Another assistant ventured forth with a platter of leftover shrimp and oysters, but Fitch waved him off. There was a rumor that he sometimes ate, but he'd never been caught in the process. The evidence was there, the thick chest and ample waistline, the fleshy roll under his goatee, the general squattiness of his frame. But he wore dark suits and kept the jackets buttoned, and did a fine job of carrying his bulk with importance.

"A brief update," he said when he felt he'd waited long enough for the honchos to settle in. "At this moment, the entire defense team is working nonstop, and this will continue through the weekend. Jury research is on schedule. Trial counsel are ready. All witnesses are prepped, all experts are already in town. Nothing unusual has yet to be encountered."

There was a pause, just a little gap as they waited long enough to make sure Fitch had finished for a bit.

"What about those jurors?" asked D. Martin Jankle, the most nervous of the bunch. He ran U-Tab, as it was formerly known, an abbreviation for an old company which for years was called Union Tobacco but after a marketing cleansing was now traded as

Pynex. The lawsuit at hand was *Wood v. Pynex,* so the roulette wheel had placed Jankle on the hot seat. Pynex was number three in size with sales of almost two billion last year. It also happened to possess, as of the last quarter, the largest cash reserves of any of the four. The timing of this trial was lousy. With a bit of bad luck, the jury might soon be shown blowups of Pynex' financials, nice neat columns which would indicate in excess of eight hundred million in cash.

"We're working on them," Fitch said. "We have soft data on eight. Four of whom might either be dead or gone. The other four are alive and expected to be in court Monday."

"One rogue juror can be poison," Jankle said. He'd been a corporate lawyer in Louisville before joining U-Tab, and he always insisted on reminding Fitch that he knew more about the law than the other three.

"I'm well aware of that," Fitch snapped.

"We have to know these people."

"We're doing our best. We can't help it if the jury lists here are not as current as other states'."

Jankle took a long drink and stared at Fitch. Fitch, after all, was a well-paid security thug, nothing remotely near the level of CEO of a major company. Call him whatever you want—consultant, agent, contractor—fact was, he worked for them. Sure he had some clout right now, liked to swagger and bark because he was pushing the buttons, but dammit he was just a glorified thug. These thoughts Jankle kept to himself.

"Anything else?" Fitch demanded of Jankle, as if his initial inquiry were thoughtless, as though if he had nothing productive to say then maybe he should just keep his mouth shut.

"Do you trust these lawyers?" Jankle asked, not for the first time.

"We've covered this before," Fitch answered.

"We can certainly cover it again if I choose."

"Why are you worried about our lawyers?" Fitch asked.

"Because, well, because they're from around here."

"I see. And you think it'd be wise to bring in some New York lawyers to talk to our jury? Maybe some from Boston?"

"No, it's just that, well, they've never defended a tobacco case."

"There's never been a tobacco case on the Coast before. Are you complaining?"

"They just worry me, that's all."

"We've hired the best in this area," Fitch said.

"Why do they work so cheap?"

"Cheap. Last week you were worried about defense costs. Now our lawyers are not charging enough. Make up your mind."

"Last year we paid four hundred bucks an hour for Pittsburgh lawyers. These guys work for two hundred. That worries me."

Fitch frowned at Luther Vandemeer, CEO of Trellco. "Am I missing something here?" he asked. "Is he serious? We're at five million bucks for this case, and he's afraid I'm pinching pennies." Fitch waved in the direction of Jankle. Vandemeer smiled and took a drink.

"You spent six million in Oklahoma," Jankle said.

"And we won. I don't recall any complaints after the verdict came in."

"I'm not complaining now. I'm just voicing a concern."

"Great! I'll go back to the office, gather all the lawyers together, and tell them my clients are upset about the bills. I'll say, 'Look, fellas, I know you're getting rich off us, but that's not good enough. My clients want you to bill more, okay. Stick it to us. You guys are working too cheap.' That sound like a good idea?"

"Relax, Martin," Vandemeer said. "The trial hasn't started yet. I'm confident we'll be sick of our own lawyers before we leave here."

"Yeah, but this trial's different. We all know that." Jankle's words trailed off as he lifted his glass. He had a drinking problem, the only one of the four. His company had quietly dried him out six months ago, but the pressure of the lawsuit was too much. Fitch, a former drunk himself, knew Jankle was in trouble. He would be forced to testify in a few weeks.

As if Fitch didn't have enough to worry about, he was now saddled with the burden of keeping D. Martin Jankle sober until then. Fitch hated him for his weakness.

"I assume the plaintiff's lawyers are ready," asked another CEO.

"Safe assumption," Fitch said with a shrug. "There are enough of them."

Eight, at last count. Eight of the largest tort firms in the country had allegedly put up a million bucks each to finance this show-down with the tobacco industry. They had picked the plaintiff, the widow of a man named Jacob L. Wood. They had picked the forum, the Gulf Coast of Mississippi, because the state had beautiful tort laws and because juries in Biloxi could at times be generous. They hadn't picked the judge, but they couldn't have been luckier. The Honorable Frederick Harkin had been a plaintiff's lawyer before a heart attack sent him to the bench.

It was no ordinary tobacco case, and everyone in the room knew it.

"How much have they spent?"

"I'm not privy to that information," Fitch said. "We've heard rumors that their war chest may not be as loaded as advertised, maybe a small problem collecting the up-front money from a few of the lawyers. But they've spent millions. And they have a dozen consumer groups hanging around ready to pitch in advice."

Jankle rattled his ice, then drained the last drop of liquid from his glass. It was his fourth drink. The room was silent for a moment as Fitch stood and waited and the CEO's watched the carpet.

"How long will it last?" Jankle finally asked.

"Four to six weeks. Jury selection goes fast here. We'll probably seat a jury by Wednesday."

"Allentown lasted three months," Jankle said.

"This ain't Kansas, Toto. You want a three-month trial?"

"No, I was just, well . . ." Jankle's words trailed off sadly.

"How long should we stay in town?" Vandemeer said, instinctively glancing at his watch.

"I don't care. You can leave now, or you can wait until the jury is picked. You all have those big jets. If I need you, I can find you." Fitch set his water on the mantel and looked around the room. He was suddenly ready to leave. "Anything else?"

Not a word.

"Good."

He said something to José as he opened the front door, then he was gone. They stared in silence at the posh carpet, worrying about Monday, worrying about lots of things.

Jankle, his hands quivering slightly, finally lit a cigarette.

□ □ □ □

WENDALL ROHR made his first fortune in the suing game when two offshore oil workers were burned on a Shell rig in the Gulf. His cut was almost two million, and he quickly considered himself a trial lawyer to be reckoned with. He spread his money around, picked up more cases, and by the age of forty had an aggressive firm and a decent reputation as a courtroom brawler. Then drugs, a divorce, and some bad investments ruined his life for a while, and at the age of fifty he was checking titles and defending shoplifters like a million other lawyers. When a wave of asbestos litigation swept the Gulf Coast, Wendall was once again in the right place. He made his second fortune, and vowed never to lose it. He built a firm, refurbished a grand suite of offices, even found a young wife. Free of booze and pills, Rohr directed his considerable energies into suing corporate America on behalf of injured people. On his second trip, he rose even quicker in trial lawyer circles. He grew a beard, oiled his hair, became a radical, and was beloved on the lecture circuit.

Rohr met Celeste Wood, the widow of Jacob Wood, through a young lawyer who had prepared Jacob's will in anticipation of death. Jacob Wood died at the age of fifty-one after smoking three packs a day for almost thirty years. At the time of his death, he was a production supervisor in a boat factory, earning forty thousand a year.

In the hands of a less ambitious lawyer, the case appeared to be nothing more than a dead smoker, one of countless others. Rohr, though, had networked his way into a circle of acquaintances who were dreaming the grandest dreams ever known to trial lawyers. All were specialists in product liability, all had made millions collecting on breast implants, Dalkon Shields, and asbestos. Now they met several times a year and plotted ways to mine the mother lode of American torts. No legally manufactured product in the history of the world had killed as many people as the cigarette. And their makers had pockets so deep the money had mildewed.

Rohr put up the first million, and was eventually joined by seven others. With no effort, the group quickly recruited help from the Tobacco Task Force, the Coalition for a Smoke Free World, and the Tobacco Liability Fund, plus a handful of other consumer groups and industry watchdogs. A plaintiff's trial council was organized, not surprisingly with Wendall Rohr as the chairman and designated point man in the courtroom. Amid as much fanfare as it could generate, Rohr's group had filed suit four years earlier in the Circuit Court of Harrison County, Mississippi.

According to Fitch's research, the Wood case against Pynex was the fifty-fifth of its kind. Thirty-six had been dismissed for a multitude of reasons. Sixteen had gone to trial and ended with verdicts in favor of the tobacco companies. Two had ended in mistrials. None had been settled. Not one penny had ever been paid to a plaintiff in a cigarette case.

According to Rohr's theory, none of the other fifty-four had been pushed by so formidable a plaintiff's group. Never had the plaintiff been represented by lawyers with enough money to level the playing field.

Fitch would admit this.

Rohr's long-term strategy was simple, and brilliant. There were a hundred million smokers out there, not all with lung cancer but certainly a sufficient number to keep him busy until retirement. Win the first one, then sit back and wait for the stampede. Every main street ham-and-egger with a grieving widow would be calling with lung cancer cases. Rohr and his group could pick and choose.

He operated from a suite of offices which took the top three floors of an old bank building not far from the courthouse. Late Friday night, he opened the door to a dark room and stood along the back wall as Jonathan Kotlack from San Diego operated the projector. Kotlack was in charge of jury research and selection, though Rohr would do most of the questioning. The long table in the center of the room was littered with coffee cups and wadded paper. The people around the table watched bleary-eyed as another face flashed against the wall.

Nelle Robert (pronounced Roh-bair), age forty-six, divorced, once raped, works as a bank teller, doesn't smoke, very overweight and thus disqualified under Rohr's philosophy of jury selection. Never take fat women. He didn't care what the jury experts would tell him. He didn't care what Kotlack thought. Rohr never took fat women. Especially single ones. They tended to be tightfisted and unsympathetic.

He had the names and faces memorized, and he couldn't take any more. He had studied these people until he was sick of them. He eased from the room, rubbed his eyes in the hallway, and walked down the stairs of his opulent offices to the conference room, where the Documents Committee was busy organizing thousands of papers under the supervision of André Durond from New Orleans. At this moment, at almost ten o'clock on Friday night, more than forty people were hard at work in the law offices of Wendall H. Rohr.

He spoke to Durond as they watched the paralegals for a few minutes. He left the room and headed for the next with a quicker pace now. The adrenaline was pumping.

The tobacco lawyers were down the street working just as hard.

Nothing rivaled the thrill of big-time litigation.

Three

T HE MAIN COURTROOM of the Biloxi courthouse was on the second floor, up the tiled staircase to an atrium where sunlight flooded in. A fresh coat of white paint had just been applied to the walls, and the floors gleamed with new wax.

By eight Monday a crowd was already gathering in the atrium outside the large wooden doors leading to the courtroom. One small group was clustered in a corner, and was comprised of young men in dark suits, all of whom looked remarkably similar. They were well groomed, with oily short hair, and most either wore horn-rimmed glasses or had suspenders showing from under their tailored jackets. They were Wall Street financial analysts, specialists in tobacco stocks, sent South to follow the early developments of *Wood v. Pynex*.

Another group, larger and growing by the minute, hung loosely together in the center of the atrium. Each member awkwardly held a piece of paper, a jury summons. Few knew one another, but the papers labeled them and conversation came easy. A nervous chatter rose quietly outside the courtroom. The dark suits from the first group became still and watched the potential jurors.

The third group wore frowns and uniforms and guarded the doors. No fewer than seven deputies were assigned to keep things secure on opening day. Two fiddled with the metal detector in front of the door. Two more busied themselves with paperwork behind a makeshift desk. They were expecting a full house. The other three sipped coffee from paper cups and watched the crowd grow.

The guards opened the courtroom doors at exactly eight-thirty, checked the summons of each juror, admitted them one by one through the metal detector, and told the rest of the spectators they would have to wait awhile. Same for the analysts and same for the reporters.

With a neat ring of folding chairs in the aisles around the padded benches, the courtroom could seat about three hundred people. Beyond the bar, another thirty or so would soon crowd around the counsel tables. The Circuit Clerk, popularly elected by the people, checked each summons, smiled, and even hugged a few of the jurors she knew, and in a much experienced way herded them into the pews. Her name was Gloria Lane, Circuit Clerk for Harrison County for the past eleven years. She wouldn't dare miss this opportunity to point and direct, to put faces with names, to shake hands, to politic, to enjoy a brief moment in the spotlight of her most notorious trial yet. She was assisted by three younger women from her office, and by nine the jurors were all properly seated by number and were busy filling out another round of questionnaires.

Only two were missing. Ernest Duly was rumored to have moved to Florida, where he supposedly died, and there was not a clue to the whereabouts of Mrs. Tella Gail Ridehouser, who registered to vote in 1959 but hadn't visited the polls since Carter beat Ford. Gloria Lane declared the two to be nonexistent. To her left, rows one through twelve held 144 prospective jurors, and to her right, rows thirteen through sixteen held the remaining 50. Gloria consulted with an armed deputy, and pursuant to Judge Harkin's written edict, forty spectators were admitted and seated in the rear of the courtroom.

The questionnaires were finished quickly, gathered by the assistant clerks, and by ten the first of many lawyers began easing into the courtroom. They came not through the front door, but from somewhere in the back, behind the bench, where two doors led to a maze of small rooms and offices. Without exception they wore dark suits and intelligent frowns, and they all attempted the impossible feat of gawking at the jurors while trying to appear uninterested. Each tried vainly to seem preoccupied with weightier matters as files were examined and whispered conferences took place. They trickled in and took their places around the tables. To the right was the plaintiff's table. The defense was next to it. Chairs were packed tightly into every possible inch between the tables and the wooden rail which separated them from the spectators.

Row number seventeen was empty, again Harkin's orders, and in eighteen the boys from Wall Street sat stiffly and studied the backs of the jurors. Behind them were some reporters, then a row of local lawyers and other curious types. Rankin Fitch pretended to read a newspaper in the back row.

More lawyers filed in. Then the jury consultants from both sides took their positions in the cramped seats between the railing and the counsel tables. They began the uncomfortable task of staring into the inquiring faces of 194 strangers. The consultants studied the jurors because, first, that was what they were being paid huge sums of money to do, and second, because they claimed to be able to thoroughly analyze a person through the telltale revelations of body language. They watched and waited anxiously for arms to fold across the chest, for fingers to pick nervously at teeth, for heads to cock suspiciously to one side, for a hundred other gestures that supposedly would lay a person bare and expose the most private of prejudices.

They scribbled notes and silently probed the faces. Juror number fifty-six, Nicholas Easter, received more than his share of concerned looks. He sat in the middle of the fifth row, dressed in starched khakis and a button-down, a nice-looking young man. He glanced around occasionally, but his attention was directed at a paperback he'd brought for the day. No one else had thought to bring a book.

More chairs were filled near the railing. The defense had no fewer than six jury experts examining facial twitches and hemorrhoidal clutches. The plaintiff was using only four.

For the most part, the prospective jurors didn't enjoy being appraised in such a manner, and for fifteen awkward minutes they returned the glaring with scowls of their own. A lawyer told a private joke near the bench, and the laughter eased the tension. The lawyers gossiped and whispered, but the jurors were afraid to say anything.

The last lawyer to enter the courtroom was, of course, Wendall Rohr, and as usual, he could be heard before he was seen. Since he didn't own a dark suit, he wore his favorite opening-day ensemble—a gray checkered sports coat, gray slacks that didn't match, a white vest, blue shirt with red-and-yellow paisley bow tie. He was barking at a paralegal as they strode in front of the defense lawyers, ignoring them as if they'd just finished a heated skirmish somewhere in the rear. He said something loudly to another plaintiff's lawyer, and once he had the attention of the courtroom, he gazed upon his potential jurors. These were his people. This was his case, one he'd filed in his hometown so he could one day stand in this, his courtroom, and seek justice from his people. He nodded at a couple, winked at another. He knew these folks. Together, they would find the truth.

His entrance rattled the jury experts on the defense side, none of whom had actually met Wendall Rohr, but all of whom had been briefed extensively on his reputation. They saw the smiles on the faces of some of the jurors, people who actually knew him. They read the body language as the entire panel seemed to relax and respond to a familiar face. Rohr was a local legend. Fitch cursed him from the back row.

Finally, at ten-thirty, a deputy burst from the door behind the bench and shouted, "All rise for the court!" Three hundred people jumped to their feet as the Honorable Frederick Harkin stepped up to the bench and asked everyone to be seated.

For a judge he was quite young, fifty, a Democrat appointed by the governor to fill an unexpired term, then elected by the people. Because he'd once been a plaintiff's lawyer, he was now rumored to be a plaintiff's judge, though there was no truth to this. Just gossip deliciously spread by members of the defense bar. In reality, he'd been a decent general practitioner in a small firm not noted for its courtroom victories. He'd worked hard, but his passion had always been local politics, a game he'd played skillfully. His luck had paid off with an appointment to the bench, where he now earned eighty thousand dollars a year, more than he'd ever made as a lawyer.

The sight of a courtroom packed with so many qualified voters would warm the heart of any elected official, and His Honor couldn't conceal a broad grin as he welcomed the panel to his lair as if they were volunteers. The smile slowly vanished as he completed a short welcoming speech, impressing upon them the importance of their presence. Harkin was not known for either his warmth or his humor, and he quickly turned serious.

And with good reason. Seated before him were more lawyers than could actually fit around the tables. The court file listed eight as counsel of record for the plaintiff, and nine for the defense. Four days earlier, in a closed courtroom, Harkin had assigned seating for both sides. Once the jury was selected and the trial started, only six lawyers per side could sit with feet under the table. The others were assigned to a row of chairs where the jury consultants now huddled and watched. He also designated seats for the parties—Celeste Wood, the widow, and the Pynex representative. The seating arrangement had been reduced to writing and included in a small booklet of rules His Honor had written just for this occasion.

The lawsuit had been filed four years ago, and actively pursued and defended since its inception. It now filled eleven storage boxes. Each side had already spent millions to reach this point. The trial would last at least a month. Assembled at this moment in his courtroom were some of the brightest legal minds and largest egos in the country. Fred Harkin was determined to rule with a heavy hand.

Speaking into the microphone on the bench, he gave a quick synopsis of the trial, but only for informational purposes. Nice to let these folks know why they're here. He said the trial was scheduled to last for several weeks, and that the jurors would not be sequestered. There were some specific statutory excuses from jury duty, he explained, and asked if anyone over the age of sixty-five had slipped through the computer. Six hands shot upward. He seemed surprised and looked blankly at Gloria Lane, who shrugged as if this happened all the time. The six had the option of leaving immediately, and five chose to do so. Down to 189. The jury consultants scribbled and X'ed off names. The lawyers gravely made notes.

"Now, do we have any blind people here?" the Judge asked. "I mean, legally blind?" It was a light question, and brought a few smiles. Why would a blind person show up for jury duty? It was unheard of.

Slowly, a hand was raised from the center of the pack, row

seven, about halfway down. Juror number sixty-three, a Mr. Herman Grimes, age fifty-nine, computer programmer, white, married, no kids. What the hell was this? Did anybody know this man was blind? The jury experts huddled on both sides. The Herman Grimes photos had been of his house and a shot or two of him on the front porch. He'd lived in the area about three years. His questionnaires didn't indicate any handicap.

"Please stand, sir," the Judge said.

Mr. Herman Grimes stood slowly, hands in pockets, casually dressed, normal-looking eyeglasses. He didn't appear to be blind.

"Your number please," the Judge asked. He, unlike the lawyers and their consultants, had not been required to memorize every available tidbit about every juror.

"Uh, sixty-three."

"And your name?" He was flipping the pages of his computer printout.

"Herman Grimes."

Harkin found the name, then gazed into the sea of faces. "And you're legally blind?"

"Yes sir."

"Well, Mr. Grimes, under our law, you are excused from jury duty. You're free to go."

Herman Grimes didn't move, didn't even flinch. He just looked at whatever he could see and said, "Why?"

"I beg your pardon."

"Why do I have to leave?"

"Because you're blind."

"I know that."

"And, well, blind people can't serve on juries," Harkin said, glancing to his right and then to his left as his words trailed off. "You're free to go, Mr. Grimes."

Herman Grimes hesitated as he contemplated his response. The courtroom was still. Finally, "Who says blind people can't serve on juries?"

Harkin was already reaching for a lawbook. His Honor was meticulously prepared for this trial. He'd stopped hearing other matters a month ago, and had secluded himself in his chambers, where he pored over pleadings, discovery, the applicable law, and the latest in the rules of trial procedure. He'd picked dozens of juries during his tenure on the bench, all kinds of juries for all kinds of cases, and he thought he'd seen it all. So of course he'd get ambushed during the first ten minutes of jury selection. And of course the courtroom would be packed.

"You want to serve, Mr. Grimes?" he said, trying to force a lighthearted moment as he flipped pages and looked at the wealth of legal talent assembled nearby.

Mr. Grimes was growing hostile. "You tell me why a blind person can't be on a jury. If it's written in the law, then the law is discriminatory, and I'll sue. If it ain't written in the law, and if it's just a matter of practice, then I'll sue even faster."

There was little doubt that Mr. Grimes was no stranger to litigation.

On one side of the bar were two hundred little people, those dragged into court by the power of the law. On the other side was the law itself—the Judge sitting elevated above the rest, the packs of stuffy lawyers looking down their nasty noses, the clerks, the deputies, the bailiffs. On behalf of the draftees, Mr. Herman Grimes had struck a mighty blow at the establishment, and he was rewarded with chuckles and light laughter from his colleagues. He didn't care.

Across the railing, the lawyers smiled because the prospective jurors were smiling, and they shifted in their seats and scratched their heads because no one knew what to do. "I've never seen this before," they whispered.

The law said that a blind person *may* be excused from jury service, and when the Judge saw the word *may* he quickly decided to placate Mr. Grimes and deal with him later. No sense getting sued in your own courtroom. There were other ways to exclude him from jury duty. He'd discuss it with the attorneys. "On second thought, Mr. Grimes, I think you'd make an excellent juror. Please be seated."

Herman Grimes nodded and smiled and politely said, "Thank you, sir."

How do you factor in a blind juror? The experts mulled this question as they watched him slowly bend and sit. What are his prejudices? Which side will he favor? In a game with no rules, it was a widely held axiom that people with handicaps and disabilities made great plaintiff's jurors because they better understood the meaning of suffering. But there were countless exceptions.

From the back row, Rankin Fitch strained to his right in a vain effort to make eye contact with Carl Nussman, the man who'd already been paid $1,200,000 to select the perfect jury. Nussman sat in the midst of his jury consultants, holding a legal pad and studying the faces as if he'd known perfectly well that Herman Grimes was blind. He hadn't, and Fitch knew he hadn't. It was a minor fact that had slipped through their vast web of intelligence. What else had they missed? Fitch asked himself. He'd peel the hide off Nussman as soon as they broke for a recess.

"Now, ladies and gentlemen," the Judge continued, his voice suddenly sharper and anxious to move on now that an on-the-spot discrimination suit had been averted. "We enter into a phase of jury selection that will be somewhat time-consuming. It deals with physical infirmities which might prevent you from serving. We are not going to embarrass you, but if you have a physical problem, we need to discuss it. We'll start with the first row."

As Gloria Lane stood in the aisle by row one, a man of about sixty raised his hand, then got to his feet and walked through the small swinging gate of the bar. A bailiff led him to the witness chair and shoved the microphone away. The Judge moved to the end of the bench and leaned downward so that he could whisper to the man. Two lawyers, one from each side, took their places directly in front of the witness stand and blocked the view from the spectators. The court reporter completed the tight huddle, and when everyone was in place the Judge softly asked about the man's affliction.

It was a herniated disc, and he had a letter from his doctor. He was excused and left the courtroom in a hurry.

When Harkin broke for lunch at noon, he had dismissed thirteen people for medical reasons. The tedium had set in. They would resume at one-thirty, for much more of the same.

NICHOLAS EASTER left the courthouse alone, and walked six blocks to a Burger King, where he ordered a Whopper and a Coke. He sat in a booth near the window, watching kids swing in the small playground, scanning a USA Today, eating slowly because he had an hour and a half.

The same blonde who first met him at the Computer Hut in tight jeans now wore baggy Umbros, a loose T-shirt, new Nikes, and carried a small gym bag over her shoulder. She met him for the second time as she walked by his booth carrying her tray and stopped when she seemed to recognize him.

"Nicholas," she said, feigning uncertainty.

He looked at her, and for an awkward second knew they'd met somewhere before. The name escaped him.

"You don't remember me," she said with a pleasant smile. "I was in your Computer Hut two weeks ago looking for—"

"Yeah, I remember," he said with a quick glance at her nicely tanned legs. "You bought a digital radio."

"Right. The name is Amanda. If I remember correctly, I left you my phone number. I guess you lost it."

"Would you like to sit down?"

"Thank you." She sat quickly and took a french fry.

"I still have the number," he said. "In fact—"

"Don't bother. I'm sure you've called several times. My answering machine is broken."

"No. I haven't called, yet. But I was thinking about it."

"Sure," she said, almost giggling. She had perfect teeth, which she delighted in showing him. Her hair was in a ponytail. She was too cute and too put together to be a jogger. And there was no evidence of sweat on her face.

"So what are you doing here?" he asked.

"On my way to aerobics."

"You're eating french fries before you do aerobics?"

"Why not?"

"I don't know. It just doesn't seem right."

"I need the carbohydrates."

"I see. Do you smoke before aerobics?"

"Sometimes. Is that why you haven't called? Because I smoke?"

"Not really."

"Come on, Nicholas. I can take it." She was still smiling and trying to be coy.

"Okay, it crossed my mind."

"Figures. Have you ever dated a smoker?"

"Not that I recall."

"Why not?"

"Maybe I don't want to breathe it secondhand. I don't know. It's not something I spend time worrying about."

"Have you ever smoked?" She nibbled on another fry and watched him intently.

"Sure. Every kid tries it. When I was ten, I stole a pack of Camels from a plumber working around our house. Smoked them all in two days, got sick, and thought I was dying of cancer." He took a bite of his burger.

"And that was it?"

He chewed and thought it over before saying, "I think so. I can't remember another cigarette. Why did you start?"

"Stupid. I'm trying to quit."

"Good. You're too young."

"Thanks. And let me guess. When I quit, you'll give me a call, right?"

"I may call you anyway."

"I've heard this before," she said, all toothy and teasing. She took a long drink from her straw, then said, "Can I ask what you're doing here?"

"Eating a Whopper. And you?"

"I've told you. I'm headed to the gym."

"Right. I was just passing through, had some business downtown, got hungry."

"Why do you work in a Computer Hut?"

"You mean, like, why am I wasting my life working for minimum wage in a mall?"

"No, but close."

"I'm a student."

"Where?"

"Nowhere. I'm between schools."

"Where was the last school?"

"North Texas State."

"Where's the next one?"

"Probably Southern Mississippi."

"What are you studying?"

"Computers. You ask a lot of questions."

"But they're easy ones, aren't they?"

"I suppose. Where do you work?"

"I don't. I just divorced a rich man. No kids. I'm twenty-eight, single, and would like to stay that way, but a date every now and then would be nice. Why don't you give me a call?"

"How rich?"

She laughed at this, then checked her watch. "I need to go. My class starts in ten minutes." She was on her feet, getting her bag but leaving her tray. "I'll see you around."

She drove off in a small BMW.

THE REST of the sick folks were hastily cleared from the panel, and by 3 P.M. the number was down to 159. Judge Harkin ordered a fifteen-minute recess, and when he returned to the bench he announced they were entering into a different phase of jury selection. He delivered a strong lecture on civic responsibility, and practically dared anyone to claim a nonmedical hardship. The first attempt was by a harried corporate executive who sat in the witness chair and softly explained to the Judge, the two lawyers, and the court reporter that he worked eighty hours a week for a large company that was losing lots of money, and any time away from the office would be disastrous. The Judge instructed him to return to his seat and await further directions.

The second attempt was by a middle-aged woman who operated an unlicensed day care center in her home. "I keep kids, Your Honor," she whispered, fighting back tears. "It's all I can do. I collect two hundred dollars a week, and I barely get by. If I have to serve on this jury, then I'll have to hire a stranger to keep the kids. Their parents won't like this, plus I can't afford to hire anyone. I'll go busted."

The prospective jurors watched with great interest as she walked down the aisle, past her row, and out of the courtroom. Her story must've been a good one. The harried corporate executive fumed.

By five-thirty, eleven people had been excused, and sixteen others had been sent back to their seats after failing to sound sufficiently pitiful. The Judge instructed Gloria Lane to pass out another, lengthier questionnaire, and told the remaining jurors to have it answered by nine in the morning. He dismissed them, with firm warnings against discussing the case with strangers.

Rankin Fitch was not in the courtroom when it adjourned Monday afternoon. He was in his office down the street. There was no record of any Nicholas Easter at North Texas State. The blonde had recorded their little chat at Burger King, and Fitch had listened to it twice. It had been his decision to send her in for a chance meeting. The meeting was risky, but it worked. She was now on a plane back to Washington. Her answering machine in Biloxi was on and would remain so until after the jury was selected. If Easter decided to call, something Fitch doubted, he wouldn't be able to reach her.

Four

I T ASKED QUESTIONS like, Do you now smoke cigarettes? And if so, how many packs a day? And if so, how long have you smoked? And if so, do you want to stop? Have you ever smoked cigarettes as a habit? Has any member of your family, or someone you know well, suffered any disease or illness directly associated with smoking cigarettes? If so, who? (Space provided below. Please give person's name, nature of disease or illness, and state whether or not the person was successfully treated.) Do you believe smoking causes (a) lung cancer; (b) heart disease; (c) high blood pressure; (d) none of the above; (e) all of the above?

Page three held the weightier matters: State your opinion on the issue of tax dollars being used to fund medical care for smoking-related health problems. State your opinion on the issue of tax dollars being used to subsidize tobacco farmers. State your opinion on the issue of banning smoking in all public buildings. What rights do you think smokers should have? Large empty spaces were available for these answers.

Page four listed the names of the seventeen lawyers who were officially attorneys of record, then it listed the names of eighty more who happened to be in some related practice with the first seventeen. Do you personally know any of these lawyers? Have you ever been represented by any of these lawyers? Have you ever been involved in any legal matter with any of these lawyers?

No. No. No. Nicholas made quick check marks.

Page five listed the names of potential witnesses, sixty-two people including Celeste Wood, the widow and plaintiff. Do you
know any of these people? No.

He mixed another cup of instant coffee and added two packs of
sugar. He'd spent an hour with these questions last night, and
another hour had already passed this morning. The sun was
barely up. Breakfast had been a banana and a stale bagel. He ate a
small bite of the bagel, thought about the last question, then answered it with a pencil in a neat, almost tedious hand—all caps
printed, because his cursive was ragged and barely legible. And he
knew that before dark today an entire committee of handwriting
experts on both sides would be poring over his words, not caring
so much about what he said but more about how he formed his
letters. He wanted to appear neat and thoughtful, intelligent and
open-minded, capable of hearing with both ears and deciding
matters fairly, an arbitrator they would clamor for.

He'd read three books on the ins and outs of handwriting analysis.

He flipped back to the tobacco subsidy question because it was
a tough one. He had an answer ready because he'd given much
thought to the issue, and he wanted to write it clearly. Or maybe
vaguely. Maybe in such a way that he wouldn't betray his feelings, yet wouldn't scare either side.

Many of these same questions had been used in the Cimmino
case last year in Allentown, Pennsylvania. Nicholas had been
David then, David Lancaster, a part-time film student with a genuine dark beard and fake horn-rimmed glasses who worked in a
video store. He'd copied the questionnaire before turning it in on
the second day of jury selection. It was a similar case, but with a
different widow and a different tobacco company, and though
there'd been a hundred lawyers involved, they were all different
from this bunch. Only Fitch remained the same.

Nicholas/David had made the first two cuts then, but was four
rows away when the panel was seated. He shaved his beard,
ditched the pharmacy eyeglasses, and left town a month later.

The folding card table vibrated slightly as he wrote. This was
his dinette—the table and three mismatched chairs. The tiny den
to his right was furnished with a flimsy rocker, a TV mounted on
a wooden crate, and a dusty sofa he'd purchased at a flea market
for fifteen dollars. He probably could have afforded to rent some

nicer pieces, but renting required forms and left a trail. There were people out there practically digging through his garbage to find out who he was.

He thought of the blonde and wondered where she might turn up today, no doubt with a cigarette close at hand and an eagerness to draw him into another banal chat about smoking. The idea of calling her hadn't crossed his mind, but the question of which side she worked for was quite intriguing. Probably the tobacco companies, because she was exactly the type of agent Fitch liked to use.

Nicholas knew from his studies of the law that it was highly unethical for the blonde, or any other hireling for that matter, to directly approach a potential juror. He also knew that Fitch had enough money to make the blonde disappear from here, without a trace, only to surface at the next trial as a redhead with a different brand and an interest in horticulture. Some things were impossible to uncover.

The one bedroom was consumed almost entirely with a king-size mattress, lying directly on the floor with nothing under it, another purchase from the flea market. A series of cardboard boxes served as the chest of drawers. Clothing littered the floor.

It was a temporary home, with the look of a place one might use for a month or two before leaving town in the middle of the night; which was exactly what he had in mind. He'd lived there for six months already, and the apartment number was his official address, at least the one used when he registered to vote and obtained his Mississippi driver's license. He had nicer quarters four miles away, but couldn't run the risk of being seen there.

So he lived happily in poverty, just another broke student with no assets and few responsibilities. He was almost certain Fitch's snoops had not entered his apartment, but he took no chances. The place was cheap, but carefully arranged. Nothing revealing could be found.

At eight, he finished the questionnaire and proofed it one last time. The one in the Cimmino case had been written in longhand, in a different style altogether. After months of practicing his printing he was certain he would not be detected. There had been three hundred potential jurors then, and almost two hundred now, and why would anyone suspect that he would be in both pools?

From behind a pillowcase stretched over the kitchen window,

he quickly checked the parking lot below for photographers or other intruders. He'd seen one three weeks ago sitting low behind the wheel of a pickup.

No snoops today. He locked his apartment door and left on foot.

GLORIA LANE was much more efficient with her herding on the second day. The remaining 148 prospective jurors were seated on the right side, packed tightly twelve to a row, twelve deep with four in the aisle. They were easier to handle when seated on one side of the courtroom. The questionnaires were gathered as they entered, then quickly copied and given to each side. By ten, the answers were being analyzed by jury consultants locked away in windowless rooms.

Across the aisle, a well-mannered throng of financial boys, reporters, the curious, and other miscellaneous spectators sat and stared at the crowds of lawyers, who sat and studied the faces of the jurors. Fitch had quietly moved to the front row, nearer to his defense team, with a nicely dressed flunkie on each side just waiting for his latest command.

Judge Harkin was a man on a mission on Tuesday, and took less than an hour to complete the nonmedical hardships. Six more were excused, leaving 142 on the panel.

Finally, it was showtime. Wendall Rohr, wearing apparently the same gray checkered sports coat, white vest, and red-and-yellow bow tie, stood and walked to the railing to address his audience. He cracked his knuckles loudly, opened his hands, and displayed a dark, broad grin. "Welcome," he said dramatically, as if what was about to follow was an event the memory of which they would cherish forever. He introduced himself, the members of his team who would be participating in the trial, and then he asked the plaintiff, Celeste Wood, to stand. He managed to use the word "widow" twice as he displayed her to the prospects. A petite woman of fifty-five, she wore a plain black dress, dark hose, dark shoes that could not be seen below the railing, and she offered a painfully proper little smile as if she had yet to exit the mourning stage, though her husband had been dead for four years. In fact, she'd almost remarried, an event Wendall got canceled at the last moment, as soon as he learned of it. It's okay to love the guy, he had explained to her, but do so quietly and you can't marry him until after the trial. The sympathy factor. You're supposed to be suffering, he had explained.

Fitch knew about the aborted nuptials, and he also knew there was little chance of getting the matter before the jury.

With everyone on his side of the courtroom officially introduced, Rohr gave his brief summary of the case, a recitation that attracted immense interest from the defense lawyers and the Judge. They seemed ready to pounce if Rohr stepped over the invisible barrier between fact and argument. He didn't, but he enjoyed tormenting them.

Then a lengthy plea for the potential jurors to be honest, and open, and unafraid to raise their timid little hands if something bothered them in the least. How else can they, the lawyers, explore thoughts and feelings unless they, the would-be jurors, speak up? "We certainly can't do it simply by looking at you," he said with another flash of teeth. At the moment, there were no less than eight people in the courtroom trying desperately to read every lifted eyebrow and curled lip.

To get things rolling, Rohr picked up a legal pad, glanced at it, then said, "Now, we have a number of people who've served on civil juries before. Please raise your hands." A dozen hands rose obediently. Rohr scanned his audience and settled on the nearest one, a lady on the front row. "Mrs. Millwood, is it?" Her cheeks reddened as she nodded. Every person in the courtroom was either staring at or straining to see Mrs. Millwood.

"You were on a civil jury a few years back, I believe," Rohr said warmly.

"Yes," she said, clearing her throat and trying to be loud.

"What kind of case was it?" he asked, though he knew virtually every detail—seven years ago, this very courtroom, different judge, zero for the plaintiff. The file had been copied weeks ago. Rohr had even talked to the plaintiff's lawyer, a friend of his. He started with this question and this juror because it was an easy warm-up, a soft pitch to show the others how painless it was to raise one's hand and discuss matters.

"A car wreck case," she said.

"Where was the trial?" he asked sincerely.

"Right here."

"Oh, in this courtroom." He sounded quite surprised, but the defense lawyers knew he was faking.

"Did the jury reach a verdict in that case?"

"Yes."

"And what was that verdict?"

"We didn't give him anything."

"Him being the plaintiff?"

"Yes. We didn't think he was really hurt."

"I see. Was this jury service a pleasant experience for you?"

She thought a moment, then, "It was okay. Lot of wasted time, though, you know, when the lawyers were wrangling about this or that."

A big smile. "Yes, we tend to do that. Nothing about that case would influence your ability to hear this one?"

"No, don't think so."

"Thank you, Mrs. Millwood." Her husband was once an accountant for a small county hospital that was forced to close after being nailed in a medical malpractice case. Large verdicts were something she secretly loathed, and for good reason. Jonathan Kotlack, the plaintiff's lawyer in charge of final jury selection, had long since removed her name from consideration.

However, around the table not ten feet from Kotlack, the defense lawyers regarded her highly. JoAnn Millwood would be a prize catch.

Rohr asked the same questions of the other veterans of jury service, and things quickly became monotonous. He then tackled the thorny issue of tort reform, and asked a string of rambling questions about the rights of victims, and frivolous lawsuits, and the price of insurance. A few of his questions were wrapped around mini-arguments, but he stayed out of trouble. It was almost lunchtime, and the panel had lost interest for a while. Judge Harkin recessed for an hour, and the deputies cleared the courtroom.

The lawyers remained though. Box lunches containing soggy little sandwiches and red apples were passed out by Gloria Lane and her staff. This was to be a working lunch. Pending motions of a dozen varieties needed resolution, and His Honor was ready for argument. Coffee and iced tea were poured.

THE USE of questionnaires greatly facilitated the selection of the jury. While Rohr asked questions inside the courtroom, dozens of people elsewhere examined the written answers and marked names off their lists. One man's sister had died of lung cancer. Seven others had close friends or family members with serious health problems, all of which they attributed to smoking. At least half the panel either smoked now or had been regular smokers in the past. Most of those smoking admitted their desire to quit.

The data were analyzed, then put in computers, and by mid-afternoon of the second day the printouts were being passed around and edited. After Judge Harkin recessed at four-thirty on Tuesday, he again cleared the courtroom and conducted proceedings on the record. For almost three hours, the written answers were discussed and debated, and in the end thirty-one additional names were removed from consideration. Gloria Lane was instructed to immediately phone these newest deletions and tell them the good news.

Harkin was determined to complete jury selection on Wednesday. Opening statements were scheduled for Thursday morning. He had even hinted at some Saturday work.

At eight o'clock Tuesday night he heard one last motion, a quickie, and sent the lawyers home. The lawyers for Pynex met Fitch at the offices of Whitney & Cable & White, where another delicious feast of cold sandwiches and greasy chips awaited them. Fitch wanted to work, and while the weary lawyers slowly filled their paper plates, two paralegals distributed copies of the latest handwriting analyses. Eat quickly, Fitch demanded, as if the food could be savored. The panel was down to 111, and the picking would start tomorrow.

THE MORNING belonged to Durwood Cable, or Durr as he was known up and down the Coast, a place he'd never really left in his sixty-one years. As the senior partner for Whitney & Cable & White, Sir Durr had been carefully selected by Fitch to handle the bulk of the courtroom work for Pynex. As a lawyer, then a judge, and now a lawyer again, Durr had spent most of the past thirty years looking at and speaking to juries. He found courtrooms to be relaxing places because they were stages—no phones, no foot traffic, no secretaries scurrying about—everyone with a role, everyone following a script with the lawyers as the stars. He moved and talked with great deliberation, but between steps and sentences his gray eyes missed nothing. Where his adversary, Wendall Rohr, was loud and gregarious and gaudy, Durr was buttoned up and quite starched. The obligatory dark suit, a rather bold gold tie, the standard issue white shirt, which contrasted nicely with his deeply tanned face. Durr had a passion for saltwater fishing, and spent many hours on his boat, in the sun. The top of his head was bald, and very bronzed.

He once went six years without losing a case, then Rohr, his foe and sometime friend, popped him for two million in a three-wheeler case.

He stepped to the railing and looked seriously into the faces of 111 people. He knew where each lived and the number of children and grandchildren, if any. He crossed his arms, pinched his chin like a pensive professor, and said in a pleasantly rich voice, "My name is Durwood Cable, and I represent Pynex, an old company that's been making cigarettes for ninety years." There, he was not ashamed of it! He talked about Pynex for ten minutes, and did a masterful job of softening up the company, of making his client warm and fuzzy, almost likable.

Finished with that, he plunged fearlessly into the issue of choice. Whereas Rohr had dwelt on addiction, Cable spent his time on the freedom to choose. "Can we all agree that cigarettes are potentially dangerous if abused?" he asked, then watched most of the heads shake in agreement. Who could argue with this? "There, fine. Now since this is common knowledge, can we all agree that a person who smokes should know the dangers?" More nodding, no hands, yet. He studied the faces, especially the blank one belonging to Nicholas Easter, now seated on row three, eighth from the aisle. Because of the dismissals, Easter was no longer juror number fifty-six. He was now number thirty-two, and advancing with each session. His face revealed nothing but rapt attention.

"This is a very important question," Cable said slowly, his words echoing in the stillness. With a pointed finger, he delicately jabbed at them and said, "Is there a single person on this panel who doesn't believe that a person who chooses to smoke should know the dangers?"

He waited, watching and tugging at the line a bit, and finally caught one. A hand was slowly raised from the fourth row. Cable smiled, took a step closer, said, "Yes, I believe you're Mrs. Tutwiler. Please stand." If he was truly eager to have a volunteer, his joy was short-lived. Mrs. Tutwiler was a fragile little lady of sixty, with an angry face. She stood straight, lifted her chin, and said, "I got a question for you, Mr. Cable."

"Certainly."

"If everybody knows cigarettes are dangerous, then why does your client keep making them?"

There were a few grins from her colleagues in the pool. All eyes were on Durwood Cable as he kept smiling, never flinching in the least. "Excellent question," he said loudly. He was not about to answer it. "Do you think the making of all cigarettes should be banned, Mrs. Tutwiler?"

"I do."

"Even if people want to exercise their right to choose to smoke?"

"Cigarettes are addictive, Mr. Cable, you know that."

"Thank you, Mrs. Tutwiler."

"The manufacturers load up the nicotine, get folks hooked, then advertise like crazy to keep selling."

"Thank you, Mrs. Tutwiler."

"I'm not finished," she said loudly, clutching the pew in front of her and standing ever taller. "The manufacturers have always denied that smoking is addictive. That's a lie, and you know it. Why don't they say so on their labels?"

Durr's face never changed expression. He waited patiently, then asked quite warmly, "Are you finished, Mrs. Tutwiler?" There were other things she wanted to say, but it dawned on her that perhaps this was not the place. "Yes," she said, almost in a whisper.

"Thank you. Responses such as yours are vital to the jury selection process. Thank you very much. You may now sit down."

She glanced around as if some of the others should stand and fight with her, but left alone, she dropped to her seat. She might as well have left the courtroom.

Cable quickly pursued less sensitive matters. He asked a lot of questions, provoked a few responses, and gave his body language experts much to chew on. He finished at noon, just in time for a quick lunch. Harkin asked the panel to return at three, but told the lawyers to eat fast and return in forty-five minutes.

At one o'clock, with the courtroom empty and locked and the lawyers crowded tightly in bunches around their tables, Jonathan Kotlack stood and informed the court that "The plaintiff will accept juror number one." No one seemed surprised. Everyone wrote something on a printout, including His Honor, who, after a slight pause, asked, "The defense?"

"The defense will accept number one." Not much of a surprise. Number one was Rikki Coleman, a young wife and mother of two who'd never smoked and worked as a records administrator in a hospital. Kotlack and crew rated her as a 7 out of 10 based on her written answers, her background in health care, her college degree, and her keen interest in everything that had been said so far. The defense rated her as a 6, and would've passed on her but for a string of serious undesirables forthcoming further down row one.

"That was easy," Harkin mumbled under his breath. "Moving right along. Juror number two, Raymond C. LaMonette." Mr. LaMonette was the first strategical skirmish of jury selection. Neither side wanted him—both rated him 4.5. He smoked heavily but was desperate to quit. His written answers were thoroughly indecipherable and utterly useless. The body linguists on both sides reported that Mr. LaMonette hated all lawyers and all things related to them. He'd nearly been killed years earlier by a drunk driver. His lawsuit netted him nothing.

Under the rules of jury selection, each side was granted a number of peremptory challenges, or strikes as they were called, which could be used to ax potential jurors for no reason whatsoever. Because of the importance of this case, Judge Harkin had granted each side ten strikes, up from the customary four. Both wanted to cut LaMonette, but both needed to save their strikes for more objectionable faces.

The plaintiff was required to go first, and after a brief delay, Kotlack said, "The plaintiff will strike number two."

"That's peremptory challenge number one for the plaintiff," Harkin said, making a note. A small victory for the defense. Based on a last-second decision, Durr Cable had been prepared to strike him as well.

The plaintiff used a strike on number three, the wife of a corporate executive, and also on number four. The strategic strikes continued, and practically decimated row one. Only two jurors survived. The carnage lessened with row two, with five of the twelve surviving various challenges, two by the court itself. Seven jurors had been chosen when the selection moved to row three.

Eight spots down sat the great unknown, Nicholas Easter, juror number thirty-two, who'd so far paid good attention and seemed to be somewhat palatable, though he gave both sides the jitters.

Wendall Rohr, now speaking for the plaintiff because Kotlack was deep in a hushed conference with an expert about two of the faces on row four, used a peremptory strike on number twenty-five. It was the plaintiff's ninth strike. The last one was reserved for a much-feared and notorious Republican on the fourth row, if they got that far. The defense struck number twenty-six, burning its eighth peremptory. Jurors number twenty-seven, twenty-eight, and twenty-nine were accepted. Juror number thirty was challenged by the defense for cause, a plea for the court to excuse the juror for mutual reasons without requiring either side to exhaust a strike. Durr Cable asked the court to go off the record because he had something he wished to discuss in private. Rohr was a bit perplexed, but did not object. The court reporter stopped recording. Cable handed a thin brief to Rohr and the same to His Honor. He lowered his voice, and said, "Your Honor, we have learned, through certain sources, that juror number thirty, Bonnie Tyus, is addicted to the prescription drug Ativan. She has never been treated, never been arrested, never admitted her problem. She certainly didn't disclose it on the questionnaires or during our little Q and A. She manages to live quietly, keep a job and a husband, though he's her third."

"How'd you learn this?" Harkin asked.

"Through our rather extensive investigation of all potential jurors. I assure you, Your Honor, that there has been no unauthorized contact with Mrs. Tyus."

Fitch had found it. Her second husband had been located in Nashville, where he washed tractor-trailer rigs at an all-night truck stop. For one hundred dollars cash, he'd happily told all he could remember about his ex.

"What about it, Mr. Rohr?" asked His Honor.

Without a second's hesitation, Rohr said, lying, "We have the same information, Your Honor." He cast a pleasant glance at Jonathan Kotlack, who in turn glared at another lawyer who'd been in charge of the group which included Bonnie Tyus. They'd spent over a million bucks so far on jury selection, and they'd missed this crucial fact!

"Fine. Juror number thirty is excused for cause. Back on the record. Juror number thirty-one?"

"Could we have a few minutes, Your Honor?" Rohr asked.

"Yes. But be brief."

After thirty names, ten had been selected; nine had been struck by the plaintiff, eight by the defense, and three had been excused by the court. It was unlikely the selection would reach the fourth row, so Rohr, with one strike remaining, looked at jurors thirty-one through thirty-six, and whispered to his huddled group, "Which one stinks the most?" The fingers pointed unanimously to number thirty-four, a large, mean white woman who had scared them from day one. Wilda Haney was her name, and for a month now they had all vowed to avoid Wide Wilda. They studied their master sheet a few minutes longer, and agreed to take numbers thirty-one, thirty-two, thirty-three, and thirty-five, not all of whom were terribly attractive, but far more so than Wide Wilda.

In a denser huddle just a few feet away, Cable and his troops agreed to strike thirty-one, take thirty-two, challenge thirty-three because thirty-three was Mr. Herman Grimes, the blind man, then take thirty-four, Wilda Haney, and strike, if necessary, number thirty-five.

NICHOLAS EASTER thus became the eleventh juror selected to hear *Wood v. Pynex*. When the courtroom was opened at three and the panel was seated, Judge Harkin began calling out the names of the chosen twelve. They walked through the gate in the railing and took their assigned seats in the jury box. Nicholas had chair number two on the front row. At twenty-seven, he was the second youngest juror. There were nine whites, three blacks, seven women, five men, one blind. Three alternates were seated in padded folding chairs wedged tightly together in one corner of the jury box. At four-thirty, the fifteen stood and repeated their oaths as jurors. They then listened for half an hour as Judge Harkin issued a series of stern warnings to them, and to the lawyers and parties involved. Contact with the jurors of any type or manner would result in stiff sanctions, monetary penalties, maybe a mistrial, perhaps disbarment and death.

He forbade the jurors from discussing the case with anyone, even their spouses and mates, and with a cheery smile bid them farewell, a pleasant night, see you at nine sharp tomorrow morning.

The lawyers watched and wished they could leave too. But there was work to do. When the courtroom was cleared of everyone but lawyers and clerks, His Honor said, "Gentlemen, you filed these motions. Now we must argue them."

Five

PARTIALLY out of a mixture of eagerness and boredom, and partially on a hunch that someone would be waiting, Nicholas Easter slipped through the unlocked rear door of the courthouse at eight-thirty, up the seldom-used back stairs, and into the narrow hallway behind the courtroom. Most of the county offices opened at eight, so there was movement and noise to be heard on the first floor. But little on the second. He peeked into the courtroom, and found it empty of people. The briefcases had arrived and been parked haphazardly on the tables. The lawyers were probably in the back, near the coffee machine, telling jokes and preparing for battle.

He knew the turf well. Three weeks earlier, the day after he'd received his precious summons for jury duty, he had come poking around the courtroom. Finding it unused and vacant for the moment, he had explored the alleys and spaces around it; the Judge's cramped chambers; the coffee room where the lawyers gossiped while sitting on ancient tables strewn with old magazines and current newspapers; the makeshift witness rooms with folding chairs and no windows; the holding room where the handcuffed and dangerous waited for their punishment; and, of course, the jury room.

This morning, his hunch was correct. Her name was Lou Dell, a squatty woman of sixty in polyester pants and old sneakers and gray bangs in her eyes. She was sitting in the hallway by the door to the jury room, reading a battered romance and waiting for someone to enter her domain. She jumped to her feet, whipped out a sheet of paper from under her, and said, "Good morning. Can I help you?" Her entire face was one massive smile. Her eyes glowed with mischief.

"Nicholas Easter," he said, as he reached for her outstretched hand. She squeezed tightly, shook with a vengeance, and found his name on her paperwork. Another, larger smile, then, "Welcome to the jury room. This your first trial?"

"Yes."

"Come on," she said, virtually shoving him through the door and into the room. "Coffee and doughnuts are over here," she said, tugging at his arm, pointing to a corner. "I made these myself," she said proudly, lifting a basket of oily black muffins. "Sort of a tradition. I always bring these on the first day, call 'em my jury muffins. Take one."

The table was covered with several varieties of doughnuts arranged neatly on trays. Two coffeepots were filled and steaming. Plates and cups, spoons and forks, sugar, cream, sweeteners of several varieties. And in the center of the table were the jury muffins. Nicholas took one because he had no choice.

"Been making them for eighteen years," she said. "Used to put raisins in them, but had to quit." She rolled her eyes up at him as if the rest of the story was just too scandalous.

"Why?" he asked, because he felt compelled.

"Gave 'em gas. Sometimes every sound can be heard in the courtroom. Know what I mean?"

"I guess."

"Coffee?"

"I can get my own."

"Fine then." She whirled around and pointed to a stack of papers in the center of the long table. "There's a list of instructions from Judge Harkin. He wants every juror to take one, read it carefully, and sign at the bottom. I'll collect them later."

"Thanks."

"I'll be in the hall by the door if you need me. That's where I stay. They're gonna put a damned deputy with me for this one, can you believe it? Just makes me sick. Probably some clod who can't hit a barn with a shotgun. But anyway, I guess this is about the biggest one we've ever had. Civil, that is. You wouldn't believe some of the criminal ones we've had." She took the doorknob and yanked it toward her. "I'm out here, dear, if you need me."

The door closed, and Nicholas gazed at the muffin. Slowly, he took a small bite. It was mostly bran and sugar, and he thought for a second about the sounds in the courtroom. He tossed it in the wastebasket and poured black coffee into a plastic cup. The plastic cups would have to go. If they planned for him to camp here for four to six weeks, then they'd have to provide real cups. And if the county could afford pretty doughnuts, then it could certainly afford bagels and croissants.

There was no decaf coffee. He made a note of this. And no hot water for tea, just in case some of his new friends weren't coffee drinkers. Lunch had better be good. He would not eat tuna salad for the next six weeks.

Twelve chairs were arranged neatly around the table, which was in the center of the room. The thick layer of dust he had noticed three weeks ago had been removed; the place was much tidier, and ready for use. On one wall was a large blackboard, with erasers and fresh chalk. Across the table, on the opposite wall, three large windows, from floor to ceiling, looked upon the courthouse lawn, still green and fresh though summer had ended over a month ago. Nicholas looked through a window and watched the foot traffic on the sidewalks.

The latest from Judge Harkin was a list of a few things to do, and many to avoid: Get organized. Elect a foreman, and if you are unable to do so, notify His Honor and he will be happy to select one. Wear the red-and-white Juror buttons at all times. Lou Dell would dispense these. Bring something to read during downtimes. Do not hesitate to ask for anything. Do not discuss the case among yourselves until you are instructed to do so by His Honor. Do not discuss the case with anyone, period. Do not leave the courthouse without permission. Do not use the telephones without permission. Lunch will be catered and eaten in the jury room. A daily menu will be provided each day before the trial resumes at nine. Notify the court immediately if you or anyone you know is in any way contacted with regard to your involvement in this trial. Notify the court immediately if you see or hear or notice anything suspicious which may or may not be related to your service as a juror in this case.

Odd directions, these last two. But Nicholas knew the details of a tobacco trial in east Texas, a trial which blew up after only one week when it was discovered that mysterious agents were slinking through the small town and offering huge sums of money to relatives of jurors. The agents disappeared before they were caught, and it was never learned which side they worked for, though both made heated accusations. Cooler heads laid heavy odds that it was the work of the tobacco boys. The jury appeared to have a strong sympathy bent to it, and the defense was delighted when the mistrial was declared.

Though there was no way to prove it, Nicholas was certain Rankin Fitch was the phantom behind the payoffs. And he knew Fitch would quickly go to work on his new set of friends.

He signed the bottom of the sheet and left it on the table. There were voices in the hallway, and Lou Dell was meeting another juror. The door opened with a kick and a thud, and Mr. Herman Grimes entered first with his walking stick tapping along in front of him. His wife was close behind, not touching him but instantly inspecting the room and describing it under her breath. "Long room, twenty-five by fifteen, length in front of you, width from left to right, long table running lengthwise in center with chairs around it, nearest chair to you is eight feet." He froze as he gathered this in, his head moving in whatever direction she was describing. Behind her, Lou Dell stood in the doorway with hands on hips and just dying to feed the blind man a muffin.

Nicholas took a few steps and introduced himself. He grabbed Herman's outstretched hand and they exchanged pleasantries. He said hello to Mrs. Grimes, then led Herman to the food and coffee where he poured him a cup and stirred in sugar and cream. He described the doughnuts and the muffins, a preemptive strike against Lou Dell, who lingered near the door. Herman was not hungry.

"My favorite uncle is blind," Nicholas said for the benefit of all three. "I'd consider it an honor if you'd allow me to assist you during the trial."

"I'm perfectly capable of handling myself," Herman said with a trace of indignation, but his wife couldn't conceal a warm smile. Then she winked and nodded.

"I'm sure you are," Nicholas said. "But I know there are lots of little things. I just want to help."

"Thank you," he said after a brief pause.

"Thank you, sir," his wife said.

"I'll be outside in the hallway if you need anything," Lou Dell said.

"What time should I come get him?" Mrs. Grimes asked.

"Five. If sooner, I'll call." Lou Dell was closing the door as she rattled off instructions.

Herman's eyes were covered with dark glasses. His hair was brown, thick, well greased, and barely yielding to gray.

"There's a bit of paperwork," Nicholas said when they were alone. "Take a seat there in front of you and I'll go over it." Herman felt the table, set down his coffee, then groped for a chair. He outlined it with his fingertips, got his bearings, and sat down. Nicholas took an instruction sheet and began reading.

AFTER SPENDING FORTUNES on the selection, the opinions came cheap. Everybody had one. The experts for the defense congratulated themselves on picking such a fine jury, though most of the puffing and posturing was done for the benefit of the legion of lawyers working round the clock. Durr Cable had seen worse juries, but he'd seen much friendlier ones too. He'd also learned many years ago that it was virtually impossible to predict what any jury would do. Fitch was happy, or as happy as he could allow himself, though that didn't stop his bitching and snarling about everything. Four smokers were on the jury. Fitch clung to the unspoken belief that the Gulf Coast, with its topless joints and casinos and proximity to New Orleans, was not a bad place to be right now because of its tolerance for vice.

On the other side of the street, Wendall Rohr and his trial counsel declared themselves satisfied with the composition of the jury. They were especially delighted with the unexpected addition of Mr. Herman Grimes, the first blind juror in the history of anyone's memory. Mr. Grimes had insisted on being evaluated just the same as those "with sight," and had threatened legal action if treated differently. His hair-trigger reliance on lawsuits greatly warmed the hearts of Rohr and company, and his handicap was a plaintiff's lawyer's dream. The defense had objected on all imaginable grounds, including the inability to see the forthcoming exhibits. Judge Harkin had allowed the lawyers to quietly quiz Mr. Grimes about this, and he assured them he could see the exhibits if the exhibits could be sufficiently described in writing.

His Honor then decided that a separate court reporter would be used to type descriptions of the exhibits. A disc could then be fed into Mr. Grimes' braille computer, and he could read at night. This made Mr. Grimes very happy, and he quit talking about discrimination suits. The defense softened a bit, especially when it learned that he had once smoked for many years and had no problems being around people who continued the habit.

So, both sides were cautiously pleased with their jury. No radicals had been seated. No bad attitudes had been detected. All twelve had high school diplomas, two had college degrees, and another three had accumulated credits. Easter's written answers admitted completion of high school, but his college studies were still a mystery.

And as both sides prepared for the first full day of real trial activities, they quietly pondered the great question, the one they loved to guess about. As they looked at the seating charts and studied the faces for the millionth time, they asked over and over, "Who will be the leader?"

Every jury has a leader, and that's where you find your verdict. Will he emerge quickly? Or will she lie back and take charge during deliberations? Not even the jurors knew at this point.

AT TEN SHARP, Judge Harkin studied the packed courtroom and decided everyone was in place. He pecked his gavel lightly and the whispers ceased. Everyone was ready. He nodded at Pete, his ancient bailiff in a faded brown uniform, and said simply, "Bring in the jury." All eyes watched the door beside the jury box. Lou Dell appeared first, leading her flock like a mother hen, then the chosen twelve filed in and went to their assigned seats. The three alternates took their positions in folding chairs. After a moment of settling in—adjusting seat cushions and hem lengths and placing purses and paperbacks on the floor—the jurors grew still and of course noticed that they were being gawked at.

"Good morning," His Honor said with a loud voice and a large smile. Most of them nodded back.

"I trust you've found the jury room and gotten yourselves organized." A pause, as he lifted for some reason the fifteen signed forms Lou Dell had dispensed then collected. "Do we have a foreman?" he asked.

The twelve nodded in unison.

"Good. Who is it?"

"It's me, Your Honor," Herman Grimes said from the first row, and for a quick second the defense, all its lawyers and jury consultants and corporate representatives, suffered a collective chest pain. Then they breathed, slowly, but never allowing the slightest indication that they had anything but the greatest love and affection for the blind juror who was now the foreman. Perhaps the other eleven just felt sorry for the old boy.

"Very well," His Honor said, relieved that his jury was able to reach this routine selection without apparent acrimony. He'd seen much worse. One jury, half white and half black, had been unable to elect a foreman. They later brawled over the lunch menu.

"I trust you've read my written instructions," he continued, then launched into a detailed lecture in which he repeated twice everything he'd already put in print.

Nicholas Easter sat on the front row, second seat from the left. He froze his face into a mask of noncommitment, and as Harkin droned on he began to take in the rest of the players. With little movement of the head, he cut his eyes around the courtroom. The lawyers, packed around their tables like vultures ready to pounce on roadkill, were, without exception, staring unabashedly at the jurors. Surely they'd tire of this, and soon.

On the second row behind the defense sat Rankin Fitch, his fat face and sinister goatee looking straight into the shoulders of the man in front of him. He was trying to ignore Harkin's admonitions and pretending to be wholly unconcerned about the jury, but Nicholas knew better. Fitch missed nothing.

Fourteen months earlier, Nicholas had seen him in the Cimmino courtroom in Allentown, Pennsylvania, looking then much the same as he looked now—thick and shadowy. And he'd seen him on the sidewalk outside the courthouse in Broken Arrow, Oklahoma, during the Glavine trial. Two sightings of Fitch were enough. Nicholas knew that Fitch now knew that he'd never attended college at North Texas State. He knew Fitch was more concerned about him than about any of the other jurors, and with very good reason.

Behind Fitch were two rows of suits, sharply dressed clones with scowling faces, and Nicholas knew these to be the worried boys from Wall Street. According to the morning paper, the market had chosen not to react to the jury's composition. Pynex was holding steady at eighty bucks a share. He couldn't help but smile. If he suddenly jumped to his feet and shouted, "I think the plaintiff should get millions!" the suits would bolt for the door and Pynex would drop ten points by lunch.

The other three—Trellco, Smith Greer, and ConPack—were also trading evenly.

On the front rows were little pockets of distressed souls who Nicholas was certain had to be the jury experts. Now that the selecting was done, they moved to the next phase—the watching. It fell to their miserable lot to hear every word of every witness and predict how the jury absorbed the testimony. The strategy was that if a particular witness made a feeble or even damaging impression on the jury, then he or she could be yanked off the stand and sent home. Perhaps another, stronger witness could then be used to repair the damage. Nicholas wasn't sure about this. He'd read a lot about jury consultants, even attended a seminar in St. Louis where trial lawyers told war stories about big verdicts, but he still wasn't convinced these "cutting edge" experts were little more than con artists.

They claimed to evaluate jurors just by watching their bodily reactions, however slight, to what was said. Nicholas managed another smile. What if he stuck his finger up his nose and left it there for five minutes? How would that little expression of body language be interpreted?

He couldn't classify the rest of the spectators. No doubt there were a number of reporters, and the usual collection of bored local lawyers and other courthouse regulars. The wife of Herman Grimes sat midway back, beaming with pride in the fact that her husband had been elected to such a lofty position. Judge Harkin stopped his rambling and pointed at Wendall Rohr, who stood slowly, buttoned his plaid jacket while flashing his false teeth at the jurors, and strode importantly to the lectern. This was his opening statement, he explained, and in it he would outline his case for the jury. The courtroom was very quiet.

They would prove that cigarettes cause lung cancer, and, more precisely, that the deceased, Mr. Jacob Wood, a fine fellow, developed lung cancer after smoking Bristols for almost thirty years. The cigarettes killed him, Rohr announced solemnly, tugging at a pointed patch of gray beard below his chin. His voice was raspy but precise, capable of floating up and down to hit the right dramatic pitch. Rohr was a performer, a seasoned actor whose crooked bow tie and clicking dentures and mismatched clothing were designed to endear him to the average man. He wasn't perfect. Let the defense lawyers, in their impeccable dark suits and rich silk ties, talk down their long noses at these jurors. But not Rohr. These were his people.

But how would they prove cigarettes cause lung cancer? There'd be lots of proof, really. First, they would bring in some of the most distinguished cancer experts and researchers in the country. Yes, that's right, these great men were on their way to Biloxi to sit and chat with this jury and explain unequivocally and with mountains of statistics that cigarettes do in fact cause cancer.

Then, and Rohr couldn't suppress a wicked smile as he prepared to reveal this, the plaintiff would present to the jury people who'd once worked for the tobacco industry. Dirty laundry would be aired, right there in that very courtroom. Damning evidence was on the way.

In short, the plaintiff would prove cigarette smoke, because it contains natural carcinogens, and pesticides, and radioactive particles, and asbestos-like fibers, causes lung cancer.

At this point, there was little doubt in the courtroom that Wendall Rohr could not only prove this, but would be able to prove it without much trouble. He paused, tugged at the ends of his bow tie with all ten chubby fingers, and glanced at his notes, then, very solemnly, began talking about Jacob Wood, the deceased. Beloved father and family man, hard worker, devout Catholic, member of the church softball team, veteran. Started smoking when he was just a kid who, like everyone else back then, was not aware of the dangers. A grandfather. And so on.

Rohr got overly dramatic for a moment, but seemed to know it. He briefly covered the area of damages. This was a big trial, he announced, one of vast importance. The plaintiff expected, and would certainly ask for, a lot of money. Not just actual damages—the economic value of Jacob Wood's life, plus his family's loss of his love and affection—but also punitive damages.

Rohr rambled on a bit about punitive damages, seemed to lose his place a few times, and it was clear to most of the jurors that he was so inspired by the prospect of a huge punitive verdict that he lost his concentration.

Judge Harkin, in writing, had allowed one hour for each side's opening statement. And had promised, in writing, to cut off any lawyer who ran over. Though he suffered from the common law-yerly affliction of overkill, Rohr knew not to mess with His Honor's clock. He finished in fifty minutes with a somber appeal for justice, thanked the jurors for their attention, smiled and clicked his dentures, and sat down.

Fifty minutes in a chair with no conversation and precious little movement feels like hours, and Judge Harkin knew it. He an-nounced a recess for fifteen minutes, to be followed by the defen-dant's opening statement.

DURWOOD CABLE finished his remarks in under thirty minutes. He coolly and deliberately assured the jurors that Pynex had ex-perts of its own, scientists and researchers who would clearly ex-plain that cigarettes in fact do not cause lung cancer. The skepti-cism of the jurors was expected, and Cable asked only for their patience and open-mindedness. Sir Durr spoke without the benefit of notes, and each word was drilled into the eyes of a juror. His eyes moved down the first row, then up slightly to the second, taking in their curious gazes one at a time. His voice and stare were almost hypnotic, but honest. You wanted to believe this man.

Six

THE FIRST CRISIS occurred at lunch. Judge Harkin announced the noon recess at twelve-ten, and the courtroom sat still as the jurors filed out. Lou Dell met them in the narrow hallway and couldn't wait to shuffle them to the jury room. "Just have a seat," she said, "and lunch will be here in a moment. Coffee's fresh." Once all twelve were in the room, she shut them in and left to check on the three alternates, who were kept separated in a smaller room down the hall. With all fifteen in place, she returned to her post and glared at Willis, the mentally deficient deputy assigned to stand nearby with a loaded gun on his belt and protect somebody.

The jurors slowly scattered about the jury room, some stretching or yawning, others continuing formal introductions—most making small talk about the weather. For some, the movements and small talk were stiff; demeanor to be expected from people suddenly thrown into a room with perfect strangers. With nothing to do but eat, the noon meal loomed as a major event. What were they going to be fed? Surely, the food would be decent.

Herman Grimes took a seat at the head of the table, fitting for the foreman, he thought, and was soon chatting away with Millie Dupree, a kindly soul of fifty who actually knew another blind person. Nicholas Easter introduced himself to Lonnie Shaver, the only black male on the jury, and a man who clearly did not want to serve. Shaver managed a grocery store for a large regional chain, and was the highest-ranking black in the company. He was wiry and nervous, and found it difficult to relax. The idea of spending the next four weeks away from the store was frightening.

Twenty minutes passed, and no lunch appeared. At exactly twelve-thirty, Nicholas said from across the room, "Hey, Herman, where's our lunch?"

"I'm just the foreman," Herman replied with a smile as the room was suddenly quiet.

Nicholas walked to the door, opened it, and summoned Lou Dell. "We're hungry," he said.

She slowly lowered her paperback, looked at the eleven other faces, and said, "It's on the way."

"Where is it coming from?" he demanded.

"O'Reilly's Deli. Just around the corner." Lou Dell didn't appreciate the questions.

"Listen, we're penned up in here like a bunch of house pets," Nicholas said. "We can't leave like normal people to go eat. I don't understand why we can't be trusted to walk down the street and enjoy a nice lunch, but the Judge has spoken." Nicholas took a step closer and glared down at the gray bangs hanging over Lou Dell's eyes. "Lunch is not going to be a hassle every day, okay?"

"Okay."

"I suggest you get on the phone and find out where our lunch is, or I'll discuss it with Judge Harkin."

"Okay."

The door closed, and Nicholas walked to the coffeepot.

"That was a bit harsh, don't you think?" asked Millie Dupree. The others were listening.

"Maybe, and if it was, then I'll apologize. But if we don't get things straight up front, then they'll forget about us."

"It's not her fault," Herman said.

"Her job is to take care of us." Nicholas walked to the table and sat near Herman. "Do you realize that in virtually every other trial they allow the jurors to leave like normal people and go eat? Why do you think we wear these Juror buttons?" The others moved closer to the table.

"How do you know?" asked Millie Dupree from directly across the table.

Nicholas shrugged as if he knew plenty but maybe couldn't talk about it. "I know a little about the system."

"And how's that?" Herman asked.

Nicholas paused for effect, then said, "I had two years of law school." He took a long sip of coffee as the others weighed this engaging bit of background.

Easter's stature among his peers rose immediately. He'd already proved himself to be friendly and helpful, courteous and bright. Now, though, he was silently elevated because he knew the law.

No food had arrived by twelve forty-five. Nicholas abruptly stopped a conversation and opened the door. Lou Dell was glancing at her watch in the hallway. "I've sent Willis," she said nervously. "Should be here any minute now. I'm really sorry."

"Where's the men's room?" Nicholas asked.

"Around the corner, to your right," she said, relieved and pointing. He didn't stop at the men's room, but instead walked quietly down the rear staircase and out of the courthouse. He made his way along Lamuese Street for two blocks until he came to the Vieux Marche, a pedestrian mall lined with neat shops along what was once the central business section of Biloxi. He knew the area well because it was only a quarter of a mile from his apartment building. He liked the cafés and delis along the Vieux Marche. There was a good bookstore.

He turned left and was soon entering a large, old white building that housed Mary Mahoney's, a locally famous restaurant where most of the town's legal community usually gathered for lunch when court was in session. He'd rehearsed this walk a week ago, and had even had his lunch at a table close to the Honorable Frederick Harkin.

Nicholas entered the restaurant, and asked the first waitress he saw if Judge Harkin was eating. Yes. And where might he be? She pointed, and Nicholas walked quickly through the bar, through a small foyer, and into a large dining room with windows and sunshine and lots of fresh flowers. It was crowded, but he saw His Honor at a table of four. Harkin saw him coming, and his fork froze halfway up with a meaty grilled shrimp stuck to the end of it. He recognized the face as one of his jurors, and he saw the bold red-and-white Juror button.

"Sorry to interrupt, sir," Nicholas said, stopping at the edge of the table, a table covered with warm bread and leafy salads and large glasses of iced tea. Gloria Lane, the Circuit Clerk, was also momentarily speechless. A second woman was the court reporter, and a third was Harkin's law clerk.

"What are you doing here?" Harkin asked, a speck of goat cheese on his lower lip.

"I'm here on behalf of your jury."

"What's the matter?"

Nicholas leaned down so he wouldn't create a scene. "We're hungry," he said, his anger apparent through clenched teeth and clearly absorbed by the four stricken faces. "While you folks are sitting here having a nice lunch, we're sitting over there in a cramped room waiting on deli food that, for some reason, can't find its way to us. We're hungry, sir, with all due respect. And we're upset."

Harkin's fork hit his plate hard, the shrimp bouncing off and tumbling to the floor. He tossed his napkin on the table while mumbling something completely indecipherable. He looked at the three women, arched his eyebrows, and said, "Well, let's go see." He stood, followed by the women, and the five of them stormed out of the restaurant.

Lou Dell and Willis were nowhere to be seen when Nicholas and Judge Harkin and the three women entered the hallway and opened the door to the jury room. The table was bare—no food. The time was five minutes after one. The jurors stopped their chatting and stared at His Honor.

"It's been almost an hour," Nicholas said, waving at the empty table. If the other jurors were astonished to see the Judge, their surprise quickly turned to anger.

"We have the right to be treated with dignity," snapped Lonnie Shaver, and with that Harkin was thoroughly defeated.

"Where's Lou Dell?" he said in the general direction of the three women. Everyone looked at the door, and suddenly Lou Dell was rushing forth. She stopped cold when she saw His Honor. Harkin faced her squarely.

"What's going on?" he asked firmly, but with control.

"I just talked to the deli," she said, out of breath and scared, beads of sweat on her cheeks. "There's been a mixup. They claim someone called and said we wouldn't need lunch until one-thirty."

"These people are starving," Harkin said, as if by now Lou Dell didn't know this. "One-thirty?"

"It's just a mixup at the deli. Somebody got their wires crossed."

"Which deli?"

"O'Reilly's."

"Remind me to speak to the owner of the deli."

"Yes sir."

The Judge turned his attention to his jury. "I'm very sorry. This will not happen again." He paused for a second, looked at his watch, then offered them a pleasant smile. "I'm inviting you to follow me to Mary Mahoney's and join me for lunch." He turned to his law clerk, and said, "Call Bob Mahoney and tell him to prepare the back room."

They dined on crab cakes and grilled snapper, fresh oysters and Mahoney's famous gumbo. Nicholas Easter was the man of the hour. When they finished dessert a few minutes after two-thirty, they followed Judge Harkin, at a leisurely pace, back to the courtroom. By the time the jury was seated for the afternoon session, everyone present had heard the story of their splendid lunch.

Neal O'Reilly, owner of the deli, later met with Judge Harkin and swore on a Bible that he had talked to someone, a young female claiming to be with the Circuit Clerk's office, and that she had specifically instructed him to deliver lunch at precisely one-thirty.

THE TRIAL'S FIRST WITNESS was the deceased, Jacob Wood, testifying by a video deposition taken a few months before his death. Two twenty-inch monitors were rolled into place before the jury, and a series of six others were situated around the courtroom. The wiring had been completed while the jury feasted at Mary Mahoney's.

Jacob Wood was propped up with pillows in what appeared to be a hospital bed. He wore a plain white T-shirt with a sheet covering him from the waist down. He was thin, gaunt, and pale, and took oxygen from a tiny tube running from behind his bony neck into his nose. He was told to begin, and he looked at the camera and stated his name and address. His voice was raspy and sick. He was also suffering from emphysema.

Though he was surrounded by lawyers, Jacob's face was the

only one to be seen. Occasionally a small skirmish would erupt off-camera among the lawyers, but Jacob didn't seem to care. He was fifty-one, looked twenty years older, and was clearly pounding at death's door.

With prompting from his lawyer, Wendall Rohr, he shared his biography beginning with his birth, and this took almost an hour. Childhood, early education, friends, homes, Navy, marriage, jobs, kids, habits, hobbies, adult friends, travel, vacation, grandkids, thoughts of retirement. Watching a dead man talk was quite compelling at first, but the jurors soon learned that his life had been just as boring as theirs. The heavy lunch settled in, and they began to twitch and fidget. Brains and eyelids grew sluggish. Even Herman, who could only hear the voice and imagine the face, got bored. Fortunately, His Honor began to suffer from the same post-lunch sinking spell, and after an hour and twenty minutes he called for a quick recess.

The four smokers on the jury needed a break, and Lou Dell happily walked them to a room with an open window, a room next to the men's toilet, a small cubicle normally used to hold juvenile delinquents awaiting court appearances. "If you can't quit smoking after this trial, something's wrong," she said, in a very flat effort at humor. Not a smile from the four. "Sorry," she said, closing the door behind her. Jerry Fernandez, thirty-eight, a car salesman with heavy casino debts and a bad marriage, lit his first, then waved his lighter in the faces of the three women. They pulled heavy puffs and blew large clouds at the window. "Here's to Jacob Wood," Jerry said as a toast. Nothing from the three women. They were too busy smoking.

Mr. Foreman Grimes had already delivered one brief lecture on the illegalities of discussing the case; he simply wouldn't tolerate it because Judge Harkin was harping on it so strenuously. But Herman was in the next room, and Jerry was curious. "Wonder if ole Jacob ever tried to quit?" he said, to no one in particular.

Sylvia Taylor-Tatum, drawing ferociously on the end of a slender, emancipated cigarette, replied, "I'm sure we're about to find out," then released an impressive torrent of bluish vapors from her long, pointed nose. Jerry loved nicknames, and he had already secretly tagged her as Poodle because of her narrow face, sharp protruding nose, and shaggy thick graying hair that parted perfectly in the center and fell in heavy layers to her shoulders. She was at least six feet tall, very angular, with a constant frown that kept people away. Poodle intended to be left alone.

"I wonder who's next," Jerry said, trying to start a conversation.

"I guess all those doctors," Poodle said, staring through the window.

The other two ladies simply smoked, and Jerry gave it up.

THE WOMAN'S NAME was Marlee, at least that was the alias she'd chosen to use for this period of her life. She was thirty, short brown hair, brown eyes, medium height, slim build with simple clothing carefully selected to avoid attention. She looked great in tight jeans and short skirts, she looked great in anything or nothing, really, but for the moment she wanted no one to notice her. She'd been in the courtroom on two prior occasions—once two weeks earlier when she'd sat through another trial, and once during jury selection in the tobacco case. She knew her way around. She knew where the Judge kept his office and where he ate lunch. She knew the names of the plaintiff's lawyers and those of the defense—no small task. She'd read the court file. She knew in which hotel Rankin Fitch was hiding during the trial.

During the recess, she got herself cleared through the metal detector at the front door, and eased into the rear row of the courtroom. Spectators were stretching and lawyers were huddling and conferencing. She saw Fitch standing in a corner, chatting with two people she believed to be jury consultants. He did not notice her. There were about a hundred people present.

A few minutes passed. She carefully watched the door behind the bench, and when the court reporter came out with a cup of coffee, Marlee knew the Judge could not be far behind. She took an envelope from her purse, waited a second, then walked a few feet to one of the deputies guarding the front door. She flashed a comely smile and said, "Could you do me a favor?"

He almost smiled in return and noticed the envelope. "I'll try."

"I've gotta run. Could you hand this to that gentleman over there in the corner? I don't want to interrupt him."

The deputy squinted in the direction she was pointing, across the courtroom. "Which one?"

"The heavyset man in the middle, with the goatee, dark suit."

At this moment, the bailiff entered from behind the bench and shouted, "Court come to order!"

"What's his name?" the deputy asked, his voice lower.

She handed him the envelope and pointed to the name on it. "Rankin Fitch. Thanks." She patted him on the arm and vanished from the courtroom.

Fitch leaned down the row and whispered something to an associate, then made his way to the rear of the courtroom as the jury returned. He'd seen enough for one day. Fitch typically spent little time in the courtroom once the juries were selected. He had other means of monitoring the trial.

The deputy stopped him at the door and handed him the envelope. Fitch was startled to see his name in print. He was an unknown, a nameless shadow who introduced himself to no one and lived under an assumed name. His D.C. firm was called Arlington West Associates, about as bland and nondescript as he could imagine. No one knew his name—except of course his employees, his clients, and a few of the lawyers he hired. He glared at the deputy without muttering a "Thank you," then stepped into the atrium, still staring in disbelief at the envelope. The printed letters were no doubt from a feminine hand. He slowly opened it, and removed a single sheet of white paper. Printed neatly in the center was a note: "Dear Mr. Fitch: Tomorrow, juror number two, Easter, will wear a gray pullover golf shirt with red trim, starched khakis, white socks, and brown leather shoes, lace-up."

José the driver sauntered over from a water fountain and stood like an obedient watchdog beside his boss. Fitch reread the note, then looked blankly at José. He walked to the door, opened it slightly, and asked the deputy to step outside the courtroom.

"What's the matter?" the deputy asked. His position was inside, against the door, and he was a man who followed orders.

"Who gave you this?" Fitch asked as nicely as was possible for him. The two deputies manning the metal detector were watching curiously.

"A woman. I don't know her name."

"When did she give it to you?"

"Just before you left. Just a minute ago."

With that, Fitch looked quickly around. "Do you see her here?"

"Nope," he answered after a cursory look.

"Can you describe her for me?"

He was a cop, and cops are trained to notice things. "Sure. Late twenties. Five six, maybe five seven. Short brown hair. Brown eyes. Pretty damned good-looking. Slim."

"What was she wearing?"

He hadn't noticed, but he couldn't admit it. "Uhm, a light-colored dress, sort of a beige, cotton, buttons down the front."

Fitch absorbed this, thought a second, asked, "What did she say to you?"

"Not much. Just asked me to hand this to you. Then she was gone."

"Anything unusual about the way she talked?"

"No. Look, I need to get back inside."

"Sure. Thanks."

Fitch and José descended the steps and roamed the corridors of the first floor. They walked outside and strolled around the court-house, both smoking and acting as if they were out for a bit of fresh air.

THE VIDEO DEPOSITION of Jacob Wood had taken two and a half days to complete while he was alive. Judge Harkin, after editing the fights among the lawyers, the interruptions of the nurses, and the irrelevant portions of testimony, had pared it down nicely to a mere two hours and thirty-one minutes.

It seemed like days. Listening to the poor man give his personal history of smoking was interesting, to a point, but the jurors soon wished Harkin had cut more. Jacob started smoking Redtops at the age of sixteen because all of his buddies smoked Redtops. He soon had the habit and was up to two packs a day. He quit Redtops when he left the Navy because he got married, and his wife convinced him to smoke something with a filter. She wanted him to quit. He couldn't, so he started smoking Bristols because the ads claimed lower tar and nicotine. By the age of twenty-five he was smoking three packs a day. He remembered this well because their first child was born when Jacob was twenty-five, and Celeste Wood warned him he wouldn't live to see his grandchildren if he didn't stop smoking. She refused to buy cigarettes when she shopped, so Jacob did it himself. He averaged two cartons a week, twenty packs, and he usually picked up another pack or two until he could purchase by the carton.

He'd been desperate to quit. He once put 'em down for two

weeks, then sneaked out of bed at night to start again. He'd cut back a few times; to two packs a day, then to one pack a day, then before he knew it he was back to three. He'd been to doctors and he'd been to hypnotists. He tried acupuncture and nicotine gum. But he simply couldn't stop. He couldn't after he was diagnosed with emphysema, and he couldn't after he was told he had lung cancer.

It was the dumbest thing he'd ever done, and now at the age of fifty-one, he was dying for it. Please, he implored between coughs, if you're smoking, stop.

Jerry Fernandez and Poodle glanced at each other.

Jacob turned melancholy when he talked about the things he'd miss. His wife, kids, grandkids, friends, trolling for redfish around Ship Island, etc. Celeste started crying softly next to Rohr, and before long Millie Dupree, number three, next to Nicholas Easter, was rubbing her eyes with a Kleenex.

Finally, the first witness spoke his last words and the monitors went blank. His Honor thanked the jury for a fine first day, and promised more of the same tomorrow. He turned serious and launched into a dire warning against discussing this case with anyone, not even a spouse. Also, and more importantly, if anyone in any way tried to initiate contact with a juror, please report it immediately. He hammered them on this point for a good ten minutes, then dismissed them until 9 A.M.

FITCH HAD TOYED with the idea of entering Easter's apartment before, but now it was necessary. And it was easy. He sent José and an operative named Doyle to the apartment building where Easter lived. Easter, of course, was at the time confined to the jury box and suffering along with Jacob Wood. He was being watched closely by two of Fitch's men, just in case court was suddenly adjourned.

José stayed in the car, near the phone, and watched the front entryway as Doyle disappeared inside. Doyle walked up one flight of stairs and found Apartment 312 at the end of a semi-lit hallway. There was not a sound from the neighboring apartments. Everyone was at work.

He shook the loose-fitting doorknob, then held it firmly as he slid an eight-inch plastic strip down the facing. The lock clicked, the knob turned. He gently pushed the door open two inches, and waited for the alarm to either beep or sound. Nothing. The apartment building was old and low-rent, and the fact that Easter had no alarm system didn't surprise Doyle.

He was inside in an instant. Using a small camera with a flash attachment, he quickly photographed the kitchen, den, bathroom, and bedroom. He took close-ups of the magazines on the cheap coffee table, the books stacked on the floor, the CD's on top of the stereo, and the software littered around the rather fancy PC. Being careful what he touched, he found a gray pullover golf shirt with red trim hanging in the closet, and took a photo of it. He opened the refrigerator and took a photo of the contents, then the cabinets and under the sink.

The apartment was small and cheaply furnished, but an effort was being made to keep it clean. The air conditioning was either turned off or out of order. Doyle photographed the thermostat. He was in the apartment less than ten minutes, long enough to shoot two rolls of film and determine that Easter in fact lived alone. There was clearly no trace of another person, especially a female.

He carefully locked the door and silently left the apartment. Ten minutes later, he was in Fitch's office.

Nicholas left the courthouse on foot, and stopped, coincidentally, at O'Reilly's Deli on the Vieux Marche, where he purchased a half-pound of smoked turkey and a container of pasta salad. He took his time walking home, no doubt enjoying the sunshine after a day inside. He bought a bottle of cold mineral water at a corner grocery and drank it as he walked. He watched some black kids play a fierce game of basketball in a church parking lot. He ducked through a small park, and for a moment almost lost his shadow. But he exited on the other side, still sipping the water and now certain he was being followed. One of Fitch's goons, Pang, a small Asian with a baseball cap, had nearly panicked in the park. Nicholas had seen him through a row of elevated boxwoods.

At his apartment door, he removed a small keypad and punched in the four-digit code. The tiny red light turned green, and he unlocked the door.

The surveillance camera was hidden in an air vent directly above the refrigerator, and from its silent perch had a complete view of the kitchen, den, and door to the bedroom. Nicholas went straight to his computer, and within seconds determined that, first, no one had attempted to turn it on, and, second, that an UAEA—unauthorized entry/apartment—had occurred at exactly 4:52 P.M.

He took a deep breath, glanced around, and decided to inspect the place. He expected to find no evidence of entry. The door appeared no different, the knob loose and easy to force open. The kitchen and den were precisely as he'd left them. His only assets— the stereo and CD's, the TV, the computer—appeared untouched. In the bedroom, he found no evidence of either a burglar or a crime. Back at the computer, he held his breath and waited for the show. He went through a series of files, found the correct program, then stopped the surveillance video. He punched two keys to rewind it, then sent it to four fifty-two. *Voilà!* In black and white, on the sixteen-inch monitor, the apartment door opened, and the camera turned directly to it. A narrow crack, as his visitor waited for the alarm to shriek. No alarm, then the door opened and a man entered. Nicholas stopped the video and stared at the face on his monitor. He'd never seen him before.

The video continued as the man rapidly pulled a camera from his pocket and began flashing away. He nosed around the apartment, disappeared for a moment in the bedroom, where he continued to take photos. He studied the computer for a moment, but didn't touch it. Nicholas smiled at this. His computer was impossible to enter. This thug couldn't find the power switch.

He was in the apartment for nine minutes and thirteen seconds, and Nicholas could only speculate on why he came today. His best guess was that Fitch knew the apartment would be empty until court adjourned.

The visit was not frightening, but rather expected. Nicholas watched the video again, chuckled to himself, then saved it for future use.

Seven

FITCH HIMSELF was sitting in the back of the surveillance van at eight the next morning when Nicholas Easter walked into the sunshine and looked around the parking lot. The van had a plumber's logo on the door and a fake phone number stenciled in green. "There he is," Doyle announced and they all jumped. Fitch grabbed the scope, focused it quickly through a blackened porthole, and said, "Damn."

"What is it?" asked Pang, the Korean technician who had pursued Nicholas yesterday.

Fitch leaned toward the round window, his mouth open, top lip curled upward. "I'll be damned. Gray pullover, khakis, white socks, brown leather shoes."

"Same shirt in the photo?" Doyle asked.

"Yep."

Pang pressed a button on a portable radio and alerted another shadow two blocks away. Easter was on foot, probably headed in the general direction of the courthouse.

He bought a large cup of black coffee and a newspaper at the same corner grocery, and sat in the same park for twenty minutes scanning the news. He wore dark sunglasses and noticed anyone who walked nearby.

Fitch went straight to his office down the street from the courthouse and huddled with Doyle, Pang, and an ex-FBI agent named Swanson. "We have to find the girl," Fitch said over and over. A plan was devised to keep one person in the back row of the court-room, one outside near the top of the stairs, one near the soft-drink machines on the first floor, and one outside with a radio. They would change posts with every recess. The flimsy description of her was passed around. Fitch decided to sit exactly where he'd sat yesterday, and go through the same motions.

Swanson, an expert on surveillance, was unsure of all the fuss. "It won't work," he said.

"Why not?" Fitch demanded.

"Because she'll find you. She has something she wants to talk about, so she'll make the next move."

"Maybe. But I wanna know who she is."

"Relax. She'll find you."

Fitch argued with him until almost nine o'clock, then walked briskly back to the courthouse. Doyle talked to the deputy, and persuaded him to point out the girl if she happened to appear again.

NICHOLAS had selected Rikki Coleman to chat with over coffee and croissants Friday morning. She was thirty and cute, married with two young children, and worked as a records administrator in a private hospital in Gulfport. She was a health nut who avoided caffeine, alcohol, and, of course, nicotine. Her flaxen hair was short, cut like a boy's, and her pretty blue eyes looked even cuter behind designer frames. She was sitting in a corner, sipping an orange juice and reading USA Today, when Nicholas zeroed in and said, "Good morning. I don't think we officially met yester-day."

She smiled, something she did easily, and offered a hand. "Rikki Coleman."

"Nicholas Easter. Nice to meet you."

"Thanks for lunch yesterday," she said with a quick laugh.

"Don't mention it. Can I sit down?" he asked, nodding at a folding chair next to her.

"Sure." She laid the paper in her lap.

All twelve jurors were accounted for, and most were engaged in quiet pockets of early morning chatter. Herman Grimes sat alone at the table, in his beloved head chair, holding his coffee with both hands and no doubt listening for wayward words about the trial. Lonnie Shaver also sat alone at the table, his eyes poring over computer printouts from his supermarket. Jerry Fernandez had gone down the hall for a quick smoke with the Poodle.

"So how's jury service?" Nicholas asked.

"Overrated."

"Did anyone attempt to bribe you last night?"

"No. You?"

"No. It's too bad, because Judge Harkin will be terribly disappointed if no one tries to bribe us."

"Why does he go on about this unauthorized contact?"

Nicholas leaned forward a bit, though not too close. She leaned too and cast a wary eye at the Foreman as if he could see them. They enjoyed the closeness and privacy of their little chat, the way two physically attractive people are sometimes drawn to one another. Just a little harmless flirting. "It's happened before. Several times," he said, almost in a whisper. Laughter erupted by the coffeepots as Mrs. Gladys Card and Mrs. Stella Hulic found something funny in the local paper.

"What's happened before?" Rikki asked.

"Contaminated juries in tobacco cases. In fact, it almost always happens, usually at the hands of the defense."

"I don't understand," she said, believing all and wanting much more information from the guy with two years of law school under his belt.

"There have been several of these cases around the country, and the tobacco industry has yet to get hit with a verdict. They pay millions for defense because they can't afford to lose the first time. One big plaintiff's verdict, and the floodgates open." He paused, looked around, and sipped his coffee. "So, they use all sorts of dirty tricks."

"Such as?"

"Such as offering money to family members of jurors. Such as spreading rumors in the community that the deceased, whoever he was, had four girlfriends, beat his wife, stole from his friends, went to church only for funerals, and had a homosexual son."

She frowned in disbelief, so he continued. "It's true, and it's well known in legal circles. Judge Harkin knows it, I'm sure, that's why we're getting the warnings."

"Can't they be stopped?"

"Not yet. They're very smart, and shrewd, and crooked, and

they leave no trail. Plus, they have millions." He paused as she studied him. "They watched you before jury selection."

"No!"

"Of course they did. It's standard procedure in big trials. The law forbids them to directly contact any prospective juror before selection, so they do everything else. They probably photographed your house, car, kids, husband, place of employment. They might have talked to co-workers, or eavesdropped on conversations at the office or wherever you eat lunch. You never know."

She set her orange juice on a windowsill. "That sounds illegal, or unethical, or something."

"Something. But they got by with it because you had no idea they were doing it."

"But you knew?"

"Yep. I saw a photographer in a car outside my apartment. And they sent a woman into the store where I work to pick a fight over our no-smoking policy. I knew exactly what they were doing."

"But you said direct contact was prohibited."

"Yes, but I didn't say they played fair. Just the opposite. They'll break any rule to win."

"Why didn't you tell the Judge?"

"Because it was harmless, and because I knew what they were doing. Now that I'm on the jury, I'm watching every move."

With her curiosity piqued, Nicholas thought it best to save more dirt for later. He glanced at his watch and abruptly stood. "I think I'll run to the boys' room before we get back in the box."

Lou Dell burst into the room, rattling the door on its hinges. "Time to go," she said firmly, not unlike a counselor at camp with much less authority than she assumed.

The crowd had thinned to about half of yesterday's number. Nicholas scanned the spectators as the jurors sat and adjusted themselves on the worn cushions. Fitch, predictably, was sitting in the same spot, now with his head partially behind a newspaper as if he couldn't care less about the jury; couldn't give a damn what Easter was wearing. He'd stare later. The reporters had all but vanished, though they'd trickle in during the day. The Wall Street types looked to be thoroughly bored already; all were young, fresh college grads sent South because they were rookies and their bosses had better things to do. Mrs. Herman Grimes held her same position, and Nicholas wondered if she'd be there every day, hearing everything and ever ready to help her husband cast his lot.

Nicholas fully expected to see the man who'd entered his apartment, maybe not today, but at some point during the trial. The man was not in the courtroom at the moment.

"Good morning," Judge Harkin said warmly to the jury when everyone was still. Smiles everywhere: from the Judge, the clerks—even the lawyers, who had stopped their huddling and whispering long enough to look at the jury with phony grins. "I trust everyone is well today." He paused and waited for fifteen faces to nod awkwardly. "Good. Madam Clerk has informed me that everyone is ready for a full day." It was hard to picture Lou Dell as Madam anything.

His Honor then lifted a sheet of paper which contained a list of questions the jurors would learn to hate. He cleared his voice and stopped smiling. "Now, ladies and gentlemen of the jury. I'm about to ask you a series of questions, very important questions, and I want you to respond if you feel the slightest need to. Also, I'd like to remind you that your failure to respond, if a response is in order, could be deemed by me as an act of contempt, punishable by a jail term."

He allowed this grievous warning to float around the courtroom; the jurors felt guilty just for receiving it. Convinced he'd found his mark, he then started the questions: Did anyone attempt to discuss this trial with you? Did you receive any unusual phone calls since we adjourned yesterday? Did you see any strangers watching you or any members of your family? Did you hear any rumors or gossip about any of the parties in the trial? Any of the lawyers? Any of the witnesses? Did any person contact any of your friends or family members in an effort to discuss this trial? Did any friend or family member attempt to discuss this trial with you since yesterday's adjournment? Did you see or receive any piece of written material which in any way mentioned anything to do with this trial?

Between each question in this script, the Judge would stop, look hopefully at each juror, then seemingly with disappointment, return to his list.

What struck the jurors as odd was the air of expectation surrounding the questions. The lawyers hung on every word, certain that damning responses were forthcoming from the panel. The clerks, usually busy shuffling papers or exhibits or doing a dozen things unrelated to the trial, were completely still and watching to see which juror would confess. The Judge's glowering face and arched eyebrows after each question challenged the integrity of every juror, and he took their silence as nothing short of deceit.

When he finished, he quietly said, "Thank you," and the courtroom seemed to breathe. The jurors felt assaulted. His Honor sipped coffee from a tall cup and smiled at Wendall Rohr. "Call your next witness, Counselor."

Rohr stood, a large brown stain in the center of his wrinkled white shirt, bow tie as crooked as ever, shoes scuffed and getting dirtier by the day. He nodded and smiled warmly at the jurors, and they couldn't help but smile at him.

Rohr had a jury consultant assigned to record everything the jurors wore. If one of the five men happened to wear cowboy boots one day, then Rohr had an old pair at the ready. Two pairs actually—pointed toe or round. He was prepared to wear sneakers if the time was right. He'd done so once before when sneakers appeared in the jury box. The Judge, not Harkin, had complained in chambers. Rohr had a foot ailment, he'd explained, and had produced a letter from his podiatrist. He could wear starched khakis, knit ties, polyester sports coats, cowboy belts, white socks, penny loafers (either shined or battered). His eclectic wardrobe was designed to connect with those now forced to sit nearby and listen to him for six hours a day.

"We'd like to call Dr. Milton Fricke," he announced.

Dr. Fricke was sworn and seated and the bailiff adjusted his microphone. It was soon learned that his résumé could be measured by the pound—lots of degrees from many schools, hundreds of published articles, seventeen books, years of teaching experience, decades of research into the effects of tobacco smoke. He was a small man with a perfectly round face with black horn-rimmed glasses; he looked like a genius. It took Rohr almost an hour to cover his astounding collection of credentials. When Fricke was finally tendered as an expert, Durr Cable wanted no part of him. "We stipulate that Dr. Fricke is qualified in his field," Cable said, in what sounded like a major understatement.

His field had been narrowed over the years, so that Dr. Fricke now spent ten hours a day studying the effects of tobacco smoke on the human body. He was the director of the Smoke Free Research Institute in Rochester, New York. The jury soon learned that he had been hired by Rohr before Jacob Wood died, and that he had been present during an autopsy performed on Mr. Wood four hours after his death. And that he had taken some photos of the autopsy.

Rohr emphasized the existence of the photos, leaving no doubt that the jurors would see them eventually. But Rohr was not ready yet. He needed to spend time with this extraordinary expert on the chemistry and pharmacology of smoking. Fricke proved quite the professor. He treaded cautiously through ponderous medical and scientific studies, weeding out the big words and giving the jurors what they could understand. He was relaxed and thoroughly confident.

When His Honor announced the lunch recess, Rohr informed the court that Dr. Fricke would be on the stand for the remainder of the day.

Lunch was waiting in the jury room, with Mr. O'Reilly himself in charge of its presentation and readily offering apologies for what had happened the day before.

"These are paper plates and plastic forks," Nicholas said as they took their seats around the table. He did not sit. Mr. O'Reilly looked at Lou Dell, who said, "So?"

"So, we specifically said we wanted to eat on real china with real forks. Didn't we say that?" His voice was rising, and a few of the jurors looked away. They just wanted to eat.

"What's wrong with paper plates?" Lou Dell asked nervously, her bangs shaking.

"They soak up grease, okay? They get spongy and leave stains on the table, you understand? That's why I specifically asked for real plates. And real forks." He took a white plastic fork, snapped it in two, and threw it in a waste can. "And what really makes me mad, Lou Dell, is that right now the Judge and all the lawyers and their clients and the witnesses and the clerks and the spectators and everybody else involved with this trial are sitting down to a nice lunch in a nice restaurant with real plates and real glasses and forks that don't snap in two. And they're ordering good food from a thick menu. That's what makes me mad. And we, the jurors, the most important people of the whole damned trial, we're stuck here like first-graders waiting to be fed our cookies and lemonade."

"The food's pretty good," Mr. O'Reilly said in self-defense.

"I think you're overdoing it a bit," said Mrs. Gladys Card, a prim little lady with white hair and a sweet voice.

"Then eat your soggy sandwich and stay out of this," Nicholas snapped, much too harshly.

"Are you gonna show your ass every day at lunch?" asked Frank Herrera, a retired colonel from somewhere up North. Herrera was short and portly with tiny hands and an opinion, so far, on just about everything. He was the only one who was truly disappointed when he wasn't elected foreman.

Jerry Fernandez had already nicknamed him Napoleon. Nap for short. The Retarded Colonel as an alternative.

"There were no complaints yesterday," Nicholas shot back.

"Let's eat. I'm starving," Herrera said, unwrapping a sandwich. A few of the others did the same.

The aroma of baked chicken and french fries rose from the table. As Mr. O'Reilly finished unpacking a container of pasta salad, he said, "I'll be happy to bring over some plates and forks on Monday. No problem."

Nicholas quietly said, "Thanks," and sat down.

THE DEAL was an easy one to make. The details were wrapped up between two old friends over a three-hour lunch at the '21' Club on Fifty-second. Luther Vandemeer, CEO of Trellco, and his former protégé, Larry Zell, now CEO of Listing Foods, had discussed the basics on the phone, but needed to meet face-to-face over food and wine so no one could hear them. Vandemeer gave him the background of the latest serious threat down in Biloxi, and didn't hide the truth that he was worried. Sure, Trellco was not a named defendant, but the entire industry was under fire and the Big Four was standing firm. Zell knew this. He'd worked for Trellco for seventeen years, and had learned to hate trial lawyers a long time ago.

There was a small regional grocery chain, Hadley Brothers, out of Pensacola, which just happened to own a few stores along the Mississippi Coast. One such store was in Biloxi, and its manager was a sharp young black man named Lonnie Shaver. Lonnie Shaver just happened to be on the jury down there. Vandemeer wanted SuperHouse, a much larger grocery chain in Georgia and the Carolinas, to purchase, at whatever premium necessary, Hadley Brothers. SuperHouse was one of twenty or so divisions of Listing Foods. It would be a small transaction—Vandemeer's people had already done the numbers—and would cost Listing no more than six million. Hadley Brothers was privately owned, so the deal would create virtually no attention. Listing Foods had grossed two billion last year, so six million was no sweat. The company had eighty million in cash and little debt. And to sweeten the deal, Vandemeer promised that Trellco would quietly purchase Hadley Brothers in two years if Zell wished to unload it.

Nothing could go wrong. Listing and Trellco were totally independent of each other. Listing was already in the business of owning grocery chains. Trellco was not directly involved in the litigation down there. It was a simple handshake deal between two old friends.

Later, of course, there would need to be a personnel shakeup within Hadley Brothers, one of the usual realignments inherent in any buyout or merger or whatever it was to be called. Vandemeer would need to pass along some instructions for Zell to send down the line until the right amount of pressure could be placed on Lonnie Shaver.

And it needed to be done quickly. The trial was scheduled to last for four more weeks. Week one would end in just a few hours.

After a brief nap in his office in downtown Manhattan, Luther Vandemeer called the number in Biloxi and left a message for Rankin Fitch to call him in the Hamptons over the weekend.

FITCH'S OFFICE was in the back of an empty store, a five-and-dime that had closed years earlier. The rent was low, parking was plentiful, no one noticed the place, and it was just a short walk from the courthouse. There were five large rooms, all hastily built with unpainted plywood walls; the sawdust was still on the floor. The furniture was cheap, rented, and consisted primarily of folding tables and plastic chairs. The lighting was fluorescent and plentiful. The outer doors were heavily secured. Two men with guns guarded the suite at all times.

If pennies had been pinched throwing the place together, nothing had been spared in getting it plugged in. Computers and monitors were everywhere. Wires to faxes and copiers and phones ran over the floor in no apparent design. Fitch had the latest technology, and he had the people to operate it.

The walls of one room were covered with large photos of the fifteen jurors. Computer printouts were tacked to another wall. A huge seating chart was on another wall, and an employee was adding data to the block under Gladys Card's name.

The room in the back was the smallest, and it was strictly off-limits for the regular employees, though they all knew what was happening in it. The door locked automatically from the inside, and Fitch had the only key. It was a viewing room, with no windows, a large screen on one wall, and half a dozen comfortable chairs. Friday afternoon, Fitch and two jury experts sat in the dark and stared at the screen. The experts preferred not to engage in small talk with Fitch, and Fitch wasn't about to entertain them. Silence.

The camera was a Yumara XLT-2, a tiny unit capable of fitting almost anywhere. The lens was half an inch in diameter, and the camera itself weighed less than a pound. It had been meticulously installed by one of Fitch's boys, and was now situated in a well-worn brown leather satchel sitting on the floor in the courtroom under the defense table, and being covertly guarded by Oliver McAdoo, a lawyer from Washington and the only foreigner selected by Fitch to sit alongside Cable and the rest. McAdoo's job was to think strategy, smile at the jurors, and feed documents to Cable. His real job, known only to Fitch and a few others, was to walk into the courtroom each day, heavily laden with the tools of warfare, including two large, identical brown briefcases, one of which held the camera, and to sit at approximately the same spot at the defense table. He was the first defense lawyer in the courtroom each morning. He would set the satchel upright, aim it at the jury box, then quickly call Fitch on a cellphone to get things adjusted.

At any given moment during the trial, there were twenty or so briefcases scattered through the courtroom, most congregated on or under the counsel tables, but some were stacked together near the clerk's bench, some were under chairs where the lower-tier lawyers labored, some were even leaning against the bar, seemingly abandoned. While they varied in size and color, as a collection they all looked pretty much the same, including McAdoo's. One he opened occasionally to retrieve papers, but the other, the one holding the camera, was locked so tight that explosives would be required to open it. Fitch's strategy was simple—if, for some unimaginable reason, the camera attracted attention, then in the ensuing fracas McAdoo would simply switch briefcases and hope for the best.

Detection was extremely remote. The camera made no noise and sent signals no human could hear. The briefcase sat near several others, and it occasionally got itself jostled or even kicked over, but readjustment was easy. McAdoo would simply find a quiet spot and call Fitch. They'd perfected the system during the Cimmino trial last year in Allentown.

The technology was amazing. The tiny lens captured the width and depth of the jury box, and sent all fifteen faces, in color, down the street to Fitch's little viewing room where two jury consultants sat throughout the day and studied every slight twitch and yawn.

Depending on what was happening in the jury box, Fitch would then chat with Durr Cable, and tell him their people in the courtroom had picked up on this and that. Neither Cable nor any of the local defense lawyers would ever know about the camera.

The camera recorded dramatic responses Friday afternoon. Unfortunately, it was frozen on the jury box. The Japanese had yet to design one that could scan from inside a locked briefcase and focus on other points of interest. So the camera couldn't see the enlarged photos of the shriveled, blackened lungs of Jacob Wood, but the jurors certainly saw them. As Rohr and Dr. Fricke worked through their script, the jurors, without exception, gawked with unrestrained horror at the ghastly wounds slowly inflicted over thirty-five years.

Rohr's timing was perfect. The two photos were mounted on a large tripod in front of the witness stand, and when Dr. Fricke finished his testimony at fifteen minutes after five, it was time to adjourn for the weekend. The last image the jurors had, the one they'd think about for the next two days and the one that would prove to be unshakable, was of the charred lungs, removed from the body and posed on a white sheet.

Eight

EASTER LAID AN EASY TRAIL to follow throughout the weekend. He left the courtroom Friday, and walked again to O'Reilly's Deli, where he had a quiet conversation with Mr. O'Reilly. They could be seen smiling. Easter purchased a sack full of food and a tall beverage. He then walked straight to his apartment and didn't leave. At eight Saturday morning, he drove to the mall, where he worked a twelve-hour shift selling computers and gadgets. He ate tacos and fried beans in the food garden with a teenager named Kevin, a co-worker. There was no visible communication with any female who remotely resembled the girl they were looking for. He returned to his apartment after work, and didn't leave.

Sunday brought a pleasant surprise. At 8 A.M., he left his apartment and drove to the Biloxi small-craft harbor, where he met none other than Jerry Fernandez. They were last seen leaving the pier in a thirty-foot fishing boat with two others, presumably friends of Jerry's. They returned eight and a half hours later with red faces, a large cooler of some undetermined species of saltwater fish, and a boat full of empty beer cans.

The fishing was the first discernible hobby of Nicholas Easter. And Jerry was the first friend they'd been able to discover.

There was no sign of the girl, not that Fitch really expected to find her. She was proving to be quite patient, and this in itself was maddening. Her first little clue was most assuredly a setup for the second, and the third. The waiting was a torment.

However, Swanson, the ex-FBI agent, was now convinced she would reveal herself to them within the week. Her scheme, whatever it was, was predicated on more contact.

She waited only until Monday morning, thirty minutes before the trial resumed. The lawyers were already in place, plotting in small groups around the courtroom. Judge Harkin was in chambers dealing with an emergency matter in a criminal case. The jurors were gathering in the jury room. Fitch was down the street in his office, in his command bunker. An assistant, a young man named Konrad, who was a whiz with phones, wires, tapes, and high-tech surveillance gadgets, stepped through the open door and said, "There's a phone call you might want to take."

Fitch, as always, stared at Konrad and instantly analyzed the situation. All of his phone calls, even from his trusted secretary in Washington, were taken at the front desk and cleared to him by use of an intercom system built into the phones. It worked this way every time.

"Why?" he asked with a great deal of suspicion.

"She says she has another message for you."

"Her name?"

"She won't say. She's very coy, but she insists it's important."

Another long pause as Fitch looked at the blinking light on one of the phones. "Any idea how she got the number?"

"No."

"Are you tracing it?"

"Yes. Give us a minute. Keep her on the line."

Fitch punched the button and lifted the receiver. "Yeah," he said as nicely as possible.

"Is this Mr. Fitch?" she asked, quite pleasantly.

"It is. And who is this?"

"Marlee."

A name! He paused a second. Every phone call was automatically recorded, so he could analyze it later. "Good morning, Marlee. And do you have a last name?"

"Yeah. Juror number twelve, Fernandez, will walk into the courtroom in about twenty minutes holding a copy of *Sports Illustrated*. It's the October 12 issue with Dan Marino on the cover."

"I see," he said as if he were taking notes. "Anything else?"

"Nope. Not now."

"And when might you call again?"

"Don't know."

"How'd you get the phone number?"

"Easy. Remember, number twelve, Fernandez." There was a click, and she was gone. Fitch punched another button, then a two-digit code. The entire conversation was replayed on a speaker above the phones.

Konrad raced in with a printout. "Came from a pay phone in Gulfport, a convenience store."

"What a surprise," Fitch said as he grabbed his jacket and began straightening his tie. "Guess I'll run to court."

NICHOLAS WAITED until most of his colleagues were either sitting at the table or standing nearby, and he waited until there was a lull in the chatter. He said loudly, "Well, did anyone get bribed or stalked over the weekend?" There were some grins and light laughs but no confessions.

"My vote's not for sale, but it can certainly be rented," said Jerry Fernandez, repeating a punchline he'd heard from Nicholas on the fishing boat yesterday. This was humorous to everyone but Herman Grimes.

"Why does he keep lecturing us like that?" asked Millie Dupree, obviously delighted someone had broken the ice and anxious to start the gossip. Others moved in closer and leaned forward to hear what the ex–law student thought about it. Rikki Coleman stayed in the corner with a newspaper. She'd already heard this.

"These cases have been tried before," Nicholas explained reluctantly. "And there have been some shenanigans with the juries."

"I don't think we should discuss this," Herman said.

"Why not? It's harmless. We're not discussing evidence or testimony." Nicholas was authoritative. Herman was not sure.

"Judge said not to talk about the trial," he protested, waiting for someone to come to his aid. There were no volunteers. Nicholas had the floor, and said, "Relax, Herman. This is not about evidence or the things we'll eventually deliberate over. This is about . . ." He hesitated a second for effect, then continued, "This is about jury tampering."

Lonnie Shaver lowered his computer printout of grocery inventory and eased closer to the table. Rikki was now listening. Jerry Fernandez had heard it all on the boat yesterday, but it was irresistible.

"There was a tobacco trial, a very similar one in Quitman County, Mississippi, about seven years ago, up in the Delta. Some of you may remember it. It was a different tobacco company, but some of the players are the same, on both sides. And there was some pretty outrageous behavior both before the jury was picked and after the trial started. Judge Harkin, of course, has heard all the stories, and he is watching us very closely. Lots of people are watching us."

Millie glanced around the table for a second. "Who?" she asked.

"Both sides." Nicholas had decided to play it fair, because both sides had been guilty of misconduct in the other trials. "Both sides hire these guys called jury consultants, and they come in here from all over the country to help pick the perfect jury. The perfect jury, of course, is not one that will be fair, but one that'll deliver the verdict they want. They study us before we're selected. They—"

"How do they do that?" interrupted Mrs. Gladys Card.

"Well, they photograph our homes and apartments, our cars, our neighborhoods, our offices, our kids and their bikes, even ourselves. This is all legal and ethical, but they come close to crossing the line. They check public records, things such as court files and tax rolls, in an effort to get to know us. They might even talk to our friends and co-workers and neighbors. This happens in every big trial nowadays."

All eleven were listening and staring, inching closer and trying to remember if they'd seen any strangers lurking around corners with cameras. Nicholas took a sip of coffee, then continued: "After the jury is picked, they change gears a little. The panel has been narrowed from two hundred to fifteen, and so we're much easier to watch. Throughout the trial each side will keep a group of jury consultants in the courtroom, watching us and trying to read our reactions. They usually sit on the first two rows, though they move around a lot."

"You know who they are?" Millie asked in disbelief.

"I don't know their names, but they're fairly easy to spot. They're well dressed, and they stare at us constantly."

"I thought those folks were reporters," said Retired Colonel Frank Herrera, unable to ignore the conversation.

"I hadn't noticed," said Herman Grimes, and everyone smiled, even Poodle.

"Watch them today," Nicholas said. "They usually start off behind their respective counsel. In fact, I have a great idea. There's this one woman whom I'm almost positive is a jury consultant for the defense. She's about forty, heavyset with thick short hair. Every morning so far she's been on the front row behind Durwood Cable. When we go out this morning, let's stare at her. All twelve of us, just glare at her real hard and watch her unravel."

"Even me?" Herman asked.

"Yes, Herm, even you. Just turn to ten o'clock, and stare with the rest of us."

"Why are we playing games?" asked Sylvia "Poodle" Taylor-Tatum.

"Why not? What else have we got to do for the next eight hours?"

"I like it," said Jerry Fernandez. "Maybe it'll make 'em stop staring at us."

"How long do we stare?" asked Millie.

"Let's do it while Judge Harkin is reading us the riot act this morning. That'll take ten minutes." They more or less agreed with Nicholas.

Lou Dell came for them at exactly nine, and they left the jury room. Nicholas held two magazines—one of which was the October 12 issue of *Sports Illustrated*. He walked beside Jerry Fernandez until they came to the door leading into the courtroom, and as they began to file in he casually turned to his new friend and said, "Want something to read?"

The magazine was slightly pressing his stomach, so Jerry just as casually took it and said, "Sure, thanks." They walked through the door into the courtroom.

Fitch knew Fernandez, number twelve, would have the magazine, but the sight of it was still a jolt. He watched him shuffle along the back row and take his seat. Fitch had seen the cover on a newsstand four blocks from the courthouse, and he knew it was Marino in the aquamarine jersey, number thirteen, arm cocked and ready to drill one.

The surprise quickly gave way to excitement. The girl Marlee was working the outside while someone on the jury was working the inside. Maybe there were two or three or four on the jury who were conspiring with her. Didn't matter to Fitch. The more the better. These people were setting the table, and Fitch was ready to deal.

The jury consultant's name was Ginger, and she worked for Carl Nussman's firm in Chicago. She had sat through dozens of trials. She usually spent half of each day in the courtroom, changing places during recesses, removing her jacket, removing her eyeglasses. She was an old pro at studying juries, and she'd seen it all. She was on the front row behind the defense lawyers; a colleague sat a few feet down scanning a newspaper as the jury settled in.

Ginger looked at the jury and waited for His Honor to greet them, which he did. Most of the jurors nodded and smiled at the Judge, then all of them, every one of them including the blind man, turned and stared directly at her. A couple had smiles, but most seemed rather perturbed about something.

She looked away.

Judge Harkin trudged through his script—one ominous question after another—and he too quickly noticed that his jury was preoccupied with one of the spectators.

They kept staring, in perfect unison.

Nicholas struggled to keep from howling. His luck was incredible. There were about twenty people sitting on the left side of the courtroom, behind the defense lawyers, and two rows behind Ginger sat the hulking figure of Rankin Fitch. From the jury box, Fitch was in the same line of vision as Ginger, and from fifty feet away it was difficult to tell exactly who the jurors were staring at—Ginger or Fitch.

Ginger certainly thought it was her. She found some notes to study while her colleague scooted farther away.

Fitch felt naked as the twelve faces studied him from the jury box. Small beads of sweat popped through above his eyebrows. The Judge asked more questions. A couple of the lawyers turned awkwardly to look behind them.

"Keep staring," Nicholas said softly without moving his lips.

Wendall Rohr glanced over his shoulder to see who was sitting out there. Ginger's shoelaces caught her attention. They kept staring.

It was unheard of for a trial judge to ask a jury to pay attention. Harkin had been tempted before, but it was usually a juror who'd become so bored with the testimony that he'd fallen asleep and was snoring. And so he raced through the rest of his tampering questions, then loudly said, "Thank you, ladies and gentlemen. Now we will continue with Dr. Milton Fricke."

Ginger suddenly had to visit the ladies' room, and she scurried from the courtroom as Dr. Fricke entered from a side door and resumed his place on the witness stand.

Cable had just a few questions on cross-examination, he said politely, with great deference to Dr. Fricke. He was not about to argue science with a scientist, but he hoped to score a few minor points with the jury. Fricke admitted that not all of the damage to Mr. Wood's lungs could be attributed to smoking Bristols for almost thirty years. Jacob Wood worked in an office for many years with other smokers, and, yes, it's true that some of the destruction of his lungs could have been caused by exposure to other smokers. "But it's still cigarette smoke," Dr. Fricke reminded Cable, who readily agreed.

And what about air pollution? Is it possible that breathing dirty air added to the condition of the lungs? Dr. Fricke admitted that this was certainly a possibility.

Cable asked a dangerous question, and he got by with it. "Dr. Fricke, if you look at all of the possible causes—direct cigarette smoke, indirect cigarette smoke, air pollution, and any others that we've failed to mention—is it possible for you to say how much of the damage to the lungs was caused by smoking Bristols?"

Dr. Fricke concentrated on this for a moment, then said, "The majority of the damage."

"How much—sixty percent, eighty percent? Is it possible for a medical scientist such as yourself to give us an approximate percentage?"

It was not possible, and Cable knew it. He had two experts ready for rebuttal in the event Fricke stepped out of bounds and speculated too much.

"I'm afraid I can't do that," Fricke said.

"Thank you. One final question, Doctor. What percentage of cigarette smokers suffer from lung cancer?"

"Depends on which study you believe."

"You don't know?"

"I have a good idea."

"Then answer the question."

"About ten percent."

"No further questions."

"Dr. Fricke, you are excused," said His Honor. "Mr. Rohr, please call your next witness."

"Dr. Robert Bronsky."

As the witnesses were passing each other in front of the bench, Ginger reentered the courtroom and took a seat on the back row, as far from the jurors as possible. Fitch took advantage of the brief break to leave. He attracted José in the atrium, and they hurried out of the courthouse and back to the dime store.

BRONSKY TOO was a superbly educated medical researcher who had almost as many degrees and published almost as many articles as Fricke. They knew each other well because they worked together at the research center in Rochester. Rohr took great pleasure in walking Bronsky through his marvelous pedigree. Once he was qualified as an expert, they launched into a clinic on the basics:

Tobacco smoke is extremely complex in makeup, with over four thousand compounds identified in its composition. A total of sixteen known carcinogens, fourteen alkalis, and numerous other compounds with known biological activity are included in the four thousand plus compounds. Tobacco smoke is a mixture of gases in tiny droplets, and when a person inhales, about fifty percent of the inhaled smoke is retained in the lungs, and some of the droplets are deposited directly in the walls of the bronchial tubes.

Two lawyers from Rohr's team quickly set up a large tripod in the center of the courtroom, and Dr. Bronsky left the witness stand to lecture a bit. The first chart was a list of all the compounds known to exist in tobacco smoke. He didn't name them all, because he didn't have to. Each of the names looked menacing, and when viewed as a group they looked downright deadly.

The next chart was a list of the known carcinogens, and Bronsky gave each one a brief summary. In addition to these sixteen, he said, tapping his pointing stick in his left hand, there may well be other, yet undetected, carcinogens present in tobacco smoke. And it's quite possible that two or more of these might act in combination to reinforce each other to cause cancer.

They dwelt on the carcinogens for the entire morning. With each new chart, Jerry Fernandez and the other smokers felt sicker and sicker until Sylvia the Poodle was almost light-headed as they left the jury box to eat lunch. Not surprisingly, the four of them first went to the "smoke hole," as Lou Dell called it, for a quick one before they joined the rest to eat.

Lunch was waiting and evidently the wrinkles had been ironed out. The table was set with china and the iced tea was poured into real glasses. Mr. O'Reilly served custom-made sandwiches to those who'd ordered them, and he opened large bowls of steaming vegetables and pasta for the others. Nicholas spared no compliment.

FITCH WAS IN THE VIEWING ROOM with two of his jury people when the call came. Konrad nervously knocked on the door. There were strict orders against getting near the room without authorization from Fitch.

"It's Marlee. Line four," Konrad whispered, and Fitch froze at the news. He then walked quickly to his office door down a makeshift hallway.

"Trace it," he ordered.

"We are."

"I'm sure she's at a pay phone."

Fitch punched button four on his phone, said, "Hello."

"Mr. Fitch?" came the familiar voice.

"Yes."

"Do you know why they were staring at you?"

"No."

"I'll tell you tomorrow."

"Tell me now."

"No. Because you're tracing the call. And if you keep tracing the calls, then I'll stop calling."

"Okay. I'll stop tracing."

"And you expect me to believe you?"

"What do you want?"

"Later, Fitch." She hung up. Fitch replayed the conversation as he waited for her phone to be located. Konrad appeared with the expected news that it was indeed a pay phone, this one in a mall in Gautier, thirty minutes away.

Fitch fell into a large, rented swivel chair and studied the wall for a moment. "She wasn't in the courtroom this morning," he said softly, thinking aloud, tugging at the tip of his goatee. "So how did she know they were staring at me?"

"Who was staring?" asked Konrad. His duties did not include sentry work in the courtroom. He never left the dime store. Fitch explained the curious incident of being stared at by the jury.

"So who's talking to her?" Konrad asked.

"That's the question."

THE AFTERNOON was spent on nicotine. From one-thirty until three, then from three-thirty until adjournment at five, the jurors learned more than they cared to about nicotine: It is a poison contained in tobacco smoke. Each cigarette contains from one to three milligrams of nicotine, and for smokers who inhale, as did Jacob Wood, up to ninety percent of the nicotine is absorbed into the lungs. Dr. Bronsky spent most of his time on his feet, pointing at various parts of the human body displayed in a brightly colored, life-size drawing mounted on the tripod. He explained in great detail how nicotine causes constriction of the superficial vessels in the limbs; it raises the blood pressure; it increases the pulse rate; it makes the heart work harder. Its effects on the digestive tract are insidious and complex. It can cause nausea and vomiting, especially when one begins to smoke. Secretions of saliva and movement of the gut are first stimulated and then depressed. It acts as a stimulant on the central nervous system. Bronsky was methodical yet sincere; he made a single cigarette sound like a dose of lethal poison.

And the worst thing about nicotine is that it's addictive. The last hour—again timed perfectly by Rohr—was spent convincing the jurors that nicotine was wildly addictive, and that this knowledge had been around for at least four decades.

The levels of nicotine can easily be manipulated during the manufacturing process.

If, and Bronsky stressed the word "if," the levels of nicotine were artificially increased, then smokers would naturally become addicted much faster. More addicted smokers means more cigarettes sold.

It was a perfect spot to end the day.

Nine

ON TUESDAY MORNING, Nicholas arrived at the jury room early, as Lou Dell was brewing the first pot of decaf and carefully arranging the daily platter of fresh rolls and dough-nuts. A collection of sparkling new cups and saucers sat near the food. Nicholas claimed to hate coffee from a plastic cup, and fortunately two of his colleagues held similar prejudices. A list of requests had been quickly acceded to by His Honor.

Lou Dell hastily finished her business when he entered the room. He smiled and greeted her pleasantly, but she held a grudge from their earlier skirmishes. He poured coffee and opened a newspaper.

As Nicholas expected, Retired Colonel Frank Herrera arrived shortly after eight, almost a full hour before they were due, clutching two newspapers, one *The Wall Street Journal*. He wanted the room to himself, but managed a smile at Easter.

"Mornin', Colonel," Nicholas said warmly. "You're here early."

"So are you."

"Yeah, I couldn't sleep. Found myself dreaming of nicotine and black lungs." Nicholas studied the sports page.

Herrera stirred his coffee and sat down across the table. "I smoked for ten years in the Army," he said, sitting stiffly, shoul-ders square, chin up, always ready to bolt to attention. "But I had the good sense to quit."

"Some people can't, I guess. Like Jacob Wood."

The Colonel grunted with disgust, and opened a newspaper. For him, the kicking of a bad habit was nothing but a simple act of willpower. Get the head straight, and the body can do anything.

Nicholas turned a page, said, "Why'd you quit?"

"Because it's bad for you. Doesn't take a genius, you know. Cigarettes are deadly. Everybody knows that."

If Herrera had been so blunt on at least two of the pretrial questionnaires, he wouldn't be sitting where he was now. Nicholas remembered the questions well. The fact that Herrera felt so strongly probably meant only one thing: He wanted to be on the jury. He was retired military, probably bored with golf, tired of his wife, looking for something to do, and obviously carrying a grudge about something.

"So you think cigarettes should be outlawed?" Nicholas asked. The question was one he'd posed to the mirror a thousand times, and he had all the right comebacks to all the possible answers.

Herrera slowly placed the newspaper on the table and took a long drink of black coffee. "No. I think people should have more sense than to smoke three packs a day for almost thirty years. What the hell do you expect? Perfect health?" His tone was sarcastic, and left no doubt that he'd walked into jury service with his mind made up.

"When did you become convinced of this?"

"Are you dense? It ain't that hard to figure out."

"Maybe that's your opinion. But you certainly should've expressed yourself during voir dire."

"What's voir dire?"

"The jury selection process. We were asked questions covering these very matters. I don't recall you saying a word."

"Never felt like it."

"You should have."

Herrera's cheeks flushed red, but he hesitated for a second. This guy Easter after all knew the law, or at least knew more than the rest of them. Maybe he had done something wrong. Maybe there was a way Easter could report him and get him bumped from the jury. Maybe he would be held in contempt, sent to jail, or fined.

And then another thought hit him. They weren't supposed to be discussing the case, right? So how could Easter report anything to the Judge? Seemed like Easter would risk getting in trouble himself if he went and repeated anything he heard in the jury room. Herrera relaxed a bit. "Lemme guess. You're gonna push hard for a big verdict, lots of punitives and stuff like that."

"No, Mr. Herrera. Unlike you, I haven't made up my mind. I think we've listened to three witnesses, all for the plaintiff, so there are many yet to come. I think I'll wait until all the evidence is in, from both sides, then I'll try to sort things out. I thought that's what we promised to do."

"Yeah, well, me too. I can be persuaded, you know." He suddenly had an interest in the editorials. The door burst open, and Mr. Herman Grimes entered with his walking stick tapping away in front of him. Lou Dell and Mrs. Grimes followed. Nicholas, as usual, rose to prepare his foreman's coffee, a ritual now.

FITCH STARED at his phones until nine. She'd mentioned a possible call today.

Not only did she play games, but evidently she was not above lying. He had no desire to be stared at again, so he locked his door and walked to the viewing room where two of his jury experts were sitting in the dark, staring at a crooked scene on the wall, waiting for the courtroom adjustment. Someone had kicked McAdoo's briefcase, and the camera was off by ten feet. Jurors one, two, seven, and eight were out of the picture, and only half of Millie Dupree and Rikki Coleman behind her were visible.

The jury had been seated for two minutes, and so McAdoo was pinned to his seat and couldn't use his cellphone. He didn't know some bigfoot under the table had kicked the wrong briefcase. Fitch swore at the screen, then returned to his office where he scribbled a note. He gave it to a well-dressed errand boy, who dashed up the street, entered the courtroom like one of a hundred young associates or paralegals, and slipped the note to the defense table.

The camera inched to the left, and the full jury came into view. McAdoo pushed a bit too hard and cut off half of Jerry Fernandez and Angel Weese, juror number six. Fitch cursed again. He'd wait until the morning recess and get McAdoo on the phone.

DR. BRONSKY was rested and ready for another day of thoughtful discourse on the ravages of tobacco smoke. Having discussed the carcinogens in tobacco smoke, and the nicotine, he was ready to move to the next compounds of medical interest: irritants.

Rohr served up the fat pitches, Bronsky swung from the heels. Tobacco smoke contains a variety of compounds—ammonia, volatile acids, aldehydes, phenols, and ketones—and these have an irritant effect on the mucous membrane. Bronsky once again left the witness stand and walked to a fresh cutaway diagram of the upper torso and head of a human. This showed the jury the respiratory tract, the throat, the bronchial tubes, and the lungs. In this area of the body, tobacco smoke stimulates secretion of mucus. At the same time, it delays the removal of the mucus by retarding the action of the ciliated lining of the bronchial tubes.

Bronsky had been remarkably adept at keeping the medical jargon on a level reachable by the average layman, and he slowed a notch to explain what happens to the bronchial tubes when smoke is inhaled. Two other large, colorful diagrams were mounted in front of the bench, and Bronsky went to work with his pointer. He explained to the jury that the bronchial tubes are lined with a membrane equipped with fine, hairlike fibers called cilia, which move together in waves and control the movement of the mucus on the surface of the membrane. This movement of the cilia acts to free the lungs from virtually all the dust and germs that are inhaled.

Smoking, of course, wreaks havoc with this process. Once Bronsky and Rohr were as certain as they could be that the jurors understood how things were supposed to work, they quickly moved forward to explain just precisely how smoking irritated the filtering process and caused all sorts of damage in the respiratory system.

They went on about mucus and membranes and cilia.

The first visible yawn came from Jerry Fernandez in the back row. He'd spent his Monday night at one of the casinos watching the football game and drinking more than he'd planned. He smoked two packs a day, and he was well aware that the habit was unhealthy. Still, he needed one now.

More yawns followed, and at eleven-thirty, Judge Harkin sent them out for a badly needed two-hour lunch.

The stroll through downtown Biloxi had been Nicholas' idea, one he'd put in a letter to the Judge on Monday. It seemed absurd to keep them confined to a small room all day with no hope of fresh air. It wasn't as if their lives were in jeopardy, or that they'd be assailed by unknown conspirators if let loose on the sidewalks. Just simply put Madam Lou Dell and Willis the guard with another lethargic deputy, give them a route, say, six or eight city blocks, forbid the jurors from speaking to anyone, as usual, and, well, turn them loose for thirty minutes after lunch so the food could settle. It seemed like a harmless idea, and in fact upon further reflection Judge Harkin embraced it as his own.

Nicholas, however, had shown the letter to Lou Dell, and so when lunch was being finished, she was explaining that a walk was planned, thanks to Mr. Easter, who had written the Judge. It seemed such a humble idea to receive such unbridled admiration.

The temperature was in the low eighties, the air clear and fresh, the trees trying their best to turn colors. Lou Dell and Willis led the way while the four smokers—Fernandez, Poodle, Stella Hulic, and Angel Weese—hung at the back thoroughly enjoying the deep inhaling and long exhaling. To hell with Bronsky and his mucus and his membranes, and to hell with Fricke and his gross pictures of Mr. Wood's sticky black lungs. They were outdoors now. The light, salt air, and conditions were perfect for a smoke.

Fitch sent Doyle and a local operative named Joe Boy to take pictures from a distance.

BRONSKY WORE THIN as the afternoon progressed. He lost his talent for keeping things simple, and the jurors lost their struggle to stay tuned. The fancy and obviously expensive charts and diagrams ran together, as did the body parts and compounds and poisons. The opinions of superbly trained and hideously expensive jury consultants were not needed to know that the jurors were bored, that Rohr was engaging in a practice lawyers simply can't avoid—overkill.

His Honor adjourned early, at four, his reason being that two hours were needed to hear some motions and other things not involving the jury. He discharged the jurors with the same dire warnings, admonitions they now had memorized and barely heard. They were delighted to escape.

Lonnie Shaver was particularly thrilled to leave early. He drove straight to his supermarket, ten minutes away, parked in his special place in the rear, and made a quick entrance through the stockroom, secretly hoping to catch a wayward sacker napping by the lettuce. His office was upstairs above the dairy and meats, and from behind a two-way mirror he could see most of the floor.

Lonnie was the only black manager in a chain of seventeen stores. He earned forty thousand dollars a year, with health insurance and an average pension plan, and was due for a raise in three months. He'd also been led to believe he'd be promoted to the level of a district supervisor, assuming his tenure as manager produced satisfactory results. The company was anxious to promote a black, he'd been told, but, of course, none of these commitments were in writing.

His office was always open, and usually occupied with any one of a half-dozen subordinates. An assistant manager greeted him, then nodded toward a door. "We have guests," he said, with a frown.

Lonnie hesitated and looked at the closed door, which led to a large room used for everything—birthday parties, staff meetings, visits from bosses. "Who is it?" he asked.

"Home office. They want to see you."

Lonnie rapped on the door, entering as he knocked. It was, after all, his office. Three men with their sleeves rolled up to their elbows sat at the end of the table, amid a pile of papers and printouts. They stood awkwardly.

"Lonnie, good to see you," said Troy Hadley, son of one of the owners, and the only face Lonnie recognized. They shook hands as Hadley made hasty introductions. The other two men were Ken and Ben; Lonnie wouldn't remember their last names until later. It had been planned that Lonnie would sit at the end of the table, in the chair eagerly vacated by the young Hadley, with Ken on one side and Ben on the other.

Troy started the conversation, and he sounded somewhat nervous. "How's jury duty?"

"A pain."

"Right. Look, Lonnie, the reason we're here is that Ken and Ben are from an outfit called SuperHouse, a large chain out of Charlotte, and, well, for lots of reasons, my dad and my uncle have decided to sell out to SuperHouse. The whole chain. All seventeen stores and the three warehouses."

Lonnie noticed that Ken and Ben were watching him breathe, so he took the news with a straight face, even offered a very slight shrug, as if to say, "So what?" He was, however, finding it hard to swallow. "Why?" he managed to ask.

"Lots of reasons, but I'll give you the top two. My dad is sixty-eight, and Al, as you know, just had surgery. That's number one. Number two is the fact that SuperHouse is offering a very fair price." He rubbed his hands together as if he couldn't wait to spend the new money. "It's just time to sell, Lonnie, pure and simple."

"I'm surprised, I never—"

"You're right. Forty years in the business, from a mom-and-pop fruit stand to a company in five states with sixty million in sales last year. Hard to believe they're throwing in the towel." Troy was not the least bit convincing in his effort at sentiment. Lonnie knew why. He was a witless dunce, a rich kid who played golf every day while trying to project the image of a hard-charging, ass-kicking corporate honcho. His father and his uncle were selling now because in a few short years Troy would take the reins and forty years of toil and prudence would get spent on racing boats and beach property.

There was a pause as Ben and Ken continued staring at Lonnie. One was in his mid-forties with a bad haircut and a pocket liner stuffed with cheap ballpoints. Maybe he was Ben. The other was a little younger, a slim-faced, executive type with better clothes and hard eyes. Lonnie looked at them, and it was obvious it was his turn to say something.

"Will this store be closed?" he asked, almost in defeat.

Troy jumped at the question. "In other words, what happens to you? Well, let me assure you, Lonnie, that I've said all the right things about you, all the truth, and I've recommended that you be kept here in the same position." Either Ben or Ken nodded very slightly. Troy was reaching for his coat. "But that's not my business anymore. I'm gonna step outside for a bit while you guys talk things over." Like a flash, Troy was out of the room.

For some reason his departure brought smiles to Ken and Ben. Lonnie asked, "Do you guys have business cards?"

"Sure," both said, and they pulled cards from pockets and slid them to the end of the table. Ben was the older, Ken the younger.

Ken was also in charge of this meeting. He began, "Just a bit about our company. We're out of Charlotte, with eighty stores in the Carolinas and Georgia. SuperHouse is a division of Listing

Foods, a conglomerate based in Scarsdale with about two billion in sales last year. A public company, traded on NASDAQ. You've probably heard of it. I'm Vice President for Operations for SuperHouse, Ben here is regional VP. We're expanding south and west, and Hadley Brothers looked attractive. That's why we're here."

"So you're keeping the store?"

"Yes, for now, anyway." He glanced at Ben, as if there was a lot more to the answer.

"And what about me?" Lonnie asked.

They actually squirmed, almost in tandem, and Ben removed a ballpoint from his collection. Ken did the talking. "Well, you have to understand, Mr. Shaver—"

"Please call me Lonnie."

"Sure, Lonnie, there are always shakeups along the line when acquisitions occur. Just part of the business. Jobs are lost, jobs are created, jobs are transferred."

"What about my job?" Lonnie pressed. He sensed the worst and was anxious to get it over with.

Ken deliberately picked up a sheet of paper and gave the appearance of reading something. "Well," he said, ruffling the paper, "you have a solid file."

"And very strong recommendations," Ben added helpfully.

"We would like to keep you in place, for now anyway."

"For now? What does that mean?"

Ken slowly returned the paper to the table, and leaned forward on both elbows. "Let's be perfectly candid, Lonnie. We see a future for you with our company."

"And it's a much better company than the one you're with now," Ben added, the tag-team working to perfection. "We offer higher salaries, better benefits, stock options, the works."

"Lonnie, Ben and I are ashamed to admit that our company does not have an African-American in a management position. We, along with our bosses, would like for this to change, immediately. We want it to change with you."

Lonnie studied their faces, and suppressed a thousand questions. In the span of a minute, he'd gone from the brink of unemployment to the prospect of advancement. "I don't have a college degree. There's a limit to—"

"There are no limits," Ken said. "You have two years of junior college, and, if necessary, you can finish your studies. Our company will cover the cost of college."

Lonnie had to smile, as much from relief as from good fortune. He decided to proceed cautiously. He was dealing with strangers. "I'm listening," he said.

Ken had all the answers. "We've studied the personnel at Hadley Brothers, and, well, let's say most of the upper- and mid-management people will soon be looking for work elsewhere. We spotted you, and another young manager from Mobile. We'd like for both of you to come to Charlotte as soon as possible and spend a few days with us. You'll meet our people, learn about our company, and we'll talk about the future. I must warn you, though, you can't spend the rest of your life here in Biloxi if you want to advance. You must be willing to move around."

"I'm willing."

"We thought so. When can we fly you up?"

The image of Lou Dell closing the door on them flashed before his eyes, and he frowned. He breathed deeply, and said with great frustration, "Well, I'm tied up in court right now. Jury duty. I'm sure Troy told you."

Ken and Ben appeared to be confused by this. "It's just a couple of days, isn't it?"

"No. The trial's scheduled for a month, and we're in week two."

"A month?" Ben asked, on cue. "What kind of trial is it?"

"The widow of a dead smoker is suing a tobacco company."

Their reactions were almost identical and left no doubt how they personally felt about such lawsuits.

"I tried to get out of it," Lonnie said in an effort to smooth things.

"A product liability suit?" Ken asked, thoroughly disgusted.

"Yeah, something like that."

"For another three weeks?" Ben asked.

"That's what they say. I can't believe I got stuck," he said, his words trailing away.

There was a long pause in which Ben opened a fresh pack of Bristols and lit one. "Lawsuits," he said bitterly. "We get sued every week by some poor clod who trips and falls and then blames it on the vinegar or the grapes. Last month a bottle of carbonated water exploded at a private party in Rocky Mount.

Guess who sold 'em the water? Guess who got sued last week for ten million? Us and the bottler. Product liability." A long puff, then a quick chew on a thumbnail. Ben was steaming. "Gotta seventy-year-old woman in Athens claiming she wrenched her back when she allegedly reached up high to get a can of furniture polish. Her lawyer says she's entitled to a coupla mill."

Ken stared at Ben as if he wanted him to shut up, but Ben evidently exploded easily when the topic was broached. "Stinkin' lawyers," he said, smoke pouring from his nostrils. "We paid over three million last year for liability insurance, money just thrown away because of all the hungry lawyers circling above."

Ken said, "That's enough."

"Sorry."

"What about the weekends?" Lonnie asked anxiously. "I'm free from Friday afternoon until late Sunday."

"I was just thinking of that. Tell you what we'll do. We'll send one of our planes to get you Saturday morning. We'll fly you and your wife to Charlotte, give you the grand tour of the home office, and we'll introduce you to our bosses. Most of these guys work Saturdays anyway. Can you do it this weekend?"

"Sure."

"Done. I'll arrange the plane."

"You sure there's no conflict with the trial?" Ben asked.

"None that I can foresee."

Ten

AFTER MOVING ALONG with impressive punctuality, the trial hit a snag on Wednesday morning. The defense filed a motion to prohibit the testimony of Dr. Hilo Kilvan, an alleged expert from Montreal in the field of statistical summaries of lung cancer, and a small battle erupted over the motion. Wendall Rohr and his team were particularly enraged at the defense tactic; the defense so far had tried to bar the testimony of every plaintiff's expert. Indeed, the defense had proved quite effective at delaying and attempting to bar everything for four years. Rohr insisted that Cable and his client were once again stalling, and he made an angry plea to Judge Harkin for the imposition of sanctions against the defense. The war over sanctions, with each side demanding monetary penalties from the other and the Judge so far denying same, had been raging almost since the initial suit was filed. As with most large civil cases, the subplot of sanctions often consumed as much time as the real issues.

Rohr ranted and stomped in front of the empty jury box as he explained that this latest motion by the defense was the seventy-first—"count 'em, seventy-one!"—to be filed by the tobacco company seeking to exclude evidence. "We've had motions to exclude evidence of other diseases caused by smoking, motions to prevent evidence of warnings, motions to prevent evidence of advertising, motions to exclude evidence of epidemiological studies and statistical theories, motions to preclude reference to patents not used by the defendant, motions to exclude evidence of subsequent or remedial measures taken by the tobacco company, motions to preclude our evidence of the testing of cigarettes, motions to strike portions of the autopsy report, motions to exclude addiction evidence, motions—"

"I've seen these motions, Mr. Rohr," His Honor interrupted when it appeared as if Rohr might name them all.

Rohr hardly missed a beat. "And, Your Honor, in addition to the seventy-one—count 'em, seventy-one!—motions to exclude evidence, they've filed exactly eighteen motions for continuances."

"I'm very much aware of this, Mr. Rohr. Please move along."

Rohr walked to his cluttered table and was handed a thick brief by an associate. "And, of course, each defense filing is accompanied by one of these damned things," he said loudly as he dropped the brief onto the table. "We don't have time to read these, as you know, because we're too busy preparing for trial. They, on the other hand, have a thousand lawyers billing by the hour and working even as we speak on another harebrained motion, which will, no doubt, weigh six pounds and doubtless take up more of our time."

"Can we get to the merits, Mr. Rohr?"

Rohr didn't hear him. "Since we don't have time to read these, Your Honor, we simply weigh them, and so our rather brief answer goes something like this: 'Please allow this letter memorandum to serve as our response to the defendant's four-and-a-half-pound, typically overdone brief in support of its latest frivolous motion.'"

With the jury out of the courtroom, smiles and manners and pleasant behavior were forgotten by everyone. The strain was evident on the faces of all the players. Even the clerks and the court reporter looked edgy.

Rohr's legendary temper was boiling, but he had long since learned to use it to his advantage. His occasional friend Cable kept his distance without holding his tongue. The spectators were treated to a loosely controlled brawl.

At nine-thirty, His Honor sent word to Lou Dell to inform the jurors that he was finishing up a motion, and the trial would start in a few moments, hopefully by ten. Since this was the first delay in which the jurors were told to wait after being set to go, they took it well. The little groups reconvened themselves, and the idle chitchat of folks waiting against their wishes continued. The divisions were along the lines of sex, not race. The men tended to group together at one end of the room, the women at the other. The smokers came and went. Only Herman Grimes kept the same position, at the head of the table, where he played hunt-and-peck with a laptop braille computer. He had let it be known that he was up until all hours of the morning plowing through the narrative descriptions of Bronsky's diagrams.

The other laptop was plugged into a socket in a corner where Lonnie Shaver had established a makeshift office with three folding chairs. He analyzed printouts of grocery stock, studied inventories, checked a hundred other details, and was generally content to be ignored. He was not unfriendly, just preoccupied.

Frank Herrera sat near the braille computer, poring over the closing quotations in *The Wall Street Journal,* and occasionally chatting with Jerry Fernandez, who sat across the table grappling with the latest Vegas line on Saturday's college games. The only male who enjoyed talking to the women was Nicholas Easter, and on this day he was quietly discussing the case with Loreen Duke, a large jovial black lady who worked as a secretary at Keesler Air Force Base. As juror number one, she sat next to Nicholas, and the two had developed a habit of whispering during the trial, at the expense of almost everybody. Loreen was thirty-five with no husband and two kids, and a nice federal job which she missed not in the least. She had confessed to Nicholas that she could be absent from the office for a year and no one would care. He told her wild stories of bad deeds by the tobacco companies in trials past, and he confessed to her that he had studied tobacco litigation at great length during his two years of law school. Said he dropped out due to financial reasons. Their low voices were carefully gauged to land just outside the ear-range of Herman Grimes, who at the moment was slapping his laptop.

Time passed and at ten Nicholas went to the door and jolted Lou Dell from her paperback. She had no idea when the Judge might send for them, and there was simply nothing she could do.

Nicholas took a seat at the table and began discussing strategy with Herman. It was not fair to keep them locked up during delays such as this, and Nicholas was of the opinion that they should be allowed to leave the building, with escorts, and engage in morning walks, as opposed to those of the noontime variety. It was agreed that Nicholas should put this request in writing, as usual, and present it to Judge Harkin during the noon recess.

AT TEN-THIRTY, they finally walked into the courtroom, the air still heavy with the heat of battle, and the first person Nicholas saw was the man who'd broken into his apartment. He was out there on the third row, plaintiff's side, in a shirt and tie with a newspaper spread before him and resting on the back of the pew in front. He was alone, and he barely looked at the jurors as they took their seats. Nicholas didn't stare; two long glances and the identification was complete.

For all of his guile and cunning, Fitch could do some stupid things. And sending this goon into the courtroom was a risky move with little potential benefit. What was he supposed to see or hear that would not be seen or heard by one of the dozen lawyers, or half-dozen jury consultants, or handful of other flunkies Fitch kept in the courtroom?

Though he was surprised to see the man, Nicholas had already thought about what to do. He had several plans, depending upon where the man surfaced. The courtroom was a surprise, but it took only a minute to sort through things. It was imperative for Judge Harkin to know that one of the thugs he'd been so overly concerned about was now sitting in the courtroom pretending to be just another casual observer. Harkin needed to see the face, because later he would see it on video.

The first witness was Dr. Bronsky, now in his third day but his first on cross-examination by the defense. Sir Durr started slowly, politely, as if in awe of this great expert, and asked a few questions that most of the jurors could have answered. Things changed rapidly. Whereas Cable had been deferential to Dr. Milton Fricke, he was ready to battle Bronsky.

He started with the over four thousand compounds identified in tobacco smoke, picked one seemingly at random, and asked what effect benzol(a)pyrene would have on the lungs. Bronsky said he didn't know, and tried to explain that the damage inflicted by a single compound was impossible to measure. What about the bronchial tubes and the membranes and the cilia? What did benzol(a)pyrene do to them? Bronsky again tried to explain that research could not determine the effect of a single compound in tobacco smoke.

Cable hammered away. He picked another compound and forced Bronsky to admit that he couldn't tell the jury what it would do to lungs or bronchial tubes or membranes. Not specifically, anyway.

Rohr objected, but His Honor overruled on the grounds that it was a cross-examination. Virtually anything relevant or even semirelevant could be thrown at the witness.

Doyle stayed in place, out there on the third row, looking bored and waiting for a chance to leave. His assigned duty was to look for the girl, something he'd been doing for four days now. He'd loitered in the hallway below for hours. He'd spent one full afternoon sitting on a Dr. Pepper crate near the vending machines, chatting with a janitor while watching the front door. He'd consumed gallons of coffee in the small cafés and delis nearby. He and Pang and two others had been hard at work, wasting their time but satisfying their boss.

After four days of sitting in one place for six hours a day, Nicholas had a sense of Fitch's routine. His people, whether the jury consultants or run-of-the-mill operatives, moved around. They used the entire courtroom. They sat in groups and they sat alone. They came and went silently when there were short breaks in the action. They rarely spoke to one another. They would pay strict attention to the witnesses and the jurors, and the next minute they would work crosswords and stare at the windows.

He knew the man would be gone before long.

He scribbled a note, folded it, and convinced Loreen Duke to hold it without reading it. He then convinced her to lean forward, during a pause in the cross-examination when Cable was consulting his notes, and hand it to Willis the deputy, who was standing against the wall guarding the flag. Willis, suddenly awakened, paused a second to collect himself, then realized he was supposed to hand the note to the Judge.

Doyle saw Loreen hand the note over, but he didn't see it originate from Nicholas.

Judge Harkin gathered the note while barely acknowledging it, and slid it across the bench close to his robe as Cable fired another question. Harkin slowly unfolded it. It was from Nicholas Easter, number two, and it said:

Judge:
That man out there, left side, third row from front, on the
aisle, white shirt, blue and green tie, was following me
yesterday. It was the second time I've seen him. Can we find
out who he is?

Nicholas Easter

His Honor looked at Durr Cable before he looked at the spectators. The man was sitting alone, staring back at the bench as if he
knew someone was watching.

This was a new challenge for Frederick Harkin. In fact, at the
moment he couldn't recall an incident even remotely similar. His
options were limited, and the more he pondered the situation the
fewer choices he had. He, too, knew both sides had plenty of
consultants and associates and operatives lurking either in the
courtroom or very nearby. He watched his courtroom closely, and
he noticed a lot of quiet movement by people who had experience
in such trials and didn't want to be noticed. He knew the man was
likely to disappear in an instant.

If Harkin suddenly called a short recess, the man would probably vanish.

This was a terribly exciting moment for the Judge. After all the
tales and rumors and lore from other trials, and after all the seemingly empty admonitions to the jury, there in the courtroom at
this very moment was one of the mystery agents, a sleuth hired by
one side or the other to monitor his jurors.

Courtroom deputies, as a general rule, are uniformed and
armed and normally quite harmless. The younger men are kept on
the streets to battle the elements, and trial duty tends to attract
the seniors bearing down hard on retirement. Judge Harkin
glanced about and his options shrank again.

There was Willis, leaning against the wall near the flag, and it
appeared he had already lapsed into his usual state of semi-
slumber with his mouth open partially at the right corner and
saliva dripping. Down the aisle, directly in front of Harkin but at
least a hundred feet away, Jip and Rasco guarded the main door.
Jip, at the moment, was sitting on the back bench, near the door,
with his reading glasses perched on the end of his beefy nose,
scanning the local paper. He'd had hip surgery two months earlier, found it difficult to stand for long periods, and had received

permission to sit during the proceedings. Rasco was in his late fifties, the youngest of the crew, and was not known for his quick movements. A younger deputy was usually assigned to the main door, but at the moment he was on the atrium side manning the metal detector.

During voir dire, Harkin had requested uniforms everywhere, but after a week of testimony the initial excitement had disappeared. It was now just another tedious civil trial, though one with enormous stakes.

Harkin took the measure of the available troops, and decided against approaching the target. He quickly scribbled a note, held it for a moment while ignoring the man, then slid it to Gloria Lane, the Circuit Clerk, who was at her small desk below the bench, opposite the witness stand. The note indicated the man, instructed Gloria to get a good look at him without being obvious, then to ease away through a side door and go fetch the Sheriff. There were other instructions to the Sheriff, but, unfortunately, they were never needed.

After more than an hour of watching the merciless cross-examination of Dr. Bronsky, Doyle was ready to move. The girl was nowhere in sight; not that he'd expected to find her. He was just following orders. Plus, he didn't like the note-passing around the bench. He quietly gathered his newspaper, and slipped unchallenged from the courtroom. Harkin watched in disbelief. He even grabbed his mounted microphone with his right hand as if he might yell at the man to stop, sit down, and answer some questions. But he kept his cool. Chances were the man would return.

Nicholas looked at His Honor and both men were frustrated. Cable paused between questions, and the Judge suddenly rapped his gavel. "Ten-minute recess. I think the jurors need a short break."

WILLIS RELAYED THE MESSAGE to Lou Dell, who stuck her head through a crack in the door and said, "Mr. Easter, could I see you for a minute?"

Nicholas followed Willis through a maze of narrow hallways until they came to the side door of Harkin's chambers. The Judge was alone, robe off, coffee in hand. He excused Willis and locked the door. "Please sit down, Mr. Easter," he said, waving at a chair across from his cluttered desk. The room was not his permanent office, in fact he shared it with two other judges who used the courtroom. "Coffee?"

"No thanks."

Harkin dropped into his chair and leaned forward on his elbows. "Now, tell me, where did you see this man?"

Nicholas would save the video for a more crucial moment. He'd already carefully planned the next tale. "Yesterday, after we adjourned, I was walking back to my apartment when I stopped to get an ice cream at Mike's, around the corner. I walked in the place, then looked out, back on to the sidewalk, and I saw this guy peeking in. He didn't see me, but I realized I'd seen him somewhere before. I got the ice cream, and began walking home. I thought the guy was following me, so I doubled back and took odd turns, and sure enough, I caught him tracking me."

"And you've seen him before?"

"Yes sir. I work at a computer store in the mall, and one night this guy, same guy I'm sure, kept walking by the door and looking in. Later, I took a break and he showed up at the other end of the mall where I was drinking a Coke."

The Judge relaxed a bit and adjusted his hair. "Be honest with me, Mr. Easter, have any of your colleagues mentioned anything like this?"

"No sir."

"Will you tell me if they do?"

"Certainly."

"There's nothing wrong with this little chat we're having, and if something happens in there, I need to know it."

"How do I contact you?"

"Just send a note through Lou Dell. Just say we need to talk without giving specifics because God knows she'll read it."

"Okay."

"Is it a deal?"

"Sure."

Harkin took a deep breath and began fishing through an open briefcase. He found a newspaper and slid it across the desk. "Have you seen this? It's today's *Wall Street Journal*."

"No. I don't read it."

"Good. There's a big story about this trial and the potential impact a plaintiff's verdict might have on the tobacco industry."

Nicholas couldn't allow the opportunity to pass. "There's only one person who reads the *Journal*."

"Who's that?"

"Frank Herrera. He reads it every morning, cover to cover."

"This morning?"

"Yes. While we were waiting, he read every word twice."

"Did he comment on anything?"

"Not to my knowledge."

"Damn."

"Doesn't matter, though," Nicholas said, looking at a wall.

"Why not?"

"His mind's made up."

Harkin leaned forward again and squinted hard. "What do you mean?"

"He should never have been picked for jury service, in my opinion. I don't know how he answered the written questions, but he didn't tell the truth or else he wouldn't be here. And I distinctly remember questions during voir dire that he should've responded to."

"I'm listening."

"Okay, Your Honor, but don't get mad. I had a conversation with him early yesterday morning. We were the only ones in the jury room, and, I swear, we weren't discussing this case in particular. But somehow we got around to cigarettes, and Frank quit smoking years ago and he has no sympathy for anybody who can't quit. He's retired military, you know, rather stiff and hard about—"

"I'm an ex-Marine."

"Sorry. Shall I shut up?"

"No. Keep going."

"Okay, but I'm nervous about this and I'll be happy to stop at any time."

"I'll tell you when to stop."

"Sure, well anyway, Frank's of the opinion that anyone who smokes three packs a day for almost thirty years deserves what he gets. No sympathy whatsoever. I argued with him a little, just for the sake of it, and he accused me of wanting to give the plaintiff a huge punitive award."

His Honor took it hard, sinking in his chair a bit, closing then rubbing his eyes as his shoulders sagged. "This is just great," he mumbled.

"Sorry, Judge."

"No, no, I asked for it." He sat straight again, made another adjustment to his hair with his fingers, forced a smile, said, "Look, Mr. Easter. I'm not asking you to become a snitch. But I'm concerned about this jury because of pressures from the outside. This type of litigation has a sordid history. If you see or hear anything even remotely related to unauthorized contact, please let me know. We'll deal with it then."

"Sure, Judge."

THE STORY, on the front page of the *Journal*, had been written by Agner Layson, a senior reporter who'd sat through most of jury selection and all of the testimony. Layson had practiced law for ten years and had been in many courtrooms. His story, the first of a series, gave the basics of the issues and the specifics on the players. There was no opinion of how the trial was progressing, no guess as to who was winning or losing, just a fair summary of the rather convincing medical proof offered so far by the plaintiff.

In response to the story, Pynex' stock dipped a dollar at the opening bell, but by noon had found itself sufficiently corrected and adjusted and was deemed to be weathering the brief storm.

The story prompted a flood of phone calls from brokerage houses in New York to their analysts on the ground in Biloxi. Minutes of meaningless gossip accumulated into hours of hopeless speculation as the harried souls in New York quizzed and inquired and pondered about the only question that mattered: "What's the jury gonna do?"

The young men and women assigned to monitor the trial and predict what the jury might do had no collective clue.

Eleven

THE CROSS-EXAMINATION of Bronsky ended late Thursday afternoon and Marlee struck with a fury Friday morning. Konrad took the first call at seven twenty-five, routed it quickly to Fitch, who was on the phone to Washington, then listened as it played on the speakerphone: "Good morning, Fitch," she said sweetly.

"Good morning, Marlee," Fitch answered with a happy voice, his best effort at pleasantness. "And how are you?"

"Fabulous. Number two, Easter, will wear a light blue denim shirt, faded jeans, white socks, old running shoes, Nikes, I think. And he'll bring with him a copy of *Rolling Stone,* October issue, Meat Loaf on the cover. Got that?"

"Yes. When can we get together and talk?"

"When I get ready. Adios." She hung up. The call was traced to the lobby of a motel in Hattiesburg, Mississippi, at least ninety minutes away by car.

Pang was sitting in a coffee shop three blocks from Easter's apartment, and within minutes he was loitering under a shade tree fifty yards from the ancient VW Beetle. On schedule, Easter exited through the front entranceway at seven forty-five, and began his customary twenty-minute walk to the courthouse. He stopped at the same corner grocery for the same newspapers and the same coffee.

Of course, he was wearing exactly what she'd promised.

Her second call also came from Hattiesburg, though from a different number. "Got a new wrinkle for you, Fitch. And you're gonna love it."

Fitch, barely breathing, said, "I'm listening."

"When the jurors come out today, instead of sitting, guess what they're gonna do?"

Fitch's brain froze. He couldn't move his lips. He knew he wasn't expected to make an intelligent guess. "I give up," he said.

"They're gonna do the Pledge of Allegiance."

Fitch shot Konrad a bewildered look.

"Got that, Fitch?" she asked, almost mocking.

"Yeah."

Her line went dead.

HER THIRD CALL went to the law offices of Wendall Rohr, who, according to a secretary, was quite busy and unavailable. Marlee understood perfectly well, but explained that she had an important message for Mr. Rohr. The message would arrive in about five minutes on the fax machine, so would the secretary be so kind as to receive it and take it straight to Mr. Rohr before he left for court. The secretary reluctantly agreed, and five minutes later found a plain sheet of paper lying alone in the receiving tray of the fax. There was no transmitting number, no indication of from where or from whom the fax came. In typed, single-spaced words in the center of the page, the message read:

> WR: Juror number 2, Easter, will today wear a blue denim shirt, faded jeans, white sox, old Nikes. He likes *Rolling Stone* and he will prove to be quite patriotic.
>
> MM

The secretary rushed it to Rohr's office where he was packing a bulky briefcase for the day's battle. Rohr read it, quizzed the secretary, then called in his co-counsel for an emergency session.

THE MOOD couldn't quite be classified as festive, especially for twelve people being held against their will, but it was Friday and the chatter was noticeably lighter as they gathered and greeted one another. Nicholas held a seat at the table, near Herman Grimes and across from Frank Herrera, and he waited for what he thought to be a lull in the idle talk. He looked at Herman, who was hard at work with his laptop. He said, "Hey, Herman. I have an idea."

By now Herman had the eleven voices committed to memory, and his wife had spent hours providing matching descriptions. He especially knew Easter's tone.

"Yes, Nicholas."

Nicholas raised his voice in an effort to catch everyone's attention. "Well, when I was a kid, I went to a little private school, and we were trained to begin each day with the Pledge of Allegiance. Every time I see a flag early in the morning, I have this desire to give the pledge." Most of the jurors were listening. Poodle had gone out for a smoke. "And in the courtroom out there we have this beautiful flag standing behind the Judge, and all we do is sit and look at it."

"I hadn't noticed," Herman said.

"You wanna do the Pledge of Allegiance, out there, in open court?" asked Herrera, Napoleon, the Retired Colonel.

"Yeah. Why not do it once a week?"

"Nothing wrong with that," said Jerry Fernandez, who had secretly been recruited for the event.

"But what about the Judge?" asked Mrs. Gladys Card.

"Why should he care? In fact, why should anyone be bothered if we stand for a moment and honor our flag?"

"You're not playing games, are you?" asked the Colonel.

Nicholas was suddenly wounded. He gazed across the table with aching eyes, and said, "My father was killed in Vietnam, okay. He was decorated. That flag means a lot to me."

And with that, the deal was sealed.

Judge Harkin greeted them with a warm Friday smile as they came through the door one by one. He was prepared to zip through his standard routine about unauthorized contact, and get on with the testimony. It took a second to realize they were not sitting, as usual. They remained standing until all twelve were in place, then they looked at the wall to his left, behind the witness stand, and they covered their hearts with their hands. Easter opened his mouth first and led them in a vigorous recitation of the Pledge of Allegiance.

Harkin's initial reaction was one of total disbelief; it was certainly a ceremony he'd never witnessed, not in a courtroom, not by a group of jurors. Nor had he ever *heard* of such a thing, and by now he thought he'd heard or seen it all. It was not a part of the daily ritual, had not been approved by him, did not in fact appear in any manual or handbook. And so his first impulse, after the jolt, was to call them down, make 'em stop it; and they'd talk about it later. Then he instantly realized that it seemed horribly unpatriotic and maybe even downright sinful to interrupt a group of well-meaning citizens as they took a moment to honor their flag. He glanced at Rohr and Cable and saw nothing but open mouths and slack jaws.

So then he stood. About halfway through the pledge, he lurched forward and upward, his black robe floating around him, and turned to the wall, clutched his chest, and picked up the chant.

With the jury and the Judge honoring the Stars and Stripes, it suddenly seemed imperative for everyone else to do likewise, especially the lawyers, who couldn't chance disfavor or show the slightest hint of disloyalty. They jumped to their feet, kicking over briefcases and knocking back chairs. Gloria Lane and her deputy clerks, and the court reporter, and Lou Dell, sitting out there on the first row, far side, likewise stood and turned and followed along. The fervor lost its momentum, though, somewhere beyond the third row of spectators, and Fitch was thus fortunately saved from having to stand like a Cub Scout and mumble words he barely remembered.

He was in the back row with José on one side and Holly, a comely young associate, on the other. Pang was out in the atrium. Doyle was back on his Dr. Pepper crate on the first floor near the Coke machines, dressed like a laborer, joking with the janitors and watching the front lobby.

Fitch watched and listened in utter amazement. The sight of a jury, on its own initiative and working as a group, assuming control of a courtroom in such a manner was simply hard to believe. The fact that Marlee knew it was coming was bewildering.

The fact that she was playing games with it was exhilarating.

At least Fitch, though, had some inkling of what was coming. Wendall Rohr felt thoroughly ambushed. He was so stunned by the sight of Easter dressed precisely as promised, and holding the exact magazine, which he placed under his chair, and then leading his fellow jurymen in the pledge, that he could only mouth the remaining words. And he did so without looking at the flag. He stared at the jury, especially at Easter, and he wondered what the hell was going on.

As the final phrase ". . . and justice for all" echoed up to the ceiling, the jurors settled into their seats and, as a group, looked quickly around the courtroom to assess the reactions. Judge Harkin adjusted his robe while shuffling some papers and seemed determined to act as if all juries were supposed to do the same thing. What could he say? It had taken thirty seconds.

Most of the lawyers were secretly embarrassed by the silly display of patriotism, but, Hey!, if the jurors were happy, then they were happy too. Only Wendall Rohr kept staring, seemingly speechless. An associate nudged him and they fell into a hushed conversation as His Honor raced through the standard comments and questions for the jury.

"I believe we're ready for a new witness," the Judge said, anxious to speed things along.

Rohr stood, still dazed, and said, "The plaintiff calls Dr. Hilo Kilvan."

As the next expert was retrieved from a witness holding room in the back, Fitch quietly slipped out of the courtroom with José fast behind him. They walked down the street and into the old dime store.

The two jury wizards in the viewing room were silent. On the main screen, one was watching the initial questioning of Dr. Kilvan. On a smaller monitor, the other was watching a replay of the Pledge of Allegiance. Fitch hovered over the monitor, and asked, "When was the last time you saw that?"

"It's Easter," the nearest expert said. "He led them into it."

"Of course it was Easter," Fitch snapped. "I could see that from the back row of the courtroom." Fitch, as usual, was not playing fair. Neither of these consultants knew of Marlee's phone calls because Fitch had yet to share the information with anyone but his agents—Swanson, Doyle, Pang, Konrad, and Holly.

"So what does that do to your computer analysis?" Fitch asked with heavy sarcasm.

"Blows it to hell."

"That's what I figured. Keep watching." He slammed the door and went to his office.

□ □ □ □

THE DIRECT EXAMINATION of Dr. Hilo Kilvan was handled by a new plaintiff's lawyer, Scotty Mangrum from Dallas. Mangrum had made his fortune suing petrochemical companies for toxic torts, and now at the age of forty-two he was deeply concerned about consumer products that caused injuries and death. After Rohr, he'd been the first lawyer to pony up his million bucks to finance the Wood case, and it had been decided that he would become fluent in statistical summaries of lung cancer. In the past four years, he'd spent countless hours reading every possible study and report on the subject, and he'd traveled extensively to meet with the experts. With great care and no regard for expense, he'd selected Dr. Kilvan as the man to visit Biloxi and share his knowledge with the jury.

Dr. Kilvan spoke perfect but deliberate English, with a touch of an accent that made an instant impression on the jury. Few things can be more persuasive in a courtroom than an expert who's traveled a great distance to be there, and has an exotic name and accent to boot. Dr. Kilvan was from Montreal, where he'd lived the past forty years, and the fact that he was from another country only added to his credibility. The jury was on board long before he got around to his testimony. He and Mangrum tag-teamed through an intimidating résumé, with particular emphasis placed on the volume of books Dr. Kilvan had published on the statistical probabilities of lung cancer.

When finally asked, Durr Cable conceded that Dr. Kilvan was qualified to testify in his field. Scotty Mangrum thanked him, and then began with the first study—one comparing ratios of lung cancer mortality between cigarette smokers and nonsmokers. Dr. Kilvan had been studying this for the past twenty years at the University of Montreal, and he relaxed in his chair as he explained the basics of this research to the jury. For American men, and he'd studied groups of men and women from around the world but primarily Canadians and Americans, the risk of getting lung cancer for one who smokes fifteen cigarettes a day for ten years is ten times greater than for one who doesn't smoke at all. Increase it to two packs a day, and the risk is twenty times greater. Increase it to three packs a day, the quantity smoked by Jacob Wood, and the risk is twenty-five times greater than for a nonsmoker.

Brightly colored charts were produced and mounted on three

tripods, and Dr. Kilvan, carefully and without a trace of hurry, demonstrated his findings to the jurors.

The next study was a comparison of the death rates from lung cancer in men in relation to the type of tobacco smoked. Dr. Kilvan explained the basic differences in pipe and cigar smoke and the rates of cancer for American men who used those forms of tobacco. He'd published two books on these comparisons, and was quite ready to show the jury the next series of charts and graphs. The numbers piled up, and they began to blur.

LOREEN DUKE was the first person with the nerve to remove her plate from the table and take it to a corner where she balanced it on her knees and ate alone. Because the lunches were ordered by menu at nine each morning, and because Lou Dell and Willis the deputy and the folks at O'Reilly's Deli and anyone else involved in the serving of the food were determined to have the food on the table at the crack of noon, a certain order was necessary. A seating arrangement was developed. Loreen's seat was directly across the table from Stella Hulic, who smacked as she talked and allowed large chunks of bread to hang from her teeth. Stella was a poorly dressed social climber who'd spent most of her time in recess working desperately to convince the other eleven that she and her husband, a retired plumbing executive named Cal, possessed more than the rest. Cal had a hotel, and Cal had an apartment complex, and Cal had a car wash. There were other investments, most of which managed to pop out with the food as if both were accidents. They took trips, just traveled all the time. Greece was a favorite. Cal had an airplane and several boats.

According to widely accepted knowledge along the Coast, Cal, a few years earlier, had used an old shrimping boat to haul marijuana from Mexico. True or not, the Hulics were now flush, and it was Stella's burden to discuss it with anyone who would listen. She rattled on with an obnoxious nasal twang, one foreign to the Coast, and waited until everyone had filled their mouths and an intense quiet had settled over the table.

She said, "I sure hope we finish early today. Me and Cal are headed to Miami for the weekend. There are some fabulous new shops down there." All heads were bowed because no one could stomach the sight of half a dinner roll packed tightly in a jaw and clearly visible. Each syllable came forth with added sounds of food sticking to teeth.

Loreen left before taking the first bite. She was followed by Rikki Coleman, who offered the feeble excuse that she had to sit by the window. Lonnie Shaver suddenly needed to work during lunch. He excused himself and huddled with his computer while munching on a chicken club.

"Dr. Kilvan certainly is an impressive witness, isn't he?" Nicholas asked the remaining jurors at the table. A few glanced at Herman, who was eating his usual turkey sandwich on white bread with no mayonnaise or mustard or any condiment capable of sticking to his mouth or lips. A sliced turkey sandwich and a nice little pile of ridged potato chips could be easily handled and consumed without the benefit of sight. Herman's jaws slowed for a second, but he said nothing.

"Those statistics are hard to ignore," Nicholas said while smiling at Jerry Fernandez. It was a deliberate attempt to provoke the foreman.

"That's enough," Herman said.

"Enough of what, Herm?"

"Enough talk about the trial. You know the Judge's rules."

"Yeah, but the Judge isn't in here, is he, Herm? And he has no way of knowing what we discuss, does he? Unless, of course, you tell him."

"I might just do that."

"Fine, Herm. What would you like to discuss?"

"Anything but the trial."

"Pick a topic. Football, the weather . . ."

"I don't watch football."

"Ha, ha."

There was a heavy pause, a stillness broken only by the slapping of food around the mouth of Stella Hulic. Evidently the quick exchange between the two men had rattled nerves, and Stella chewed even faster.

But Jerry Fernandez had had enough. "Could you please stop smacking your food like that!" he snapped viciously.

He caught her in mid-bite, mouth open, food perceptible. He glared at her as if he might slap her, then he said, after a deep breath, "I'm sorry, okay. It's just that you have these terrible table manners."

She was stunned for a second, then embarrassed. Then she attacked. Her cheeks turned red and she managed to swallow the large portion already in her mouth. "Maybe I don't like yours either," she said, bristling as the other heads lowered. Everyone wanted the moment to pass.

"At least I eat quietly and keep my food in my mouth," Jerry said, very aware of how childish he sounded.

"So do I," Stella said.

"No you don't," said Napoleon, who had the misfortune of sitting next to Loreen Duke and across from Stella. "You make more racket than a three-year-old."

Herman cleared his throat loudly, said, "Let's all take a deep breath now. And let's finish our lunch in peace."

Not another word was spoken as they strained to quietly finish the remains of their lunch. Jerry and Poodle left first for the smoke room, followed by Nicholas Easter, who didn't smoke but needed a change of scenery. A light rain was falling, and the daily walk around the town would have to be canceled.

They met in the small, square room with folding chairs and a window that opened. Angel Weese, the quietest of all jurors, soon joined them. Stella, the fourth smoker, was wounded and had decided to wait behind.

Poodle didn't mind talking about the trial. Neither did Angel. What else did they have in common? They seemed to agree with Jerry that everybody knows cigarettes cause cancer. So if you smoke, you do so at your own risk.

Why give millions to the heirs of a dead man who smoked for thirty-five years? One should know better.

Twelve

THOUGH THE HULICS longed for a jet, a small cute one with leather seats and two pilots, they were temporarily stuck with an old twin-engine Cessna, which Cal could fly if the sun was up and the clouds were gone. He wouldn't dare fly it at night, especially to a crowded place like Miami, so they boarded a commuter flight at the Gulfport Municipal Airport and flew to Atlanta. From there they flew to Miami International, first class, with Stella knocking down two martinis and a glass of wine in less than an hour. It had been a long week. Her nerves were ragged from the stress of civic service.

They poured their luggage into a cab and headed for Miami Beach, where they checked into a new Sheraton.

Marlee followed them. She'd sat behind them on the commuter, and she'd flown coach from Atlanta. Her cab waited as she loitered about the lobby to make sure they were checked in. She then found a room a mile down the beach at a resort hotel. She waited until almost eleven, Friday night, before she called.

Stella had been tired and simply wanted a drink and dinner in the room. Several drinks. She'd shop tomorrow, but for now she needed liquids. When the phone rang, she was flat on the bed, barely conscious. Cal, clad only in drooping boxers, grabbed the phone. "Hello."

"Yes, Mr. Hulic," came the very crisp, professional voice of a young lady. "You need to be careful."

"Say what?"

"You're being followed."

Cal rubbed his red eyes. "Who is this?"

"Listen carefully please. Some men are watching your wife. They're here in Miami. They know you took flight 4476 from Biloxi to Atlanta, flight 533 on Delta to Miami, and they know exactly which room you're in now. They're watching every move."

Cal looked at the phone and slapped himself lightly on the forehead. "Wait a minute. I—"

"And they'll probably wire your phones tomorrow," she added helpfully. "So, please be very careful."

"Who are these guys?" he asked loudly, and Stella perked up slightly. She managed to swing her bare feet onto the floor and focus on her husband through foggy eyes.

"They're agents hired by the tobacco companies," was the reply. "And they're vicious."

The young lady hung up. Cal again looked at the receiver, then looked at his wife, a pathetic sight. She was reaching for the cigarettes. "What is it?" she demanded with a thick tongue, and Cal repeated every word.

"Oh my god!" she shrieked and walked to the table by the TV where she clutched a wine bottle and poured another glass. "Why are they after me?" she asked, falling into a chair and spilling cheap cabernet on her hotel bathrobe. "Why me?"

"She didn't say they were gonna kill you," he explained, with a slight trace of regret.

"Why are they following me?" She was near tears.

"I don't know, dammit," Cal growled as he took another beer from the mini-bar. They drank in silence for a few minutes, neither wanting to look at the other, both bewildered.

Then, the phone rang again and she let out a yelp. Cal took the receiver, slowly said, "Hello."

"Hi, it's me again," came the same voice, this time quite merry. "Something I forgot to mention. Don't call the cops or anything. These guys are doing nothing illegal. It's best just to pretend as if nothing is wrong, okay?"

"Who are you?" he asked.

"Bye." And she was gone.

□ □ □ □

LISTING FOODS owned not one but three jets, one of which was dispatched early Saturday morning to collect Mr. Lonnie Shaver and fly him to Charlotte, alone. His wife had been unable to find a baby-sitter for the three kids. The pilots greeted him warmly and offered him coffee and fruit before takeoff.

Ken met him at the airport in a company van with a company driver, and fifteen minutes later they arrived at the SuperHouse headquarters in suburban Charlotte. Lonnie was greeted by Ben, the other pal from the first meeting in Biloxi, and together Ben and Ken gave Lonnie a quick tour of their corporate center. The building was new, a one-story brick with lots of glass and completely indistinguishable from a dozen others they'd passed on the drive from the airport. The hallways were wide and tiled and spotless; the offices were sterile and filled with technology. Lonnie could almost hear the sound of money being printed.

They shared coffee with George Teaker, CEO, in his large office with a view of a small courtyard filled with plastic greenery. Teaker was youthful, energetic, clad in denim (his usual Saturday office dress, he explained). On Sundays he wore a jogging suit. He fed Lonnie the party line—the company was growing like crazy and they wanted him on board. Then Teaker was off to a meeting.

In a small, white boardroom with no windows, Lonnie was placed at a table with coffee and doughnuts before him. Ben disappeared, but Ken stuck close as the lights dimmed and an image appeared on the wall. It was a thirty-minute video about SuperHouse—its brief history, its current position in the market, its ambitious growth plans. And its people, the "real assets."

According to the script, SuperHouse planned to increase both gross sales and number of stores by fifteen percent a year for the next six years. Profits would be stunning.

The lights came on, and an earnest young man with a name that was quickly forgotten appeared and took a position across the table. He was a benefits specialist, and had all the answers to all the questions about health care, pension plans, vacations, holidays, sick leave, employee stock options. Everything was covered in one of the packages on the table before Lonnie, so he could mull over it later.

After a long lunch with Ben and Ken in a swanky suburban restaurant, Lonnie went back to the boardroom for a few more meetings. One covered the training program they were contemplating for him. The next, presented by video, outlined the structure of the company in relation to its parent and to its competitors. Boredom hit hard. For a man who'd spent the entire week sitting on his rear listening to lawyers haggle with experts, this was no way to spend a Saturday afternoon. Excited though he was about his visit and its prospects, he suddenly needed fresh air.

Ken, of course, knew this, and the moment the video ended he suggested they go play golf, a sport Lonnie had yet to try. Ken, of course, knew this too, so he suggested they get some sunshine anyway. Ken's BMW was blue and spotless, and he drove it with great care into the countryside, past manicured farms and estates and tree-lined roads until they reached the country club.

For a black guy from a lower-middle-class family in Gulfport, the thought of stepping foot in a country club was intimidating. Lonnie at first resented the idea, and vowed to leave if he saw no other black faces. On second thought, however, he was somewhat flattered that his new employers would think so highly of him. They were really nice guys, genuine and seemingly anxious for him to adjust to their corporate culture. There'd been no mention of money yet, but how could it be less than he was earning now?

They stepped into the Club Lounge, a sprawling room of leather chairs, stuffed game on the walls, and a cloud of blue cigar smoke hanging near the pitched ceiling. A serious boy room. At a large table near the window, with the eighteenth green just below, they found George Teaker, now in golf attire, having a drink with two black gentlemen, also nicely dressed and apparently not long off the links. All three stood and warmly greeted Lonnie, who was relieved to see kindred spirits. In fact, a huge weight left his chest, and he was suddenly ready for a drink, though he was careful with alcohol. The burly black man was Morris Peel, a loud and hearty soul who smiled constantly and introduced the other, a Percy Kellum from Atlanta. Both men were in their mid-forties, and as the first round of drinks was ordered, by Peel, he explained that he was a vice president with Listing Foods, the parent company in New York, and that Kellum was a regional something or other for Listing.

No pecking order was established; none was needed. It was

obvious that Peel, from the parent in New York, ranked higher than Teaker, who carried the title of CEO but only ran a division. Kellum was positioned somewhere further down the pole. Ken, even lower. And Lonnie was just happy to be there. Over the second drink, with the formalities and polite chitchat out of the way, Peel, with great relish and humor, offered his biography. Sixteen years earlier, he had been the first black mid-level manager to enter the world of Listing Foods, and he had been a pain in the ass. He'd been hired as a token, not as a talent, and he'd been forced to claw his way upward. Twice he'd sued the company, and twice he'd won. And once the boys upstairs realized he was determined to join them, and that he had the brains to do so, they accepted him as a person. It still wasn't easy, but he had their respect. Teaker, now on his third scotch, leaned in and offered, confidentially of course, that Peel was being groomed for the big job. "You could be talking to a future CEO," he said to Lonnie. "One of the first black CEO's of a Fortune 500 company."

Because of Peel, Listing Foods had implemented an aggressive program of recruiting and promoting black managers. This is where Lonnie would fit in. Hadley Brothers was a decent company, but quite old-fashioned and quite Southern, and Listing was not surprised to find but a few blacks with more authority than floor sweepers.

For two hours, as darkness fell across the eighteenth green and a piano player sang in the lounge, they drank and talked and planned the future. Dinner was just down the hall, in a private dining room with a fireplace and a moosehead above the mantel. They ate thick steaks flavored with sauce and mushrooms. Lonnie slept that night in a suite on the third floor of the country club, and awoke to a splendid fairway view, and a slight hangover.

Only two brief meetings were planned for late Sunday morning. The first, again with Ken present, was a planning session with George Teaker, in a jogging suit, and fresh from a five-miler. "Best thing in the world for a hangover," he said. He wanted Lonnie to run the store in Biloxi under a new contract for a period of ninety days, after which they would evaluate his performance. Assuming everyone was pleased, and they certainly expected to be, then he would be transferred to a larger store, probably in the Atlanta area. A larger store meant more responsibility, and more compensation. After a year there, he would be reevaluated, and probably moved again. During this fifteen-month period, he would be required to spend at least one weekend each month in Charlotte in a management trainee program, one that was outlined in excruciating detail in a packet on the table.

Teaker finally finished, and ordered more black coffee.

The last guest was a wiry young black man with a bald head and a meticulous suit and tie. His name was Taunton, and he was a lawyer from New York, from Wall Street, actually. His firm represented Listing Foods, he explained gravely, and in fact, he worked on nothing but Listing's business. He was there to present a proposed contract of employment, a rather routine matter but nonetheless an important one. He handed Lonnie a document, only three or four pages, but it seemed much heavier after having traveled from Wall Street. Lonnie was impressed beyond words.

"Look it over," Taunton said, tapping his chin with a designer pen. "And we'll talk next week. It's fairly standard. The compensation paragraph has several blanks. We'll fill them in later."

Lonnie glanced at the first page, then placed it with the other papers and packets and memos in a pile that was growing by the moment. Taunton whipped out a legal pad and seemed to prepare himself for a nasty cross-examination. "Just a few questions," he said.

Lonnie had a painful flashback to the courtroom in Biloxi where the lawyers always had "just a few more questions."

"Sure," Lonnie said, glancing at his watch. He couldn't help it.

"No criminal record of any sort?"

"No. Just a few speeding tickets."

"No lawsuits pending against you personally?"

"No."

"Any against your wife?"

"No."

"Have you ever filed for bankruptcy?"

"No."

"Ever been arrested?"

"No."

"Indicted?"

"No."

Taunton flipped a page. "Have you, in your capacity as a store manager, ever been involved in litigation?"

"Yeah, lemme see. About four years ago, an old man slipped and fell on a wet floor. He sued. I gave a deposition."

"Did it go to trial?" Taunton asked with great interest. He had reviewed the court file, had a copy of it in his thick briefcase, and knew every detail of the old man's claim.

"No. The insurance company settled out of court. I think they paid him twenty thousand or so."

It was twenty-five thousand, and Taunton wrote this figure on his legal pad. The script called for Teaker to speak at this point. "Damned trial lawyers. They're a blight on society."

Taunton looked at Lonnie, then at Teaker, then said defensively, "I'm not a trial lawyer."

"Oh, I know that," Teaker said. "You're one of the good guys. It's those greedy ambulance chasers I hate."

"Do you know what we paid last year for liability insurance coverage?" Taunton asked Lonnie, as if he might be able to provide an intelligent guess. He just shook his head.

"Listing paid over twenty million."

"Just to keep the sharks away," Teaker added.

There was a dramatic pause in the conversation, or at least a pause aimed at drama as Taunton and Teaker bit their lips and showed their disgust and seemed to appear to contemplate the money wasted for protection against lawsuits. Then Taunton looked at something on his legal pad, glanced at Teaker, and asked, "I don't suppose you've discussed the trial, have you?"

Teaker looked surprised. "I don't think it's necessary. Lonnie's on board. He's one of us."

Taunton appeared to ignore this. "This tobacco trial in Biloxi has serious implications throughout the economy, especially for companies like ours," he said to Lonnie, who nodded gently and tried to understand how the trial might affect anyone other than Pynex.

Teaker said to Taunton, "I'm not sure you're supposed to discuss it."

Taunton continued, "It's okay. I know trial procedure. You

don't mind, do you, Lonnie? I mean, we can trust you on this, can't we?"

"Sure. I won't say a word."

"If the plaintiff wins this case and there's a big verdict, it will open the floodgates of tobacco litigation. Trial lawyers will go crazy. They'll bankrupt the tobacco companies."

"We make a lot of money off tobacco sales, Lonnie," Teaker said with perfect timing.

"Then they'll probably sue dairy companies claiming cholesterol kills people." Taunton's voice was rising and he was leaning forward across the table. The issue had struck a nerve. "There has to be an end to these trials. The tobacco industry has never lost one of them. I think their record is something like fifty-five wins, no losses. Folks on juries have always understood that you smoke at your own risk."

"Lonnie understands this," Teaker said, almost defensively.

Taunton took a deep breath. "Sure. Sorry if I said too much. It's just that this Biloxi trial has a lot at stake."

"No problem," Lonnie said. And he really wasn't bothered by the talk. Taunton was, after all, a lawyer, and he certainly knew the law, and perhaps it was okay if he spoke of the trial in broad terms without going into specifics. Lonnie was satisfied. He was on board. No problem out of him.

Taunton was suddenly all smiles as he packed away his notes and promised to give Lonnie a call midweek. The meeting was over and Lonnie was a free man. Ken drove him to the airport where the same Lear with the same pleasant pilots sat idling and ready.

THE WEATHERMAN promised a chance of afternoon showers, and that was all Stella wanted to hear. Cal insisted there wasn't a cloud to be seen, but she wouldn't take a look. She pulled the shades and watched movies until noon. She ordered a grilled cheese and two bloody marys, then slept for a while with the door chained and a chair propped against it. Cal was off to the beach, specifically a topless one he'd heard about but never got the chance to visit on account of his wife. With her safely boarded up inside their room on the tenth floor, he was free to roam the sands and admire young flesh. He sipped a beer at a thatched-roof bar and thought how wonderful the trip had become. She was afraid to be seen, thus the credit cards were safe for the weekend.

They caught an early flight Sunday morning and returned to Biloxi. Stella was hungover and weary from a weekend of being watched. She was apprehensive about Monday and the courtroom.

Thirteen

THE HELLOS and howdies were muffled Monday morning. The routine of gathering by the coffeepot and inspecting the doughnuts and rolls was growing tiresome, not so much from repetition but more from the burdensome mystery of not knowing how long this all might drag on. They broke into small groups, and recounted what happened during their freedom over the weekend. Most ran their errands and shopped and visited with family and went to church, and the humdrum took on new importance for people about to be confined. Herman was late so there were whispers about the trial, nothing important, just a general consensus that the plaintiff's case was sinking in a mire of charts and graphs and statistics. They all believed smoking caused lung cancer. They wanted new information.

Nicholas managed to isolate Angel Weese early in the morning. They had exchanged brief pleasantries throughout the trial, but had talked of nothing substantive. She and Loreen Duke were the only two black women on the jury, and oddly kept their distance from each other. Angel was slender and quiet, single, and worked for a beer distributor. She kept the permanent look of someone in silent pain, and she proved difficult to talk to.

Stella arrived late and looked like death; her eyes were red and puffy, her skin pale. Her hands shook as she poured coffee, and she went straight to the smoke room down the hall, where Jerry

Fernandez and Poodle were chatting and flirting as they were now prone to do.

Nicholas was anxious to hear Stella's weekend report. "How about a smoke?" he said to Angel, the fourth official smoker on the jury.

"When did you start?" she asked with a rare smile.

"Last week. I'll quit when the trial's over." They left the jury room under the prying gaze of Lou Dell, and joined the others— Jerry and Poodle still talking; Stella stone-faced and teetering on the brink of a breakdown.

Nicholas bummed a Camel from Jerry, and lit it with a match. "Well, how was Miami?" he asked Stella.

She jerked her head toward him, startled, and said, "It rained." She bit her filter and inhaled fiercely. She didn't want to talk. The conversation lagged as they concentrated on their cigarettes. It was ten minutes before nine, time for the last hit of nicotine.

"I think I was followed this weekend," Nicholas said after a minute of silence.

The smoking continued without interruption, but the minds were working. "Say what?" Jerry asked.

"They followed me," he repeated and looked at Stella, whose eyes were wide and filled with fear.

"Who?" asked Poodle.

"I don't know. It happened Saturday when I left my apartment and went to work. I saw a guy lurking near my car, and I saw him later at the mall. Probably some agent hired by the tobacco boys."

Stella's mouth dropped open and her jaw quivered. Gray smoke leaked from her nostrils. "Are you gonna tell the Judge?" she asked, holding her breath. It was a question she and Cal had fought over.

"No."

"Why not?" asked Poodle, only mildly curious.

"I don't know for certain, okay. I mean, I'm sure I was followed, but I don't know for sure who it was. What am I supposed to tell the Judge?"

"Tell him you were followed," said Jerry.

"Why would they follow you?" asked Angel.

"Same reason they're following all of us."

"I don't believe that," Poodle said.

Stella certainly believed it, but if Nicholas, the ex–law student, planned to keep it from the Judge, then so did she.

"Why are they following us?" Angel asked again, nervously.

"Because it's just what they do. The tobacco companies spent millions selecting us, and now they're spending even more to watch us."

"What are they looking for?"

"Ways to get to us. Friends we might talk to. Places we might go. They typically start gossip in the various communities where we live, little rumors about the deceased, bad things he did while he was alive. They're always looking for a weak spot. That's why they've never lost a jury trial."

"How do you know it's the tobacco company?" asked Poodle, lighting another one.

"I don't. But they have more money than the plaintiff. In fact, they have unlimited funds to fight these cases with."

Jerry Fernandez, always ready to help with a joke or assist in a gag, said, "You know, come to think of it, I remember seeing this strange little dude peeking around a corner at me this weekend. Saw him more than once." He glanced at Nicholas for approval, but Nicholas was watching Stella. Jerry winked at Poodle, but she didn't see.

Lou Dell knocked on the door.

NO PLEDGES or anthems Monday morning. Judge Harkin and the lawyers waited, ready to spring forward with unabashed patriotism at the slightest hint the jurors might be in the mood, but nothing happened. The jurors took their seats, already a bit tired it seemed and resigned to another long week of testimony. Harkin flashed them a warm welcoming smile, then proceeded with his patented monologue about unauthorized contact. Stella looked at the floor without a word. Cal was watching from the third row, present to give her support.

Scotty Mangrum rose and informed the court that the plaintiff would like to resume with the testimony of Dr. Hilo Kilvan, who was fetched from the rear somewhere and placed on the witness stand. He nodded politely at the jury. No one nodded back.

For Wendall Rohr and the plaintiff's team of lawyers, the weekend had brought no break in their labors. The trial itself presented enough challenges, but the distraction of the fax from MM on

Friday had wrecked all pretense of order. They had traced its origin to a truck stop near Hattiesburg, and after accepting some cash, a clerk had given a weak description of a young woman, late twenties maybe early thirties, with dark hair tucked under a brown fishing cap and a face half-hidden behind large dark sunshades. She was short, but then maybe she was average. Maybe she was about five six or five seven. She was slender, that was for sure, but after all it had been before nine on a Friday morning, one of their busiest periods. She'd paid five bucks for a one-page fax to a number in Biloxi, a law office, which in itself seemed odd and thus remembered by the clerk. Most of their faxes dealt with fuel permits and special loads.

No sign of her vehicle, but then again the place was packed.

It was the collective opinion of the eight principal plaintiff's lawyers, a group with a combined total of 150 years of trial experience, that this was something new. Not a one could recall a single trial in which a person on the outside contacted the lawyers involved with hints of what the jury might do. They were unanimous in their belief that she, MM, would be back. And though they at first denied it, through the weekend they grudgingly arrived at the belief that she would probably ask for money. A deal. Money for a verdict.

They could not, however, muster the courage to plot a strategy to deal with her when she wanted to negotiate. Maybe later, but not now.

Fitch, on the other hand, thought of little else. The Fund currently had a balance of six and a half million dollars, with two of that budgeted for the remaining trial expenses. The money was quite liquid and very movable. He'd spent the weekend monitoring jurors and meeting with lawyers and listening to summaries from his jury people, and he'd spent time on the phone with D. Martin Jankle at Pynex. He'd been pleased with the results of the Ken and Ben show in Charlotte, and had been assured by George Teaker that Lonnie Shaver was a man they could trust. He'd even watched a secret video of the last meeting in which Taunton and Teaker had all but convinced Shaver to sign a pledge.

Fitch slept four hours Saturday and five Sunday, about average for him though sleep was difficult. He dreamed of the girl Marlee and of what she might bring him. This could be the easiest verdict yet.

He watched the opening ceremonies Monday from the viewing room with a jury consultant. The hidden camera had been working so well they had decided to try a better one, one with a larger lens and clearer picture. It was locked in the same briefcase and placed under the same table, and no one in the busy courtroom had a clue.

No Pledge of Allegiance, nothing out of the ordinary, but then Fitch had expected this. Surely Marlee would've called if something special was planned.

He listened as Dr. Hilo Kilvan resumed his testimony, and almost smiled to himself as the jurors seemed to dread it. His consultants and his lawyers were unanimous in the belief that the plaintiff's witnesses had yet to capture the jury. The experts were impressive with credentials and visual aids, but the tobacco defense had seen it all before.

The defense would be simple and subtle. Their doctors would argue strenuously that smoking does not cause lung cancer. Other impressive experts would argue people make informed choices about smoking. Their lawyers would argue that if cigarettes are allegedly so dangerous, then you smoke at your own risk.

Fitch had been through it many times before. He'd memorized the testimony. He'd suffered through the arguments of the lawyers. He'd sweated while the juries deliberated. He'd quietly celebrated the verdicts, but he'd never had the chance to purchase one.

CIGARETTES kill four hundred thousand Americans each year, according to Dr. Kilvan, and he had four large charts to prove it. It is the single deadliest product on the market, nothing else comes close. Except for guns, and they, of course, are not designed to be aimed and fired at people. Cigarettes are designed to be lit and puffed; thus they are used properly. They are deadly if used exactly as intended.

This point hit home with the jury, and it would not be forgotten. But by ten-thirty they were ready for the morning coffee and potty break. Judge Harkin recessed for fifteen minutes. Nicholas slipped a note to Lou Dell, who gave it to Willis, who happened to be awake for the moment. He took the note to the Judge. Easter wanted a private conference at noon, if possible. It was urgent.

□ □ □ □

NICHOLAS EXCUSED HIMSELF from lunch with the explanation that his stomach was queasy and he'd lost his appetite. He needed to visit the boys' room, he said, and he'd be back in a moment. No one cared. Most were leaving the table anyway to avoid being near Stella Hulic.

He cut through the narrow back hallways and entered the chambers where the Judge was waiting, alone with a cold sandwich. They greeted each other tensely. Nicholas carried a small brown leather handbag. "We need to talk," he said, sitting.

"Do the others know you're here?" Harkin asked.

"No. But I need to be quick."

"Go." Harkin ate a corn chip and pushed his plate away.

"Three things. Stella Hulic, number four, front row, went to Miami this weekend, and she was followed by unknown persons believed to be working for the tobacco company."

His Honor stopped chewing. "How do you know?"

"I overheard a conversation this morning. She was trying to whisper this to another juror. Don't ask me how she knew she was being followed—I didn't hear all of it. But the poor woman is a wreck. Frankly, I think she had a coupla drinks before court this morning. Vodka, I'd say. Probably bloody marys."

"Keep going."

"Secondly, Frank Herrera, number seven, we talked about him last time, well his mind is made up and I'm afraid he's trying to influence other people."

"I'm listening."

"He came into this trial with a fixed opinion. I think he wanted to serve; he's retired military or something, probably bored to death, but he is very pro-defense and, well, he just worries me. I don't know what you do with jurors like that."

"Is he discussing the case?"

"Once, with me. Herman is very proud of his title of foreman, and he won't tolerate any talk about the trial."

"Good for him."

"But he can't monitor everything. And as you know, well, it's just human nature to gossip. Anyway, Herrera is poison."

"Okay. And third?"

Nicholas opened his leather bag and removed a videocassette.

"Does this thing work?" he asked, nodding to a small-screened TV/VCR on a roller stand in the corner.

"I think so. It did last week."

"May I?"

"Please."

Nicholas punched the ON button and inserted the tape. "You remember the guy I saw in court last week? The one who was following me?"

"Yes." Harkin stood and walked to within two feet of the TV screen. "I remember."

"Well, here he is." In black and white, a little fuzzy but certainly clear enough to distinguish, the door opened and the man entered Easter's apartment. He looked around anxiously, and for one very long second seemed to look in the precise direction of the camera, hidden in an air vent above the refrigerator. Nicholas stopped the video in full frontal shot of the man's face, and said, "That's him."

Judge Harkin repeated without breathing, "Yeah, that's him."

The tape continued with the man (Doyle) coming and going from view, taking pictures, leaning close to the computer, then leaving in less than ten minutes. The screen went black.

"When did—" Harkin asked slowly, still staring.

"Saturday afternoon. I worked an eight-hour shift, and this guy broke in while I was on the job." Not entirely true, but Harkin would never know the difference. Nicholas had reprogrammed the video to reflect last Saturday's time and date in the lower right corner.

"Why do you—"

"I was robbed and beaten five years ago when I lived in Mobile, almost died. Happened during a break-in of my apartment. I'm careful about security, that's all."

And this made it all perfectly plausible; the existence of sophisticated surveillance equipment in a run-down apartment; the computers and cameras on a minimum wage salary. The man was terrified of violence. Everybody could understand that. "You want to see it again?"

"No. That's him."

Nicholas removed the tape and handed it to the Judge. "Keep it. I have another copy."

□ □ □ □

FITCH'S ROAST BEEF SANDWICH was interrupted when Konrad pecked on the door and uttered the words Fitch longed to hear: "The girl's on the phone."

He wiped his mouth and his goatee with the back of a hand, and grabbed the phone. "Hello."

"Fitch baby," she said. "It's me, Marlee."

"Yes dear."

"Don't know the guy's name, but he's the goon you sent into Easter's apartment on Thursday, the nineteenth, eleven days ago, at 4:52 P.M. to be exact." Fitch gasped for breath and coughed up specks of sandwich. He cursed silently and stood up straight. She continued, "It was just after I gave you the note about Nicholas wearing a gray golf shirt and starched khakis, you remember?"

"Yes," he said hoarsely.

"Anyway, you later sent the goon into the courtroom, probably to look for me. It was last Wednesday, the twenty-fifth. Pretty stupid move because Easter recognized the man and he sent a note to the Judge, who also got an eyeful. Are you listening, Fitch?"

Listening, but not breathing. "Yes!" he snapped.

"Well, now the Judge knows the guy broke into Easter's apartment, and he's signed a warrant for the guy's arrest. So, get him out of town immediately or you're about to be embarrassed. Maybe arrested yourself."

A hundred questions raced wildly through Fitch's brain, but he knew they wouldn't be answered. If Doyle somehow got recognized and taken in, and if he said too much, then, well, it was unthinkable. Breaking and entering was a felony anywhere on the planet, and Fitch had to move fast. "Anything else?" he said.

"No. That's all for now."

Doyle was supposed to be eating at a window table in a dinky Vietnamese restaurant four blocks from the courthouse, but was in fact playing two-dollar blackjack at the Lucy Luck when the beeper erupted on his belt. It was Fitch, at the office. Three minutes later, Doyle was headed east on Highway 90, east because the Alabama state line was closer than Louisiana. Two hours later he was flying to Chicago.

It took Fitch an hour to dig and determine that no arrest warrant had been issued for Doyle Dunlap, nor for any unnamed person resembling him. This was of no comfort. The fact remained that Marlee knew they'd entered Easter's apartment.

But how did she know? That was the great and troubling question. Fitch yelled at Konrad and Pang behind locked doors. It would be three hours before they found the answer.

AT THREE-THIRTY, Monday, Judge Harkin called a halt to Dr. Kilvan's testimony and sent him home for the day. He announced to the surprised lawyers that there were a couple of serious matters involving the jury that had to be dealt with immediately. He sent the jurors back to their room and ordered all spectators out of the courtroom. Jip and Rasco herded them away, then locked the door.

Oliver McAdoo gently slid the briefcase under the table with his long left foot until the camera was aimed at the bench. Next to it were four other assorted satchels and cases, along with two large cardboard boxes filled with bulky depositions and other legal refuse. McAdoo was not sure what was about to happen, but he assumed, correctly, that Fitch would want to see it.

Judge Harkin cleared his throat and addressed the horde of lawyers watching him intently. "Gentlemen, it has come to my attention that some if not all of our jurors feel as if they're being watched and followed. I have clear proof that at least one of our jurors has been the victim of a break-in." He allowed this to sink in, and sink in it did. The lawyers were stunned, each side knowing full well it was innocent of any wrongdoing and immediately placing guilt where it belonged—at the other table.

"Now, I have two choices. I can declare a mistrial, or I can sequester the jury. I'm inclined to pursue the latter, as distasteful as it will be. Mr. Rohr?"

Rohr was slow to rise, and for a rare moment could think of little to say. "Uh, gee, Judge, we'd sure hate to see a mistrial. I mean, I'm certain that we've done nothing wrong." He glanced at the defense table as he said this. "Someone broke in on a juror?" he asked.

"That's what I said. I'll show you the proof in a moment. Mr. Cable?"

Sir Durr stood and buttoned his jacket right properly. "This is quite shocking, Your Honor."

"Certainly is."

"I'm really in no position to respond until I hear more," he said, returning the look of utter suspicion to the lawyers who were obviously guilty, the plaintiff's.

"Very well. Bring in juror number four, Stella Hulic," His Honor instructed Willis. Stella was stiff with fear and already pale by the time she reentered the courtroom.

"Please take a seat in the witness stand, Mrs. Hulic. This won't take but a minute." The Judge smiled with great assurance and waved at the chair in the witness box. Stella shot wild looks in all directions as she sat down.

"Thank you. Now, Mrs. Hulic, I want to ask you just a few questions."

The courtroom was still and silent as the lawyers held their pens and ignored their sacred legal pads and waited for a great secret to be revealed. After four years of pretrial warfare, they knew virtually everything that every witness would say beforehand. The prospect of unrehearsed statements coming from the witness stand was fascinating.

Surely she was about to reveal some heinous sin committed by the other side. She looked up pitifully at the Judge. Someone had smelled her breath and squealed on her.

"Did you go to Miami over the weekend?"

"Yes sir," she answered slowly.

"With your husband?"

"Yes." Cal had left the courtroom before lunch. He had deals to attend to.

"And what was the purpose of this visit?"

"To shop."

"Did anything unusual happen while you were there?"

She took a deep breath and looked at the eager lawyers packed around the long tables. Then she turned to Judge Harkin and said, "Yes sir."

"Please tell us what happened."

Her eyes watered, and the poor woman was about to lose control. Judge Harkin seized the moment, and said, "It's okay, Mrs. Hulic. You've done nothing wrong. Just tell us what happened."

She bit her lip and clenched her teeth. "We got in Friday night, to the hotel, and after we'd been there for two maybe three hours the phone rang, and it was some woman who told us that these men from the tobacco companies were following us. She said they had followed us from Biloxi, and they knew our flight numbers and everything. Said they'd follow us all weekend, might even try to bug our phones."

Rohr and his squad breathed in relief. One or two shot nasty looks at the other table, where Cable et al. were frozen.

"Did you see anybody following you?"

"Well, frankly, I never left the room. It upset me so. My husband Cal ventured out a few times, and he did see this one guy, some Cuban-looking man with a camera on the beach, then he saw the same guy on Sunday as we were checking out." It suddenly hit Stella that this was her exit, her one moment to appear so overcome she just couldn't continue. With little effort, the tears began to flow.

"Anything else, Mrs. Hulic?"

"No," she said, sobbing. "It's just awful. I can't keep . . ." and the words were lost in anguish.

His Honor looked at the lawyers. "I'm going to excuse Mrs. Hulic, and replace her with alternate number one." A small wail went up from Stella, and with the poor woman in such misery it was impossible to argue that she should be kept. Sequestration was looming, and there was no way she could keep pace.

"You may return to the jury room, get your things, and go home. Thank you for your service, and I'm sorry this has happened."

"I'm so sorry," she managed to whisper, then rose from the witness chair and left the courtroom. Her departure was a blow for the defense. She'd been rated highly during selection, and after two weeks of nonstop observation the jury experts on both sides were of the near-unanimous opinion that she was not sympathetic to the plaintiff. She had smoked for twenty-four years, without once trying to stop.

Her replacement was a wild card, feared by both sides but especially by the defense.

"Bring in juror number two, Nicholas Easter," Harkin said to Willis, who was standing with the door open. As Easter was being called for, Gloria Lane and an assistant rolled a large TV/VCR to the center of the courtroom. The lawyers began chewing their pens, especially the defense.

Durwood Cable pretended to be preoccupied with other matters on the table, but the only question on his mind was, What has Fitch done now? Before the trial, Fitch directed everything; the composition of the defense team, the selection of expert witnesses, the hiring of jury consultants, the actual investigation of all prospective jurors. He handled the delicate communications with the client, Pynex, and he watched the plaintiff's lawyers like a hawk. But most of what Fitch did after the trial began was quite secretive. Cable didn't want to know. He took the high road and tried the case. Let Fitch play in the gutter and try to win it.

Easter sat in the witness chair and crossed his legs. If he was scared or nervous, he didn't show it. The Judge asked him about the mysterious man who'd been following him, and Easter gave specific times and places where he'd seen the man. And he explained in perfect detail what happened last Wednesday when he glanced across the courtroom and saw the same man sitting out there, on the third row.

He then described the security measures he'd taken in his apartment, and he took the videotape from Judge Harkin. He inserted it in the VCR, and the lawyers sat on the edge of their seats. He ran the tape, all nine and a half minutes of it, and when it stopped he sat again in the witness chair and confirmed the identity of the intruder—it was the same man who'd been following him, the same guy who'd shown up in court last Wednesday.

Fitch couldn't see the damned monitor through his hidden camera because bigfoot McAdoo or some other klutz had kicked the briefcase under the table. But Fitch heard every word Easter said, and he could close his eyes and see precisely what was happening in the courtroom. A severe headache was forming at the base of his skull. He gulped aspirin and washed it down with mineral water. He'd love to ask Easter a simple question: For one concerned enough about security to install hidden cameras, why didn't you install an alarm system on your door? But the question occurred to no one but himself.

His Honor said, "I can also verify that the man in the video was in this courtroom last Wednesday." But the man in the video was now long gone. Doyle was safely tucked away in Chicago when the courtroom saw him enter the apartment and slink around as if he'd never get caught.

"You may return to the jury room, Mr. Easter."

AN HOUR PASSED as the lawyers made their rather feeble and unprepared arguments for and against sequestration. Once things warmed up, allegations of wrongdoing began to fly back and forth, with the defense catching the most flak. Both sides knew things they couldn't prove and thus couldn't say, so the accusations were left somewhat broad.

The jurors got a full report from Nicholas, an embellished account of everything that happened both in court and in the video. In his haste, Judge Harkin had failed to prohibit Nicholas from discussing the matter with his colleagues. It was an omission Nicholas had immediately caught, and he couldn't wait to structure the story to suit himself. He also took the liberty of explaining Stella's rapid departure. She'd left them in tears.

Fitch narrowly averted two minor strokes as he stomped around his office, rubbing his neck and his temples and tugging at his goatee and demanding impossible answers from Konrad, Swanson, and Pang. In addition to those three, he had young Holly, and Joe Boy, a local private eye with incredibly soft feet, and Dante, a black ex-cop from D.C., and Dubaz, another Coast boy with a lengthy record. And he had four people in the office with Konrad, another dozen he could summon to Biloxi within three hours, and loads of lawyers and jury consultants. Fitch had lots of people, and they cost lots of money, but he damned sure didn't send anyone to Miami over the weekend to watch Stella and Cal shop.

A Cuban? With a camera? Fitch actually threw a phonebook against a wall as he repeated this.

"What if it's the girl?" asked Pang, raising his head slowly after lowering it to miss the phonebook.

"What girl?"

"Marlee. Hulic said the phone call came from a girl." Pang's composure was a sharp contrast to his boss's explosiveness. Fitch froze in mid-step, then sat for a moment in his chair. He took another aspirin and drank more mineral water, and finally said, "I think you're right."

And he was. The Cuban was a two-bit "security consultant" Marlee found in the yellow pages. She'd paid him two hundred dollars to look suspicious, not a difficult task, and to get caught with a camera as the Hulics left the hotel.

THE ELEVEN JURORS and three alternates were reassembled in the courtroom. Sylvia's empty chair on the first row was filled by

Phillip Savelle, a forty-eight-year-old misfit neither side had been able to read. He described himself as a self-employed tree surgeon, but no record of this profession had been found on the Gulf Coast for the past five years. He was also an avant-garde glass-blower whose forte was brightly colored, shapeless creations to which he gave obscure aquatic and marine names and occasionally exhibited at tiny, neglected galleries in Greenwich Village. He boasted of being an expert sailor, and had in fact once built his own ketch, which he sailed to Honduras where it sank in calm waters. At times he fancied himself an archaeologist, and after the boat dropped he spent eleven months in a Honduran prison for illegal excavations.

He was single, agnostic, a graduate of Grinnell, a nonsmoker. Savelle scared the hell out of every lawyer in the courtroom.

Judge Harkin apologized for what he was about to do. Sequestration of a jury was a rare, radical event, made necessary by extraordinary circumstances, and almost always used in sensational murder cases. But he had no choice in this case. There had been unauthorized contact. There was no reason to believe it would cease, regardless of his warnings. He didn't like it one bit, and he was very sorry for the hardship it would cause, but his job at this point was to guarantee a fair trial.

He explained that months earlier he had developed a contingency plan for this very moment. The county had reserved a block of rooms at a nearby, unnamed motel. Security would be increased. He had a list of rules which he would cover with them. The trial was now entering its second full week of testimony, and he would push the lawyers hard to finish as soon as possible.

The fifteen jurors were to leave, go home, pack, get their affairs in order, and report to court the next morning prepared to spend the next two weeks sequestered.

There were no immediate reactions from the panel; they were too stunned. Only Nicholas Easter thought it was funny.

Fourteen

BECAUSE OF JERRY'S FONDNESS for beer and gambling and football and rowdiness in general, Nicholas suggested they meet at a casino Monday night to celebrate their last few hours of freedom. Jerry thought it was a wonderful idea. As the two left the courthouse, they toyed with the idea of inviting a few of their colleagues. The idea sounded good, but it didn't work. Herman was out of the question. Lonnie Shaver left hurriedly, quite agitated and not speaking to anyone. Savelle was new and unknown, and apparently the kind of guy you'd keep at a distance. That left Herrera, Nap the Colonel, and they simply weren't up to it. They were about to spend two weeks locked up with him.

Jerry invited Sylvia Taylor-Tatum, the Poodle. The two were becoming friends of a sort. She was divorced for the second time, and Jerry was about to be divorced for the first. Since Jerry knew all the casinos along the Coast, he suggested they meet at a new one called The Diplomat. It had a sports bar with a large screen, cheap drinks, a little privacy, and cocktail waitresses with long legs and skimpy outfits.

When Nicholas arrived at eight, Poodle was already there, holding a table in the crowded bar, sipping a draft beer and smiling pleasantly, something she never did inside the courthouse. Her flowing curly hair was pulled back. She wore tight faded jeans, a bulky sweater, and red cowboy boots. Still far from pretty, she looked much better in a bar than in the jury box.

Sylvia had the dark, sad, worldly eyes of a woman beaten by life, and Nicholas was determined to dig as fast and as deep as possible before Fernandez arrived. He ordered another round, and dispensed with the chitchat. "Are you married?" he asked, knowing she wasn't. The first marriage had occurred when she was nineteen, had produced twin boys, now twenty. One worked offshore on an oil rig, the other was a junior in college. Very opposite. Husband One left after five years, and she raised the boys herself. "What about you?" she asked.

"No. Technically I'm still a student, but I'm working now."

Husband Two was an older man, and thankfully they produced no children. The marriage lasted seven years, then he traded her in for a newer model. She vowed to never marry again. The Bears kicked off to the Packers and Sylvia watched the game with interest. She loved football because her boys had been all-conference picks in high school.

Jerry arrived in a rush, casting wary glances behind him before apologizing for being late. He gulped down the first beer in a matter of seconds, and explained that he thought he was being followed. Poodle scoffed at this, and offered the opinion that right now every member of the jury was jerking at the neck, certain that shadows were not far behind.

"Forget the jury," Jerry said. "I think it's my wife."

"Your wife?" said Nicholas.

"Yeah. I think she's got some private snoop trailing me."

"You should look forward to being sequestered," Nicholas said.

"Oh I am," Jerry said, winking at Poodle.

He had five hundred dollars on the Packers, plus six points, but the bet was only for the combined score in the first half. He'd place another bet at halftime. Any pro or college game offered an amazing array of bets, he explained to the two novices seated with him, virtually none of which had anything to do with the ultimate winner. Jerry sometimes bet on who'd fumble first, who'd make the first field goal, who'd throw the most interceptions. He watched the game with the edginess of a man wagering money he could ill afford to lose. He drank four draft beers in the first quarter. Nicholas and Sylvia fell quickly behind.

In the gaps of Jerry's incessant chatter about football and the art of successful betting, Nicholas made a few awkward forays into the subject of the trial, without success. Sequestration was a sore subject, and since they had not yet experienced it there was little to say. The day's testimony had been painful enough to sit through, and the thought of rehashing Dr. Kilvan's opinions during leisure seemed cruel. Nor was there interest in the bigger picture. Sylvia in particular was disgusted by a simple inquiry into the general concept of liability.

MRS. GRIMES had been ushered from the courtroom and was in the atrium when Judge Harkin announced his rules for sequestration. As she drove Herman home he explained that he'd be spending the next two weeks in a motel room, on strange turf, without her around. Shortly after they reached their house, she had Judge Harkin on the phone, and gave him an earful of her thoughts on these most recent developments. Her husband was blind, she reminded him more than once, and he needed special assistance. Herman sat on the sofa, drinking his one beer of the day and fuming at his wife's intrusion.

Judge Harkin quickly found middle ground. He would allow Mrs. Grimes to stay with Herman in his room at the motel. She could eat breakfast and dinner with Herman, and care for him, but she had to avoid contact with the other jurors. Also, she could no longer watch the trial because it was imperative that she not be able to discuss it with Herman. This didn't sit well with Mrs. Grimes, one of the few spectators who'd heard every word so far. And, though she didn't reveal this to His Honor, or to Herman, she had already developed some rather strong opinions about the case. The Judge was firm. Herman was furious. But Mrs. Grimes prevailed, and set off to the bedroom to begin packing.

LONNIE SHAVER did a week's work Monday night at the office. After numerous attempts, he found George Teaker at home in Charlotte, and explained that the jury was about to be locked away for the duration of the trial. He was scheduled to talk to Taunton later in the week, and he was worried about being inaccessible. He explained that the Judge was prohibiting any direct phone calls to and from the motel room, and it would be impossible to correspond again until after the trial. Teaker was sympathetic, and as the conversation progressed he expressed somber concerns about the outcome of the trial.

"Our people in New York think an adverse verdict could send shock waves through the retail economy, especially in our business. God knows where insurance rates will go."

"I'll do what I can," Lonnie promised.

"Surely the jury isn't serious about a big verdict, is it?"

"Hard to tell right now. We're halfway through the plaintiff's case, it's just too early."

"You've gotta protect us on this, Lonnie. I know it puts you in the bull's-eye, but, damn, you just happen to be there, know what I mean?"

"Yeah, I understand. I'll do what I can."

"We're counting on you up here. Hang in there."

THE CONFRONTATION with Fitch was brief and went nowhere. Durwood Cable waited until almost nine, Monday night, when the offices were still busy with trial preparation and a late, catered dinner was being completed in the conference room. He asked Fitch to step into his office. Fitch obliged, though he wanted to leave and return to the dime store.

"I'd like to discuss a matter," Durr said stiffly, standing on his side of his desk.

"What is it?" Fitch barked, choosing also to stand with hands on hips. He knew exactly what Cable had in mind.

"We were embarrassed in court this afternoon."

"You were not embarrassed. As I recall, the jury was not present. So whatever happened was of no consequence to the final verdict."

"You got caught, and we got embarrassed."

"I did not get caught."

"Then what do you call it?"

"I call it a lie. We did not send people to follow Stella Hulic. Why would we do that?"

"Then who called her?"

"I don't know, but it certainly wasn't any of our people. Any more questions?"

"Yeah, who was the guy in the apartment?"

"He was not one of my men. I didn't get to see the video, you understand. So I didn't see his face, but we have reason to believe he was a goon employed by Rohr and his boys."

"Can you prove this?"

"I don't have to prove a damned thing. And I don't have to answer any more questions. Your job is to try this lawsuit, and you let me worry about security."

"Don't embarrass me, Fitch."

"And don't you embarrass me by losing this trial."

"I rarely lose."

Fitch turned and headed for the door. "I know. And you're doing a fine job, Cable. You just need a little help from the outside."

NICHOLAS ARRIVED FIRST with two gym bags stuffed with clothes and toiletries. Lou Dell and Willis and another deputy, a new one, were waiting in the hallway outside the jury room to collect the bags and store them for a while in an empty witness room. It was eight-twenty, Tuesday.

"How do the bags get from here to the motel?" Nicholas asked, still holding his and quite suspicious.

"We'll haul them over sometime during the day," Willis said. "But we have to inspect them first."

"I'll be damned."

"I beg your pardon."

"No one is inspecting these bags," Nicholas pronounced and stepped into the empty jury room.

"Judge's orders," said Lou Dell, following.

"I don't care what the Judge has ordered. No one is inspecting my bags." He placed them in a corner, walked to the coffeepot, and said to Willis and Lou Dell in the doorway, "Leave, okay. This is the jury room."

They shuffled backward and Lou Dell closed the door. A minute passed before there were words in the hallway. Nicholas opened the door and saw Millie Dupree, sweat lining her forehead, confronting Lou Dell and Willis with two huge Samsonite suitcases. "They think they're gonna inspect our bags, but they're not," Nicholas explained. "Let's put them in here." He grabbed the nearest, and with great effort lifted it and hauled it to the same corner in the jury room.

"Judge's orders," Lou Dell was heard to mumble.

"We're not terrorists," Nicholas snapped, heaving. "What's he think we're gonna do, smuggle in some guns or drugs or something?" Millie grabbed a doughnut and expressed her gratitude to Nicholas for protecting her privacy. There were things in there that, well, she just wouldn't want men such as Willis or anybody for that matter to touch or feel.

"Leave," Nicholas yelled, pointing at Lou Dell and Willis, who again retreated into the hallway.

By eight forty-five, all twelve jurors were present and the room was cramped with baggage Nicholas had rescued and stored. He'd ranted and raved and grown angrier with each new load, and had done a fine job of whipping the jury into a nasty bunch ready for a showdown. At nine, Lou Dell knocked on the door, then turned the knob to enter.

The door was locked from the inside.

She knocked again.

In the jury room, no one moved but Nicholas. He walked to the door, said, "Who is it?"

"Lou Dell. It's time to go. The Judge is ready for you."

"Tell the Judge to go to hell."

Lou Dell turned to Willis, who was bug-eyed and reaching for his rusty revolver. The harshness of his reply startled even some of the angrier jurors, but there was no break in their unity.

"What did you say?" Lou Dell asked.

There was a loud click, then the doorknob turned. Nicholas walked into the hallway and closed the door behind him. "Tell the Judge we're not coming out," he said, glaring down at Lou Dell and her dirty gray bangs.

"You can't do that," Willis said as aggressively as possible, which was not aggressive at all but rather feeble.

"Shut up, Willis."

THE EXCITEMENT of jury trouble lured people back to the courtroom Tuesday morning. Word had spread quickly that one juror had been bounced and that another had had his apartment broken into, and that the Judge was angry and had ordered the entire panel locked up. Rumors ran wild, the most popular of which was the one about a tobacco snoop actually getting caught in a juror's apartment and a warrant being issued for his arrest. Cops and FBI were looking everywhere for the man.

The morning papers from Biloxi, New Orleans, Mobile, and Jackson ran large stories either on the front page or front page—Metro.

The courthouse regulars were back in droves. Most of the local bar suddenly had pressing business in the courtroom and loitered about. A half-dozen reporters from various papers held the front row, plaintiff's side. The boys from Wall Street, a group that had been dwindling as its members discovered casinos and deep sea fishing and long nights in New Orleans, were back in full force.

And so there were many witnesses to the sight of Lou Dell nervously tiptoeing through the jury door, across the front of the courtroom to the bench, where she leaned up and Harkin leaned down, and they conferred. Harkin's head cocked sideways as if he didn't catch it at first, then he looked blankly at the jury door where Willis was standing with his shoulders up in a frozen shrug.

Lou Dell finished delivering her message and walked quickly back to where Willis was waiting. Judge Harkin studied the inquiring faces of the lawyers, then looked at all the spectators out there. He scribbled something he couldn't read himself. He pondered about what to do next.

His jury was on strike!

And what exactly did his judge's handbook say about that?

He pulled his microphone closer and said, "Gentlemen, there is a small problem with the jury. I need to go speak with them. I'll ask Mr. Rohr and Mr. Cable to assist me. Everyone else is to remain in place."

The door was locked again. The Judge knocked politely, three light raps followed by a twist of the doorknob. It wouldn't open. "Who is it?" came a male voice from inside.

"It's Judge Harkin," he said loudly. Nicholas was standing at the door. He turned and smiled at his colleagues. Millie Dupree and Mrs. Gladys Card were hovering in a corner near a pile of luggage, fidgeting nervously, afraid of jail or whatever the Judge might throw at them. But the other jurors were still indignant.

Nicholas unlocked the door and opened it. He smiled pleasantly as if nothing were wrong, as if strikes were a routine part of trials. "Come in," he said.

Harkin, in a gray suit, no robe, entered with Rohr and Cable in tow. "What's the problem here?" he asked while surveying the room. Most of the jurors were seated at the table with coffee cups and empty plates and newspapers scattered everywhere. Phillip Savelle stood alone at one window. Lonnie Shaver sat in a corner with a laptop on his knees. Easter was no doubt the spokesman, and probably the instigator.

"We don't think it's fair for the deputies to search our bags."

"And why not?"

"It should be obvious. These are our personal effects. We're not terrorists or drug smugglers, and you're not a customs agent." Easter's tone was authoritative, and the fact that he spoke so boldly to a distinguished judge made most of the jurors very proud. He was one of them, undoubtedly their leader regardless of what Herman thought, and he had told them more than once that they—not the Judge, not the lawyers, not the parties—but they the jurors were the most important people in this trial.

"It's routine in all sequestration cases," His Honor said, taking a step closer to Easter, who was four inches taller and not about to be cowered.

"But it's not in black and white, is it? In fact, I'll bet it's a simple matter of discretion with the presiding judge. True?"

"There are some good reasons for it."

"Not good enough. We're not coming out, Your Honor, until you promise our bags will be left alone." Easter said this with a tight jaw and semi-snarl, and it was evident to the Judge and the lawyers that he meant it. He was also speaking for the group. No one else had moved.

Harkin made the mistake of glancing over his shoulder at Rohr, who couldn't wait to add a few thoughts. "Oh hell, Judge, what's the big deal?" he blurted. "These folks aren't carrying plastic explosives."

"That's enough," Harkin said, but Rohr had managed to curry a slight favor with the jury. Cable, of course, felt the same, and wanted to convey his heartfelt trust in whatever the jurors had packed in their American Touristers, but Harkin didn't give him the chance.

"Very well," His Honor said. "The bags will not be searched. But if it comes to my attention that any juror possesses any item prohibited by the list I handed out yesterday, then that juror will be in contempt of court and subject to being jailed. Do we understand?"

Easter looked around the room, took the measure of each of his fellow jurors, most of whom appeared relieved and a few of whom were actually nodding. "That's fine, Judge," he said.

"Good. Now can we get on with the trial?"

"Well, there's one other problem."

"What is it?"

Nicholas lifted a sheet of paper from the table, read something, then said, "According to your rules here, we're allowed one conjugal visit per week. We think we should get more."

"How many?"

"As many as possible."

This was news to most of the jurors. There had been some grumbling among some of the men, Easter and Fernandez and Lonnie Shaver in particular, about the number of conjugal visits, but the women had not discussed it. Particularly, Mrs. Gladys Card and Millie Dupree were downright embarrassed to have His Honor think they were insisting on having as much sex as they could get. Mr. Card had had prostate trouble years earlier, and, well, Mrs. Gladys Card thought about divulging this to clear her good name when Herman Grimes said, "Two'll do me."

The image of old Herm feeling his way around under the covers with Mrs. Grimes could not be denied, and provoked laughter that broke the tension.

"I don't think we should take a survey," Judge Harkin said. "Can we agree on two? We're just talking about a couple of weeks, folks."

"Two, with a possible third," Nicholas counteroffered.

"That's fine. Does that suit everyone?" His Honor looked around the room. Loreen Duke was giggling to herself at the table. Mrs. Gladys Card and Millie were trying their best to disappear into the walls and would not under any circumstances look the Judge in the eyes.

"Yes, that's fine," said Jerry Fernandez, red-eyed and hung over. If Jerry went a day without sex he developed headaches, but he knew two things: his wife was delighted to have him out of the house for the next two weeks, and he and Poodle would work out an arrangement.

"I object to the wording of this," Phillip Savelle said from the window, his first words of the trial. He was holding the sheet of rules. "Your definition of the persons eligible to participate in conjugal visits leaves something to be desired."

In clear English, the offending section read: "During each conjugal visit, each juror may spend two hours, alone and in his or her room, with his or her spouse, girlfriend, or boyfriend."

Judge Harkin, along with the two lawyers looking over his shoulder, and every juror in the room read the language carefully and wondered what in the world this weirdo had in mind. But Harkin was not about to find out. "I assure you, Mr. Savelle and members of the jury, I have no plans to restrict any of you in any way with respect to your conjugal visits. I don't care what you do, or whom you do it with, frankly."

This seemed to satisfy Savelle as much as it humiliated Mrs. Gladys Card.

"Now, anything else?"

"That's all, Your Honor, and thank you," Herman said loudly, reasserting himself as the leader.

"Thanks," Nicholas said.

SCOTTY MANGRUM announced to the court, as soon as the jury was settled and happy, that he was finished with Dr. Kilvan. Durr Cable began a cross-examination so delicate that he seemed thoroughly intimidated by the great expert. They agreed on a few statistics that were undoubtedly meaningless. Dr. Kilvan stated that, through his plethora of numbers, he believed that about ten percent of all smokers actually get lung cancer.

Cable reinforced the point, something he'd done from the beginning and something he would do to the very end. "So Dr. Kilvan, if smoking causes lung cancer, then why do so few smokers get lung cancer?"

"Smoking greatly increases the risk of lung cancer."

"But it doesn't cause it every time, does it?"

"No. Not every smoker gets lung cancer."

"Thank you."

"But for those who smoke, the risk of lung cancer is much greater."

Cable warmed to the task and began to press. He asked Dr. Kilvan if he was familiar with a twenty-year-old study from the University of Chicago in which researchers found a greater incidence of lung cancer for smokers who lived in metropolitan areas than for smokers who lived in rural areas. Kilvan was very familiar with the study, though he had nothing to do with it.

"Can you explain it?" Cable asked.

"No."

"Can you venture a guess?"

"Yes. It was a controversial study when it came out because it indicated factors other than tobacco smoke might cause lung cancer."

"Such as air pollution?"

"Yes."

"Do you believe this?"

"It's possible."

"So you admit that air pollution causes lung cancer."

"It might. But I stand by my research. Rural smokers get lung cancer more than rural nonsmokers, and urban smokers get cancer more than urban nonsmokers."

Cable lifted another thick report and made an event of flipping pages. He asked Dr. Kilvan if he was familiar with a 1989 study at the University of Stockholm in which researchers determined that there was a link between heredity and smoking and lung cancer.

"I read that report," Dr. Kilvan said.

"Do you have an opinion on it?"

"No. Heredity is not my specialty."

"So you can't say yes or no on the issue of whether heredity might be related to smoking and lung cancer."

"I cannot."

"But you don't contest this report, do you?"

"I don't have a position on the report."

"Do you know the experts who conducted the research?"

"No."

"So you can't tell us if they're qualified or not?"

"No. I'm sure you've talked to them."

Cable walked to his table, swapped reports, and walked back to the lectern.

AFTER TWO WEEKS of severe scrutiny but little movement, Pynex stock suddenly had a reason to stir. Other than the impromptu Pledge of Allegiance, a phenomenon that so baffled the courtroom no one could decipher its meaning, the trial had produced virtually no high drama until late Monday afternoon when the jury was shaken. One of the many defense lawyers let it slip to one of the many financial analysts that Stella Hulic was generally deemed to be a decent defense juror. This got repeated a few times, and with each telling Stella's significance to the tobacco industry rose to new heights. By the time the calls were made to New York, the defense had lost its most prized possession—Stella Hulic, who was by then home on the sofa in a martini-induced coma.

Added to the rumor mill was the delicious bit about the break-in of juror Easter's apartment. It was easy to assume the intruder was paid by the tobacco industry, and since they'd been caught or at least were highly suspected, things looked bad all around for the defense. They'd lost a juror. They'd got caught cheating. The sky was falling.

Pynex opened Tuesday morning at seventy-nine and a half, quickly fell to seventy-eight in trading that became heavier as the morning progressed and the rumors mushroomed. It was at seventy-six and a quarter by mid-morning when a fresh report was received from Biloxi. An analyst who was *actually in the courtroom* down there called his office with the news that the jury had refused to come out this morning, had in fact gone on strike because it was sick and tired of the boring testimony being offered by the plaintiff's experts.

In seconds, the report was repeated a hundred times, and it became a simple fact on the Street that the jury down there was revolting against the plaintiff. The price jumped to seventy-seven, flew past seventy-eight, hit seventy-nine, and was nearing eighty by lunch.

Fifteen

OF THE SIX WOMEN remaining on the jury, the one Fitch
wanted most to nail was Rikki Coleman, the wholesome,
pretty, thirty-year-old mother of two. She earned twenty-one
thousand dollars a year as a records administrator in a local hospital. Her husband earned thirty-six thousand dollars as a private
pilot. They lived in a nice suburb with a manicured lawn and a
ninety-thousand-dollar mortgage, and they each drove Japanese
cars, both of which were paid for. They saved frugally and invested conservatively—eight thousand dollars last year alone in
mutual funds. They were very active in a neighborhood church—
she taught small kids in Sunday School and he sang in the choir.

Apparently the Colemans had acquired no bad habits. Neither
smoked, and there was no evidence they drank. He liked to jog
and play tennis, she spent an hour a day at a health club. Because
of the clean life and because of her background in health care,
Fitch feared her as a juror.

The medical records obtained from her ob-gyn revealed nothing
remarkable. Two pregnancies, with perfect deliveries and recov-
eries. The annual checkups were done on time. A mammography
two years ago showed nothing unusual. She was five feet five
inches, 116 pounds.

Fitch had medical records for seven of the twelve jurors.
Easter's couldn't be found for obvious reasons. Herman Grimes
was blind and had nothing to hide. Savelle was new and Fitch was

digging. Lonnie Shaver hadn't been to the doctor in at least twenty years. Sylvia Taylor-Tatum's doctor had been killed months earlier in a boating accident, and his successor was a rookie who didn't know how the game was played.

The game was serious hardball, and Fitch had written most of the rules. Each year, The Fund contributed a million dollars to an organization known as the Judicial Reform Alliance, a noisy presence in Washington funded primarily by insurance companies, medical associations, and manufacturing groups. And tobacco companies. The Big Four reported annual contributions of a hundred thousand each, with Fitch and The Fund sliding another million under the door. The purpose of JRA was to lobby for laws to restrict the size of awards in damage suits. Specifically, to eliminate the nuisance of punitive damages.

Luther Vandemeer, CEO of Trellco, was a vocal member of the JRA board, and with Fitch quietly calling the shots, Vandemeer often ran roughshod over the members of the organization. Fitch wasn't seen, but he got what he wanted. Through Vandemeer and JRA, Fitch put enormous pressure on the insurance companies, which in turn put pressure on various local doctors, who in turn leaked sensitive and thoroughly confidential records of selected patients. So when Fitch wanted Dr. Dow in Biloxi to accidentally send the medical records for Mrs. Gladys Card to a nondescript post office box in Baltimore, he told Vandemeer to lean on contacts at St. Louis Mutual, Dr. Dow's malpractice carrier. Dr. Dow was told by St. Louis Mutual that his liability coverage might be dropped if he didn't play the game, and he became altogether happy to comply.

Fitch had quite a collection of medical records, but nothing so far that might turn a verdict. His luck changed during lunch on Tuesday.

When Rikki Coleman was still Rikki Weld, she attended a small Bible college in Montgomery, Alabama, where she was very popular. Some of the prettier girls at the school were known to date boys from Auburn. As the routine investigation into her background progressed, Fitch's investigator in Montgomery got a hunch that Rikki probably had plenty of dates. Fitch pursued the hunch with serious arm-twisting through JRA, and after two weeks of dead-end probing they finally found the right clinic.

It was a small, private women's hospital in downtown Montgomery, one of only three places abortions were performed in the city at that time. During her junior year, a week after her twentieth birthday, Rikki Weld had an abortion.

And Fitch had the records. A phone call told him they were coming, and he laughed to himself as he picked the sheets off his fax machine. No name for the father, but that was fine. Rikki had met Rhea, her husband, a year after she finished college. At the time of the abortion, Rhea was a senior at Texas A & M, and it was doubtful the two had ever met.

Fitch was willing to bet a ton of money the abortion was a dark secret, all but forgotten by Rikki and definitely never revealed to her husband.

THE MOTEL was a Siesta Inn in Pass Christian, thirty minutes west along the Coast. The trip was made by charter bus with Lou Dell and Willis riding up front with the driver and the fourteen jurors scattered throughout the seats. No two sat together. Conversation was nonexistent. They were tired and disheartened, already isolated and imprisoned, though they had yet to see their new temporary home. For the first two weeks of the trial, adjournment at five meant escape; they left hurriedly and raced back to reality, back to homes and kids and hot meals, back to errands and maybe the office. Adjournment now meant a chartered ride to another cell where they were to be watched and monitored and protected from evil shadows out there somewhere.

Only Nicholas Easter was delighted with sequestration, but he managed to look as dispirited as the rest.

Harrison County had rented for them the entire first floor of one wing, twenty rooms in all, though only nineteen would be needed. Lou Dell and Willis had separate rooms by the door leading to the main building where the reception and restaurant were located. A large young deputy named Chuck had a room at the other end of the hallway, ostensibly to guard the door leading to a parking lot.

The rooms were assigned by Judge Harkin himself. The bags had already been transported and placed, unopened and definitely uninspected. Keys were passed out like candy by Lou Dell, whose self-importance grew by the hour. Beds were kicked and inspected—doubles in every room for some reason. TV's were turned on, to no avail. No programs, no news during sequestration. Only movies from the motel's station. Bathrooms were scrutinized, faucets checked, toilets flushed. Two weeks here would seem like a year.

The bus was of course followed by Fitch's boys. It left the courthouse with a police escort, cops in front and back on motorcycles. It was easy to track the cops. Two detectives working for Rohr also followed along. No one expected the location of the motel to remain a secret.

Nicholas had Savelle on one side and Colonel Herrera on the other. The men's rooms were next to each other; the women were across the hall as if segregation was necessary to prevent unauthorized frolicking. Five minutes after unlocking the door the walls began to close in, and ten minutes later Willis knocked loudly and inquired as to whether everything was okay. "Just beautiful," Nicholas said without opening the door.

The telephones had been removed, as had the mini-bars. A room at the end of the hall had been stripped of the beds and furnished with two round tables, phones, comfortable chairs, a large-screen TV, and a bar fully equipped with every possible nonalcoholic beverage. Someone dubbed it the Party Room, and it stuck. Each phone call had to be approved by one of their guardians, and no incoming calls were permitted. Emergencies would be handled through the front desk. In Room 40, directly across the hall from the Party Room, the beds had also been removed and a makeshift dining table had been set up.

No juror could leave the wing without prior approval from Judge Harkin, or on-the-spot approval from Lou Dell or one of the deputies. There was no curfew because there was no place to go, but the Party Room closed at ten.

Dinner was from six to seven, breakfast from six to eight-thirty, and they were not expected to eat en masse. They could come and go. They could fix a plate and go back to their rooms. Judge Harkin was deeply concerned about the quality of the food, and wanted to be told each morning if there were complaints.

Tuesday's smorgasbord was either fried chicken or broiled snapper, with salads and plenty of vegetables. They were amazed at their appetites. For people who'd done nothing all day but remain seated and listen, most were weak with starvation by the time the food arrived at six. Nicholas fixed the first plate and sat at the end of the table where he engaged everyone in conversation and insisted they eat as a group. He was hyper and chipper and acted as if sequestration were nothing but an adventure. His enthusiasm was slightly contagious.

Only Herman Grimes ate in his room. Mrs. Grimes prepared two plates and left in a rush. Judge Harkin had strict written instructions prohibiting her from eating with the jury. Same for Lou Dell and Willis and Chuck. So when Lou Dell entered the room with dinner in mind and found Nicholas in the middle of a tale, the conversation suddenly ceased. She flung a few green beans alongside a chicken breast and a dinner roll, and left.

They were a group now, isolated and exiled, cut off from reality and banished against their wishes to a Siesta Inn. They had no one but themselves. Easter was determined to keep them happy. They would be a fraternity, if not a family. He would work to avoid divisions and cliques.

They watched two movies in the Party Room. By ten, they were all asleep.

"I'M READY for my conjugal visit," Jerry Fernandez announced over breakfast, in the general direction of Mrs. Gladys Card, who blushed.

"Really," she said, rolling her eyes toward the ceiling. Jerry smiled at her as if she might be the object of his longing. Breakfast was a veritable feast of everything from fried ham to cornflakes.

Nicholas arrived mid-meal with a soft hello to the group and a troubled countenance. "I don't understand why we can't have telephones," were the first words from his mouth, and the pleasant morning mood suddenly turned sour. He sat across from Jerry, who read his face and caught on immediately.

"Why can't we have a cold beer?" Jerry asked. "I have a cold beer every night when I'm home, maybe two. Who has the right to dictate what we can drink here?"

"Judge Harkin," said Millie Dupree, a woman who avoided alcohol.

"I'll be damned."

"And what about television?" Nicholas asked. "Why can't we watch television? I've been watching television since the trial started, and I don't recall much excitement." He turned to Loreen Duke, a large woman with a plate full of scrambled eggs. "Have you seen any sudden newsbreaks with the latest from the trial?"

"Nope."

He looked at Rikki Coleman, who was sitting behind a tiny bowl of harmless flakes. "And what about a gym, someplace to go sweat after eight hours in the courtroom? Surely they could've found a motel with a gym." Rikki nodded her complete agreement.

Loreen swallowed her eggs and said, "What I don't understand is, why can't we be trusted with a telephone? My kids might need to call me. It's not like some goon's gonna call my room and threaten me."

"I'd just like a cold beer, or two," Jerry said. "Any maybe a few more conjugal visits," he added, again looking at Mrs. Gladys Card.

The grumbling gathered speed around the table, and within ten minutes of Easter's arrival, the jurors were on the verge of revolt. The random irritations were now a full-fledged list of abuses. Even Herrera, the Retired Colonel who'd camped in jungles, was not pleased with the selection of beverages offered in the Party Room. Millie Dupree objected to the absence of newspapers. Lonnie Shaver had pressing business, and deeply resented the notion of sequestration in the first place. "I can think for myself," he said. "No one can influence me." At the least, he needed an unrestricted telephone. Phillip Savelle did yoga in the woods each morning at dawn, alone, just himself communing with nature, and there wasn't a tree within two hundred yards of the motel. And what about church? Mrs. Card was a devout Baptist who never missed prayer meeting on Wednesday nights and visitation on Tuesdays and WMU on Fridays and of course the Sabbath was crammed full of meetings.

"We'd better get things straight now," Nicholas said solemnly. "We're gonna be here for two weeks, maybe three. I say we get Judge Harkin's attention."

Judge Harkin had nine lawyers packed into his chambers haggling over the daily issues to be kept away from the jury. He required the lawyers to appear each morning at eight for the warm-up bouts, and he often made them stay an hour or two after the jury left. A heavy knock interrupted a heated debate between Rohr and Cable. Gloria Lane pushed the door open until it hit a chair occupied by Oliver McAdoo.

"We have a problem with the jury," she said gravely.

Harkin jumped to his feet. "What!"

"They want to talk to you. That's all I know."

Harkin looked at his watch. "Where are they?"

"At the motel."

"Can't we get them over here?"

"No. We've tried. They're not coming until they talk to you."

His shoulders sagged and his mouth hung open. "This is getting ridiculous," Wendall Rohr offered to no one in particular. The lawyers watched the Judge, who looked absently at the pile of papers on his desk and collected his thoughts. Then he rubbed his hands together and gave them all a huge phony smile. "Let's go see them."

KONRAD TOOK THE FIRST CALL at 8:02. She didn't want to talk to Fitch, just wanted to give him the message that the jury was once again perturbed and not coming out until Harkin hauled himself over to the Siesta Inn and unruffled their feathers. Konrad ran to Fitch's room and delivered the message.

At 8:09, she called again and gave Konrad the information that Easter would be wearing a dark denim shirt over a tan T-shirt, with red socks and the usual starched khakis. Red socks, she repeated.

At 8:12, she called for the third time and asked to speak to Fitch, who was pacing around his desk and pulling on his goatee. He clenched the receiver. "Hello."

"Good morning, Fitch," she said.

"Good morning, Marlee."

"You ever been to the St. Regis Hotel in New Orleans?"

"No."

"It's on Canal Street in the French Quarter. There's an open-air bar on the roof. It's called the Terrace Grill. Get a table overlooking the Quarter. Be there at seven tonight. I'll be there later. Are you with me?"

"Yes."

"And come by yourself, Fitch. I'll watch you enter the hotel, and if you bring friends the meeting's off. Okay?"

"Okay."

"And if you attempt to trail me, then I disappear."

"You have my word."

"Why am I not comforted by your word, Fitch?" She hung up.

□ □ □ □

CABLE, ROHR, AND JUDGE HARKIN were met at the front
desk by Lou Dell, who was flustered and scared and rattling on
about how this had never happened to her; she'd always kept her
juries under control. She led them to the Party Room where thirteen of the fourteen jurors were holed up. Herman Grimes was
the lone dissenter. He had argued with the group about their
tactics, and had angered Jerry Fernandez to the point of getting
himself insulted. Jerry had pointed out that Herman had his wife
with him, that he had no use for either televisions or newspapers,
didn't drink anymore, and probably didn't need a gym. Jerry
apologized after Millie Dupree asked him to.

If His Honor had a chip on his shoulder, it didn't last long.
After a few uncertain hellos and good mornings, he said, starting
badly, "I'm a little bit disturbed by this."

To which Nicholas Easter responded, "We're not in the mood
to take any abuse."

Rohr and Cable had been expressly forbidden from speaking,
and they hung near the door and watched with great amusement.
Both knew this was a scene unlikely to be repeated in their litigat-
ing careers.

Nicholas had written down their list of complaints. Judge Harkin removed his coat, took a seat, and was soon hammered from
all directions. He was pitifully outnumbered and virtually de-
fenseless.

Beer was no problem. Newspapers could be censored by the
front desk. Unrestricted phone calls made perfect sense. Same for
televisions, but only if they promised not to watch the local news.
The gym might be a problem, but he'd look into it. Visits to
church could be arranged.

In fact, everything was flexible.

"Can you explain why we're here?" Lonnie Shaver demanded.

He tried. He cleared his throat and reluctantly attempted to
justify his reasons for locking them away. He rambled for a bit
about unauthorized contact, about what had happened so far
with this jury, and he made some vague references to events that
had occurred in other tobacco trials.

The misconduct was well documented, and both sides had been
guilty in the past. Fitch had left a wide trail across the landscape
of tobacco litigation. Operatives for some of the plaintiffs' law-

yers in other cases had done dirty deeds. But Judge Harkin couldn't talk about them in front of his jury. He had to be careful and not prejudice either side.

The meeting lasted an hour. Harkin asked for a no-strike guarantee in the future, but Easter wouldn't commit.

PYNEX OPENED DOWN two points on news of a second strike, which according to an analyst waiting in the courtroom was caused by an ill-defined negative reaction by the jurors to certain tactics employed the day before by the defense team. The tactics were also ill-defined. A second rumor by another analyst in Biloxi cleared things up a little by speculating that no one in the courtroom knew for certain exactly why the jury was on strike. The stock moved half a point lower before correcting itself and inching upward in the early morning trading.

THE TAR in cigarettes causes cancer, at least in laboratory rodents. Dr. James Ueuker from Palo Alto had worked with mice and rats for the past fifteen years. He'd conducted many studies himself and he'd studied extensively the work of researchers around the world. At least six major studies had, in his opinion, conclusively linked cigarette smoking with lung cancer. In great detail, he explained to the jury exactly how he and his team had taken tobacco smoke condensates, usually referred to simply as "tars," and rubbed them directly onto the skin of what looked like a million white mice. The pictures were large and in color. The lucky mice got just a touch of tar, the others got fairly painted. To no one's surprise, the heavier the tar, the quicker skin cancer developed.

It's a long way from surface tumors on rodents to lung cancer in humans, and Dr. Ueuker, with Rohr leading the way, couldn't wait to link the two. Medical history is filled with studies in which laboratory findings have ultimately been proven to apply to humans. Exceptions have been rare. Though mice and humans live in vastly different environments, the results in some animal tests are fully consistent with the epidemiologic findings in humans.

Every available jury consultant was in the courtroom during Ueuker's testimony. Disgusting little rodents were one thing, but rabbits and beagles could be cuddly pets. Ueuker's next study involved a similar plastering of tar on rabbits, with virtually the same results. His last test involved thirty beagles which he taught to smoke through tubes in their tracheas. The heavy smokers worked their way up to nine cigarettes a day; the equivalent of about forty cigarettes for a 150-pound man. In these dogs, serious lung damage in the form of invasive tumors was detected after 875 consecutive days of smoking. Ueuker used dogs because they exhibit the same reaction to cigarette smoking as do humans.

He would not, however, get to tell this jury about his rabbits and his beagles. An untrained amateur could look at Millie Dupree's face and tell she felt very sorry for the mice, and held a grudge against Ueuker for killing them. Sylvia Taylor-Tatum and Angel Weese also expressed overt signs of displeasure. Mrs. Gladys Card and Phillip Savelle emitted subtle evidence of disapproval. The other men were unmoved.

Rohr and company made the decision during lunch to forgo more testimony from James Ueuker.

Sixteen

JUMPER, the courtroom deputy who took the note from Marlee thirteen days earlier and handed it to Fitch, was approached during lunch and offered five thousand dollars cash to call in sick with stomach cramps or diarrhea or some such affliction, and travel in plain clothes with Pang to New Orleans for a night of food, fun, perhaps a call girl if Jumper was so inclined. Pang needed only a few hours of light work from him. Jumper needed the money.

They left Biloxi around twelve-thirty in a rented van. By the time they arrived in New Orleans two hours later, Jumper had been convinced to temporarily retire his uniform and work for Arlington West Associates for a while. Pang offered him twenty-five thousand dollars for six months' work, nine thousand more than he was presently earning for an entire year.

They checked into their rooms at the St. Regis, two single rooms on each side of Fitch, who'd been able to extort only four from the hotel. Holly's room was down the hall. Dubaz, Joe Boy, and Dante were four blocks away in the Royal Sonesta. Jumper was first parked on a bar stool in the lounge, where he had a view of the front entrance of the hotel.

The waiting began. There was no sign of her as the afternoon dragged toward dark, and no one was surprised. Jumper was moved four times, and swiftly tired of shadow work.

Fitch left his room a few minutes before seven and rode the

elevator to the roof. His table was in a corner with a nice view of the Quarter. Holly and Dubaz were at a table ten feet away, both well dressed and seemingly oblivious to everyone. Dante and a hired escort in a black mini-skirt had another table. Joe Boy would take the pictures.

At seven-thirty, she appeared from nowhere. Neither Jumper nor Pang reported seeing her anywhere near the front lobby. She simply emerged through the open French doors on the roof and was at Fitch's table in an instant. He later speculated that she did what they had done—got a room at the hotel under another name and used the stairs. She was dressed in slacks and jacket, and very pretty—dark short hair, brown eyes, strong chin and cheeks, very little makeup but then little was needed. He guessed her age to be between twenty-eight and thirty-two. She sat quickly, so fast in fact that Fitch didn't get the chance to offer her a chair. She sat directly across from him with her back to the other tables.

"A pleasure to meet you," he said softly, glancing around at the other tables to see if anyone was listening.

"Yes, a real pleasure," she replied, leaning on her elbows.

The waiter appeared with rapid efficiency and asked if she wanted something to drink. No, she did not. The waiter had been bribed with hard cash to carefully remove anything she touched with her fingers—glasses, plates, silver, ashtrays, anything. He would not get the chance.

"Are you hungry?" Fitch asked, sipping a mineral water.

"No. I'm in a hurry."

"Why?"

"Because the longer I sit here the more photos your goons can take."

"I came alone."

"Of course you did. How'd you like the red socks?" A jazz band began across the roof, but she ignored it. Her eyes never left Fitch's.

Fitch rolled his head back and offered a snort. It was still difficult to believe he was chatting with the lover of one of his jurors. He'd had indirect contact with jurors before, several times in different forms, but never this close.

And she came to him!

"Where's he from?" Fitch asked.

"What difference does it make? He's here."

"Is he your husband?"

"No."

"Boyfriend?"

"You ask a lot of questions."

"You present a lot of questions, young lady. And you expect me to ask them."

"He's an acquaintance."

"When did he assume the name Nicholas Easter?"

"What difference does it make? That's his legal name. He's a legal resident of Mississippi, a registered voter. He can change his name once a month if he wants."

She kept her hands tucked together under her chin. He knew she would not make the mistake of leaving prints. "What about you?" Fitch asked.

"Me?"

"Yeah, you're not registered to vote in Mississippi."

"How do you know?"

"Because we checked. Assuming, of course, your real name is Marlee, and that it's spelled properly."

"You're assuming too much."

"It's my job. Are you from the Coast?"

"No."

Joe Boy leaned down low between two plastic boxwoods just long enough to take six shots of the side of her face. A decent view would require a tightrope act on top of the brick banister, eighteen floors above Canal. He'd stay in the greenery and hope for something better when she left.

Fitch rattled the ice in his glass. "So why are we here?" he asked.

"One meeting leads to another."

"And where do all the meetings lead us?"

"To the verdict."

"For a fee, I'm sure."

"Fee has an awfully small ring to it. Are you recording this?" She knew perfectly well Fitch was recording every sound.

"Of course not."

He could play the tape in his sleep for all she cared. He had nothing to gain by sharing it with anyone. He carried too much baggage to run to the cops or to the Judge, and that didn't fit into his modus operandi anyway. The thought of blackmailing her with the authorities never occurred to Fitch, and she knew this too.

He could take all the photos he wanted, and he and his thugs scattered around the hotel could follow and watch and listen. She'd play along for a while, dodging and darting and making them work for their money. They'd find nothing.

"Let's not talk about money now, okay, Fitch?"

"We'll talk about whatever you want to talk about. This is your show."

"Why'd you break into his apartment?"

"That's just what we do."

"How do you read Herman Grimes?" she asked.

"Why do you ask me? You know exactly what's happening in the jury room."

"I want to see how smart you are. I'm interested in knowing if you're getting your money's worth from all those jury experts and lawyers."

"I've never lost, so I always get my money's worth."

"So what about Herman?"

Fitch thought for a second and motioned for another glass of water. "He'll have a lot to do with the verdict because he is a man of strong opinions. Right now, he's open-minded. He absorbs every word in court and probably knows more than every other juror, with the exception, of course, of your friend. Am I right?"

"You're pretty close."

"That's good to hear. How often do you chat with your friend?"

"Occasionally. Herman objected to the strike this morning, did you know that?"

"No."

"He was the only one of the fourteen."

"Why'd they strike?"

"Conditions. Phones, TV, beer, sex, church, the usual yearnings of mankind."

"Who led the strike?"

"Same one who's been leading from day one."

"I see."

"That's why I'm here, Fitch. If my friend was not in control, I'd have nothing to offer."

"And what are you offering?"

"I said we wouldn't talk about money now."

The waiter set the fresh glass in front of Fitch and again asked Marlee if she wanted something to drink. "Yes, a diet cola in a plastic cup, please."

"We, uh, well, we don't have any plastic cups," the waiter said with a puzzled look at Fitch.

"Then forget it," she said, grinning at Fitch.

Fitch decided to press on. "What's the mood of the jury right now?"

"Getting bored. Herrera's a big fan. Thinks trial lawyers are dirt and severe restrictions should be placed on frivolous lawsuits."

"My hero. Can he convince his pals?"

"No. He has no pals. He is despised by all, definitely the most disliked member of the panel."

"Who's the friendliest girl?"

"Millie is everybody's mother, but she won't be a factor. Rikki is cute and popular, and very health conscious. She's trouble for you."

"That's no surprise."

"Do you want a surprise, Fitch?"

"Yeah, surprise me."

"Which juror has actually started smoking cigarettes since the trial started?"

Fitch squinted and cocked his head a little to the left. Did he hear her correctly? "Started smoking?"

"Yep."

"I give up."

"Easter. Surprised?"

"Your friend."

"Yeah. Look, Fitch, gotta run. I'll call you tomorrow." She was on her feet and gone, disappearing as quickly as she'd come.

Dante with the hired woman reacted before Fitch, who was stunned for a second with the speed of her departure. Dante radioed Pang in the lobby, who saw her exit the elevator and leave the hotel. Jumper tracked her on foot for two blocks before losing her in a crowded alley.

For an hour they watched the streets and parking garages and hotel lobbies and bars but did not see her. Fitch was in his room at the St. Regis when the call came from Dubaz, who'd been dispatched to the airport. She was waiting for a commuter flight that left in an hour and a half and landed in Mobile at ten-fifty. Don't follow her, Fitch instructed him, then called two standbys in Biloxi, who raced to the airport in Mobile.

Marlee lived in a rented condo facing the Back Bay of Biloxi. When she was twenty minutes from home, she called the Biloxi police by dialing 911 on her cellphone and explained to the dispatcher that a Ford Taurus with two thugs in it was following her, had been in fact since she left Mobile, that they were stalkers of some odious variety and she was fearful for her life. With the dispatcher coordinating movements, Marlee did a series of turns through a quiet subdivision and abruptly stopped at an all-night gas station. As she filled her tank, a police car pulled behind the Taurus, which was trying to hide around the corner of a closed dry cleaner. The two thugs were ordered out, then marched across the parking lot to face the woman they'd been stalking.

Marlee performed superbly as the terrified victim. The cops got angrier the more she cried. Fitch's goons were hauled away to jail.

AT TEN, Chuck, the large deputy with a sullen attitude, unfolded a chair at the end of the hallway near his room, and set up watch for the night. It was Wednesday, the second night of sequestration, and time to breach security. As planned, Nicholas phoned Chuck's room at eleven-fifteen. The instant he left his post to answer it, Jerry and Nicholas slipped from their rooms and walked casually through the exit door near Lou Dell's room. Lou Dell was in bed sound asleep. And though Willis had slept most of the day in court, he too was under the covers, snoring furiously.

Avoiding the front lobby, they eased through the shadows and found the taxi waiting precisely as instructed. Fifteen minutes later they entered the Nugget Casino on Biloxi Beach. They drank three beers in the sports bar as Jerry lost a hundred dollars on a hockey game. They flirted with two married women whose husbands were either winning or losing a fortune at the crap tables. The flirting took a turn toward serious, and at 1 A.M. Nicholas left the bar to play five-dollar blackjack and drink decaf coffee. He played and waited and watched as the crowd dwindled.

Marlee slipped into the chair next to him and said nothing. Nicholas pushed a short stack of chips in front of her. A drunk college boy was the only other player. "Upstairs," she whispered between hands as the dealer turned to talk to the pit boss.

They met on an outdoor mezzanine with a view of the parking lot and the ocean in the distance. November had arrived and the air was light and cool. There was no one else around. They kissed and huddled together on a bench. She replayed her trip to New Orleans; every detail, every word. They laughed at the two boys from Mobile who were now in the county jail. She'd call Fitch after daybreak and get his men released.

They talked business briefly because Nicholas wanted to return to the bar and collect Jerry before he drank too much and lost all his money or got caught with somebody's wife.

They each had slim pocket cellphones which could not be completely secured. New codes and passwords were exchanged.

Nicholas kissed her good-bye and left her alone on the mezzanine.

WENDALL ROHR had a hunch the jury was tired of listening to researchers tout their findings and lecture from their charts and graphs. His consultants were telling him the jurors had heard enough about lung cancer and smoking, that they had probably been convinced before the trial started that cigarettes were addictive and dangerous. He was confident he had established a strong causal relationship between the Bristols and the tumors that killed Jacob Wood, and it was now time to ice the case. Thursday morning he announced that the plaintiff would like to call Lawrence Krigler as its next witness. A noticeable tension seized the defense table for the moment it took to call Mr. Krigler from somewhere in the rear. Another plaintiff's lawyer, John Riley Milton from Denver, rose and smiled sweetly at the jury.

Lawrence Krigler was in his late sixties, tanned and fit, well dressed and quick in step. He was the first witness without Doctor stuck to the front of his name since the video of Jacob Wood. He lived now in Florida, where he'd retired after he left Pynex. John Riley Milton rushed him through the preliminaries because the juicy stuff was just around the corner.

An engineering graduate of North Carolina State, he'd worked for Pynex for thirty years before leaving in the midst of a lawsuit thirteen years earlier. He'd sued Pynex. The company'd countersued him. They settled out of court with terms being nondisclosed.

When he was first hired, the company, then called Union Tobacco, or simply U-Tab, had shipped him to Cuba to study tobacco production down there. He'd worked in production ever since, or at least until the day he left. He'd studied the tobacco leaf and a thousand ways to grow it more efficiently. He considered himself an expert in this field, though he was not testifying as an expert and would not offer opinions. Only facts.

In 1969, he completed a three-year, in-house study on the feasibility of growing an experimental tobacco leaf known only as Raleigh 4. It had one third the nicotine of regular tobacco. Krigler concluded, with a wealth of research to support him, that Raleigh 4 could be grown and produced as efficiently as all other tobaccos then grown and produced by U-Tab.

It was a monumental work, one he was quite proud of, and he was devastated when his study was at first ignored by higher-ups within his company. He slogged his way through the entrenched bureaucracy above him, with disheartening results. No one seemed to care about this new strain of tobacco with much less nicotine.

Then he learned that he was very wrong. His bosses cared a great deal about nicotine levels. In the summer of 1971 he got his hands on an intercompany memo instructing upper management to quietly do whatever possible to discredit Krigler's work with Raleigh 4. His own people were silently knifing him in the back. He kept his cool, told no one he had the memo, and began a clandestine project to learn the reasons for the conspiracy against him.

At this point in his testimony, John Riley Milton introduced into evidence two exhibits—the thick study Krigler completed in 1969, and the 1971 memo.

The answer became crystal clear, and it was something he'd come to suspect. U-Tab could not afford to produce a leaf with markedly lower nicotine, because nicotine meant profits. The industry had known since the late thirties that nicotine was physically addictive.

"How do you know the industry knew?" Milton asked, very deliberately. With the exception of the defense lawyers, who were doing their best to appear bored and indifferent, the entire court-room was listening with rapt attention.

"It's common knowledge within the industry," Krigler answered. "There was a secret study in the late 1930s, paid for by a tobacco company, and the result was clear proof that the nicotine in cigarettes is addictive."

"Have you seen this report?"

"No. As you might guess, it has been well concealed." Krigler paused and looked at the defense table. The bombshell was coming, and he was thoroughly enjoying the moment. "But I saw a memo—"

"Objection!" Cable shouted as he rose. "This witness cannot state what he may or may not have seen in a written document. The reasons are plentiful and are set out more fully in the brief we filed on this point."

The brief was eighty pages long and had been argued over for a month now. Judge Harkin had already ruled, in writing. "Your objection is noted, Mr. Cable. Mr. Krigler, you may continue."

"In the winter of 1973, I saw a one-page memo summarizing the nicotine study from the 1930s. The memo had been copied many times, was very old, and had been slightly altered."

"Altered in what way?"

"The date had been deleted, as had the name of the person sending it."

"To whom was it sent?"

"It was addressed to Sander S. Fraley, who at that time was the president of Allegheny Growers, the predecessor of a company now called ConPack."

"A tobacco company."

"Yes, basically. It calls itself a consumer products company, but the bulk of its business is manufacturing cigarettes."

"When did he serve as president?"

"From 1931 to 1942."

"Is it then safe to assume the memo was sent prior to 1942?"

"Yes. Mr. Fraley died in 1942."

"Where were you when you saw this memo?"

"At a Pynex facility in Richmond. When Pynex was still Union Tobacco, its corporate headquarters were in Richmond. In 1979, it changed its name and moved to New Jersey. But the buildings are still in use in Richmond, and that's where I worked until I left.

Most of the company's old records are there, and a person I know showed me the memo."

"Who was this person?"

"He was a friend, and he's now dead. I promised him I'd never reveal his identity."

"Did you actually hold the memo?"

"Yes. In fact, I made a copy of it."

"And where is your copy?"

"It didn't last long. The day after I locked it in my desk drawer, I was called out of town on business. While I was out, someone went through my desk and removed a number of things, including my copy of the memo."

"Do you recall what the memo said?"

"I remember very well. Keep in mind, for a long time I'd been digging for some confirmation of what I suspected. Seeing the memo was an unforgettable moment."

"What did it say?"

"Three paragraphs, maybe four, brief and to the point. The writer explained that he had just read the nicotine report that was secretly shown to him by the head of research at Allegheny Growers, a person who went unnamed in the memo. In his opinion, the study proved conclusively and beyond any doubt that nicotine is addictive. As I recall, this was the gist of the first two paragraphs."

"And the next paragraph?"

"The writer suggested to Fraley that the company take a serious look at increasing the nicotine levels in its cigarettes. More nicotine meant more smokers, which meant more sales and more profits."

Krigler delivered his lines with a fine flair for the dramatic, and every ear soaked up his words. The jurors, for the first time in days, watched every move the witness made. The word "profits" floated over the courtroom and hung like a dirty fog.

John Riley Milton paused for a bit, then said, "Now, let's keep this straight. The memo was prepared by someone at another company, and sent to the president of that company, right?"

"That's correct."

"A company that was then and is now a competitor of Pynex?"

"That's correct."

"How did the memo find its way to Pynex in 1973?"

"I never found out. But Pynex certainly knew about the study. In fact, the entire tobacco industry knew about the study by the early 1970s, if not sooner."

"How do you know this?"

"I worked in the industry for thirty years, remember. And I spent my career in production. I talked to a lot of people, especially my counterparts at other companies. Let's just say that the tobacco companies at times can stick together."

"Did you ever attempt to obtain another copy of the memo from your friend?"

"I tried. It didn't work. Let's leave it at that."

EXCEPT for the usual fifteen-minute coffee break at ten-thirty, Krigler testified nonstop for the three-hour morning session. His testimony passed by as if it were only a matter of minutes, and was a crucial moment in the trial. The drama of an ex-employee spilling dirty secrets was played to perfection. The jurors even ignored their customary longings for lunch. The lawyers watched the jurors more closely than ever, and the Judge seemed to write down every word the witness said.

The reporters were unusually reverent; the jury consultants unusually attentive. The watchdogs from Wall Street counted the minutes until they could bolt from the room and make breathless phone calls to New York. The bored local lawyers hanging around the courtroom would talk about the testimony for years. Even Lou Dell stopped her knitting on the front row.

Fitch watched and listened from the viewing room next to his office. Krigler had been scheduled to testify early next week, and then there'd been the chance that he wouldn't testify at all. Fitch was one of the few people still alive who'd actually seen the memo, and Krigler had described it with amazing recollection. It was clear to everyone, even Fitch, that the witness was telling the truth.

One of Fitch's first assignments nine years ago when he'd first been hired by the Big Four was to track down *every* copy of the memo, and destroy each one. He was still working on it.

Neither Cable nor any defense lawyer retained by Fitch so far had seen the memo.

The admissibility of its existence in court had caused a small war. The rules of evidence normally prevent such verbal descriptions of lost documents, for obvious reasons. The best evidence is the document itself. But, as with every area of the law, there are exceptions and exceptions to the exceptions, and Rohr et al. had done a masterful job of convincing Judge Harkin that the jury should hear Krigler's description of what was, in effect, a lost document.

Cable's cross-examination that afternoon would be brutal, but the damage was done. Fitch skipped lunch and locked himself in his office.

IN THE JURY ROOM, the atmosphere over lunch was remarkably different. The ordinary drivel about football and recipes was replaced by a virtual silence. As a deliberative body, the jury had been lulled into stupor with two weeks of tedious scientific testimony from experts who were being paid large sums of money to travel to Biloxi and lecture. Now the jury had been shaken back to life with Krigler's sensational inside dirt.

They ate less and stared more. Most wanted to ease into another room with their favorite friend and replay what they'd just heard. Did they hear it right? Did everyone understand what the man just said? They intentionally kept nicotine high so people got hooked!

They managed to do just that. The smokers, only three now since Stella had departed, though Easter was a semi-smoker because he preferred to spend time with Jerry and Poodle and Angel Weese, ate quickly then excused themselves. They all sat on folding chairs, staring and puffing at the open window. With the weighted nicotine, the cigarettes felt a bit heavier. But when Nicholas said so, no one laughed.

Mrs. Gladys Card and Millie Dupree managed to leave for the rest room at the same moment. They took a long pee then spent fifteen minutes washing their hands and speaking to each other in front of the mirror. They were joined in mid-conversation by Loreen Duke, who leaned by the towel dispenser and quickly threw in her amazement and disgust with tobacco companies.

After the table was cleared, Lonnie Shaver opened his laptop two chairs down from Herman, who had his braille machine plugged in and was typing away. The Colonel said to Herman, "Don't guess you need a translator for that testimony, do you?" To which Herman replied with a grunt and said, "Pretty amazing,

I'd say." That was the nearest Herman Grimes came to discussing any aspect of the case.

Lonnie Shaver was not amazed or impressed by anything.

Phillip Savelle had politely asked for and received permission from Judge Harkin to spend part of his lunch break doing yoga under a large oak tree behind the courthouse. He was escorted by a deputy to the oak tree, where he removed his shirt, socks, and shoes, then sat on the soft grass and creased himself into a pretzel. When he began chanting, the deputy slid away to a nearby concrete bench and lowered his face so no one would recognize him.

CABLE SAID HELLO to Krigler as if the two were old friends. Krigler smiled and said "Good afternoon, Mr. Cable," with an abundance of confidence. Seven months earlier, in Rohr's office, Cable and company had spent three days taking a video deposition of Krigler. The video had been watched and studied by no fewer than two dozen lawyers and several jury experts and even two psychiatrists. Krigler was telling the truth, but the truth needed to be blurred at this point. This was a cross-examination, a crucial one, so to hell with the truth. The witness had to be discredited!

After hundreds of hours of plotting, a strategy had been developed. Cable began by asking Krigler if he was angry with his former employer.

"Yes," he answered.

"Do you hate the company?"

"The company is an entity. How do you hate a thing?"

"Do you hate war?"

"Never been."

"Do you hate child abuse?"

"I'm sure it's sickening, but luckily I've never had any connection with it."

"Do you hate violence?"

"I'm sure it's awful, but, again, I've been lucky."

"So you don't hate anything?"

"Broccoli."

A gentle laugh came from all quarters of the courtroom, and Cable knew he had his hands full.

"You don't hate Pynex?"

"No."

"Do you hate anyone who works there?"

"No. I dislike some of them."

"Did you hate anyone who worked there when you worked there?"

"No. I had some enemies, but I don't remember hating anyone."

"What about the people against whom you directed your lawsuit?"

"No. Again, they were enemies, but they were just doing their jobs."

"So you love your enemies?"

"Not really. I know I'm supposed to try, but it sure is difficult. I don't recall saying I loved them."

Cable had hoped to score a minor point by injecting the possibility of retribution or revenge on the part of Krigler. Maybe if he used the word "hate" enough, it might stick with some of the jurors.

"What is your motive for testifying here?"

"That's a complicated question."

"Is it money?"

"No."

"Are you being paid by Mr. Rohr or anyone working for the plaintiff to come and testify?"

"No. They've agreed to reimburse me for my travel expenses, but that's all."

The last thing Cable wanted was an open door for Krigler to expound upon his reasons for testifying. He had touched on them briefly during Milton's direct examination, and he'd spent five hours detailing them during the video deposition. It was crucial to keep him occupied with other matters.

"Have you ever smoked cigarettes, Mr. Krigler?"

"Yes. Unfortunately I smoked for twenty years."

"So you wished you'd never smoked?"

"Of course."

"When did you start?"

"When I went to work for the company, 1952. Back then they encouraged all their employees to smoke cigarettes. They still do."

"Do you believe you damaged your health by smoking for twenty years?"

"Of course. I feel lucky I'm not dead, like Mr. Wood."

"When did you quit?"

"In 1973. After I learned the truth about nicotine."

"Do you feel your present health has been diminished in some way because you smoked for twenty years?"

"Of course."

"In your opinion, was the company responsible in any way for your decision to smoke cigarettes?"

"Yes. As I said, it was encouraged. Everybody else smoked. We could purchase cigarettes at half price in the company store. Every meeting began with a bowl of cigarettes passed around. It was very much a part of the culture."

"Were your offices ventilated?"

"No."

"How bad was the secondhand smoke?"

"Very bad. There was always a blue fog hanging not far over your head."

"So you blame the company today because you're not as healthy as you think you should be?"

"The company had a lot to do with it. Fortunately, I was able to kick the habit. It wasn't easy."

"And you hold a grudge against the company for this?"

"Let's just say I wish I'd gone to work in another industry when I finished college."

"Industry? Do you carry a grudge against the entire industry?"

"I'm not a fan of the tobacco industry."

"Is that why you're here?"

"No."

Cable flipped his notes and quickly changed direction. "Now, you had a sister at one time, didn't you, Mr. Krigler?"

"I did."

"What happened to her?"

"She died in 1970."

"How'd she die?"

"Lung cancer. She smoked two packs a day for about twenty-three years. Smoking killed her, Mr. Cable, if that's what you want."

"Were you close to her?" Cable asked with enough compassion to deflect some of the ill will for bringing up the tragedy in the first place.

"We were very close. She was my only sibling."

"And you took her death very hard?"

"I did. She was a very special person, and I still miss her."

"I'm sorry to bring this up, Mr. Krigler, but it is relevant."

"Your compassion is overwhelming, Mr. Cable, but there's nothing relevant about it."

"How did she feel about your smoking?"

"She didn't like it. As she was dying she begged me to stop. Is that what you want to hear, Mr. Cable?"

"Only if it's the truth."

"Oh it's true, Mr. Cable. The day before she died I promised I would quit smoking. And I did, though it took me three long years to do it. I was hooked, you see, Mr. Cable, as was my sister, because the company that manufactured the cigarettes that killed her, and could've killed me, intentionally kept the nicotine at a high level."

"Now—"

"Don't interrupt me, Mr. Cable. Nicotine in itself is not a carcinogen, you know that, it's just a poison, a poison that gets you addicted so the carcinogens can one day take care of you. That's why cigarettes are inherently dangerous."

Cable watched him with complete composure. "Are you finished?"

"I'm ready for the next question. But don't interrupt me again."

"Certainly, and I apologize. Now, when did you first become convinced that cigarettes were inherently dangerous?"

"I don't know exactly. It's been known for some time, you know. It did not then and does not now take a genius to figure it out. But I'd say at some point in the early seventies, after I finished my study, after my sister had died, and shortly before I saw the infamous memo."

"In 1973?"

"Somewhere in there."

"When did your employment with Pynex cease? What year?"

"In 1982."

"So you continued working for a company which made products you considered to be inherently dangerous?"

"I did."

"What was your salary in 1982?"

"Ninety thousand dollars a year."

Cable paused and walked to his table where he was handed yet another yellow legal pad which he studied for a second as he bit a stem of his reading glasses, then he returned to the lectern and asked Krigler why he'd sued the company in 1982. Krigler didn't appreciate the question, and looked at Rohr and Milton for help. Cable pursued details of the events leading up to the litigation, hopelessly complicated and personal litigation, and the testimony slowed to a virtual halt. Rohr objected and Milton objected, and Cable acted as if he couldn't understand why in the world they'd object. The lawyers met at the sidebar to haggle in private in front of Judge Harkin, and Krigler grew weary of the witness stand.

Cable hammered away at Krigler's performance record during his last ten years with Pynex, and hinted strongly that other witnesses might be called to contradict him.

The ploy almost worked. Unable to shake the damaging aspects of Krigler's testimony, the defense chose instead to blow smoke at the jury. If a witness is unshakable, then beat him up with insignificant details.

The ploy was explained to the jury, however, by young Nicholas Easter, who'd had two years of law school and chose to remind his colleagues of his experiences during a late afternoon coffee break. Over Herman's objections, Nicholas voiced his resentment at Cable for throwing mud and trying to confuse the jury. "He thinks we're stupid," he said bitterly.

Seventeen

IN RESPONSE to frantic calls from Biloxi, the price of Pynex shares dipped as low as seventy-five and a half by closing Thursday, down almost four points in heavy trading attributed to the dramatic events in the courtroom.

In other tobacco trials, former employees had testified about pesticides and insecticides sprayed on the crops, and experts had linked the chemicals to cancer. The juries had not been impressed. In one trial, a former employee had spilled the news that his former employer had targeted young teenagers with ads showing thin and glamorous idiots with perfect chins and perfect teeth having all manner of fun with tobacco. The same employer had targeted older teenaged males with ads depicting cowboys and stock car drivers seriously pursuing life with cigarettes stuck between their lips.

But the juries in those trials did not award the plaintiffs.

No former employee, though, did as much damage as Lawrence Krigler. The infamous memo from the 1930s had been seen by a handful of people, but never produced in litigation. Krigler's version of it for the jury was as close as any plaintiff's lawyer had come to the real thing. The fact that he'd been allowed by Judge Harkin to describe it to the jury would be hotly contested on appeal, regardless of who won at trial.

Krigler was quickly escorted out of town by Rohr's security people, and an hour after finishing his testimony he was on a private plane back to Florida. Several times since leaving Pynex he had been tempted to contact a plaintiff's lawyer in a tobacco trial, but had never mustered the courage.

Pynex had paid him three hundred thousand dollars out of court, just to get rid of him. The company had insisted he agree never to testify in trials similar to Wood, but he refused. And when he refused, he became a marked man.

They, whoever they had been, said they'd kill him. The threats had been few and scattered over the years, always from unknown voices and always dropping in when least expected. Krigler was not one to hide. He'd written a book, an exposé he said would be published in the event of his untimely death. A lawyer had it in Melbourne Beach. The lawyer was a friend who'd arranged the initial meeting with Rohr. The lawyer had also opened a dialogue with the FBI, just in case something happened to Mr. Krigler.

MILLIE DUPREE'S HUSBAND, Hoppy, owned a struggling realty agency in Biloxi. Certainly not the aggressive sort, he had few listings and few leads, but he worked diligently with what little business came his way. One wall in the front room had pictures of available OPPORTUNITIES thumbtacked to a corkboard—mainly little brick houses with neat lawns and a few run-down duplexes.

Casino fever had brought to the Coast a new herd of real estate swingers unafraid to borrow heavily and develop accordingly. Once again, Hoppy and the little guys had played it safe and got themselves squeezed even further into markets they knew all too well—darling little STARTERS for the newlyweds and hopeless FIXUPS for the desperate and MOTIVATED SELLERS for those who couldn't qualify for a bank loan.

But he paid his bills and somehow provided for his family—his wife Millie and their five kids, three at the junior college and two in high school. At any given time he had attached to his office the licenses of a half a dozen part-time sales associates, for the most part a downhearted bunch of losers who shared his aversion to debt and forcefulness. Hoppy loved pinochle, and many hours were passed at his desk in the back over cards as subdivisions sprang up all around him. Realtors, regardless of their talent, love to dream of the big score. Hoppy and his motley gang were not above taking a late-afternoon nip and talking big business over cards.

Just before six on Thursday, as the pinochle was winding down and preparations were being made to end another nonproductive day, a well-dressed young businessman with a shiny black attaché entered the office and asked for Mr. Dupree. Hoppy was in the back, rinsing his mouth with Scope and hurrying to get home since Millie was locked away. Introductions were made. The young man presented a business card which declared him to be Todd Ringwald of KLX Property Group out of Las Vegas, Nevada. The card impressed Hoppy enough to shoo off the last of the lingering sales associates, and lock his office door. The mere presence of one dressed so well and having traveled such a great distance could only mean serious matters were possible.

Hoppy offered a drink, then coffee, which could be brewed in an instant. Mr. Ringwald declined, and asked if he'd come at a bad time.

"No, not at all. We work crazy hours, you know. It's a crazy business."

Mr. Ringwald smiled and agreed because he too was once in business for himself, not too many years ago. First a bit about his company. KLX was a private outfit with holdings in a dozen states. While it did not own casinos, and had no plans to do so, it had developed a related specialty, a lucrative one. KLX tracked casino development. Hoppy nodded furiously as if this type of enterprise was altogether familiar to him.

Typically, when casinos move in, the local real estate market changes dramatically. Ringwald was certain Hoppy knew all about this, and Hoppy agreed wholeheartedly as if he'd made a fortune recently. KLX moved in quietly, and Ringwald emphasized just how utterly secretive the company was, a step behind the casinos, and developed shopping areas and expensive condos and apartment complexes and upper-end subdivisions. Casinos pay well, employ many, things change in the local economy, and, well, there's just a helluva lot more money floating around and KLX wanted its share. "Our company is a vulture," Ringwald explained with a devious smile. "We sit back and watch the casinos. When they move, we go in for the kill."

"Brilliant," Hoppy offered, unable to control himself.

However, KLX had been slow to move on the Coast, and, confidentially, this had cost a few jobs back in Vegas. There were still incredible opportunities, though, to which Hoppy said, "There certainly are."

Ringwald opened his briefcase and removed a folded property map, which he held on his knees. He, as Vice President of Development, preferred to deal with smaller realty agents. The big firms had too many people hanging around, too many overweight housewives reading classifieds and waiting for the slightest morsel of gossip. "You got that right!" Hoppy said, staring at the property map. "Plus you get better service from a small agency, like mine."

"You have been highly recommended," Ringwald said, and Hoppy couldn't suppress a smile. The phone rang. It was the senior in high school wanting to know what was for supper and when might Mother be coming home. Hoppy was pleasant but short. He was very busy, he explained, and there might be some old lasagna in the freezer.

The property map was unfolded on Hoppy's desk. Ringwald pointed to a large red-colored plot in Hancock County, next door to Harrison and the westernmost of the three coastal counties. Both men hovered over the desk from different sides.

"MGM Grand is coming here," Ringwald said, pointing to a large bay. "But no one knows it yet. You certainly can't tell anyone."

Hoppy's head was shaking Hell No! before Ringwald finished.

"They're gonna build the biggest casino on the Coast, probably middle of next year. They'll announce in three months. They'll buy a hundred acres or so of this land here."

"That's beautiful land. Virtually untouched." Hoppy had never been near the property with a real estate sign, but he had lived on the Coast for forty years.

"We want this," Ringwald said, pointing again to the land marked in red. It was adjacent to the north and west of the MGM land. "Five hundred acres, so we can do this." He pulled the top sheet back to reveal an artist's rendering of a rather splendid Planned Unit Development. It was labeled Stillwater Bay with bold blue letters across the top. Condos, office buildings, big homes, smaller homes, playgrounds, churches, a central square, a shopping mall, a pedestrian mall, a dock, a marina, a business block, parks, jogging paths, bike trails, even a proposed high school. It was utopia, all planned for Hancock County by some wonderfully farsighted people in Las Vegas.

"Wow," Hoppy said. There was a bloody fortune on his desk.

"Four different phases over five years. The whole thing will cost thirty million. It's by far the biggest development ever seen in these parts."

"Nothing can touch it."

Ringwald flipped another page and revealed another drawing of the dock area, then another for a close-up of the residential section. "These are just the preliminary drawings. I'll show you more if you can come to the home office."

"Vegas."

"Yes. If we can reach an agreement on your representation, then we'd like to fly you out for a few days, you know, meet our people, see the whole project from the design end."

Hoppy's knees wobbled and he took a breath. Slow down, he told himself. "Yes, and what type of representation did you have in mind?"

"Initially, we need a broker to handle the purchase of the land. Once we buy it, we have to convince the local authorities to approve the development. This, as you know, can take time and become controversial. We spend a lot of time before planning commissions and zoning boards. We even go to court when necessary. But it's just part of our business. You'll be involved to some extent at this point. Once it's approved, we'll need a real estate firm to handle the marketing of Stillwater Bay."

Hoppy backed into his chair and pondered figures for a moment. "How much will the land cost?" he asked.

"It's expensive, much too expensive for this area. Ten thousand an acre, for land worth about half that much."

Ten thousand an acre for five hundred acres added up to five million bucks, six percent of which was three hundred thousand dollars for Hoppy's commission, assuming of course no other realtors were to be involved. Ringwald watched poker-faced as Hoppy did the mental math.

"Ten thousand's too much," Hoppy said with authority.

"Yes, but the land is not on the market. The sellers don't really want to sell, so we have to sneak in quickly, before the MGM story leaks, and snatch it. That's why we need a local agent. If word hits the street that a big company from Vegas is looking at the land, it'll go to twenty thousand an acre. Happens all the time."

The fact that the land was not on the market caused Hoppy's heart to stutter. No other realtors were involved! Just him. Just little Hoppy and his full six percent commission. His ship had finally come in. He, Hoppy Dupree, after decades of selling duplexes to pensioners, was about to make a killing.

Not to mention the "marketing of Stillwater Bay." All those houses and condos and commercial properties, hell thirty million dollars' worth of red-hot property with Dupree Realty signs hanging all over it. Hoppy could be a millionaire in five years, he decided on the spot.

Ringwald moved in. "I'm assuming your commission is eight percent. That's what we normally pay."

"Of course," Hoppy said, the words rushing forward over a very dry tongue. From three hundred thousand to four hundred thousand, just like that. "Who are the sellers?" he asked, quickly changing the subject now that they'd agreed on eight percent.

Ringwald allowed a noticeable sigh and his shoulders sagged, but only for an instant. "This is where it gets complicated." Hoppy's heart sank.

"The property is in the sixth district of Hancock County," Ringwald said slowly. "And the sixth district is the domain of a county supervisor by the name of—"

"Jimmy Hull Moke," Hoppy interrupted, with no small measure of sadness.

"You know him?"

"Everybody knows Jimmy Hull. He's been in office for thirty years. Slickest crook on the Coast."

"Do you know him personally?"

"No. Only by reputation."

"Which we've heard is rather shady."

"Shady is a compliment to Jimmy Hull. On a local level, the man controls everything in his end of the county."

Ringwald offered a puzzled look as if he and his company had no clue about how to proceed. Hoppy rubbed his sad eyes and plotted to keep his fortune. They made no eye contact for a full minute, then Ringwald said, "It's not wise to buy the land unless we can get some assurances from Mr. Moke and the local people.

As you know, there will be a maze of regulatory approvals for the project."

"Planning, zoning, architectural review, soil erosion, you name it," Hoppy said, as if he fought these wars every day.

"We've been told that Mr. Moke controls all of this."

"With an iron fist."

Another pause.

"Perhaps we should arrange a meeting with Mr. Moke," Ringwald said.

"I don't think so."

"Why not?"

"Meetings don't work."

"I'm not following you."

"Cash. Pure and simple. Jimmy Hull likes it under the table, large sacks of it in unmarked bills."

Ringwald nodded with a solemn grin as if this was unfortunate but not unexpected. "So we've heard," he said, almost to himself. "Actually, this is not unusual, especially in areas where casinos have appeared. There's lots of fresh foreign money and people get greedy."

"Jimmy Hull was born greedy. He was stealing thirty years before casinos appeared here."

"He doesn't get caught?"

"No. For a local supervisor, he's pretty bright. Everything's in cash, no trail, he covers himself carefully. Then again, it doesn't take a rocket scientist." Hoppy tapped his forehead lightly with a handkerchief. He bent forward and removed two tumblers from a lower drawer, then a bottle of vodka. He poured two stiff drinks and placed one across the desk in front of Ringwald. "Cheers," he said before Ringwald touched his glass.

"So what do we do?" Ringwald asked.

"What do you normally do in situations like this?"

"We normally find a way to work with the local authorities. There's too much money involved to pack up and go home."

"How do you work with local authorities?"

"We have ways. We have contributed money to reelection campaigns. We have honored our friends with expensive vacations. We've paid consulting fees to spouses and children."

"You ever paid bribes in hard cash?"

"Well, I'd rather not say."

"That's what it'll take. Jimmy Hull is a simple man. Just cash."
Hoppy took a long sip and smacked his lips.

"How much?"

"Who knows. But it'd better be enough. You low-ball him up front, he'll kill your project later. And he'll keep the cash. Jimmy Hull doesn't do refunds."

"You sound like you know him rather well."

"Those of us who wheel and deal along the Coast know how he plays the game. He's sort of a local legend."

Ringwald shook his head in disbelief. "Welcome to Mississippi," Hoppy said, then took another sip. Ringwald had not touched his drink.

For twenty-five years Hoppy had played it straight, and he had no plans to compromise himself now. The money wasn't worth the risk. He had kids, a family, a reputation, standing in the community. Church occasionally. The Rotary Club. And just exactly who was this stranger sitting across his desk in the fancy suit and designer loafers, offering the world if only one minor agreement could be reached? He, Hoppy, would certainly get on the phone and check out KLX Property Group and Mr. Todd Ringwald as soon as he left the office.

"This is not unusual," Ringwald said. "We see it all the time."

"Then what do you do?"

"Well, I think our first step is to approach Mr. Moke and determine the likelihood of a deal."

"He'll be ready to deal."

"Then we determine the terms of the deal. As you put it, we'll decide how much cash." Ringwald paused and took a tiny sip of his drink. "Are you willing to be involved?"

"I don't know. In what way?"

"We don't know anyone in Hancock County. We try to keep a low profile. We're from Vegas. If we start asking questions, then the entire project gets blown."

"You want me to talk to Jimmy Hull?"

"Only if you want to be involved. If not, then we'll be forced to find someone else."

"I have a clean reputation," Hoppy said, with astounding firmness, then swallowed hard at the thought of a competitor raking in his four hundred thousand.

"We don't expect you to get dirty." Ringwald paused and

groped for the right words. Hoppy was pulling for him. "Let's just say that we have ways of delivering what Mr. Moke wants. You won't have to touch it. In fact, you won't know when it happens."

Hoppy sat straighter as a burden lifted itself from his shoulders. Perhaps there was some middle ground here. Ringwald and his company did this all the time. They'd probably dealt with crooks much more sophisticated than Jimmy Hull Moke. "I'm listening," he said.

"Your fingers are on the pulse here. We're obviously outsiders, so we'll rely on you. Let me give you a scenario. You tell me if it'll work. What if you meet with Mr. Moke, just the two of you, and you tell him in broad strokes about the development? Our names are not mentioned, you simply have this client who wants to work with him. He'll name his price. If it's within our range, then you tell him it's a deal. We'll take care of the delivery, and you never know for certain if the cash actually changes hands. You've done nothing wrong. He's happy. We're happy because we're about to make a pot full of money, along with you, I might add."

Hoppy liked it! None of the mud could stick to his hands. Let his client and Jimmy Hull do their dirty work. He'd stay out of the gutter and simply turn his head. Still, he was overcome by caution. He said he'd like to think about it.

They chatted some more, looked at the plans once again, and said good-bye at eight. Ringwald was to call early Friday morning.

Before heading home, Hoppy dialed the number on Ringwald's business card. An efficient receptionist in Las Vegas said, "Good afternoon, KLX Property Group." Hoppy smiled, then asked to speak to Todd Ringwald. The call was routed, with soft rock in the background, to Mr. Ringwald's office where Hoppy spoke to Madeline, an assistant of some variety who explained that Mr. Ringwald was out of town and not expected back until Monday. She asked who was calling, and Hoppy quickly hung up.

There now. KLX was indeed legitimate.

INCOMING PHONE CALLS were stopped at the front desk where they were recorded on yellow message slips and forwarded to Lou Dell, who then distributed them like the Easter Bunny passing out chocolate eggs. The one from George Teaker arrived at seven-forty Thursday night, and was delivered to Lonnie Shaver, who was skipping the movie and working with his computer. He called Teaker at once, and for the first ten minutes answered nothing but questions about the trial. Lonnie confessed that it had been a bad day for the defense. Lawrence Krigler had made a noticeable impact on the jurors, all except for Lonnie, of course. Lonnie had not been impressed, he assured Teaker. The folks in New York were certainly worried, Teaker said more than once. They're awfully relieved that Lonnie was on the jury and could be counted on no matter what, but things looked dim. Or did they?

Lonnie said it was too early to tell.

Teaker said they needed to tie up the loose ends of the employment contract. Lonnie could think of only one loose end, and that was how much his new salary would be. He currently made forty thousand dollars. Teaker said SuperHouse would raise him to fifty thousand with some stock options, and a performance-based bonus that might hit twenty thousand.

They wanted him to start a management training course in Charlotte as soon as the trial was over. Mention of the trial brought on another round of questions about the mood of the jury.

An hour later, Lonnie stood at his window, watched the parking lot, and tried to convince himself he was about to earn seventy thousand dollars a year. Three years ago, he made twenty-five thousand.

Not bad for a kid whose father drove a milk truck for three bucks an hour.

Eighteen

ON FRIDAY MORNING, *The Wall Street Journal* ran a front-page story about Lawrence Krigler and his testimony of the day before. Written by Agner Layson, who'd so far not missed a word of the trial, the story did a fair job of describing what the jury heard. Then Layson speculated about Krigler's impact on the jury. The remaining half of the article tried to peel skin off Krigler with quotes from the good old boys at ConPack, formerly Allegheny Growers. Not surprisingly, there were vehement denials of almost everything Krigler said. The company had not conducted a study of nicotine in the 1930s, or at least no one around now knew about any such study. It was a long time ago. No one at ConPack had ever seen the infamous memo. Probably just a figment of Krigler's imagination. It was not common knowledge in the tobacco industry that nicotine was addictive. Levels of the poison were not kept artificially high by ConPack, or any other manufacturer for that matter. The company would not admit, in fact denied again in print, that nicotine was addictive in the first place.

Pynex also delivered a few potshots, all from unnamed sources. Krigler was a corporate misfit. He fancied himself a serious scientific researcher when in fact he was just an engineer. His work with Raleigh 4 was seriously flawed. Production of that leaf was totally impractical. The death of his sister seriously affected his work and conduct. He was quick to threaten litigation. There was a strong hint that the out-of-court settlement thirteen years earlier had been heavily weighted in Pynex' favor.

A short, related story tracked the movement of Pynex common, which had closed at seventy-five and a half, down three points in heavy trading after a late rally.

Judge Harkin read the story an hour before the jury arrived. He called Lou Dell at the Siesta Inn to make sure there was no way any of the jurors could see it. She assured him they would get only the local dailies, all censored as per his instructions. She rather enjoyed cutting out the stories about the trial. Occasionally she would scissor out an unrelated story, just for the fun of it, just to make them wonder what they were missing. How could they ever know?

HOPPY DUPREE slept little. After washing the dishes and vacuuming the den, he talked to Millie on the phone for almost an hour. She was in good spirits.

He left his bed at midnight to sit on the porch and ponder KLX and Jimmy Hull Moke and the fortune that was out there, almost within reach. The money would be used for the kids, he had determined before he left the office. No more junior colleges. No more part-time jobs. They'd have the best schools. A larger house would be nice, but only because the kids were cramped. He and Millie could live anywhere; such simple tastes.

No debt whatsoever. After taxes, he'd put the money in two places—mutual funds and real estate. He'd buy small commercial properties with solid leases. He could think of a half-dozen already.

The agreement with Jimmy Hull Moke worried him to no end. He'd simply never been involved with graft, never, to his knowledge, gotten near it. He had a cousin who sold used cars and got himself sent away for three years for double and triple mortgaging his inventory. Wrecked his marriage. Ruined his children.

At some point before dawn, he became oddly comforted by the reputation of Jimmy Hull Moke. The man had fine-tuned the practice of corruption and made it an art form. He had become quite wealthy on a meager public servant's salary. And everybody knew it!

Surely Moke would know precisely how to handle the agreement without getting caught. Hoppy wouldn't get near the cash, wouldn't even know for sure if and when it was delivered.

He ate a Pop-Tart for breakfast and determined the risk to be minimal. He'd have a safe chat with Jimmy Hull, let the conversation run whatever course Jimmy Hull wanted because they'd soon enough get to the issue of cash, and then he'd report to Ringwald. He thawed frozen cinnamon swirls for the kids, left their lunch money on the kitchen counter, and went to the office at eight.

FOR THE DAY after Krigler the defense adopted a gentler style. It was imperative to seem relaxed, unbothered by the severe blow the plaintiff had delivered yesterday. The pack of them wore suits of lighter shades, soft grays and blues and even a khaki. Gone were the harsh blacks and navys. Gone too were the serious frowns of men overburdened with their own importance. The instant the door opened and the first juror appeared, wide toothy smiles appeared from behind the defense table. Even a couple of chuckles. What a laid-back bunch.

Judge Harkin said hello, but there were few smiles inside the jury box. It was Friday, which meant the weekend started soon, a weekend to be spent incarcerated at the Siesta Inn. It had been decided over breakfast that Nicholas would pass a note to the Judge and ask him to explore the possibility of working Saturday. The jurors would rather be in court trying to finish this ordeal than sitting around their rooms doing nothing but thinking about it.

Most of them noticed the stupid grins from Cable and company. They noticed the summer suits, the jovial air, the humorous whispers. "Why are they so damned happy?" Loreen Duke whispered under her breath as Harkin read his list of questions.

"They want us to think everything's under control," Nicholas whispered back. "Just glare at them."

Wendall Rohr stood and called the next witness. "Dr. Roger Bunch," he said with an air of greatness. He watched the jury for reactions to the name.

It was Friday. There would be no reactions from the jury.

Bunch had gained fame a decade earlier when, as Surgeon General of the United States, he had been a relentless critic of the tobacco industry. For the six years he'd served, he had instigated countless studies, directed frontal assaults, given a thousand antismoking speeches, written three books on the subject, and pushed agencies for tougher regulatory controls. His victories had been few and far between. Since leaving office, he had continued his crusade with a talent for publicity.

He was a man of many opinions and he was anxious to share them with the jury. The evidence was conclusive—cigarettes caused lung cancer. Every professional medical organization in the world that had addressed the issue had determined that smoking cigarettes caused lung cancer. The only organizations with contrary opinions were the manufacturers themselves and their hired mouthpieces—lobbying groups and the like.

Cigarettes are addictive. Ask any smoker who's tried to quit. The industry claims smoking is a matter of free choice. "Typical hogwash from the tobacco companies," he said with disgust. In fact, during his six years as Surgeon General he released three separate studies, each of which proved conclusively that cigarettes are addictive.

Tobacco companies spend billions misleading the public. They conduct studies which claim to prove smoking is virtually harmless. They spend 2 billion a year on advertising alone, then claim people make informed choices about whether or not to smoke. It's simply not true. People, especially teenagers, receive confusing signals. Smoking appears to be fun, sophisticated, even healthy.

They spend tons of money on all sorts of screwball studies which they claim will prove whatever they're asserting. The industry as a whole is notorious for lying and covering up. The companies refuse to stand behind their products. They advertise and promote like mad, but when one of their customers dies from lung cancer they claim the person should have known better.

Bunch did a study proving cigarettes contain insecticide and pesticide residue, asbestos fibers, unidentified junk and trash swept from floors. While sparing no expense on advertising, the companies do not go to the trouble and expense of properly cleaning poisonous residues from their tobacco.

He directed a project which showed how tobacco companies elusively target the young; how they target the poor; how they develop and advertise certain brands for the different sexes and classes.

Because he was once the Surgeon General, Dr. Bunch was permitted to share his opinions on a wide range of subjects. At times throughout the morning he was unable to conceal his loathing for the tobacco industry, and when the bitterness leaked through his credibility suffered. But he connected with the jury. There were no yawns or blank stares.

TODD RINGWALD was of the firm opinion that the meeting should take place in Hoppy's office, on his turf where Jimmy Hull Moke would be caught off guard. Hoppy presumed this made sense. He was really at a loss for the proper customs in these matters. He got lucky and found Moke at home, puttering with his bush-hog and heading on over to Biloxi later in the day anyway. Moke claimed he knew of Hoppy, had heard of him at some point. Hoppy said it was a very important matter involving a potentially big development in Hancock County. They agreed on lunch, a quick sandwich in Hoppy's office. Moke said he knew exactly where Hoppy was located.

For some reason, three part-time sales associates loitered in the front of the office as noon approached. One chatted with a boy-friend on the phone. One scanned the classifieds. One was apparently waiting for the pinochle. With great difficulty, Hoppy dispatched them to the streets where the real estate was to be found. He didn't want anyone around when Moke appeared.

The offices were deserted when Jimmy Hull walked through the door in jeans and cowboy boots. Hoppy greeted him with a nervous handshake and a jittery voice and showed him to his office in the back where his desk was set with two deli sandwiches and iced teas. They talked about local politics, casinos, and fishing as they ate, though Hoppy's appetite was nil. His stomach flipped with fear and his hands wouldn't stop shaking. He then cleared the desk and produced the artist's rendering of Stillwater Bay. Ringwald had delivered it earlier, and it contained no clue as to who was behind the project. Hoppy gave a quick ten-minute summary of the proposed development, and found himself getting stronger. He made a very nice presentation, if he said so himself.

Jimmy Hull stared at the drawing, rubbed his chin, and said, "Thirty million dollars huh?"

"At least," Hoppy answered. His bowels were suddenly loose. "And who's doing it?"

Hoppy had practiced his answer, and he delivered it with convincing authority. He simply couldn't divulge the name, not at this point. Jimmy Hull liked the secrecy. He asked questions, all of which had to do with money and financing. Hoppy answered most of them.

"Zoning could be a real problem," Jimmy Hull said with a frown.

"Certainly."

"And the planning commission will put up a nasty fight."

"We expect this."

"Of course, the supervisors make the final decision. As you know, the recommendations from zoning and planning are merely advisory. Bottom line is the six of us do whatever we want." He snickered and Hoppy laughed along. In Mississippi, the six county supervisors ruled supreme.

"My client understands how things work. And my client is anxious to work with you."

Jimmy Hull removed his elbows from the desk and sat back in his chair. His eyelids narrowed. His forehead wrinkled. He stroked his chin and his beady black eyes shot lasers across the desk and hit poor Hoppy like hot bullets deep in the chest. Hoppy pressed all ten fingers onto the desk so his hands wouldn't tremble.

How many times had Jimmy Hull been at this particular moment, sizing up the prey before going in for the kill?

"You know I control everything in my district," he said, his lips barely moving.

"I know exactly how things work," Hoppy replied as coolly as possible.

"If I want this to be approved, it'll slide right through. If I don't like it, it's dead right now."

Hoppy only nodded.

Jimmy Hull was curious about what other locals were involved at this point, who knew what, just how secret was the project right then. "No one but me," Hoppy assured him.

"Is your client in gambling?"

"No. But they're from Vegas. They know how to get things done at the local level. And they're anxious to move fast."

Vegas was the operative word here, and Jimmy Hull savored it. He looked around the shabby little office. It was spare and spartan and conveyed a certain innocence, as if not much happened here and not much was expected. He had called two friends in

Biloxi, both of whom reported that Mr. Dupree was a harmless sort who sold fruitcakes at Christmas for the Rotary Club. He had a large family and managed to avoid controversy, and commerce generally, for that matter. The obvious question was, why would the boys behind Stillwater Bay associate themselves with a mom-and-pop outfit like Dupree Realty?

He decided not to ask the question. He said, "You know, my son is a very fine consultant for projects like this?"

"Didn't know that. My client would love to work with your son."

"He's over in Bay St. Louis."

"Shall I give him a call?"

"No. I'll handle it."

Randy Moke owned two gravel trucks and spent most of his time tinkering with a fishing boat he advertised for saltwater charters. He had dropped out of high school two months before his first drug conviction.

Hoppy pressed on. Ringwald had insisted he try and pin down Moke as soon as possible. If a deal wasn't reached initially, then Moke might race back to Hancock County and start talking about the development. "My client is anxious to determine the preliminary fees before purchasing the land. How much might your son charge for his services?"

"A hundred thousand."

Hoppy didn't flinch a muscle and was quite proud of his coolness. Ringwald had predicted a shakedown in the neighborhood of one to two hundred thousand. KLX would gladly pay it. Frankly, it was cheap compared to New Jersey. "I see. Payable—"

"In cash."

"My client is willing to discuss this."

"No discussion. Cash up front, or no deal."

"And the deal being?"

"A hundred thousand cash now, and the project sails through. My guarantee. A penny less, and I'll kill it with one phone call."

Remarkably, there was not the slightest trace of menace in his voice or face. Hoppy told Ringwald later that Jimmy Hull simply laid out the terms of the deal as if he were selling used tires at a flea market.

"I need to make a phone call," Hoppy said. "Just sit tight." He walked to the front room, which was thankfully still deserted, and called Ringwald, who was sitting by the phone in his hotel. The terms were relayed, discussed only for a few seconds, and Hoppy returned to his office. "It's a deal. My client will pay it." He said this slowly, and frankly it felt good to finally broker a deal that would lead to millions. KLX on one end, Moke on the other, and Hoppy in the middle of it all, in the fire and totally immune from the dirty work.

Jimmy Hull's face relaxed and he managed a smile. "When?"

"I'll call you Monday."

Nineteen

FITCH IGNORED the trial Friday afternoon. There were urgent matters at hand with one of his jurors. He, along with Pang and Carl Nussman, locked themselves in a conference room at Cable's office and stared at the wall for an hour.

The idea had been Fitch's and his alone. It was a shot in the dark, one of his wildest hunches yet, but he got paid to dig under rocks no one else could find. Money gave him the luxury of dreaming the improbable.

Four days earlier he had ordered Nussman to ship overnight to Biloxi the entire jury file from the Cimmino trial a year before in Allentown, Pennsylvania. The Cimmino jury had listened to four weeks of testimony, then handed the tobacco company another verdict. Three hundred potential jurors had been summoned for duty in Allentown. One of them was a young man named David Lancaster.

The file on Lancaster was thin. He worked in a video store and claimed to be a student. He lived in an apartment over a struggling Korean deli, and apparently traveled by bicycle. There was no evidence of another vehicle, and the county rolls reflected no taxes levied on any car or truck titled in his name. His jury information card stated he was born in Philadelphia on May 8, 1967, though this had not been verified at the time of the trial. There had been no reason to suspect he was lying. Nussman's people had just determined that the birthdate was in fact fictitious. The card also stated he was not a convicted felon, had not served on jury duty in the county in the past year, had no medical reasons not to serve, and was a duly qualified elector. He had registered to vote five months before the trial started.

There was nothing strange in the file except a handwritten memo from a consultant which said that when Lancaster appeared for jury duty on the first day, the clerk had no record of his being summoned. He then produced what appeared to be a valid summons, and he was seated with the pool. One of Nussman's consultants noted that Lancaster seemed quite anxious to serve.

The only photo of the young man was one taken from a distance as he rode his mountain bike to work. He wore a cap, dark sunglasses, long hair, and a heavy beard. One of Nussman's operatives chatted with Lancaster as she rented videos, and reported him to be dressed in faded jeans, Birkenstocks, wool socks, and a flannel shirt. The hair was pulled back severely in a ponytail and tucked under his collar. He was polite but not talkative.

Lancaster got a bad draw when the numbers were pulled, but made the first two cuts and was four rows away when the jury was chosen.

His file was closed immediately.

Now it was open again. In the past twenty-four hours, it had been determined that David Lancaster had simply vanished from Allentown a month after the trial was over. His Korean landlord knew nothing. His boss at the video store said he failed to show up for work one day and was never heard from again. Not another person in town could be found who would admit to knowing Lancaster ever existed. Fitch's people were checking, but no one expected to find anything. He was still registered to vote, but the rolls wouldn't be purged for another five years, according to the county registrar.

By Wednesday night, Fitch was all but certain David Lancaster was Nicholas Easter.

Early Thursday morning, Nussman had received from his office in Chicago two large boxes which contained the jury file from the Glavine trial in Broken Arrow, Oklahoma. Glavine had been a vicious courtroom brawl two years earlier against Trellco, with Fitch securing his verdict long before the lawyers stopped arguing. Nussman had not slept Thursday as he plowed through the Glavine jury research.

There had been a young white male in Broken Arrow named Perry Hirsch, age twenty-five at the time, allegedly born in St. Louis on a date which was ultimately determined to be false. He said he worked in a lamp factory and delivered pizzas on the weekend. Single, Catholic, college dropout, no prior jury service, all according to his own words recorded on a brief questionnaire which was given to the lawyers before the trial. He had registered to vote four months before the trial, and supposedly lived with an aunt in a trailer park. He was one of two hundred people who answered the call for jury service.

There were two photos of Hirsch. In one he was hauling a stack of pizzas to his car, a battered Pinto, in a colorful blue-and-red Rizzo's shirt and matching cap. He wore wire-rimmed glasses and a beard. The other was a shot of him standing beside the trailer where he lived, but his face could hardly be seen.

Hirsch almost made the Glavine jury, but was cut by the plaintiff for reasons that were unclear at the time. Evidently he left town at some point after the trial. The factory where he worked employed a man named Terry Hurtz, but no Perry Hirsch.

Fitch was paying a local investigator to dig furiously. The unnamed aunt had not been found; there were no records from the trailer park. No one at Rizzo's remembered a Perry Hirsch.

Fitch and Pang and Nussman sat in the dark and stared at the wall Friday afternoon. The photos of Hirsch, Lancaster, and Easter were blown up and focused as clearly as possible. Easter of course was now clean-shaven. His photo was taken as he worked, so there were no sunglasses, no cap.

The three faces were of the same person.

Nussman's handwriting expert arrived after lunch Friday. He was flown in on a Pynex jet from D.C. He took fewer than thirty minutes to form a few opinions. The only handwriting samples available were the jury information cards from Cimmino and Wood, and the short questionnaire from Glavine. It was more than enough. The expert had no doubt that Perry Hirsch and David Lancaster were the same person. Easter's handwriting was quite dissimilar from Lancaster's, but he'd made a mistake in running from Hirsch. The carefully printed, block-style hand Easter had used was obviously designed to distinguish itself from earlier trails. He had worked hard to create an entirely new style of writing, one that could not be linked to the past. His mistake came at the bottom of the card when Easter signed his name. The "t" was crossed low and angled down from left to right, very distinguishable. Hirsch had used a sloppy cursive style, no doubt designed to portray a lack of education. The "t" in St. Louis, his alleged place of birth, was identical to the "t" in Easter, though to the untrained eye nothing about the two appeared remotely similar.

He announced without the slightest doubt, "Hirsch and Lancaster are the same people. Hirsch and Easter are the same people. Therefore, Lancaster and Easter must be the same."

"All three are the same," Fitch said slowly as it sunk in.

"That's correct. And he's very, very bright."

The handwriting expert left Cable's. Fitch returned to his office where he met with Pang and Konrad for the rest of Friday afternoon and into the night. He had people on the ground in both Allentown and Broken Arrow digging and bribing and hoping to pry loose employment records and tax withholding forms on Hirsch and Lancaster.

"Have you ever known a person to stalk a trial?" Konrad asked.

"Never," Fitch growled.

THE RULES for conjugal visits were simple. Between 7 P.M. and 9 P.M. Friday night, each juror could entertain spouses or mates or whomever in their rooms. The guests could come and go at any time, but they first had to be registered by Lou Dell, who sized them up and down as if she and she alone possessed the power to approve what they were about to do.

The first to arrive, promptly at seven, was Derrick Maples, the handsome boyfriend of young Angel Weese. Lou Dell took his name, pointed down the hall, said, "Room 55." He was not seen again until nine, when he came up for air.

Nicholas would not have a guest Friday night. Neither would Jerry Fernandez. His wife had moved into a separate bedroom a month ago, and she wasn't about to waste her time visiting a man she despised. Besides, Jerry and the Poodle were exercising conjugal rights every night. Colonel Herrera's wife was out of town. Lonnie Shaver's wife couldn't find a baby-sitter. So the four men watched John Wayne in the Party Room and lamented the sorry states of their romances. Blind old Herman was getting some, but they weren't.

Phillip Savelle had a guest, but Lou Dell refused to divulge to the rest of the boys the sex, race, age, or anything else about his visitor. It happened to be a very nice young lady who appeared to be Indian or Pakistani.

Mrs. Gladys Card watched TV in her room with Mr. Nelson Card. Loreen Duke, who was divorced, visited with her two young teenaged daughters. Rikki Coleman exercised conjugal relations with her husband Rhea, then talked about their kids for the remaining one hour and forty-five minutes.

And Hoppy Dupree brought Millie some flowers and a box of chocolates, which she ate most of while he jumped around the room in a fit of excitement, the likes of which she'd rarely seen. The kids were fine, all out on dates, and business was going full speed. In fact, business had never been better. He had a secret, a large wonderful rich secret about a deal he'd stepped into, but he couldn't tell her just yet. Maybe Monday. Maybe later. But he just couldn't now. He stayed an hour and rushed back to the office for more work.

Mr. Nelson Card left at nine, and Gladys made the mistake of stepping into the Party Room where the boys were drinking beer and eating popcorn and watching boxing matches now. She found a soft drink and sat at the table. Jerry eyed her suspiciously. "You little devil," he said. "Come on, tell us about it."

Her mouth fell open and her cheeks flushed. She couldn't speak.

"Come on, Gladys. We didn't get any."

She grabbed her Coke and jumped to her feet. "Maybe there's a good reason you didn't," she snapped angrily, then marched from the room. Jerry managed a laugh. The other men were too tired and despondent to care.

MARLEE'S CAR was a Lexus leased from a dealer in Biloxi, a three-year lease at six hundred a month with the lessee being Rochelle Group, a brand-spanking-new corporation Fitch had been able to learn nothing about. A transmitter weighing almost a pound had been attached by a magnet under the rear left tire well, so Marlee could now be tracked by Konrad sitting at his desk. Joe

Boy had stuck it under there a few hours after they'd followed her from Mobile and seen her license plates.

Her large new condo was leased by the same corporation. Almost two thousand dollars a month. Marlee had some serious overhead, but Fitch and company couldn't find a trace of a job.

She called late Friday night, just minutes after Fitch had stripped to his XX-Large boxers and black socks and sprawled on his bed like a beached whale. For now he owned the Presidential Suite on the top floor of the Colonial Hotel in Biloxi, on Highway 90, the Gulf a hundred yards away. When he bothered to look, he had a nice view of the beach. No one outside his little circle knew where he was.

The call went to the front desk, an urgent message for Mr. Fitch, and it posed a dilemma for the night clerk. The hotel was being paid large sums of money to protect the privacy and identity of Mr. Fitch. The clerk could not admit he was a guest. The young lady had it all figured out.

When Marlee called back ten minutes later, she was put straight through, pursuant to Mr. Fitch's orders. Fitch was now standing with his boxers pulled almost to his chest but still sagging down past his fleshy thighs, scratching his forehead and wondering how she'd found him. "Good evening," he said.

"Hi, Fitch. Sorry to call so late." She wasn't sorry about a damned thing. The "i" in "Hi" was deliberately flat, something that happened occasionally with Marlee. It was an effort to sound a little Southern. The recordings of all eight phone conversations, however brief, along with the recording of their chat in New Orleans, had been scrutinized by voice and dialect experts in New York. Marlee was a Midwesterner, from eastern Kansas or western Missouri, probably from somewhere within a hundred miles of Kansas City.

"No problem," he said, checking the recorder on a narrow folding table near his bed. "How's your friend?"

"Lonely. Tonight was conjugal night, you know?"

"So I heard. Did everybody get conjugated?"

"Not exactly. It's pretty sad, really. The men watched John Wayne movies while the women knitted."

"Nobody got laid?"

"Very few. Angel Weese, but she's in the middle of a hot romance. Rikki Coleman. Millie Dupree's husband showed up but didn't stay long. The Cards were together. Can't tell about Herman. And Savelle had a guest."

"What manner of humanity did Savelle attract?"

"Don't know. It was never seen."

Fitch lowered his wide rear to the edge of the bed and pinched the bridge of his nose. "Why didn't you visit your friend?" he asked.

"Who said we're lovers?"

"What are you?"

"Friends. Guess which two jurors are sleeping together?"

"Now how would I know that?"

"Guess."

Fitch smiled at himself in the mirror and marveled at his wonderful luck. "Jerry Fernandez and somebody."

"Good guess. Jerry's about to get a divorce, and Sylvia is lonely too. Their rooms are just across the hall, and, well, there's little else to do at the Siesta Inn."

"Ain't love grand?"

"I gotta tell you, Fitch, Krigler worked for the plaintiff."

"They listened to him, huh?"

"Every word. They listened and they believed. He turned them around, Fitch."

"Tell me some good news."

"Rohr's worried."

His spine stiffened noticeably. "What's bugging Rohr?" he asked, studying his puzzled face in the mirror. He shouldn't be surprised that she was talking to Rohr, so why the hell was he shocked to hear it? He felt betrayed.

"You. He knows you're loose on the streets scheming up all sorts of ways to get to the jury. Wouldn't you be worried, Fitch, if some guy like you was hard at work for the plaintiff?"

"I'd be terrified."

"Rohr isn't terrified. He's just worried."

"How often do you talk to him?"

"A lot. He's sweeter than you, Fitch. He's a very pleasant man to talk to, plus he doesn't record my calls, doesn't send in goons to follow my car. None of that sort of stuff."

"Really knows how to charm a girl, huh?"

"Yeah. But he's weak where it counts."

"Where's that?"

"In the wallet. He can't match your resources."

"How much of my resources do you want?"

"Later, Fitch. Gotta run. There's a suspicious-looking car sitting across the street. Must be some of your clowns." She hung up.

Fitch showered and tried to sleep. At 2 A.M., he drove himself to the Lucy Luck, where he played blackjack at five hundred dollars a hand, sipped Sprite until dawn, when he left with close to twenty thousand dollars in fresh winnings.

Twenty

THE FIRST SATURDAY in November arrived with temperatures in the low sixties, unseasonably cool for the Coast and its near-tropical climate. A gentle breeze from the north rattled trees and scattered leaves on the streets and sidewalks. Fall usually arrived late and lasted until the first of the year, when it yielded to spring. The Coast did not experience winter.

A few joggers were on the street just after dawn. No one noticed the plain black Chrysler as it pulled into the driveway of a modest brick split-level. It was too early for the neighbors to see the two young men in matching dark suits exit the car, walk to the front door, ring the buzzer, and wait patiently. It was too early, but in less than an hour the lawns would be busy with leaf rakers and the sidewalks busy with children.

Hoppy had just poured the water into the Mr. Coffee when he heard the buzzer. He tightened the belt of his ragged terry-cloth bathrobe and tried to straighten his unkempt hair with his fingers. Must be the Boy Scouts selling doughnuts at this ungodly hour. Surely it wasn't the Jehovah's Witnesses again. He'd let them have it this time. Nothing but a cult! He moved quickly because the upstairs was filled with comatose teenagers. Six at last count. Five of his and a guest someone had dragged home from junior college. A typical Friday night at the Dupree home.

He opened the front door and met two serious young men, both of whom instantly reached into their pockets and whipped out gold medallions stuck to black leather. In the quick rush of syllables, Hoppy caught "FBI" at least twice, and nearly fainted.

"Are you Mr. Dupree?" Agent Nitchman asked.

Hoppy gasped. "Yes, but—"

"We'd like to ask you some questions," said Agent Napier as he somehow managed to take a step even closer.

"About what?" Hoppy asked, his voice dry. He tried to look between them, at the street, across it where Mildred Yancy was no doubt watching all of this.

Nitchman and Napier exchanged a harsh, conspiratorial look. Then Napier said to Hoppy, "We can do it here, or perhaps somewhere else."

"Questions about Stillwater Bay, Jimmy Hull Moke, things like that," Nitchman said for clarification, and Hoppy clutched the door frame.

"Oh my god," he said as the air was sucked from his lungs and most vital organs froze.

"May we come in?" Napier said.

Hoppy lowered his head and rubbed his eyes as if to weep. "No, please, not here." The children! Normally they'd sleep till nine or ten, or even noon for that matter if Millie let them, but with voices downstairs they'd be up in a minute. "My office," he managed to say.

"We'll wait," Napier said.

"Make it quick," Nitchman said.

"Thank you," Hoppy said, then quickly closed the door, and locked it. He fell onto a sofa in the den, and stared at the ceiling, which was spinning clockwise. No sounds from upstairs. The kids were still sleeping. His heart pounded fiercely and for a full minute he thought he might just lie there and die. Death would be welcome now. He could close his eyes and float away, and in a couple of hours the first kid down would see him and call 911. He was fifty-three, and bad hearts ran in his family, on his mother's side. Millie would get a hundred thousand in life insurance.

When he realized his heart was determined to continue, he slowly swung to his feet. Still dizzy, he groped his way to the kitchen and poured a cup of coffee. It was five minutes after seven, according to the digital on the oven. Fourth day of November. Undoubtedly one of the worst days of his life. How could he have been so stupid!

He thought about calling Todd Ringwald, and he thought about calling Millard Putt, his lawyer. He decided to wait. He was suddenly in a hurry. He wanted to leave the house before the kids got up, and he wanted those two agents out of his driveway before the neighbors noticed. Besides, Millard Putt did nothing but real estate law, and was not very good at that. This was a criminal matter.

A criminal matter! He skipped a shower and dressed in seconds. He was halfway through the brushing of his teeth when he finally looked at himself in the mirror. Betrayal was written all over his face, stamped in his eyes for all to see. He couldn't lie. Deceit was not in him. He was just Hoppy Dupree, an honest man with a fine family, good reputation, and all. He'd never cheated on his tax returns!

So why, Hoppy, were there two FBI agents waiting outside for a trip downtown, not to jail yet, though that would surely come, but to a private place where they could eat him for breakfast and lay bare his fraud? He decided not to shave. Perhaps he should call his minister. He brushed his swirling hair and thought of Millie, and the public disgrace, and the kids, and what would everybody think.

Before leaving the bathroom, Hoppy vomited.

Outside, Napier insisted that he ride with Hoppy. Nitchman in the black Chrysler followed. Not a word was spoken.

DUPREE REALTY was not the sort of commercial enterprise that attracted early risers. This was true on Saturday, as it was for the rest of the week. Hoppy knew the place would be deserted until at least nine, maybe ten. He unlocked doors, turned on lights, said nothing until it was time to ask if they wanted coffee. Both declined and seemed quite anxious to proceed to the slaughter. Hoppy sat on his side of the desk. They huddled together like twins across from him. He was unable to hold their gaze.

Nitchman got it started by saying, "Are you familiar with Stillwater Bay?"

"Yes."

"Have you met a man by the name of Todd Ringwald?"

"Yes."

"Have you signed any type of contract with him?"

"No."

Napier and Nitchman looked at each other as if they knew this to be false. Napier said, smugly, "Look, Mr. Dupree, this will go a lot smoother for you if you tell the truth."

"I swear I'm telling the truth."

"When did you first meet Todd Ringwald?" Nitchman asked as he pulled a narrow notepad from his pocket and began scribbling.

"Thursday."

"Do you know Jimmy Hull Moke?"

"Yes."

"When did you first meet him?"

"Yesterday."

"Where?"

"Right here."

"What was the purpose of the meeting?"

"To discuss the development of Stillwater Bay. I'm supposed to represent a company called KLX Properties. KLX wants to develop Stillwater Bay, which is in Mr. Moke's supervisor's district in Hancock County."

Napier and Nitchman stared at Hoppy and pondered this for what seemed like an hour. Hoppy silently repeated his words to himself. Had he said something? Something that would speed along his journey to prison? Perhaps he should stop this right now and seek legal counsel.

Napier cleared his throat. "We've been investigating Mr. Moke for the past six months, and two weeks ago he agreed to enter into a plea bargain arrangement whereby he will receive a light sentence in exchange for his assistance."

This legal crap-speak meant little to Hoppy. He heard it, but things weren't registering clearly right now.

"Did you offer money to Mr. Moke?" Napier asked.

"No," Hoppy said because there was no way he could say yes. He said it quickly, without force or conviction, it just came out. "No," he said again. He hadn't actually offered money. He had cleared the way for his client to offer money. At least, that was his interpretation of what he'd done.

Nitchman slowly reached into his coat pocket, slowly felt around until his fingers were just right, slowly removed a slender pocket something or other which he slowly placed in the center of the desk. "Are you sure?" he asked, almost taunting.

"Sure I'm sure," Hoppy said, staring slack-jawed at the sleek hideous device.

Nitchman gently pressed a button. Hoppy held his breath and clenched his fists. Then, there was his voice, chirping along nervously about local politics and casinos and fishing with an occasional entry by Moke. "He was wired!" Hoppy exclaimed, breathless and totally defeated.

"Yes," one of them said gravely.

Hoppy could only stare at the recorder. "Oh no," he mumbled. The words had been uttered and recorded less than twenty-four hours earlier, right there at that very desk over chicken clubs and iced tea. Jimmy Hull had sat where Nitchman was and arranged a bribe for a hundred grand, and he did so with an FBI wire stuck somewhere to his body.

The tape dragged painfully on until the damage was done and Hoppy and Jimmy Hull were offering their hurried good-byes. "Shall we listen to it again?" Nitchman asked as he touched a button.

"No, please," Hoppy said, pinching the bridge of his nose. "Should I talk to a lawyer?" he asked without looking up.

"Not a bad idea," Napier said sympathetically.

When he finally looked at them his eyes were red and wet. His lip quivered but he thrust his chin outward and tried to be bold. "So what am I looking at?" he asked.

Napier and Nitchman relaxed in unison. Napier stood and walked to a bookcase. "It's hard to say," Nitchman said, as if the issue would be determined by someone else. "We've busted a dozen supervisors in the past year. The judges are sick of it. The sentences are getting longer."

"I'm not a supervisor," Hoppy said.

"Good point. I'd say three to five years, federal, not state."

"Conspiracy to bribe a government official," Napier added helpfully. Napier then returned to his seat next to Nitchman. Both men sat on the edges of their chairs as if ready to leap across the desk and flog Hoppy for his sins.

The mike was the cap of a blue Bic disposable ballpoint sitting harmlessly with a dozen other pencils and cheap pens in a dusty fruit jar on Hoppy's desk. Ringwald had left it there Friday morning when Hoppy had gone to the rest room. The pens and pencils gave the appearance of never being used, the type of collection which would sit untouched for months before being rearranged. In the event Hoppy or someone else decided to use the blue Bic, it was out of ink and would find itself immediately in the wastebasket. Only a technician could disassemble it and discover the bug.

From the desk, the words were relayed to a small, powerful transmitter hidden behind the Lysol and air freshener under a rest room vanity, next to Hoppy's office. From the transmitter, the words were sent to an unmarked van across the street in a shopping center. In the van, the words were recorded on tape and delivered to Fitch's office.

Jimmy Hull had not been wired, was not working with the feds, had in fact been doing what he did best—hustling bribes.

Ringwald, Napier, and Nitchman were all ex-cops who were now private agents employed by an international security firm in Bethesda. It was a firm Fitch used often. The Hoppy sting would cost The Fund eighty thousand dollars.

Chicken feed.

HOPPY MENTIONED the possibility of legal counsel again. Napier stonewalled it with a lengthy recitation of the FBI's efforts to stop rampant corruption on the Coast. He blamed all ills on the gambling industry.

It was imperative to keep Hoppy away from a lawyer. A lawyer would want names and phone numbers, records and paperwork. Napier and Nitchman had enough fake credentials and quick lies to bluff poor Hoppy, but a good lawyer would force them to disappear.

What had begun as a routine probe of Jimmy Hull and graft of the local garden variety had turned into a much broader investigation into gaming and, the magic words, "organized crime," according to Napier's lengthy narrative. Hoppy listened when he could. It was difficult though. His mind raced away with concerns for Millie and the kids and how they would survive for the three to five years he was gone.

"So we didn't target you," Napier said, wrapping things up.

"And, frankly, we'd never heard of KLX Properties," added Nitchman. "We sort of just stumbled into this."

"Can't you just stumble out?" Hoppy asked, and actually managed a soft, helpless smile.

"Maybe," Napier said deliberately, then glanced at Nitchman as if they had something even more dramatic to lay on Hoppy.

"Maybe what?" he asked.

They withdrew from the edge of the desk in unison, their timing perfect as if they'd either rehearsed for hours or done this a hundred times. They both stared hard at Hoppy, who wilted and looked at the desktop.

"We know you're not a crook, Mr. Dupree," Nitchman said softly.

"You just made a mistake," added Napier.

"You got that right," Hoppy mumbled.

"You're being used by some awfully sophisticated crooks. They roll in here with big plans and big bucks, and well, we see it all the time in drug cases."

Drugs! Hoppy was shocked but said nothing. Another pause as the stares continued.

"Can we offer you a twenty-four-hour deal?" Napier asked.

"How can I say no?"

"Let's keep this quiet for twenty-four hours. You don't tell a soul, we don't tell a soul. You keep it from your lawyer, we don't pursue you. Not for twenty-four hours."

"I don't understand."

"We can't explain everything right now. We need some time to evaluate your situation."

Nitchman leaned forward again, elbows on desk. "There might be a way out for you, Mr. Dupree."

Hoppy was rallying, however faintly. "I'm listening."

"You're a small, insignificant fish caught in a large net," Napier explained. "You might be expendable."

Sounded good to Hoppy. "What happens in twenty-four hours?"

"We meet again right here. Nine o'clock in the morning."

"It's a deal."

"One word to Ringwald, one word to anyone, even your wife, and your future is in serious jeopardy."

"You have my word."

THE CHARTERED BUS left the Siesta Inn at ten with all fourteen jurors, Mrs. Grimes, Lou Dell and her husband Benton, Willis and his wife Ruby, five part-time deputies in plain clothes, Earl

Hutto, the Sheriff of Harrison County, and his wife Claudelle, and two assistant clerks from Gloria Lane's office. Twenty-eight in all, plus the driver. All approved by Judge Harkin. Two hours later they rolled along Canal Street in New Orleans, then exited the bus at the corner of Magazine. Lunch was in a reserved room in the back of an old oyster bar on Decatur in the French Quarter, and paid for by the taxpayers of Harrison County.

They were allowed to scatter throughout the Quarter. They shopped at outdoor markets; strolled with the tourists through Jackson Square; gawked at naked bodies in cheap dives on Bourbon; bought T-shirts and other souvenirs. Some rested on benches along the Riverwalk. Some ducked into bars and watched football. At four, they gathered at the river and boarded a paddle wheeler for a sight-seeing trip. At six they ate dinner at a pizza and po-boy deli on Canal.

By ten they were locked in their rooms in Pass Christian, tired and ready for sleep. Busy jurors are happy jurors.

Twenty-one

WITH THE HOPPY SHOW proceeding flawlessly, Fitch made the decision late Saturday to launch the next assault against the jury. It was a strike made without the advantage of meticulous planning, and it would be as severe as the Hoppy sting was slick.

Early Sunday morning, Pang and Dubaz, both dressed in tan shirts with a plumber's logo above the pockets, picked the lock on the door of Easter's apartment. No alarm sounded. Dubaz went straight to the vent above the refrigerator, removed the screen, and yanked out the hidden camera that had caught Doyle earlier. He placed it in a large toolbox he'd brought to remove the goods.

Pang went to the computer. He had studied the hurried photos taken by Doyle during the first visit, and he had practiced on an identical unit which had been installed in an office next to Fitch's. He twisted screws and removed the back cover panel of the computer. The hard drive was precisely where he'd been told. In less than a minute it was out. Pang found two stacks of 3.5-inch discs, sixteen in all, in a rack by the monitor.

While Pang performed the delicate removal of the hard drive, Dubaz opened drawers and quietly turned over the cheap furniture in the search for more discs. The apartment was so small and had so few places to hide anything, his task was easy. He searched the kitchen drawers and cabinets, the closets, the cardboard boxes Easter used to store his socks and underwear. He found nothing.

All computer-related paraphernalia were apparently stored near the computer.

"Let's go," Pang said, ripping cords from the computer, monitor, and printer.

They practically threw the system on the ragged sofa, where Dubaz piled on cushions and clothing, then poured charcoal lighter fluid from a plastic jug. When the sofa, chair, computer, cheap rugs, and assorted clothing were sufficiently doused, the two men walked to the door and Dubaz threw a match. The ignition was rapid and virtually silent, at least to anyone who might have been listening outside. They waited until the flames were lapping the ceiling and black smoke was boiling throughout the apartment, then made a hasty departure, locking the door behind them. Down the stairs, on the first level, they pulled a fire alarm. Dubaz ran back upstairs where the smoke was seeping from the apartment, and began yelling and beating on doors. Pang did the same on the first level. Screams followed quickly as the hallways filled with panicked people in bathrobes and sweatsuits. The shrill clanging of ancient firebells added to the hysteria.

"Make damned sure you don't kill anyone," Fitch had warned them. Dubaz pounded on doors as the smoke thickened. He made certain every apartment near Easter's was empty. He pulled people by the arms; asked if everyone was out; pointed to the exits.

As the crowd spilled into the parking lot, Pang and Dubaz separated and slowly retreated. Sirens could be heard. Smoke appeared in the windows of two upstairs apartments—Easter's and one next door. More people scrambled out, some wrapped in blankets and clutching babies and toddlers. They joined the crowd and waited impatiently for the fire trucks.

When the firemen arrived, Pang and Dubaz dropped farther back, then vanished.

NO ONE DIED. No one was injured. Four apartments were completely destroyed, eleven severely damaged, nearly thirty families homeless until cleanup and restoration.

Easter's hard drive proved impenetrable. He had added so many passwords, secret codes, antitampering and antiviral barriers that Fitch's computer experts were stumped. He'd flown them in Saturday from Washington. They were honest people with no idea where the hard drive and the discs came from. He simply locked them in a room with a system identical to Easter's and told them what he wanted. Most of the discs had similar protections. About halfway through the stack, though, the tension was broken when they were able to evade passwords on an older disc Easter had neglected to adequately secure. The files list showed sixteen entries with document names which revealed nothing. Fitch was notified as the first document was being printed. It was a six-page summary of current news items about the tobacco industry, dated October 11, 1994. Stories from *Time, The Wall Street Journal,* and *Forbes* were mentioned. The second document was a rambling two-page narrative describing a documentary Easter had just seen about breast implant litigation. The third was a gawky poem he'd written about rivers. The fourth was another compilation of recent news articles about lung cancer trials.

Fitch and Konrad read each page carefully. The writing was clear and straightforward, obviously hurriedly done because the typos were almost cumbersome. He wrote like an unbiased reporter. It was impossible to determine whether Easter was sympathetic to smokers or just keenly interested in mass tort litigation.

There were more dreadful poems. An aborted short story. And finally, pay dirt. Document number fifteen was a two-page letter to his mother, a Mrs. Pamela Blanchard in Gardner, Texas. Dated April 20, 1995, it began: "Dear Mom: I'm now living in Biloxi, Mississippi, on the Gulf Coast," and proceeded to explain how much he loved salt water and beaches and could never again live in farm country. He apologized at length for not writing sooner, apologized for two long paragraphs about his tendency to drift, and promised to do better with his letter writing. He asked about Alex, said he hadn't talked to him in three months and couldn't believe he'd finally made it to Alaska and found a job as a fishing guide. Alex appeared to be a brother. There was no mention of a father. No mention of a girl, certainly not anyone named Marlee.

He said he'd found a job working in a casino, and it was fun for the moment but not much of a future. He still thought about being a lawyer, and was sorry about law school, but he doubted he'd ever go back. He confessed to being happy, living simply with little money and even fewer responsibilities. Oh well, gotta run now. Lots of love. Say hello to Aunt Sammie and he'd call soon.

He signed off simply as "Jeff." "Love Jeff." No last name appeared anywhere in the letter.

Dante and Joe Boy left on a private jet an hour after the letter was first read. Fitch instructed them to go to Gardner and hire every private snoop in town.

The computer people cracked one more disc, the next to the last of the bunch. Again, they were able to sidestep the antitampering barriers with a complicated series of password clues. They were very impressed by Easter's hacking ability.

The disc was filled with part of one document—the voter registration rolls of Harrison County. Starting with A and running through K, they printed over sixteen thousand names with addresses. Fitch checked on them periodically throughout the printing. He too had a complete printout of all registered voters in the county. It was not a secret list, in fact it could be purchased from Gloria Lane for thirty-five dollars. Most political candidates made the purchase during election years.

But two things were odd about Easter's list. First, it was on a computer disc, which meant he had somehow managed to enter Gloria Lane's computer and steal the information. Second, what did a part-time computer hack/part-time student need with such a list?

If Easter accessed the clerk's computer, then he certainly could tamper with it enough to have his own name entered as a prospective juror in the *Wood* case.

The more Fitch thought about it, the more it made perfect sense.

HOPPY'S EYES were red and puffy as he drank thick coffee at his desk early Sunday and waited for 9 A.M. He hadn't eaten a bite since a banana Saturday morning while the Folger's brewed in his kitchen just minutes before the doorbell rang and Napier and Nitchman entered his life. His gastrointestinal system was shot. His nerves were ragged. He'd sneaked too much vodka Saturday night, and he'd done it at the house, something Millie prohibited.

The kids had slept through it all Saturday. He hadn't told a soul, hadn't been tempted to, really. The humiliation helped keep the loathsome secret safe.

At precisely nine, Napier and Nitchman entered with a third man, an older man who also wore a severe dark suit and severe facial expressions as if he'd come to personally whip and flay poor Hoppy. Nitchman introduced him as George Cristano. From Washington! Department of Justice!

Cristano's handshake was cold. He didn't make small talk.

"Say, Hoppy, would you mind if we had this little chat somewhere else?" Napier asked as he looked scornfully around the office.

"It's just safer," Nitchman added for clarification.

"You never know where bugs might show up," Cristano said.

"Tell me about it," Hoppy said, but no one caught the humor. Was he in a position to say no to anything? "Sure," he said.

They left in a spotless black Lincoln Town Car, Nitchman and Napier in the front, Hoppy in the back with Cristano, who matter-of-factly began to explain that he was some type of high-ranking Assistant Attorney General from deep inside Justice. The closer they got to the Gulf the more odious his position became. Then he was silent.

"Are you a Democrat or a Republican, Hoppy?" Cristano asked softly during one particularly long lull in the conversation. Napier turned at the shore and headed west along the Coast.

Hoppy surely didn't want to offend anyone. "Oh, I don't know. Always vote for the man, you know. I don't get hung up on parties, know what I mean?"

Cristano looked away, out the window, as if this wasn't what he wanted. "I was hoping you were a good Republican," he said, still looking through the window at the sea.

Hoppy could be any damned thing these boys wanted. Absolutely anything. A card-carrying, wild-eyed, fanatical Communist, if it would please Mr. Cristano.

"Voted for Reagan and Bush," he said proudly. "And Nixon. Even Goldwater."

Cristano nodded ever so slightly, and Hoppy managed to exhale.

The car became silent again. Napier parked it at a dock near Bay St. Louis, forty minutes from Biloxi. Hoppy followed Cristano down a pier and onto a deserted sixty-foot charter boat named *Afternoon Delight*. Nitchman and Napier waited by the car, out of sight.

"Sit down, Hoppy," Cristano said, pointing to a foam-padded bench on the deck. Hoppy sat. The boat rocked ever so slightly.

The water was still. Cristano sat across from him and leaned forward so that their heads were three feet apart.

"Nice boat," Hoppy said, rubbing the imitation leather seat.

"It's not ours. Listen, Hoppy, you're not wired, are you?"

Instinctively, he bolted upright, shocked by the suggestion. "Of course not!"

"Sorry, but these things do happen. I guess I should frisk you." Cristano looked him up and down quickly. Hoppy was horrified at the thought of being fondled by this stranger, alone on a boat.

"I swear I am not wired, okay," Hoppy said, so firmly that he was proud of himself. Cristano's face relaxed. "You wanna frisk me?" he asked. Hoppy glanced around to see if anyone was within view. Look sorta odd, wouldn't it? Two grown men rubbing each other in broad daylight on an anchored boat?

"Are you wired?" Hoppy asked.

"No."

"Swear?"

"I swear."

"Good." Hoppy was relieved and quite anxious to believe the man. The alternative was simply unthinkable.

Cristano smiled then abruptly frowned. He leaned in. The small talk was over. "I'll be brief, Hoppy. We have a deal for you, a deal which will enable you to walk away from this without a scratch. Nothing. No arrest, no indictment, no trial, no prison. No face in the newspaper. In fact, Hoppy, no one will ever know."

He paused to catch his breath, and Hoppy charged in. "So far so good. I'm listening."

"It's a bizarre deal, one we've never attempted. Has nothing to do with law and justice and punishment, nothing like that. It's a political deal, Hoppy. Purely political. There'll be no record of it in Washington. No one will ever know, except for me, you, those two guys waiting by the car, and less than ten people deep inside Justice. We cut the deal, you do your part, and everything is forgotten."

"You got it. Just point me in the right direction."

"Are you concerned about crime, drugs, law and order, Hoppy?"

"Of course."

"Are you sick of graft and corruption?"

Odd question. At this very moment, Hoppy felt like the poster child for the campaign against corruption. "Yes!"

"There are good guys and bad guys in Washington, Hoppy. There are those of us at Justice who've devoted our lives to fighting crime. I mean serious crime, Hoppy. I mean drug payoffs to judges and congressmen who take money from foreign enemies, criminal activity that could threaten our democracy. Know what I mean?"

If Hoppy didn't know for sure, then he certainly was sympathetic to Cristano and his fine friends in Washington. "Yes, yes," he said, hanging on every word.

"But everything's political these days, Hoppy. We're constantly fighting with Congress and we're fighting with the President. Do you know what we need in Washington, Hoppy?"

Whatever it was, Hoppy wanted them to have it.

Cristano didn't give him the chance to answer. "We need more Republicans, more good, conservative Republicans who'll give us money and get out of our way. The Democrats are always meddling, always threatening budget cuts, restructuring, always concerned about the rights of these poor criminals we're picking on. There's a war raging up there, Hoppy. We fight it every day."

He looked at Hoppy as if he should say something, but Hoppy was momentarily trying to adjust to the war. He nodded gravely, then looked at his feet.

"We have to protect our friends, Hoppy, and this is where you come in."

"Okay."

"Again, this is a strange deal. Take it, and our tape of you bribing Mr. Moke will be destroyed."

"I'll take the deal. Just tell me what it is."

Cristano paused and looked up and down the pier. Some fishermen were making noises far away. He leaned closer and actually touched Hoppy on the knee. "It's about your wife," he said, almost under his breath, then reared back to let it sink in.

"My wife?"

"Yes. Your wife."

"Millie?"

"That's her."

"What the hell—"

"I'll explain."

"Millie?" Hoppy was flabbergasted. What could sweet Millie have to do with a mess like this?

"It's the trial, Hoppy," Cristano said, and the first piece of the puzzle plunged roughly into place.

"Guess who contributes the most money to Republican congressional candidates?"

Hoppy was too stunned and confused to offer an intelligent guess.

"That's right. The tobacco companies. They pour millions into races because they're afraid of the FDA and they're fed up with government regulations. They're free-enterprise people, Hoppy, same as you. They believe people smoke because they choose to smoke, and they're sick of the government and the trial lawyers trying to run them out of business."

"It is political," Hoppy said, staring at the Gulf in disbelief.

"Nothing but politics. If Big Tobacco loses this trial, then there will be an avalanche of litigation the likes of which this country has never seen. The companies will lose billions, and we'll lose millions in Washington. Can you help us, Hoppy?"

Jolted back to reality, Hoppy could only manage, "Say what?"

"Can you help us?"

"Sure, I guess, but how?"

"Millie. You talk to your wife, make sure she understands how senseless and how dangerous this case is. She needs to take charge in that jury room, Hoppy. She needs to stand her ground against those liberals on the jury who might want to bring back a big verdict. Can you do it?"

"Of course I can."

"But will you, Hoppy? We don't want to use the tape, okay. You help us, and the tape goes down the toilet."

Hoppy suddenly remembered the tape. "Yeah, you gotta deal. I'll see her tonight, as a matter of fact."

"Go to work on her. It's terribly important—important for us at Justice, for the good of the country, and, of course, it'll keep you outta prison for five years." Cristano delivered the last line with a horselaugh and a slap on the knee. Hoppy laughed too.

They talked about strategy for half an hour. The longer they sat on the boat, the more questions Hoppy had. What if Millie voted with the tobacco company but the rest of the jury disagreed and delivered a big verdict? What would happen to Hoppy then?

Cristano promised to hold his end of the deal regardless of the verdict, as long as Millie voted right.

Hoppy virtually skipped along the pier as they returned to the car. He was a new man when he saw Napier and Nitchman.

AFTER DELIBERATING on his decision for three days, Judge Harkin reversed himself late Saturday and decided the jurors would not be permitted to attend their churches Sunday. He was convinced all fourteen would suddenly possess an amazing desire to commune with the Holy Spirit, and the idea of them fanning out to all parts of the county was simply unworkable. He called his minister, who in turn made more calls, and a young divinity student was located. A chapel service was planned for eleven o'clock Sunday morning, in the Party Room at the Siesta Inn.

Judge Harkin sent a personal note to each juror. The notes were slid under their doors before they returned from New Orleans Saturday night.

Six people attended the service, a rather dull affair. Mrs. Gladys Card was there, in a surprisingly nasty mood for the Sabbath. She hadn't missed Sunday School at the Calvary Baptist Church in sixteen years, the last absence caused by the death of her sister in Baton Rouge. Sixteen straight years without a miss. She had the Perfect Attendance Pins lined up on her dresser. Esther Knoblach in the Women's Mission Union had twenty-two years, the current record at Calvary, but she was seventy-nine and was afflicted with high blood pressure. Gladys was sixty-three, in fine health, and thus considered Esther catchable. She couldn't admit this to anyone, but everyone at Calvary suspected it.

But now she'd blown it, thanks to Judge Harkin, a man she didn't like from the start and now despised. And she didn't like the divinity student either.

Rikki Coleman came in a jogging suit. Millie Dupree brought her Bible. Loreen Duke was a devout churchgoer, but was appalled at the brevity of the service. On at eleven and over by eleven-thirty, typical hurried style of white folks. She'd heard of such foolishness, but had never worshiped in such a manner. Her pastor never got to the pulpit before one, and often didn't leave it until three, when they broke for lunch, which they ate on the grounds if the weather was nice, then trooped back inside for another dose. She nibbled on a sweet roll and suffered in silence.

Mr. and Mrs. Herman Grimes attended, not through any calling of faith but because the walls in Room 58 were closing in. Herman in particular had not voluntarily gone to church since childhood.

Throughout the course of the morning, it had come to be known that Phillip Savelle was angered at the notion of worship. He told someone he was an atheist, and this news had spread in a flash. To protest, he positioned himself on his bed, apparently nude or certainly close to it, folded and tucked his wiry legs and arms into some type of yoga drill, and hollered chants at full volume. He did this with the door open.

He could be heard faintly in the Party Room, during the service, and this no doubt was a factor in the young divinity student's rather hastened wrap-up and benediction.

Lou Dell marched down the first time to tell Savelle to shut up, but backed away quickly when she noticed Savelle's nakedness. Willis tried next, but Savelle kept his eyes closed and his mouth open and simply ignored the deputy. Willis kept his distance.

The nonworshiping jurors hunkered down behind locked doors and watched loud televisions.

At two, the first relatives began to arrive with fresh clothing and supplies for the week. Nicholas Easter was the only juror with no close contact on the outside. It was determined by Judge Harkin that Willis would drive Easter in a squad car to his apartment.

The fire had been out for several hours. The trucks and firemen were long gone. The narrow front lawn and sidewalk in front of the building were strewn with charred debris and piles of soggy clothing. Neighbors milled about, stunned, but busily going about the cleanup.

"Which one's yours?" Willis asked as he stopped the car and gaped at the burnt crater in the center of the building.

"Up there," Nicholas said, trying to point and nod at the same time. His knees were weak as he left the car and walked to the first cluster of people, a family of Vietnamese who were mutely studying a melted plastic table lamp.

"When did this happen?" he asked. The air was thick with the acrid smell of freshly burnt wood and paint and carpet.

They said nothing.

"This morning, about eight," answered a woman as she walked

by with a heavy cardboard box. Nicholas looked at the people and realized he didn't know a single name. In the small foyer, a busy lady with a clipboard was scribbling notes while talking on a cellphone. The main staircase to the second level was guarded by a private security guard who at the moment was helping an elderly woman drag a wet throw rug down the steps.

"Do you live here?" the woman asked when she finished her conversation.

"Yes. Easter, in 312."

"Wow. Totally destroyed. That's probably where it started."

"I'd like to see it."

The security guard led Nicholas and the woman up the steps to the second floor, where the damage was quite apparent. They stopped at a yellow caution tape at the edge of the crater. The fire had gone upward, through the plaster ceilings and cheap rafters, and had managed to burn two large holes in the roof, directly over the spot where his bedroom used to be, as far as he could tell. And it had burned downward, severely damaging the apartment directly under him. Nothing was left of number 312, except for the kitchen wall, where the sink hung by one end and seemed ready to fall. Nothing. No sign of the cheap furniture in the den, no sign of the den itself. Nothing from the bedroom except blackened walls.

And, to his horror, no computer.

Virtually all the floors, ceilings, and walls of the apartment had vanished, leaving nothing but a gaping hole.

"Anybody hurt?" Nicholas asked softly.

"No. Were you home?" she asked.

"No. Who are you?"

"I'm with the management company. I have some forms for you to fill out."

They returned to the foyer where Nicholas hurriedly did the paperwork and left with Willis.

Twenty-two

IT WAS POINTED OUT to Judge Harkin by Phillip Savelle, in a tersely worded, hardly legible message, that the word "conjugal" as defined by Webster covered husband and wife only, and he objected to the term. He did not have a wife, and had little regard for the institution of marriage. He suggested "Communal Interludes," and he went on to bitch about the worship service held that morning. He faxed the letter to Harkin, who received it at home during the fourth quarter of the Saints game. Lou Dell arranged the fax through the front desk. Twenty minutes later she received a return fax from His Honor changing the word "conjugal" to "personal," and relabeling the whole thing "Personal Visits." He directed her to make copies for all jurors. Because it was Sunday, he threw in another hour, from 6 P.M. to 10, instead of 9. He then called her to ask what else Mr. Savelle might want, and inquired as to the general mood of his jury.

Lou Dell just couldn't tell him about seeing Mr. Savelle all nude and perched on his bed like that. She figured the Judge had enough things to worry about. Everything was fine, she assured him.

Hoppy was the first guest to arrive and Lou Dell whisked him away quickly to Millie's room, where he once again delivered chocolates and a small bouquet of flowers. They kissed briefly on the cheeks, never considered anything conjugal, and lounged on the beds during "60 Minutes." Hoppy slowly brought the conversation around to the trial, where he struggled to keep it for a while. "Just doesn't make sense, you know, for people to sue like this. I mean, it's silly, really. Everybody knows cigarettes are addictive and dangerous, so why smoke? Remember Boyd Dogan, smoked Salems for twenty-five years, quit just like that," he said, snapping his fingers.

"Yeah, he quit five minutes after the doctor found that tumor on his tongue," Millie reminded him, then added a mocking snap of her own.

"Yeah, but lots of people quit smoking. It's mind over matter. Not right to keep smoking then sue for millions when the damned things kill you."

"Hoppy, your language."

"Sorry." Hoppy asked about the other jurors and their reactions so far to the plaintiff's case. Mr. Cristano thought it would be best to try and win Millie over with the merits, instead of terrorizing her with the truth. They'd talked about this over lunch. Hoppy felt treacherous plotting against his own wife, but each time the guilt hit him so did the thought of five years in prison.

Nicholas left his room during halftime of the Sunday-night game. The hall was empty of jurors and guards. Voices were heard in the Party Room, generally male voices it seemed. Once again the men drank beer and watched football while the women made the most of their personal visits and communal interludes.

He slid silently through the double glass doors at the end of the hallway, ducked around the corner, past the soft-drink machines, then bounded up the stairs to the second floor. Marlee was waiting in a room she'd paid cash for and registered under the name of Elsa Broome, one of her many aliases.

They went straight to bed, with a minimum of words and preliminaries. Both had agreed that eight consecutive nights apart was not only a record for them, but also unhealthy.

MARLEE MET NICHOLAS when both had other names. The point of contact was a bar in Lawrence, Kansas, where she worked as a waitress and he spent late nights with pals from law school. She had collected two degrees by the time she settled in Lawrence, and because she wasn't eager to initiate a career, she was pondering the option of law school, that great American baby-sitter for directionless postgrads. She was in no hurry. Her mother had died a few years before she met Nicholas, and Marlee had inherited almost two hundred thousand dollars. She served drinks because the hangout was cool and she would've been bored otherwise. It kept her in shape. She drove an old Jaguar, watched her money closely, and dated only law students.

They noticed each other long before they spoke. He'd come in late with a small group, the usual faces, sit in a booth in a corner, and debate abstract and incredibly boring legal theories. She'd deliver draft beer in pitchers, and try to flirt, with varying degrees of success. During his first year, he was enamored with the law and paid little attention to girls. She asked around and learned he was a good student, top third in his class, but nothing outstanding. He survived the first year and returned for the second. She cut her hair and lost ten pounds, though it wasn't necessary.

He had finished college and applied to thirty law schools. Eleven said yes, though none were top ten. He flipped a coin and drove to Lawrence, a place he'd never seen. He found a two-room apartment stuck to the rear of a spinster's crumbling house. He studied hard and had little time for a social life, at least during the first two semesters.

The summer after his first year he clerked for a large firm in Kansas City where he pushed interoffice mail from floor to floor with a cart. The firm had three hundred lawyers under one roof, and at times it seemed as though all were working on one trial—the defense of Smith Greer in a tobacco/lung cancer case down in Joplin. The trial lasted five weeks and ended with a defense verdict. Afterward, the firm threw a party and a thousand people showed up. Rumor was that the catered celebration cost Smith Greer eighty grand. Who cared? The summer was a miserable experience.

He hated the big firm, and midway through his second year he was fed up with the law in general. No way he would spend five years locked in a cubbyhole writing and rewriting the same briefs so rich corporate clients could be bilked.

Their first date was to a law school keg party after a football game. The music was loud, the beer plentiful, the pot passed around like candy. They left early because he didn't like noise and she didn't like the smell of cannabis. They rented videos and cooked spaghetti in her apartment, a rather spacious and well-furnished layout. He slept on the sofa.

A month later he moved in and first broached the subject of dropping out of law school. She was thinking about applying. As the romance blossomed, his interest in things academic diminished to the point of barely completing his fall exams. They were madly in love, and nothing else mattered. Plus, she had the benefit of a little cash, so the pressure was off. They spent Christmas in Jamaica between semesters of his second, and final, year.

By the time he quit, she'd been in Lawrence for three years, and was ready to move on. He would follow her anywhere.

MARLEE HAD BEEN ABLE to learn little about the fire Sunday afternoon. They suspected Fitch, but couldn't pinpoint a reason. The only asset of value was the computer, and Nicholas was certain no one could breach its security system. The important discs were locked away in a vault in Marlee's condo. What could Fitch gain by burning a run-down apartment? Intimidation maybe, but it didn't fit. Fire officials were conducting a routine investigation. Arson seemed unlikely.

They'd slept in finer places than the Siesta Inn, and they'd slept in worse. In four years they'd lived in four towns, traveled to a half-dozen countries, seen most of North America, backpacked in Alaska and Mexico, rafted the Colorado twice, and floated the Amazon once. They had also tracked tobacco litigation, and that journey had forced them to set up housekeeping in places such as Broken Arrow, Allentown, and now Biloxi. Together, they knew more about nicotine levels, carcinogens, statistical probabilities of lung cancer, jury selection, trial tactics, and Rankin Fitch than any group of high-powered experts.

After an hour under the covers, a light came on beside the bed and Nicholas emerged, hair ruffled, reaching for clothing. Marlee got dressed and peeked through the shades at the parking lot.

Directly below them, Hoppy was trying his best to discount the scandalous revelations of Lawrence Krigler, testimony Millie seemed quite impressed with. She dished it out to Hoppy in heavy doses, and was puzzled by his desire to argue so much.

Just for the fun of it, Marlee had left her car parked on the street a half a block from the offices of Wendall Rohr. She and Nicholas were operating under the assumption that Fitch was following every move she made. It was amusing to imagine Fitch squirming with the idea that she was in there, in Rohr's office, actually meeting with him face-to-face and agreeing to who knew what. For the personal visit, she had arrived in a rental car, one of several she'd used in the past month.

Nicholas was suddenly weary of the room, an exact replica of the one he was confined to. They went for a long drive along the Coast; she drove, he sipped beer. They walked down a pier above the Gulf, and kissed as the water rocked gently below them. They talked little of the trial.

At ten-thirty, Marlee emerged from the car at a point two blocks from Rohr's office. As she walked hurriedly along the sidewalk, Nicholas followed nearby. Her car was parked alone. Joe Boy saw her get into it and radioed Konrad. After she drove away, Nicholas hurried back to the motel in the rental car.

Rohr was in the midst of a heated council meeting, the daily gathering of the eight trial lawyers who'd put up a million each. The issue Sunday night was the number of witnesses left to be called by the plaintiff, and as usual, there were eight separate opinions about what to do next. Two schools of thought, but eight very firm and very different inclinations about precisely what would be effective.

Including the three days spent selecting the jury, the trial was now three weeks old. Tomorrow would start week four, and the plaintiff had enough experts and other witnesses to go on for at least two more weeks. Cable had his own army of experts, though typically the defense in these cases used less than half the time of the plaintiff. Six weeks was a reasonable prediction, which meant the jury would be sequestered for almost four weeks, a scenario that troubled everyone. At some point the jury would rebel, and since the plaintiff used the bulk of the court time, the plaintiff had the most to lose. But on the other hand, since the defense went last, and the jury would tire at the end, then perhaps the jury's venom would be aimed at Cable and Pynex. This argument raged for an hour.

Wood v. Pynex was unique because it was the first tobacco trial featuring a sequestered jury. It was, in fact, the first sequestered civil jury in the history of the state. Rohr was of the opinion that the jury had heard enough. He wanted to call only two more witnesses, finish their case by noon Tuesday, then rest and wait for Cable. He was joined by Scotty Mangrum of Dallas and André Durond of New Orleans. Jonathan Kotlack of San Diego wanted three more witnesses.

The opposing view was vigorously pushed by John Riley Milton of Denver and Rayner Lovelady of Savannah. Since they'd spent so damned much money on the world's greatest collection of experts, why be in a hurry, they argued. There remained some crucial testimony from outstanding witnesses. The jury wasn't going anywhere. Sure they'd get tired, but didn't every jury? It was far safer to stick to the game plan and try the case thoroughly than to jump ship in midstream because a few jurors were getting bored.

Carney Morrison of Boston harped repeatedly on the weekly summaries from the jury consultants. This jury was not convinced! Under Mississippi law, it would take nine of the twelve to get a verdict. Morrison was certain they didn't have nine. Rohr especially paid little attention to the current analyses of how Jerry Fernandez rubbed his eyes and how Loreen Duke shifted her weight and how poor old Herman twisted at the neck when Dr. So-and-So was testifying. Frankly, Rohr was sick of the jury experts and especially sick of the obscene sums of money they were getting. It was one thing to have their assistance while investigating potential jurors. It was a far different matter to have them lurking everywhere during the trial, always anxious to prepare a daily report to tell the lawyers how the case was trying. Rohr could read a jury far better than any consultant.

Arnold Levine of Miami said little because the group knew his feelings. He'd once taken on General Motors in a trial that lasted eleven months, so six weeks was a warm-up for him.

There was no coin toss when the vote was even. It had been agreed long before jury selection that this was Wendall Rohr's trial, filed in his hometown, fought in his courtroom before his judge and his jurors. The plaintiff's trial council was a democratic body to a point, but Rohr had veto power which could not be overridden.

He made his decision late Sunday, and the serious egos left bruised but not permanently damaged. There was too much at stake for bickering and second-guessing.

Twenty-three

THE FIRST ORDER of business Monday morning was a private meeting between Judge Harkin and Nicholas, the topic being the fire and his well-being. They met alone in chambers. Nicholas assured him he was fine and had enough clothing at the motel to wash and rewash. He was just a student with little to lose, with the exception of a fine computer and some expensive surveillance equipment, all of which was, of course, uninsured along with everything else.

The fire was dispensed with quickly, and since they were alone Harkin asked, "So how are the rest of our friends doing?" Chatting off the record like this with a juror was not improper, but was certainly in the gray area of trial procedure. The better practice was to have the lawyers present and to record every word with a court reporter. But Harkin wanted just a few minutes of gossip. He could trust this kid.

"Everything's fine," Nicholas said.

"Nothing unusual?"

"Not that I can think of."

"Is the case being discussed?"

"No. In fact, when we're together, we try to avoid it."

"Good. Any spats or squabbles?"

"Not yet."

"Food's okay?"

"Food's fine."

"Enough personal visits?"

"I think so. I haven't heard any complaints."

Harkin would have loved to know if there was any hanky-panky among the jurors, not that it would carry any legal significance. He just had a dirty mind. "Good. Let me know if there's a problem. And let's keep this quiet."

"Sure," Nicholas said. They shook hands and he left.

Harkin greeted the jurors warmly and welcomed them back for another week. They seemed eager to get to work and finish this ordeal.

Rohr rose and called Leon Robilio as the next witness, and the players settled down to business. Leon was led from a side door into the courtroom. He shuffled gingerly in front of the bench to the witness stand, where the deputy assisted him in having a seat. He was old and pale, dressed in a dark suit, white shirt, no tie. He had a hole in his throat, an opening covered by a thin white dressing and camouflaged with a white linen neckerchief. When he swore to tell the truth, he did so by holding a pencil-like mike to his neck. The words were the flat, pitchless monotone of a throat cancer victim without a larynx.

But the words were audible and understandable. Mr. Robilio held the microphone close to his throat and his voice rattled around the courtroom. This was how he talked, dammit, and he did so every day of his life. He meant to be understood.

Rohr got quickly to the point. Mr. Robilio was sixty-four years old, a cancer survivor who'd lost his voice box eight years earlier and had learned to talk through his esophagus. He had smoked heavily for nearly forty years, and his habits had almost killed him. Now, in addition to the aftereffects of the cancer, he suffered from heart disease and emphysema. All because of the cigarettes.

His listeners quickly adjusted to his amplified, robotlike voice. He grabbed their attention for good when he told them he'd made his living for two decades as a lobbyist for the tobacco industry. He quit the job when he got cancer and realized that even with the disease he couldn't stop smoking. He was addicted, physically and psychologically addicted to the nicotine in cigarettes. For two years after his larynx was removed and the chemotherapy ravaged his body, he continued to smoke. He finally quit after a near-fatal heart attack.

Though obviously in bad health, he still worked full-time in Washington, but now he was on the other side of the fence. He had the reputation of a fiercely committed antismoking activist. A guerrilla, some called him.

In a prior life, he had been employed at the Tobacco Focus Council. "Which was nothing more than a slick lobbying outfit funded entirely by the industry," he said with disdain. "Our mission was to advise the tobacco companies on current legislation and attempts to regulate them. We had a fat budget with unlimited resources to wine and dine influential politicians. We played hardball, and we taught other tobacco apologists the ins and outs of political fistfighting."

At the Council, Robilio had access to countless studies of cigarettes and the tobacco industry. In fact, part of the mission of the Council was the meticulous assimilation of all known studies, projects, experiments. Yes, Robilio had seen the infamous nicotine memo Krigler had described. He'd seen it many times, though he did not keep a copy. It was well known at the Council that all tobacco companies kept nicotine at high levels to ensure addiction.

Addiction was a word Robilio used over and over. He'd seen studies paid for by the companies in which all sorts of animals had been quickly addicted to cigarettes through nicotine. He'd seen and helped hide studies proving beyond any doubt that once young teenagers were hooked on cigarettes the rates of kicking the habit were much lower. They became customers for life.

Rohr produced a box of thick reports for Robilio to identify. The studies were admitted into evidence, as if the jurors would find the time to plow through ten thousand pages of documents before making their decision.

Robilio regretted many things he'd done as a lobbyist, but his greatest sin, one he struggled with daily, had been the artfully worded denials he'd issued claiming the industry did not target teenagers through advertising. "Nicotine is addictive. Addiction means profits. The survival of tobacco depends upon each new generation picking up the habit. Kids receive mixed messages through advertising. The industry spends billions portraying cigarettes as cool and glamorous, even harmless. Kids get hooked easier, and stay hooked longer. So it's imperative to seduce the young." Robilio managed to convey bitterness through his man-made voice box. And he managed to sneer at the defense table while looking warmly at the jurors.

"We spent millions studying kids. We knew that they could name the three most heavily advertised brands of cigarettes. We knew that almost ninety percent of the kids under eighteen who smoked preferred the top three advertised brands. So what did the companies do? They increased the advertising."

"Did you know how much money the tobacco companies were making off cigarette sales to children?" Rohr asked, certain of the answer.

"About two hundred million a year. And that's in sales to kids eighteen or under. Of course we knew. We studied it annually, kept our computers filled with the data. We knew everything." He paused and waved his right hand at the defense table, sneering as if it were surrounded by lepers. "They still know. They know that three thousand kids start smoking every day, and they can give you an accurate breakdown of the brands they're buying. They know that virtually all adult smokers began as teenagers. Again, they have to hook the next generation. They know that one third of the three thousand kids who start smoking today will eventually die from their addiction."

The jury was captivated with Robilio. Rohr flipped pages for a second so the drama wouldn't be rushed. He took a few steps back and forth behind the lectern as if his legs needed limbering. He scratched his chin, looked at the ceiling, then asked, "When you were with the Tobacco Focus Council, how did you counter the arguments that nicotine is addictive?"

"The tobacco companies have a party line; I helped formulate it. It goes something like this: Smokers choose the habit. So it's a matter of choice. Cigarettes are not addictive, but, hey, even if they are, no one forces anybody to smoke. It's all a matter of choice.

"I could make this sound real good, back in those days. And they make it sound good today. Trouble is, it's not true."

"Why isn't it true?"

"Because the issue is addiction, and the addict cannot make choices. And kids become addicted much quicker than adults."

Rohr for once avoided the natural lawyerly compulsion of

overkill. Robilio was efficient with words, and the strain of being clear and being heard tired him after an hour and a half. Rohr tendered him to Cable for cross-examination, and Judge Harkin, who needed coffee, called a recess.

Hoppy Dupree made his first visit to the trial Monday morning, slipping into the courtroom midway through Robilio's testimony. Millie caught his eye during a lull, and was thrilled he would stop by. His sudden interest in the trial was odd, though. He'd talked of nothing else for four hours last night.

After a twenty-minute coffee break, Cable stepped to the lectern and tore into Robilio. His tone was strident, almost mean, as if he viewed the witness as a traitor to the cause, a turncoat. Cable scored immediately with the revelation that Robilio was being paid to testify, and that he had sought out the plaintiff's lawyers. He was also on retainer in two other tobacco cases.

"Yes, I'm being paid to be here, Mr. Cable, same as you," Robilio said, delivering the typical expert's response. But the stain of money slightly tainted his character.

Cable got him to confess that he started smoking when he was almost twenty-five, married, with two children, hardly a teenager who could've been seduced by slick work from Madison Avenue. Robilio had a temper, a fact proven to all the lawyers during a two-day marathon deposition five months earlier, and Cable was determined to exploit it. His questions were sharp, rapid, and designed to provoke.

"How many children do you have?" Cable asked.

"Three."

"Did any of them ever smoke cigarettes regularly?"

"Yes."

"How many?"

"Three."

"How old were they when they started?"

"It varies."

"On the average?"

"Late teens."

"Which ads do you blame for getting them hooked on cigarettes?"

"I don't recall exactly."

"You can't tell the jury which ads were responsible for getting your own kids hooked on cigarettes?"

"There were so many ads. Still are. It would be impossible to pinpoint one or two or five that worked."

"So it was the ads?"

"I'm sure the ads were effective. Still are."

"So it was somebody else's fault?"

"I didn't encourage their smoking."

"Are you sure? You're telling this jury that your own children, the children of a man whose job for twenty years was to encourage the world to smoke, began smoking because of slick advertising?"

"I'm sure the ads helped. They were designed to."

"Did you smoke in the home, in front of your children?"

"Yes."

"Did your wife?"

"Yes."

"Did you ever tell a guest he couldn't smoke in your home?"

"No. Not then."

"Safe to say, then, that the environment of your home was smoker friendly?"

"Yes. Then."

"But your children started smoking because of devious advertising? Is that what you're telling this jury?"

Robilio took a deep breath, counted slowly to five, then said, "I wish I'd done a lot of things differently, Mr. Cable. I wish I'd never picked up the first cigarette."

"Did your children stop smoking?"

"Two of them did. With great difficulty. The third has been trying to quit for ten years now."

Cable had asked the last question on an impulse, and wished for a second he hadn't. Time to move on. He shifted gears. "Mr. Robilio, are you aware of efforts by the tobacco industry to curb teenage smoking?"

Robilio chuckled, which sounded like a gargle when amplified through his little mike. "No serious efforts," he said.

"Forty million dollars last year to Smoke Free Kids?"

"Sounds like something they'd do. Makes 'em seem warm and fuzzy, doesn't it?"

"Are you aware that the industry is on record supporting legislation to restrict vending machines in areas where kids congregate?"

"I think I've heard of that. Sounds lovely, doesn't it?"

"Are you aware that the industry last year gave ten million dollars to California for a statewide kindergarten program designed to warn youngsters about underage smoking?"

"No. What about overage smoking? Did they tell the little fellas that it was okay to smoke after their eighteenth birthdays? Probably did."

Cable had a checklist, and seemed content to fire off the questions while ignoring the answers.

"Are you aware that the industry supports a bill in Texas to ban smoking in all fast-food establishments, places frequented by teenagers?"

"Yeah, and do you know why they do things like that? I'll tell you why. So they can hire people like you to tell jurors like these about it. That's the only reason—it sounds good in court."

"Are you aware that the industry is on record supporting legislation which imposes criminal penalties against convenience stores which sell tobacco products to minors?"

"Yeah, I think I heard that one too. It's window dressing. They'll drop a few bucks here and there to preen and posture and buy respectability. They'll do this because they know the truth, and the truth is that two billion dollars a year in advertising will guarantee addiction by the next generation. And you're a fool if you don't believe this."

Judge Harkin leaned forward. "Mr. Robilio, that is uncalled-for. Don't do it again. I want it stricken from the record."

"Sorry, Your Honor. And sorry to you, Mr. Cable. You're just doing your job. It's your client I can't stand."

Cable was thrown off track. He offered up a lame "Why?" and wished immediately he'd kept his mouth shut.

"Because they're so devious. These tobacco people are bright, intelligent, educated, ruthless, and they'll look you in the face and tell you with all sincerity that cigarettes are not addictive. And they know it's a lie."

"No further questions," Cable said, halfway to his table.

GARDNER WAS A TOWN of eighteen thousand an hour from Lubbock. Pamela Blanchard lived in the old section of town, two blocks off Main Street in a house built at the turn of the century and nicely renovated. Brilliant red and gold maple trees covered the front lawn. Children roamed the street on bikes and skate-boards.

By ten Monday, Fitch knew the following: She was married to the president of a local bank, a man who'd been married once before and whose wife had died ten years ago. He was not the father of Nicholas Easter or Jeff or whoever the hell he was. The bank had almost collapsed during the oil bust of the early eighties, and many locals were still afraid to use it. Pamela's husband was a native of the town. She was not. She may have come from Lubbock, or maybe it was Amarillo. They got married in Mexico eight years ago, and the local weekly barely recorded it. No wedding picture. Just an announcement next to the obituaries that N. Forrest Blanchard, Jr., had married Pamela Kerr. After a brief honeymoon in Cozumel, they would reside in Gardner.

The best source in town was a private investigator named Rafe who'd been a cop for twenty years and claimed to know everyone. Rafe, after being paid a sizable retainer in cash, worked without sleep Sunday night. No sleep, but plenty of bourbon, and by dawn he reeked of sour mash. Dante and Joe Boy worked beside him, in his grungy office on Main, and repeatedly declined the whiskey.

Rafe talked to every cop in Gardner, and finally found one who could talk to a lady who lived across the street from the Blanchards. Bingo. Pamela had two sons by a previous marriage; it ended in divorce. She didn't talk much about them, but one was in Alaska and one was a lawyer, or was studying to be a lawyer. Something like that.

Since neither son grew up in Gardner, the trail soon ran cold. No one knew them. In fact, Rafe couldn't find anyone who'd ever seen Pamela's sons. Then Rafe called his lawyer, a sleazy divorce specialist who routinely used Rafe's primitive surveillance services, and the lawyer knew a secretary at Mr. Blanchard's bank. The secretary talked to Mr. Blanchard's personal secretary, and it was discovered that Pamela was from neither Lubbock nor Amarillo, but Austin. She'd worked there for a bankers' association, and that's how she'd met Mr. Blanchard. The secretary knew of the prior marriage, and was of the opinion that it had ended many years ago. No, she had never seen Pamela's sons. Mr.

Blanchard never discussed them. The couple lived quietly and almost never entertained.

Fitch received reports every hour from Dante and Joe Boy. Late Monday morning, he called an acquaintance in Austin, a man he'd worked with six years earlier in a tobacco trial in Marshall, Texas. It was an emergency, Fitch explained. Within minutes, a dozen investigators were scouring phone books and making calls. It wasn't long before the bloodhounds picked up the trail.

Pamela Kerr had been an executive secretary for the Texas Bankers Association, in Austin. One phone call led to another, and a former co-worker was located working as a private school guidance counselor. Using the ruse that Pamela was a prospective juror in a capital murder case in Lubbock, the investigator described himself as an assistant district attorney who was trying to gather legitimate information about the jurors. The co-worker felt obligated to answer a few questions, though she hadn't seen or talked to Pamela in years.

Pamela had two sons, Jeff and Alex. Alex was two years older than Jeff, and had graduated from high school in Austin, then drifted to Oregon. Jeff had also finished high school in Austin, with honors, then gone to college at Rice. The boys' father had abandoned the family when they were toddlers, and Pamela had done an outstanding job as a single mother.

Dante, fresh off the private jet, accompanied an investigator to the high school, where they were allowed to rummage through old yearbooks in the library. Jeff Kerr's 1985 senior picture was in color—a blue tux, large blue bow tie, short hair, earnest face looking directly at the camera, the same face Dante had studied for hours in Biloxi. Without hesitation he said, "This is our man," then quietly ripped the page from the yearbook. He immediately called Fitch on a cellphone from between the stacked tiers of books.

Three phone calls to Rice revealed that Jeff Kerr graduated there in 1989 with a degree in psychology. Posing as a representative from a prospective employer, the caller found a Rice professor of political science who'd taught and who remembered Kerr. He said the young man went to law school at Kansas.

With the guarantee of serious cash, Fitch found by phone a security firm willing to drop everything and began scouring Lawrence, Kansas, for any trace of Jeff Kerr.

□ □ □ □

FOR ONE normally so chipper, Nicholas was quite reserved during lunch. He didn't say a word as he ate a heavily stuffed baked potato from O'Reilly's. He avoided glances and looked downright sad.

The mood was shared. Leon Robilio's voice stayed with them, a robotic voice substituted for a real one lost to the ravages of tobacco, a robotic voice which delivered the sickening dirt he once helped hide. It still rang in their ears. Three thousand kids a day, one third of whom die from their addiction. Gotta hook the next generation!

Loreen Duke tired of picking at her chicken salad. She looked across the table at Jerry Fernandez, and said, "Can I ask you something?" Her voice broke a weary silence.

"Sure," he said.

"How old were you when you started smoking?"

"Fourteen."

"Why did you start?"

"The Marlboro Man. Every kid I hung around with smoked Marlboros. We were country kids, liked horses and rodeos. The Marlboro Man was too cool to resist."

At that moment, every juror could see the billboards—the rugged face, the chin, the hat, the horse, the worn leather, maybe the mountains and some snow, the independence of lighting up a Marlboro while the world left him alone. Why wouldn't a young boy of fourteen want to be the Marlboro Man?

"Are you addicted?" asked Rikki Coleman, playing with her usual fat-free plate of lettuce and boiled turkey. The "addicted" rolled off her tongue as if they were discussing heroin.

Jerry thought for a moment and realized his friends were listening. They wanted to know what powerful urges kept a person hooked.

"I don't know," he said. "I guess I could quit. I've tried a few times. Sure would be nice to stop. Such a nasty habit."

"You don't enjoy it?" Rikki asked.

"Oh, there are times when a cigarette hits the spot, but I'm doing two packs a day now and that's too much."

"What about you, Angel?" Loreen asked Angel Weese, who sat next to her and generally said as little as possible. "How old were you when you started?"

"Thirteen," Angel said, ashamed.

"I was sixteen," Sylvia Taylor-Tatum admitted before anyone could ask.

"I started when I was fourteen," Herman offered from the end in an effort at conversation. "Quit when I was forty."

"Anybody else?" Rikki asked, finishing the confessional.

"I started at seventeen," the Colonel said. "When I joined the Army. But I kicked the habit thirty years ago." As usual, he was proud of his self-discipline.

"Anybody else?" Rikki asked again, after a long, silent pause.

"Me. I started when I was seventeen and quit two years later," Nicholas said, though it was not true.

"Did anybody here start smoking after the age of eighteen?" Loreen asked.

Not a word.

NITCHMAN, in plain clothes, met Hoppy for a quick sandwich. Hoppy was nervous about being seen in public with an FBI agent, and was quite relieved when Nitchman appeared in jeans and a plaid shirt. Wasn't like Hoppy's pals and acquaintances around town could instantly spot the local feds, but he was still nervous nevertheless. Besides, Nitchman and Napier were from a special unit in Atlanta, they'd told Hoppy.

He replayed what he'd heard in court that morning, said the voiceless Robilio made quite an impression and seemed to have the jury in his pocket. Nitchman, not for the first time, professed little interest in the trial and explained again he was just doing what his bosses in Washington told him to do. He handed Hoppy a folded sheet of paper, plain white with tiny numbers and words scattered on the top and bottom, and said this had just come from Cristano at Justice. They wanted Hoppy to see it.

It was really a creation of Fitch's document people, two retired CIA boys who puttered around D.C. enjoying the mischief.

It was a faxed copy of a sinister-looking report on Leon Robilio. No source, no date, just four paragraphs under the ominous headline of CONFIDENTIAL MEMO. Hoppy read it quickly while chomping on french fries. Robilio was being paid half a million dollars to testify. Robilio had been fired from the Tobacco Focus Council for embezzling funds; had even been indicted, though charges were later dropped. Robilio had a history of psychiatric problems. Robilio had sexually harassed two secretaries at the Council. Robilio's throat cancer had probably been caused by his alcoholism, and not by tobacco. Robilio was a notorious liar who hated the Council and was on a crusade of revenge.

"Wow," Hoppy said, showing a mouthful of potatoes.

"Mr. Cristano thought you should sneak this to your wife," Nitchman said. "She should show it only to those she can trust on the jury."

"Right about that," Hoppy said, quickly folding and stuffing it into a pocket. He looked around the crowded dining room as if he was completely guilty of something.

WORKING from law school yearbooks and the limited records the registrar would release, it was learned that Jeff Kerr enrolled as a first-year law student at Kansas in the fall of 1989. His unsmiling face appeared with the second-year class in 1991, but there was no trace of him after that. He did not receive a law degree.

He played rugby for the law school team his second year. A team photo showed him arm in arm with two pals—Michael Dale and Tom Ratliff—both of whom had finished law school the following year. Dale was working for Legal Services in Des Moines. Ratliff was an associate for a firm in Wichita. Investigators were sent to both places.

Dante arrived in Lawrence and was taken to the law school, where he confirmed the identity of Kerr in the yearbooks. He spent an hour looking at faces from 1985 through 1994, and saw no female resembling the girl known as Marlee. It was a shot in the dark. Many law students skipped the picture taking. Yearbooks were sophomoric. These were serious young adults. Dante's work was nothing but a series of shots in the dark.

Late Monday, the investigator named Small found Tom Ratliff hard at work in his tiny windowless office at Wise & Watkins, a large firm in downtown Wichita. They agreed to meet in a bar in an hour.

Small talked to Fitch and gathered as much background as he could, or as much as Fitch would give him. Small was an ex-cop with two ex-wives. His title was security specialist, which in Lawrence meant he did everything from motel watching to polygraph exams. He was not bright, and Fitch realized this immediately.

Ratliff arrived late and they ordered drinks. Small did his best to bluff and act knowledgeable. Ratliff was suspicious. He said little at first, which was what could be expected from a person unexpectedly asked by a stranger to talk about an old acquaintance.

"I haven't seen him in four years," Ratliff said.

"Have you talked to him?"

"No. Not a word. He dropped out of school after our second year."

"Were you close to him?"

"I knew him well our first year, but we were not the best of friends. He withdrew after that. Is he in trouble?"

"No. Not at all."

"Perhaps you should tell me why you're so interested."

Small recited in general terms what Fitch had told him to say, got most of it right and it was close to the truth. Jeff Kerr was a prospective juror in a large trial somewhere, and he, Small, had been hired by one of the parties to dig through his background.

"Where's the trial?" Ratliff asked.

"I can't say. But I assure you, none of this is illegal. You're a lawyer. You understand."

Indeed he did. Ratliff had spent most of his brief career slaving under a litigation partner. Jury research was a chore he'd already learned to hate. "How can I verify this?" he asked, like a real lawyer.

"I don't have the authority to divulge specifics about the trial. Let's do it like this. If I ask something which you think might be harmful to Kerr, then don't answer. Fair enough?"

"We'll give it a shot, okay? But if I get nervous, then I'm outta here."

"Fair enough. Why did he quit law school?"

Ratliff took a sip of his beer and tried to remember. "He was a good student, very bright. But after the first year, he suddenly hated the idea of being a lawyer. He clerked in a firm that summer, a big firm in Kansas City, and it soured him. Plus, he fell in love."

Fitch desperately wanted to know if there was a girl. "Who was the woman?" Small asked.

"Claire."

"Claire who?"

Another sip. "I can't remember right now."

"You knew her?"

"I knew who she was. Claire worked at a bar in downtown Lawrence, a college hangout favored by law students. I think that's where she met Jeff."

"Could you describe her?"

"Why? I thought this was about Jeff."

"I was asked to get a description of his girlfriend in law school. That's all I know." Small shrugged as if he couldn't help it.

They studied each other for a bit. What the hell, thought Ratliff. He'd never see these people again. Jeff and Claire were distant memories anyway.

"Average height, about five six. Slender. Dark hair, brown eyes, pretty girl, all the bells and whistles."

"Was she a student?"

"I'm not sure. I think maybe she had been. Maybe a grad student."

"At KU?"

"I don't know."

"What was the name of the hangout?"

"Mulligan's, downtown."

Small knew it well. At times he went there himself to drown his worries and admire the college girls. "I've knocked back a few at Mulligan's," he said.

"Yeah. I miss it," Ratliff said wistfully.

"What did he do after he dropped out?"

"I'm not sure. I heard that he and Claire left town, but I never heard from him again."

Small thanked him and asked if he could call him at the office if he had more questions. Ratliff said he was awfully busy, but give it a try.

Small's boss in Lawrence had a friend who knew the guy who'd owned Mulligan's for fifteen years. The advantages of a small town. Employment records weren't exactly confidential, especially for the owner of a bar who reported fewer than half of his cash sales. Her name was Claire Clement.

□ □ □ □

FITCH RUBBED his stubby hands together with glee as he took the news. He loved the chase. Marlee was now Claire, a woman with a past who'd worked hard to cover it up.

"Know thine enemy," he said aloud to his walls. The first rule of warfare.

Twenty-four

THE NUMBERS RETURNED with a vengeance Monday afternoon. The messenger was an economist, a man trained to look at the life of Jacob Wood and put a concise dollar figure on it. His name was Dr. Art Kallison, a retired professor from a private school in Oregon no one had heard of. The math was not complicated, and Dr. Kallison had obviously seen a courtroom before. He knew how to testify, how to keep the figures simple. He placed them on a chalkboard with a neat hand.

When he died at fifty-one, Jacob Wood's base salary was $40,000 a year, plus a retirement plan funded by his employer, plus other benefits. Assuming he would live and work until the age of sixty-five, Kallison placed his lost future earnings at $720,000. The law also allowed the factoring of inflation into this projection, and this upped the total to $1,180,000. Then the law required that this total be reduced to its present value, a concept that muddied the water a bit. Here, Kallison delivered a quick, friendly lecture to the jury on present value. The money might be worth $1,180,000 if paid out over fifteen years, but for purposes of the lawsuit he had to determine what it was worth at the moment. Thus, it had to be discounted. His new figure was $835,000.

He did a superb job of assuring the jury that this figure dealt only with lost salary. He was an economist, quite untrained to place a value on the noneconomic value of one's life. His job had nothing to do with the pain and suffering Mr. Wood endured as he died; had nothing to do with the loss his family had endured.

A young defense lawyer named Felix Mason uttered his first word of the trial. He was one of Cable's partners, a specialist in economic forecasts, and, unfortunately for him, his only appearance would be brief. He began his cross-examination of Dr. Kallison by asking him how many times a year he testified. "That's all I do these days. I've retired from teaching," Kallison answered. He took the question in every trial.

"Are you being paid to testify?" Mason asked. The question was as tired as the answer.

"Yes. I'm paid to be here. Same as you."

"How much?"

"Five thousand dollars for consultation and testimony." No doubt among the lawyers that Kallison was by far the cheapest expert of the trial.

Mason had a problem with the rate of inflation Kallison used in his calculations, and they haggled over the historical rise of the consumer price index for thirty minutes. If Mason scored a point, no one noticed. He wanted Kallison to agree that a more reasonable figure for Mr. Wood's lost wages would be $680,000.

It really didn't matter. Rohr and his blue-ribbon pack of trial lawyers would take either number. Lost wages were merely the starting point. Rohr would add to it pain and suffering, loss of enjoyment of life, loss of companionship, and a few incidentals such as the cost of Mr. Wood's medical care and the price of his funeral. Then Rohr would go for the gold. He would show the jury how much cash Pynex owned and would ask them for a large chunk of it as punitive damages.

With an hour to go, Rohr proudly announced to the court that "The plaintiff will call its last witness. Mrs. Celeste Wood."

The jury had been given no warning that the plaintiff was almost finished. A burden was suddenly lifted. The sluggish air of the late afternoon was immediately lighter. Several jurors couldn't conceal smiles. Several more lost their frowns. Their chairs rocked as they came to life.

Tonight would be their seventh in sequestration. According to Nicholas' latest theory, the defense would take no more than three days. They did the math. They could be home by the weekend!

In the three weeks she'd been sitting silently at the table, with hordes of lawyers around her, Celeste Wood had barely uttered a whisper. She'd shown an amazing ability to ignore the lawyers, ignore the faces of the jurors, and stare straight ahead with a blank face at the witnesses. She'd worn every shade of black and gray dress, always with black hose and black shoes.

Jerry had dubbed her Widow Wood during the first week.

She was now fifty-five, the same age her husband would have been but for the lung cancer. She was very thin, diminutive, with short gray hair. She worked for a regional library and had raised three children. Family portraits were passed to the jury.

Celeste had given her deposition a year earlier, and she had been rehearsed by the professional handlers Rohr had brought in. She was under control, nervous but not fidgety, and determined to show no emotion. After all, her husband had been dead for four years.

She and Rohr walked through their script without a flaw. She talked of her life with Jacob, how happy they'd been, the early years, the kids, then the grandchildren, their dreams of retirement. A few bumps in the road but nothing serious, nothing until he got sick. He had wanted to quit smoking so badly, had tried many times with little success. The addiction was just too powerful.

Celeste was sympathetic without working too hard for it. Her voice never waivered. Rohr had guessed, correctly, that false tears might not be well received by the jury. She didn't cry easily anyway.

Cable passed on any cross-examination. What could he ask her? He rose and with a sad countenance and humble air, said simply, "Your Honor, we have no questions for this witness."

Fitch had a bunch of questions for the witness, but he couldn't get them asked in open court. After a proper grieving period, in fact it was over a year after the funeral, Celeste had started seeing a divorced man who was seven years younger. According to good sources, they were planning a quiet wedding as soon as the trial was over. Fitch knew that Rohr himself had ordered her not to get married until after the trial.

The jury wouldn't hear this in the courtroom, but Fitch was working on a plan to sneak it through the back door.

"The plaintiff rests," Rohr announced after he'd seated Celeste at the table. The lawyers on both sides clutched one another and huddled into small groups of serious whispering.

Judge Harkin studied some of the clutter on his bench, then he looked at his weary jury. "Ladies and gentlemen, I have good news and bad. The good news is obvious. The plaintiff has rested, and we're more than halfway finished. The defense is expected to call fewer witnesses than the plaintiff. The bad news is that we're required at this point in the trial to argue a bunch of motions. We'll do that tomorrow, probably all day. I'm sorry, but we have no choice."

Nicholas raised his hand. Harkin looked at him for a few seconds, then managed to say, "Yes, Mr. Easter?"

"You mean we have to sit around the motel all day tomorrow?"

"I'm afraid so."

"I don't understand why."

The lawyers unclutched and stopped their tiny conferences and gawked at Easter. It was rare for a juror to speak in open court.

"Because we have a list of things to do outside the presence of the jury."

"Oh, I understand that. But why do we have to sit around?"

"What do you want to do?"

"I can think of a lot of things. We could charter a big boat, go for a ride in the Gulf, fish if we want to."

"I can't ask the taxpayers of this county to pay for that, Mr. Easter."

"I thought we were taxpayers."

"The answer is no. I'm sorry."

"Forget the taxpayers. I'm sure these lawyers here wouldn't mind passing the plate. Look, ask each side to put up a thousand dollars. We can charter a huge boat and have a wonderful time."

Though Cable and Rohr both reacted at the same instant, Rohr managed to speak first as he jumped to his feet. "We'd be more than happy to pay half, Your Honor."

"It's a great idea, Judge!" Cable added quickly, and loudly.

Harkin raised both hands, palms out. "Hold it," he said. Then he rubbed his temples and searched his brain for a precedent. Of course there was none. No rule or law prohibiting it. No conflicts of interest.

Loreen Duke tapped Nicholas on the arm and whispered something in his ear.

His Honor said, "Well, I've certainly never heard of this. It seems to fall into the discretionary category. Mr. Rohr?"

"It's harmless, Your Honor. Each side pays half. No problem."

"Mr. Cable?"

"I can think of no statute or rule of procedure which would prevent it. I agree with Mr. Rohr. If both sides split the cost, what's the harm?"

Nicholas raised his hand again. "Excuse me, Your Honor. It's come to my attention that perhaps some of the jurors would rather shop in New Orleans than take a boat ride in the Gulf."

Again, Rohr was a beat quicker. "We'll be happy to split the cost of a bus, Your Honor. And lunch."

"Same here," Cable said. "Dinner too."

Gloria Lane hustled to the jury box with a clipboard. Nicholas, Jerry Fernandez, Lonnie Shaver, Rikki Coleman, Angel Weese, and Colonel Herrera opted for the boat. The rest chose the French Quarter.

INCLUDING THE VIDEO of Jacob Wood, Rohr and company presented ten witnesses to the jury and took thirteen days to do it. A solid case was built; now it was up to the jury to determine not if cigarettes were dangerous but if it was time to punish their makers.

Had the jury not been sequestered, Rohr would have called at least three more experts: one to discuss the psychology of advertising; one an expert on addiction; one ready to describe in detail the application of insecticides and pesticides to tobacco leaves.

But the jury was very sequestered, and Rohr knew it was time to stop. It was obvious this was no ordinary jury. A blind man. A misfit who did yoga at lunch. At least two strikes so far. Lists of demands at every turn. China and silver for lunch. Beer after work, paid for by the taxpayers. Communal interludes and personal visits. Judge Harkin was finding sleep difficult.

It was certainly not ordinary for Fitch, a man who'd sabotaged more juries than any person in the history of American jurisprudence. He'd laid the usual traps and gathered the usual dirt. His scams were proceeding flawlessly. Only one fire, so far. No broken bones. But the girl Marlee had changed everything. Through her he'd be able to purchase a verdict, a slam-dunk defense judgment that would humiliate Rohr and frighten away the legion of hungry trial lawyers circling like vultures, waiting for the carcass.

In this, the biggest tobacco trial yet, with the biggest plaintiff's lawyers lined up with millions, his beloved little Marlee would hand him a verdict. Fitch believed this, and it consumed him. He thought of her every minute and he saw her in his dreams.

If not for Marlee, Fitch wouldn't be sleeping at all. The time was right for a plaintiff's verdict; right courtroom, right judge, right mood. The experts were by far the best Fitch had encountered in his nine years of directing the defense. Nine years, eight trials, eight defense verdicts. As much as he hated Rohr, he could admit, only to himself, that he was the right lawyer to nail the industry.

A victory over Rohr in Biloxi would be a huge barricade to future tobacco litigation. It might very well save the industry.

When Fitch tallied the jury's vote, he always started with Rikki Coleman, because of the abortion. He had her vote in his pocket, she just didn't know it yet. Then he added Lonnie Shaver. Then Colonel Herrera. Millie Dupree would be easy. His jury people were convinced that Sylvia Taylor-Tatum was virtually incapable of sympathy, and besides she smoked. But his jury people didn't know she was sleeping with Jerry Fernandez. Jerry and Easter were buddies. Fitch was predicting the three of them—Sylvia, Jerry, and Nicholas—would vote the same. Loreen Duke sat next to Nicholas, and the two were often seen whispering during the trial. Fitch thought she would follow Easter. And if Loreen did, then so would Angel Weese, the only other black female. Weese was impossible to read.

No one doubted that Easter would dominate the deliberations. Now that Fitch knew Easter had two years of law school, he was willing to bet that this information had been shared with the entire jury.

It was impossible to predict how Herman Grimes might vote. But Fitch wasn't counting on him. Likewise with Phillip Savelle. Fitch felt good about Mrs. Gladys Card. She was old and conservative and likely to be turned off when Rohr asked them for twenty million or so.

So Fitch had four in the bag, with Mrs. Gladys Card being a possible fifth. Flip a coin on Herman Grimes. Concede Savelle on the grounds that anyone so in tune with nature had to dislike tobacco companies. That left Easter and his gang of five. Nine votes were needed by either side for a verdict. Anything less would hang the jury and force Harkin to declare a mistrial. Mistrials become retrials, something Fitch did not want in this case.

The horde of legal analysts and scholars closely watching the trial agreed on little, but they were unified in their prediction that a unanimous, twelve-vote verdict in favor of Pynex would chill, if not completely freeze, tobacco litigation for a decade.

Fitch was determined to deliver one, whatever the cost.

THE MOOD in Rohr's office was much lighter Monday night. With no more witnesses to call, the pressure was momentarily off. Some fine scotch was poured in the conference room. Rohr sipped his mineral water and nibbled on cheese and crackers.

The ball was now in Cable's court. Let him and his crew spend a few days prepping witnesses and labeling documents. Rohr had only to react, to cross-examine, and he had watched every video-taped deposition of every defense witness a dozen times.

Jonathan Kotlack, the lawyer in charge of jury research, like-wise drank only water and speculated with Rohr about Herman Grimes. Both felt they had him. And they felt good about Millie Dupree and Savelle, the strange one. Herrera worried them. All three of the blacks—Lonnie, Angel, and Loreen—were solidly on board. It was, after all, a case of a little person against a large powerful corporation. Surely the blacks would come through. They always did.

Easter was the key because he was the leader, everybody knew that. Rikki would follow him. Jerry was his pal. Sylvia Taylor-Tatum was passive and she'd follow the crowd. As would Mrs. Gladys Card.

They only needed nine, and Rohr was convinced he had them.

Twenty-five

BACK IN LAWRENCE, Small, the investigator, worked his list of leads diligently and got nowhere. He loafed around Mulligan's Monday night, drinking against orders, chatting occasionally with the waitresses and law students and succeeding at nothing but arousing suspicion among the youth.

Early Tuesday morning, he made one visit too many. The woman's name was Rebecca, and a few years back, while still a grad student at KU, she had worked at Mulligan's with Claire Clement. They had been friends, according to a source dug up by Small's boss. Small found her in a downtown bank, where she worked as manager. He introduced himself awkwardly, and she was immediately suspicious.

"Didn't you work with Claire Clement a few years back?" he asked, looking at a notepad, standing on one side of her desk because she was standing on the other. He had not been invited in, and she was busy.

"Maybe. Who wants to know?" Rebecca asked, arms crossed, head cocked, phone buzzing somewhere behind her. In marked contrast to Small, she was sharply dressed and missed nothing.

"Do you know where she is now?"

"No. Why are you asking?"

Small repeated the narrative he'd memorized. It was all he had. "Well, see, she's a potential juror in a big trial, and my firm has been hired to conduct a thorough investigation into her background."

"Where's the trial?"

"Can't tell you that. You guys worked together at Mulligan's, right?"

"Yes. That was a long time ago."

"Where was she from?"

"Why is that important?"

"Well, to be honest, it's on my list of questions. We're just checking her out, okay? Do you know where she came from?"

"No."

This was an important question because Claire's trail had started and stopped in Lawrence. "Are you sure?"

She cocked her head the other way and glared at this klutz. "I don't know where she came from. When I met her, she was working at Mulligan's. The last time I saw her, she was working at Mulligan's."

"Have you talked to her recently?"

"Not in the last four years."

"Did you know Jeff Kerr?"

"No."

"Who were her friends here in Lawrence?"

"I don't know. Look, I'm very busy, and you're wasting your time. I didn't know Claire that well. Nice girl and all, but we were not close. Now, please, I have things to do." She was pointing to the door by the time she finished, and Small reluctantly left her office.

With Small out of the bank, Rebecca closed her office door and dialed the number to an apartment in St. Louis. The recorded voice on the other end belonged to her friend Claire. They chatted at least once a month, though they hadn't seen each other in a year. Claire and Jeff lived an odd life, drifting and never staying long in one place, never anxious to reveal their whereabouts. Only the apartment in St. Louis remained the same. Claire had warned her that people might come poking around with curious questions. She had hinted more than once that she and Jeff were working for the government in some mysterious capacity.

At the sound of the tone, Rebecca left a brief message about Small's visit.

□ □ □ □

MARLEE CHECKED her voice mail each morning, and the message from Lawrence made her blood run cold. She wiped her face with a moist cloth, and tried to calm herself.

She called Rebecca and managed to sound perfectly normal, though her mouth was dry and her heart was pounding. Yes, the man named Small had specifically asked about Claire Clement. And he had mentioned Jeff Kerr. With Marlee's prompting, Rebecca managed to replay the entire conversation.

Rebecca knew not to ask too many questions. "Are you okay?" was about the extent of her inquiry.

"Oh we're fine," Marlee assured her. "Living on the beach for a while."

Which beach would be nice, but Rebecca let it pass. No one dug too deep with Claire. They said their good-byes with the usual promises to keep in touch.

Neither she nor Nicholas had believed they would ever be tracked to Lawrence. Now that they had, the questions fell like hard rain around her. Who had found them? Which side, Fitch or Rohr? Most likely Fitch, simply because he had more money and more cunning. What had been their mistake? How did the trail ever leave Biloxi? How much did they know?

And how far would they go? She needed to speak to Nicholas, but he was, at the moment, on a boat somewhere in the Gulf trolling for mackerel and bonding with his fellow jurors.

FITCH, OF COURSE, was not fishing. In fact he hadn't taken a day of rest or pleasure in three months. He was at his desk, neatly arranging piles of paperwork, when the call came. "Hello, Marlee," he said into the receiver, to the girl of his dreams.

"Hey, Fitch. You've lost another one."

"Another what?" he asked, biting his tongue to keep from calling her Claire.

"Another juror. Loreen Duke was enthralled by Mr. Robilio, and now she's leading the parade to reward the plaintiff."

"But she hasn't heard our case yet."

"True. You have four smokers now—Weese, Fernandez, Taylor-Tatum, and Easter. Guess how many started smoking after the age of eighteen."

"Don't know."

"None. They all started as kids. Herman and Herrera used to smoke. Guess how old they were when they started."

"Don't know."

"Fourteen and seventeen. That's half of your jury, Fitch, and all started smoking as minors."

"What am I supposed to do about it?"

"Keep lying, I guess. Look, Fitch, what are the chances of us getting together for a little chat, private you know, without all your goons ducking behind bushes?"

"The chances are excellent."

"Another lie. Let's do it this way. Let's meet and talk, and if my people see your people anywhere near us, then it will be our last conversation."

"Your people?"

"Anybody can hire goons, Fitch. You should know this."

"It's a deal."

"You know Casella's, the little seafood joint with outdoor tables at the end of the Biloxi pier."

"I can find it."

"That's where I am now. So when you walk down the pier, I'll be watching. And if I see any character who looks the least bit suspicious, deal's off."

"When?"

"Right now. I'm waiting."

JOSÉ SLOWED for a second in the parking lot near the small-craft harbor, and Fitch practically jumped from the Suburban. It drove away, and Fitch, very much alone and unwired, strolled down the wooden pier with the heavy wooden planks shifting gently in the tide. Marlee sat at a wooden table with an umbrella above it, with her back to the Gulf, her face to the pier. Lunch was an hour away and the place was deserted.

"Hello, Marlee," Fitch said as he approached, stopped, then sat across from her. She wore jeans and a denim shirt, a fishing cap, and sunglasses. "A pleasure, Fitch," she said.

"Are you always so surly?" he asked, settling his squatty frame into a narrow chair, trying his best to smile and be chummy.

"Are you wired, Fitch?"

"No. Of course not."

Slowly, she removed from her bulky purse a thin black device resembling a small Dictaphone. She pushed a button and placed it on the table, aimed at Fitch's ample gut. "Pardon me, Fitch, just checking to see if you had time to stick a bug here or there."

"I said I wasn't wired, okay," Fitch said, very relieved. Konrad had suggested a small body mike with a tech van parked nearby, but Fitch, in a hurry, had said no.

She glanced at the tiny digital monitor on the end of the sensor-scan, then placed it back in her purse. Fitch smiled, but only for a second.

"I got a call from Lawrence this morning," she said, and Fitch swallowed hard. "Evidently you've got some real meatheads up there banging on doors and kicking over trash cans."

"I don't know what you're talking about," Fitch said, somewhat unsteadily and without sufficient conviction.

It was Fitch! His eyes betrayed him; they fluttered and dropped and darted away quickly before returning to see her, then dropped again, all in an instant but with plenty of proof that she'd caught him. His breath was short for a second, and his shoulders jerked ever so slightly. He'd been nailed.

"Right. One more phone call from old friends and you'll never hear my voice again."

He rallied adequately though. "What's in Lawrence?" he demanded as if his integrity had been questioned.

"Give it up, Fitch. And call off the dogs."

He exhaled heavily while shrugging in utter bewilderment. "Fine. Whatever. I just wish I knew what you were talking about."

"You do. One more phone call and it's over, okay?"

"Okay. Whatever you say."

Though Fitch couldn't see her eyes, he could feel them beaming at him from behind the thick glasses. She said nothing for a minute. A waiter busied himself at a nearby table, but made no effort to serve them.

Finally, Fitch leaned forward and said, "When do we stop playing games?"

"Now."

"Wonderful. What do you want?"

"Money."

"I figured. How much?"

"I'll name a price later. I take it you're ready to deal."

"I'm always ready to deal. But I gotta know what I get in return."

"It's very simple, Fitch. It depends on what you want. As far as you're concerned this jury can do one of four things. It can deliver a verdict for the plaintiff. It can split and hang and go home, and you'll be back down here in a year or so doing this again. Rohr isn't going away. It can come back nine to three for you, and you get a huge victory. And it can come back twelve to zero, and your clients can relax for several years."

"I know all this."

"Of course you do. If we rule out a plaintiff's verdict, then we have three choices."

"What can you deliver?"

"Anything I want. Including a plaintiff's verdict."

"So the other side is willing to pay."

"We're talking. Let's just leave it at that."

"Is this an auction? Your verdict to the highest bidder?"

"It's whatever I want it to be."

"I'd feel better if you'd stay away from Rohr."

"I'm not too concerned with your feelings."

Another waiter appeared and noticed them. He reluctantly asked if they'd like something to drink. Fitch wanted iced tea. Marlee asked for a Diet Coke in a can.

"Tell me how the deal works," he said when the waiter left.

"It's very simple. We agree on the verdict you want, just look at the menu and place your order. Then we agree on the price. You get your money ready. We wait until the very end, until the lawyers finish their closing arguments and the jury retires to deliberate. At that point, I furnish you with wiring instructions and the money is immediately sent to a bank in, say, Switzerland. Once I get confirmation the money has been received, then the jury returns with your verdict."

Fitch had spent hours predicting a scenario remarkably similar to this, but to hear it come from Marlee's lips with such a cool precision made his heart pound and his head spin. This could be the easiest one yet!

"Won't work," he said smugly, like a man who'd negotiated many such verdict deals.

"Oh really. Rohr thinks it will."

Damn, she was quick! She knew just exactly where to stick the knife.

"But there's no guarantee," he protested.

She adjusted her sunglasses and leaned forward on her elbows. "So you doubt me, Fitch?"

"That's not the issue. You're asking me to wire what I'm sure will be a large sum of money on the hope and prayer that your friend will control the deliberations. Juries are so unpredictable."

"Fitch, my friend is controlling the deliberations even as we speak. He'll have his votes long before the lawyers stop talking."

Fitch would pay. He'd made the decision a week earlier to pay whatever she wanted, and he knew that when the money left The Fund there were no guarantees. He didn't care. He trusted his Marlee. She and her friend Easter or whatever the hell his name was had patiently stalked Big Tobacco to reach this point, and they would happily hand over a verdict for the right price. They had lived for this moment.

Oh, the questions he wanted to ask. He'd love to start with the two of them and ask whose idea this was, such an ingenious, devious plan to study litigation, then follow it across the country, then plant oneself on the jury so a deal could be cut for a verdict. It was nothing short of brilliant. He could grill her for hours, maybe days, about the specifics, but he knew there would be no answers.

He also knew she'd deliver. She had worked too hard and had come too far with their plot to fail.

"I'm not totally helpless in this matter, you know," he said, still holding his ground.

"Of course not, Fitch. I'm sure you've laid enough traps to snag at least four jurors. Shall I name them?"

The drinks arrived and Fitch gulped his tea. No, he did not want her to name them. He would not play a guessing game with someone who had the hard facts. Talking with Marlee was like talking to the leader of the jury, and though Fitch cherished the moment it made the conversation quite one-sided. How was he to know if she was bluffing or telling the truth? It simply wasn't fair.

"I sense you doubt whether I'm in control," she said.

"I doubt everything."

"What if I get a juror bumped?"

"You've already bumped Stella Hulic," Fitch said, and drew the first and only very small smile from her.

"I can do it again. What if, say, I decided to send home Lonnie Shaver? Would you be impressed?"

Fitch almost choked on his tea. He wiped his mouth with the back of a hand, said, "I'm sure Lonnie would be happy. He's probably the most bored of the twelve."

"Shall I bump him?"

"No. He's harmless. Plus, since we'll be working together, I think we should keep Lonnie."

"He and Nicholas talk a lot, you know?"

"Is Nicholas talking to everyone?"

"Yes, at various levels. Give him time."

"You seem confident."

"I'm not confident in the ability of your lawyers. But I am confident in Nicholas, and that's all that matters."

They sat quietly and waited for two waiters to set the table next to them. Lunch began at eleven-thirty, and the café was coming to life.

When the waiters finished and left, Fitch said, "I can't cut a deal if I don't know the terms."

Without the slightest hesitation, she said, "And I'm not cutting a deal as long as you're digging through my past."

"Got something to hide?"

"No. But I have friends, and I don't like getting phone calls from them. Stop it now, and this meeting will lead to the next. One more phone call, and I'll never speak to you again."

"Don't say that."

"I mean it, Fitch. Call off the dogs."

"They're not my dogs, I swear."

"Call them off anyway, or I'll spend more time with Rohr. He might want to cut a deal, and a verdict for him means you're out of work and your clients lose billions. You can't afford it, Fitch."

She was certainly right about that. Whatever she planned to ask for would be a tiny sum compared to the ultimate cost of a plaintiff's verdict.

"We'd better move fast," he said. "This trial won't last much longer."

"How long?" she asked.

"Three or four days for the defense."

"Fitch, I'm hungry. Why don't you leave and retrace your steps? I'll call you in a couple of days."

"What a coincidence. I'm hungry too."

"No thanks. I'll eat alone. Plus, I want you away from here."

He rose, said, "Sure, Marlee. Whatever you want. Good day."

She watched him saunter back down the pier to the parking lot next to the beach. He stopped there and called someone from a cellphone.

AFTER REPEATED ATTEMPTS to reach Hoppy by phone, Jimmy Hull Moke dropped in unannounced on Dupree Realty Tuesday afternoon and was told by a sleepy-eyed receptionist that Mr. Dupree was somewhere in the back. She left to fetch him, and returned fifteen minutes later with the apology that she had been wrong, that Mr. Dupree was not in his office and had in fact left for an important meeting.

"I see his car out there," Jimmy Hull said, agitated, pointing to the small parking lot just outside the door. Sure enough, there was Hoppy's old station wagon.

"He rode with someone else," she said, obviously lying.

"Where'd he go?" Jimmy Hull asked as if he might go after him.

"Somewhere near Pass Christian. That's all I know."

"Why won't he return my phone calls?"

"I have no idea. Mr. Dupree is a very busy man."

Jimmy Hull shoved both hands deep in the pockets of his jeans and glared down at the woman. "You tell him I stopped by, that I'm very irritated, and that he'd better call me. You got that?"

"Yes sir."

He left the office, got in his Ford pickup, and drove away. She watched to be safe, then raced to the back to free Hoppy from the broom closet.

THE SIXTY-FOOTER with Captain Theo at the helm traveled fifty miles into the Gulf, where under a cloudless sky and amid gentle sea breezes, half the jury fished for mackerel, snapper, and redfish. Angel Weese had never been on a boat, couldn't swim, and got sick two hundred yards from shore, but with the help of a seasoned deckhand and a bottle of Dramamine she recovered and actually caught the first fish of any size. Rikki looked splendidly cute with shorts, Reeboks, tanned legs. The Colonel and the Captain were inevitably kindred spirits, and it wasn't long before Nap was on the bridge talking naval strategy and exchanging war stories.

Two deckhands prepared a fine lunch of boiled shrimp, fried oyster sandwiches, crab claws, and chowder. The first round of beer was served with lunch. Only Rikki abstained and drank water.

The beer continued throughout the afternoon as the fishing alternated between frenzy and boredom, and as the sun grew warmer on the deck. The boat was large enough to find privacy. Nicholas and Jerry made certain that Lonnie Shaver kept a cold beer in hand. They were determined to chat him up for the first time.

Lonnie had an uncle who'd worked on a shrimp boat for many years, before it sank in a storm and the entire crew was never found. When he was a kid, he'd fished these waters with his uncle, and, frankly, he'd had his share of fishing. Despised it, really, and hadn't been in years. Still, the boat trip sounded a bit more tolerable than the bus ride to New Orleans.

It took four beers to knock the edge off and loosen the tongue. They lounged in a small upper-deck cabin, open on all sides. On the main deck below them Rikki and Angel were watching the deckhands clean their catch.

"I wonder how many experts the defense will call," Nicholas said, changing the subject from fishing with near total exasperation. Jerry was lying on a plastic cot, his socks and shoes off, his eyes closed, cold beer in hand.

"They don't have to call any as far as I'm concerned," Lonnie said, gazing at the sea.

"You've had enough, huh?" Nicholas said.

"Pretty damned ridiculous. Man smokes for thirty-five years, then wants millions for his estate after he kills himself."

"See what I told you," Jerry said without opening his eyes.

"What?" Lonnie asked.

"Jerry and I had you pegged as a defense juror," Nicholas explained. "It was difficult though, because you've had so little to say."

"And what are you?" Lonnie asked.

"Me, I'm still open-minded. Jerry's leaning toward the defense, right, Jerry?"

"I have not discussed the case with anyone. I have had no unauthorized contact. I have not taken any bribes. I am a juror Judge Harkin can be proud of."

"He's leaning toward the defense," Nicholas said to Lonnie. "Because he's addicted to nicotine, can't kick the habit, but he's convinced himself he can throw them away whenever he wants. He can't, because he's a wimp. But he wants to be a real man like Colonel Herrera."

"Who doesn't?" Lonnie said.

"Jerry thinks that because he can quit, if he really wanted to, then anyone should be able to quit, which he can't do himself, and therefore Jacob Wood should've stopped long before he got cancer."

"That's about right," Jerry said. "But I object to the part about the wimp."

"Makes good sense to me," Lonnie said. "How can you be open-minded?"

"Gee, I don't know. Maybe it's because I haven't heard all the testimony yet. Yeah, that's it. The law says that we must refrain from reaching verdicts until all the evidence is in. Forgive me."

"You're forgiven," Jerry said. "Now it's your turn to fetch another round." Nicholas drained his can and walked down the narrow stairway to the cooler on the main deck.

"Don't worry about him," Jerry said. "He'll be with us when it counts."

Twenty-six

THE BOAT RETURNED a few minutes after five. The hearty band of fishermen staggered from the deck onto the pier, where they posed for photos with Captain Theo and their trophies, the largest of which was a ninety-pound shark hooked by Rikki and landed by a deckhand. They were gathered by two deputies and led down the pier, leaving behind their catch because there was certainly no use for it at the motel.

The bus with the shoppers would be another hour. Its arrival, as was the arrival of the boat, was duly watched, recorded, and relayed to Fitch, but for whatever purpose no one was sure. Fitch just wanted to know. They had to watch something. It was a slow day, not much to do but sit and wait for the jury to return.

Fitch was locked in his office with Swanson, who'd spent most of the afternoon on the phone. The "meatheads," as Marlee had described them, had been called off. In their place, Fitch was sending in the professionals, the same Bethesda firm he was using for the Hoppy sting. Swanson had once worked there, and many of the agents were either ex-FBI or ex-CIA.

Results were guaranteed. It was hardly a job to get them excited—the uncovering of a young woman's past. Swanson was to leave in an hour and fly to Kansas City, where he would monitor things.

There was also a guarantee not to get caught. Fitch was in a quandary—he had to hold Marlee, yet he also had to know who she was. Two factors pushed him to keep digging. First, it was terribly important to her that he stop. There was something hidden back there that was crucial. And second, she had gone to such lengths to leave no trail.

Marlee had left Lawrence, Kansas, four years ago, after living there for three years. She was not Claire Clement until she arrived, and she certainly was not when she left. In the meantime, she met and recruited Jeff Kerr, who was now Nicholas Easter and was now doing hell knows what to the jury.

ANGEL WEESE was in love with and planned to marry Derrick Maples, a strapping young man of twenty-four who was between jobs and between wives. He'd lost his job selling car phones when the company merged, and he was now in the process of dispensing with his first wife, the result of a teenage romance gone bad. They had two young children. His wife and her lawyer wanted six hundred dollars a month in child support. Derrick and his lawyer waved his unemployment like a burning flag. The negotiations had turned bitter and a final divorce was months away.

Angel was two months pregnant, though she'd told no one but Derrick.

Derrick's brother Marvis had once been a deputy sheriff and was now a part-time minister and community activist. Marvis was approached by a man named Cleve, who said he'd like to meet Derrick. Introductions were made.

For lack of a better job description, Cleve was known as a runner. He ran cases for Wendall Rohr. Cleve's task was to find good, solid death and injury claims and make sure they found their way to Rohr's office. Good running was an art form, and of course Cleve was a fine runner because Rohr would have nothing but the best. Like all good runners, Cleve moved in shadowy circles because the soliciting of clients was still technically an unethical practice, though any decent car wreck would attract more runners than emergency personnel. In fact, Cleve's business card pronounced him to be an "Investigator."

Cleve also delivered papers for Rohr, served summonses, checked on witnesses and potential jurors, and spied on other lawyers, the usual functions of a runner when he wasn't running. He received a salary for his investigating, and Rohr paid him cash bonuses when he landed a particularly good case.

Over a beer in a tavern, he talked with Derrick and realized quickly the guy had financial problems. He then steered the conversation toward Angel, and asked if anyone had beaten him to the punch. No, said Derrick, no one had come around asking about the trial. But then, Derrick had been living with a brother, sort of laying low and trying to avoid his wife's greedy lawyer.

Good, said Cleve, because he'd been hired as a consultant by some of the lawyers, and, well, the trial was awfully important. Cleve ordered a second round and talked awhile about just how damned important the trial was.

Derrick was bright, had a year of junior college and a desire to make a buck, and he picked it up quickly. "Why don't you get to the point?" he asked.

Cleve was ready to do just that. "My client is willing to purchase influence. For cash. No trail whatsoever."

"Influence," Derrick repeated, then took a long sip. The smile on his face encouraged Cleve to press the deal.

"Five thousand cash," Cleve said, glancing around. "Half now, half when the trial is over."

The smile widened with another sip. "And I do what?"

"You talk with Angel when you see her during the personal visits, and make sure she understands how important this case is to the plaintiff. Just don't tell her about the money, or about me or any of this. Not now. Maybe later."

"Why not?"

"Because this is illegal as hell, okay? If the Judge somehow found out that I was talking to you, offering you money to talk to Angel, then both of us would go to jail. Understand?"

"Yeah."

"It's important for you to realize that this is dangerous. If you don't wanna pursue it, then say so now."

"Ten thousand."

"What?"

"Ten. Five now, five when the trial is over."

Cleve grunted as if slightly disgusted. If only Derrick knew the stakes. "Okay. Ten."

"When can I get it?"

"Tomorrow." They ordered sandwiches and talked for another hour about the trial, and the verdict, and how best to persuade Angel.

□ □ □ □

THE CHORE of keeping D. Martin Jankle away from his cherished vodka fell to Durwood Cable. Fitch and Jankle had fought bitterly over the question of whether or not Jankle could drink Tuesday night, the night before he testified. Fitch, the former drunk, accused Jankle of having a problem. Jankle cursed Fitch viciously for trying to tell him, the CEO of Pynex, a Fortune 500 company, if and when and how much he could drink.

Cable was dragged into the brawl by Fitch. Cable insisted that Jankle hang around his office throughout the night to prepare for his testimony. A mock direct exam was followed by a lengthy cross, and Jankle performed adequately. Nothing spectacular. Cable made him watch the video of it with a panel of jury experts.

When he was finally taken to his hotel room after ten, he found that Fitch had removed all liquor from the mini-bar and replaced it with soft drinks and fruit juices.

Jankle cursed and went to his overnight bag, where he kept a flask hidden in a leather pouch. But there was no flask. Fitch had removed it too.

AT 1 A.M., Nicholas silently opened his door and looked up and down the hall. The guard was gone, no doubt asleep in his room.

Marlee was waiting in a room on the second floor. They embraced and kissed but never got around to anything else. She had hinted on the phone that there was trouble, and she hurriedly spilled the story, beginning with her early morning chat with Rebecca in Lawrence. Nicholas took it well.

Other than the natural passion of two young lovers, their relationship rarely saw emotion. And when it surfaced, it was almost always from Nicholas, who had a slight temper, which, regardless of how slight, was certainly more than she possessed. He might raise his voice when angry, but that almost never occurred. Marlee wasn't cold, just calculating. He'd never seen her cry, the one exception being at the end of a movie he'd hated. They had never been through a difficult fight, and the usual squabbles were snuffed out quickly because Marlee had taught him to bite his tongue. She didn't tolerate wasted sentiment, didn't pout or carry petty grudges, and didn't put up with him when he tried to.

She replayed her conversation with Rebecca, and she tried to recall every word from her meeting with Fitch.

The realization that they'd been partially discovered hit hard. They were sure it was Fitch, and they wondered how much he knew. They were convinced, and always had been, that Jeff Kerr would have to be discovered in order to find Claire Clement. Jeff's background was harmless. Claire's had to be protected or they might as well flee now.

There was little to do but wait.

DERRICK ENTERED Angel's room by wedging himself through the fold-out window. He hadn't seen her since Sunday, a gap of almost forty-eight hours, and he simply couldn't wait until tomorrow night because he loved her madly and missed her and had to hold her. She immediately noticed he had been drinking. They fell into bed, where they quietly consummated an unauthorized personal visit.

Derrick rolled over and fell fast asleep.

They awoke at dawn, and Angel panicked because she had a man in her room and this was, of course, against the Judge's orders. Derrick was unconcerned. He said he'd simply wait until they left for court, then sneak out of the room. This did little to calm her nerves. Angel took a long shower.

Derrick had taken Cleve's plan and improved on it immensely. After leaving the tavern, he bought a six-pack and drove along the Gulf for hours. Slowly, up and down Highway 90, past the hotels and casinos and boat docks, from Pass Christian to Pascagoula he had driven, sipping beer and expanding the scheme. Cleve, after a few drinks, had let it slip that the lawyers for the plaintiff were seeking millions. It took only nine of the twelve for a verdict, so Derrick figured Angel's vote was worth a helluva lot more than ten thousand dollars.

Ten thousand sounded great at the tavern, but if they would pay that much, and agree to do it so quickly, then they would pay more with pressure. The more he drove, the more her vote was worth. It was now at fifty, and rising almost by the hour.

Derrick was intrigued by the notion of percentages. What if the verdict was ten million, for example? One percent, one lousy little percent, would be a hundred thousand dollars. A twenty-million-dollar verdict? Two hundred thousand dollars. What if Derrick proposed to Cleve a deal whereby they paid him cash up front and a percentage of the verdict? That would motivate Derrick, and of course his girlfriend, to press hard during deliberations for a large verdict. They'd become players. It was a chance they'd never see again.

Angel returned in her bathrobe and lit a cigarette.

Twenty-seven

PYNEX' DEFENSE of its good corporate name got off to a
miserable start Wednesday morning, through no fault of its
own. An analyst named Walter Barker, writing in *Mogul,* a popular weekly financial, laid two-to-one odds that the jury down in
Biloxi would find against Pynex, and return a large verdict.
Barker was no lightweight. Trained as a lawyer, he had developed
a formidable reputation on Wall Street as the man to watch when
litigation affected commerce. His specialty was monitoring trials
and appeals and settlements, and predicting their outcomes before
they were final. He was usually right, and had made a fortune
with his research. He was widely read, and the fact that he was
betting against Pynex shocked Wall Street. The stock opened at
seventy-six, dropped to seventy-three, and by mid-morning was at
seventy-one and a half.

The courtroom crowd was larger Wednesday. The Wall Street
boys were back in force, each reading a copy of *Mogul* and all
suddenly agreeing with Barker, though over breakfast an hour
earlier the consensus had been that Pynex had weathered the
plaintiff's witnesses and should close strongly. Now they read
with worried faces and revised their reports to their offices.
Barker had actually been in the courtroom last week. He'd sat
alone on the back row. What had he seen that they'd missed?

The jurors filed in promptly at nine, with Lou Dell proudly
holding the door as if she'd collected her brood after they'd scat-

tered yesterday and was now delivering them back to where they belonged. Harkin welcomed them as if they'd been gone for a month, made some flat crack about fishing, then raced through his standard "Have you been molested?" questions. He promised the jurors a speedy end to the trial.

Jankle was called as a witness, and the defense began. Free of the effects of alcohol, Jankle was primed and sharp. He smiled easily and seemed to welcome the chance to defend his tobacco company. Cable waltzed him through the preliminaries without a hitch.

Seated on the second row was D. Y. Taunton, the black lawyer from the Wall Street firm who'd met with Lonnie in Charlotte. He listened to Jankle while cutting his eyes at Lonnie, and it didn't take long to connect. Lonnie glanced once, couldn't help it as he glanced again, and on the third look managed to nod and smile because it seemed like the proper thing to do. The message was clear—Taunton was an important person who'd traveled all the way down to Biloxi because this was an important day. The defense was now speaking, and it was critical for Lonnie to understand that he should listen and believe every word now being said from the witness stand. No problem with Lonnie.

Jankle's first defensive thrust was on the issue of choice. He conceded that a lot of people think cigarettes are addictive, but only because he and Cable realized he would sound foolish otherwise. But, then, maybe they're not addictive. No one really knows, and the folks in research are just as confused as anyone. One study leans this way, the next one leans another, but he'd never seen positive proof that smoking was addictive. Personally, he just did not believe it. Jankle had smoked for twenty years, but only because he enjoyed it. He smoked twenty cigarettes a day, by choice, and he'd chosen a lower-tar brand. No, he most certainly was not addicted. He could quit whenever he wanted. He smoked because he liked to. He played tennis four times a week and his annual physical revealed nothing to worry about.

Seated one row behind Taunton was Derrick Maples, making his first appearance at the trial. He'd left the motel just minutes after the bus, and had planned to spend the day looking for work. Now, he was dreaming of an easy payday. Angel saw him, but kept her eyes on Jankle. Derrick's sudden interest in the trial was baffling. He'd done nothing but complain since they'd been sequestered.

Jankle described the various brands his company made. He stepped down and stood before a colorful chart with each of the eight brands, each with its tar and nicotine levels labeled beside it. He explained why some cigarettes have filters, some don't, some have more tar and nicotine than others. It all boiled down to choice. He was proud of his product line.

A crucial point was made here, and Jankle conveyed it well. By offering such a wide selection of brands, Pynex allowed each consumer to decide how much tar and nicotine he or she wanted. Choice. Choice. Choice. Choose the level of tar and nicotine. Choose the number of cigarettes you smoke each day. Choose whether or not to inhale. Make the intelligent choice of what you do to your body with cigarettes.

Jankle pointed to a bright drawing of a red pack of Bristols, the brand with the second-highest level of tar and nicotine. He conceded that if Bristols were "abused" then the results could be damaging.

Cigarettes were responsible products, if used with restraint. Like many other products—alcohol, butter, sugar, and handguns, just to name a few—they could become dangerous if abused.

Seated across the aisle from Derrick was Hoppy, who had stopped by for a quick update on what was happening. Plus he wanted to see and smile at Millie, who was delighted to see him but also curious about his sudden obsession with the trial. Tonight the jurors were allowed personal visits, and Hoppy couldn't wait to spend three hours in Millie's room with sex the last thing on his mind.

When Judge Harkin stopped for lunch, Jankle was completing his thoughts about advertising. Sure his company spent tons of money, but not as much as beer companies or car companies or Coca-Cola. Advertising was crucial to survival in a fiercely competitive world, regardless of the product. Of course children saw his company's ads. How do you design a billboard ad so that it won't be seen by children? How do you keep kids from looking at the magazines their parents subscribe to? Impossible. Jankle readily admitted he'd seen the statistics showing eighty-five percent of the kids who smoke buy the three most heavily advertised brands. But so do adults! Again, you can't design an ad campaign that targets adults without affecting kids.

FITCH WATCHED ALL of Jankle's testimony from a seat near the back. To his right was Luther Vandemeer, CEO of Trellco, the largest tobacco company in the world. Vandemeer was the unofficial head of the Big Four, and the only one Fitch could tolerate. He, in return, had the perplexing gift of being able to tolerate Fitch.

They ate lunch at Mary Mahoney's, alone at a table in a corner. They were relieved by Jankle's success so far, but knew the worst was yet to come. Barker's column in *Mogul* had ruined their appetites.

"How much influence do you have with the jury?" Vandemeer asked, picking at his food.

Fitch wasn't about to answer truthfully. He wasn't expected to. His dirty deeds were kept from everyone except his own agents.

"The usual," Fitch said.

"Maybe the usual is not enough."

"What are you suggesting?"

Vandemeer didn't answer, but instead studied the legs of a young waitress taking an order at the next table.

"We're doing everything possible," Fitch said, with uncharacteristic warmth. But Vandemeer was scared, and rightly so. Fitch knew the pressure was enormous. A large plaintiff's verdict wouldn't bankrupt Pynex or Trellco, but the results would be messy and far-reaching. An in-house study predicted an immediate twenty percent loss in shareholder value for all four companies, and that was just for starters. In the same study, a worst-case scenario predicted one million lung cancer lawsuits filed during the five years after such a verdict, with the average lawsuit costing a million dollars in legal fees alone. The study didn't dare predict the cost of a million verdicts. The doomsday scenario called for the certification of a class-action suit, the class being any person who had ever smoked and felt injured because of it. Bankruptcy would be a possibility at that point. And it would be probable that serious efforts would be made in Congress to outlaw the production of cigarettes.

"Do you have enough money?" Vandemeer asked.

"I think so," Fitch said, asking himself for the hundredth time just how much his dear Marlee might have in mind.

"The Fund should be in good shape."

"It is."

Vandemeer chewed on a tiny piece of grilled chicken. "Why don't you just pick out nine jurors and give them a million bucks apiece?" he said, with a quiet laugh as if he were only joking.

"Believe me, I've thought about it. It's just too risky. People would go to jail."

"Just kidding."

"We have ways."

Vandemeer stopped smiling. "We have to win, Rankin, you understand? We have to win. Spend whatever it takes."

A WEEK EARLIER, Judge Harkin, pursuant to another written request from Nicholas Easter, had changed the lunch routine a bit and declared that the two alternate jurors could eat with the twelve. Nicholas had argued that since all fourteen now lived together, watched movies together, ate breakfast and dinner together, then it was almost ludicrous to separate them at lunch. The two alternates were both men, Henry Vu and Shine Royce.

Henry Vu had been a South Vietnamese fighter pilot who ditched his plane in the China Sea the day after Saigon fell. He was picked up by an American rescue vessel and treated at a hospital in San Francisco. It took a year to smuggle his wife and kids through Laos and Cambodia and into Thailand, and finally to San Francisco, where the family lived for two years. They settled in Biloxi in 1978. Vu bought a shrimp boat and joined a growing number of Vietnamese fishermen who were squeezing out the natives. Last year his youngest daughter was the valedictorian of her senior class. She accepted a full scholarship to Harvard. Henry bought his fourth shrimp boat.

He made no effort to avoid jury service. He was as patriotic as anyone, even the Colonel.

Nicholas, of course, had befriended him immediately. He was determined that Henry Vu would sit with the chosen twelve, and be present when the deliberations began.

WITH A JURY blindsided by sequestration, the last thing Durwood Cable wanted was to prolong the case. He had pared his list of witnesses to five, and he had planned for their testimony to run no more than four days.

It was the worst time of the day for a direct examination—the first hour after lunch—when Jankle took his seat on the witness stand and resumed his testimony.

"What is your company doing to combat underage smoking?" Cable asked him, and Jankle rambled for an hour. A million here for this do-gooder cause, and a million there for that ad campaign. Eleven million last year alone.

At times, Jankle sounded as if he almost despised tobacco.

After a very long coffee break at three, Wendall Rohr was given his first crack at Jankle. He started with a vicious question, and matters went from bad to worse.

"Isn't it true, Mr. Jankle, that your company spends hundreds of millions trying to convince people to smoke, yet when they get sick from your cigarettes your company won't pay a dime to help them?"

"Is that a question?"

"Of course it is. Now answer it!"

"No. That's not true."

"Good. When was the last time Pynex paid a penny of one of your smoker's medical bills?"

Jankle shrugged and mumbled something.

"I'm sorry, Mr. Jankle. I didn't catch that. The question is, when was the last time—"

"I heard the question."

"Then answer it. Just give us one example where Pynex offered to help with the medical bills of someone who smoked your products."

"I can't recall one."

"So your company refuses to stand behind its products?"

"We certainly do not."

"Good. Give the jury just one example of Pynex standing behind its cigarettes."

"Our products are not defective."

"They don't cause sickness and death?" Rohr asked incredulously, arms flopping wildly at the air.

"No. They don't."

"Now lemme get this straight. You're telling this jury that your cigarettes do not cause sickness and death?"

"Only if they are abused."

Rohr laughed as he spat out the word "abused" in thorough disgust. "Are your cigarettes supposed to be lit with some type of lighter?"

"Of course."

"And is the smoke produced by the tobacco and the paper supposed to be sucked through the end opposite the end that is lit?"

"Yes."

"And is this smoke supposed to enter the mouth?"

"Yes."

"And is it supposed to be inhaled into the respiratory tract?"

"Depends on the choice of the smoker."

"Do you inhale, Mr. Jankle?"

"Yes."

"Are you familiar with studies showing ninety-eight percent of all cigarette smokers inhale?"

"Yes."

"So it's accurate to say that you know the smoke from your cigarettes will be inhaled?"

"I suppose so."

"Is it your opinion that people who inhale the smoke are actually abusing the product?"

"No."

"So tell us, please, Mr. Jankle, how does one abuse a cigarette?"

"By smoking too much."

"And how much is too much?"

"I guess it depends on each individual."

"I'm not talking to each individual smoker, Mr. Jankle. I'm talking to you, the CEO of Pynex, one of the largest cigarette producers in the world. And I'm asking you, in your opinion, how much is too much?"

"I'd say more than two packs a day."

"More than forty cigarettes a day?"

"Yes."

"I see. And what study do you base this on?"

"None. It's just my opinion."

"Below forty, and smoking is not unhealthy. Above forty, and the product is being abused. Is this your testimony?"

"It's my opinion." Jankle was starting to squirm and cast his eyes at Cable, who was angry and looking away. The abuse theory was a new one, a creation of Jankle's. He insisted on using it.

Rohr lowered his voice and studied his notes. He took his time for the setup because he didn't want to spoil the kill. "Would you describe for the jury the steps you've taken as CEO to warn the public that smoking more than forty cigarettes a day is dangerous?"

Jankle had a quick retort, but he thought the better of it. His mouth opened, then he hung in mid-thought for a long, painful pause. After the damage was done, he gathered himself and said, "I think you misunderstand me."

Rohr wasn't about to let him explain. "I'm sure I do. I don't believe I've ever seen a warning on any of your products to the effect that more than two packs a day is abusive and dangerous. Why not?"

"We're not required to."

"Required by whom?"

"The government."

"So if the government doesn't make you warn folks that your products can be abused, then you're certainly not going to do it voluntarily, are you?"

"We follow the law."

"Did the law require Pynex to spend four hundred million dollars last year in advertising?"

"No."

"But you did, didn't you?"

"Something like that."

"And if you wanted to warn smokers of potential dangers you could certainly do it, couldn't you?"

"I suppose."

Rohr switched quickly to butter and sugar, two products Jankle had mentioned as being potentially dangerous. Rohr took great delight in pointing out the differences between them and cigarettes, and made Jankle look silly.

He saved the best for last. During a short recess, the video monitors were once again rolled into place. When the jury returned, the lights were dimmed and there was Jankle on-screen, right hand raised while being asked to tell the truth and nothing but the truth. The occasion was a hearing before a congressional subcommittee. Standing next to Jankle were Vandemeer and the other two CEO's of the Big Four, all summoned against their will to give testimony to a bunch of politicians. They looked like four Mafia dons about to tell Congress there was no such thing as organized crime. The questioning was brutal.

The tape was heavily edited. One by one, they were asked point-blank if nicotine was addictive, and each emphatically said no. Jankle went last, and by the time he made his angry denial, the jury, just like the subcommittee, knew he was lying.

Twenty-eight

DURING A TENSE forty-minute meeting with Cable in his office, Fitch unloaded most of what had been bothering him about the way the case was being defended. He started with Jankle and his brilliant new tobacco defense, the abused-cigarette strategy, a harebrained approach that just might doom them. Cable, in no mood to be scolded, especially by a nonlawyer he loathed anyway, repeatedly explained that they had begged Jankle not to raise the issue of abuse. But Jankle had been a lawyer in another life and fancied himself as an original thinker who'd been given the golden chance to save Big Tobacco. Jankle was now on a Pynex jet en route to New York.

And Fitch thought the jury might be tired of Cable. Rohr had spread the courtroom work among his gang of thieves. Why couldn't Cable allow another defense lawyer besides Felix Mason to handle a few witnesses? God knew there were enough of them. Was it ego? They yelled at each other from across the desk.

The article in *Mogul* had unraveled nerves and added another, much heavier layer of pressure.

Cable reminded Fitch that he was the lawyer, and he had thirty rather outstanding years in the courtroom. He could better read the mood and texture of the trial.

And Fitch reminded Cable that this was the ninth tobacco trial he'd directed, not to mention the two mistrials he'd engineered, and he'd certainly seen more effective courtroom advocacy than what was being offered by Cable.

When the yelling and cursing died down, and after both men made efforts to pull themselves together, they did agree that the defense should be brief. Cable projected three more days, and that included whatever cross-examination Rohr would offer. Three days and no more, Fitch said.

He slammed the door as he left the office, and gathered José in the hallway. Together they stormed through the offices, offices still very much alive with lawyers in shirtsleeves and paralegals eating pizza and harried secretaries darting about trying to finish and get home to the kids. The mere sight of Fitch swaggering at full speed and the beefy José stomping after him made grown men cower and duck into doorways.

In the Suburban, José handed Fitch a stack of faxes, which he scanned as they sped away to headquarters. The first was a list of Marlee's movements since the meeting on the pier yesterday. Nothing unusual.

Next was the recap of what was happening in Kansas. A Claire Clement had been found in Topeka, but she was a resident of a nursing home. The one in Des Moines actually answered the phone at her husband's used-car lot. Swanson said they were pursuing many leads, but the report was rather scant on details. One of Kerr's law school chums had been found in Kansas City, and they were trying to arrange a meeting.

They drove past a convenience store, and in the front window a neon beer sign caught Fitch's attention. The smell and taste of a cold beer filled his senses, and Fitch ached for a drink. Just one. Just a sweet, frosty beer in a tall mug. How long had it been?

The urge to stop hit hard. Fitch closed his eyes and tried to think of something else. He could send José in to buy just one, one cold bottle and that would be it. Wouldn't it? Surely, after nine years of sobriety he could handle a single drink. Why couldn't he have just one?

Because he'd had a million. And if José stopped here then he'd stop again two blocks away. And by the time they eventually reached the office the Suburban would be filled with empty bottles and Fitch would be throwing them at passing cars. He was not a pretty drunk.

But just one to settle his nerves, to help forget this miserable day.

"You okay, boss?" José asked.

Fitch grunted something, and stopped thinking about beer. Where was Marlee, and why hadn't she called today? The trial was winding down. A deal would take time to negotiate and execute.

He thought of the column in *Mogul,* and he longed for Marlee. He heard Jankle's idiotic voice expounding a brand-new defense theory, and he longed for Marlee. He closed his eyes and saw the faces of the jurors, and he longed for Marlee.

SINCE DERRICK now considered himself to be a major player, he chose a new meeting place for Wednesday night. It was a rough bar in the black section of Biloxi, a place Cleve had actually been before. Derrick figured he'd have the upper hand if the rendezvous occurred on his turf. Cleve insisted they meet in the parking lot first.

The lot was almost filled. Cleve was late. Derrick spotted him when he parked, and walked to the driver's side.

"I don't think this is a good idea," Cleve said, peeking through the crack in his window and looking at the dark, cinder-block building with steel rods across the windows.

"It's okay," said Derrick, himself a bit worried but unwilling to show it. "It's safe."

"Safe? They've had three stabbings here in the last month. I've got the only white face here, and you expect me to walk in there with five thousand bucks in cash and hand it over to you. Reckon who'd get cut first? Me or you?"

Derrick saw his point, but was unwilling to concede so quickly. He leaned closer to the window, glanced around the parking lot, suddenly more fearful.

"I say we go in," he said, in his best tough-guy routine.

"Forget it," Cleve said. "If you want the money, meet me at the Waffle House on 90." Cleve started his engine and raised the window. Derrick watched him drive away, with the five thousand dollars in cash somewhere within his reach, then ran to his car.

THEY ATE PANCAKES and drank coffee at the counter. Conversation was low because the cook was flipping eggs and sausage on a grill less than ten feet away and seemed to be straining to hear every word.

Derrick was nervous and his hands were jittery. Runners handled cash payoffs daily. The affair was of little significance to Cleve.

"So I'm thinking that maybe ten grand ain't enough, know what I mean?" Derrick said finally, repeating a line he'd rehearsed most of the afternoon.

"Thought we had a deal," Cleve said, unmoved, chomping on pancakes.

"I think you're trying to screw me, though."

"Is this your way of negotiating?"

"You ain't offering enough, man. I've been thinking about it. I even went by the courtroom this morning and watched some of the trial. I know what's going on now. I got it figured out."

"You do?"

"Yeah. And you guys ain't playing fair."

"There were no complaints last night when we agreed on ten."

"Things are different now. You caught me off guard last night."

Cleve wiped his mouth with a paper napkin and waited for the cook to serve someone at the far end of the counter. "Then what do you want?" he asked.

"A lot more."

"We don't have time to play games. Tell me what you want."

Derrick swallowed hard and glanced over his shoulder. Under his breath he said, "Fifty thousand, plus a percentage of the verdict."

"What percentage?"

"I figure ten percent would be fair."

"Oh you do." Cleve tossed his napkin onto his plate. "You're outta your mind," he said, then put a five-dollar bill beside his plate. He stood and said, "We cut a deal for ten. That's it. Anything larger and we'll get caught."

Cleve left in a hurry. Derrick searched both pockets and found nothing but coins. The cook was suddenly hovering nearby watching the desperate search for money. "I thought he was gonna pay," Derrick said, checking his shirt pocket.

"How much you got?" the cook asked, picking the five-dollar bill from beside Cleve's plate.

"Eighty cents."

"That's enough."

Derrick raced into the parking lot where he caught Cleve waiting with his engine running and his window down. "I'll bet the other side'll pay more," he said, leaning over.

"Then go try. Walk up to them tomorrow and tell them you want fifty thousand bucks for one vote."

"And ten percent."

"You're clueless, son." Cleve slowly switched off the ignition and got out of the car. He lit a cigarette. "You don't understand. A defense verdict means no money changes hands. Zero for the plaintiff means zero for the defense. It means no percentages for anybody. The plaintiff's lawyers get forty percent of zero. Does that make sense?"

"Yeah," Derrick said slowly, though obviously still confused.

"Look, what I'm offering you is something that's illegal as hell. Don't get greedy. If you do, then you'll get caught."

"Ten thousand seems cheap for something this big."

"No, don't look at it that way. Think of it like this. She's entitled to nothing, okay. Zero. She's doing her civic duty, getting fifteen bucks a day from the county for being a good citizen. The ten thousand is a bribe, a dirty little gift that has to be forgotten as soon as it's received."

"But if you offer a percentage, then she'll be motivated to work harder in the jury room."

Cleve drew a long puff and exhaled slowly, shaking his head. "You just don't understand. If there's a plaintiff's verdict, it will be years before the money changes hands. Look, Derrick, you're making this too complicated. Take the money. Talk to Angel. Help us out."

"Twenty-five thousand."

Another long puff, then the cigarette fell to the asphalt, where Cleve ground it with his boot. "I'll have to talk to my boss."

"Twenty-five thousand, per vote."

"Per vote?"

"Yeah. Angel can deliver more than one."

"Who?"

"I ain't saying."

"Lemme talk to my boss."

□ □ □ □

IN ROOM 54, Henry Vu read letters from his daughter at Harvard while his wife Qui studied new insurance policies for their fleet of fishing boats. Because Nicholas was watching movies down the hall, 48 was empty. In 44, Lonnie and his wife cuddled under the covers for the first time in almost a month, but they had to hurry since her sister had the kids. In 58, Mrs. Grimes watched sitcoms while Herman loaded trial narratives into his computer. Room 50 was empty because the Colonel was in the Party Room, alone again because Mrs. Herrera was off in Texas visiting a cousin. And 52 was also empty because Jerry was drinking beer with the Colonel and Nicholas and waiting until later to sneak across the hall to Poodle's room. In 56, Shine Royce, alternate number two, worked on a large bag of rolls and butter he'd taken from the dining room, watched TV, and once again thanked God for his good fortune. Royce was fifty-two, unemployed, lived in a rented trailer with a younger woman and her six kids, and hadn't earned fifteen dollars a day doing anything in years. Now, he simply had to sit and listen to a trial and the county would not only pay him but feed him too. In 46, Phillip Savelle and his Pakistani mate drank herbal tea and smoked pot with the windows open.

Across the hall in Room 49, Sylvia Taylor-Tatum talked on the phone with her son. In 45, Mrs. Gladys Card played gin rummy with Mr. Nelson Card, he of the prostate history. In 51, Rikki Coleman waited for Rhea, who was running late and might not make it because the baby-sitter hadn't called. In 53, Loreen Duke sat on her bed, eating a brownie and listening with wretched envy as Angel Weese and her boyfriend rattled the walls next door in 55.

And in 47, Hoppy and Millie Dupree made love like never before. Hoppy had arrived early with a large sack of Chinese food and a bottle of cheap champagne, something he hadn't tried in years. Under normal circumstances, Millie would've fussed about the alcohol, but these days were far from normal. She sipped a little of the beverage from a plastic motel cup, and ate a generous portion of sweet and sour pork. Then Hoppy attacked her.

When they finished, they lay in the darkness and talked softly about the kids and school and the home in general. She was quite weary of this ordeal, and anxious to get back to her family.

Hoppy spoke forlornly of her absence. The kids were testy. The house was a wreck. Everybody missed Millie.

He dressed and turned on the television. Millie found her bathrobe and poured another tiny bit of champagne.

"You're not gonna believe this," Hoppy said, fishing through a coat pocket and retrieving a folded piece of paper.

"What is it?" she asked, taking the paper and unfolding it. It was a copy of Fitch's bogus memo listing the many sins of Leon Robilio. She read it slowly, then looked suspiciously at her husband. "Where did you get this?" she demanded.

"It came across the fax yesterday," Hoppy said sincerely. He'd practiced his answer because he couldn't stand the thought of lying to Millie. He felt like a wretch, but then Napier and Nitchman were out there somewhere, just waiting.

"Who sent it?" she asked.

"Don't know. It looks like it came from Washington."

"Why didn't you throw it away?"

"I don't know. I—"

"You know it's wrong to show me stuff like this, Hoppy." Millie flung the paper on the bed and walked closer to her husband, hands on hips. "What are you trying to do?"

"Nothing. It just got faxed to my office, that's all."

"What a coincidence! Somebody in Washington just happened to know your fax number, just happened to know your wife was on the jury, just happened to know Leon Robilio testified, and just happened to suspect that if they sent you this you'd be stupid enough to bring it over here and try to influence me. I want to know what's going on!"

"Nothing. I swear," Hoppy said, on his heels.

"Why have you taken such a sudden interest in this trial?"

"It's fascinating."

"It was fascinating for three weeks and you hardly mentioned it. What's going on, Hoppy?"

"Nothing. Relax."

"I can tell when something's bothering you."

"Get a grip, Millie. Look, you're edgy. I'm edgy. This thing has all of us somewhat out of whack. I'm sorry for bringing it."

Millie finished off her champagne and sat on the edge of the bed. Hoppy sat next to her. Mr. Cristano at Justice had suggested in rather strong terms that Hoppy get Millie to show the memo to all of her friends on the jury. He dreaded telling Mr. Cristano that this probably wouldn't happen. But then, how would Mr. Cristano know for sure what happened to the damned thing?

As Hoppy pondered this Millie started crying. "I just want to go home," she said, eyes red, lip quivering. Hoppy put his arm around her and squeezed tightly.

"I'm sorry," he said. She cried even harder.

Hoppy felt like crying too. This meeting had proved worthless, the sex notwithstanding. According to Mr. Cristano, the trial would end in a few short days. It was imperative that Millie soon be convinced that the only verdict was one for the defense. Since their time together was scarce, Hoppy would be forced to tell her the awful truth. Not now, not tonight, but surely during the next personal visit.

Twenty-nine

THE COLONEL'S ROUTINE never varied. Like a good soldier, he rose at precisely five-thirty every morning for fifty pushups and situps before a quick, cold shower. At six, he went to the dining room, where there'd damned well better be some fresh coffee and plenty of newspapers. He ate toast with jam and no butter, and greeted each of his colleagues with a hale and hearty good morning as they drifted in and out. They were sleepy-eyed and anxious to return to their rooms where they could sip coffee and watch the news in private. It was a helluva way to start the day, being forced to greet the Colonel and return his verbal barrage. The longer they were sequestered, the more hyper he became before sunrise. Several of the jurors waited until eight, when he was known to promptly leave and return to his room.

At six-fifteen Thursday morning, Nicholas said hello to the Colonel as he poured a cup of coffee, then endured a brief discussion about the weather. He left the makeshift dining room and eased quietly down the empty, darkened hall. Several TV's could already be heard. Someone was talking on the phone. He unlocked his door and quickly set the coffee on the dresser, removed a stack of newspapers from a drawer, then left the room.

Using a key he'd stolen from the rack under the front desk, Nicholas entered Room 50, the Colonel's. The smell of cheap aftershave lingered heavily. Shoes were assembled in a perfect row against one wall. The clothes in the closet were neatly hung and precisely starched. Nicholas fell to his knees, lifted the edge of the bedspread, and deposited the newspapers and magazines under the bed. One was a copy of yesterday's *Mogul*.

He silently left the room and returned to his. An hour later he called Marlee. Assuming Fitch was listening to all of her calls, he simply said, "Darlene, please." To which she said, "Wrong number." Both hung up. He waited five minutes and dialed the number to a cellphone Marlee kept hidden in a closet. They expected Fitch to tap her phones and wire her apartment.

"Delivery's complete," he said.

Thirty minutes later Marlee left her apartment and found a pay phone at a biscuit drive-through. She called Fitch, and waited for her call to be routed.

"Good morning, Marlee," he said.

"Hey, Fitch. Look, I'd love to talk on the phone, but I know all this is getting recorded."

"No it's not. I swear."

"Right. There's a Kroger at the corner of Fourteenth and Beach Boulevard, five minutes from your office. There are three pay phones near the front entrance, right side. Go to the one in the middle. I'll call in seven minutes. Hurry, Fitch." She hung up.

"Sonofabitch!" Fitch screamed as he threw down the receiver and bolted for the door. He yelled at José and together they raced out the back door and jumped into the Suburban.

As expected, the pay phone was ringing when Fitch got there.

"Hey, Fitch. Look, Herrera, number seven, is really getting on Nick's nerves. I think we'll lose him today."

"What!"

"You heard me."

"Don't do it, Marlee!"

"Guy's a real pain. Everybody's sick of him."

"But he's on our side!"

"Oh, Fitch. They'll all be on our side when it's over. Anyway, be there at nine for the suspense."

"No, listen, Herrera is vital to—" Fitch got himself cut off in mid-sentence when he heard the click on her end. Then the line was dead. He gripped the receiver and began pulling on it, as if he'd slowly rip it from the phone and hurl it across the parking lot. Then he released it, and without cursing or yelling he calmly walked back to the Suburban and told José to go to the office.

Whatever she wanted. It didn't matter.

JUDGE HARKIN lived in Gulfport, fifteen minutes from the courthouse. For obvious reasons, his phone number was not listed in the local directory. Who needed convicts from the jail calling at all hours of the night?

As he was in the process of kissing his wife and gathering his cup of coffee for the road, the phone in the kitchen rang and Mrs. Harkin took it. "It's for you, dear," she said, handing it to His Honor, who set down his coffee and briefcase and glanced at his watch.

"Hello," he said.

"Judge, I'm sorry to bother you at home like this," said a nervous voice, one almost in a whisper. "This is Nicholas Easter, and if you want me to hang up right now, I'll do it."

"Not yet. What's the matter?"

"We're still at the motel, getting ready to leave, and, well, I think I need to talk to you first thing this morning."

"What is it, Nicholas?"

"I hate to call you, but I'm afraid some of the other jurors might be getting suspicious of our notes and chats in chambers."

"Maybe you're right."

"So I thought I'd call you. This way they'll never know we've talked."

"Let's try it. If I think we should stop the conversation, then I'll do so." Harkin wanted to ask how a sequestered juror obtained his phone number, but decided to wait.

"It's about Herrera. I think maybe he's reading some stuff that isn't on the approved list."

"Like what?"

"Like *Mogul*. I walked into the dining room early this morning. He was there all alone, and he tried to hide a copy of *Mogul* from me. Isn't that some kind of business magazine?"

"Yes, it is." Harkin had read yesterday's column by Barker. If Easter was telling the truth, and why should he doubt him, then Herrera would be sent home immediately. The reading of any unauthorized material was grounds for dismissal, maybe even contempt. The reading of yesterday's *Mogul* by any juror bordered on grounds for a mistrial. "Do you think he's discussed it with anyone else?"

"I doubt it. Like I said, he was trying to hide it from me. That's why I got suspicious. I don't think he'd discuss it with anyone. But I'll listen carefully."

"You do that. I'll call Mr. Herrera in first thing this morning and interrogate him. We'll probably search his room."

"Please don't tell him I'm the snitch. I feel rotten doing this."

"It's okay.

"If the other jurors get word we're talking, then my credibility is gone."

"Don't worry."

"I'm just nervous, Judge. We're all tired and ready to go home."

"It's almost over, Nicholas. I'm pushing the lawyers as hard as I can."

"I know. Sorry, Judge. Just make sure no one knows I'm playing the mole here. I can't believe I'm doing this."

"You're doing the right thing, Nicholas. And I thank you for it. I'll see you in a few minutes."

Harkin kissed his wife much quicker the second time, and left the house. By car phone, he called the Sheriff and asked him to go to the motel and wait. He called Lou Dell, something he did most mornings while driving to court, and asked her if *Mogul* was sold at the motel. No, it wasn't. He called his law clerk and asked her to locate both Rohr and Cable and have them waiting in chambers when he arrived. He listened to a country station and wondered how in the world a sequestered juror got a copy of a business magazine not readily available on the streets of Biloxi.

Cable and Rohr were waiting with the law clerk when Judge Harkin entered his chambers and closed his door. He removed his jacket, took his seat, and summarized the allegations against Herrera without divulging his source. Cable was annoyed because Herrera was deemed by all to be a solid defense juror. Rohr was irritated because they were losing another juror and a mistrial couldn't be far away.

With both lawyers unhappy, Judge Harkin felt much better. He sent his law clerk to the jury room to fetch Mr. Herrera, who was sipping his umpteenth cup of decaf and chatting with Herman over his braille computer. Frank glanced around quizzically after

Lou Dell called his name, and left the room. He followed Willis the deputy through the back corridors behind the courtroom. They stopped at a side door, where Willis knocked politely before entering.

The Colonel was greeted warmly by the Judge and the lawyers, and he was shown a chair in the cramped room, a chair sitting snugly next to one occupied by the court reporter, who sat ready with her stenographic machine.

Judge Harkin explained that he had a few questions which would require responses under oath, and the lawyers suddenly produced yellow legal pads and started their scribbling. Herrera immediately felt like a criminal.

"Have you been reading any materials not expressly authorized by me?" Judge Harkin asked.

A pause as the lawyers looked at him. The law clerk and the court reporter and the Judge himself were poised to pounce on his response. Even Willis by the door was awake and paying remarkable attention.

"No. Not to my knowledge," the Colonel said, truthfully.

"Specifically, have you been reading a business weekly called *Mogul*?"

"Not since I've been sequestered."

"Do you normally read *Mogul*?"

"Once, maybe twice a month."

"In your room at the motel, do you possess any reading materials not authorized by me?"

"Not to my knowledge."

"Will you consent to a search of your room?"

Frank's cheeks went red and his shoulders jerked. "What're you talking about?" he demanded.

"I have reason to believe you've been reading unauthorized materials, and that this has occurred at the motel. I think a quick search of your room might settle the matter."

"You're questioning my integrity," Herrera said, wounded and angry. His integrity was vital to him. A glance at the other faces revealed that they all thought he was guilty of some heinous transgression.

"No, Mr. Herrera. I simply believe a search will allow us to proceed with this trial."

It was just a motel room, not like a home where all sorts of private things are hidden. And, besides, Frank knew damned well there was nothing in his room that could incriminate him. "Then search it," he said with clenched teeth.

"Thank you."

Willis led Frank into the hallway outside chambers, and Judge Harkin called the Sheriff at the motel. The manager opened the door to Room 50. The Sheriff and two deputies conducted a delicate search of the closet and drawers and bathroom. Under the bed, they found a stack of *Wall Street Journals* and *Forbes* magazines, and also a copy of yesterday's *Mogul*. The Sheriff called Judge Harkin, relayed what they'd found, and was instructed to bring the unauthorized items to chambers at once.

Nine-fifteen, no jury. Fitch sat rigid on a back pew, eyes peering just barely over the top of a newspaper and staring hard at the door near the jury box, knowing full and damned well that when they finally emerged, juror number seven would not be Herrera but rather Henry Vu. Vu was mildly tolerable from a defense view because he was Asian, and Asians typically weren't the big spenders of other people's moneys in tort cases. But Vu was no Herrera, and Fitch's jury people had been telling him for weeks now that the Colonel was with them and would be a force during deliberations.

If Marlee and Nicholas could bounce Herrera on a whim, who might be next? If they were doing this solely to get Fitch's attention, then they were surely successful.

THE JUDGE and the lawyers stared in disbelief at the newspapers and magazines now lined neatly across Harkin's desk. The Sheriff dictated into the record a brief narrative of how and where the items were found, then left.

"Gentlemen, I have no choice but to excuse Mr. Herrera," His Honor said, and the lawyers said nothing. Herrera was brought back into the room and directed to the same chair.

"On the record," Judge Harkin said to the court reporter. "Mr. Herrera, what is your room number at the Siesta Inn?"

"50."

"These items were found under the bed in Room 50 just minutes ago." Harkin waved at the periodicals. "All are recent, most are dated after the date of sequestration."

Herrera was dumbfounded.

"All, of course, are unauthorized, some are highly prejudicial."

"They're not mine," Herrera said slowly, his anger building.

"I see."

"Somebody put them there."

"Who might have done this?"

"I don't know. Maybe the same person who gave you the tip."

A very good point, thought Harkin, but not one to be pursued right now. Both Cable and Rohr looked at the Judge as if to ask, Okay, who gave you the tip?

"We can't escape the fact that these were found in your room, Mr. Herrera. For this reason, I have no choice but to excuse you from further jury service."

Frank's mind was focusing now, and there were many questions he wanted to ask. He wanted to raise his voice and get in Harkin's face when he suddenly realized he was about to be set free. After four weeks of trial and nine nights at the Siesta Inn, he was about to walk out of this courthouse and go home. He'd be on the golf course by lunchtime.

"I don't think this is right," he said halfheartedly, trying not to push too hard.

"I'm very sorry. I'll deal with the contempt of court issue at a later date. As for now, we need to get on with the trial."

"Whatever you say, Judge," Frank said. Dinner tonight at Vrazel's, fresh seafood and a wine list. He could see his grandson tomorrow.

"I'll have a deputy take you back to the motel so you can pack. I am instructing you not to repeat any of this to anyone, especially members of the press. You are under a gag order until further notice. Do you understand this?"

"Yes sir."

The Colonel was escorted down the rear stairway and out the back door of the courthouse, where the Sheriff was waiting for Herrera's quick and final trip to the Siesta Inn.

"I hereby move for a mistrial," Cable said, in the direction of the court reporter. "On the grounds that this jury may have been improperly influenced by the story appearing in *Mogul* yesterday."

"Motion denied," Judge Harkin said. "Anything else?"

The lawyers shook their heads and stood.

□ □ □ □

THE ELEVEN JURORS and two alternates took their seats at a few minutes after ten, as the courtroom watched silently. Frank's seat on the second row, far left, was empty, and this was immediately noticed by everyone. Judge Harkin greeted them with a solemn face and got quickly to the point. He held a copy of yesterday's *Mogul* and asked if anyone had seen or read it, or if anyone had heard anything about what was in it. No volunteers.

He then said, "For reasons that have been made clear in chambers, and placed in the record, juror number seven, Frank Herrera, has been dismissed and will now be replaced by the next alternate, Mr. Henry Vu." At this point, Willis said something to Henry, who left his padded folding chair and took four steps to seat number seven, where he became an official member of the panel and left Shine Royce as the sole remaining alternate.

Desperate to move things along and divert attention away from his jury, Judge Harkin said, "Mr. Cable, call your next witness."

Fitch's newspaper dropped six inches, down to his chest, and his mouth dropped too as he stared at the new composition with bewilderment. He was scared because Herrera was gone, and he was thrilled because his girl Marlee had waved her wand and delivered exactly what she'd promised. Fitch couldn't help but look at Easter, who must have felt it because he turned slightly and caught Fitch's eyes with his own. For five or six seconds, an eternity for Fitch, they stared at each other from ninety feet. Easter's face was smirking and proud, as if to say, "Look what I can do. Are you impressed?" Fitch's face said, "Yes. Now, what do you want?"

In the pretrial order, Cable had listed twenty-two possible witnesses, virtually all with the word Doctor somewhere in their names, and all with solid credentials. His stable included battle-tested veterans of other cigarette trials, and prickly researchers funded by Big Tobacco, and myriad other mouthpieces assembled to counterattack what the jury had already heard.

During the past two years, all twenty-two had been deposed by Rohr and his gang. There would be no surprises.

The consensus was that the plaintiff's heaviest blows had been landed by Leon Robilio and his claims that kids were targeted by the industry. Cable thought it best to attack there first. "The defense calls Dr. Denise McQuade," he announced.

She presented herself through a side door, and the courtroom, heavily dominated by middle-aged men, seemed to stiffen a bit as she strolled in front of the bench, smiled up at His Honor, who was most definitely smiling down, and took her seat in the witness chair. Dr. McQuade was a beautiful woman, tall and thin with a short red dress just inches above her knees, and blond hair pulled severely back and tucked away behind her head. She took her oath with a comely smile, and when she crossed her legs she had an audience. She seemed much too young and much too pretty to be involved in a nasty brawl like this.

The six men on the jury, especially Jerry Fernandez, along with Shine Royce, the alternate, paid very close attention as she gently pulled the microphone close to her mouth. Red lipstick. Long red fingernails.

If they were expecting a bimbo they were quickly disappointed. Her husky voice detailed her education, background, training, field of expertise. She was a behavioral psychologist with her own firm in Tacoma. She'd written four books, published over three dozen articles, and Wendall Rohr had no objection when Cable moved to have Dr. McQuade declared as an expert.

She got right to the point. Advertising permeates our culture. Ads directed at one age group or one class of people quite naturally are heard and seen by those not in the target group. This cannot be prevented. Kids see tobacco ads because kids see newspapers and magazines and billboards and flashing neon lights in convenience store windows, but this doesn't mean the kids are targeted. Kids also see beer commercials on TV, commercials often made by their favorite sports heroes. Does this mean beer companies are subliminally trying to hook the next generation? Of course not. They're simply trying to sell more beer to their market. The kids just get in the way, but there's nothing that can be done about it short of banning all advertising for all offensive products. Cigarettes, beer, wine, liquor, what about coffee and tea and condoms, and butter? Do ads by credit card companies encourage people to spend more and save less? Dr. McQuade made the point repeatedly that in a society where free speech is a valued right, restrictions on advertising are carefully scrutinized.

Cigarette ads are no different from others. Their purpose is to reinforce a person's desire to buy and use the product. Good ads stimulate the natural response to rush out and purchase what's being advertised. Ineffective ads do not, and normally are quickly pulled. She used the example of McDonald's, a company she had studied, and she just happened to have a report handy in the event the jury wanted to peruse it. By the time a child is three, the child can hum, whistle, or sing whatever the current McDonald's jingle happens to be. The child's first trip to McDonald's is a momentous occasion. This is no accident. The corporation spends billions to hook children before its competitors do. American children consume more fat and cholesterol than the last generation. They eat more cheeseburgers, fries, and pizza, and drink more sodas and sugared fruit drinks. Do we charge McDonald's and Pizza Hut with devious advertising practices for targeting the young? Do we sue them because our kids are fatter?

No. We as consumers make informed choices about the foods we feed our children. No one can argue that we make the best choices.

And we as consumers make informed choices about smoking. We are bombarded with ads for thousands of products, and we respond to those ads which reinforce our needs and desires.

She crossed and recrossed her legs every twenty minutes or so, and each crossing was duly noted by the packs of lawyers around both tables and by the six male jurors and most of the females as well.

Dr. McQuade was pleasant to look at and easy to believe. Her testimony made perfect sense, and she connected with most of the jurors.

Rohr sparred with her politely for an hour on cross but didn't land a serious punch.

Thirty

ACCORDING to Napier and Nitchman, Mr. Cristano at Justice desperately wanted a full report on what had happened last night when Hoppy met Millie for their latest personal visit. "Everything?" Hoppy asked. The three were huddled over a rickety table in a smoky diner, sipping boiled coffee from paper cups and waiting for greasy grilled cheese sandwiches.

"Skip the personal stuff," Napier said, doubtful if there was much personal stuff to skip.

If they only knew, Hoppy thought, still quite proud of himself. "Well, I showed Millie the memo on Robilio," he said, not knowing how much of the truth he should tell.

"And?"

"And, well, she read it."

"Of course she read it. Then what did she do?" Napier asked.

"What was her response?" Nitchman asked.

Sure, he could lie and tell them she was stunned by the memo, believed every word of it, and couldn't wait to show it to her pals on the jury. That's what they wanted to hear. But Hoppy didn't know what to do. Lying could only make matters worse. "She didn't respond too well," he said, then told them the truth.

When the sandwiches arrived, Nitchman left to call Mr. Cristano. Hoppy and Napier ate without looking at each other. Hoppy felt like such a failure. Surely he was one step closer to prison.

"When do you see her again?" asked Napier.

"Not sure. The Judge hasn't said yet. There's a chance the trial could be over this weekend."

Nitchman returned and took his seat. "Mr. Cristano is on his way," he said gravely, and Hoppy's stomach began to churn. "He'll be here late tonight and wants to meet with you first thing in the morning."

"Sure."

"He is not a happy man."

"Neither am I."

ROHR SPENT his lunch hour locked in his office with Cleve, doing the dirty work that had to be kept to themselves. Most of the other lawyers used runners like Cleve to spread cash and chase cases and perform dark little deeds not taught in law school, but none of them would ever admit to such unethical activity. Trial lawyers keep their runners to themselves.

Rohr had several choices. He could tell Cleve to tell Derrick Maples to get lost. He could pay Derrick Maples $25,000 in cash, and he could promise another $25,000 for each plaintiff's vote in the final verdict, assuming there would be at least nine. This would cost $225,000 at most, a sum Rohr was perfectly willing to pay. But he was extremely doubtful Angel Weese could deliver more than two votes—her own and maybe Loreen Duke's. She was not a leader. He could manipulate Derrick into approaching the lawyers for the defense, then try to catch them in bed together. This would probably result in Angel's getting removed, an event Rohr did not want.

Rohr could wire Cleve, capture incriminating statements from Derrick, then threaten the kid with criminal prosecution if he didn't lean on his girlfriend. This was risky, because the bribery plot had been hatched in Rohr's own office.

They covered each scenario with the seasoned judgment of men who'd done it before. A hybrid was developed.

"Here's what we'll do," Rohr said. "We'll give him fifteen grand now, promise the other ten after the verdict, and we'll also get him on tape now. We'll mark some of the bills, set him up for later. We'll promise him twenty-five for the other votes, and if we get our verdict, then we'll screw him when he demands the rest.

We'll have him on tape, and when he makes noise we'll threaten to call the FBI."

"I like it," Cleve said. "He gets his money, we get our verdict, he gets screwed. Sounds like justice to me."

"Get yourself wired and get the cash. This needs to be done this afternoon."

BUT DERRICK had other plans. They met in a lounge at the Resort Casino, a dark bar sadly filled with losers massaging their losses with cheap drinks while outside the sun was shining brightly and the temperature was inching toward seventy.

Derrick wasn't about to get a postverdict screwing. He wanted Angel's twenty-five thousand in cash, now, up front, and he also wanted a "deposit," as he called it, for each of the other jurors. A preverdict deposit. In cash too, of course, something reasonable and fair, say, five thousand per juror. Cleve did the quick math, and got it wrong. Derrick was figuring on a unanimous verdict, so the deposit of five grand times eleven other jurors worked out nicely to fifty-five thousand dollars. Add Angel's, and all Derrick wanted was eighty thousand cash now.

He knew a girl in the clerk's office, and this friend had looked at the file. "You guys are suing the tobacco company for millions," he said, every word getting captured by a body mike in Cleve's shirt pocket. "Eighty thousand is a drop in the bucket."

"You're crazy," Cleve said.

"And you're crooked."

"There's no way we can pay eighty thousand cash. Like I said before, when the money gets too big, then we run the risk of getting caught."

"Fine. I'll go talk to the tobacco company."

"You do that. I'll read about it in the newspapers."

They didn't finish their drinks. Cleve again left early, but this time Derrick did not chase him.

THE PARADE of beauties continued Thursday afternoon as Cable put on the stand Dr. Myra Sprawling-Goode, a black professor and researcher at Rutgers who turned every head in the depraved courtroom as she presented herself for testimony. She was almost six feet tall, as striking and slender and well dressed as the last witness. Her creamy light brown skin creased perfectly as she smiled at the jurors, a smile that lingered on Lonnie Shaver, who actually smiled back.

Cable had an unlimited budget when he began his search for experts, so he was not compelled to use people who weren't sharp and glib and able to connect with average folk. He had video-taped Dr. Sprawling-Goode twice before he hired her, then once during her deposition in Rohr's office. Like all his witnesses, she had spent two days getting grilled in a mock courtroom setting a month before the trial began. She crossed her legs and the court-room took a collective deep breath.

She was a professor of marketing with two doctorates and im-pressive credentials, no surprise. She'd spent eight years in adver-tising on Madison Avenue after she had completed her education, then returned to academia, where she belonged. Her field of ex-pertise was consumer advertising, a subject she taught at the grad-uate level and one she researched continually. Her purpose at the trial soon became clear. A cynic might have claimed she was there to look pretty, to connect with Lonnie Shaver and Loreen Duke and Angel Weese, to make them proud that a fellow African-American was perfectly capable of projecting expert opinions in this crucial trial.

She was actually there because of Fitch. Six years earlier, after a scare in New Jersey in which a jury stayed out three days before returning with a defense verdict, Fitch had hatched the plan to find an attractive female researcher, preferably at a reputable uni-versity, to take a chunk of grant money and study cigarette adver-tising and its effects on teenagers. The parameters of the project would be vaguely defined by the source of the money, and Fitch was hoping the study would one day be useful in a trial.

Dr. Sprawling-Goode had never heard of Rankin Fitch. She had received an eight-hundred-thousand-dollar grant from the Con-sumer Product Institute, an obscure and previously unheard of think tank in Ottawa which existed, it claimed, to study the mar-keting trends of thousands of consumer products. She knew little about the Consumer Product Institute. Neither did Rohr. He and his investigators had been digging for two years. It was very pri-vate, protected to some degree by Canadian law, and apparently funded by large consumer product companies, none of which ap-peared to be cigarette manufacturers.

Her findings were contained in a handsome, bound, two-inch-thick report, which Cable got admitted into evidence. It joined a stack of other exhibits as an official piece of the record. Exhibit number eighty-four, to be exact, adding to the twenty thousand or so pages already in evidence and expected to be reviewed by the jury during deliberations.

After the thorough and efficient setup, her findings were succinct and unsurprising. With certain clearly defined and obvious exceptions, all advertising for consumer products is aimed at young adults. Cars, toothpaste, soap, cereal, beer, soft drinks, apparel, cologne—all of the most heavily advertised products have young adults as their target audience. The same is true for cigarettes. Sure, they are portrayed as the products of choice of the thin and beautiful, the active and carefree, the rich and glamorous. But so are countless other products.

She then ticked off a list of specifics, starting with automobiles. When was the last time you saw a TV ad for a sports car with a fat fifty-year-old man behind the wheel? Or a mini-van driven by an obese housewife with six kids and a dirty dog hanging out the windows? Never happens. Beer? You got ten guys sitting in a den watching the Super Bowl. Most have hair, strong chins, perfect jeans, and flat stomachs. This is not reality, but it's successful advertising.

Her testimony became quite humorous as she went through her list. Toothpaste? Ever see an ugly person with ugly teeth grinning at you through the TV? Of course not. They all have perfect teeth. Even in the acne commercials the troubled teens have only a pimple or two.

She smiled easily and even giggled at times at her own comments. The jury smiled along with her. Her point found its mark repeatedly. If successful advertising depends on targeting young adults, why shouldn't tobacco companies be allowed to do it?

She stopped smiling when Cable moved her to the issue of targeting kids. She and her research team had found no evidence of this, and they had studied thousands of tobacco ads over the past forty years. They had watched, studied, and cataloged every cigarette ad used during the TV days. And she noted, almost in an aside, that smoking had increased since such ads were banned from TV. She had spent almost two years searching for evidence that tobacco companies target teens, because she had started the project with this unfounded bias. But it simply wasn't true.

In her opinion, the only way to prevent kids from being influenced by cigarette ads was to ban all of them—billboards, buses, newspapers, magazines, coupons. And, in her opinion, this would do nothing to slow tobacco sales. It would have no impact whatsoever on underage smoking.

Cable thanked her as if she were a volunteer. She'd already been paid sixty thousand dollars to testify, and would send a bill for another fifteen. Rohr, who was anything but a gentleman, knew the pitfalls of attacking such a pretty lady in the Deep South. He delicately probed instead. He had lots of questions about the Consumer Product Institute, and the eight hundred thousand dollars it had paid for this study. She told him everything she knew. It was an academic body established to study trends and formulate policy. It was funded by private industry.

"Any tobacco companies?"

"Not that I'm aware of."

"Any subsidiaries of tobacco companies?"

"I'm not sure."

He asked her about companies related to tobacco companies, parent companies, sister companies, and divisions and conglomerates, and she knew nothing.

She knew nothing because that was the way Fitch had planned it.

CLAIRE'S TRAIL took an unexpected turn Thursday morning. The ex-boyfriend of a friend of Claire's took a thousand dollars in cash and said his ex-girlfriend was now in Greenwich Village working as a waitress while aspiring to do serious work in soap operas. His ex-girlfriend and Claire had worked together at Mulligan's and allegedly had been close friends. Swanson flew to New York, arrived late Thursday afternoon, and took a cab to a small hotel in SoHo where he paid cash for one night and started making calls. He found Beverly at work in a pizzeria. She answered the phone in a hurry.

"Is this Beverly Monk?" Swanson asked, in his best imitation of Nicholas Easter. He'd listened to his recorded voice many times.

"It is. Who is this?"

"The Beverly Monk who once worked at Mulligan's in Lawrence?"

A pause, then, "Yes. Who is this?"

"This is Jeff Kerr, Beverly. It's been a long time." Swanson and Fitch were gambling that after Claire and Jeff left Lawrence they had not kept in touch with Beverly.

"Who?" she asked, and Swanson was relieved.

"Jeff Kerr. You know, I went with Claire. I was a law student."

"Oh yeah," she said as if maybe she remembered him and maybe she didn't.

"Look, I'm in the city, and I was wondering if you've heard from Claire recently."

"I don't understand," she said slowly, obviously trying to place the name with the face and figure out who was who and why was he here.

"Yeah, it's a long story, but Claire and I split six months ago. I'm sorta looking for her."

"I haven't talked to Claire in four years."

"Oh, I see."

"Look, I'm real busy. Maybe some other time."

"Sure." Swanson hung up and called Fitch. They decided it was worth the risk to approach Beverly Monk, with cash, and ask about Claire. If she hadn't talked to her in four years, it would be impossible for her to quickly find Marlee and report the contact. Swanson would follow her, and wait until tomorrow.

EACH JURY CONSULTANT was required by Fitch to prepare a one-page report at the close of trial each day. One page, double-spaced, straightforward, with no words beyond four syllables and setting forth in clear language that expert's impressions of the day's witnesses and how their testimony was received by the jury. Fitch demanded honest opinions, and had berated his experts before when the language was too sugary. He insisted on pessimism. The reports were due on his desk precisely one hour after Judge Harkin recessed for the day.

Wednesday's reports on Jankle were mixed to bad, but Thursday's summaries of Dr. Denise McQuade and Dr. Myra Sprawling-Goode were nothing short of magnificent. Aside from brightening up a drab courtroom packed with boring men in dull suits, both women had performed well on the stand. The jurors paid attention, and seemed to believe what they heard. Especially the men.

Still, Fitch was not consoled. He had never felt worse at this point in a trial. The defense had lost one of its most sympathetic jurors with the exit of Herrera. The New York financial press had suddenly declared the defense to be on the ropes and was openly concerned about a plaintiff's verdict. Barker's column in *Mogul* was the week's hottest topic. Jankle had been a disaster. Luther Vandemeer of Trellco, the smartest and most influential of the Big Four CEO's, had called with harsh words during lunch. The jury was sequestered, and the longer the trial dragged on, the more blame the jurors would heap upon the party now calling the witnesses.

THE TENTH NIGHT of sequestration passed without incident. No wayward lovers. No unauthorized trips to casinos. No spontaneous yoga at full volume. Herrera was missed by no one. He had packed in minutes and left, telling the Sheriff repeatedly he was being framed and vowing to get to the bottom of it.

An impromptu checkers tournament began in the dining room after dinner. Herman had a braille board with numbered spaces, and the night before, he'd whipped Jerry eleven straight games. Challenges were issued, and Herman's wife brought his board to the room and a crowd gathered. In less than an hour, he took three straight from Nicholas, three more from Jerry, three from Henry Vu, who'd never played the game, three straight from Willis, and was about to play Jerry again, this time for a small wager, when Loreen Duke entered the room in search of another dessert. She'd played the game as a child with her father. When she beat Herman in the first game, there was not the slightest trace of sympathy for the blind man. They played until curfew.

Phillip Savelle stayed in his room, as usual. He spoke occasionally during meals at the motel and during coffee breaks in the jury room, but he was perfectly content to keep his nose in a book and ignore everyone.

Nicholas had tried twice to reach him, to no avail. He would not suffer small talk, and wanted no one to know anything about him.

Thirty-one

AFTER ALMOST TWENTY YEARS of shrimping, Henry Vu seldom slept past four-thirty. He got his hot tea early on Friday, and with the Colonel gone he sat alone at the table and scanned a newspaper. Nicholas soon joined him. As he often did, Nicholas hurried through the pleasantries and asked about Vu's daughter at Harvard. She was the source of immense pride, and Henry's eyes danced when he told of her last letter.

Others came and went. The conversation turned to Vietnam and the war. Nicholas confided in Henry for the first time that his father had been killed there in 1972. It wasn't true, but Henry was deeply touched by the story. Then, when they were alone, Nicholas asked, "So what do you think about this trial?"

Henry took a long drink of heavily creamed tea, and licked his lips. "Is it okay to talk about it?"

"Sure. It's just me and you. Everybody's talking, Henry. That's the nature of a jury. Everybody but Herman."

"What does everybody else think?"

"I think most of us have an open mind. The most important thing is that we stick together. It's crucial that this jury reach a verdict, preferably unanimous, but at least a vote of nine to three one way or the other. A hung jury would be disastrous."

Henry took another drink and pondered this. He understood English perfectly, could speak it well though with an accent, but like most laymen, natives and immigrants alike, had little grasp of the law. "Why?" he asked. He trusted Nicholas, as did virtually all the jurors, because Nicholas had studied the law and seemed incredibly adept at comprehending facts and issues the rest of them missed.

"Very simple. This is the mother of all tobacco trials—Gettysburg, Iwo Jima, Armageddon. This is where the two sides have met to unload their heaviest ammo. There's gotta be a winner, and there's gotta be a loser. Clear and decisive. The issue of whether tobacco companies are to be held liable for cigarettes has to be settled right here. By us. We've been chosen, and it's up to us to reach a verdict."

"I see," Henry said, nodding, still confused.

"The worst thing we can do is hang ourselves, split down the middle and have a mistrial declared."

"Why would that be so bad?"

"Because it's a cop-out. We'd simply be passing the buck to the next jury. If we get hung up and go home, it'll cost each side millions of dollars because they'll have to come back in two years and replay the whole thing. Same judge, same lawyers, same witnesses, everything will be the same but the jury. We will, in effect, be saying that we didn't have enough sense to reach a decision, but the next jury from Harrison County will be smarter."

Henry leaned to his right a bit, in the direction of Nicholas. "What're you gonna do?" he asked, just as Millie Dupree and Mrs. Gladys Card entered giggling and went for the coffee. They chatted with the guys for a moment, then left to watch Katie on the "Today Show." They just loved Katie.

"What're you gonna do?" Henry whispered again, eyes on the door.

"I don't know right now, and it's not important. The important thing is for us to stick together. All of us."

"You're right," Henry said.

DURING THE COURSE of the trial, Fitch had developed the habit of keeping himself busy at his desk during the hours before court while staring at the phone. His eyes seldom left it. He knew she would call Friday morning, though he had no idea what scheme or ploy or heart-stopping prank she'd be up to.

At eight sharp, Konrad interrupted on the intercom with the simple words "It's her."

Fitch lunged for the phone. "Hello," he said pleasantly.

"Hey, Fitch. Look, guess who's bothering Nicholas now?"

He stifled a groan and closed his eyes hard. "I don't know," he said.

"I mean, this guy is really giving Nicholas a hard time. We might have to bump him."

"Who?" Fitch pleaded.

"Lonnie Shaver."

"Oh! Damn! No! You can't do that!"

"Gee, Fitch."

"Don't do it, Marlee! Dammit!"

She paused to let him despair for a second. "You must be fond of Lonnie."

"You gotta stop this, Marlee, okay? This is getting us nowhere." Fitch was very aware of how desperate he sounded, but he was no longer in control.

"Nicholas has to have harmony on his jury. That's all. Lonnie has become a thorn."

"Don't do it, please. Let's talk about this."

"We're talking, Fitch, but not for long."

Fitch took a deep breath, then another. "The game is almost over, Marlee. You've had your fun, now what do you want?"

"Got a pen?"

"Sure."

"There's a building on Fulton Street, Number 120. White brick, two stories, an old building chopped into tiny offices. Upstairs, Number 16, belongs to me, for at least another month. It's not pretty, but that's where we'll meet."

"When?"

"In an hour. Just the two of us. I'll watch you come and go, and if I see any of your goons then I'll never speak to you again."

"Sure. Whatever."

"And I'll check you for bugs and mikes."

"There won't be any."

EVERY LAWYER on Cable's defense team held the opinion that Rohr had spent too much time with his scientists; nine full days in all. But with the first seven, the jury had at least been free to go home at night. The mood was vastly different now. The decision was made to pick their two best researchers, get them on the stand, and get them off as quickly as possible.

They had also made the decision to ignore the issue of nicotine addiction, a radical departure from the normal defense in cigarette cases. Cable and his crew had studied each of the sixteen previous trials. They had talked to many of the jurors who had decided those cases, and they were repeatedly told that the weakest part of the defense came when the experts put forth all sorts of fancy theories to prove that nicotine was in fact not addictive. Everyone knew the opposite to be true. It was that simple.

Don't try to convince jurors otherwise.

The decision required Fitch's approval, which he grudgingly gave.

The first witness Friday morning was a shaggy-headed nerd with a thin red beard and heavy bifocals. The beauty show was apparently over. His name was Dr. Gunther, and it was his opinion that cigarette smoking really didn't cause cancer after all. Only ten percent of smokers get cancer, so what about the other ninety percent? Not surprisingly, Gunther had a stack of relevant studies and reports, and couldn't wait to stand before the jury with a tripod and a pointer and explain in breathless detail his latest findings.

Gunther was not there to prove anything. His job was to contradict Dr. Hilo Kilvan and Dr. Robert Bronsky, experts for the plaintiff, and to muddy the waters so there would be considerable doubt in the minds of the jurors about just how deadly smoking really was. He couldn't prove smoking didn't cause lung cancer, and he argued that no amount of research had proved that smoking absolutely does cause it. "More research is needed," he said every ten minutes.

ON THE CHANCE that she might be watching, Fitch walked the last block to 120 Fulton Street, a pleasant stroll along the shaded sidewalk with leaves dropping gently from above. The building was in the old part of town, four blocks from the Gulf, in a neat line of carefully painted two-stories, most of which seemed to be offices. José was told to wait three streets over.

No chance of a body mike or a wire. She'd broken him of that habit at their last meeting, on the pier. Fitch was alone, wireless, mikeless, bugless, without a camera or an agent nearby. He felt liberated. He would have to survive by brains and wit, and he welcomed the challenge.

He climbed the sagging wooden stairs, stood before her unmarked office door, took notice of the other unmarked doors in the cramped hallway, and gently knocked. "Who is it?" came her voice.

"Rankin Fitch," he answered just loud enough to be heard.

A dead bolt rattled from the inside, then Marlee appeared in a gray sweatshirt and blue jeans, no smile at all, no greeting of any sort. She closed the door behind Fitch, locked it, and walked to one side of a rented folding table. Fitch took the measure of the room, a cubbyhole with no window, one door, peeling paint, three chairs, and a table. "Nice place," he said, looking at the brown water spots on the ceiling.

"It's clean, Fitch. No phones for you to tap, no vents for cameras, no wires in the walls. I'll check it every morning, and if I find your trail, then I'll simply walk out the door and never come back."

"You have a low impression of me."

"It's one you deserve."

Fitch looked again at the ceiling, then the floor. "I like the place."

"It'll serve its purpose."

"Its purpose being?"

Her purse was the only item on the table. She removed the same sensor-scan from it, and aimed it at Fitch from head to toe.

"Come on, Marlee," he protested. "I promised."

"Yeah right. You're clean. Have a seat," she said, nodding at one of two chairs on his side of the table. Fitch shook the folding chair, a rather thin job that might not meet his challenge. He lowered himself onto it, then leaned forward with his elbows on the table, which was also not too stable, so he was perched precariously at both ends. "Are we ready to talk money?" he asked with a nasty grin.

"Yes. It's a simple deal, really, Fitch. You wire me a bunch of money, and I promise to deliver you a verdict."

"I think we should wait until after the verdict."

"You know I'm not that stupid."

The folding table was three feet wide. Both were leaning on it, their faces not far apart. Fitch often used his bulk and his nasty eyes and his sinister goatee to physically intimidate those around him, especially the younger lawyers in the firms he hired. If Marlee was intimidated, she certainly didn't show it. Fitch admired her poise. She stared straight into his eyes, never blinking, a most difficult task.

"Then there are no guarantees," he said. "Juries are unpredictable. We could give you the money—"

"Drop it, Fitch. You and I both know the money will be paid before the verdict."

"How much money?"

"Ten million."

He managed a guttural discharge, as if choking on a golf ball, then he coughed loudly as his elbows flew up and his eyes rolled and his fat jowls shook in utter, sheer disbelief. "You must be kidding," he managed to say in a raspy voice, glancing around for a cup of water or a bottle of pills or anything to help him through this horrible shock.

She watched the show calmly, never blinking, never taking her eyes off him. "Ten million, Fitch. It's a bargain. And it's nonnegotiable."

He coughed again, his face slightly redder. Then he gathered his composure and thought of a response. He'd guessed in the millions, and he knew he'd sound foolish trying to negotiate down as if his client couldn't afford it. She probably had the latest quarterly reports for each of the Big Four.

"How much is in The Fund?" she asked, and Fitch's eyes instinctively narrowed. As far as he could tell, she hadn't blinked yet.

"The what?" he asked. No one knew about The Fund!

"The Fund, Fitch. Don't play games with me. I know all about your little slush fund. I want the ten million wired from The Fund account to a bank in Singapore."

"I don't think I can do that."

"You can do anything you want, Fitch. Stop playing games. Let's cut the deal now and get on with our business."

"What if we wire five now and five after the verdict?"

"Forget it, Fitch. It's ten million now. I don't like the idea of tracking you down and trying to collect the last installment after the trial. For some reason, I think I'd waste a lot of time."

"When do we wire it?"

"I don't care. Just make sure it's received before the jury gets the case. Otherwise the deal is off."

"What happens if the deal is off?"

"One of two things. Either Nicholas will hang the jury, or he'll send it nine to three for the plaintiff."

The veneer cracked above the eyebrows, two long wrinkles pinched together as he absorbed these predictions, delivered so matter-of-factly. Fitch had no doubts about what Nicholas could do because Marlee had no doubts. He slowly rubbed his eyes. The game was over. No more exaggerated reactions to anything she said. No more feigned disbelief at her demands. She was in control.

"It's a deal," he said. "We'll wire the money, pursuant to your instructions. I must warn you, though, that wires can take time."

"I know more about wiring money than you do, Fitch. I'll explain precisely how I want it done. Later."

"Yes ma'am."

"So we have a deal?"

"Yes," he said, extending his hand across the table. She shook it limply. Both smiled at the absurdity. Two crooks shaking hands over an agreement no court of law could enforce because no court of law would ever know about it.

BEVERLY MONK'S APARTMENT was a fifth-floor loft in a dingy Village warehouse. She shared it with four other starving actresses. Swanson followed her to a corner coffee shop and waited until she had settled at a window table with an espresso, a bagel, and a newspaper with want ads. With his back to the other tables, he approached her and asked, "Excuse me. Are you Beverly Monk?"

She looked up, startled, and said, "Yes. Who are you?"

"A friend of Claire Clement's," he said as he quickly slid into the chair across from her.

"Have a seat," she said. "What do you want?" She was nervous but the shop was crowded. She was safe, she thought. He looked nice enough.

"Information."

"You called me yesterday, didn't you?"

"Yes, I did. I lied, said I was Jeff Kerr. I'm not."

"Then who are you?"

"Jack Swanson. I work for some lawyers in Washington."

"Is Claire in trouble?"

"None whatsoever."

"Then what's all the fuss?"

Swanson gave a quick version of Claire's summons for jury service in a huge trial and his duty to track down the backgrounds of certain prospective jurors. This time it was a contaminated landfill case in Houston where billions were at stake, thus the expense of digging so deeply.

Swanson and Fitch were gambling on two things. The first was Beverly's slow recognition of Jeff Kerr's name on the phone yesterday. The second was her assertion that she hadn't talked to Claire in four years. They were assuming both to be genuine.

"We'll pay for information," Swanson said.

"How much?"

"A thousand dollars cash to tell me everything you know about Claire Clement." Swanson quickly removed an envelope from his coat pocket and laid it on the table.

"Are you sure she's in no trouble?" asked Beverly, staring at the gold mine before her.

"I'm sure. Take the money. If you haven't seen her in four or five years, why should you care?"

Good point, thought Beverly. She grabbed the envelope and stuck it in her purse. "There's not much to tell."

"How long did you work with her?"

"Six months."

"How long did you know her?"

"Six months. I was working as a waitress at Mulligan's when she started. We got to be friends. Then I left town and drifted east. I called her once or twice when I lived in New Jersey, then we sorta just forgot about each other."

"Did you know Jeff Kerr?"

"No. She wasn't dating him at the time. She told me about him later, after I'd left town."

"Did she have other friends, male and female?"

"Yeah, sure. Don't ask me to name them. I left Lawrence five, maybe six years ago. I really don't remember when I left."

"You can't name any of her friends?"

Beverly drank some espresso and thought for a minute. Then

she rattled off the names of three people who'd worked with Claire. One had been checked out with no results. One was being tracked at the moment. One had not been found.

"Where did Claire go to college?"

"Somewhere in the Midwest."

"You don't know the name of the school?"

"I don't think so. Claire was very quiet about her past. You got the impression something bad happened back there, and she didn't talk about it. I never knew. I thought maybe it was a bad romance, maybe even a marriage, or maybe a bad family, rotten childhood, or something. But I never knew."

"Did she discuss it with anybody?"

"Not to my knowledge."

"Do you know her hometown?"

"She said she moved around a lot. Again, I didn't ask a lot of questions."

"Was she from the Kansas City area?"

"I don't know."

"Are you sure her real name was Claire Clement?"

Beverly withdrew and frowned. "You think maybe it wasn't?"

"We have reason to believe she was someone else before she arrived in Lawrence, Kansas. Do you remember anything about another name?"

"Wow. I just assumed she was Claire. Why would she change her name?"

"We'd love to know." Swanson removed a small notepad from a pocket and studied a checklist. Beverly was another dead end.

"Did you ever go to her apartment?"

"Once or twice. We'd cook and watch movies. She didn't party much, but she invited me over with friends."

"Anything unusual about her apartment?"

"Yeah. It was very nice, a modern condo, well furnished. It was obvious she had money from sources other than Mulligan's. I mean, we got paid three bucks an hour plus tips."

"So she had money?"

"Yeah. A lot more than we did. But, again, she was very secretive. Claire was a casual friend and a fun person to be around. You just didn't ask a lot of questions."

Swanson pressed her on other details and came up dry. He

thanked her for her help and she thanked him for the cash, and as he was leaving she offered to make a few calls. It was an obvious solicitation for more money. Swanson said fine, but then cautioned her about revealing what she was doing.

"Look, I'm an actress, okay. This is a piece of cake."

He left her a business card with his Biloxi hotel number written on the back.

HOPPY THOUGHT Mr. Cristano was a bit too harsh. But then, the situation was deteriorating, according to the mysterious folks in Washington whom Mr. Cristano answered to. There was discussion at Justice about simply aborting the whole scheme and sending Hoppy's case on to the federal grand jury.

If Hoppy couldn't convince his own wife, how the hell was he supposed to influence an entire jury?

They sat in the back of the long black Chrysler and drove along the Gulf toward nowhere in particular but Mobile in general. Nichtman drove and Napier rode shotgun and both managed to act completely oblivious to the mauling of Hoppy in the backseat.

"When do you see her again?" Cristano asked.

"Tonight, I think."

"The time has come, Hoppy, for you to tell her the truth. Tell her what you've done, tell her everything."

Hoppy's eyes watered and his lip quivered as he stared at the tinted window and saw his wife's pretty eyes as he laid bare his soul. He cursed himself for his stupidity. If he had a gun he could almost shoot Todd Ringwald and Jimmy Hull Moke, but he could most definitely shoot himself. Maybe he'd take these three clowns out first, but, no doubt about it, Hoppy could blow his own brains out.

"I guess so," he mumbled.

"Your wife must become an advocate, Hoppy. Do you realize this? Millie Dupree has to be a force in that jury room. Since you've been unable to convince her with the merits, now you have to motivate her with the fear of seeing you go off to prison for five years. You have no choice."

At the moment, he'd rather face prison than face Millie with the truth. But he didn't have that choice. If he didn't convince her, she'd learn the truth *and* he'd go off to prison.

Hoppy started crying. He bit his lip and covered his eyes and tried to stop the damned tears, but he couldn't help it. As they drove peacefully along the highway, the only sounds for several miles were the pitiful whimperings of a broken man.

Only Nitchman couldn't conceal a tiny grin.

Thirty-two

THE SECOND MEETING in Marlee's office began an hour after the first one ended. Fitch arrived again on foot with a briefcase and a large cup of coffee. Marlee scanned the briefcase for hidden devices, much to his amusement.

When she finished, he closed his briefcase and sipped his coffee. "I have a question," he announced.

"What?"

"Six months ago, neither you nor Easter lived in this county, probably not in this state. Did you move here to watch this trial?" He knew the answer, of course, but he wanted to see how much she would admit, now that they were business partners and supposedly working on the same side.

"You could say that," she said. Marlee and Nicholas were assuming that Fitch had now tracked them back to Lawrence, and this was not altogether bad. Fitch had to appreciate their ability to hatch such a plot, and their commitment to carry it out. It was Marlee's pre-Lawrence days that had them losing sleep.

"You're both using aliases, aren't you?" he asked.

"No. We're using our legal names. No more questions about us, Fitch. We're not important. Time is short, and we have work to do."

"Perhaps we should begin by your telling me how far you've gone with the other side. How much does Rohr know?"

"Rohr knows nothing. We danced and shadowboxed, but never connected."

"Would you have cut a deal with him had I not been willing?"

"Yes. I'm in it for the money, Fitch. Nicholas is on that jury because we planned it that way. We have worked for this moment. It'll work because all the players are corrupt. You're corrupt. Your clients are corrupt. My partner and I are corrupt. Corrupt but smart. We pollute the system in such a way that we cannot be detected."

"What about Rohr? He'll be suspicious when he loses. In fact, he'll suspect you've cut a deal with the tobacco company."

"Rohr doesn't know me. We never met."

"Come on."

"I swear it, Fitch. I made you think I had met him, but it never happened. It would have, though, had you not been willing to negotiate."

"You knew I'd be willing."

"Of course. We knew you'd be more than anxious to purchase a verdict."

Oh, he had so many questions. How did they learn of his existence? How did they get his phone numbers? How did they make certain Nicholas would be summoned for jury duty? How did they get him on the jury? And how in hell did they learn about The Fund?

He would ask them one day when this was behind them and the pressure was off. He'd love to chat with Marlee and Nicholas over a long dinner and get all his questions answered. His admiration for them grew by the moment.

"Promise me you won't bump Lonnie Shaver," he said.

"I'll make the promise, Fitch, if you'll tell why you're so fond of Lonnie."

"He's on our side."

"How do you know this?"

"We have ways."

"Look, Fitch, if we're both working for the same verdict, then why can't we be honest?"

"You know, you're right. Why'd you bump Herrera?"

"I told you. He's an ass. He didn't like Nicholas and Nicholas didn't like him. Plus, Henry Vu and Nicholas are buddies. So we didn't lose anything."

"Why'd you bump Stella Hulic?"

"Just to get her out of the jury room. She was horribly obnoxious. Everything about her was disruptive."

"Who's next?"

"I don't know. We have one left. Who should we get rid of?"

"Not Lonnie."

"Then tell me why."

"Let's just say Lonnie has been bought and paid for. His employer is someone who'll listen to us."

"Who else have you bought and paid for?"

"No one."

"Come on, Fitch. Do you want to win or not?"

"Of course I do."

"Then come clean. I'm your easiest way to a quick verdict."

"And most expensive."

"You didn't expect me to be cheap. What do you gain by withholding information from me?"

"What do I gain by giving it to you?"

"That should be obvious. You tell me. I tell Nicholas. He has a better handle on where the votes are. He knows where to spend his time. What about Gladys Card?"

"She's a follower. We have nothing on her. What does Nicholas think?"

"The same. What about Angel Weese?"

"She smokes and she's black. Flip a coin. Another follower. What does Nicholas think?"

"She'll follow Loreen Duke."

"And who will Loreen Duke follow?"

"Nicholas."

"How many followers does he have now? How many members are in his little cult?"

"Jerry for starters. Since Jerry is sleeping with Sylvia, then count her in. Add Loreen and you get Angel."

Fitch held his breath and counted rapidly. "That's five. Is that all?"

"And Henry Vu makes six. Six in the bank. You do the math, Fitch. Six and counting. What do you have on Savelle?"

Fitch actually glanced at some notes as if he wasn't sure. Everything brought to the meeting in his briefcase had been read a dozen times. "Nothing. He's too much of a weirdo," he said sadly, as if he'd been a miserable failure in his efforts to find some way to coerce Savelle.

"Any dirt on Herman?"

"No. What does Nicholas think?"

"Herman will be listened to, but not necessarily followed. He hasn't made a lot of friends, but then he's not disliked either. His vote will probably stand alone."

"Which way is he leaning?"

"He's the one juror who's hardest to read now because he is determined to follow the Judge's orders against discussing the case."

"Of all the nerve."

"Nicholas will have nine votes before the closing arguments, maybe more. He just needs a little leverage with some of his friends."

"Like who?"

"Rikki Coleman."

Fitch took a drink without looking at the cup. He set it down and pressed the whiskers around his mouth. She watched every move. "We, uh, may have something there."

"Why are you playing games, Fitch? Either you have something or you don't. Either you tell me so I can tell Nicholas so we can nail her vote, or you sit there hiding your memos and hoping she jumps on board."

"Let's just say it's a nasty personal secret she'd prefer to keep from her husband."

"Why keep the secret from me, Fitch?" Marlee said angrily. "Are we working together?"

"Yes, but I'm not sure I need to tell you at this point."

"Great, Fitch. Something in her past, right? An affair, an abortion, a DUI?"

"I'll think about it."

"You do that, Fitch. You keep playing games, I'll keep playing games. What about Millie?"

Fitch was reeling while appearing cool and calm. How much should he tell her? His instincts said to be cautious. They'd meet again tomorrow, and the next day, and if he chose to he could tell her about Rikki and Millie and maybe even Lonnie. Go slow, he told himself. "Nothing on Millie," he said, glancing at his watch and thinking that at that very moment poor Hoppy was locked inside a big black car with three FBI men and probably bawling by now.

"Are you sure, Fitch?"

Nicholas had met Hoppy in the hallway of the motel, just outside his room, a week ago as Hoppy was arriving with flowers and fudge for his wife. They had chatted for a moment. The next day Nicholas had noticed Hoppy sitting in the courtroom, a new face filled with wonder, a new face suddenly interested after almost three weeks of trial.

With Fitch in the game, Nicholas and Marlee were assuming that any juror was a potential target for outside influence. So Nicholas watched everyone. He sometimes loitered in the hallway as the guests were arriving for the personal visits, and he sometimes loitered there as they left. He eavesdropped on the gossip in the jury room. He listened to three conversations at once during the daily walks around town after lunch. He took notes on every person in the courtroom, even had nicknames and code names for them all.

It was only a hunch that Fitch was working on Millie through Hoppy. They seemed like such a nice, good-hearted pair; the type Fitch could easily snare in one of his insidious plots.

"Of course I'm sure. Nothing on Millie."

"She's been acting strange," Marlee said, lying.

Wonderful, thought Fitch. The Hoppy sting was working.

"What does Nicholas think about Royce, the last alternate?" he asked.

"White trash. Not bright at all. Easily manipulated. The type we could slip five grand to and we'd own him. That's another reason Nicholas wants to bump Savelle. We get Royce, and he'll be easy."

Her casualness about bribery warmed Fitch's heart. Many times, in other trials, he'd dreamed of finding angels like Marlee, little saviors with sticky hands who were anxious to fix his juries for him. This was almost unbelievable!

"Who else might take cash?" he asked eagerly.

"Jerry's broke, lots of gambling debts, plus a messy divorce around the corner. He'll need twenty thousand or so. Nicholas hasn't cut the deal with him yet, but it'll happen over the weekend."

"This could get expensive," Fitch said, trying to be serious.

Marlee laughed loudly, and continued to laugh until Fitch was forced to snicker at his own humor. He'd just promised her ten million, and he was in the process of spending another two million for the defense. His clients had a net worth of something close to eleven billion.

The moment passed, and they spent a while ignoring each other. Finally, Marlee looked at her watch, and said, "Write this down, Fitch. It's now three-thirty, Eastern Time. The money's not going to Singapore. I want the ten million wired to the Hanwa Bank in the Netherlands Antilles, and I want it done immediately."

"Hanwa Bank?"

"Yes. It's Korean. The money is not going to my account, but to yours."

"I don't have an account there."

"You'll open one with the wire." She pulled folded papers from her purse and slid them across the table. "Here are the forms and instructions."

"It's too late in the day to do this," he said, taking the papers. "And tomorrow is Saturday."

"Shut up, Fitch. Just read the instructions. Everything'll work fine if you simply do as you're told. Hanwa is always open for preferred customers. I want the money parked there, in your account, over the weekend."

"How will you know it's there?"

"You'll show me a confirmation of the wire. The money is diverted briefly until the jury retires, then it leaves Hanwa and goes to my account. This should happen Monday morning."

"What if the jury gets the case sooner?"

"Fitch, I assure you, there will be no verdict until the money is in my account. That's a promise. And if for some reason you try to screw us, then I can also promise you there'll be a nice verdict for the plaintiff. A huge verdict."

"Let's not talk about that."

"No, let's not. This has all been carefully planned, Fitch. Don't mess it up. Just do as you're told. Start the wire now."

WENDALL ROHR yelled at Dr. Gunther for an hour and a half, and when he finished there were no calm nerves anywhere in the courtroom. Rohr himself was probably the most relaxed person because his own badgering bothered him not in the least. Everybody else was sick of it. It was almost five, Friday, another week finished. Another weekend planned at the Siesta Inn.

Judge Harkin was worried about his jury. They were obviously bored and irritated, weary of sitting captive and listening to words they no longer cared about.

The lawyers were worried about them too. They weren't responding to testimony as expected. When they weren't fidgeting they were nodding off. When they weren't gazing about with blank looks they were pinching themselves to stay awake.

But Nicholas wasn't the least bit concerned about his colleagues. He wanted them fatigued and on the verge of revolt. A mob needs a leader.

During a late afternoon recess, he had prepared a letter to Judge Harkin in which he requested the trial be continued on Saturday. The issue had been debated during lunch, a debate which lasted only a few minutes because he had planned it and had all the answers. Why sit around the motel room when they could be sitting in the jury box trying to finish this marathon?

The other twelve readily added their signatures, under his, and Harkin had no choice. Saturday court was rare but not unheard of, especially in sequestration trials.

His Honor quizzed Cable as to what they might expect tomorrow, and Cable confidently predicted the defense would finish its case. Rohr said the plaintiff would have no rebuttal. Sunday court was out of the question.

"This trial should be over Monday afternoon," Harkin said to the jury. "The defense will finish tomorrow, then we'll have closing arguments Monday morning. I anticipate you'll receive the case before noon Monday. That's the best I can do, folks."

There were suddenly smiles throughout the jury box. With the end in sight, they could endure one last weekend together.

Dinner would be at a notorious rib place in Gulfport, followed by four hours of personal visits both tonight, tomorrow night, and Sunday. He sent them away with apologies.

After the jury left, Judge Harkin reconvened the lawyers for two hours of arguments on a dozen motions.

Thirty-three

HE ARRIVED LATE with no flowers or chocolates, no champagne or kisses, nothing but his tortured soul, which he wore on his sleeve. He took her by the hand at the door, led her to the bed, where he sat on the edge and tried to utter something before choking up. He buried his face in his hands.

"What's the matter, Hoppy?" she asked, fully alarmed and certain she was about to hear some dreadful confession. He had not been himself lately. She sat beside him, patted his knee, and listened. He began by blurting out just how stupid he'd been. He said repeatedly she wouldn't believe what he'd done, and he rambled on about how stupid it was until she finally said, firmly, "What have you done?"

He was suddenly angry—angry at himself for such a ridiculous stunt. He clenched his teeth, curled his upper lip, scowled, and launched into Mr. Todd Ringwald and KLX Property Group and Stillwater Bay and Jimmy Hull Moke. It was a setup! He'd been minding his own business, not out looking for trouble, just hustling with his sad little properties, just trying to help newlyweds into their first charming little starters. Then this guy walked in, from Vegas, nice suit, thick wad of architect's plans which, when unraveled on Hoppy's desk, looked like a gold mine.

Oh how could he have been so stupid! He lost his edge and began sobbing.

When he got to the part about the FBI coming to the house, Millie couldn't contain herself. "To our house?!"

"Yes, yes."

"Oh my god! Where were the kids?"

So Hoppy told her how it happened, how he deftly maneuvered Agents Napier and Nitchman away from the house and down to his office, where they presented him with—the tape!

It was awful. He forged ahead.

Millie began crying too, and Hoppy was relieved. Maybe she wouldn't scold him so bad. But there was more.

He got to the part where Mr. Cristano came to town and they met on the boat. Lots of folks, good folks really, in Washington were concerned about the trial. The Republicans and all that. The crime stuff. And, well, they cut a deal.

Millie wiped her cheeks with the back of a hand, and abruptly stopped the crying. "But I'm not sure I want to vote for the tobacco company," she said, dazed.

Hoppy dried it up quickly too. "Oh that's just great, Millie. Send me away for five years just so you can vote your conscience. Wake up."

"This is not fair," she said, looking at herself in the mirror on the wall behind the dresser. She was stunned.

"Of course it's not fair. Won't be fair either when the bank forecloses on the house because I'm locked away. What about the kids, Millie? Think of the kids. We got three in junior college and two in high school. The humiliation will be bad enough, but who'll educate the kids?"

Hoppy, of course, had the benefit of many hours of rehearsal for this. Poor Millie felt as though she'd been hit by a bus. She couldn't think quickly enough to ask the right questions. Under different circumstances, Hoppy might have felt sorry for her.

"I just can't believe it," she said.

"I'm sorry, Millie. I'm so sorry. I've done a terrible thing, and it's not fair to you." He was leaning forward, elbows on knees, head drooping low in utter defeat.

"It's not fair to the people in this trial."

Hoppy couldn't have cared less about the other people involved in the trial, but he bit his tongue. "I know, honey. I know. I'm a total failure."

She found his hand and squeezed it. Hoppy decided to go for

the kill. "I shouldn't tell you this, Millie, but when the FBI came to the house, I thought about getting the gun and ending it all right there."

"Shooting them?"

"No, myself. Blowing my brains out."

"Oh, Hoppy."

"I'm serious. I've thought about it many times in the past week. I'd rather pull the trigger than humiliate my family."

"Don't be silly," she said, and started to weep again.

FITCH AT FIRST had considered faking the wire, but after two phone calls and two faxes with his forgers in Washington, he was not convinced it would be safe. She seemed to know everything about wire transfers, and he had no idea how much she knew about the bank in the Netherlands Antilles. With her precision, she probably had someone down there waiting for the wire. Why run the risk?

In a flurry of phone calls, he located in D.C. an ex-Treasury official who now ran his own consulting firm, a man who allegedly knew everything about the rapid movements of money. Fitch gave him the bare essentials, hired him by fax, then sent him a copy of Marlee's instructions. She definitely knew what she was doing, the man said, and assured Fitch his money would be safe, at least during its first leg. The new account would belong to Fitch; she would have no access to it. Marlee was requiring a copy of the confirmation, and the man warned Fitch not to show her the account number either from the originating bank or from Hanwa in the Caribbean.

The Fund had a balance of six and a half million when Fitch cut his deal with Marlee. Throughout Friday, Fitch had called each of the Big Four CEO's and instructed them to immediately wire another two million dollars each. And he had no time for questions. He would explain later.

At five-fifteen Friday, the money left The Fund's untitled account in a bank in New York and within seconds landed at Hanwa in the Netherlands Antilles, where it was expected. The new account, numbered only, was created upon arrival, and a confirmation was immediately faxed to the originating bank.

Marlee called at six-thirty, and, not surprisingly, knew the wire was complete. She instructed Fitch to erase the account numbers on the confirmation, something he planned to do anyway, and fax it to the front desk of the Siesta Inn at precisely 7:05.

"That's a bit risky, isn't it?" Fitch asked.

"Just do as you're told, Fitch. Nicholas will be standing by the fax machine. The clerk thinks he's cute."

At seven-fifteen, Marlee called back to report that Nicholas had received the confirmation, and that it looked authentic. She instructed Fitch to be at her office at ten in the morning. Fitch quite happily agreed.

Though no money had changed hands, Fitch was elated with his success. He collected José and went for a silent stroll, something he rarely did. The air was crisp and invigorating. The sidewalks were deserted.

At this very moment, there was a sequestered juror holding a piece of paper with the amount "$10,000,000" printed twice on it. This juror, and this jury, belonged to Fitch. This trial was over. For certain, he would skip sleep and sweat bullets until he heard the verdict, but for all practical purposes, the trial was over. Fitch had won again. He'd snatched another victory from near defeat. The cost was much greater this time, but so were the stakes. He'd be forced to listen to some pointed bitching from Jankle and the others about the price of this operation, but it would just be a formality. They had to bitch about costs. They were corporate executives.

The real costs were the ones they wouldn't mention: the price of a plaintiff's verdict, certainly with the potential to exceed ten million, and the incalculable cost of a torrent of lawsuits.

He deserved this rare moment of pleasure, but his work was far from finished. He couldn't rest until he knew the real Marlee, where she came from, what motivated her, how and why she hatched this plot. There was something back there that Fitch had to know, and the unknown scared him immensely. If and when he found the real Marlee, then he would have his answers. Until then, his precious verdict was not safe.

Four blocks into his walk, Fitch was once again his angry, pouting, tormented self.

DERRICK MADE IT to the front lobby and was poking his head through an open door when a young woman politely asked him what he wanted. She held a stack of files and looked quite busy. It was almost eight, Friday night, and the law offices were still swarming.

What he wanted was a lawyer, one of those he'd seen in court who represented the tobacco company, one he could sit down with and cut a deal behind closed doors. He'd done his homework and learned the names of Durwood Cable and a few of his partners. He'd found this place, and he'd waited outside in his car for two hours, rehearsing his lines, steadying his nerves, mustering the guts to leave the car and walk through the front door.

There wasn't another black face to be seen.

Weren't all lawyers crooks? He figured that if Rohr would offer cash, then it made sense that all lawyers involved in the trial would offer cash. He had something to sell. There were rich buyers out there. It was a golden opportunity.

But the right words failed him as the secretary lingered and looked, and then began glancing around as if she might need some help with the situation. Cleve had said more than once that this was highly illegal, that he'd get caught if he got too greedy, and the fear suddenly hit like him a brick.

"Uh, is Mr. Gable in?" he asked with great uncertainty.

"Mr. Gable?" she said, eyebrows arched.

"Yeah, that's him."

"There is no Mr. Gable here. Who are you?"

A group of young coatless honkies walked slowly behind her, sizing him up and down, each knowing he didn't belong. Derrick had nothing else to offer. He was sure he had the right firm, but the wrong name, the wrong game, and he wasn't about to go to jail.

"I guess I have the wrong place," he said, and she gave him an efficient little smile. Of course you have the wrong place; now please leave. He stopped at a table in the front lobby and gathered five business cards from a small bronze rack. He'd show these to Cleve as proof of his visit.

He thanked her and left in a hurry. Angel was waiting.

MILLIE WEPT and tossed and flung sheets until midnight, then she changed into her favorite outfit, a well-worn red sweat suit, size XX-Large, a Christmas gift from one of the kids years ago, and quietly opened her door. Chuck, the guard at the far end, called softly to her. She was just going down for a snack, she explained, then eased down the semi-lit hall to the Party Room, where she heard a faint noise. Inside, Nicholas sat alone on a sofa, eating microwave popcorn and sipping carbonated water. He was watching rugby from Australia. Harkin's Party Room curfew had long since been forgotten.

"Why are you up so late?" he asked, muting the wide-screen TV with the remote. Millie sat nearby in a chair, her back to the door. Her eyes were red and puffy. Her short gray hair was tousled. She didn't care. Millie lived in a house which was continually filled with teenagers. They came and went, stayed, slept, ate, watched TV, cleaned out the fridge, saw her all the time in her red sweats, and she wouldn't have it any other way. Millie was everybody's mother.

"Can't sleep. You?" she said.

"It's hard to sleep here. You want some popcorn?"

"No thanks."

"Did Hoppy stop by tonight?"

"Yes."

"Seems like a nice man."

She paused, then said, "He is."

There was a longer pause as they sat in silence and thought about what they should say next. "You wanna watch a movie?" he finally asked.

"No. Can I ask you something?" she said, very seriously, and Nicholas punched the remote and the TV was off. The room was now lit only by a shadowy table lamp.

"Sure. You look troubled."

"I am. It's a legal question."

"I'll try to answer."

"Okay." She took a deep breath and squeezed her hands together. "What if a juror becomes convinced she cannot be fair and impartial? What should she do?"

He looked at the wall, the ceiling, then took a sip of water. Slowly, he said, "I think it would depend on the reasons behind her decision."

"I don't follow you, Nicholas." He was such a sweet boy, and so sharp. Her youngest son wanted to be a lawyer, and she'd caught herself hoping he'd turn out as smart as Nicholas.

"For the sake of simplicity, let's skip the hypotheticals," he said. "Let's say this juror is actually you, okay?"

"Okay."

"So something has happened since the trial started to affect your ability to be fair and impartial?"

Slowly, she said, "Yes."

He pondered this for a moment, then said, "I think it would depend on whether it was something you heard in court, or something that has happened out of court. As jurors, we're expected to become biased and partial as the trial progresses. That's how we reach our verdict. There's nothing wrong with that. It's part of the decision-making process."

She rubbed her left eye, and slowly asked, "What if it's not that? What if it's something out of court?"

He seemed shocked by this. "Wow. That's a lot more serious."

"How serious?"

For dramatic effect, Nicholas stood and walked a few steps to a chair, which he pulled close to Millie, their feet almost touching.

"What's the matter, Millie?" he asked softly.

"I need help, and there's no one to turn to. I'm locked up here in this awful place, away from my family and friends, and there's just nowhere to turn. Can you help me, Nicholas?"

"I'll try."

Her eyes watered for the umpteenth time that night. "You're such a nice young man. You know the law and this is a legal matter, and there's just no one else I can talk to." She was crying now, and he handed her a cocktail napkin from the table.

She told him everything.

LOU DELL AWOKE for no reason at 2 A.M., and took a quick patrol of the hallway in her cotton nightgown. In the Party Room, she found Nicholas and Millie with the TV off, deep in conversation, with a large bowl of popcorn between them. Nicholas was actually polite to her as he explained they couldn't sleep, were just talking about families, everything was fine. She left, shaking her head.

Nicholas suspected a scam, but he did not indicate that to Millie. Once her tears stopped, he grilled her on the details and took a few notes. She promised to do nothing until they could talk again. They said good night.

He went to his room, dialed Marlee's number, and hung up when she answered the phone with a rather sleepy hello. He waited two minutes, then dialed the same number. It rang six times, unanswered, then he hung up. After another two minutes, he dialed the number of her hidden cellphone. She answered it in the closet.

He gave her the full Hoppy story. Her night's rest was over. There was much work to be done, and quickly.

They agreed to start with the names of Napier, Nitchman, and Cristano.

Thirty-four

THE COURTROOM didn't change on Saturday. The same clerks wore the same clothes and busied themselves with the same paperwork. Judge Harkin's robe was just as black. The lawyers' faces all blurred, same as Monday through Friday. The deputies were just as bored, maybe more so. Minutes after the jury was seated and Harkin finished his questions, the monotony settled in, same as Monday through Friday.

After Gunther's tedious performance on Friday, Cable and crew thought it best to start the day with a bit of action. Cable called forward and got qualified as an expert a Dr. Olney, a researcher no less, who'd done some amazing things with laboratory mice. He had a video of his cute little subjects, all of them alive and seemingly filled with energy, certainly not diseased and dying. They were in several groups, boxed in glass cages, and it was Olney's task to apply various quantities of cigarette smoke each day to each cage. This he did over a period of years. Massive doses of cigarette smoke. The prolonged exposure failed to produce a single case of lung cancer. He'd tried everything short of suffocation to force death upon his little creatures, but it just wouldn't work. He had the stats and details. And he had lots of opinions about how cigarettes do not cause lung cancer, either in mice or in humans.

Hoppy was listening, from what was now his usual seat in the courtroom. He had promised to stop by, to wink at her, to give moral support, to once again let her know how awfully sorry he was. It was the least he could do. And after all it was Saturday, a busy day for realtors, but Dupree Realty seldom got cranked up until late in the morning. Since the disaster of Stillwater Bay, Hoppy had lost his drive. The thought of several years in prison sapped his will to hustle.

Taunton was back, on the front row now behind Cable, still wearing an immaculate dark suit, taking important notes and glancing at Lonnie, who did not need the reminder.

Derrick sat near the rear, watching it all and scheming. Rikki's husband Rhea sat on the rear seat with both kids. They tried to wave at their mother when the jury was seated. Mr. Nelson Card sat next to Mrs. Herman Grimes. Loreen's two teenaged daughters were present.

The families were there to be supportive, and to satisfy their curiosities. They'd heard enough to form their own opinions about the issues, the lawyers, the parties, the experts, and the Judge. They wanted to listen, so that perhaps they could later share an insight into what ought to be done.

BEVERLY MONK slipped out of her coma mid-morning, the remnants of gin and crack and what else she couldn't remember still lingering hard and blinding her as she covered her face and realized she was lying on a wooden floor. She wrapped herself in a dirty blanket, stepped over a snoring male she didn't recognize, and found her sunglasses on a wooden crate she used as a dresser. With the glasses on, she could see. The open loft was a mess—bodies sprawled on beds and floors, empty liquor bottles perched on every stick of cheap furniture. Who were these people? She shuffled toward a small loft window, stepping over a roommate here and a stranger there. What had she done last night?

The window was frosted; an early light snow was falling on the streets, where the flakes melted as they landed. She pulled the blanket around her emaciated body and sat on a beanbag near the window, watching the snow and wondering how much of the thousand bucks was left.

She inhaled the chilly air close to a windowpane, and her eyes began to clear. The throbbing in her temples ached but the dizziness was fading. Before she'd met Claire years ago, she'd chummed with a KU student named Phoebe, a flaky girl with a substance problem who'd spent time in recovery but was always on the brink of succumbing. Phoebe had worked briefly at Mulligan's with Claire and Beverly, then left the place under a cloud. Phoebe was from Wichita. She had once told Beverly that she knew something about Claire's past, something she'd learned from a boy who'd dated Claire. It wasn't Jeff Kerr, but some other guy, and if her head wasn't pounding she maybe could remember more of the details.

It was a long time ago.

Someone grunted under a mattress. Then there was silence again. Beverly had spent a weekend with Phoebe and her large, Catholic family in Wichita. Her father was a physician there. Should be easy to find. If that nice thug Mr. Swanson would fork over a thousand bucks for a few harmless answers, how much would he pay for some real background on Claire Clement?

She'd find Phoebe. Last she heard, she was in L.A. playing the same game Beverly was playing in New York. She'd shake down Swanson for all she could, then maybe find another place to live, a larger flat with nicer friends who'd keep the riffraff out.

Where was Swanson's card?

FITCH SKIPPED the morning's testimony to engage in a rare briefing, an event he despised. His guest was important, though. The man's name was James Local, head of the private investigation company to which Fitch was paying a fortune. Hidden in Bethesda, Local's firm hired lots of former government intelligence agents, and in the normal course of things an excursion into the heartland to locate a lone American female with no criminal record would be a nuisance. Their specialty was monitoring illegal arms shipments, tracking terrorists, and the like.

But Fitch had plenty of money, and the work involved only the slightest risk of flying bullets. The work had also been quite fruitless, and this was the reason Local was in Biloxi.

Swanson and Fitch listened as Local, without the slightest trace of apology, detailed their efforts of the past four days. Claire Clement had not existed before she appeared in Lawrence in the summer of 1988. Her first apartment was a two-bedroom condo she rented by the month and paid for with cash. The utilities were in her name—water, electric, gas. If she'd used the courts of Kansas for a legal name change, there was no record of it. Such files are kept locked, but they had managed to access them nonetheless. She didn't register to vote, didn't purchase car tags, didn't purchase real estate, but she did possess a Social Security number, which she'd used for employment purposes at two places—Mulligan's and a clothing boutique just off campus. A Social Security card is relatively easy to get, and it makes life much easier for a person on the run. They had managed to obtain a copy of her application for it, which revealed nothing useful. She had not applied for a passport.

It was Local's opinion that she had legally changed her name in another state, just pick one of the other forty-nine, then moved to Lawrence with a fresh identity.

They had her phone records for the three years she lived in Lawrence. There were no long distance calls billed to her. He repeated this twice so it would sink in. No long distance calls in three years. At the time, the phone company did not keep records of incoming long distance calls, so the printouts revealed nothing but the local activity. They were checking numbers. She used her phone sparingly.

"How does a person live with no long distance calls? What about family, old friends?" Fitch asked incredulously.

"There are ways," Local said. "Lots of ways, really. Maybe she borrowed a friend's phone. Maybe she went to a motel once a week, some budget place where they let you charge calls to your room, then pay for them with the bill when you check out. There's no way to trace that."

"Unbelievable," Fitch mumbled.

"I gotta tell you, Mr. Fitch, this girl is good. If she made a mistake, we haven't found it yet." The respect was obvious in Local's voice. "A person like this plans every move from the viewpoint that someone will come looking later."

"Sounds like Marlee," Fitch said, as if he were admiring a daughter.

She had two credit cards in Lawrence—a Visa and a Shell gas card. Her credit history revealed nothing remarkable or helpful. Evidently, most of her expenditures were in cash. No telephone cards either. She wouldn't dare make that mistake.

Jeff Kerr was a different story. His trail to law school at KU had been easy to follow, most of the work having been done by Fitch's initial operatives. Only after he met Claire did he pick up her habits of secrecy.

They left Lawrence in the summer of 1991, after his second year of law school, and Local's men had yet to find anyone who knew exactly when they left or where they were going. Claire had paid cash for the June rent that year, then vanished. They had spot-checked a dozen cities for signs of a Claire Clement after May of 1991, but so far had found nothing helpful. For obvious reasons, it was not possible to check every city.

"My guess is that she ditched Claire as soon as she left town, and became someone else," Local said.

Fitch had figured this out long ago. "This is Saturday. The jury gets the case on Monday. Let's forget what happened after Lawrence, and concentrate on finding out who she really is."

"We're working on that now."

"Work harder."

Fitch glanced at his watch and explained that he had to go. Marlee would be expecting him in a matter of moments. Local left for a private plane and a quick trip back to Kansas City.

MARLEE HAD BEEN in her little office since six. She slept little after Nicholas called her around three. They talked four times before he left for the courtroom.

The Hoppy scam had Fitch stamped all over it—why else would Mr. Cristano threaten to crush Hoppy if he didn't pressure Millie to vote right? Marlee had scribbled pages of notes and flow charts, and she'd made dozens of calls on her cellphone. Information was trickling in. The only George Cristano with a listed phone number in the metropolitan D.C. area lived in Alexandria. Marlee had called him around 4 A.M., and explained she was so-and-so with Delta Airlines, a plane had gone down near Tampa, a Mrs. Cristano was on board, and was this the George Cristano who worked with the Justice Department. No, he worked at Health and Human Services, thank God. She apologized, hung up, and snickered at the thought of the poor man racing to CNN to see the story.

Dozens of similar calls had led her to believe that there were no FBI agents working out of Atlanta named Napier and Nitchman. Nor were there any in Biloxi, New Orleans, Mobile, or any nearby city. At eight, she made contact with an investigator in

Atlanta who was now pursuing leads on Napier and Nitchman. Marlee and Nicholas were almost positive the two were stooges, but this had to be confirmed. She called reporters, cops, FBI hotlines, government information services.

When Fitch arrived promptly at ten, the table was clear and the phone was hidden in a small closet. They barely said hello. Fitch was wondering who she was before she was Claire, and she was still analyzing the next move to uncover his Hoppy scam.

"You'd better wrap it up, Fitch. The jury is numb."

"We'll be through by five this afternoon. That soon enough?"

"Let's hope so. You're not making it easier on Nicholas."

"I've told Cable to hurry. That's all I can do."

"We got problems with Rikki Coleman. Nicholas has spent time with her, and she'll be a hard sell. She's well respected on the jury, by the men and women alike, and Nicholas says she's slowly becoming a major player. He's surprised by this, actually."

"She wants a big verdict?"

"It looks that way, though they haven't discussed specifics. Nicholas detects a real bitterness toward the industry for duping kids into addiction. She doesn't appear to have much sympathy for the Wood family, she's more inclined to punish Big Tobacco for hooking the younger generation. Anyway, you said we might have a surprise for her."

Without comment or formality, Fitch lifted a single sheet of paper from his briefcase and slid it across the table. Marlee scanned it quickly. "Abortion, huh?" she said, still reading, unsurprised.

"Yep."

"You're sure this is her?"

"Positive. She was in college."

"This should do it."

"Does he have the guts to show it to her?"

Marlee released the paper and glared at Fitch. "Would you, for ten million bucks?"

"Of course. And why not? She sees this, she votes right, this is forgotten, and her dirty little secret is safe. She leans the other way, then threats are made. It's an easy sell."

"Precisely." She folded the piece of paper and removed it from the table. "Don't worry about Nick's courage, okay? We've been planning this for a long time."

"How long?"

"That's not important. You have nothing on Herman Grimes?"

"Not a thing. Nicholas will have to deal with him during deliberations."

"Gee thanks."

"He's damned sure getting paid for it, don't you think? For ten million, you'd think he should be able to sway a few votes."

"He's got the votes, Fitch. They're in his pocket right now. He wants it unanimous. Herman might be a problem."

"Then bump the sonofabitch. Seems to be a game you enjoy."

"We're thinking about it."

Fitch shook his head in amazement. "Do you realize how utterly corrupt this is?"

"Yes, I think so."

"I love it."

"Go love it somewhere else, Fitch. That's all for now. I have work to do."

"Yes dear," Fitch said, bouncing to his feet and closing his briefcase.

EARLY SATURDAY AFTERNOON, Marlee located an FBI agent in Jackson, Mississippi, who happened to be at the office catching up with paperwork when the phone rang. She gave an alias, said she was employed by a real estate company in Biloxi, and suspected two men of posing as FBI agents when in fact they were not. The two men had been harassing her boss, making threats, flashing badges, etc. She thought they had something to do with the casinos, and for good measure she threw in the name of Jimmy Hull Moke. He gave her the home number of a young FBI agent in Biloxi named Madden.

Madden was in bed with flu, but willing to talk nonetheless, especially when Marlee informed him she might have confidential information about Jimmy Hull Moke. Madden had never heard of either Napier or Nitchman, and hadn't heard of Cristano either. He was unaware of any special crime-fighting unit from Atlanta now operating on the Coast, and the more she talked, the more excited he became. He wanted to investigate a bit, and she promised to call him back in an hour.

He sounded much stronger when he phoned later. There was no FBI agent named Nitchman. There was a Lance Napier in the

San Francisco office, but he would have no business on the Coast. Cristano was likewise a bogus identity. Madden had talked to the agent in charge of the investigation into Jimmy Hull Moke, and confirmed that Nitchman, Napier, and Cristano, whoever they might be, were certainly not FBI agents. He'd love to talk to these boys, and Marlee said she'd try to arrange a meeting.

THE DEFENSE rested at three Saturday afternoon. Judge Harkin announced proudly, "Ladies and gentlemen, you've just heard the last witness." There would be some last-minute motions and arguments for him and the lawyers to tend to, but the jurors were free to go. For their Saturday night entertainment, one bus would travel to a junior college football game, and the other would go to a local movie theater. Afterward, personal visits would be allowed until midnight. For tomorrow, each juror would be allowed to leave the motel from 9 A.M. until 1 for worship services, unsupervised as long as they promised not to say a word to anybody about the trial. For Sunday night, personal visits from seven until ten. First thing Monday they would hear closing arguments, and receive the case before lunch.

Thirty-five

EXPLAINING FOOTBALL to Henry Vu was more trouble than it was worth. But then, everyone seemed to be an expert. Nicholas had played high school junior varsity, in Texas, no less, where the sport is something only slightly less than a religion. Jerry followed twenty games a week, followed in fact with his wallet and thus claimed to know the game intimately. Lonnie, sitting behind Henry, had also played in high school and was quick to lean over his shoulder and point. The Poodle, sitting next to Jerry, closely under the quilt, had learned the game thoroughly when her two sons played. Even Shine Royce didn't hesitate to throw in a few pointers. He'd never played the game but watched a lot of television.

They sat in a tiny huddled group on the visitors' side, on cold aluminum bleachers, away from the rest of the crowd, watching a Gulf Coast school play one from Jackson. It was a perfect football setting—cool weather, nice crowd on the home side, a rowdy band in the stands, cute cheerleaders, close score.

Henry asked all the wrong questions: Why are their trousers so tight? What do they say when they group together between plays and why do they hold hands? Why do they pile up like that? He claimed it was his first live football game.

Across an aisle, Chuck and another deputy watched the game in plain clothes, ignoring six of the jurors in the most important civil trial in the country.

□ □ □ □

IT WAS EXPRESSLY FORBIDDEN for any juror to have contact with another juror's visitors. The prohibition had been in writing since the beginning of sequestration, and Judge Harkin had harped on it repeatedly. But an occasional hello in the hallway was unavoidable, and Nicholas had been especially determined to violate the rule whenever possible.

Millie had no interest in movies and certainly none in football. Hoppy arrived with a sack of burritos, which they ate slowly with few words. After dinner, they tried to watch a TV show but finally gave it up and began to rehash Hoppy's mess. There were more tears, more apologies, even a few of Hoppy's casual references to suicide, which Millie found a bit overly dramatic. She finally confessed she'd spilled her guts to Nicholas Easter, a fine young man who knew the law and could be trusted implicitly. Hoppy at first was shocked and angry, then his curiosity got the better of him and he longed to know what someone else thought of his situation. Especially someone who'd studied the law, as Millie said. More than once she'd mentioned her admiration for the young man.

Nicholas had promised to make a few calls, and this alarmed Hoppy. Oh how Nitchman and Napier and Cristano lectured him on the necessity of silence! Nicholas could be trusted, Millie repeated, and Hoppy eventually warmed to the idea.

The phone rang at ten-thirty; it was Nicholas, back from the game, settled in his room, and anxious to meet with the Duprees. Millie unlocked the door. Willis watched with great surprise from the end of the hall as Easter sneaked into Millie's room. Was her husband still in there? He couldn't remember. Many of the guests had yet to leave, and he'd been napping anyway. Surely Easter and Millie weren't seeing each other! Willis made a mental note of it, then drifted back to sleep.

Hoppy and Millie sat on the edge of the bed facing Nicholas, who leaned on the dresser near the TV. He began by lecturing them kindly on the need for silence, as if Hoppy hadn't heard this in the past week. They were violating a Judge's orders, enough said.

He broke the news gently. Napier, Nitchman, and Cristano were minor players in a large fraud, a conspiracy orchestrated by the tobacco company to pressure Millie. They were not government agents. The names were aliases. Hoppy had been duped.

He took it well. At first he felt even more stupid, if that was possible, then the room began to spin as Hoppy got yanked this way and that. Was it good news or bad? What about the tape? What was his next move? What if Nicholas was wrong? A hundred thoughts raced through his overloaded brain as Millie squeezed his knee and started crying.

"Are you sure?" he was able to ask, his voice on the verge of cracking.

"Positive. They have no connection with either the FBI or the Department of Justice."

"But, but they had badges and—"

Nicholas raised both hands, nodded compassionately, and said, "I know, Hoppy. Believe me, that stuff was easy. The cover was simple to create."

Hoppy rubbed his forehead and tried to arrange things. Nicholas went on to explain that KLX Property Group in Las Vegas was a sham. They had been unable to find a Mr. Todd Ringwald, which was almost certainly an alias too.

"How do you know all this?" Hoppy asked.

"Good question. I have a close friend on the outside who's very good at digging for information. He is completely trustworthy. Took about three hours on the phone, which is not bad considering it's Saturday."

Three hours. On a Saturday. Why hadn't Hoppy made a few calls? He'd had a week. He sunk lower until his elbows rested on his knees. Millie wiped her cheeks with a tissue. A quiet minute passed.

"What about the tape?" Hoppy asked.

"Of you and Moke?"

"Yes. That tape."

"I'm not worried about it," Nicholas said confidently, as if he was now Hoppy's lawyer. "Legally, there are lots of problems with the tape."

Tell me about it, Hoppy thought but said nothing. Nicholas continued, "It was obtained by false pretenses. It's a clear case of entrapment. It's in the possession of men who themselves are violating the law. It was not obtained by law enforcement officials.

There was no search warrant for it, no court order allowing your words to be recorded. Forget it."

What sweet words! Hoppy's shoulders jerked upward and he exhaled mightily. "You're serious?"

"Yes, Hoppy. The tape will never be played again."

Millie leaned over and clutched Hoppy, and they hugged without shame or embarrassment. Her tears were now of unbridled joy. Hoppy jumped to his feet and bounced around the room. "So what's the game plan?" he asked, cracking his knuckles, ready for battle.

"We have to be careful."

"Just point me in the right direction. The bastards."

"Hoppy!"

"Sorry, dear. I'm just ready to kick some ass."

"Your language!"

SUNDAY BEGAN with a birthday cake. Loreen Duke had mentioned to Mrs. Gladys Card that her thirty-sixth birthday was approaching. Mrs. Card called her sister out in the free world, and early Sunday her sister delivered a thick chocolate caramel cake. Three layers with thirty-six candles. The jurors met in the dining room at nine and ate the cake for breakfast. Most then left in a hurry for four hours of much-awaited worship. Some had not been to church in years, but felt drawn by the Spirit.

One of Poodle's boys picked her up, and Jerry tagged along. They headed in the general direction of some unnamed church, but as soon as they realized no one was watching they went to a casino instead. Nicholas left with Marlee, and they attended Mass. Mrs. Gladys Card made a grand entrance at the Calvary Baptist Church. Millie went home with good intentions of dressing for church, but she was overcome with emotion at the sight of her kids. No one was watching, so she spent her time in the kitchen, cooking and cleaning and doting on her brood. Phillip Savelle remained behind.

Hoppy went to his office at ten. He had called Napier at eight Sunday morning with the news that he had important trial developments to discuss; said he'd made much progress with his wife and she was now scoring major points with other jurors. He wanted to meet with Napier and Nitchman at his office to give a full report, and to receive further instructions.

Napier took the call in a run-down two-room apartment he and Nitchman were using as a front for the scam. Two phone lines were temporarily installed—one as the office number, the other as their residence for the duration of their hard-charging investigation into corruption along the Gulf Coast. Napier chatted with Hoppy, then called Cristano for orders. Cristano's room was at a Holiday Inn near the beach. Cristano in turn called Fitch, who was delighted with the news. Finally, Millie was off dead-center and moving their way. Fitch had begun to wonder if his investment would pay off. He green-lighted the meeting at Hoppy's office.

Wearing their standard dark suits and dark sunshades, Napier and Nitchman arrived at the office at eleven to find Hoppy brewing coffee and in great spirits. They settled around his desk and waited for the coffee. Millie was in there fighting like hell to save her husband, Hoppy said, and she felt quite confident she had already convinced Mrs. Gladys Card and Rikki Coleman. She had shared the Robilio memo with them, and they had been shocked at the man's deceit.

He poured coffee as Napier and Nitchman dutifully took notes. Another guest quietly entered the building through the front door, which had been left unlocked by Hoppy. He eased along the hall behind the open reception area, stepping lightly on the worn carpet until he came to a wooden door with HOPPY DUPREE painted on it. He listened for a moment, then knocked loudly.

Inside, Napier jumped and Nitchman set down his coffee, and Hoppy stared at them as if startled. "Who is it?" he growled loudly. The door opened suddenly, and Special Agent Alan Madden stepped in, said loudly, "FBI!" while walking to the edge of Hoppy's desk and glaring at all three. Hoppy kicked his chair back and stood as if he might have to get frisked.

Napier would've fainted had he been standing. Nitchman's mouth dropped open. Both turned pale as their hearts stopped.

"Agent Alan Madden, FBI," he said as he opened his badge for all to inspect. "Are you Mr. Dupree?" he demanded.

"Yes. But the FBI is already here," Hoppy said, looking at Madden, then at the other two, then back at Madden.

"Where?" he asked, scowling down at Napier and Nitchman.

"These two guys," Hoppy said, acting brilliantly. It was his finest moment. "This is Agent Ralph Napier, and this is Agent Dean Nitchman. You guys don't know each other?"

"I can explain," Napier started, nodding confidently as if he could in fact make everything satisfactory.

"FBI?" Madden said. "Show me some identification," he demanded, shoving forward an empty palm.

They hesitated, and Hoppy pounced on them. "Go ahead. Show him your badges. Same ones you showed me."

"Identification please," Madden insisted, his anger growing by the second.

Napier started to stand, but Madden returned him to his seat by pressing down on his shoulder. "I can explain," Nitchman said, his voice an octave higher than normal.

"Go ahead," Madden said.

"Well, you see, we're not really FBI agents, but instead—"

"What!" Hoppy screamed from across the desk. He was wild-eyed and ready to throw something. "You lying sonofabitch! You've been telling me for the last ten days that you're FBI agents!"

"Is that true?" Madden demanded.

"Not, not really," Nitchman said.

"What!" Hoppy screamed again.

"Cool it!" Madden snapped at him. "Now continue," he said to Nitchman.

Nitchman didn't want to continue. He wanted to bolt through the door, kiss Biloxi good-bye, and never be seen again. "We're private investigators, and, well—"

"We work for a firm in D.C.," Napier chimed in helpfully. He was about to add something else when Hoppy lunged for a desk drawer, yanked it open, and removed two business cards—one for Ralph Napier, one for Dean Nitchman, both labeled as FBI agents, both from the Southeast Regional Unit in Atlanta. Madden studied both cards, saw the local numbers scrawled on the back.

"What's going on here?" Hoppy demanded.

"Who's Nitchman?" Madden asked. There was no answer.

"He's Nitchman," Hoppy yelled, pointing at Nitchman.

"Not me," Nitchman said.

"What!" Hoppy screamed.

Madden took two steps toward Hoppy and pointed at his

chair. "I want you to sit down and shut up, okay? Not another word until I ask for it." Hoppy fell into his seat, his eyes glaring fiercely at Nitchman.

"Are you Ralph Napier?" Madden asked.

"Nope," Napier said, looking down, away from Hoppy.

"Sonofabitches," Hoppy mumbled.

"Then who are you?" Madden asked. He waited, but there was no response.

"They gave me those cards, okay?" Hoppy said, not about to keep quiet. "I'll go to the grand jury and swear on a stack of Bibles that they gave me those cards. They've held themselves out as FBI agents, and I want them prosecuted."

"Who are you?" Madden asked the one previously known as Nitchman. No response. Madden then removed a service revolver, an action that greatly impressed Hoppy, and made the two stand and spread their legs and lean forward on the desk. A quick frisk of each revealed nothing but pocket change, some keys, and a few dollars. No wallets. No fake FBI badges. No identification whatsoever. They were too well trained to make that mistake.

He handcuffed them and led them from the office to the front of the building, where another FBI agent was sipping coffee from a paper cup and waiting. Together, they loaded Napier and Nitchman into the back of a real FBI car. Madden said good-bye to Hoppy, promised to call him later, and drove away with the two stooges in the backseat, sitting on their hands. The other FBI agent followed in the fake FBI car Napier always drove.

Hoppy waved farewell.

Madden drove along Highway 90, in the direction of Mobile. Napier, the quicker wit of the two, concocted a fairly reasonable story, which Nitchman added to slightly. They explained to Madden that their firm had been hired by some vague and unnamed casino interests to investigate various parcels of real estate along the Coast. This is where they'd run into Hoppy, who was quite corrupt and had tried to shake 'em down for cash. One thing led to another, and their boss made them pose as FBI agents. No harm had been done, really.

Madden listened with hardly a word. They would later tell Fitch that he seemed not to have a clue about Hoppy's wife Millie and her current civic responsibilities. He was a young agent, obviously amused with his catch and not certain what to do with them.

For his part, Madden deemed it a minor offense, unworthy of prosecution, certainly not worth any more effort on his part. His caseload was staggering anyway. The last thing he needed was to waste time pursuing convictions for two small-time liars. When they crossed into Alabama, he delivered a stern lecture on the penalties for impersonating a federal officer. They were truly sorry. It would never happen again.

He stopped at a rest station, uncuffed them, gave them their car, and told them to stay out of Mississippi. They thanked him profusely, promised never to return, and sped away.

FITCH BROKE A LAMP with his fist when he got the call from Napier. Blood dripped from a knuckle as he seethed and cursed and listened to the story, as told from a noisy truck stop somewhere in Alabama. He sent Pang to collect the two.

Three hours after they were first handcuffed, Napier and Nitchman were seated in a room next to Fitch's office in the rear of the old dime store. Cristano was present.

"Start at the beginning," Fitch said. "I want to hear every word." He punched a button and a recorder started. They painstakingly collaborated on the narrative until they'd recollected virtually all of it.

Fitch dismissed them and sent them back to Washington.

Alone, he dimmed the lights in his office and sulked in the darkness. Hoppy would tell Millie tonight. Millie would be lost as a defense juror; in fact, she'd probably swing so far to the other side she'd want billions in damages for the poor widow Wood.

Marlee could salvage this disaster. Only Marlee.

Thirty-six

IT WAS THE STRANGEST THING, Phoebe said not long into the surprise call from Beverly, because the day before yesterday some guy had called her too, claimed he was Jeff Kerr looking for Claire. She knew immediately the guy was faking, but she strung him along anyway to see what he wanted. She hadn't talked to Claire in four years.

Beverly and Phoebe compared notes about their calls, though Beverly didn't mention the meeting with Swanson or the jury trial he was investigating. They reminisced about the college days in Lawrence, which seemed so long ago. They lied about their acting careers and the speed with which each was progressing. They promised to get together at the first opportunity. Then they said good-bye.

Beverly called back an hour later, as if she'd forgotten something. She'd been thinking about Claire. They'd parted on less than good terms, and this bothered her. It was a trivial matter they'd never resolved. She wanted to see Claire, to patch things up, if for no other reason than to relieve the guilt. But she didn't have a clue where to find her. Claire had disappeared so fast and so thoroughly.

At this point, Beverly decided to take a chance. Since Swanson had mentioned the possibility of a prior name, and since she remembered the mystery surrounding Claire's past, she decided to cast the bait and see if Phoebe would take it. "Claire was not her real name, you know?" she said, acting quite effectively.

"Yeah, I know," Phoebe said.

"She told me once, but I can't remember now."

Phoebe hesitated. "She had the prettiest name, not that Claire was bad."

"What was it?"

"Gabrielle."

"Oh yes, Gabrielle. And what was her last name?"

"Brant. Gabrielle Brant. She was from Columbia, Missouri, that's where she went to school, at the university there. Did she tell you the story?"

"Maybe, but I don't remember."

"She had a boyfriend who was abusive and crazy. She tried to ditch him, and he began stalking her. That's why she left town and changed her name."

"Never heard that. What's her parents' name?"

"Brant. I think her father's dead. Her mother was a professor of medieval studies at the university."

"Is she still there?"

"I have no idea."

"I'll try to find her through her mom. Thanks, Phoebe."

It took an hour to get Swanson on the phone. Beverly asked him how much the information was worth. Swanson called Fitch, who needed some good news. He authorized a ceiling of five thousand dollars, and Swanson called her back with an offer of half that. She wanted more. They negotiated for ten minutes and settled on four thousand, which she wanted in cash and in hand before she'd say a word.

All four of the CEO's were in town for the closing arguments and the verdict, so Fitch had a small fleet of finely appointed corporate jets at his disposal. He sent Swanson to New York on the Pynex plane.

Swanson arrived in the city at dusk and checked into a small hotel near Washington Square. According to a roommate, Beverly was not in, was not working, but she might be at a party. He called the pizzeria where she worked, and was told she had been fired. He called the roommate again, and got himself hung up on when he asked too many questions. He slammed the phone down and stomped around his room. How the hell do you find a person on the streets of Greenwich Village? He walked a few blocks to her apartment, his feet freezing in the cold rain. He drank coffee where he'd met her before while his shoes thawed and dried. He used a pay phone for another fruitless chat with the same roommate.

MARLEE WANTED one last meeting before the big Monday. They met in her little office. Fitch could've kissed her feet when he saw her.

He decided to tell her everything about Hoppy and Millie and his great scam gone bad. Nicholas had to work on Millie immediately, to soothe her before she contaminated her friends. After all, Hoppy had told Napier and Nitchman early Sunday that Millie was now a fierce advocate for the defense, that she was in there showing copies of the Robilio memo to her comrades. Was this true? If so, what in the world would she do now when she learned the truth about Hoppy? She'd be furious, no doubt. She'd flip-flop immediately. She'd probably tell her friends what a heinous thing the defense had done to her husband in an effort to pressure her.

It would be a disaster, no question about it.

Marlee listened straight-faced as Fitch unraveled the story. She wasn't shocked, but quite amused to see Fitch sweat.

"I think we should bump her," Fitch declared when he was finished.

"Do you have a copy of the Robilio memo?" she asked, completely unmoved.

He picked one out of his briefcase and handed it to her. "Some of your work?" she asked after she'd read it.

"Yes. It's completely bogus."

She folded it and placed it under her chair. "A helluva scam, Fitch."

"Yeah, it was beautiful until we got caught."

"Is this something you do in every tobacco trial?"

"We certainly try."

"Why'd you pick Mr. Dupree?"

"We studied him carefully, and decided he'd be easy. Small-town realtor, barely paying his bills, lots of money changing hands with the casinos and all, lots of his friends making big bucks. He fell for it immediately."

"Have you been caught before?"

"We've had to abort scams, but we've never been caught red-handed."

"Until today."

"Not really. Hoppy and Millie might suspect it was somebody working for the tobacco company, but they don't know who. So, in that respect, there's still some doubt."

"What's the difference?"

"None."

"Relax, Fitch. I think her husband may have been exaggerating her effectiveness. Nicholas and Millie are quite close, and she hasn't become an advocate for your client."

"Our client."

"Right. Our client. Nicholas hasn't seen the memo."

"You think Hoppy was lying?"

"Would you blame him? Your boys had him convinced he was about to be indicted."

Fitch breathed a little easier and almost smiled. He said, "It's imperative Nicholas talk to Millie tonight. Hoppy will go over in a couple of hours and tell her all about it. Can Nicholas get to her quickly?"

"Fitch, Millie will vote the way he wants. Relax."

Fitch relaxed. He removed his elbows from the table and tried to smile again. "Just out of curiosity, how many votes do we have right now?"

"Nine."

"Who are the other three?"

"Herman, Rikki, and Lonnie."

"He hasn't discussed Rikki's past with her?"

"Not yet."

"That'll make ten," Fitch said, his eyes dancing, his fingers suddenly twitching. "We can get eleven if we can bump somebody and pick up Shine Royce, right?"

"Look, Fitch, you're worrying too much. You've paid your money, you've hired the best, now relax and wait on your verdict. It's in very good hands."

"Unanimous?" Fitch asked gleefully.

"Nicholas is determined to bring it back unanimous."

Fitch sprang down the steps of the sagging building and bounced along the short sidewalk until he hit the street. For six blocks he whistled and almost skipped in the night air. José met him on foot and tried to keep up. He'd never seen his boss in such good spirits.

ON ONE SIDE of the conference room sat seven lawyers who'd each paid a million dollars for the privilege of sharing this event. No one else was in the room, no one but Wendall Rohr, who stood on the other side of the conference table and paced slowly back and forth, speaking softly with measured words, to his jury. His voice was warm and rich, filled with compassion one second and harsh words for Big Tobacco the next. He lectured and he cajoled. He was comical and he was angry. He showed them photographs, and he wrote figures on a chalkboard.

He finished in fifty-one minutes, the shortest rehearsal so far. The closing had to be an hour or less, Harkin's orders. The comments from his peers were fast and mixed, some complimentary but most probing for ways to improve. No tougher audience could be found. The seven had combined for hundreds of closing arguments, arguments which had produced close to half a billion dollars in verdicts. They knew how to extract large sums of money from juries.

They had agreed to park their egos outside the door. Rohr took another beating, something he didn't do well, and agreed to perform again.

It had to be perfect. Victory was so close.

CABLE UNDERWENT similar abuse. His audience was much larger—a dozen lawyers, several jury consultants, lots of paralegals. He was videotaped so he could study himself. He was determined to do it in half an hour. The jury would be appreciative. Rohr would no doubt run longer. The contrast would be nice— Cable the technician sticking to the facts versus Rohr the flamboyant mouthpiece tugging at their emotions.

He delivered his closing, then watched the video. Again and again, throughout Sunday afternoon and deep into the night.

BY THE TIME Fitch arrived at the beach house, he had managed to work himself back into his usual state of cautious pessimism. The four CEO's were waiting, having just finished a fine meal. Jankle was drunk and kept to himself by the fireplace. Fitch took some coffee and analyzed the last-minute efforts of the defense.

The questions quickly got around to the wire transfers he'd demanded on Friday; two million from each of the four.

Prior to Friday, The Fund had a balance of six and a half million, certainly more than enough to complete the trial. What was the additional eight million for? And how much was in The Fund now?

Fitch explained that the defense had had a sudden, unplanned expenditure of the grandest proportions.

"Stop the games, Fitch," said Luther Vandemeer of Trellco. "Have you managed to finally purchase a verdict?"

Fitch tried not to lie to these four. They were, after all, his employers. He never told them the complete truth, and they didn't expect him to. But in response to a direct question, especially one of this magnitude, he felt compelled to make some effort at honesty. "Something like that," he said.

"Do you have the votes, Fitch?" asked another CEO.

Fitch paused and looked carefully at each of the four, including Jankle, who was suddenly attentive. "I believe I do," he said.

Jankle jumped to his feet, unsteady but quite focused, and stepped into the center of the room. "Say it again, Fitch," he demanded.

"You heard me," Fitch said. "The verdict has been purchased." His voice couldn't resist a touch of pride.

The other three stood too. All four eased toward Fitch, forming a loose semicircle. "How?" one of them asked.

"I'll never tell," Fitch said coolly. "The details are not important."

"I demand to know," Jankle said.

"Forget it. Part of my job is to do the dirty work while protecting you and your companies. If you want to terminate me, fine. But you'll never know the details."

They stared at him during a long pause. The circle grew tighter. They slowly sipped their drinks and admired their hero. Eight times they'd been to the brink of disaster, and eight times Rankin Fitch had worked his dirty tricks and saved them. Now he'd done it for the ninth time. He was invincible.

And he'd never promised victory before, not like this. Just the opposite. He'd always anguished before each verdict, always predicting defeat and taking pleasure in making them miserable. This was so uncharacteristic.

"How much?" Jankle demanded.

It was something Fitch couldn't hide. For obvious reasons, these four had the right to know where the money went. They had installed a primitive accounting format for The Fund. Each company contributed equal amounts when Fitch said so, and each CEO was entitled to a monthly list of all expenses.

"Ten million," Fitch said.

The drunk barked first. "You've paid ten million dollars to a juror!" The other three were equally shocked.

"No. Not to a juror. Let's put it this way. I've purchased the verdict for ten million dollars, okay? That's all I will say. The Fund now has a balance of four-point-five million. And I'm not going to answer any questions about how the money changed hands."

Maybe a sack of cash under the table might make sense. Five, ten thousand bucks maybe. But it was impossible to picture any of these small-town hicks on the jury possessing brains big enough to dream of ten million dollars. Surely it wasn't all going to one person.

They hung together near Fitch in stunned silence, each having the same thoughts. Surely Fitch had worked his wizardry on ten of them. That would make sense. He'd gotten ten and offered them a million each. That made a helluva lot more sense. Ten fresh new millionaires on the Gulf Coast. But how do you hide that kind of money?

Fitch savored the moment. "Of course, nothing is guaranteed," he said. "You never know until the jury comes back."

Well, it damned sure better be guaranteed, at the rate of ten million bucks. But they said nothing. Luther Vandemeer backed away first. He poured a stiffer brandy and sat on the piano bench near the baby grand. Fitch would tell him later. He'd wait a month or two, get Fitch up to New York on business, and pick the story out of him.

Fitch said he had things to do. He wanted each of the four in the courtroom tomorrow for closing arguments. Don't sit together, he instructed.

Thirty-seven

THERE WAS A GENERAL FEELING among the jurors that
Sunday night would be their last in sequestration. They
whispered that perhaps if they got the case by noon Monday, then
certainly they could reach a verdict by Monday night and go
home. This wasn't discussed openly because it necessarily involved speculation about the verdict, something Herman was
quick to stifle.

The mood was light, though, and many of the jurors quietly
packed and tidied up their rooms. They wanted their last visit to
the Siesta Inn to be quick—a dash in from court to gather packed
bags and grab toothbrushes.

Sunday was the third consecutive night of personal visits, and
collectively they'd had enough of their mates. Especially the married ones. Three straight nights of coziness in a small room was
trying for most marriages. Even the singles needed a night off.
Savelle's woman friend stayed away. Derrick told Angel he might
stop by later, but had some important business first. Loreen didn't
have a boyfriend, but she'd had enough of her teenaged daughters
for one weekend. Jerry and Poodle were having their first little
spat.

The motel was quiet Sunday night; no football and beer in the
Party Room, no checkers tournaments. Marlee and Nicholas ate
pizza in his room. They covered their checklists and made final

plans. Both were nervous and tense, and managed only slight humor at her recounting of Fitch's sad story about Hoppy.

Marlee left at nine. She drove her leased car to her rented condo, where she finished packing her own things.

Nicholas walked across the hall where Hoppy and Millie were waiting like a couple of honeymooners. They couldn't thank him enough. He had exposed this horrible fraud and set them free again. It was shocking to think of the extreme measures the tobacco industry would go to just to pressure a juror.

Millie expressed her concern about remaining on the jury. She and Hoppy had already discussed it, and she didn't feel she could be fair and impartial in light of what they'd done to her husband. Nicholas had anticipated this. It was his opinion that he needed Millie.

And there was a more compelling reason. If Millie told Judge Harkin about the Hoppy scam, then he'd probably declare a mistrial. And that would be a tragedy. A mistrial would mean that in a year or two another jury would be picked to hear the same case. Each side would spend another fortune doing what they were doing right now. "It's up to us, Millie. We've been chosen to decide this case, and it's our responsibility to reach a verdict. The next jury will be no smarter than us."

"I agree," Hoppy said. "This trial will be over tomorrow. It'd be a shame to have a mistrial declared here at the last minute."

So Millie bit her lip and found new resolve. Her friend Nicholas made everything easier.

CLEVE MET DERRICK in the sports bar of the Nugget Casino Sunday night. They drank a beer, watched a football game, said little because Derrick was pouting and trying to appear angry at the screwing he claimed to be receiving. The fifteen thousand in cash was in a small brown packet that Cleve slid across the table and which Derrick took and stuffed in a pocket, without saying thanks or anything. Pursuant to their latest deal, the other ten thousand would be paid after the verdict, assuming of course that Angel voted with the plaintiff.

"Why don't you leave now?" Derrick said a few minutes after the money landed near his heart.

"Great idea," Cleve said. "Go see your girlfriend. Explain things carefully."

"I can handle her."

Cleve took his longneck with him, and disappeared.

Derrick drained his beer and rushed to the men's room, where he locked himself in a stall and counted the money, a hundred and fifty fresh, new, neatly packed hundred-dollar bills. He pressed the stack together and was amazed at its size—less than an inch thick. He divided it in quarters, and placed a folded wad in each pocket of his jeans.

The casino was bustling. He'd learned to shoot craps from an older brother who'd served in the Army, and for some reason, as if drawn by a magnet, he wandered near the crap tables. He watched for a minute, then decided to resist the temptation and go see Angel. He stopped for a quick beer at a small bar overlooking the roulette pit. Everywhere below him fortunes were being won and lost. It takes money to make money. It was his lucky night.

He bought a thousand dollars' worth of chips at a crap table, and enjoyed the attention that all big spenders command. The pit boss examined the unused bills, then smiled at Derrick. A blond waitress appeared from nowhere and he ordered another beer.

Derrick bet heavily, heavier than any white person at the table. The first batch of chips disappeared in fifteen minutes, and he never hesitated before cashing in for a thousand more.

Another thousand soon followed, then the dice got hot and Derrick won eighteen hundred dollars in five minutes. He bought more chips. The beers kept coming. The blond started flirting. The pit boss asked if he wanted to become a gold member of the Nugget.

He lost track of the money. He pulled it from all four pockets, then he replaced some of it. He bought more chips. After an hour, he was down six thousand dollars and wanted desperately to quit. But his luck had to change. The dice had been hot earlier; they'd get hot again. He decided to keep betting heavily, and when his luck turned he'd get it all back. Another beer, and he switched to scotch.

After a bad run, he pulled himself away from the table and returned to the men's room, same stall. He locked it and pulled loose bills from all four pockets. Down to seven thousand dollars, and he felt like crying. But he had to get it back. He decided to go out there and reclaim his money. He'd try a different table. He'd alter his betting. And, regardless of what happened, he would throw up his hands and bolt from the floor if, God help him, his pot dwindled down to five thousand. There was no way he'd lose the last five thousand.

He walked past a roulette table with no players, and on a whim placed five hundred-dollar chips on red. The dealer spun, red played, Derrick made five hundred dollars. He left the chips on red, and won again. With no hesitation, he left the twenty hundred-dollar chips on red, and won for the third straight time. Four thousand dollars in less than five minutes. He got a beer in the sports bar and watched a boxing match. Wild shouting from the crap pit told him to stay away. He felt fortunate to have almost eleven thousand dollars in his pocket.

It was past time for visiting Angel, but he had to see her. He purposely walked through the rows of slot machines, as far away from the crap tables as he could get. He walked fast, hoping to reach the front door before changing his mind and racing toward the dice. He made it.

He'd driven for only a minute, it seemed, when he saw blue lights behind him. It was a City of Biloxi police car, fast on his bumper, headlights flickering. Derrick had no mints or gum. He stopped, got out of the car, and waited for orders from the cop, who got up close and immediately smelled alcohol.

"Been drinking?" he asked.

"Oh, you know, couple of beers at the casino."

The cop checked Derrick's eyes with a blinding flashlight, then made him walk a straight line and touch his nose with his fingers. Derrick was obviously drunk. He was handcuffed and taken to jail. He consented to a breath test and registered .18.

There were lots of questions about the cash stuffed in his pockets. The explanation made sense—he'd had a good night at the casino. But he had no job. He lived with a brother. No criminal record. The jailer listed his cash and other pocket items and locked it all away in a vault.

Derrick sat on a top bunk in the drunk tank, with two winos moaning on the floor. A phone would not help because he couldn't call Angel direct. A five-hour stay was mandatory for drunk drivers. He had to reach Angel before she left for court.

□ □ □ □

THE PHONE woke Swanson at three-thirty Monday morning. The voice on the other end was thick and groggy, the words slurred but obviously belonging to Beverly Monk. "Welcome to the Big Apple," she said loudly, then laughed crazily, bombed out of her mind.

"Where are you?" Swanson demanded. "I've got the money."

"Later," she said, then he heard two angry male voices in the background. "We'll do it later." Someone turned up the music.

"I need the information fast."

"And I need the money."

"Great. Tell me when and where."

"Oh, I don't know," she said, then yelled an obscenity at someone in the room.

Swanson gripped the receiver tighter. "Look, Beverly, listen to me. You remember that little coffee shop where we met last time?"

"Yeah, I think."

"On Eighth, near Balducci's."

"Oh yeah."

"Good. Meet me there as soon as you can."

"How soon is that?" she asked, then erupted in laughter.

Swanson was patient. "How about seven o'clock?"

"What time is it now?"

"Three-thirty."

"Wow."

"Look, why don't I come get you right now? Tell me where you are, and I'll grab a cab."

"Naw, I'm okay. Just having some fun."

"You're drunk."

"So."

"So, if you want this four thousand bucks, you'd better stay sober enough to meet me."

"I'll be there, baby. What's your name again?"

"Swanson."

"Right, Swanson. I'll be there at seven, or close to it." She laughed as she hung up.

Swanson didn't bother to sleep again.

AT FIVE-THIRTY, Marvis Maples presented himself to the jailer and asked if he could collect his brother Derrick. The five hours were up. The jailer retrieved Derrick from the drunk tank, then unlocked a metal tray and placed it on the counter. Derrick inventoried the contents of the tray—eleven thousand dollars in cash, car keys, pocketknife, lip balm—as his brother stared in disbelief.

In the parking lot, Marvis asked about the cash and Derrick explained he'd had a good night at the crap tables. He gave Marvis two hundred dollars and asked if he could borrow his car. Marvis took the money and agreed to wait at the jail until Derrick's car was brought from the city lot.

Derrick raced to Pass Christian and parked behind the Siesta Inn just as the sky was dawning in the east. He crouched low, in case anyone happened by, and sneaked through shrubbery until he came to the window of Angel's room. It was locked, of course, and he began pecking on it. There was no response, and so he picked up a small rock and tapped louder. Daylight was landing all around him, and he was beginning to panic.

"Freeze!" came a loud voice very near his back.

Derrick jerked around to see Chuck, the uniformed deputy, aiming a long shiny black pistol at his forehead. He waved the gun. "Get away from that window! Hands up."

Derrick raised his hands and stepped through the shrubbery. "On the ground" was the next command, and Derrick went spread-eagle on the cold sidewalk, hands behind him. Chuck radioed for help.

Marvis was still loitering around the jail waiting for Derrick's car when his brother returned for his second arrest of the night.

Angel slept through it all.

Thirty-eight

I T WAS A SHAME the juror who'd been the most diligent, listened more carefully than the others, remembered more of what had been said, and obeyed every one of Judge Harkin's rules would be the last one bumped and thus prevented from affecting the verdict.

As reliable as the clock itself, Mrs. Herman Grimes arrived in the dining room at exactly seven-fifteen, took a tray, and began gathering the same breakfast items she had been gathering for almost two weeks. Bran cereal, skim milk, and a banana for Herman. Cornflakes, two percent milk, a strip of bacon, and apple juice for herself. As he often did, Nicholas met her at the buffet and offered to help. He still prepared Herman's coffee throughout the day in the jury room, and he felt obligated to help in the morning. Two sugars and one cream for Herman. Black for Mrs. Grimes. They chatted about whether or not they were packed and ready to go. She seemed genuinely excited at the prospect of eating dinner at home Monday night.

The mood had been downright festive throughout the morning as Nicholas and Henry Vu held court at the dining table and greeted the early stragglers. They were going home!

Mrs. Grimes reached for the silverware, and Nicholas quickly dropped four small tablets into Herman's coffee while saying something about the lawyers. It wouldn't kill him. It was Methergine, an obscure prescription drug used primarily in emergency rooms to revive bodies which were all but dead. Herman would be a sick man for four hours, then recover completely.

As he often did, Nicholas followed her down the hall to their room, carrying the tray and chatting on about this and that. She thanked him generously; such a nice young man.

The commotion hit thirty minutes later, and Nicholas was in the middle of it. Mrs. Grimes stepped into the hallway and yelled at Chuck, who was sitting at his post, sipping coffee and reading the newspaper. Nicholas heard her call, and rushed from his room. Something was wrong with Herman!

Lou Dell and Willis arrived amid panicked voices, and soon most of the jurors were outside the Grimeses' room, where the door was open and people were swarming. Herman was on the bathroom floor, bent double at the waist, clutching his stomach and in terrible pain. Mrs. Grimes and Chuck crouched over him. Lou Dell ran to the phone and called 911. Nicholas said gravely to Rikki Coleman that it was chest pains, maybe a heart attack. Herman had already had one, six years earlier.

Within minutes, everyone knew Herman was suffering from cardiac arrest.

The paramedics arrived with a stretcher, and Chuck pushed the other jurors farther down the hall. Herman was stabilized and given oxygen. His blood pressure was only slightly above normal. Mrs. Grimes said repeatedly it reminded her of his first heart attack.

They rolled him out and pushed him rapidly down the hall. In the confusion, Nicholas managed to knock over Herman's coffee cup.

The sirens wailed as Herman was sped away. The jurors retreated to their rooms to try and settle their frazzled nerves. Lou Dell called Judge Harkin to tell him Herman had fallen violently ill. The consensus was he'd had another heart attack.

"They're dropping like flies," she said, then went on to recollect how she'd never lost so many jurors in her eighteen years as the jury madam. Harkin cut her off.

HE REALLY didn't expect her to arrive promptly at seven for coffee and the cash. Just a few hours earlier she'd been smashed and gave no indication of relenting, so how could he expect her to keep this appointment. He ate a long breakfast and read the first of many newspapers. Eight o'clock came and went. He moved to a better table near the window so he could watch the people on the sidewalk hustle by.

At nine, Swanson called her apartment and managed to pick another fight with the same roommate. No, she was not there, had not been there all night, and maybe she'd moved anyway.

This is someone's daughter, he told himself, living from loft to loft, day to day, scrounging for food and enough money to stay alive and buy the next round of chemicals. Did her parents know what she was doing?

He had plenty of time to consider these matters. At ten, he ordered dry toast because the waiter was staring now, obviously irritated that Swanson had evidently camped out for the day.

FUELED BY RUMORS that were apparently well founded, Pynex' common opened strong. After closing Friday at seventy-three, it jumped to seventy-six at the opening bell and was at seventy-eight within minutes. There was good news out of Biloxi, though no one seemed to know the source. All tobacco stocks rose quickly in early, heavy trading.

JUDGE HARKIN didn't appear until almost nine-thirty, and when he stepped to the bench he noted, without surprise, that his courtroom was packed. He'd just finished a heated argument with Rohr and Cable, the latter of whom wanted a mistrial because another juror had been removed. There were insufficient grounds for a mistrial. Harkin had done his homework. He'd even found an old case allowing eleven jurors to decide a civil case. Nine votes had been required, but the jury's verdict had been upheld by the Supreme Court.

As expected, news of Herman's cardiac arrest spread quickly among the many watching the trial. The jury consultants hired by the defense quietly declared it a major victory for their side because Herman was obviously pro-plaintiff. The jury consultants hired by the plaintiff assured Rohr and company that Herman's removal was a major blow to the defense because Herman was obviously pro-tobacco. All jury experts claimed to welcome the addition of Shine Royce, though most had difficulty with their reasoning.

Fitch just sat in stunned amazement. How in hell do you give someone a heart attack? Was Marlee cold-blooded enough to poison a blind man? Thank God she was on his side.

The door opened. The jurors filed in. Everyone watched to make sure Herman was in fact not among them. His seat was empty.

Judge Harkin had talked to a doctor at the hospital, and he began by telling the jurors that Herman appeared to be responding well, that perhaps it was not as serious as initially thought. The jurors, especially Nicholas, were mightily relieved. Shine Royce became juror number five, and took Herman's old seat on the front row between Phillip Savelle and Angel Weese.

Shine was right proud of himself.

When all was settled and still, His Honor instructed Wendall Rohr to begin his final summation. Keep it under an hour, he warned. Rohr, wearing his favorite gaudy jacket but with a starched shirt and clean bow tie, began softly by apologizing for the length of the trial, and thanking them for being such a wonderful jury. With the friendly remarks behind him, he launched into a vicious description of ". . . the deadliest consumer product ever manufactured. The cigarette. It kills four hundred thousand Americans each year, ten times more than illegal drugs. No other product comes close."

He hit the high points of the testimony of Drs. Fricke, Bronsky, and Kilvan, and he did so without belaboring what they'd said. He reminded them of Lawrence Krigler, a man who'd worked in the industry and knew its dirty secrets. He spent ten minutes talking casually about Leon Robilio, the voiceless one who'd worked for twenty years promoting tobacco, then realized how corrupt the industry was.

Rohr hit his stride when he got around to the kids. For Big Tobacco to survive, it must hook teenagers and ensure the next generation will buy its products. As if he'd been listening in the jury room, Rohr asked the jurors to ask themselves how old they'd been when they started smoking.

Three thousand kids a day pick up the habit. A third of these will eventually die from it. What else had to be said? Wasn't it time to force these rich corporations to stand behind their products? Time to get their attention? Time to make them leave our children alone? Time to make them pay for the damages caused by their products?

He turned nasty when he dwelt on nicotine and Big Tobacco's stubborn insistence that it is not addictive. Former drug addicts had testified that it was easier to quit marijuana and cocaine than cigarettes. He got even meaner when he mentioned Jankle and his abuse theory.

Then he blinked once and was a different person. He talked about his client, Mrs. Celeste Wood, a fine wife, mother, friend, a real victim of the tobacco industry. He talked about her husband, the deceased Mr. Jacob Wood, who'd gotten hooked on Bristols, the star of the Pynex product line, and tried to kick the habit for twenty years. He left behind children and grandchildren. Dead at the age of fifty-one because he'd used a legally manufactured product precisely in the manner in which it was supposed to be used.

He stepped to a white marker board on a tripod and did some quick math. The monetary value of Jacob Wood's life was, say, a million dollars. He added in some other damages and the total became two million. These were the actual damages, monetary amounts the family was entitled to because of Jacob's death.

But the case wasn't about actual damages. Rohr delivered a mini-lecture on punitive damages and their role in keeping corporate America in line. How do you punish a company that has eight hundred million dollars in cash?

You get the company's attention.

Rohr was careful not to suggest a figure, though legally he could have. He simply left $800,000,000 CASH in bold print on the board as he returned to the lectern and finished his remarks. He thanked the jury again, and sat down. Forty-eight minutes.

His Honor declared a ten-minute recess.

SHE WAS FOUR HOURS LATE, but Swanson could've hugged her nonetheless. He didn't, though, because he feared infectious diseases, and because she was escorted by a grimy young man in black leather from toe to cap, jet black hair and goatee, dyed. The word JADE was tattooed impressively in the center of his forehead, and he wore a handsome collection of earrings on both sides of his head.

Jade said nothing as he pulled a chair close and perched on guard like a Doberman.

Beverly appeared to have been beaten. Her lower lip was cut

and puffy. She'd tried to cover a bruise on her cheek with makeup. The corner of her right eye was swollen. She smelled of rancid pot smoke and cheap bourbon, and she was on something, probably speed.

With little provocation, Swanson could've slapped Jade across his tattoo and slowly ripped out the earrings.

"Have you got the money?" she asked, glancing at Jade, who stared blankly at Swanson. No doubt where the money was going.

"Yes. Tell me about Claire."

"Lemme see the money."

Swanson removed a small envelope, opened it slightly to reveal the bills, then tucked it under both hands on the table. "Four thousand bucks. Now talk quickly," he said, glaring at Jade.

Beverly looked at Jade, who nodded like a bad actor and said, "Go ahead."

"Her real name is Gabrielle Brant. She's from Columbia, Missouri. She went to college at the university there, where her mother taught medieval studies. That's all I know."

"What about her father?"

"I think he's dead."

"Anything else?"

"No. Gimme the money."

Swanson slid it across the table, and immediately jumped to his feet. "Thanks," he said, and disappeared.

IT TOOK DURWOOD CABLE slightly more than half an hour to skillfully discount the ridiculous notion of giving millions to the family of a man who'd voluntarily smoked for thirty-five years. The trial was hardly more than a naked grab for money.

What he resented most about the plaintiff's case was that they had attempted to shift the issues away from Jacob Wood and his habits, and turn the trial into an emotional debate on teenage smoking. What did Jacob Wood have to do with current cigarette advertising? There wasn't an ounce of proof that the late Mr. Wood had been influenced by an ad campaign. He had started smoking because he chose to start.

Why bring the kids into this fight? Emotion, that's why. We respond angrily when we think children are being hurt or manipulated. And before the plaintiff's lawyers can convince you, the jurors, to hand them a fortune, they must first make you angry.

Cable deftly appealed to their sense of fairness. Decide the case on its facts, not on emotions. When he finished, he had their complete attention.

As he took his seat, Judge Harkin thanked him and said to the jury, "Ladies and gentlemen, the case now belongs to you. I suggest you select a new foreman to take the place of Mr. Grimes, who I'm told is doing much better. I talked to his wife during the last recess, and he is still quite ill but expected to recover fully. If for any reason you need to speak to me, please notify madam clerk. The rest of your instructions will be handed to you in the jury room. Good luck."

As Harkin bid them farewell, Nicholas turned slightly to the audience and locked eyes with Rankin Fitch, just a brief acknowledgment of where matters were at the moment. Fitch nodded, and Nicholas stood with his colleagues.

It was almost noon. Court was in recess subject to the call of the bench, which meant that those who wanted to were free to loiter about until the jury reached a verdict. The horde from Wall Street sprinted out to call their offices. The Big Four CEO's mingled with underlings for a moment, then made their way out of the courtroom.

Fitch left immediately and went to his office. Konrad was hovering over a bank of phones. "It's her," he said anxiously. "She's calling from a pay phone." Fitch walked even faster to his office, where he grabbed his phone. "Hello."

"Fitch, look. New wiring instructions. Put me on hold and go to your fax." Fitch looked at his private fax, which was transmitting.

"It's right here," he said. "Why new instructions?"

"Shut up, Fitch. Just do as I say, and do it immediately."

Fitch yanked the fax from his machine and skimmed the handwritten message. The money was now headed to Panama. Banco Atlántico, in Panama City. She had routing instructions and account numbers.

"You have twenty minutes, Fitch. The jury is eating lunch. If I don't have a confirmation by twelve-thirty, then the deal is off and Nicholas changes directions. He has a cellphone in his pocket, and he's waiting for me to call."

"Call back at twelve-thirty," Fitch said, hanging up. He told Konrad to hold all calls. No exceptions. He immediately faxed her message to his wiring expert in D.C., who in turn faxed the necessary authorization to Hanwa Bank in the Netherlands Antilles. Hanwa had been on standby all morning, and within ten minutes the money left Fitch's account and bounced across the Caribbean to the bank in Panama City, where it had been expected. A confirmation from Hanwa was faxed to Fitch, who, at the moment, would've loved to fax it to Marlee, but he didn't have her number.

At twelve-twenty, Marlee called her banker in Panama, who confirmed the receipt of ten million dollars.

Marlee was in a motel room five miles away, working with a portable fax. She waited five minutes, then sent instructions to the same banker to wire the money to a bank in the Cayman Islands. All of it, and once it's gone, close the account in Banco Atlántico.

Nicholas called at exactly twelve-thirty. He was hiding in the men's room. Lunch was over, and it was time to start the deliberations. Marlee said the money was safe, and that she was leaving.

Fitch waited until almost one. She called from another pay phone. "The money has arrived, Fitch," she said.

"Great. How about lunch?"

"Maybe later."

"So when can we expect a verdict?"

"Late afternoon. I hope you're not worried, Fitch."

"Me. Never."

"Just relax. It'll be your finest hour. Twelve to zip, Fitch. How does that sound?"

"Like music. Why'd you bump poor old Herman?"

"Don't know what you're talking about."

"Yeah right. When can we celebrate?"

"I'll call you later."

She sped away in a rented car, watching every movement behind her. Her leased car was sitting in front of her condo, abandoned for all she cared. In the backseat she had two bags stuffed with clothing, the only personal items she could pack, along with the portable fax. The furniture in the condo would belong to whoever bought it at a sidewalk sale.

She looped through a subdivision, a run she'd practiced yesterday in case anyone wanted to follow. Fitch's boys weren't behind her. She zigzagged through side streets until she came to the Gulf-port Municipal Airport, where the small Lear Jet was waiting. She grabbed her two bags and locked the keys in the car.

SWANSON CALLED ONCE, but couldn't get through. He called the supervisor in Kansas City, and three agents were immediately dispatched to Columbia, an hour away. Two more worked the phones, making rapid calls to the University of Missouri, to the medieval studies department, in a desperate attempt to locate someone who knew something and was willing to talk. Six Brants were listed in the Columbia phone book. All were called more than once and none claimed to know Gabrielle Brant.

He finally got Fitch on the phone just after one. Fitch had been barricaded in his office for an hour, taking no calls. Swanson was on his way to Missouri.

Thirty-nine

WHEN THE LUNCH DISHES were cleared and all the smokers had returned from the smoke room, it became apparent that they were now supposed to do what they'd been dreaming about for a month. They took their places around the table, and stared at the empty seat at the end, the one Herman had so proudly occupied.

"Guess we need a new foreman," Jerry said.

"And I think it should be Nicholas," Millie added quickly.

There really wasn't any doubt about who the new foreman would be. No one else wanted the job, and Nicholas seemed to know as much about the trial as the lawyers themselves. He was elected by acclamation.

He stood by Herman's old chair and summarized a list of suggestions from Judge Harkin. He said, "He wants us to carefully consider all the evidence, including the exhibits and documents, before we start voting." Nicholas turned to his left and stared at a table in a corner piled high with all those wonderful reports and studies they'd been collecting for the last four weeks.

"I'm not planning on staying here for three days," Lonnie said as they all looked at the table. "In fact, I'm ready to vote now."

"Not so fast," Nicholas said. "This is a complicated, very important case, and it would be wrong to rush things without thoughtful deliberation."

"I say we vote," Lonnie said.

"And I say we do what the Judge says. We can call him in for a chat, if necessary."

"We're not going to read all that stuff, are we?" asked Sylvia the Poodle. Reading was not one of her favorite pastimes.

"I have an idea," Nicholas said. "Why don't we each take a report, skim it, then summarize it for everyone else? We can then honestly tell Judge Harkin that we reviewed all the exhibits and documents."

"Do you really think he'll want to know?" asked Rikki Coleman.

"Probably so. Our verdict must be based on the evidence before us—the testimony we heard and the exhibits we've been given. We at least have to make an effort to follow his orders."

"I agree," said Millie. "We all want to go home, but our duty demands that we carefully consider what's before us."

With that, the other protests were snuffed out. Millie and Henry Vu lifted the bulky reports and placed them in the center of the table, where they were slowly taken by the jurors.

"Just skim through them," Nicholas said, coaxing them along like a flustered schoolteacher. He grabbed the thickest one, a study by Dr. Milton Fricke on the effects of cigarette smoke on the respiratory tract, and he read it as if he'd never seen such dynamic prose.

In the courtroom, a few of the curious hung around for a spell in hopes there might be a quick verdict. This often happened—get the jury back there, feed 'em lunch, let 'em vote, and you've got yourself a verdict. The jury had made up its mind before the first witness.

But not this one.

AT FORTY-ONE THOUSAND FEET and at five hundred miles per hour, the Lear made the trip from Biloxi to George Town, Grand Cayman, in ninety minutes. Marlee cleared customs with a new Canadian passport, one issued to Lane MacRoland, a pretty young lady from Toronto who was down for a week of pleasure, no business. As required by Caymanian law, she also possessed a return air ticket, which showed her booked on a Delta flight to Miami in six days. The Caymanians were delighted to have tourists, but had other thoughts about new citizens.

The passport was part of a perfect set of new papers she'd

purchased from a noted forger in Montreal. Passport, driver's license, birth certificate, voter's registration card. Cost: three thousand dollars.

She took a cab into George Town and found her bank, the Royal Swiss Trust, in a stately old building a block from the seafront. She'd never been to Grand Cayman before, though it felt like a second home. She'd been studying the place for two months. Her financial affairs there had been carefully arranged by fax.

The tropical air was heavy and warm, but she hardly noticed. She wasn't there for the sun and beaches. It was three o'clock in George Town and New York. Two P.M. in Mississippi.

She was greeted by a receptionist and led to a small office where another form had to be completed, one that couldn't be faxed. Within minutes, a young man named Marcus introduced himself. They had spoken many times on the phone. He was slender, well groomed, well tailored, very European, with a slight accent to his perfect English.

The money had arrived, he informed her, and Marlee managed to take the news while suppressing any sign of a smile. It was difficult. The paperwork was in order. She followed him upstairs to his office. Marcus' title was vague, like a lot of bankers' titles in Grand Cayman, but he was a vice president of this or that, and he managed portfolios.

A secretary brought coffee and Marlee ordered a sandwich.

Pynex was at seventy-nine, up strongly all day in heavy trading, Marcus reported while pecking at his computer. Trellco was up three and a quarter to fifty-six. Smith Greer was up two to sixty-four and a half. ConPack was trading even at around thirty-three.

Working from notes which were virtually memorized, Marlee made her first trade by selling short fifty thousand shares of Pynex at seventy-nine. Hopefully, she would buy it back in the very near future at a much lower price. Short selling was a tricky maneuver normally used by only the most sophisticated investors. If the price of a stock was about to fall, trading rules allowed the stock to be sold first at the higher price, then purchased later at a lower one.

With ten million in cash, Marlee would be allowed to sell approximately twenty million dollars' worth of stocks.

Marcus confirmed the trade with a flurry of keypunching, and he excused himself for a second while he put on his headset. Her second trade was the short selling of Trellco—thirty thousand shares at fifty-six and a quarter. He confirmed it, and then came the flurry. She sold forty thousand shares of Smith Greer at sixty-four and a half; sixty thousand more of Pynex at seventy-nine and an eighth; thirty thousand more of Trellco at fifty-six and an eighth; fifty thousand of Smith Greer at sixty-four and three-eighths.

She paused and instructed Marcus to watch Pynex closely. She had just unloaded one hundred and ten thousand shares of its stock, and was very concerned about the immediate response on Wall Street. It stalled at seventy-nine, dropped to seventy-eight and three-quarters, then eased back to seventy-nine.

"I think it's safe now," said Marcus, who'd been watching the stock closely for two weeks.

"Sell fifty thousand more," she said without hesitation.

Marcus skipped one beat, then nodded at his monitor and completed the trade.

Pynex dipped to seventy-eight and a half, then down another quarter. She sipped her coffee and fiddled with her notes as Marcus watched and Wall Street reacted. She thought about Nicholas, and what he was doing right now, but she wasn't worried. In fact, she was remarkably calm at the moment.

Marcus removed his headset. "That's approximately twenty-two million dollars, Ms. MacRoland. I think we should stop. More sales will require approval from my superior."

"That's enough," she said.

"The market closes in fifteen minutes. You're welcome to wait in our client lounge."

"No thanks. I'll go to the hotel, maybe get some sun."

Marcus stood and buttoned his jacket. "One question. When do you anticipate movement on these stocks?"

"Tomorrow. Early."

"Significant movement?"

Marlee stood and held her notes. "Yes. If you want your other clients to think you're a genius, then short sell tobacco right now."

He sent for a company car, a small Mercedes, and Marlee was driven to a hotel on Seven Mile Beach, not far from downtown and the bank.

□ □ □ □

IF MARLEE'S PRESENT seemed under control, her past was rapidly catching up with her. An operative digging for Fitch at the University of Missouri found a collection of old admissions manuals in the main library. In 1986, a Dr. Evelyn Y. Brant was listed and briefly described as a professor of medieval studies, but she was absent from the 1987 handbook.

He immediately called an associate who was checking through tax rolls at the Boone County Courthouse. The associate went straight to the clerk's office and within minutes found the Wills and Estates register. Evelyn Y. Brant's will had been received for probate in April of 1987. A clerk helped him find the file.

It was pay dirt. Mrs. Brant had died on March 2, 1987, in Columbia, at the age of fifty-six. She left no husband and one child, Gabrielle, age twenty-one, who inherited everything under a will Dr. Brant signed three months before her death.

The file was an inch thick, and the agent scanned it with great speed. The inventory consisted of a house valued at $180,000 with a mortgage of half that, a car, an unimpressive list of furniture and furnishings, a certificate of deposit at a local bank in the amount of $32,000, and a stock and bond portfolio valued at $202,000. There were only two creditors' claims filed; evidently Dr. Brant had known death was imminent and obtained legal advice. With the approval of Gabrielle, the house was sold, the estate was reduced to cash, and after estate taxes, legal fees, and court costs, the sum of $191,500 was placed in a trust. Gabrielle was the only beneficiary.

The estate had been handled without the slightest hint of acrimony. The lawyer appeared to be prompt and quite competent. Thirteen months after Dr. Brant's death, the estate was closed.

He flipped through again, making notes. Two pages stuck together, and he delicately pulled them apart. The bottom one was a half sheet with an official stamp on it.

It was the death certificate. Dr. Evelyn Y. Brant had died of lung cancer.

He stepped into the hallway and called his supervisor.

BY THE TIME the call was placed to Fitch, they knew more. A careful reading of the file by another operative, this one a former FBI agent with a law degree, revealed a series of donations to such groups as the American Lung Association, the Coalition for a Smoke Free World, the Tobacco Task Force, the Clean Air Campaign, and a half-dozen other antismoking causes. One of the creditors' claims was a bill for almost twenty thousand dollars for her last hospital stay. Her husband, the late Dr. Peter Brant, was listed on an old insurance policy. A quick search of the register listed the opening of his estate in 1981. His file was located on the other side of the clerk's office. He died in June of 1981 at the age of fifty-two, leaving his beloved wife and cherished daughter, Gabrielle, then age fifteen. He died at home, according to his death certificate, which was signed by the same doctor who'd signed Evelyn Brant's. An oncologist.

Peter Brant had also succumbed to the ravages of lung cancer.

Swanson made the call, but only after being repeatedly assured that the facts were correct.

FITCH TOOK THE CALL in his office, alone, with the door locked, and he took it calmly because he was too shocked to react. He was seated at his desk with his jacket off, tie undone, shoes unlaced. He said little.

Both of Marlee's parents had died of lung cancer.

He actually scribbled this on a yellow pad, then drew a circle around it, with lines branching off, as if he could flow-chart this news, break it down, analyze it; somehow he could make it fit with her promise to deliver a verdict.

"Are you there, Rankin?" Swanson asked after a long silence.

"Yeah," Fitch said, then continued saying nothing for a while. The flow chart grew but went nowhere.

"Where's the girl?" Swanson asked. He was standing in the cold outside the county courthouse in Columbia with an impossibly small phone pressed to his jaw.

"Don't know. We'll have to find her." He said this with no conviction whatsoever, and Swanson knew the girl was gone.

Another long pause.

"What shall I do?" Swanson asked.

"Get back here, I guess," Fitch said, then abruptly hung up. The numbers on his digital clock were blurred, and Fitch closed his eyes. He massaged his pounding temples, pressed his goatee hard against his chin, contemplated an eruption with the desk flying against the wall and phones ripped from sockets, but thought the better of it. A cool head was needed.

Short of burning the courthouse or tossing grenades at the jury room, there was nothing he could do to stop the deliberations. They were in there, the last twelve, with deputies by the door. Perhaps if their work was slow, and if they had to retire for another night in sequestration, then perhaps Fitch could pull a rabbit from his hat and spark a mistrial.

A bomb threat was a possibility. The jurors would be evacuated, sequestered some more, led away to some hidden place so they could continue.

The flow chart fizzled and he made lists of possibilities—outrageous acts, all of which would be dangerous, illegal, and destined for failure.

The clock was ticking.

The chosen twelve—eleven disciples and their master.

He slowly rose to his feet and took the cheap ceramic lamp with both hands. It was a lamp Konrad had earlier wanted to remove because it sat on Fitch's desk, a place of great chaos and violence.

Konrad and Pang were loitering in the hallway, waiting for instructions. They knew something had gone terribly wrong. The lamp crashed with great force against the door. Fitch screamed. The plywood walls rattled. Another object hit and splintered; maybe it was a telephone. Fitch yelled something about "the money!" and then the desk landed loudly against a wall.

They backed away, petrified and not wanting to be near the door when it opened. Bam! Bam! Bam! It sounded like a jackhammer. Fitch was punching the plywood with his fists.

"Find the girl!" he screamed in anguish. Bam! Bam!

"Find the girl!"

Forty

AFTER A PAINFUL STRETCH of forced concentration, Nicholas sensed some debate was needed. He elected to go first, and briefly summarized Dr. Fricke's report on the condition of Jacob Wood's lungs. He passed around the autopsy photos, none of which attracted much attention. This was old territory and the audience was bored.

"Dr. Fricke's report says that prolonged cigarette smoking causes lung cancer," Nicholas said dutifully, as if this might surprise someone.

"I have an idea," Rikki Coleman said. "Let's see if we can all agree that cigarettes cause lung cancer. It'll save us a lot of time." She'd been waiting for a crack in the door, and seemed ready to quarrel.

"Great idea," Lonnie said. He was by far the most hyper and frustrated of the bunch.

Nicholas shrugged his approval. He was the foreman, but he still had only one vote. The jury could do what it pleased. "Fine with me," he said. "Does everyone believe cigarettes cause lung cancer? Raise your hands."

Twelve hands shot up, and a giant step was taken toward a verdict.

"Let's go ahead and take care of addiction," Rikki said, looking up and down the table. "Who thinks nicotine is addictive?"

Another unanimous yes.

She savored the moment and appeared on the verge of venturing onto the thin ice of liability.

"Let's keep it unanimous, folks," Nicholas said. "It's crucial that we walk out of here united. If we split, then we fail."

Most of them had already heard this little pep talk. The legal reasons behind his quest for a unanimous verdict were not clear, but they believed him nonetheless.

"Now, let's finish these reports. Is someone ready?"

Loreen Duke's was a glossy publication prepared by Dr. Myra Sprawling-Goode. She'd read the introduction, which declared the study to be a thorough review of advertising practices by tobacco companies, especially how said practices related to children under the age of eighteen, and she'd read the conclusion, which absolved the industry of targeting underage smokers. Most of the two hundred pages in between had gone untouched.

She summarized the summary. "Just says here they couldn't find any evidence of tobacco companies advertising to attract kids."

"Do you believe that?" asked Millie.

"No. I thought we'd already decided that most folks start smoking before they're eighteen. Didn't we take a poll in here one day?"

"We did," Rikki answered. "And all the smokers here started when they were young teenagers."

"And most of them quit, as I recall," Lonnie said, with no small amount of bitterness.

"Let's move along," Nicholas said. "Anybody else?"

Jerry offered a lame effort at describing the tedious findings of Dr. Hilo Kilvan, the statistical genius who'd proven the increased risks of lung cancer among smokers. Jerry's summation sparked no interest, no questions, no debate, and he left the room for a quick smoke.

Then there was silence as they continued to plow through the printed material. They came and went at will—to smoke, to stretch, to use the rest rooms. Lou Dell and Willis and Chuck guarded the door.

MRS. GLADYS CARD had once taught biology to ninth-graders. She had a grasp of science. She did a superb job of dissecting Dr. Robert Bronsky's report on the composition of cigarette smoke—

the more than four thousand compounds, the sixteen known carcinogens, the fourteen alkalis, the irritants, and all that other stuff. She used her best classroom diction and looked from face to face.

Most faces cringed as she droned on and on.

When she finished, Nicholas, still awake, thanked her warmly and stood to get more coffee.

"So what do you think about all that?" Lonnie asked. He was standing in front of the window, his back to the room, eating peanuts and holding a soft drink.

"To me, it proves cigarette smoke is pretty harmful," she answered.

Lonnie turned around and looked at her. "Right. I thought we'd already decided that." He then looked at Nicholas. "I say we get on with the voting. We've been reading now for almost three hours, and if the Judge asks me if I've looked at all that stuff, I'm gonna say, 'Hell yeah. Read every word.' "

"Do what you wanna do, Lonnie," Nicholas shot back.

"All right. Let's vote."

"Vote on what?" Nicholas asked. The two were now standing on opposites sides of the table, with the seated jurors between them.

"Let's see who's standing where. I'll go first."

"Go. Let's hear it."

Lonnie took a deep breath and everyone turned to watch him.

"My position is real easy. I believe cigarettes are dangerous products. They're addictive. They're deadly. That's why I leave them alone. Everybody knows this, in fact we've already decided it. I believe every person has a right to choose. Nobody can force you to smoke, but if you do, then you suffer the consequences. Don't puff like hell for thirty years, then expect me to make you rich. These crazy lawsuits need to be stopped."

His voice was loud and every word got absorbed.

"You finished?" Nicholas asked.

"Yeah."

"Who's next?"

"I have a question," said Mrs. Gladys Card. "How much money does the plaintiff expect us to award? Mr. Rohr sort of left it hanging."

"He wants two million in actual damages. The punitive is left to our discretion," Nicholas explained.

"Then why'd he leave eight hundred million on the board?"

"Because he'd take eight hundred million," Lonnie replied. "Are you gonna give it to him?"

"I don't think so," she said. "I didn't know there was that much money in the world. Would Celeste Wood get all of it?"

"You see all those lawyers out there?" Lonnie asked sardonically. "She'll be lucky to get anything. This trial ain't about her or her dead husband. This trial is about a bunch of lawyers getting rich suing tobacco companies. We're stupid if we fall for it."

"Do you know when I started smoking?" Angel Weese asked Lonnie, who was still standing.

"No. I don't."

"I remember the exact day. I was thirteen, and I saw this big billboard on Decatur Street, not far from my house, had this big, lean black guy, really good-looking, with his jeans rolled up, splashing water on a beach, cigarette in one hand and a slinky black chick on his back. All smiles. All perfect teeth. Salem menthols. What great fun. I thought to myself, Now there's the good life. I'd like to have some of that. So I went home, went to my drawer, got my money, walked down the street, and bought a pack of Salem menthols. My friends thought I was so cool, so I've been smoking them ever since." She paused and glanced at Loreen Duke, then back to Lonnie. "Don't try to tell me anyone can kick the habit. I'm addicted, okay. It ain't that easy. I'm twenty years old, two packs a day, and if I don't quit I won't see fifty. And don't tell me they don't target kids. They target blacks, women, kids, cowboys, rednecks, they target everybody, and you know it."

For one who'd shown no emotion in the four weeks they'd been together, the anger in Angel's voice was a surprise. Lonnie glared down at her, but said nothing.

Loreen came to her aid. "One of my girls, the fifteen-year-old, told me last week she'd started smoking at school because all of her friends are now smoking. These kids are too young to know about addiction, and by the time they realize, they'll be hooked. I asked her where she gets her cigarettes. You know what she told me?"

Lonnie said nothing.

"Vending machines. There's one next to the arcade at the mall where the kids hang out. And there's one in the lobby of the cinema where the kids hang out. A couple of the fast-food places have machines. And you're gonna tell me they don't target kids. It makes me sick. I can't wait to get home and straighten her out."

"So what're you gonna do when she starts drinking beer?" Jerry asked. "You gonna sue Budweiser for ten million because all the other kids are sneaking beer?"

"There's no proof that beer is physically addictive," Rikki responded.

"Oh, so it doesn't kill?"

"There's a difference."

"Please explain it," Jerry said. The debate now covered two of his favorite vices. Could gambling and philandering be next?

Rikki arranged her thoughts for a second, then launched into an unpleasant defense of alcohol. "Cigarettes are the only products that are deadly if used exactly as intended. Alcohol is supposed to be consumed, of course, but in reasonable amounts. And if it's taken in moderation, then it's not a dangerous product. Sure, people get drunk and kill themselves in all sorts of ways, but a strong argument can be made that the product is not being used properly in those instances."

"So if a person drinks for fifty years he's not killing himself?"

"Not if he drinks in moderation."

"Boy, that's good to hear."

"And there's something else. Alcohol has a natural warning. You get an immediate feedback when you use the product. Not so with tobacco. It takes years of smoking before you realize the damage to your body. By then, you're hooked and can't quit."

"Most people can quit," Lonnie said from the window, without looking at Angel.

"And why do you think everyone's trying to quit?" Rikki asked calmly. "Is it because they're enjoying their cigarettes? Is it because they feel young and glamorous? No, they're trying to quit to avoid lung cancer and heart disease."

"So how are you voting?" Lonnie asked.

"I guess it's pretty obvious," she answered. "I started this trial with an open mind, but I've come to realize that the only way to hold the tobacco companies responsible is for us to do it."

"What about you?" Lonnie asked Jerry, hoping to find a friend.

"I'm undecided right now. I think I'll listen to everybody else."

"And you?" he asked Sylvia Taylor-Tatum.

"I'm having a hard time understanding why we're supposed to make this woman a multimillionaire."

Lonnie walked around the table, looking at faces, most of which tried to avoid him. There was no doubt he was enjoying his role as a rebel leader. "What about you, Mr. Savelle? You don't seem to say much."

This would be interesting. No one on the panel had a clue about what Savelle was thinking.

"I believe in choice," he said. "Absolute choice. I deplore what these corporations do to the environment. I hate their products. But each person has the power to choose."

"Mr. Vu?" Lonnie said.

Henry cleared his throat, pondered things for a minute, then said, "I'm still thinking." Henry would follow Nicholas, who for the moment was incredibly quiet.

"What about you, Mr. Foreman?" Lonnie asked.

"We can finish these reports in thirty minutes. Let's do it, then we'll start voting."

After the first serious skirmish, they were relieved to read for a few more minutes. The shootout was clearly not far away.

AT FIRST he felt like roaming the streets in his Suburban with José at the wheel, up and down Highway 90 to no place in particular, no chance of catching her. At least he'd be out there doing something, trying to find her, hoping maybe to stumble upon her.

He knew she was gone.

So he stayed instead in his office, alone by the phone praying she'd call one more time and tell him a deal was a deal. Throughout the afternoon Konrad came and went, bearing the news that Fitch expected to hear: Her car was outside the condo, and it hadn't been moved in eight hours. No activity in or out of the condo. No sign of her whatsoever. She was gone.

Oddly, the longer the jury stayed out, the more hope Fitch managed to create for himself. If she planned to take the money and run, and screw Fitch with a plaintiff's verdict, then where was the verdict? Maybe it wouldn't be that easy. Nicholas could be having a hard time in there getting his votes.

Fitch had never lost one of these, and he kept reminding himself he'd been here before, sweating blood while the jury fought.

AT PRECISELY FIVE, Judge Harkin reconvened his courtroom, and sent for the jury. The lawyers scurried to get in place. Most of the spectators returned.

The jurors took their seats. They looked tired, but then all jurors did at this point.

"Just a few quick questions," His Honor said. "Have you elected a new foreman?"

They nodded, and then Nicholas raised his hand. "I have the honor," he said softly, without the slightest trace of pride.

"Good. Just so you'll know, I talked with Herman Grimes about an hour ago, and he's doing fine. Seems to be something other than a heart attack, and he's expected to be released tomorrow. He sent his best wishes."

Most of them managed a pleasant expression.

"Now, you've had the case for five hours, and I'd like to know if you're making progress."

Nicholas stood awkwardly, and stuffed his hands in his khakis. "I think so, Your Honor."

"Good. Without indicating anything that's been discussed, do you think the jury will reach a verdict, one way or the other?"

Nicholas glanced around at his peers, then said, "I think we will, Your Honor. Yes, I'm confident we'll have a verdict."

"When might you have a verdict? Mind you, I'm not rushing. You can take as much time as you wish. I just need to make plans for this courtroom if we're gonna be here into the night."

"We want to go home, Your Honor. We're determined to wrap this up and have a verdict sometime tonight."

"Wonderful. Thank you. Dinner is on the way. I'll be in my chambers if you need me."

Forty-one

MR. O'REILLY was back for the last time, serving his final meal and saying good-bye to people he now considered friends. He and three employees fed and served them as if they were royalty.

Dinner was over at six-thirty, and the jury was ready to go home. They agreed to vote first on the issue of liability. Nicholas couched the question in layman's terms: "Are you willing to hold Pynex liable for the death of Jacob Wood?"

Rikki Coleman, Millie Dupree, Loreen Duke, and Angel Weese said yes, unequivocally. Lonnie, Phillip Savelle, and Mrs. Gladys Card said no, without question. The rest fell somewhere in between. Poodle was uncertain, but leaning toward no. Jerry was suddenly vacillating, but probably leaning toward no. Shine Royce, the newest member of the panel, hadn't said three words all day and was simply drifting in the breeze. He'd jump on the nearest bandwagon, as soon as he could identify one. Henry Vu declared himself to be undecided, but he was really waiting for Nicholas, who was waiting until everybody had finished. He was disappointed that the jury was so divided.

"I think it's time for you to declare," Lonnie said to Nicholas, itching for a fight.

"Yeah, let's hear it," Rikki said, also ready to argue. All eyes were glued to the foreman.

"Okay," he said, and the room went perfectly still. After years of planning, it all came down to this. He chose his words carefully, but in his mind he'd made the speech a thousand times. "I'm convinced cigarettes are dangerous and deadly; they kill four hundred thousand people a year; they're loaded with nicotine by their makers, who've known for a long time that the stuff is addictive; they could be a lot safer if the companies wanted, but the nicotine would be reduced and thus sales would suffer. I think cigarettes killed Jacob Wood, and none of you will argue this. I'm convinced the tobacco companies lie and cheat and cover up, and do everything in their power to get kids to smoke. They're a ruthless bunch of sonofabitches, and I say we stick it to them."

"I agree," said Henry Vu.

Rikki and Millie felt like clapping.

"You want punitives?" Jerry asked, in disbelief.

"The verdict means nothing if it's not significant, Jerry. It has to be huge. A verdict for actual damages only means we don't have the guts to punish the tobacco industry for its corporate sins."

"We have to make it hurt," Shine Royce said, but only because he wanted to sound intelligent. He'd found his bandwagon.

Lonnie looked at Shine and Vu in disbelief. He counted quickly—seven votes for the plaintiff. "You can't talk money, because you don't have your votes yet."

"They're not my votes," Nicholas said.

"The hell they're not," he said bitterly. "This is your verdict."

They went around the table again—seven for the plaintiff, three for the defense, Jerry and Poodle straddling the fence but looking for a place to land. Then Mrs. Gladys Card upset the tally by saying, "I don't like voting for the tobacco company, but, at the same time, I just can't understand giving Celeste Wood all this money."

"How much money would you give her?" Nicholas asked.

She was flustered and confused. "I just don't know. I'll vote to give something, but, well, I just don't know."

"How much do you have in mind?" Rikki asked the foreman, and the room was still again. Very still and quiet.

"A billion," Nicholas said with a completely straight face. It landed like a percussion bomb on the center of the table. Mouths fell open and eyes bulged.

Before anyone could speak, Nicholas explained himself. "If we're serious about sending a message to the tobacco industry, then we have to shock them. Our verdict should be a landmark. It should be famous and known from this day forward as the moment the American public, acting through its jury system, finally stood up to the tobacco industry and said, 'Enough is enough.' "

"You're outta your mind," Lonnie said, and at the moment, most felt the same way.

"So you want to be famous," Jerry said, heavy on the sarcasm.

"Not me, but the verdict. Nobody will remember our names next week, but everyone will remember our verdict. If we're gonna do it, then let's do it right."

"I like it," Shine Royce chimed in. The thought of dispensing so much money made him giddy. Shine was the only juror ready to spend another night at the motel so he could eat free and collect another fifteen dollars tomorrow.

"Tell us what will happen," Millie said, still stunned.

"It'll be appealed, and some day, probably two years from now, a bunch of old goats in black robes will reduce it. They'll lower it to something more reasonable. They'll say it was a runaway verdict from a runaway jury, and they'll fix it. The system works most of the time."

"Then why should we do it?" Loreen asked.

"For change. We'll start the long process of making the tobacco companies accountable for killing so many people. Keep in mind, they've never lost a trial such as this. They think they're invincible. We prove otherwise, and we do it in such a way that other plaintiffs are not afraid to take on the industry."

"So you want to bankrupt them," Lonnie said.

"Wouldn't bother me. Pynex is worth one-point-two billion, and virtually all its profits have come at the expense of people who use their products but would love to quit. Yeah, come to think of it, the world would be a better place without Pynex. Who'd cry if it folded?"

"Maybe its employees," Lonnie said.

"Good point. But I have more sympathy for the thousands of people hooked on their products."

"How much will the appeals court give Celeste Wood?" Mrs. Gladys Card asked. She was troubled by the idea that one of her neighbors, albeit a person she didn't know, was going to get rich. Sure, she'd lost her husband, but Mr. Card had survived prostate cancer with no thought of suing anybody.

"I have no idea," Nicholas said. "And that's not something we should worry about. That's another day in another courtroom, and there are guidelines to be followed when reducing large verdicts."

"A billion dollars," Loreen repeated to herself, but audibly enough to be heard. It was as easy to say as "A million dollars." Most of the jurors stared at the table and repeated the word "billion."

Not for the first time, Nicholas thanked himself for Herrera's absence. At a moment like this, with a billion dollars on the table, Herrera would be raising hell and probably throwing things. But the room was quiet. Lonnie was the only advocate left for the defense, and he was busy counting and recounting votes.

Herman's absence was also important, probably more so than the Colonel's because people would listen to Herman. He was thoughtful and calculating, not prone to emotion and certainly not susceptible to an outrageous verdict.

But they were gone.

Nicholas had steered the talk away from liability and onto the issue of damages, a crucial shift that no one recognized but himself. The billion dollars had stunned them and forced them to think about money, not fault.

He was determined to keep their thoughts on money. "It's just an idea," he said. "It's important to get their attention."

Nicholas quickly winked at Jerry, who entered perfectly on cue. "I can't go that high," he said in his best car salesman routine, which was pretty effective. "It's, well, it's outrageous. I can see some damages, but, damn, this is just plain crazy."

"It's not outrageous," Nicholas argued. "The company has eight hundred million in cash. The place is like a mint. All tobacco companies print their own money."

Jerry made eight, and Lonnie withdrew to a corner, where he began clipping his fingernails.

And Poodle made nine. "It is outrageous, and I can't do that," she said. "Something lower maybe, but not a billion dollars."

"So how much?" Rikki asked.

Only five hundred million. Only one hundred million. They could not force themselves to utter these ridiculous sums of money.

"I don't know," Sylvia said. "What do you think?"

"I like the idea of putting these guys on the ropes," Rikki said. "If we're going to send a message, then let's not be shy about it."

"A billion?" Sylvia asked.

"Yeah, I can do that."

"Me too," Shine said, feeling wealthy just by being there.

There was a long pause; the only sound came from Lonnie snipping his fingernails.

Finally, Nicholas said, "Who cannot vote to return any damages whatsoever?"

Savelle raised his hand. Lonnie ignored the question, but then he didn't need to respond.

"The vote stands at ten to two," Nicholas reported, and wrote this down. "This jury has hereby reached its decision on liability. Now, let's settle the issue of damages. Can the ten of us agree that the Wood estate is entitled to the two million in actual damages?"

Savelle kicked his chair back and left the room. Lonnie poured a cup of coffee and sat by the window, his back to the group, but listening to every word.

The two million sounded like pocket change in light of the previous discussion, and it was approved by the ten. Nicholas wrote this on a form approved by Judge Harkin.

"Can the ten of us agree that punitive damages should be imposed, in some amount?" He slowly went around the table and got a "Yes" from each. Mrs. Gladys Card hesitated. She could change her mind, but it would have no impact. Only nine votes were needed for a verdict.

"All right. Now, as to the amount of punitive damages. Any ideas?"

"I have one," Jerry said. "Get everybody to write their amount on a piece of paper, fold it, keep it secret, then add them up and divide by ten. That way we'll see what the average is."

"Will it be binding?" Nicholas asked.

"No. But it'll give us an idea of where we are."

The idea of a secret ballot was very appealing, and they quickly scribbled their numbers on scraps of paper.

Nicholas slowly unfolded each ballot and called the amounts to Millie, who wrote them down. One billion, one million, fifty million, ten million, one billion, one million, five million, five hundred million, one billion, and two million.

Millie did the math. "The total is three billion, five hundred sixty-nine million. Divide by ten, and the average is three hundred fifty-six million, nine hundred thousand."

It took a moment for the zeros to settle in. Lonnie jumped to his feet and walked by the table. "You people are crazy," he said just loud enough to be heard, then left the room, slamming the door.

"I can't do this," Mrs. Gladys Card said, visibly shaken. "I'm living on a pension, okay. It's a good pension, but I cannot fathom these numbers."

"The numbers are real," Nicholas said. "The company has eight hundred million in cash, equity of over a billion. Last year our country spent six billion on medical costs directly related to smoking, and the number goes up each year. The four largest tobacco companies had combined sales last year of almost sixteen billion. And their numbers are going up. You gotta think big, okay. These guys'll laugh at a five-million-dollar verdict. They won't change a thing, business as usual. Same ads directed at kids. Same lies to Congress. Same everything, unless we wake them up."

Rikki leaned forward on her elbows, and stared across the table at Mrs. Card. "If you can't do it, then leave with the rest of them."

"Don't taunt me."

"I'm not taunting. This take guts, okay. Nicholas is right. If we don't slap them in the face and bring them to their knees, nothing will change. These are ruthless people."

Mrs. Gladys Card was nervous and shaking and ready for a breakdown. "I'm sorry. I want to help, but I just can't do this."

"It's okay, Mrs. Card," Nicholas said, trying to soothe. The poor lady was distraught and needed a friend. Sure, things were fine as long as there were nine other votes. He could afford to be comforting; he just couldn't afford to lose another vote.

There was a silence as they waited to see if she would regroup or come unglued. She took a deep breath, jutted her chin forward, and found inner strength.

"Can I ask a question?" Angel said in the direction of Nicholas, as if he were now the sole source of wisdom.

"Sure," he said, shrugging.

"What will happen to the tobacco industry if we bring back a big verdict, the kind we're talking about?"

"Legally, economically, or politically?"

"All."

He thought for a second or two, but was anxious to respond. "A lot of panic, initially. Lots of shock waves. Lots of scared executives worrying about what's next. They'll hunker down and wait to see if the trial lawyers flood them with litigation. They'll be forced to reexamine their advertising strategies. They won't go bankrupt, at least not in the near future, because they have so much money. They'll run to Congress and demand special laws, and I suspect Washington will treat them with less and less favor. In short, Angel, the industry will never be the same if we do what we should do."

"Hopefully, one day cigarettes will be outlawed," Rikki added.

"That, or the companies will not be financially able to manufacture them," said Nicholas.

"What will happen to us?" Angel asked. "I mean, will we be in any danger? You said these people have been watching us since before the trial started."

"Naw, we'll be safe," Nicholas said. "They can't do anything to us. Like I said earlier, next week they won't remember our names. But everyone will remember our verdict."

Phillip Savelle returned and took his seat. "So what have you Robin Hoods decided now?" he asked.

Nicholas ignored him. "We need to decide on an amount, folks, if we want to go home."

"I thought we'd made that decision," said Rikki.

"Do we have at least nine votes?" Nicholas asked.

"For how much, may I ask?" Savelle inquired in a mocking tone.

"Three hundred and fifty million, give or take a few," Rikki answered.

"Ah, the old distribution of wealth theory. Funny, you folks don't look like a bunch of Marxists."

"I have an idea," Jerry said. "Let's round it off to four hundred, half their cash. That shouldn't bankrupt them. They can tighten their belts, load up some more nicotine, hook some more kids, and, presto, they'll have the money back in a couple of years."

"Is this an auction?" Savelle asked, and no one answered.

"Let's do it," Rikki said.

"Count the votes," Nicholas said, and nine hands went up. He then polled them by asking each of the other eight if they were voting to return a verdict of two million dollars in actual damages and four hundred million in punitive. Each of them said yes. He filled in the verdict form, and made each of them sign it.

Lonnie returned after a long absence.

Nicholas addressed him. "We've reached a verdict, Lonnie."

"What a surprise. How much?"

"Four hundred and two million dollars," Savelle said. "Give or take a few million."

Lonnie looked at Savelle, then looked at Nicholas. "You're kidding?" he said, barely audible.

"Nope," Nicholas said. "It's true, and we have nine votes. Care to join?"

"Hell no."

"Pretty incredible, ain't it?" Savelle said. "And just think, we'll all be famous."

"This is unheard of," Lonnie said, leaning against the wall.

"Not really," Nicholas replied. "Texaco got hit with a ten-billion-dollar verdict a few years back."

"Oh, so this is a bargain?" Lonnie said.

"No," Nicholas said, standing. "This is justice." He walked to the door, opened it, and asked Lou Dell to inform Judge Harkin that his jury was ready.

While they waited for a minute, Lonnie cornered Nicholas, and in a whisper asked, "Is there any way I can keep my name out of this?" He was more nervous than angry.

"Sure. Don't worry. The Judge will poll us, ask us one at a time if this is our verdict. When he asks you, make sure everyone knows you had nothing to do with it."

"Thanks."

Forty-two

LOU DELL took the note as she had taken his previous ones and gave it to Willis, who walked down the hall, around the corner, and out of sight. He personally delivered it to His Honor, who at that moment was chatting on the phone, and anxious to hear the verdict. He heard verdicts all the time, but he had a hunch this one might have some pop to it. He felt sure he would one day preside over a grander civil trial, but one was hard to contemplate at the moment.

The note said: "Judge Harkin, Could you arrange for a deputy to escort me from the courthouse as soon as we're dismissed? I'm scared. I'll explain later. Nicholas Easter."

His Honor gave instructions to a deputy waiting outside his chambers, then strode purposefully through the door and into the courtroom, where the air seemed thick with trepidation. Lawyers, most of whom had been lounging around their offices not far away waiting for the call, were scurrying down the aisle, hustling to their seats, nerved up and wild-eyed. Spectators filtered in. It was almost eight o'clock.

"I have been informed that the jury has reached a verdict," Harkin said loudly into his microphone, and he could see the lawyers shaking. "Please bring in the jury."

They filed in with solemn faces, something jurors always do. Regardless of what good news they bear for one side or the other, and regardless of how united they might be, their eyes are always downcast, causing both sides to instinctively sink low and begin plans for appeal.

Lou Dell took the form from Nicholas, gave it to His Honor, who somehow managed to examine it while remaining remarkably straight-faced. He gave not the slightest hint of the shattering news he was holding. The verdict shocked him beyond reason, but procedurally there was nothing he could do. It was technically in order. There would be motions to reduce it later, but he was handcuffed now. He refolded it, gave it back to Lou Dell, who walked it over to Nicholas. He was standing and ready for the announcement.

"Mr. Foreman, read the verdict."

Nicholas unfolded his masterpiece, cleared his throat, glanced around quickly to see if Fitch was in the courtroom, and when he didn't see him, he read: "We, the jury, find for the plaintiff, Celeste Wood, and award compensatory damages in the amount of two million dollars."

This alone was a precedent. Wendall Rohr and his gang of trial lawyers breathed an enormous sigh of relief. They had just made history.

But the jury wasn't finished.

"And we, the jury, find for the plaintiff, Celeste Wood, and award punitive damages in the amount of four hundred million dollars."

From a lawyer's point of view, the receiving of a verdict approaches an art form. One cannot flinch or twitch. One cannot look around for either solace or jubilation. One cannot grab one's client to celebrate or to comfort. One must sit perfectly still, frown hard at a legal pad upon which one is writing, and act as though one knew precisely what the verdict would be.

The art form was desecrated. Cable slumped as if shot in the stomach. His comrades stared at the jury box with mouths gaping, air rushing out, eyes squinted in utter disbelief. An "Oh my god!" was heard from somewhere among the second-tier defense lawyers behind Cable.

Rohr was all teeth as he quickly put his arm around Celeste Wood, who had started crying. The other trial lawyers clutched each other with quiet congratulations. Oh, the thrill of victory, the prospect of splitting forty percent of this verdict.

Nicholas sat down and patted Loreen Duke on the leg. It was over, finally over.

Judge Harkin was suddenly all business, as if it were just another verdict. "Now, ladies and gentlemen, I'm going to poll the jury. This means I will ask each of you individually if this is your verdict. I'll start with Ms. Loreen Duke. Please state clearly for the record whether or not you voted for this verdict."

"I did," she said proudly.

Some of the lawyers took notes. Some simply stared blankly into space.

"Mr. Easter? Did you vote in favor of this verdict?"

"I did."

"Mrs. Dupree?"

"Yes sir. I did."

"Mr. Savelle?"

"I did not."

"Mr. Royce? Did you vote for this?"

"I did."

"Ms. Weese?"

"I did."

"Mr. Vu?"

"I did."

"Mr. Lonnie Shaver?"

Lonnie half-stood, said loudly for the world to hear, "No sir, Your Honor, I did not vote for this verdict, and I disagree with it entirely."

"Thank you. Mrs. Rikki Coleman? Is this your verdict?"

"Yes sir."

"Mrs. Gladys Card?"

"No sir."

There suddenly arose a flicker of hope for Cable and Pynex and Fitch and the entire tobacco industry. Three jurors had now disclaimed the verdict. Only one more, and the jury would be sent back for more deliberations. Every trial judge could tell stories of juries whose verdicts disintegrated after they were delivered and while the polling took place. A verdict sounded much different in open court, with lawyers and clients watching, than it did only minutes earlier in the safety of the jury room.

But the slim prospect of a miracle was stamped out by the Poodle and Jerry. Both affirmed the verdict.

"Looks like the vote is nine to three," His Honor said. "Everything else appears to be in order. Anything, Mr. Rohr?"

Rohr simply shook his head. He could not thank the jury now, though he would've loved to jump over the railing and kiss their feet. He sat smugly in his seat, one heavy arm around Celeste Wood.

"Mr. Cable?"

"No sir," Cable managed to say. Oh, the things he'd love to tell the jurors, the idiots.

The fact that Fitch was not in the courtroom worried Nicholas immensely. His absence meant he was outside, somewhere in the dark, lurking and waiting. How much did Fitch know now? Probably too much. Nicholas was anxious to leave the courtroom, and get the hell out of town.

Harkin then began a windy thank-you, interspersed it with a rowsing dose of patriotism and civic duty, threw in every cliché he'd heard from the bench, warned them against talking to anybody about their deliberations and their verdict, said he could hold them in contempt of court if they breathed a word of what had happened in the jury room, and sent them away on their final journey to the motel to gather their things.

Fitch watched and listened from the viewing room next to his office. And he watched alone, the jury consultants having been fired hours earlier and sent back to Chicago.

He could snatch Easter, and this had been discussed at length with Swanson, who'd been told everything as soon as he arrived. But what good would it do? Easter wouldn't talk and they'd run the risk of a kidnapping charge. They had enough troubles without spending time in jail in Biloxi.

They decided to follow him, hoping he would lead them to the girl. Which, of course, posed another dilemma: What would they do with the girl if they found her? They couldn't report Marlee to the police. She'd made the magnificent decision to steal dirty money. What would Fitch tell the FBI in his sworn affidavit: that he gave her ten million dollars to deliver a verdict in a tobacco trial, and she had the nerve to double-cross him? Now would somebody please prosecute her?

Fitch was screwed at every turn.

He watched the video through the lens of Oliver McAdoo's

hidden camera. The jurors stood, shuffled out, and the jury box was empty.

They gathered in the jury room to pick up books and magazines and knitting bags. Nicholas was in no mood for small talk. He slipped through the door, where Chuck, an old friend now, stopped him and told him the Sheriff was waiting outside.

Without a word to Lou Dell or Willis, or to any of the people he'd spent the last four weeks with, Nicholas hurriedly disappeared behind Chuck. They ducked out the back entrance, where the Sheriff himself was waiting behind the wheel of his big brown Ford.

"Judge said you needed some help," the Sheriff said from behind the wheel.

"Yeah. Get on Forty-nine north. I'll show you where to go. And make sure we're not followed."

"Okay. Who might be following you?"

"Bad guys."

Chuck slammed the passenger door in the front, and they sped away. Nicholas took one last look at the jury room on the second floor. He saw Millie from the waist up, hugging Rikki Coleman.

"Don't you have things at the motel?" the Sheriff asked.

"Forget it. I'll get them later."

The Sheriff radioed instructions for two cars to follow and make sure they were not being tailed. Twenty minutes later, as they raced through Gulfport, Nicholas began pointing this way and that, and the Sheriff stopped by the tennis court of a large apartment complex north of town. Nicholas said this was fine, and got out.

"You sure you're okay?" the Sheriff asked.

"I'm sure. I'll stay here with some friends. Thanks."

"Call me if you need help."

"Sure."

Nicholas disappeared into the night, and watched from a corner as the patrol car left. He waited by the pool house, a vantage point that enabled him to see all traffic to and from the apartment complex. He saw nothing suspicious.

His getaway car was brand-new, a rental Marlee had left there two days ago, one of three now abandoned in various parking lots on the outskirts of Biloxi. He safely made the ninety-minute drive to Hattiesburg while watching his rear the entire way.

The Lear was waiting at the Hattiesburg airport. Nicholas locked the keys in the car, and walked nonchalantly into the small terminal.

SOMETIME AFTER MIDNIGHT, he breezed through customs in George Town with fresh Canadian papers. There were no other passengers; the airport was practically deserted. Marlee met him by the baggage claim, and they embraced fiercely.

"Have you heard?" he asked. They stepped outside, where the humid air hit hard.

"Yeah, it's all over CNN," she said. "Was that the best you could do?" she asked with a laugh, and they kissed again.

She drove toward George Town, through the empty winding streets, around the modern bank buildings clustered near the pier. "That's ours," she said, pointing to the Royal Swiss Trust building.

"Nice."

Later, they sat in the sand, at the edge of the water, splashing in the foam as the gentle waves broke across their feet. A few boats with dim lights inched along the horizon. The hotels and condos stood quiet behind them. They owned the beach for the moment.

And what a moment it was. Their four-year quest was now over. Their plans had finally worked, and to perfection. They'd dreamed of this night for so long, had been convinced countless times that it could never happen.

The hours drifted by.

THEY THOUGHT IT BEST if Marcus the broker never laid eyes on Nicholas. There was an excellent chance authorities might ask questions later, and the less Marcus knew, the better. Marlee presented herself to the Royal Swiss Trust receptionist promptly at nine, and was escorted upstairs where Marcus was waiting with many questions he couldn't ask. He offered coffee, then closed his door.

"The shorting of Pynex seems to have been an excellent trade," he said with a grin at his own talent for understatement.

"Seems so," she said. "Where will it open?"

"Good question. I've been on the phone to New York, and things are quite chaotic. The verdict has stunned everyone. Except you, I guess." He wanted so badly to probe, but he knew there would be no answers. "There's a chance it might not open. They could suspend trading for a day or two."

She seemed to understand this perfectly. The coffee arrived. They sipped it as they reviewed yesterday's closings. At nine-thirty, Marcus slipped on his headset and focused on the two monitors on his side desk. "The market is open," he said, waiting.

Marlee listened intently while trying to appear calm. She and Nicholas wanted to make a quick killing, in and out, then be gone with the money to some faraway place they'd never seen before. She had to cover 160,000 shares of Pynex, stock she was anxious to unload.

"It's suspended," Marcus said to his computer, and she flinched slightly. He punched digits and began a conversation with someone in New York. He mumbled numbers and points, then said to her, "They're offering it at fifty, and there are no buyers. Yes or no?"

"No."

Two minutes passed. His eyes never left the screen. "It's on the board at forty-five. Yes or no?"

"No. What about the others?"

His fingers danced across the keyboard. "Wow. Trellco is down thirteen to forty-three. Smith Greer down eleven to fifty-three and a quarter. ConPack down eight to twenty-five. It's a bloodbath. The entire industry is getting shelled."

"Check Pynex."

"Still falling. Forty-two, with a few small buyers."

"Buy twenty thousand shares at forty-two," she said, looking at her notes.

A few seconds passed before he said, "Confirmed. Up to forty-three. They're paying attention up there. I'd keep it under twenty thousand shares next time."

Less commissions, the Marlee/Nicholas partnership had just made $740,000.

"Back down to forty-two," he said.

"Buy twenty thousand shares at forty-one," she said.

A minute later he said, "Confirmed."

Another $760,000 in profits.

"Steady at forty-one, now a half up," he said like a robot. "They saw your buy."

"Is anybody else buying?" she asked.

"Not yet."

"When will they start?"

"Who knows? But soon, I think. This company has too much cash to go under. Book value per share is around seventy. It's a steal at fifty. I'd tell all my clients to jump in now."

She bought another twenty thousand shares at forty-one, then waited half an hour to buy twenty thousand at forty. When Trellco fell to forty, down sixteen, she bought twenty thousand shares, for a profit of $320,000.

The quick kill was happening. She borrowed a phone at ten-thirty and called Nicholas, who was glued to the TV, watching it all unfold on CNN. They had a crew in Biloxi trying to get interviews from Rohr and Cable and Harkin, from Gloria Lane or anybody who might know something. No one wanted to talk to them. Nicholas was also watching stock quotes on a financial news channel.

Pynex found its bottom an hour after it opened. Takers were found at thirty-eight, at which point Marlee dumped the remaining eighty thousand shares.

When Trellco found resistance at forty-one, she bought forty thousand shares. She was out of the Trellco business. With the bulk of her trades covered, and covered quite brilliantly, Marlee was less inclined to hang around and be greedy with the other stocks. She worked hard at being patient. She had rehearsed this plan many times, and the opportunity would never again be hers.

A few minutes before noon, with the market still in disarray, she covered the remaining shares of Smith Greer. Marcus removed his headset and wiped his forehead.

"Not a bad morning, Ms. MacRoland. You've netted over eight million, less commissions." A printer hummed quietly on the desk, spewing out confirmations.

"I want the money wired to a bank in Zurich."

"Our bank?"

"No." She handed him a sheet of paper with wiring instructions.

"How much?" he asked.

"All of it, minus, of course, your commissions."

"Certainly. I assume this is a priority."

"Immediately, please."

□ □ □ □

SHE PACKED QUICKLY. He watched because he had nothing to pack, nothing but two golf shirts and a pair of jeans he'd purchased at a dive shop in the hotel. They promised each other new wardrobes at their next destination. Money would not be a factor.

They flew, first class, to Miami, where they waited two hours before boarding a flight to Amsterdam. The in-flight news service in first class featured none other than CNN and Financial News. They watched with great amusement as the verdict got covered in Biloxi while Wall Street ran in circles. Experts popped up everywhere. Law professors made fearless predictions about the future of tobacco liability. Stock analysts offered myriad opinions, each in sharp contrast to the preceding one. Judge Harkin had no comment. Cable could not be found. Rohr finally emerged from his office and took full credit for the victory. No one knew of Rankin Fitch, which was a shame because Marlee wanted so badly to see his suffering face.

In hindsight, her timing was perfect. The market bottomed soon after it crashed, and by the end of the day Pynex was holding steady at forty-five.

From Amsterdam, they flew to Geneva, where they leased a hotel suite for a month.

Forty-three

FITCH LEFT BILOXI three days after the verdict. He returned to his home in Arlington and to his routine in Washington. Though his future as director of The Fund was in doubt, his anonymous little firm had plenty of nontobacco work to keep it busy. Nothing, though, that paid like The Fund.

A week after the verdict, he met with Luther Vandemeer and D. Martin Jankle in New York, and confessed every detail of the deal with Marlee. It was not a pretty meeting.

He also conferred with a collection of ruthless New York lawyers on how best to attack the verdict. The fact that Easter had vanished immediately was grounds for suspicion. Herman Grimes had already agreed to release his medical records. There was no evidence of an imminent heart attack. He'd been fit and healthy until that morning. He remembered an odd taste to his coffee, then he was on the floor. Retired Colonel Frank Herrera had already given an affidavit in which he swore the unauthorized materials found under his bed were not placed there by him. He'd had no visitors. *Mogul* was not sold anywhere near the motel. The mystery surrounding the verdict swirled more each day.

The New York lawyers did not know about the Marlee deal, nor would they ever.

Cable had prepared and was almost ready to file a motion requesting permission to interview the jurors, an idea Judge Harkin seemed to like. How else could they find out what had gone on in

there? Lonnie Shaver was particularly anxious to tell all. He'd
received his promotion and was ready to defend corporate America.

There was hope for the post-trial efforts. The appellate process
would be long and arduous.

As for Rohr and the group of trial lawyers who'd funded the
case, the future was filled with unbounded opportunity. A staff
was organized just to handle the flood of calls from other lawyers
and potential victims. An 800 number was implemented. Class
actions were being considered.

Wall Street seemed more sympathetic to Rohr than to the tobacco industry. In the weeks following the verdict, Pynex couldn't
top fifty, and the other three were down at least twenty percent.
Antismoking groups openly predicted the bankruptcy and even-
tual demise of the tobacco companies.

SIX WEEKS after he left Biloxi, Fitch was eating lunch alone in a
tiny Indian diner near Dupont Circle in D.C. He huddled over a
bowl of spicy soup, still wearing his overcoat because it was
snowing outside and chilly inside.

She dropped in from nowhere, just appeared like an angel, the
same way she'd emerged on the rooftop terrace of the St. Regis in
New Orleans, over two months earlier. "Hi, Fitch," she said, and
he dropped his spoon.

He glanced around the dark restaurant, saw nothing but small
groups of Indians huddled over steaming bowls, not another spoken word of English within forty feet.

"What are you doing here?" he said without moving his lips.
Her face was lined with the fur from her coat. He remembered
how pretty she was. The hair seemed even shorter.

"Just dropped in to say hello."

"You've said it."

"And the money is being returned to you, even as we speak. I'm
wiring it back to your account at Hanwa, in the Netherlands
Antilles. All ten million, Fitch."

He could think of no quick response to this. He was looking at
the lovely face of the only person who'd ever beaten him. And she
still had him guessing. "How kind of you," he said.

"I started to give it away, you know, like to some of those
antismoking groups. But we decided against it."

"We? How's Nicholas?"

"I'm sure you miss him."

"Deeply."

"He's fine."

"So you're together?"

"Of course."

"Thought you probably just took the money and ran from everybody, including him."

"Come on, Fitch."

"I don't want the money."

"Great. Give it to the American Lung Association."

"That's not my kinda charity. Why are you returning the money?"

"It's not mine."

"So you've found ethics and morals, maybe even God."

"Skip the lecture, Fitch. It sounds rather hollow coming from you. I never planned to keep the money. I just wanted to borrow it."

"If you're gonna lie and cheat, why not go ahead and steal?"

"I'm not a thief. I lied and I cheated because that's what your client understands. Tell me, Fitch, did you find Gabrielle?"

"Yes, we did."

"And did you find her parents?"

"We know where they are."

"Do you understand now, Fitch?"

"It makes more sense, yes."

"They were both wonderful people. They were intelligent and vigorous and they loved life. They both got hooked on cigarettes when they were in college, and I watched them fight the habit until they died. They hated themselves for smoking, but could never give it up. They died horrible deaths, Fitch. I watched them suffer and shrivel and gasp for breath until they couldn't breathe anymore. I was their only child, Fitch. Did your goons learn this?"

"Yes."

"My mother died at home, on the sofa in the den because she couldn't walk to her bedroom. Just Mother and I." She paused and glanced around. Fitch noticed her eyes were remarkably clear. Sad as it must have been, he could muster no sympathy.

"When did you set this plan in motion?" he asked, finally taking a spoonful of soup.

"Grad school. I studied finance, thought about law, then I dated a lawyer for a while and heard stories of tobacco litigation. The idea evolved."

"A helluva plot."

"Thanks, Fitch. Coming from you, that's a compliment."

She pulled her gloves tighter as if she was ready to go. "Just wanted to say hello, Fitch. And to make sure you know why it happened."

"Are you finished with us?"

"No. We'll watch the appeal closely, and if your lawyers get too carried away attacking the verdict, then I've got copies of the wire transfers. Be careful, Fitch. We're kind of proud of that verdict, and we're always watching."

She stood at the edge of the table. "And remember, Fitch, next time you boys go to trial, we'll be there."